THE
MAKER'S
MARK

Roy Hattersley

SIMON & SCHUSTER

New York   London   Toronto   Sydney   Tokyo   Singapore

SIMON & SCHUSTER

SIMON & SCHUSTER BUILDING
ROCKEFELLER CENTER
1230 AVENUE OF THE AMERICAS
NEW YORK, NEW YORK 10020

DESIGNED BY LEVAVI & LEVAVI
MANUFACTURED IN THE UNITED STATES OF AMERICA

1   3   5   7   9   10   8   6   4   2

LIBRARY OF CONGRESS CATALOGING IN PUBLICATION DATA
HATTERSLEY, ROY.
THE MAKER'S MARK/ROY HATTERSLEY.
P.   CM.
I. TITLE.
PR6058.A83M35   1990
823'.914—DC20   90-28129
CIP
ISBN 0-671-73493-8

CONTENTS

1 A FAMILY CHRISTMAS 11

2 A MIRACLE ON THE

CHAPELTOWN ROAD 25

3 AMBITION 40

4 A BARGAIN 51

5 GETTING ON 66

6 PRIMARY EDUCATION 85

7 BUILDING BRIDGES 97

8 THE END OF INNOCENCE 106

9 EXCEPTIONAL ABILITY 117

10 DESTINY 130

11 THE RESOURCES OF CIVILIZATION 141

12 MISS ANNIE ELLIS TELLS A STORY 154

13 MARCHING ORDERS 161

14 BETWEEN FRIENDS 174

15 A FREE MAN 189

16 ENTERPRISE 202

17 LESSONS IN FAITH AND MORALS 219

18 TWO MEDALS 233

19 LOVED HER NOT LESS 246

20 DOING WHAT'S RIGHT 263

21 HERBERT HATTERSLEY FACES UP
TO HIS RESPONSIBILITIES 276

22 FOR RICHER, FOR POORER 289

23 CHANGING PARTNERS 306

24 MYSTERIOUS WAYS 321

25 IN SICKNESS AND IN HEALTH 337

26 BY ANY OTHER NAME 349

27 SERVICE AND SACRIFICE 367

28 WOMEN'S RIGHTS 382

29 RESPONSIBILITY 394

30 FOR KING AND FILEY 407

31 DUTY DONE 421

32 THE FAMILY GOES TO WAR 433

33 DUTY BY THE DEAD 447

34 MEN OF LETTERS 460

35 SECOND THOUGHTS 475

36 ANOTHER CHURCH: ANOTHER MIRACLE 490

37 THE LIFE AND THE RESURRECTION 505

38 MEN OF PROPERTY 521

39 LOST AND FOUND 534

40 THE FIRST CHRISTMAS 546

41 THE SALAMANDER 562

42 THE LAST MIRACLE 581

THE
MAKER'S
MARK

CHAPTER ONE

A FAMILY CHRISTMAS

At five minutes to twelve on Christmas Eve, 1929, Father Hattersley knelt in the corner of his vestry and prayed for the strength to say the Midnight Mass. That in itself was a measure of his confusion, for he no longer believed in the power of prayer. But he was still imprisoned by the habits of the past. So he prayed and his prayer was answered. After the last amen he hurried around to the front of the church and said good night to each parishioner, wondering if he was really saying goodbye. He was still afraid to choose, but he knew that he could postpone the choice no longer. The time of doubt was almost over and the new age of certainty would soon begin.

It had started to snow again, and, as he reached the presbytery door a shadowy figure in the road beyond his gate wished him a Merry Christmas and described the weather as seasonable. It was cold in the hall and colder still in the bedroom. Ice had begun to form on the inside of the windows. Father Hattersley decided that he would wear his socks in bed. He did not want to snuffle and sneeze his way into the better life which lay ahead.

He woke up before his tin alarm clock began to clang and looked up blankly into the dark limbo between bed and ceiling. Although he had slept in the same room every night for almost a year, during the few seconds when he was no longer asleep but not quite awake he always had to struggle to remember where he was. When he remembered he turned over with such a start that the old topcoat—which augmented his blankets—fell onto the floor. He reached out for the box of Swan Vestas which he had carefully placed within easy reach the night before. First he felt his spectacles, then his cigarettes, then the half-filled ashtray. When, eventually, he struck a match, he barely had time to focus on the scratched face of the old clock before the flame spluttered out. It was either twenty past five or almost half past four. Either way, he was free to go back to sleep. He had already performed his daily office. It was the one morning in the year when he was not required to rise at six. Father Hattersley retrieved the coat from the floor, rolled out onto his back, turned again on his side—and got out of bed.

Letting as little of his feet as possible touch the cold linoleum, he made a dash for the door and switched on the light. He remembered that the shabby leather chair, which he had brought from St. Philip Neri in Mansfield, had been pulled into the middle of the room. But he was still frightened to see it there. Piled into it were all the possessions he valued. They did not amount to much. A battered silver-plated cigarette case. A black lacquered papier-mâché box with white flowers painted on its lid. A sitting Buddha, designed to burn pagan incense but converted into a Christian ashtray. A framed portrait of a stout lady and her florid husband. A pile of dog-eared novels, Thackeray and Dickens side by side with light romances bought for sixpence in Boots' bargain basement. An imitation-leather pocket book. A single rolled-gold cuff link. The crucifix which usually hung over his bed. A scrapbook filled with picture postcards. Next to the chair there was a battered cardboard suitcase. Stuck to its scratched sides were the remnants of two labels. Both proclaimed the same destination—Rome.

Trying not to look at the chair, Father Hattersley pulled on the old topcoat which was used both as a counterpane and as a dressing gown. Suitably protected, he crept out onto the landing and, squeezing himself against the banister, began to tiptoe down to the living room. He had read in an Edgar Wallace novel that stairs creak only when a foot falls in the middle of the tread. Edgar Wallace was wrong. But it did not matter. The only other inhabitant of the house was already awake. His aunt—wrapped in a faded brocade housecoat—

sat in front of the fire, disturbing the dying embers in the vain hope that they would come back to life.

"God bless us and save us," said the old lady. "What in heaven's name are you doing up at this time? It's the one day in the year that you get a lie-in."

"It's no use. I can't sleep. I'm too used to getting up early. But what are you doing down here?"

"I couldn't sleep either. I was frozen to death. I've never been in such a cold house."

Father Hattersley could not bring himself to apologize. He had warned his aunt about the house and about the inconvenience. He had prayed that she would not come. For the desperate day which lay ahead could only be complicated by the companionship of an eccentric spinster. But she had insisted on spending the night in the presbytery. If she had been cold, she had only herself to blame. His aunt's disturbed night was the least of his problems. It seemed to be the greatest of hers.

"I've never known a presbytery like this one. I've never known a presbytery without a housekeeper."

She picked up a week-old newspaper from the sofa and used it to sweep some of the ashes from the tiled hearth back under the grate.

"It's like Paddy's Market. I don't know how you manage."

"I manage all right. I'm sorry if you were uncomfortable."

"Well, I was and I still am. But I wouldn't have missed it for the world. Your first Midnight Mass in your own parish. Your mother would never have forgiven me. She would have been waiting up there to complain the moment that I arrived."

Father Hattersley wanted his aunt, when the time came, to give the proper message.

"It was a very big congregation. Twice as big as anything I've had before."

"Most of them weren't Catholics. Church of England. Just come for the show. You could tell that by how many took communion."

"I've told you, it isn't a very big parish."

"If you ask me, it isn't a parish at all. The sooner you leave here, the better."

Father Hattersley winced. But his aunt was too preoccupied with her thoughts to notice.

"Give us a chance. I've not been here a year."

"If you spend another winter here, you'll die of pneumonia. Your chest isn't strong at the best of times."

"It's strong enough to survive Langwith Junction. Anyway, this is where the Bishop sent me."

"That's nothing to do with it. A man of your education should be at the cathedral. Seven years in Rome and you end up in St. Joseph's, Langwith Junction."

"I don't think that I'll end up here."

"You will if you go on like this. You've no push. You're just like your father. And look what happened to him."

"Dad's not done so badly. He enjoys himself more than anybody else I know. You're very hard on him. He's all right."

"Enjoys himself a great deal too much. You've got better things to do with your time. Your mother always knew you were meant for something special and she was right."

"I hope you won't say anything like that to Father Keogh when he comes around."

"Why not? I've said it to the Bishop and I've said it to the Vicar-General." She laughed sardonically. "Father Payne, recognized at last. What next?"

"*Monsignor* Payne! If you please." Her nephew laughed too.

"Does he ever write? He hasn't even sent you a card. I've looked."

"You can hardly blame him, after what my mother said to him."

"Heavens above, he's your godfather. He's got duties by you. Whatever would your mother have said? What if you were in some sort of trouble, who would you turn to?"

Father Hattersley winced again. "Let's make some tea."

Together they padded into the kitchen and, as Father Hattersley struggled to light the gas ring, his aunt examined the cups which hung from the plate rack. None of them was clean enough to touch her lips, so she went back into the living room to get the best china out of the glass-fronted cabinet. She called back over her shoulder, "I bet your bedroom's like a tip. I'll be upstairs to tidy it up as soon as I've had a drink."

Father Hattersley normally drank his tea lukewarm. But in the small hours of Christmas Day, 1929, he swilled it down scalding hot. He refused a second cup and announced—with absolutely no conviction—that he suddenly felt tired again. Before the sentence was finished, he was into the hall and on his way back to his bedroom. In

14

the kitchen, his aunt chased floating tea leaves with a corroded apostle spoon.

Father Hattersley closed his bedroom door like a man who had just escaped the hound of heaven. After a moment's frantic searching, he retrieved a sheet of cheap blue paper from under his pillow. He kissed it with the theatrical solemnity with which he had been taught to kiss his scapular. Then he struck the last of his matches and held the flame against the letter's edge. When all but one blue corner had burned, he caught the ashes in his hand. Opening his bedroom window for the first time in almost a year, he threw the scraps of charred paper into the wind and watched them blow into the darkness. With the same thoroughness which he had used that morning to polish away the last drop of wine from inside the chalice, he brushed the last scraps of ash from his hand. The corner which had survived the blaze he put in the innermost compartment of his wallet.

The time to decide had come. He thought of praying for guidance as he had prayed for strength in the vestry before the mass. When he decided that prayer would not help, he knew that the decision had been made. So he double-checked that the bedroom door was latched and, reaching up on top of his wardrobe, took from their hiding place two shirts with attached collars, a striped club tie and a Fair Isle pullover, knitted (apparently by hand) in extremely unclerical green and red. He dragged a pair of gray flannel trousers from underneath the mattress and—having assembled all the evidence of his guilt—began to fill his suitcase. He stuffed his spare pair of shoes with dirty socks, but before he packed them, he polished their toe caps on his sleeve as if the heavy black brogues were of special importance to him. The treasures from the easy chair he wrapped in old darned underpants, threadbare vests and worn towels. They were held secure by his best black suit, which was the last possession in the case before its lid was closed. He only just finished in time. It was barely six o'clock but his aunt was shouting from the landing.

"You'd better get up now. Father Keogh will be here any minute."

Father Keogh was late and when he arrived, the cause of the delay was not in doubt. He had said mass at ten o'clock. Then the celebration of Christ's Nativity had continued in the homes of his more gregarious parishioners.

"I mustn't stay more than a minute," he said, settling himself into the only comfortable armchair. "Mrs. Fitzpatrick says that dinner is sharp at half past one. But I wouldn't miss drinking the health of the best curate I ever had at St. Philip Neri."

Father Hattersley took the hint and brought in the bottle of whiskey which the colliery manager had sent him as a Christmas present. His guest watched appreciatively as the tumbler was half filled, and then offered a clarification of his encomium.

"I meant, of course, St. Philip Neri, Mansfield. I can't speak for St. Philip Neri in Rome. No doubt that was the one you were thinking of, Rex, being an English College man."

The use of the nickname was malicious and deliberate. It symbolized the gulf between Maynooth and the Collegio Inglese, Irish sensuality and English asceticism. It was a constant reminder of the aunt's hope and Father Keogh's suspicion that Rex was destined for higher things on earth as well as in heaven. Father Hattersley's discomfiture was too obvious to ignore. The parish priest of St. Philip Neri—in Mansfield—chose to misinterpret the signs of distress.

"I don't want to overstay my welcome. You and Miss Martin have got your own dinner to cook."

He did not move from the chair.

"We're going home to Nottingham," said Rex.

"Shouldn't you be leaving?" Another double measure of whiskey was slurped from the bottle.

"I've got a wedding at two o'clock. Don't you remember? The girl's from Mansfield."

Life still had the power constantly to surprise Miss Martin. "I've never known anything like it. Not in all my years have I ever known a wedding on Christmas Day."

"I've done them in my time. Anyway, Rex volunteered to do it today. All the young man asked was a wedding before the twenty-eighth. He's a sailor and goes back to sea the day after tomorrow. And the girl's in the family way."

Miss Martin was shocked, but not by the bride's condition or the priest's description of the young lady's delicate state. Her nephew, having officiated at midnight, could not say a second mass. Suddenly she realized the truth about the wedding.

"Is the girl not Catholic? Is that why there's no Nuptial Mass? Are you giving up Christmas Day for a mixed marriage?"

"She's C of E," her nephew told her.

16

"I wouldn't feel married," the spinster assured the two priests, "unless I'd had a Nuptial Mass."

A wave of uncharacteristic charity engulfed Father Keogh. "She can take instruction after. They need to be married quick."

Remembering that it was his habit to see the worst in everything, Father Keogh abandoned his defense of the happy couple and renewed his assault on the priest who was to marry them.

"Father Hattersley can instruct her. That's what the English College was founded for—converting England back to the true faith. They've not been very successful up to date. But Father Hattersley keeps trying, don't you, Rex?"

Miss Martin made a feeble attempt to change the direction of the conversation. "How long is it since we were in your parish at St. Mary's, Father—twenty years?"

"You were never in my parish, dear lady. You may have lived within its boundaries for a time, but you were cathedral people. All the family. Right up to poor young Bert going away."

The whiskey bottle had emptied down to the point at which Father Keogh turned maudlin.

"What a parish that was! What a parish! We did everything in that parish. These days young priests aren't the same." He turned to Rex. "They tell me you haven't even got a football team going here. They say that you don't even encourage the lads to play football."

"There wasn't one when I got here and it's hard to start one up. The lads are all playing for schools or colliery teams."

"I'm not surprised. Father Froes never bothered. It's a miracle that he didn't have the choir steeplechasing and the altar boys entered in the Newark point-to-point. Did you know Father Froes, Miss Martin?"

"Not well, Father."

"Well, I'll tell you. He was a man for the horses. Owned some in his time. He was a horse-racing and betting man. Thought of nothing else. He was a gambling man, like young Rex here is a car-driving man."

"A what?" asked Miss Martin.

"A car-driving man. Now don't tell me that you don't know about your nephew's motorcar."

"Indeed I do. I've driven in it from the station."

"You may not know the whole story. He thinks of nothing else. Nothing except driving, that is. He's no mechanic. No good with

17

engines at all. When he lived with me at Mansfield he couldn't even change a fuse. I suppose they didn't teach him how at the Gregorian University. He should have inherited something from his father. But he hasn't. Didn't your sister, God rest her soul, marry an engineer?"

Rex was about to reply that his father was the proprietor of an ironmonger's shop when his aunt assumed responsibility for answering the question.

"When we two girls first met him, Herbert was finishing his apprenticeship as a surgical-instrument maker. He was just about to become manager of his father's factory in Sheffield."

Father Hattersley decided that the time had come to edge his guest out of the door. "I'll drive you home in it, if you like."

He took Father Keogh by the elbow and guided him across the living room.

"A taxi's coming at half past twelve. But I'll step outside and view this vehicle of yours. Will you join us, Miss Martin?"

Together they walked onto the square of concrete which in Langwith Junction was known as the presbytery drive. The cold air, which cut through the coats that nephew and aunt were wise enough to wear, only enlivened Father Keogh's malice.

"The Father goes on mystery tours into the countryside on Saturday afternoons. Did you know that, Miss Martin? He's been spotted at Hucknall, Southwell, Cuckney, Clowne and"—he paused to make sure that his false teeth were capable of the alliteration—"Cresswell. He draws pictures of the churches."

"It was Syd who drew the pictures, Auntie. I just drove him."

"I hear that Sydney goes to Ratcliffe now. Another bishop's scholar."

"We're very proud of him," said the aunt. "He'll be the third. We'll have three priests in the family."

Father Keogh's smile grew increasingly malicious. "And no doubt, like his brother, he'll go to Rome and own a motorcar. No stopping them. I reckon that Rex will have red piping on his cassock one day. Ratcliffe, motorcar and the Bishop's Secretary for his best friend. He can't miss."

Father Hattersley blushed—not with the embarrassment for which Father Keogh hoped but at the absurdity of such an accusation being made on that particular day. He blushed with shame at the old man's foolishness.

"How can you afford it, Rex? That's what I would like to know."

"It's not much of a car. It cost forty pounds. It's very old and very battered. The hood lets in rain, a wheel's buckled and it only goes uphill in first gear."

He racked his brain for other deficiencies. Self-depreciation comforted him and self-criticism gave him confidence. True to his training, he quoted authority.

"Mr. Brackenbury says it's just scrap."

Father Keogh pounced. "Then why did you pay forty pounds for it? You must have been desperate to get a car."

Rex was anxious not to say anything which he would regret later, something that would be wholly inappropriate to his last meeting with Father Keogh. The old man was full of envy. And envy was a deadly sin. But if all he coveted was a forty-pound Austin, friendship with William Ellis at the cathedral, a brother at Ratcliffe College and a fancy nickname brought home from Rome, he was to be pitied.

Sensing that he had gone too far, Father Keogh tried to make amends. "I meant it all in good part. Just my little joke. You know my jokes well enough."

"I do, Father, I do," said Rex. "And I never minded them. Not even when I was at St. Philip's and heard them every day."

At the age of twenty-seven, Father Hattersley had discovered the secret of the universe. It was a day to be charitable toward an elderly Irishman who had not discovered (and would never understand) a truth far more profound than the Seven Proofs of the Existence of God or the doctrine of transubstantiation.

The Austin Seven rocked to an uncertain stop outside Hattersley's ironmongery in Alfreton Road, Nottingham, at a little after six o'clock. The son of the proprietor had felt obliged to stay at the Langwith Junction wedding while Father Keogh—who made a surprise appearance and received a hero's welcome from the groom—drank the health of virtually everybody in the room. Then the forty-pound car had refused to start. The bridegroom and best man had pushed it until the ignition fired with an explosion that made his aunt, sitting in the passenger seat, give a little shriek for which she immediately apologized. Having been forced into life, the car made uncertain progress to Nottingham.

Passing Newstead Abbey, the radiator began to hiss and steam. At Arnold, boiling water gushed out onto the bonnet. A local, who showed every sign of knowing about such things, refused to fill up the radiator until the engine had cooled down. Miss Martin looked faint but insisted that she felt perfectly well. Father Hattersley smoked five Woodbines and waited to be told that the car was in a condition to cover the last leg of its journey. The engine was boiling again by the time priest and passenger pulled into Alfreton Road. His brothers and sisters were already there.

Gus was in the kitchen washing dishes. She was being watched, in unhelpful admiration, by her husband Mac, who had earned his Scottish nickname for no better reason than that he had lost a leg while serving with a Scottish regiment at Mons. Syd, incongruous in his Ratcliffe College blazer, sat at the living-room table, playing three-handed whist with Muriel and her husband, Bill Moon. He was absentmindedly destroying the fringe on the heavy maroon cloth as he waited for one of them to play the next card.

Herbert Hattersley, the master of the house, slept in an easy chair, his legs stretched across the hearth. His waistcoat and the top buttons of his trousers were undone to accommodate the expansion that Christmas had already produced. The old lady made a studied entrance which nobody noticed. The priest sidled in beside her and was received with joy.

Gus, Muriel and Syd (his youngest brother)—although far too old for such emotional displays—all rushed at their brother, arms outstretched. Mac stood up with difficulty and hobbled in his direction. Herbert Hattersley, waking with a start, took a few seconds to comprehend what was happening.

"Well, I'll go to Trent! You really do look the part. Your mother would be proud. If only she could be here to see you today."

A faded picture of his wife, aged twenty-five, stood on the edge of the mantelpiece. It had been moved forward by his eldest daughter in order to make sure that it was not hidden by the Christmas cards. When the snap was taken, their mother was the talented Miss Martin who met and fell in love with Herbert Hattersley, the aspiring baritone. The aspirations had ended in an unprofitable ironmonger's shop with a living room too small to accommodate a piano. In almost equal pride of place, next to the picture of his wife, Herbert had arranged a second photograph. It was a posed studio portrait of Bert, their first-born. He wore the uniform of a private in the Sherwood Foresters.

On the sideboard there was a picture of old Frederick Hattersley, the father whose factory—according to his sister-in-law—Herbert had been destined to manage. Frederick Hattersley had been a real three-times-every-Sunday Methodist who hated Catholics. But Herbert had no doubt that he would have approved of his grandson. He had believed with fierce conviction in service and sacrifice and he would have admired the dedication which had made the boy a priest. For Father Hattersley had succeeded when, in their different and complicated ways, all the rest of the family had failed. Of course, Herbert decided, old Frederick Hattersley would have been proud too.

"Damn it," he said almost aloud, "I'm proud of him myself and I never thought I would be."

For an hour Herbert made Father Hattersley tell stories—stories about Rome which they had heard a dozen times before and stories about St. Joseph's at Langwith Junction which were especially invented for the occasion. Rex talked to them with his mouth full of Christmas cake and mince pie. For although they were to have Christmas dinner in the evening, Herbert had insisted that they must still have Christmas tea in the afternoon. Syd was still picking marzipan from the top of the cake when Gus said that dinner was ready and that they all must sit down at once. Herbert's judgment upon the quality of the chicken did not depress her. It was the judgment that he made on everything.

"It's nothing like the chicken we used to get in the old days in Sheffield. Nothing like."

Much of Herbert Hattersley's conversation concerned the old days. For he knew the past to be infinitely preferable to the present. It was a belief that he had held since, at the age of twelve, he had decided that it was better to be ten. The conviction that the good times had gone had caused him to impose on his children a lifetime of anecdotes about previous generations of Hattersleys. As a result of his obsession with the old days, he had raised a family of ancestor worshipers.

After dinner, Mac and his father-in-law drank bottles of Red Label Bass, and as the sighs of contented satisfaction echoed around the table Herbert Hattersley insisted that glasses be brought for the lemonade drinkers and everyone was obliged to accept two inches of beer. He told his sister-in-law how beautiful she looked, was forbidden to talk nonsense and then rose to his feet to propose a toast.

"Absent friends."

Gus and Muriel and their aunt all wept. But their father wept more. It was Mac who broke out of the moment's sadness.

"Are you going to give us a song, Dad?"

"Well, I thought of nipping out."

Gus and Muriel cried, "No, Dad, not tonight, Dad!" in perfect unison.

Mac, who was thinking of nipping out as well, suggested a compromise. "Let's have a song first."

Herbert needed no more persuading. He stood in front of the fireplace and struck the pose that he used to take up at smoking concerts in Queen Victoria's England: legs apart, left hand on bulging waistcoat and right free to wave in suitable gestures. He hummed the introduction.

> *"Then eastward ho to Trinidad*
> *And westward ho to Spain*
> *And 'Ship Ahoy' a hundred times a day."*

The first encore was "Tom Bowling." Then came "Trumpeter, What Are You Sounding Now?" with moist eyes during the verse about loved ones waiting, "till Gabriel sounds the reveille." The disciplines of tenor and baritone began to mix and merge with "The Lost Chord" and "The Holy City," until the recital ended with the whole company joining together in a chorus of "The Soldiers of the Queen." It was accompanied by the tapping of glasses with teaspoons and tasteful drumming on the table by Mac, who preferred dance music but knew how to humor his father-in-law. Then he and Herbert Hattersley nipped out.

Father Hattersley drove off at six o'clock on Boxing Day morning in order, his family assumed, to say mass. He did not even attempt to start the Austin Seven with its starting handle. Instead, he let the car roll down the steep incline of Alfreton Road and crashed it into gear just in time for its momentum to turn the engine over before it reached the flat ground at the bottom of the hill. It spluttered and coughed into reluctant life with a judder which set the dashboard quivering, before the petrol gauge settled at empty. A journey of thirty miles lay ahead—twenty miles to Langwith Junction and ten more beyond. That would require two gallons of petrol, two gallons that Father Hattersley could just afford if the almost empty tank carried him as far as the ROP garage on the Mansfield Road. For Russian Oil Products retailed at twopence a gallon cheaper than Shell and BP. There was nothing for it but to drive on in hope.

He reached the garage safely and decided that his success was a good omen. If he felt any emotion, it was surprise—surprise that he was neither frightened nor ashamed. The idea of guilt had never entered his mind. For the notion of free will, on which so much of his extended education had been built, had been totally overlaid by the knowledge that he had no choice but to drive on past Langwith Junction. All that—free will, the presbytery and daily mass—was the past. They were part of the old dream which had faded. The new dream which had taken its place might never come true. But it was the only dream he had that Boxing Day.

As he left the Nottingham suburbs behind him he realized that he was not even certain of where he would eat his next meal. Perhaps he was squandering the warm security of the Church for no more than the remote chance of gaining a prize which it was almost impossible to win. Perhaps he should have asked Gus to make him a sandwich. But that would have meant telling her that he would not be having his Boxing Day dinner in St. Joseph's presbytery, and it was best that she should find out the truth from his letter. If he did not give her time to think before she spoke, she might speak to him in a way that would separate them forever. He was prepared to lose his old family. But he was determined to hang on to the happy memories.

Refreshed with two gallons of Russian petrol, the Austin Seven began to make unusually steady progress. With some difficulty, the engine was moved into top gear and the driver, suddenly confident of completing his journey, began to think of the years that lay ahead. At first his mind was filled with thoughts of future glory. But the family which he was leaving behind kept forcing their way into his imagination. One by one they made him anticipate how they would react to the news of his great adventure.

Most of all, Father Hattersley thought about his grandfather, the grandfather after whom he had been named, the grandfather he had never met but about whose life and work he had been told so much. Old Frederick Hattersley had been the subject of most of Herbert's Christmas Day anecdotes and he had become the villain and hero of the nightmares and dreams which had disturbed his grandson's troubled sleep. The patriarch had believed in duty and discipline. Rex had heard a thousand stories about the old man's unyielding rectitude. The time had come for his grandfather to bend the knee. Up there in his Methodist heaven of choral music and guaranteed return on investment, he would have to learn to live with his grandson as his grandson had learned to live with the memory and reputation of the whole family.

The family had made Rex what he was, and they must accept the consequences of what they had created. The great leap which lay ahead was just another chapter in the family saga—the stories which had been repeated so often that not even the storytellers could draw the line between memory and folklore. And what a story that Christmas would be for Gus and Muriel to tell their children—and Syd to tell his, if he had the sense to follow his instincts and turn his back on Rome.

Father Hattersley thought with mixed feelings that he would become the best story of all—better even than the parable of the rabbit that had crossed his grandfather's path on the road between Chapeltown and Sheffield back in 1867.

CHAPTER TWO

A MIRACLE
ON THE CHAPELTOWN ROAD

On the afternoon of August 28, 1867, Frederick Hattersley prepared to set out on what he believed to be the most important journey of his life. He stood on the cobbles of the factory yard, anxiously fingering the medallions which hung from his watch chain, as the gross of hammered, ridged and treated spades was loaded into his trap. They were the first "Best Quality" spades that the Heather Works had ever forged and they were to be delivered to Urwin Statham, General Dealer, of Chapeltown.

"Gently. Lie 'em down gentle. There'll be no paint left by the time you've loaded up. Have some sense."

The workmen cursed under their breath, bent their backs and obeyed.

"Make sure that them sacks are straight. I don't want the varnish scratching. I want every spade perfect when I get to Chapeltown."

The sacks were spread out between the spades with ostentatious care.

"And put some sacks on top of 'em."

The day had started bright and clear, but gray clouds had begun to blow in from the south. There would be rain before evening. Frederick Hattersley, who had to drive to Chapeltown and back in an open trap, would normally have set out without a moment's thought about the consequences of a downpour. But the expedition to Chapeltown had been judged sufficiently important to his personal standing to justify his best suit—the suit which was usually kept for weddings, christenings, funerals and hanging in the wardrobe to give the confidence that came from knowing that it was there. When he thought of rain and its effect on the best worsted that he could afford, he began to finger the medallions on the watch chain again.

The two medallions had been presented to him by the Sheffield Sunday School Union. One, struck to commemorate its centenary, bore the noble head of James Montgomery, the "child of prayer" who was the Union's founder. The other carried a portrait of Charles Wesley, the Union's inspiration. Frederick Hattersley and the medallions were inseparable. When he rubbed them between finger and thumb, as he struggled to master a piece of music or to calculate the discount on a gross of spades, he did not think of the open Bible or the fluttering doves on their reverse sides. It was Wesley and Montgomery, the men who became great through piety, who inspired him to do more and do better. By following their example, he had discovered his destiny.

It was God's will that he should have come to make the best spades in all Sheffield and, therefore, the best in the world. Spades were not his real love. He was by trade and inclination a scissor maker. But scissors could wait. He was not quite thirty-five and already the partner in an expanding business. Spades were making him prosperous and, for the time being, spades would have to do. And as he flicked his whip over the horse's flanks he knew that by delivering his new and improved spades to Urwin Statham, he was praising Him and glorifying His works as well as making a profit of nearly five guineas a gross. Five guineas was almost twice as much as he had expected. But it was not for him to question God's will.

It was Frederick Hattersley's good fortune to detect the hand of Providence in events which less pious men attributed to chance, coincidence, mistake or sheer misfortune. And his ability to recognize divine intervention had been improved by constant, if one-sided, conversation with the Almighty. He had assumed the habit of prayer as a boy, and had, at the same time, developed the technique of declaring his prayers to be satisfactorily answered. The Lord—working in mysterious ways—sometimes tested the faith of His servant Frederick, as He had tested the faith of His servant Job. But, in the end, God always sent him a sign that his faith had been rewarded. His talent for deciphering God's cryptic messages was so well developed that when eventually he realized the significance of what had happened on the road to Chapeltown that morning, he was forced to conclude that God had made him temporarily stupid as once he had made Paul temporarily blind.

He felt no surprise at his failure instantly to recognize the hand of Providence. It was Providence which decreed that at first he saw nothing but a rabbit, making a ripple run through the barley as it fled in front of the scythes. Then it leaped the high stone wall, barely a yard in front of his horse's hooves.

As he looked back and saw the animal lying mutilated in the road with its front legs kicking convulsively, his only emotion was anger. He was short of time. Yet it was his Christian duty to put the creature out of its misery. So he pulled his horse to a steady halt and, breathing a deep sigh of resentment, stepped down into the road. Then he reached back into the cart and took a spade from one of the dozen bundles which were lying on its floor. They were beautiful. Each blade was painted a shiny black down to the polished two inches of its steel cutting edge. Each handle was varnished elm. On the handle was the maker's name and on the blade, the maker's mark.

The spades should have been delivered without a scratch on the varnish of a single handle or a stain on the matt black paint of a single blade. Yet one was going to be spattered with blood and brains. There was no escape. The Bible was explicit on this, as on every other issue. If God recorded the fall of a sparrow, He would certainly notice the suffering of one of His creatures which had ten times a sparrow's body weight and fifty times its value when hanging in a poulterer's window.

By the time he reached the rabbit it was almost dead, and he nearly turned away with the spade undefiled. But a sudden spasm in its back legs removed all hope of conscientious escape. In order to complete the odious task with a single blow, he held the spade high in front of him like a town alderman making the most of cutting the first sod at the site of a new public washhouse. Then, with all his force, he crashed it down onto the rabbit's neck. There was a flash of sparks as steel cut through flesh and hit stone. Then the varnished handle shuddered in its maker's hand as the "Hammered, Ridged and Treated" blade broke in two, just above the "Guaranteed Two-Inch Best Steel Cutting Edge."

Frederick Hattersley stood in the road bewildered and humiliated, looking at the broken piece of blade which lay, ridiculous, at his feet, and hoping that his shame had not been observed by the farm laborers who worked beyond the drystone wall. Then he picked up the piece of broken metal and pensively carried it back to the cart. Turning his horse around, he drove slowly back to Sheffield.

Being a Christian of the modern scientific school, he spent the first part of his return journey attempting to estimate the mathematical probability of the shoe of a trotting horse hitting the hind legs of a running rabbit, when horse and rabbit cross each other's path at an angle of ninety degrees. To his regret—unlike Bishop Burrows, who calculated the date of creation by adding together the ages of the Old Testament prophets—he could not produce a precise figure. But by the time he got back to the Heather Works, he had no doubts about either the rabbit's significance or his own obligations. He did not turn the cart into the works yard, but pulled it to a halt outside the gate and shouted for "the lad"—a job and title for which Billy Robinson qualified by reason of advanced age and infirmity—to hold the horse's head. Frederick was inside the factory for less than five minutes. Then, furiously shaking the reins, he drove home with the spades still clattering on the cart floor.

Frederick Hattersley looked forward to getting home and describing his day of tribulation to his wife. Emily would not understand the technical details or the subtleties of the moral dilemma. But she would not interrupt. She would listen with concentrated attention, nodding when the tale was told with particular emphasis, pursing her lips in horror at accounts of her husband's suffering and cooing encouragement on the rare occasions that he paused to await reassurance. As he drove through the gate of number 18 Alderson Road he could hardly wait to unburden his heart. Only his stern sense of duty prevented him from leaving the pony standing in its shafts. He unbuckled the harness and called for Lizzie, the maid of all work, to rub it down. It was the first time that he had thought her capable of protecting his investment against colic. He bounded through the door, ready to begin his adventure story.

Standing in the hall—apparently on the point of leaving—was Winifred Banks, his unmarried sister-in-law. Frederick never looked directly at Winifred. For she enjoyed being looked at so much that he thought it his moral duty to deny her that pleasure. But he listened to her a great deal. She was a woman of many strong opinions. Had he remembered that it was her afternoon to call, he would certainly not have returned home early. To his annoyance, she showed every sign of being genuinely pleased to see him.

"Just on your way?" he asked.

His question was almost justified by Winifred's proximity to the hat stand.

"I was. But now you're here, I'll stay for a bit. It seems ages since I saw you. Come into the parlor and sit down."

Frederick could not imagine any other woman inviting him into his own parlor.

"Is something wrong?"

Emily could not remember the last time that her husband had arrived home from work before half past six.

"Nowt important. I'll tell you after."

Emily was too nervous to wait.

"You're sure? You're not unwell? Have you been to Chapeltown?"

"I'm going next week. I'll tell you all about it later."

"Can I come with you?" Winifred's eyes lit up with delight. "I'm here next week. I'd love the trip out."

"I thought that you were coming to help your sister get that new room ready."

"I am. But it won't take every minute. Emily won't mind my being away for a day, will you, Em?"

Frederick answered for his wife. "I've no doubt that she'd be very happy for you to go. But you can't. It's work."

The irony was lost on Winifred, who assumed that the whole world was as enthusiastic to share her company as she was to see the world. She tried to hypnotize her brother-in-law with her piercing blue stare. It had no perceptible effect.

"Why does work stop me coming? I'd only just sit in the trap."

"It wouldn't be appropriate."

Any other woman, thought Frederick, would regard that as the last word on the subject. And no other woman would be allowed to come to any other conclusion. Winifred, however, was not quite finished.

"You really are the stuffiest man I ever met. But I suppose that there's no changing your mind. I'll corner you next week, though. See if I don't. I've got a dozen things to ask you and two dozen to tell you."

Winifred rose and Frederick performed a host's courtesies to a departing guest with as much grace as he could manage. When the door closed behind her, he gave a great sigh of relief and, returning to the parlor, sank back into the familiar pattern of family life.

Conversation in the Hattersley household rarely deviated from the subjects which Frederick found most interesting. It concentrated on the Heather Works, the chapel choir, the literal truth of the Bible and the history of the Hattersley family. The greatest of these was the history of the Hattersleys, a subject discussed with such indiscriminate nostalgia that the two great-grandfathers—one who had ridden out with John Wesley and the other who had retreated form Corunna in chains after attempting to desert Sir John Moore's rear guard— were spoken of with equal reverence.

Emily knew by heart how her husband had been befriended by a benevolent cutler in the days when the Cutlers Company represented not masters but men. As he progressed from journeyman to employer Frederick abandoned his prejudice against the guild being held together by the mutual interest of property rather than a common respect for skill. But he maintained the conviction that "the Cutlers Company was the only father I ever knew." His eyes always moistened at the thought of his peculiarly industrial parentage.

His real father had died when he was five, a victim of dust which killed most razor grinders before their fortieth birthday. He remembered—or believed that he remembered—a summer afternoon spent at his father's knee, learning about the Arcadian days before the coming of the factories, when Hattersley sheep grazed on the hills of South Yorkshire.

Although Frederick sentimentalized about the old days of rustic peace and rural prosperity, he never pretended that he had the slightest wish to return to the land. He was at home in the heat and grime of his forge, where—as he constantly and rightly claimed—he could do every job better than it was done by any of the men who worked for him. He was, however, never quite sure that others realized the extent of his talent. It was for that reason that he was anxious to explain to his wife how the fault in the spade had been caused by others and—with God's assistance—detected by him.

"I know what happened. It's the new forgeman that Thomas Spooner recommended. I always had my doubts about him."

He spoke of the new forgeman, but he felt much the same about the sleeping partner whose only substantial contribution to the

Heather Works was capital. It was taken for granted at Alderson Road that any able-bodied man who did not earn his daily bread by the sweat of his brow was not to be trusted.

"That new forgeman mistook t'color and skelped it straw when he should have heated it to oatmeal."

He had not yet decided whether the forgeman had been drunk or negligent. But it did not matter. The iron blade had been hammered at the wrong heat.

The conversation moved on to the Work of Providence.

"If that rabbit hadn't come running across t'road, that spade with my name on the handle would have been sold in Chapeltown before I'd found out what he'd been up to. And when it smashed, my reputation would have been smashed with it."

His wife—who was far less stupid than she found it convenient to pretend—was skeptical about the likelihood of God manifesting Himself in the form of a rodent. But if her husband believed that it was all part of the Great Plan—either God's or his own, Frederick could not distinguish between the two—she was prepared to nod in agreement. She was still signifying silent support when she was told that it was time for bed.

They made a slow ascent of the stairs. Emily, who was eight months pregnant, was only able to hoist herself up step by step. Her husband—carrying a candle, a pot mug of water and a piece of cloth (torn from the back of an old shirt) into which he would blow his hay fever throughout the night—followed so impatiently that his wife could feel the heat of the candle against her back. Having reached the safe haven of the bedroom, she rolled underneath the quilted counterpane and Frederick knelt down by the bed and began to give thanks for the Lord's bountiful mercies. He extemporized as he had been taught to do as an aspiring lay preacher at the Calver Street Methodist Chapel, and he identified his quotations as he had learned at the Mechanics' Institute was the habit of scholars.

"O God, who exalts the humble and meek, accept my sincere thanks for Your much appreciated protection. Teach me always to remember that a good name is rather to be chosen than greatness (Proverbs, chapter twenty-two, verse one)."

He prayed aloud and his wife concentrated hard on every word so that she could add her own "Amen" at exactly the right moment. When she had done her duty by her husband, she said a silent prayer of her own.

"Please, God, make this one a boy. Do not let me fail again. Please, God, make this one a boy."

Frederick Hattersley paused for a moment and then invited his wife to join him in another act of worship. Emily clambered slowly out of bed. Kneeling uncomfortably side by side, husband and wife could hardly see each other by the light of the single candle. So Emily was forced to rely on intonation alone to signal that the last prayer had ended.

"O God, help me to understand that he who maketh haste to be rich shall not be innocent (Proverbs, chapter twenty-seven, verse twenty)."

Not being prepared for so short a *nunc dimittis,* Emily was late with her "Amen." But despite her deplorable inattention, she was helped back into bed.

That single act of uncharacteristic kindness did not totally convince her that her husband had developed what her Sunday school teachers used to call the tender virtues. But his behavior over the rabbit had been admirable, and she decided to express her pride about the way in which he had sacrificed time and convenience to put the poor beast out of its misery.

"You did quite right to break the spade," she said, missing the point and contradicting it simultaneously in the way which sometimes made Frederick think that she chose to be obtuse in order to provoke him. She had begun to feel an unusual but genuine warmth toward the stern figure who was about to climb into bed beside her. His compassionate qualities, normally exhibited only to her, should become more widely known.

"Have you told the men at the factory about it?"

"I told the forgeman," her husband reassured her. "I told him when I sacked him."

Next morning, as he drove to work, Frederick Hattersley wondered if he should tell Thomas Spooner that he had sacked the forgeman. It was a brief moment of doubt. The courtesy was, he decided, both unnecessary and, in the immediate future, impossible. For however his partner might pass the day, he would not spend it in the production of spades. Perhaps he would stay at home and practice the violin or, lying on his back in his attic, carefully focus his homemade telescope in preparation for that night's inspection of the stars. In the afternoon he might walk, book in hand, around the arboretum, learning by heart the names and origins of exotic trees. And he would possibly use the early evening to prune the vines that he was attempting to cultivate in his fair imitation of the conservatory which Joseph Paxton had built for the Duke of Devonshire at Chatsworth House. But he would not be in the heat and grime of the forge. Apart from the occasional intervention on behalf of deserving cause or fashionable enthusiasm, he did not concern himself with the day-to-day running of the Heather Works.

Frederick Hattersley despised Thomas Spooner for possessing the capital, though not the character, to found a company. And he thought of him not as a partner but as a willing sacrifice sent by God as the lamb was sent to Abraham—emerging not from a burning bush but from the tenor section of the Handel Oratorio Choir. Sometimes Frederick worried that he took advantage of the innocent. Then he recalled that Abraham did not ignore the Lord's commandment just because the lamb made no objection to having its throat cut. He was, he decided, in partnership not with Thomas Spooner but with the Almighty—who accepted unlimited liability. Frederick would have enjoyed disturbing the life of thoughtless luxury which he believed was common to the residents of Ranmoor. But to ask his partner's opinion was gratuitously to admit that the opinion was of consequence. And that was a concession which he was not willing to make.

In fact, Thomas Spooner was not preparing to spend his day in the self-indulgent luxury which Frederick assumed to be the pattern of his hours. As was his usual habit, he was out and about early. He had begun the work of allocating Latin names to the cacti in his conservatory long before Frederick left home for the Heather Works. But he had barely finished identifying the various species of the genus *Cereus* when his mother appeared and stood amongst the plants as if she anticipated that her son was about to make an announcement of unusual moment.

"Good morning, Mother. You're up early."

Mrs. Thomas Spooner senior did not reply but made a half-turn, rustling her skirt and making the hem fly as she rotated through nearly ninety degrees and back again.

"Is there something wrong?" Thomas asked.

"Not with me. Nothing with me at all."

Her gyrations came to a sudden halt and she stood silent and still, obviously waiting.

"I'll have finished this first job in ten minutes. Then I'll be in to breakfast."

If Thomas had said "Go away," his meaning would not have been more plain. His mother took no notice.

"Are you sure that nothing's wrong?"

"Only that I want you to tell me that I look all right. It's very difficult without a woman to talk to. You're my son and I want to look nice for you—especially on special days."

"Of course you look nice. You always do."

"Then why is it so difficult for you to say so? Why do you want to belittle everything that I do?"

Notwithstanding twenty years of experience, Thomas Spooner was incapable of dealing with his mother's insecurity. He knew that if an emotional spasm was to be averted he must say something quickly. But he had no idea what it should be. His mother filled the vacuum.

"I put it on specially for you."

"What, Mother?"

"The new dress. It's the first time on. When Mrs. Senior saw me wearing it, she said how nice it looked. I'm tall enough to carry it. Not everybody could. Will it do?"

"Do for what, Mother?"

"For the memorial service. Canon Hill's memorial. Surely you haven't forgotten."

"It's not today. It's on Friday."

"It's no good you saying that. I've just looked at the card. It's today at St. John's."

"It's on Friday at St. George's."

"You contradict everything that I say."

"No I don't . . ." Despite his anguish, Thomas almost laughed.

"You treat me as if I was stupid. I've just seen the card with my own eyes. I don't mind if you don't want to come. I'll understand if you have something more important to do. But don't treat me like an idiot."

"It's on Friday, Mother."

Old Mrs. Spooner sniffed and looked away. Her son was not sure which impression she meant to create, the brave struggle against tears or thoughts concentrated on higher things. After some effort she managed to speak.

"Very well. There is no more to be said. But I can have my own thoughts. Nobody can deny me those. I'm only thankful your father's

34

not here to see how I'm treated. If he was here you wouldn't treat me like this."

It's going to be a terrible day, thought Thomas. It would be bad enough if she were right. But when she finds that the service is on Friday . . .

He tried to concentrate his thoughts on the cacti.

When God's partner drove into the yard of the Heather Works, the forgeman was standing, cap in hand, as he had been instructed to do. The rain which had threatened on the previous day was pouring down on all South Yorkshire. In the fields outside Chapeltown, what remained of the uncut barley was flattened against the earth. And in the yard of the Heather Works, the cobblestones were almost invisible under half an inch of flood. The forgeman, Walter Bradley, stood in the downpour, ready for work. His shirt, torn off above the elbows, was sodden, and the old rags, bound around his legs to protect them from the furnace heat, were weighed down with water.

He stood, as respect required, bareheaded. His carefully arranged kiss-curl stuck to his brow, almost covering the scar which ran across the full breadth of his forehead and proclaimed the dangers of hammering hot metal, and his meticulously shaved brindle side-whiskers clung to his cheeks as if they had been painted on his face. But he did not look like a man in despair.

During his sleepless night, Walter Bradley had convinced himself that he had not been sacked at all. He had been told that his work had proved unsatisfactory and that he was no longer in the employ of Hattersley and Spooner. But he had also been ordered to be in the yard at six o'clock sharp on the next morning. At first he could make no sense of the instructions. Then he decided that the master wanted only to frighten him, dress him down and warn him. Then he would be told to get back to his drop hammer. By half past six he would be skelping another pair of spade plates.

Frederick Hattersley neither spoke nor climbed down from the cart, but picked up one of the spades and threw it without a word to the forgeman, who—dropping his cap onto the wet yard—caught it before the paint and varnish were scratched by the cobbles.

"Hit it on the stones."

The forgeman jabbed away at the cobbles. To his relief, nothing happened.

"Hit, I said. Don't tap it. Hit it hard!"

35

n clanged away with the back of the spade. It lost
a few sparks flew. But it did not break.

pade was thrown with greater force than the first. Brad-
Once more he was told to hit it on the cobbles and once
sed the test. So did the third and the fourth—which were
ach thrown to, as at, the forgeman. For a moment, he
thoug. f attempting to disarm his assailant. But he feared that if he
approached him unarmed, he would be chopped down by a spade
wielded like a battle-ax. To face his master, hand to hand and armed
with a spade of his own, was unthinkable. He decided on retreat.

"Come back here. Don't you dare turn your back on me."

Frederick Hattersley had descended onto the cobblestones. Much
to the forgeman's relief, he had left the rest of the spades in the trap.
He waved in their direction.

"Test 'em. Test every one."

"Test them for what, Mr. Hattersley?"

The forgeman squinted through hair which the downpour had
washed over his eyes, and noticed that water was dribbling over the
edge of his master's hard hat like rain out of a broken guttering. He
hoped that the hat was ruined.

"You know full well for what. Don't try to slow-time me."

"I can't test the spades unless I know what I'm looking for."

"Them blades break like butterscotch. You know that and you
know why. You skelped 'em too soon. Didn't bother to wait for the
heat. Slapdash."

"I did no such thing."

"Arguing won't help. Impudence doesn't wash with me."

Frightened though he was, Walter Bradley's mind wandered to his
employer's absurdity. Frederick Hattersley was no more than thirty-
five years old—younger perhaps than the forgeman himself—yet he
behaved like a man of sixty. He stood in his own yard: drenched,
furious and ridiculous, cock on his own muck heap crowing to prove
that he ruled the roost.

"Take every spade out of that wagon and pile 'em in this yard. Hit
every one on them cobbles. You'll pay for every one that smashes.
You can have what's left of your wages, paid up to last night. Then
down the road."

Concerned that he might be regarded as overindulgent, he added
an excuse for his benevolence.

"If it were up to me, you wouldn't get a penny for this week, on account of all the upset you've caused. But Mr. Spooner will want you to get what's left out of your three days' pay."

Walter Bradley had been emboldened by his employer's absurdity. "And when none smash at all?"

Frederick Hattersley had no answer. So he began the bellowing for Billy which was the invariable beginning to a daily pantomime. It continued, as always, with the lad coughing his way across the yard. The gasping, like the related coughing and spitting, was entirely genuine. For Billy was dying of a disease which he, like the rest of Sheffield, called "grinder's asthma." His employment was an act not of charity but of gross sentimentality. Five years before, master and man had both been scissor makers—Fred (who then commanded less respect) had forged the circular bows and Bill (who was not then sufficiently decrepit to qualify for the dismissive diminutive) ground and polished the blades.

Despite the gulf which now divided them, in one particular of dress master and man were still identical. Billy, with bad feet to match his bad chest, always wore secondhand leather boots instead of unyielding wooden-soled clogs. Frederick Hattersley, with almost his whole lifetime spent amongst hot and heavy metal, had never trusted gentlemen's elastic-sided boots. Only at chapel and choir practice did he feel secure without toes and insteps protected by heavy leather. Boot against boot, but towering over Billy, he asked him the question that was the opening line in the pantomime which they performed several times each day.

"Have you swept this yard?"

As was his habit, Billy lied.

"Swept it first thing. All that fash"—he waved a feeble arm toward the steel parings and gobbets of pig iron which littered the cobblestones—"was dropped off a dray ten minutes since."

Frederick Hattersley knew that the yard had not been swept that day, for the fash was tarnished and spattered with overnight rain and Billy had only emerged from the hut in which he lived when he heard the master's horse and cart clatter into the yard. He had hobbled out with his boots unfastened—certain proof that they had only been pulled on when he heard the horse and cart approaching. His eyes were still full of sleep. But the sentimental convention required that the deception should not be challenged.

"Sweep it again. You know what I always say. You can tell the state of a business from the way it keeps its yard."

The pantomime was supposed to end with what was really the purpose of the whole charade, reminiscences about the standards of hygiene and housekeeping which were expected at John Skinner's of Stanley Street, where all the best apprentices served their time. Billy was then required to do no more than remain silent—not revealing by either expression or gesture that Ebenezer Skinner, son of the founder, had gone out of business, bankrupt, earlier that year. However, on the morning of the forgeman's sacking, Billy spoke.

"Can I come t'shop?"

The shop was the cutler's workshop, and at the Heather Works it served as an office. Frederick Hattersley did not hold with regular offices. They incurred rates, encouraged sloth and bred ideas far above their occupants' station. Even the cutler's shop was an extravagance. For the single craftsman who worked in it and justified its name did not pay for its keep. But while the scissor maker kept tapping away at his bench a Hattersley mark could be kept on the register at the Cutlers' Hall. Thomas Spooner's willingness to finance a part of the business which could never make a profit excited his partner's contempt, not gratitude. Spooner himself thought of the unproductive investment as an act of charity, comparable to the subscription that he made to various parish schemes for feeding the poor, housing the elderly and redeeming the fallen—a concession to his partner's insecurity. He also regarded it as a protection against Frederick's developing a sudden ambition to abandon spades and return to scissors.

He knew the real purpose of the cutler's shop. In it the still-unborn Hattersley heirs were to serve their apprenticeship. The dynasty was to be homegrown, trained to make scissors under the eye of the best scissor forger in Sheffield. The fantasy was justified—by both partners —with the pretense that there was some advantage in keeping a registered maker's mark and some saving to be made from using the office of Hattersley and Spooner as a cutler's shop.

The effrontery of Billy's request to use the shop as if he were a buyer from the London to Manchester Railway Company convinced his master that he must have some extraordinary secret to impart. The agreement was still grudging.

"Come on then if you must."

Billy Robinson tried valiantly to keep up with the giant steps which preceded him across the yard. Outside the door of the shop, he paused to regain his breath and clear his throat, first expectorating onto the cobblestone and then grinding the gobbet of spittle into the ground as a sign that he had learned the lesson about neat and tidy yards. His diligence was not rewarded. For he made the mistake of keeping Frederick Hattersley informed about the drama in the yard below.

"He's not broken another yet. Every one's all right, so far."

The news did not improve his master's temper. "Get up here, if you're coming. I've not got all day."

Billy entered the shop, his silent lips moving not in a fight for breath but in a quick rehearsal of the speech which he was about to make.

CHAPTER THREE

AMBITION

It was some time before Frederick Hattersley condescended to notice Billy. For his attention was captured by Jack Foster, the cutler, who sat at his bench staring at a sheet of paper on which he had drawn a close pattern of vertical and horizontal lines. Some of the tiny squares had been filled in with India ink. And it was clear—both from his attitude and from the pen in his hand—that he was anxious to fill in more.

"Let's look."

The paper was snatched from his hand, and the emerging pattern studied at arm's length. At the top was what looked like the twin bowls of a pair of scissors. Further down was the beginning of a coat of arms.

"Rutland?"

"Wortley."

"Wortleys would never pay for a pair like that. And nobody will get up a subscription for t'Wortleys like they did for the Duke of Devonshire. You'll have to wait to 1951 and another Great Exhibition. Then t'Cutlers Company or Parliament will put up a prize and you can win t'competition."

"I could make the Centenary Scissors today. I could make them right here in this shop."

"You might as well, for all t'business we're doing. I can't work out why Mr. Spooner lets me keep you."

Jack Foster spoke to his employer with a reckless familiarity. "He keeps this shop so that he can keep you. He knows you'd be off, if it weren't for t'shop."

"It's not half as daft an idea as thine. What sort of ambition is it to want to make a pair of scissors that looks like a shield held up by a pair of stags?"

Before Jack Foster could reply, Frederick Hattersley answered his own question.

"It's no ambition at all. You know it won't happen. You live in a dream world. All you really want to do is kick a football and back horses."

"I've not placed a bet for five years."

"That's just because your wife won't let you. You've wanted to and that's just as bad. You're not just a gambler. You're a henpecked gambler."

Billy Robinson, just a little late, echoed his master's humorless laughter.

The lad's wheezy crackle of counterfeited humor was intended as a reminder of his presence. But Jack Foster had not finished and Frederick Hattersley seemed surprisingly disposed to listen to what he had to say.

"My ambition is to keep out of trouble. You wouldn't understand that. But there's nowt wrong with it."

"There's nowt wrong with it as long as somebody else does all the worrying. Anyway, making spades is no trouble to me. I wouldn't be happy sitting in that big house in Ranmoor . . ."

Propriety prevented the completion of the sentence. Thomas Spooner was a rich sybarite. But he was also the senior partner. He could not be criticized in front of his own workmen, no matter how much the criticism was deserved. Annoyed that he could not express his feelings, it was natural enough that Frederick Hattersley should turn on Billy.

"What do you want? We've got work to do. At least I have."

"It's about the forgeman."

"What about him?"

41

"He's got a sick wife and four babbies."

"It's none of your business. You sweep the yard and I'll run the factory. Thank you very much."

Billy persisted, believing that he noticed in manner or demeanor the memory that once upon a time they had made scissors in the same hull, fished together on a Saturday afternoon and talked into the night about dreams of a great cutlery company to match Joseph Rodgers and a maker's mark to rival the Star and Maltese Cross.

"You've spoilt work. Everybody spoils work."

"I never tried to palm it off as good. I never gave you a cracked bowl to polish. He tried to cheat me, Billy. If he'd got away with it, I'd have been ruined. It would have been *my* wife and children who went hungry. I sacked him for lying. That's what it were, lying. That's the end to it."

He then added an afterthought. "Are the two of you related?"

After a period of noisy near asphyxiation, Billy insisted that he and the forgeman, far from being kin, had never even met before the new hand was taken on at Hattersley and Spooner. His only concern was justice.

Jack Foster did not concern himself with questions of justice, lest he should come to some conclusion which required action or sacrifice. He was, however, anxious that the day's troubles should not require him to stay at the Heather Works later than was his usual habit.

"Who'll forge t'spades until a new forgeman starts?"

Frederick Hattersley gave his answer with obvious and unashamed excitement.

"I shall."

For weeks he had spent part of each day in front of the furnace, watching the forgeman swing the slabs of hot steel under the skelping hammer. A skelped spade had to be made from the best Sheffield iron, which never cracked or split on the anvil. But once hammered into shape it lasted for a lifetime. Cheaper spades—pressed to the right thickness in a machine which old spade makers thought only suitable for squeezing water out of Monday's washing—were made out of cheap Staffordshire billets.

It was Frederick Hattersley's ambition to forge a blade from the sort of iron that ordinary spade makers would dare only to roll, and then sell "hammered" spades at half the usual price. He had no doubt that the cheap hammered spade was possible and that, if Hattersley and Spooner were the first firm to make one, his fortune and his name would be made. So he hammered Staffordshire iron at every temperature from purple to white. After months of trial and error, he could skelp Staffordshire iron without it cracking or splintering on the anvil. And that, he told the gawping laborers, was a very considerable achievement. The spade blades looked like first-quality forgings, but they remained as brittle as baked clay. They were known derisively in the works as "the mester's experimentations," the fantasies of a scissor maker who thought he knew about forging.

The workers laughed behind their master's back about his unattainable ambition. To his face they were full of praise for the way in which he had so swiftly taught himself to forge spade blades as well as any man in Sheffield.

Now his new skill was to be tested. Until a new forgeman was taken on, he would neglect the jobs which, in the long run, made the difference between solvency and bankruptcy. He would not count the billets as they were unloaded from the ironworks' wagon. Nor would he check the finisher's paint to make sure that he was not cheating the company by thinning it down with turpentine. He would be unable to make surprise raids on the rolling shop, where he knew for certain that the men would lean on their tongs all day if they were not bullied into work. He might not even have a chance to count every spade, rake and hoe that went into the warehouse. His unremitting campaign against the devil and all his doings—or at least those parts of them which might encourage thieving from the Heather Works—would temporarily be suspended. He would not find it easy to behave, for three days, as if he trusted his fellow man. But he would do it. He would show anybody who cared to watch (and several people who were reluctantly forced to take notice) that he could do every job in the Heather Works. He had no more time to waste on Billy.

"Off you go. Back down into the yard."

For a moment, it seemed that the lad was still going to argue, but patience had run out.

"Down those stairs before I kick you down them. And sweep that yard."

Billy left, doubled up with coughing and anxiety. Then, with his hand still on the doorknob and his foot hovering above the top step, he spoke in a stage whisper far more audible than anything that a man dying of grinder's asthma should have been able to produce.

Back in the cutler's shop, with his thought divided between the muscular challenge of forging spade plates and the old delicate art of forging scissors, Frederick Hattersley heard the warning distinctly—as he was intended to hear it.

"When t'tin of gunpowder gets dropped down t'chimney, don't say that tha wasn't warned."

"Billy! Back here. This minute."

The roar could be heard all over the Heather Works. The lad hobbled back into the cutler's shop, affecting surprise.

"What do you know? Tell me, Billy. Tell me plain or you'll be down the road in five minutes."

The lad, leaning on the workbench to recover his breath and composure, noticed a Hattersley family characteristic. The skin began to whiten on his master's knuckles. He decided to gasp out his reply at once.

"I know what happened to Mr. Baxter at Loxley. He had his works blow'd up. And I know what happened to Elijah Parker. His horse was hamstrung in Dore and then he were shot."

"That's ten years since."

Billy began to show disconcerting signs of being more frightened of violent death than he was of his master's displeasure.

"There's been trouble since then. Joseph Helliwell was blinded at t'Tower Grinding Wheel and Mr. Wilson had his house blown up. An' how much rattening 'as there been? You'll be none too happy if you get here tomorrow morning and find all t'tools broke and t'driving belts cut. I'm the one that lives here. I don't want to see my hut smashed and set fire to. I can't do nowt if they come. It'll be no good blaming me."

"Billy, you're a old coward as well as a old fool! The troubles are all but over."

"You say that, Mester Hattersley. But you can't be sure. It's not worth it. Take him back. I'll go down to Shalesmoor to get him."

"You'll do no such thing. There's too much talk in this town about outrages, and arson. It only happens to them that ask for it. And we don't ask for it here. We keep in with them that might cause trouble. I see to that. You're a daft old man. You've coughed yourself senseless. This town has got outrages on the brain. Get about thi' business and let me get on wi' mine."

As Billy turned to go his employer called him back.

"Have you been drinking again?"

"Not a drop, Mester 'attersley. Not a drop since you found the bottle last Whitsun. That bottle you smashed on the coal heap is the last I touched. I swear it."

As the lad at last tottered back to his broom and the cobblestones Frederick Hattersley began to worry. He was not in the slightest concerned about the risk of midnight marauders and the danger of sudden explosion. If he had thought such outrages to be remotely possible, he would have brought a bed into the cutler's shop and waited to break the back of the first intruder to drop over the Heather Works' wall, smiting his enemies as David smote the Philistines.

Only the previous day, God had sent the rabbit to protect him from ridicule. And the Lord—who had spoken to Frederick on the road to Chapeltown as He had spoken to Paul on the road to Damascus—would protect him from his assailants, no matter how mighty their host. But he needed an explanation for Billy's extraordinary behavior. The lad—stone-cold sober—had argued with him about his decision to sack the forgeman. First he had said that the sacking was unfair, then that it could be bad for business and finally that it was dangerous. Billy, having once ground and polished Frederick Hattersley's scissors, was allowed a familiarity denied to other workmen in the company. But even in his days of heavy drinking, he had never taken such liberties. There could be only one possible explanation. Billy was sick.

There seemed no doubt about how the dementia had started. Grinder's asthma had ravaged his body and drink had softened his brain. He was already hallucinating. Soon he would turn violent. The finished work would be damaged by his deranged sabotage. He would put laudanum, or worse, in the tea. The yard would never get swept again.

But, although he would never admit it to anyone (and barely to himself), Frederick Hattersley felt responsible for Billy. In the bad old days of his near bankruptcy, he had been known to borrow a shilling from the old grinder. And since he had begun to prosper he had made sure, in his way, that Billy benefited from his good fortune. First he had converted the old grinder to the Way of the Lord. Then he had weaned him off gin and porter. Finally he had taken him on at the works at a wage only slightly lower than that which he would have been forced to pay to an able-bodied man. Frederick Hattersley was not ready to make his second summary dismissal for the day.

Delay and compromise were usually anathema to a man whose life had been built on a misunderstanding of the injunction to "make straight the way." But in the case of Billy Robinson he would bend, perhaps even break, his usual rule. He would leave the yardman be for the rest of the year. God in His infinite mercy had brought Billy's grinder's asthma to its terminal stage. Perhaps He would relieve his employer of the trouble and responsibility by direct intervention— not with a thunderbolt or plague of locusts (which only the Primitive Methodists expected) but with the sudden massive hemorrhage which usually brought an end to phthisis.

There was always, of course, the risk that agonizing death might not be God's will for the lad. If the Lord was not yet ready to enfold him into Abraham's bosom, His servant, Frederick, would have to accept (with humble and contrite heart) the tribulations which God heaped upon him. He would also have to prepare a contingency plan. If the Almighty did not take Billy by the end of the year, he would be given a guinea and told to leave his hut in the Heather Works forever. Meanwhile he would be watched.

Having thus resolved his moral dilemma, Frederick Hattersley removed his frock coat, rolled up his sleeves, changed his collar and cravat for a cotton handkerchief, tied on a leather apron and strode out of the cutler's shop into the three days of romance that awaited him in the forge.

Billy was put out of his mind. So was his wife's constant failure to produce a son and the likelihood that she would fail again in five weeks' time. Even the injustice of the chapel in denying him election as an elder was temporarily forgotten. Nothing could spoil the adventure which lay ahead. He would stand, steel tongs in hand, in front of the great tilt hammer and he would pull the white-hot billet out of the furnace and swing it under the hammer's head. In the half-light he would turn and tilt the glowing ingot, until it began to look like the shape of a spade. Then, when the job was almost done, he would pour water onto the still-red-hot iron. Steaming and hissing, the skin of scale would peel away, leaving the plates of the perfect hammered spade blade. It was the idea of the iron, glowing in the dark like the Holy Grail, that excited Frederick Hattersley. He was about to begin on three days' hard work. It was what he did best and enjoyed most.

As Frederick left the forge at the end of his long and satisfying day, he noticed with immense pleasure that the gas was still burning in the cutler's shop. He had an audience for his account of his day's achievements. Jack Foster was still at his bench. But he was reading, not working. It was one of his training nights and he had to be at Bramall Lane, the home of the Sheffield Football Club, by seven o'clock. He was desperately anxious not to be delayed. For he prized his football prowess (and his membership in "the Gentleman's Club") above everything except his comfortable home and the unthinking admiration of his wife. It had not always been so. But Jack Foster had also been redeemed by Frederick Hattersley—redeemed from his passion for gambling and his association with a married woman. His redemption—unlike Billy Robinson's—had been genuine. Every Tuesday night he endured pangs of conscience and agonies of regret about sacrificing his family's company for three hours of ball practice and physical jerks. But it was essential to his continued membership in the team, and the Saturday afternoons of glory with Clara and the three boys watching in awe from the touchline. He was not willing to waste a moment of the evening listening to stories of how God had been present in the forge that afternoon and contributed to the record output of perfect spade blades. So as soon as he heard a heavy footstep on the stairs he stood up and started to pack his snap-tin. He was too late.

"I only spoilt one all day. Recognized it straightaway. It wasn't my fault. Just cooled quickly. Only one thrown away all day. Not bad, eh?"

"It'll be better when you get the rolling machine."

"They're not such good spades. Not the quality of them that's forged."

"Everybody's doing it now. Mester Spooner's right."

"I know he's right. I'm not a man to stand in the way of progress. I'll work the mangle and squash out cheap spades. All I'm saying is that when you skelp properly there isn't much waste. And you can recognize them that's brittle!"

Jack Foster was not in the mood to argue, but a nod was not regarded as a satisfactory response.

"I saw it at once. It was all but finished. But I could tell from the strike that it was bad. I threw it out straightaway. Bradley should have done the same!"

The merits of the case were none of Jack Foster's business. He felt sorry for the forgeman. But he did not propose to allow his evening to be spoilt by feelings of pity. As he edged out of the shop he said what was required of him.

"You did right, Master Hattersley. You had to sack him."

Jack Foster sat on the low wall which surrounded the pitch at Bramall Lane. He had limped out of the practice match after half an agonizing hour during which a nail that had worked its way up through the sole of his boot had bored a hole into the underside of his big toe. With his hand inside the boot, he was holding the nail firmly between his forefinger and thumb and was cursing that none of the workmen who had come to the evening's practice had brought their tools with them. When he was convinced that he could not wriggle the nail free, he began to search the wall for a piece of broken brick that he could use to blunt its spike. He had not found one by the time the whistle blew for halftime.

"What's up? Somebody tread on you?"

Jack Foster was in no mood to joke.

"I've got a hole in my foot big enough to put a penny in. Look."

He held his foot in the air to display the patch of blood that soaked his sock.

"You'll not be playing on Saturday."

"I'll be all right as soon as I get this bloody nail out. I've been looking forward to going to Stannington all week. I was ready to tell Master Hattersley that I wasn't going to work this weekend. If I was up to doing that, I'm not likely to let a bleeding tin tack stop me."

There were murmurs of both interest and skepticism. The news that a company was working overtime always caused excitement. The suggestion that Jack Foster had stood out against the wishes of his employer was inevitably treated with derision. Jack Foster had a reputation for being tough as the nails that held his football boots together—except when he came to his dealings with Frederick Hattersley.

"Have you got a big order in?"

"We've not had a big order for scissors since we started. I just make up a few bespoke specials. Mostly presentation work. We've lost our forgeman in the spade shop. I thought he'd try to make me skelp blade plates. But he's doing it himself and as fast as a proper bloody forgeman. Leastways he's done it all day."

"I think you're in love with that Mr. Hattersley. You never have a bad word for him."

"I have a bad word when he deserves it. But I'm just telling you he can skelp bloody spade plates as if he's been doing it all his life. Mind you, he's had a bit of practice."

"What sort?"

"He experiments with cheap steel. Going to make good spades with cheap steel one day."

"Some hopes, silly sod."

"That's what I say." For once Jack was critical of his employer. "But he thinks he will, and nobody'll make him think any different."

"What happened to your proper forgeman? Burned?"

Before Jack could answer, the concern which unites all men who share a common danger prompted half a dozen more questions.

"Is it a man called Bradley? He's had accidents before."

"Was it his fault? Is this a bad one? The poor bugger had a lot of time off."

"Was it his head again? Christ, I feel sorry for the poor sod. I was at Doncaster's when he got hit. He was doing rings then. Core just exploded. You could see his skull under the blood."

"Will he be off long? His wife's got consumption. They need every bleeding penny they can get."

"Is he at home, or did they take him to t'Infirmary?"

Jack Foster cut into the questions—which were really not questions at all but disguised statements of sympathy.

"He were sacked, not hurt."

Anxiety turned to astonishment.

"But you told us how good he were. When your forge took him on, you said he were brilliant."

"You did. You said that he spoilt nowt."

There was silence for a moment as Jack Foster decided whether to defend his original judgment or deny that it had ever been made. He decided upon the path of honor.

"I thought he were at the time, but . . ."

"But what?"

"But he spoilt a spade plate."

"And he were sacked for that? For one spade plate?"

"Not on its own. He tried to pass it off as good. And he argued with Mr. Hattersley."

"It's still not much to get the sack for."

"I know."

Jack Foster sounded guilty, as guilty as if he had sacked the forgeman himself.

"Bet you didn't speak up for him."

The small, swarthy youth who made the metaphorical wager spoke with a passion which astonished the men around him. Jack Foster answered with studied calm.

"No, I didn't, Ted. As well you know, it's not my way. Looking for trouble is not my way."

"I know that all right," said Ted. "Your way is to do what Mr. Hattersley tell you, like you did when he told you to send my sister back to her husband."

"I'm not rowing with you, Ted. We've rowed too much."

The rest of the men gave sighs of relief that the danger of real conflict was averted and mumbled their appreciation of Jack's good sense. Ted's remark, they all agreed, was uncalled for.

Jack Foster said that it was all forgotten about, over, done with. The important thing was not to make a fuss. Things usually righted themselves at the end. As, at last, he dislodged the exposed nail from the inside of his boot he offered his philosophical conclusion on the subject.

"There's nothing to be done about it. In a month or two none of us will remember about poor old Walter Bradley."

About that, Jack Foster was wrong.

CHAPTER FOUR

A BARGAIN

The scene acted out between Frederick Hattersley and his forge-man in the rainswept yard of the Heather Works quickly became the most popular topic of conversation in the places where grinders and forgemen met. The master had shouted, as masters do. But more than a couple of yards away almost all that he said was incomprehensible above the noise of hammers hitting iron, grindstones shaping steel, steam driving pistons and water turning wheels which filled the air over the valley of the river Don. Workmen, watching furtively through the broken windows of the factory, only recognized odd words. Nobody saw or heard all of what happened and everybody exaggerated what they saw and heard.

Some said that the master had run at his employee, swinging a spade around his head like a battle-ax. In the bars of public houses there were expressions of anxiety about the forgeman's wounds and even talk of a collection for his widow.

Reports of the incident delivered to the Cutlers' Hall were more accurate but they received a no less febrile response. The more folk-lore they heard, the more the Bailiffs of the Company wanted to exploit Frederick Hattersley's newfound reputation. Whether or not that reputation was justified did not matter. His reassertion of the owner's right to hire and fire came just at the right moment.

Earlier that year, the Razor Grinders' Protection Society had fought and won a battle to prevent "foreigners" being employed in the industry to perform "country work." The foreigners were British, and the country work was done in Sheffield. But the work was not done by journeymen members of the Society. For weeks, no hammer forged a razor and no grindstone sharpened a blade. Then the employers capitulated, adding humiliation to defeat by paying a "fine" to the Razor Grinders' Protection Society as punishment and apology for employing unskilled labor. The employers were in desperate need of a victory, and Frederick Hattersley had provided one.

In the Cutlers' Hall, John Brown, the Master Cutler, considered with his cronies how the new hero might be rewarded. John Brown was one of the Men of 1860—the steelmakers who had been admitted into the Company when the traditional stream of knife and scissor manufacturers had begun to dry up and subscriptions had, in consequence, begun to evaporate. He suggested that the time had come to accept Frederick Hattersley into membership.

"He's certainly eligible," said the Master.

Joseph Mappin was adamant. "Whatever it says in his advertisements, spades don't have a cutting edge."

John Brown tried again. "His mark is registered. He makes scissors."

Joseph Mappin was still unmoved. "He makes a gross a year, and puts the grinding and polishing out to home workers. Whatever he is, he isn't a Master Manufacturer."

"He makes good spades."

"It's Thomas Spooner who makes the spades." Samuel Osborn had met the sleeping partner at a meeting of the Literary and Philosophical Society.

Charles Cammell was scandalized. "But Thomas Spooner can't become a member of the Company. He is certainly a radical and probably an atheist. He has a degree from London University!"

However eloquently John Brown argued that they should reward Frederick Hattersley, the majority against formal recognition was solid. The new men—prophets of mass production and apostles of heavy industry—had spent years changing the statutes of the Cutlers Company. Now that its charter accepted their membership, they would not contemplate the slightest deviation from the rules. They had become the new establishment. They had burrowed their way inside, and they were determined that other outsiders should not be admitted.

"Are they good spades?" Samuel Osborn's interest was mostly commercial. He would like to reward the paragon. If he could do it in a way which was to his own financial advantage, he would be doubly pleased.

"They are very good." Charles Cammell seemed to concede their quality with regret.

"He sells hammered, ridged and treated for less than Bedford's or Haywood's. Forty shillings a dozen for the biggest. Christopher Johnson showed me one last Monday. Johnson's very worried. His are no better—and they costs a shilling a dozen more."

"Well, then." John Brown decided to reestablish his control over the meeting. "It's obvious what we do. We buy his spades."

"And we let people know why we buy them." Joseph Mappin had a flair for publicity.

"That's right," said Samuel Osborn. "The Cutlers Company helps God to help them that help themselves."

They all laughed uneasily at his profanity. But it was agreed that those with spades to buy would favor Hattersley and Spooner and that, whenever their reputation as shrewd businessmen allowed, they would whisper the explanation that it was style of management as much as quality of forging that prompted their purchase.

Samuel Osborn, Joseph Mappin, John Brown and Charles Cammell represented the power, wealth and influence of modern Sheffield. It was an age of industrial expansion and civic development. And it seemed that the foundations of modern Sheffield were to be dug with Hattersley and Spooner spades. Suddenly half the city were the company's customers. The new forgeman was persuaded by bullying and bribery to work a fourteen-hour day. Thomas Spooner talked of buying a second skelping hammer if demand kept up throughout the winter.

Indeed, he talked of a good deal more. To him the spade business had always been a crusade as well as a commercial opportunity. He wanted to meet the needs of families who, having been driven from the land, longed to grow flowers and vegetables on any patch of land which they could rent or lease. He was a disciple of William Cobbett and believed that England had been merry before the factories came. He hoped to make it happy again by planting cabbage patches and herb gardens between the rows of terraces, behind the back-to-back houses and around the privies, pumps and middens in the communal backyards. The great industrialists were not his ideal customers. But he hoped that success with them might provide new opportunities for his enlightened ideas to be expanded into enlightened enterprise. Enlightened was what Thomas Spooner most wanted to be.

Frederick Hattersley saw the new success quite differently. He had no patience with his partner's plan to build a new world around marigolds, sweet peas and hollyhocks. He was not a spade maker by inclination. But spades—with a little assistance from rakes and hoes —would help him fulfill all his ambition. Through spades he would become a justice of the peace, a chapel elder, the Secretary of the Choral Society and a freeman of the Cutlers Company. Thanks to spades he had escaped from William Shirtcliffe's Central Works in Bailey Lane, where he had rented a dingy room in a desperate and impecunious attempt to be his own master. Spades had taken him out of scissor making and they would take him back in style and allow him to found the great cutlery company which was still the center-piece of his elaborate ambition. But, for the time being, since he must make spades, he would make the best spades in Sheffield. He would make spades he could boast about at choir practice, spades which convinced him that he had won the spade-making prize for which he competed in his mind each day.

The only obstacle in the path of his short-term ambition was his partner, whose enlightened views of working conditions often inhib-ited the pursuit of quality and profit. The receipt of a note from Thomas Spooner warning of a visitation to the Heather Works that afternoon, "to discuss my new ideas," was, therefore, read with deep foreboding. The new ideas were even more absurd than the notion of rebuilding Arcadia in the backyards of the Wicker and Shalesmoor.

"Did Billy Robinson ever use a Grinder's Life Preserver?"

The opening question confirmed that the conversation would be detached from reality.

"Never when I saw him grind. He couldn't make a living with one of them things hanging around his neck. Nobody could."

"So he just swallowed the dust?"

"Everybody did. He knew what he was doing. His father was a razor grinder. Died at thirty. He knew about grinder's asthma before he was apprenticed. It was his choice."

Thomas Spooner sat down, a sure sign to his partner that he was going to "preach one of his sermons."

"You raise the most profound philosophical questions," he said. "Questions which I would very much enjoy discussing with you," adding, to his partner's relief, "at some future time. But, for now, I want to talk about more practical matters."

He pulled at the knees of his fashionable sponge-bag trousers to make sure that they remained in the shape which his tailor had designed, moistened a finger in order to remove a spot of mud from the toe of his left shoe and stared Frederick Hattersley in the eye.

"Sooner or later, the Factory Acts are going to cover forging and grinding. The sooner the better. I've promised that we'll help to get the idea going. I've promised Dr. Holland—"

Frederick Hattersley was appalled.

"Calvert Holland will ruin all of Sheffield and I'm not going to let him ruin us first. We can't afford fans and funnels and all the other daft paraphernalia. I must tell you, Mr. Spooner, I will not do it. I will not drive this company into the bankruptcy court."

Foolishly Thomas Spooner decided to reason with his partner. "Frederick, have you read Dr. Holland's report?"

"Indeed I have, Mr. Spooner. That's what worries me. What he says should be done, can't be done. But once a grinder reads that book, he begins to demand what no master can afford. Forgemen will do just the same. I'd sack any man I found reading anything by Calvert Holland. Thank God the unions have no sense. If they began to frighten the men with all those facts and figures, we'd be done for. If they began to preach about dust, they could ruin us all in a year. Now you want to ruin us yourself. I'll not be party to it."

"Frederick, I have given my word."

"You've not given mine. And t'Heather Works won't make spades without me. You won't get your skelping done by the Society for Bettering the Conditions of the Poor."

"I'm not going to argue with you about it now. Come to supper at Ranmoor and talk to my friend Dr. Hall. You'll like him. He's not a zealot like Dr. Holland. He's a young man like you." There was a discernible pause before he added, "He has new ideas. He keeps an eye on my little heart problem. At least promise me you'll come and talk to him."

Frederick Hattersley ungraciously agreed.

"Come this week and bring Emily. Dr. Hall's got some very interesting ideas on childbirth. He says that a doctor ought to be at every birth and that most midwives do more harm than good. I'll ask him to look after Emily when her time comes. I'll pay his bill."

He knew the sort of reply to expect, when Frederick Hattersley stood up.

"Mr. Spooner, thanks to your money you may be able to tell me how to run this works, even though thou knows nowt about rolling and skelping. But you will not tell me how to run my family. My wife's health is nobody's business but mine. And the baby that's coming is nobody's business but mine. I will thank you not to interfere with things which are none of your concern."

So Emily, free from the impertinent attentions of a doctor, gave birth to her fifth child. The previous four—only two of whom survived the trauma of entering Frederick Hattersley's family—had been girls. Mary and Martha were as pretty and as timid as their mother and they seemed, despite their infancy, to live a life of constant apology for failing in their duty to be boys. Their father loved and admired them as he loved and admired the pieces of expensive furniture with which he had gradually stuffed the house. It was almost impossible to walk around his drawing room without bumping into mahogany, oak and inlaid rosewood. But now Frederick Hattersley needed no more tables or chairs. And he needed no more daughters. In the weeks before the fifth baby was due, he began to pray openly for the blessing of a son. If Emily resented his obsession she never spoke of it. She simply prayed the same prayer in silence. She knew that she had failed to perform a wife's first duty. Her only concern was to right the wrong she had done her husband.

When Emily knew that her time had come, she woke her husband with diffidence and difficulty from his usual deep sleep. But, once awake, he assumed complete command. From the bottom of the attic stairs he bellowed for Lizzie—the fourteen-year-old maid of all work.

"Come down here this minute and keep an eye on the missus." When their sudden crying confirmed that he had woken Mary and Martha, he added, "And try to get those girls back to sleep."

Lizzie stumbled downstairs, cold and shivering under an ancient nightdress and tattered shawl.

"There's nowt to be frightened of. Mrs. Armitage will be here in ten minutes."

Mrs. Armitage was, by the standards of her trade, unusually progressive. She had absolute faith in what she called "soap and water," although her conviction extended to every sort of hygiene. She had absolute confidence in her ability to deliver, live and unmaimed, every infant who was capable of emerging, whole and healthy, into her scrubbed red hands. Her record confirmed her competence. Four out of every five babies that she delivered were born alive. Mrs. Armitage worked best when untroubled by the expectant father. It was therefore with some concern that she discovered that Frederick Hattersley did not propose to visit his place of work during the day of his wife's labor.

He had explained his intention in the horse and trap as he brought the midwife back to 18 Alderson Road. The labor pains had started several days too soon and at a time which he found highly inconvenient. The slater was due that morning to patch the roof, and the slater must come and do his work while Mrs. Armitage did hers. When he said that he would stay at home to see that the job was properly done, the midwife hoped that he spoke of the leaking roof. To her relief, she was led to the bedroom door and left, with proper modesty, to enter alone.

"I shall be in the parlor when you have something to tell me."

In the parlor's darkest corner there stood a great walnut grandfather clock. Its face, decorated with scenes from pastoral life, proudly boasted its origins at Manoah Rhodes and Sons, Clockmaker of Bradford.

He turned the brass finger below its face from "Chime Two" to "Chime Eight." So noon was heralded by a peal of bells. But the baby had not arrived. For the next hour the gold sovereign that he meant to give the midwife tarnished in the sweat of his palm. He stared out of the bay window down the windswept hill that led to the city. At two o'clock he shouted for Lizzie and demanded more bread and cheese. Anxiety made him hungry. With his mouth still stuffed full, he knelt by the horsehair sofa that stood against the wall under Emily's embroidered sampler. "Emily Banks," the stitched words read, "aged seven. This is her work. God is Love."

"Please, God," he prayed, "make it a boy."

He was still on his knees when the midwife opened the door. She did not knock or wait for him to invite her into the parlor. He knew from her manner that his prayer had not been granted.

"It was a boy, Mr. Hattersley. But the little fellow's dead. He fought like a tiger. But the breath just wasn't there."

Frederick Hattersley stayed still and silent as a marble knight kneeling at the foot of a crusader's tomb. Then he rose and walked to the back of the parlor. As if he had not even heard the midwife speak, he turned the brass finger on the grandfather clock to "Chime Silent." The midwife answered the question which she thought he should have asked.

"Your wife's very well. She's weak but very well. Come up and see them both."

Receiving no reply, Mrs. Armitage climbed wearily back to her charge in the front bedroom.

It was almost an hour before Frederick Hattersley knocked on the door. Emily had fallen into so deep a sleep that the sound of neither her husband's knuckles nor his boots could waken her. The dead baby lay beside her—purple, but no more purple than newborn babies usually are, and wrinkled, but no more wrinkled than dozens of infants who have survived to enjoy long life and happiness. It would have been easy enough to believe that it was still alive. Its huge head lay against the pillow with its watery-blue eyes still half open.

"Do you want me to dispose of it?"

Mrs. Armitage had done the job a hundred times before.

"I do not. He will be buried next to his grandfather." Frederick Hattersley emphasized the personal pronoun.

"It's not usual."

"Maybe not. But I doubt if the chapel will deny me."

"Shall I take him away before his mother wakes?"

Frederick was relieved that Mrs. Armitage had, at last, realized that his dead son had been a human being. "The undertaker will do that."

"The undertaker?"

Mrs. Armitage was whispering in the hope that she would not waken Emily. Frederick did his best to follow suit.

"Be so kind, my good woman, not to question everything that I say in my own house about my own son. If you come down into the parlor, I will pay you and you can be on your way."

Downstairs in the hall, Emily's sister Winifred Banks had just arrived from Doncaster. She stood, as was her habit, against the light, and took off her coat and bonnet in a way which ensured that her long blond hair cascaded down her back. She was at the height of her infatuation with the Pre-Raphaelite movement and correctly imagined herself to resemble the Lady of Shallot—though she had never even seen a reflection of Sir Lancelot. She had arrived to assist during her sister's confinement. But she had arrived late.

Winifred Banks wore a skirt loose enough to allow her to sit or walk upstairs easily and at will. Her sleeves were both puffed and slashed in the style of the Renaissance—which she wrongly believed to be the style of the fourteenth century. She thought of herself as the aesthetic Pre-Raphaelite woman, as nobly aquiline as Jane Morris or Lizzie Siddall. Her brother-in-law, who had never even heard of Raphael, stared coldly at what he regarded as a wholly inappropriate dress for such a solemn occasion.

"I've heard. Lizzie told me as I came in. She says that Emily is well enough."

"She is. And she'll be pleased to see you."

How could she, Frederick wondered, have come on such a day in such a getup? She could not have known that she was coming to a house of mourning. But she was well enough aware that her sister might have given birth to the family's son and heir. Yet she was dressed like a pantomime fairy. She should have shown proper respect—not for the death which it would have been wicked to anticipate but for the birth for which they had all so fervently hoped.

"Can I go and see her now?"

"The midwife is with her now. But she's about to go. Ten minutes. No more."

Winifred advanced up the stairs.

"How are you?"

"I'm well enough."

"You say that. But I know better. Frederick, I'm so sorry."

"I'm grateful. But it's God's will. It's not for us to question these things."

"I question them."

"Not to me, if you please."

Before Winifred could say that Frederick need not hide his feelings to her, Mrs. Armitage appeared out of the bedroom door. She carried, under one arm, a bundle wrapped in an old newspaper and tied with rough hemp cord.

If Frederick had caught her with his pocket watch hidden inside her muff, he would not have made a more obvious accusation. He put his hand on her shoulder and asked, "What's that? That in there?" He seemed about to tear the bundle open.

"It's the stained sheets and the afterbirth. I'm taking them home to burn. It's quite usual."

Frederick pushed the sovereign into the midwife's hand and opened the door, careful not to look at her or the bundle.

Winifred Banks took him by the hand.

"Come and sit down in the parlor. Come and sit down with me until Emily wakes up."

She was convinced that buried deep inside that great frame there was a human being. She spent a great deal of time thinking about defeating the demon that lived inside him and almost as much worrying about why she was so anxious to bring out what she told her sister was his true nature. She always came to the conclusion that she liked him. Then she remembered that her feelings were of no particular significance. She liked everyone.

There were difficulties about the funeral. The Reverend Horace Beardsley of the Calver Street Methodist Chapel was uncertain about the words which it was proper to speak over the coffin of an unbaptized infant. And the sexton at the Psalter Lane cemetery was not sure what entry he should make in his ledger for a "Male. Stillborn" who did not even need a birth or death certificate to send him on his final journey. The monumental mason had been particularly obstructive. He had gladly agreed to provide a stone slab to top the grass mound which had previously marked the Hattersley grave. But he resisted the idea of carving Frederick's chosen inscription into the black granite. He had read a book on Michelangelo which explained that sculpture and philosophy were related disciplines.

"Has the body in question really got a Christian name?" he asked. "For it was not christened and it had no birth certificate."

"Your job is to carve the stone."

Frederick Hattersley handed him two shillings wrapped in a piece of paper on which was written: "Also Frederick his dearly beloved grandson."

"How can that be?" inquired the stonemason, peering at the paper. "The grandfather died twenty years before the grandson was born. How could he have dearly beloved something he never even saw?"

Frederick Hattersley snatched the paper back and changed the message to "and Frederick his grandson, dearly beloved son of Frederick Joseph and Emily Hattersley."

The mason counted the letters and said that the extra work would cost a shilling more. The bargain was struck.

"Leave some space above his name," said the chief mourner. "Leave some space for his mother and me."

The undertaker and Frederick Hattersley agreed that a hearse—with sable horses, black plumes and accompanying mutes—would be unsuitable. So a hansom cab was hired. The father sat on the back seat, with the tiny oak coffin across his knees. There were no other mourners. Emily was adjudged too ill and Martha and Mary too young to stand in the cold churchyard.

Winifred had wanted to travel with her brother-in-law and stand, to the end, at the graveside. But she decided that propriety required her to stay at home and look after the family. She urged Frederick to prepare himself for his cold ordeal with a glass of medicinal whiskey. He declined but he declined gently. Thomas Spooner had asked to be allowed to pay his last respects but had been refused permission, with a logical but offensive comment which was based on the stonemason's philosophical quibbling.

"Since you never met him, how can you do anything for the last time?"

Various neighbors, members of the Calver Street congregation and colleagues from the Oratorio Choir had also asked about the time and place of the interment. They were all rebuffed. Father was burying son. It was no one else's business.

The solitary mourner climbed down from the hansom cab with the coffin in his arms and, carrying it before him as a shepherd might carry a lost sheep, strode through the Doric columns of the cemetery's top gate, the gate—with not quite Christian engravings on its lintel—which had been cut into the churchyard wall for the use of dissenters. The place at which the wall had been breached was intended to remind Nonconformists of their relationship to heaven. They had to approach the funeral chapel by a long and winding route. Frederick walked along the moss-covered path between the broken columns and weeping angels, past the sculptured urns and the granite crosses. Beyond the marble doors which opened into catacombs, the cemetery was overgrown and forgotten. He pushed his way through the withered rosebay willow herb and the Queen Anne's lace that had turned autumn brown. His black frock coat caught on brambles, and his boots squelched through fallen leaves that had not been swept away. The rotting undergrowth gave off a special sweet churchyard smell— decaying petals from ancient wreaths, green-slimed water in the abandoned flower vases and the dead wildflowers which nobody had dared to pick. He noticed scarlet bunches of belladonna shining against the dark green leaves of a cypress bush, and a thousand shriveled blackberries which had escaped both boys and birds only to die on the tangled brambles. Then he came to the clearing which, the previous day, he had cut around his father's grave.

Slowly, with the help of the doddering verger, he lowered his son into the damp earth while the Reverend Horace Beardsley spoke of bringing nothing into this life and taking nothing away. Frederick threw a handful of moist clay into the grave and turned his back on his firstborn son forever. It was then that he noticed that the senile verger was leaning on a Hattersley and Spooner "Hammered, Ridged and Tested Best Iron Spade with Guaranteed Two-Inch Best Steel Cutting Edge retail price forty shillings a dozen."

The verger did not realize that his life was in danger until he felt himself being lifted off his feet by demonic hands which held him by the worn collar of his shabby coat.

"Where did you get it?"

The verger could not doubt what his assailant meant. For the spade had been snatched from his feeble hands and its blade was being wiped with the piece of cloth which had been torn from his collar.

"I bought it."

"You're a liar."

"I bought it in the Hen and Chickens in Exchange Street."

"In a public house!"

The Reverend Horace Beardsley, who had accepted the assault and the accusation of theft with pious equanimity, was horrified to hear where the verger spent his spare time. Frederick was concerned with sterner matters.

"How much did you pay?"

"I gave him two shillings when I bought it and I owe him another sixpence."

"You got a bargain. Who did you buy it off?"

"A drunken old grinder called Billy Robinson."

"Well, I'm buying it off you—for its proper value."

Frederick Hattersley reached under his long black topcoat into his trouser pocket for the purse in which he kept his change. Carefully he counted out three shillings and tenpence.

"The spade's worth three and fourpence, and there's sixpence to have your coat mended."

Frederick Hattersley's return from the funeral to the Heather Works became almost as famous in local folklore as his confrontation with the forgeman. Eyewitnesses inside and outside the yard gate described how he stepped down from the hansom cab still carrying the spade with which he had buried his son. He looked, they said, like a man possessed by demons, and they attributed his hollow, staring eyes and twitching cheeks to a father's uncontrollable grief. He stood for a moment on the cobblestones, deep in thought. Then silently he walked to the shed in which Billy Robinson lived. The more sentimental onlookers, who knew that he and Billy had worked together when they were young, had no doubt of his intentions.

"He's going to see his old friend. Straight to see his old friend, still carrying the spade that laid his son to rest."

He had to bend to get through the hut door. Even inside he could not stand erect. Billy, sitting on the pile of rags he called his bed, and drinking from a green glass bottle, could not at first believe that the huge figure who shrugged and struggled through his doorway was the master. Then, even in the half-light of the hut, he recognized the spade—the spade with part of the handle broken. Billy had torn it away to convince the old man in the Hen and Chickens that it was a reject from the Heather Works, picked up (as was a lad's right) from the pile of broken iron at the back of the yard.

"How did you do it, Billy? That's what I want to know first. How did you do it? How did you get it out of the yard?"

"I took it out late at night, Mester Hattersley, and hid it in the bushes on t'canal bank by Dixons. Then I got it back next day and took it to this old chap who said he wanted a good spade."

"Why didn't we miss it? We count what we've got often enough."

"I swapped it."

Billy, reconciled to the sack and already preparing himself for the long walk to Lodge Moor Workhouse, was ready to confess everything.

"I swapped it with one of your experimentations. There were one,

Mester Hattersley, what looked so good that you nailed an 'andle on it and painted it. You said let it stand for a week and then try digging wi' it. Do you remember?"

Frederick remembered only too well. It had been the first of his experimentations which seemed like a success. He had skelped it while hot and said that there was to be no water on it from start to finish. For days he hoped that he had hammered a good blade from cheap steel. Then cracks had started to show around the nail holes.

"It looked just like a good 'un." Billy sounded as if he were attempting to be reassuring. "So I put it in your cart and took a good 'un out."

The horror which had engulfed Frederick Hattersley on the road to Chapeltown suddenly washed over him again. Somewhere, hanging in an ironmonger's shop, was a spade with a blade as fragile as glass. On its handle it proclaimed that it had been made by Hattersley and Spooner. He had no doubt that the spade had not yet struck earth or clay. If it had been sold as part of the gross that Samuel Osborn bought, it would have been used already. The Board of Guardians would have put their six dozen into the hands of able-bodied paupers on the day after they were delivered. If it had been used, the runt would have broken already. And if it had broken, a dozen loving friends—not to mention the aggrieved customer—would have told him about it by now. There was, therefore, a faint hope of getting it back into the privacy of the works—if Billy could remember the batch in which he made the swap.

Assuming that the lad could be frightened into clear thought, he forced him back onto the bed and, leaning down, pushed his great face as close to Billy's hollow cheeks.

"I want it back. I want it back for my reputation's sake and the reputation of this firm. I want it back before it smashes. Think hard, where did it go?"

"It's smashed already."

"If it was, I would know about it. I'm sick and tired of your lies, Billy. If you don't tell me where it went, I'll thrash it out of you!"

"It went to Chapeltown, Mester Hattersley, and you broke it on that rabbit—"

The sentence was never finished. It was not a heavy blow, but the blood ran slowly from the corner of Billy's mouth and down his dirty unshaved jaw as his assailant thought of the implications of the revelation. For months Frederick Hattersley had bathed in the glory of his ruthless refusal to tolerate poor work. The Lord Mayor had called him a credit to the town, and the Master Cutler himself had written to congratulate him on standing no nonsense. But the mistake was his and the forgeman was innocent. As soon as the story was known he would be ruined.

Billy, the blood still dripping from his chin, was bundling together his few possessions.

"What are you doing now, you old fool?"

"I'm on m'way, Mester Hattersley. I want to be in Lodge Moor before dark."

"You're going nowhere."

Fumbling in his coat pocket, Frederick took out a sovereign, looked at it and then put it back. When he found a florin, he gave it to Billy.

"There's a job for you here for the rest of your life. And you can keep this hut—sick or well, drunk or sober. But there's one condition."

Billy nodded without waiting to hear what it was.

"You never tell anybody what you've told me today."

Billy was garrulous with gin and relief. "I never thought you'd find out. Not after you sacked the forgeman. He's been on my conscience all these weeks. That's why I tried to stop you sacking him. What will you do about him now? He's still not got a job."

Billy was pushed back onto his bed in the hope that a winding and shaking would concentrate his mind.

"I've told you, Billy. You remember or you're out. The forgeman is a liar. He tried to pass off bad work as good. The truth was not in him. He deserved sacking and he stays sacked. You stay in a job as long as you keep your bargain with me."

CHAPTER FIVE

GETTING ON

The bargain was honored for more than two years. Then, after several months in which the yard was rarely swept, Billy Robinson finally discharged his obligations in full. The end did not come with the sudden and spectacular hemorrhage which Frederick Hattersley had hoped God, in His infinite mercy, would provide. Billy was found one Monday morning, lying on the pile of rags which he called his bed. A half-empty gin bottle was clutched in one dead hand.

The relative comfort in which the yard laborer had spent his last days was observed with a mixture of envy and astonishment by other employees of the Heather Works. At the Calver Street Methodist Chapel, where God was stern and unforgiving, they had no doubt that Billy was headed straight for an ingrate's hell. Thomas Spooner—who regarded himself as a moral philosopher as well as an engineer, zoologist, architect, botanist, astronomer and anthropologist—carefully considered the ethical implications of his partner's charity. Frederick's benevolence toward Billy Robinson solved a second moral dilemma just at the moment when he might have been forced to make the sort of difficult choice he was always desperate to avoid. When he had been told that Frederick Hattersley had beaten a forgeman with a broken spade in front of the Heather Works' employees, he had almost closed the factory there and then. But Billy's benefaction had come as a sign of grace. So for two years Thomas tried to hope that the partners could become friends.

They had been eventful years for Sheffield. A Royal Commission had inquired into the "outrages" and concluded that while some men had been intimidated and some masters had been assaulted, it had happened only rarely and was not likely to happen again. The Factory Acts had been extended to cover forging and grinding, and Thomas Spooner's enlightened notions were no longer the exclusive preserve of radical debating societies. A million working men were enfranchised by the Great Reform Bill, and trades unions met openly in Manchester for what they called "a congress."

The Heather Works expanded, prospered and expanded again while its managing partner's family grew at a less rapid rate. Emily gave birth each year. Two more babies were girls. Neither survived. At the Calver Street Methodist Chapel, it was generally agreed that a continued pattern of yearly pregnancies would leave Frederick a widower with two daughters to bring up on his own. There was universal amazement that he showed no sign of noticing that his wife was not the pink and gold girl he had married within weeks of his escape from the penury of scissor grinding into the Heather Works.

His myopia became all the more amazing after Winifred Banks moved from Doncaster and took up residence in Sheffield to be near her sister Emily. Winifred looked exactly as her sister had looked before five still and two live births. And it seemed impossible that her brother-in-law did not see in her the specter of the young wife he had married. But all he noticed was the difference in their characters —a difference as marked as their appearance had once been similar. Emily offered opinions only on cooking and sewing and child rearing. Winifred had an opinion on every subject. That, the elders of the chapel had no doubt, would be the cause of her undoing. They defined failure as remaining into old age what they tastefully described as "a maiden lady."

Winifred herself seemed wholly satisfied with a life devoted to watercolors, charcoal sketches and a conversational technique which was shocking in its boldness and awe-inspiring in the breadth of knowledge on which it was based. The only cloud in her sky was the state of her sister's health, about which she approached her brother-in-law with brash self-assurance. Her confidence was based on a belief that Frederick would accept from her intrusions and impertinence that he would tolerate from no one else.

"What are we going to do about Emily?"

"What are we going to do? Do about what?"

"Haven't you noticed how poorly she looks? You *must* have noticed."

"I've noticed her looking a bit pale. But that's nothing new."

"It's not the same as usual. She gets tired and she gets bad-tempered. That's not like her."

"She ought to see a doctor."

"If you think that a bottle of tonic will set her up like new, you'd better tell her."

Emily was not consulted about whether or not she thought medical advice necessary, or asked if she wanted to become again the girl of twenty her husband had met and married. Nor did she expect to make such decisions for herself. Such profound considerations were none of her concern. She was told that she should see a doctor, and she prepared herself for the examination because it was her husband's will. Winifred wanted her sister to walk around to Dr. Roberts's consulting rooms. But Frederick believed that tradesmen ought to call at the house. So Emily was examined in her own bedroom. She refused to allow Winifred to witness the examination and gave no hint of its outcome until the doctor had ponderously collected his hat and gloves from the hallstand and made an agonizingly slow and scrupulously courteous exit. Even then Winifred had to ask an impatient question.

"Well then, what did he say?"

"He says that there's nothing really wrong with me."

"Nothing really wrong with you?"

"It's just the babies. I'm short of iron. Frederick was right, he's given me a bottle of iron tonic."

"And what about more babies?" Winifred was a disciple of Mrs. Elizabeth Garrett Anderson.

"What about them?" Emily (who had heard of both the reformer and her radical ideas, but thought it best to feign ignorance) looked blank. She hoped to give the impression that she took it for granted that babies, like Christmas, came once a year.

"Two's enough," said Winifred, "at least for a while. You've got to tell Frederick that there mustn't be any more, at least for a while."

Emily was scandalized. "I shall do no such thing and it's shameful that you should suggest it. I'm his wife. I would never talk to him about such things."

Winifred sighed loudly enough to emphasize her frustration.

"And it's no good behaving like that. If you've got something to say, say it. But don't make noises. Best of all, say nothing."

Winifred was delighted that she had provoked her sister to such passion. She knew that, by nature, Emily was not the timid creature that Frederick dominated. In her husband's presence, Emily assumed a persona which Winifred believed to be pure invention. She did not realize that the fact of Frederick's immense presence changed his wife's character and made her genuinely, if only temporarily, timid and therefore astonished by the bold way in which he was treated by his sister-in-law.

Winifred talked to Frederick about men's subjects, but she did not talk about them as if she were a man. When they discussed serious topics, Winifred answered her brother-in-law's arguments with affectionate mockery which reminded Emily of her carefree youth. Frivolous girls of her acquaintance had gossiped in the same manner to young men who came to call. But the talk in those Doncaster soirées concerned who had danced with whom at balls in the assembly rooms and whose carriage was most smartly turned out at the race meeting—the sort of subjects which Winifred would never discuss. She despised dancing and disapproved of racing. Her conversation concerned extraordinary radical notions like compulsory education, the admission of Jews and dissenters to the universities and entry into the civil service by examination rather than patronage. All these topics she discussed with a vivacity which other women employed in conversation with eligible bachelors, promising provocatively that these things would come to pass, when the Liberal Party was no longer led by Lord John Russell. Emily sometimes worried about Winifred's facetious tone and familiar manner. Then she realized that it was not possible to flirt while discussing Mr. William Ewart Gladstone.

The arguments which—thanks to the visits of Winifred—went on across the Hattersleys' dinner table were not as incomprehensible to Emily as the casual observer might have believed. Winifred was a clever woman who flaunted her cleverness. Her sister, though less intelligent, was far from stupid. She had decided that it was best to play the part of dull wife and even duller mother. And she played the part with such determination that sometimes she convinced herself that the role was a reality.

Emily felt a terrible dread of Winifred discussing her health and maternal prospects with Frederick. The more she considered the idea of such a conversation, the more horrified she felt. It was an intrusion into her private life. It defiled the sanctity of her marriage. It would cause trouble. So she decided to use the one weapon which would certainly prevent Winifred from talking to Frederick about a subject that husband and wife had never discussed in nine years of marriage. She had meant to keep the secret for another month or more.

"It's too late. There's another baby coming in the spring."

In Ranmoor, April spread slowly between the great houses. Over the horizon were the hills of Derbyshire and beyond Baslow and Bakewell, the Pennines themselves. So the spring winds which blew over Sheffield from the west carried the chill of the last snow that huddled into hollows in the millstone grit and hid in the caves and crevices cut into the limestone by summer rain. Along the steep garden paths which ran up from the roads to the leaded and mullioned front doors, the crocuses bloomed late. And on the grass terraces that ran down from drawing-room windows to tennis courts and croquet lawns, the daffodils were still only in bud. At Riverdale Grange, only the figs and the pomegranates in the conservatory were progressing at the speed which the horticultural textbooks regarded as appropriate to spring. Thomas Spooner therefore decided to spend April indoors, studying the principles, rather than engaging in the practice of gardening. Having talked for over a year about Mr. Charles Darwin's latest work, he decided that the time had come to read it. Once he had ordered *Variation of Plants and Animals Under Domestication,* he awaited its arrival with childlike impatience. At times when postal deliveries were expected, he took up a position in the gallery above the reception hall and gazed over the privet and cypress bushes for the first sign of the familiar uniformed figure toiling up the path.

Thomas felt no need to hide his enthusiasms. So when, after almost a week of frustration, he saw the postman approaching with the lunchtime delivery and noticed a large parcel lying on the top of the canvas letter bag, he rushed downstairs and flung the door open before the bell was even rung. The parcel contained a pattern book sent to his mother by her London milliner. For him there was only a letter. It had been posted at half past six that morning and it bore the instantly recognizable copperplate script of Frederick Hattersley. Thomas could not recall his partner ever having written to him before, and the novelty of the event almost made up for his disappointment that his book had not arrived. The message inside the heavy white envelope drove all thought of Charles Darwin out of his mind. The note was cryptic to the point of mystery and Thomas found mystery exciting.

> Certain matters pertaining to the future of the Heather Works have become so pressing that it is essential that I see you at once. I therefore propose to presume upon our partnership by calling on you at your residence this afternoon. I have, Mr. Spooner, the honor to be your humble and obedient servant.

The letter ended with an additional salutation which was common at the time amongst commercial correspondents. Thomas was distracted for a moment by the thought that he really ought to persuade Frederick that "and oblige" was a valediction suitable only for letters which concluded with a request. But his mother, turning from her pattern book to inquire, "Anything wrong, dear?" brought his mind back to the day's great mystery. Before he had time to answer, she explained why she asked the question.

"It's only natural for me to worry. You tell me nothing. I am your mother, after all. I'm bound to worry about you. I'm not a fool and I know you're in trouble."

For some time he did not attempt to answer, for, as was the case with so many of his mother's questions, no answer was possible or expected. Her only object was an increase in the emotional temperature.

In a few minutes Mrs. Spooner forgot her anxiety. When the announcement that lunch was ready drove all thought of offense out of his mother's butterfly mind, Thomas felt able to remind her that a visitor was expected.

"Don't forget, Hattersley's coming for tea to discuss some business about the works."

They walked in tense silence into the dining room and sat at opposite ends of the long luncheon table, taking it in turns to guess what the pressing matters might be. The son thought that it might be a massive new order from one of the colonies which would justify the purchase of a new forging hammer or rolling machine. He then expressed the hope that he was to be presented with a proposal to buy the piece of land between the Heather Works and the river Don so that the dilapidated buildings on the present site could be pulled down and replaced by a new model factory full of light and air. His mother continued to hope that it was nothing too serious, and counseled calm. She was anxious that the hours of uncertainty should not prove a strain on Thomas's suspect heart, and urged him to rest in preparation for the evening's ordeal. Suddenly, she decided to inject a little passion into the conversation.

"It must be important. After all, he hardly ever consults you about running the business. I can't recall when he last bothered to ask you anything."

Her son, who was used to absorbing his mother's assaults, decided that a soft answer would deflect her wrath.

"Oh, he does, Mother, all the time. But most of the decisions I leave to him."

In case he was challenged to give an example, he struggled to remember any discussion on the future of the Heather Works which his partner had initiated. He could not think of one.

At their first meeting, Thomas had done all the talking. For Frederick had become one of his sudden enthusiasms from the moment he saw the scissor maker in the heavy boots struggling through his audition for membership in the Choral Society. With years of violin lessons to rely on, he recognized at once the evidence of the narrowed eyes and furrowed brow. The young man could not sight-read with the facility that membership in the Society required. But, thanks to a combination of confidence and determination, he completed the tenor solo from *Judas Maccabeus* which was his set piece. Thomas was spellbound. Confidence and determination were the characteristics necessary to revive the fortunes of the Heather Works. What slight doubts he might have retained about Frederick's qualifications were totally removed when, for the second part of the audition, the applicant chose to sing "The Londonderry Air" and confirmed the possession of a near perfect, though totally untrained, voice. The business proposition, which was made before the end of the evening, left Frederick with nothing to say except the slightly ungracious request to see the offer in writing.

Recalling each of their subsequent conversations, Thomas wondered for a moment if Frederick wanted to renegotiate the terms of the partnership. The original offer had been typically generous—so generous indeed that Frederick would have accepted it even had he not been only a month away from bankruptcy, with no orders for his scissors except those that he provided for his landlord in lieu of monthly rent. He had struggled to become his own master and he had failed. Yet suddenly he had been offered half the profits in a spade-making business. A more sophisticated man would have been suspicious and a less confident one would have doubted his own ability to perform a task for which he was wholly unprepared and entirely untrained. But having been offered his chance, he thought about nothing except grasping it. The strange young man in the foolishly fashionable clothes was clearly incapable of running the business himself. So it was not surprising that he should contract the work to a capable manager and split the profit between them. The ignorance of spade making was easily remedied. Next day, Frederick went to the Mechanics' Institute and withdrew from its circulating library Volume II of *The Cabinet Cyclopaedia,* "edited by the Reverend Dionysius Lardner, LL.D, F.R.S., L.E., M.R.I.A., F.R.A.S., F.L.S., Hon. FEDS etc. etc." Chapter Nine in the "Manufacturing of Metal" section described spade making. Frederick Hattersley read it twice. Thereafter he was a spade maker.

Thomas was not as certain about Frederick's attitude to the partnership arrangement as he was about the success with which he had become a spade maker.

"I don't think he'll want a new agreement," said Thomas.

"I should hope not!" His mother was emphatic. "You've made that man and he shows you no gratitude. I want you to tell me now that he doesn't get a penny more. You can trust your mother, can't you? My only concern is for you. I just hope you'll have enough sense to tell him not a penny more. Promise me."

"He's done very well by the company. Anyway, we don't know that he wants a penny more. The profits are three times greater than when he took over. We'd do badly without him. If he asked for a bigger percentage, I'd have to think about it. He'd have to mend some of his ways though. Extractor fans. Machine guards. He'd have to agree to that sort of thing."

"You did try to talk to him about that once. I remember. He ignored you. Do you know what Mrs. Firth said to me yesterday?"

Not even Mrs. Spooner—whose demands upon her son were limitless—really expected him to possess information about a conversation which had taken place over tea on the day before. The question was a bridging passage intended to change the subject. Mrs. Spooner had grown bored with the Heather Works. Her son had not.

"We got nowhere. He's as hard as nails. And he has absolutely no sympathy for the workmen. It's difficult to remember that he was once a workman himself."

"You can tell he was a workman just by looking at him. He certainly speaks like a workman."

"That's not quite what I meant, Mother. I meant his attitudes. He doesn't care about them in the way that I care."

"Perhaps that's because he sees so much more of them than you do."

Mrs. Spooner hoped to express her distaste for workingmen and heighten the tension simultaneously.

Thomas, always determined to do something useful but never sure what it should be, blushed with guilt like a boy of fifteen.

"I don't think that there would be much to be gained from me spending all day at the Heather Works, or at the coal yard for that matter, or at the foundry."

"Certainly not, dear. I was not suggesting for a moment that you should. I was only inventing excuses for Mr. Hattersley. I was only trying to make conversation."

What might have sounded, to an outsider, like an apology was, in fact, the beginning of an assault. Mrs. Spooner had found her casus belli.

"It's nothing to do with me. I know that. You don't have to tell me to mind my own business. The Heather Works has been no concern of mine since your father left its management to you. And how you live your life is none of my business either. I was just trying to think of something to say instead of sitting here staring out of the window. I don't know why I don't just keep quiet."

There was a moment's silence. Thomas's hope that his mother had exhausted her anguish proved wishful thinking. She simply changed the subject.

"I daren't touch a penny of my own money. I'm nothing now. I shall speak when I am spoken to. Please forgive me for interfering, but I am your mother and all I want is for you to love me."

Thomas Spooner knew that he ought to walk across to his mother, put his arms around her and tell her that he loved her and that he had valued her advice more than she would ever realize. But he knew that instead of hugging him in return and recognizing that it was his feelings, not his words that mattered, she would begin a recital of the times when he had foolishly failed to consult her. The list of slights and humiliations would be followed by demands for him to cite one, just one, occasion when he had taken notice of her about anything important. So he pushed his chair back from the table.

"I'll spend the afternoon upstairs trying to put the telescope back together. We're bound to have a clear night soon. I'll be down at about half past four and we can start tea together before he gets here."

Frederick—as the Spooners should have expected—arrived early. So the housemaid had to climb up to the top of the house to tell Mr. Thomas, as she still called him, that his guest had arrived. He hurried downstairs. But he was too late. By the time he got to the drawing room, his mother was already in full spate and Frederick Hattersley was showing every sign of drowning under the torrent of reminiscence about the old days in Newark and her father who had never sunk a new pit shaft without consulting his entire family. She moved on effortlessly into a description of her family's close association with the Manners and the Manvers families. When she made a smooth transition to the joy with which she had anticipated her only son's birth and the pains she had endured during his delivery, the ten-pound baby interrupted. For he remembered that Frederick himself would soon become a father again and he recalled that, at such times, his partner was sensitive about the subject of childbirth. The question was, therefore, asked brusquely out of embarrassment. It was answered brusquely out of habit.

"Well, Frederick, what is it that I can do for you?"

He took his visitor's arm and led him out of the drawing room.

"You can change the name of the company. I want nothing else changed. Not the money. Just the name."

Thomas was incredulous. "You want the name changed? Is that all? Just the name, nothing else?"

"I want the name changed, or you need another partner. From tomorrow it's Hattersley, Son and Spooner."

Thomas Spooner agreed. And he agreed again, just over a year later, when a second change of name was demanded. Mrs. Spooner, who had been offended by the first suggestion, was horrified by the proposition that the invoices and letterheads should be altered again. When her son reminded her, in his reasonable way, that the name of

Hattersley, Sons and Spooner would accommodate whatever other additions there might be to his partner's family, she called him a fool to himself, and added for good, if irrelevant, measure that no one would ever love him as she did and that she wished she loved him less and could thus be spared the worry about how he would get on when she was gone.

"Frederick only asked for the name to be changed," Thomas said weakly. "We still split the profit in the same way."

His mother withered him with her contemptuous stare. "You must think that I'm a complete fool. I didn't think that he expected you to pay wages to a newborn baby. But he's after something."

"What could he possibly be after? It's just sentimentality."

The explanation sounded unconvincing.

"He's after inheriting the company. That's what. For his family if not himself."

"How could that happen, Mother? The company's yours. Everything's yours."

"It's only mine in trust. And I'll die one day and you'll inherit. Then you will die—sooner rather than later if you go back to your old ways. And you will leave everything to Frederick Hattersley."

Thomas, whose complexion was always unhealthily purple, turned a deeper shade of puce at the reference to the alcoholic habits of his youth. He decided to ignore her taunts about a weakness that had attracted the sobriquet of Tot.

"Nobody plans and schemes like that. Anyway, you'll live to be a hundred and see all of us to heaven!"

"I just don't trust him."

"If you really got to know him, you'd like him. We've never asked him here. We should have asked him to call years ago. Why don't we invite the whole family for tea on the first Sunday that his wife gets out?"

The suggestion that the Hattersleys should come to visit stimulated what Thomas regarded as one of the classic motifs in his mother's conversation. In his musical way, he thought of it as a virtuoso trombone solo. First the slide was extended to its full length in order to maximize dramatic effect. Then it was gradually retracted so as to ensure a prolonged performance.

"I'm far too ill and old to have four young children here for an afternoon. The girls would enjoy seeing my embroidery. Nobody ever sees it these days. Now that I'm an old woman, I never have any visitors. Jessica Witham comes regularly because she worries about me being on my own so much. But she's such a stupid woman that she's no company. She has no real conversation. I doubt if she has even read a book. She said last week that the flowers on the pillow-cases were the best embroidery that she had ever seen. And she's quite an authority on embroidery. It just proves that not everybody thinks that your mother is a stupid old woman with nothing interesting to say."

The concerto had moved into its second movement, self-congratulation mixed with denigration of others in the hope that the result would be a stark contrast between virtue and vice, intellect and ignorance, culture and barbarism.

"Not that I take any notice of anything that *she* thinks. Your father always called her Phoebe because he thought she should have been a milkmaid. Not that she came around very often then. I suppose that she comes now because nobody bothers with her. My friends come to see me because I've kept young by keeping my interest in reading and pictures. And in poetry. When Mr. Wilson came around to tune the piano, he mentioned Robert Browning. He was very impressed by how much I knew about him. He said that he had never met anybody who could quote so well."

The recital ended with a variation on the original theme.

"You see, not everybody thinks me stupid. But it's not them that I want to respect me. It's my own son. Tell me, why is it that when so many people enjoy my company you can't spare a moment to talk to me about serious subjects?"

Compassion required Thomas to respond either with the reassurance that he admired her more than any other living woman or with a reply which was sufficiently dismissive to provoke a paroxysm of anguish. Outright rejection of his mother's plea for a sign of his love and admiration would have been the kindest course to follow. For an uninhibited demonstration of her complicated emotional relationship with her son was the best way to set up Mrs. Spooner for the whole day. But Thomas, who regarded reticence as a major virtue, simply said, "I'm sure that the Hattersleys would love to meet you."

He expected his mother to say that she was too busy to find them time or so cut off from social intercourse that she would not know how to behave if they accepted the invitation.

When she made both complaints in a single sentence, he sat back and waited to be engulfed in her resentment. For he knew that his mother could always be relied upon to fill a conversational vacuum. Often he sat in silence, counting the seconds between each of her unconnected sentences and waiting for her anxiety to exhaust itself. He assumed that the suggestion about inviting the Hattersleys to tea had awakened one of the demons of self-doubt that prodded and poked her into so much inconsequential nonsense. By chance, her monologue ended with the idea that the whole family should visit Riverdale Grange.

Mrs. Spooner wrote an effusive letter of invitation which reflected only one honest emotion—the need to be loved. It implied that every day she passed without having seen the newborn Hattersley son was an intolerable frustration and an unbearable disappointment. She did not, however, go on to describe the special attraction of the child which distinguished him from his older siblings, whom she had never seen. The letter emphasized the joy with which she looked forward to a good long talk with "all of you." The collective familiarity was employed as the result of a temporary inability to recall the name of Emily's sister.

Emily's letter of acceptance arrived by return of post. It had been written with obvious care and equally obvious difficulty. It would be ten days before she could leave home, but Riverdale Grange would be her first visit. Mrs. Spooner brandished the letter.

"Emily Hattersley says that I'm the one person that she wants to see."

The account of the reply to his mother's invitation produced in Thomas a strange mixture of delight and panic. He was anxious to see more of Frederick, whom he regarded as an interesting specimen of a dying race. But faced with the impending reality of that great scientific exhibit sitting in one of his armchairs, he began to wish that he had never planned the extended observation. The rest of the Hattersley family neither interested nor worried him. The children would be entertained by his mother in the hope that a display of maternal affection would endear her to the assembled adults. Emily he knew to be an easily satisfied guest who would sit spine erect against the back of her chair—knees and ankles together and hands folded—until she was offered another cup of tea or cucumber sandwich. Winifred, who looked as Emily had looked ten years before, he assumed to be equally docile, and he was quite prepared to be bored by both the sisters as the price he paid for a closer observation of the genus Hattersley in a domestic environment. But the thought of

Frederick himself, refusing to compromise with courtesy or convention, and correcting every one of his mother's errors, filled him with dread.

The afternoon began well enough. It was the last Saturday in June, and after the whole family had descended from the carriage which had recently replaced their horse and trap, Frederick formed them up on the path outside the great front door of Riverdale Grange, blowing his nose in order to prevent the introductions being interrupted by a bout of sneezing. First were the little girls, Mary and Martha. They were in white from head to toe—white bonnets, white muslin dresses, white calfskin shoes. Hand in hand they led the procession up the steps, followed by Winifred, carrying one-year-old Joseph, and, as rank required, the head of the household in the rear, gripping his wife's elbow while she held their newborn son in her arms. Mrs. Spooner, seeing them arrive from the window, hurried with fluttering little pretenses of pleasure into the hall. Frederick, putting his top hat under one arm in fair imitation of Prince Albert arriving to plight his troth at Windsor Castle, stepped forward and rang the bell. The maid swung the door open and to her astonishment was immediately greeted by a simultaneous curtsy from the two little girls. From the back of the hall Mrs. Spooner, in a voice several octaves lower than normal, said, "Do come in," and the girls curtsied twice more, once at the sound and once at the sight of their hostess. Everyone was charmed. The introductions, accompanied by several more curtsies, were completed in relaxed ease and the conversation got off to a flying start.

"What was he christened, my dear?"

Mrs. Spooner was jabbing the infant in the stomach with her bony finger. She stood up to ask the question, having the minute before been grimacing horribly at the child with her face only a few inches away from his.

Emily answered literally. "He's not been christened yet. This is my first day out. We came to see you on the first day."

Mrs. Spooner clucked her pleasure at having been shown such respect. Frederick had kept the meaning of the question in his mind and he interrupted the felicities to answer it.

"He is to be named Herbert."

Attention was switched to the one-year-old boy, whom Winifred was nursing. Mrs. Spooner bared her teeth at his uncomprehending face and addressed him as "Little Frederick."

"That, ma'am," said Frederick, his knuckles turning ominously white, "is Joseph."

"Is there no Frederick?" Mrs. Spooner became coy. "Perhaps the next one is to be given his father's name."

"My first son was Frederick. He is deceased."

"I am so sorry."

For a moment Thomas feared that his mother was about to take Frederick's hand.

"How old was he when he died?"

"Only a few hours."

"But surely . . ." As was her habit, she looked around the room for allies to support her cause and on whom the blame could be heaped if she was proved wrong. "Surely Emily would like one of her sons to be named after his father."

Thomas knew that duty required him just to change the subject and then to ensure that for the rest of the afternoon only safe topics were discussed. But he felt wholly incapable of holding the balance between his mother's intrusive insensitivity and Frederick's bristling pride. So he made a diversion which he hoped would both avert the impending social tragedy and allow him to escape from the next twenty minutes of discomfort. Summoning up all his reserves of courage, he turned to Emily.

"I wonder, Mrs. Hattersley, if your little girls would like to see my conservatory. There really are some very interesting plants in there. The cacti are in flower. The pollen will not be good for your husband's throat, but perhaps your sister would accompany me."

He knew that the final suggestion was scandalous and he relied on the mild shock that it would cause to set the conversation off on a new tack. To his surprise and pleasure, Winifred answered for herself.

"I would be delighted to see the conservatory. May I take the girls, Emily?"

Within the time that it took Mary and Martha to curtsy to the assembled company, curtsy to no one in particular and then curtsy to the assembled company again, the idea had been agreed. Suddenly, to his alarm, Thomas was side by side with a single woman of less than thirty, a single woman with long golden hair and the profile of a Pre-Raphaelite princess, and a single woman unchaperoned except by the presence of her two angelic but apparently dumb nieces. He took refuge in botany.

"This is a rare member of the *Opuntia* family. I have spent months keeping it alive and encouraging it to flower. I believe it is the only one to blossom outside London. There is certainly one at Kew."

But Winifred was not listening. While her nieces stood hand in hand, fascinated by the grotesque purple petals which hung from the cactus like gobbets of congealed blood, she stared at Thomas's unremarkable profile caught in sharp focus by the bright evening light which shone through the glass conservatory walls. He had hair which his mother called tawny and a complexion which she described as bronzed. At school, he had been called Sandy or Tomahawk, not because there was any suggestion of Scottish or Red Indian ancestry but because of the combination of various shades of fawn and pinkish brown which colored his head and face. At university, it had all been attributed to his sudden passion for whiskey. But when he signed the pledge, the florid complexion remained. Winifred had seen that head and face before. But then it belonged to the young muscular workman who dominated the left foreground of her favorite painting of the moment—*Work*, the allegory of noble toil on which Ford Madox Brown had labored for thirteen years. She felt a thrill of pleasure almost as great as the joy which would have gripped her had she suddenly been confronted by John Ruskin and Thomas Carlyle, who, deep in conversation at the other side of the painting, represented the glories of intellectual activity.

Winifred, for all her infatuation with the picture and her pleasure at seeing one of its characters brought to life, had wit enough to recognize the irony of the coincidence. She knew by heart all the rubrics which the painter had himself engraved around the frame.

"Neither did we eat any man's bread for nought; but wrought with labor and travail night and day." It was not a view of life with which her host was likely to agree. It was her brother-in-law Frederick who, "diligent in work," was "fit to stand before kings." She tried to avoid making a comparison between the rival virtues of the partners as Thomas continued his unsuccessful attempts to interest his guests in the collection of ugly tropical plants which lined his conservatory walls. He addressed them with such boyish eagerness to please that Winifred began to feel something like maternal sympathy for him. Sympathy turned to curiosity, and curiosity created an uncontrollable urge to discover why he passed his days in making experiments which had already been made, discovering stars which were already discovered and cultivating rare plants which were so unique that they thrived in neighboring gardens. Without thinking, she asked him the question which was in the front of her mind.

"Why do you not work, Mr. Spooner? Why do you spend your time on unimportant things?"

Thomas was highly accomplished in the art of not taking offense. And Winifred had, after much practice, perfected the art of asking impertinent questions as if they were proof of both her indestructible innocence and her burning interest in the life and work of the person who was the victim of her effrontery. She knew that behaving in such a way was a social contrivance barely less reprehensible than the wasp waist. But she justified her artifice as a necessary stratagem in the battle for female emancipation in general and her own recognition in particular. Thomas was simply fascinated by what sounded to him like the voice of unspoilt nature. He assumed that the question had come into Winifred's mind and that, in her innocence, she had seen no reason not to ask it. Inevitably, his frank explanation sounded like an excuse and his honest answer became an apology.

"I do not need to work for money and there is really very little work of that sort that I am equipped to do. I have no trade or profession. Before my father was ill, I was meant for the law. I studied law at London University, but then my mother needed me here at home. I thought of becoming a pupil to a barrister on the northern circuit, but it proved difficult to find suitable chambers. I gradually developed all my other interests—botany, music, astronomy. So I keep very busy with all that and supervising the quarry, the farm that we own and the pit."

He knew how unconvincing it all sounded. As he grew increasingly distressed Thomas talked at greater and greater speed.

"I am, of course, much engaged in the promotion of the Free Library. I am outraged by the Council's behavior."

He then began to repeat a speech which he had made, with equal passion, many times before. The town aldermen were condemned for choosing to convert the Mechanics Institute not into the library, which they had first intended, but a Council hall.

"Four hundred pounds for a place to hold Council meetings. And not a free library. It is an outrage."

He was about to explain why the site at the corner of Norfolk Street and Arundel Street was ideally situated for the convenience of the literate poor, when he saw that Winifred's attention was wandering. Weakly, he added, "And of course, there is the Heather Works."

Winifred knew that victory was assured and she pressed on to occupy the whole field of battle.

"I hear you spend precious little time there."

"Do you indeed?" Thomas, struggling for a less feeble response, inquired if he was a constant subject of conversation in the Hattersley household, adding, "I should be very flattered if that were so."

Winifred decided that even the reputation for frankness on which her social success was based could not justify an honest description of the complaint made by her brother-in-law about his partner. So she described one area of Frederick's dissatisfaction which could be revealed as if it were not a criticism. It happened to be the area of Thomas's misconduct which most interested her—and from which she hoped to benefit.

"Every night after supper I hear about your hobbies and pastimes. I knew about this conservatory and its strange plants long before you invited me to see what it held. I know about your work, too. The Society for Bettering the Conditions of the Poor. Your passion for clean water and your campaigns for better sanitation."

"Miss Banks, please. You flatter me too much with your interest."

Thomas blushed to discover that someone, unknown to him an hour ago, already knew so much about him. He decided upon a suitably self-deprecatory response. He carefully constructed his reply in a way which ensured the necessary protestation of modesty without forswearing his passion for public washhouses, factory ventilation and the separation of sewage and drinking water.

"I'm afraid that your brother-in-law disapproves of my ideas about public health."

"I am afraid that he does. But I do not. Sometimes Frederick astounds me. I cannot understand how a man of such intelligence can reject the evidence of his own eyes. I have shown him Mr. Chadwick's cholera maps. They are quite conclusive. Disease thrives in fetid water."

The cholera maps were a trump card which Winifred had hoped to play ever since, earlier that week, she had discovered their existence during a discussion at Friends' Meeting House on the subject of "Women and Medicine." The purpose of the gathering was to promote the acceptance of lady doctors. But Mr. Chadwick had been mentioned as second only to Florence Nightingale in his hatred of infection, and Winifred had clutched the fact to her in anticipation of its deployment at Riverdale Grange.

It had the desired effect. Thomas conceived in his mind a hazy picture of Frederick Hattersley sitting at the head of his dinner table while Winifred spread maps of northern England over the plates and cutlery. They proved conclusively that cholera prospered in the absence of sanitation. He was at once fascinated and terrified, bewildered and impressed, uncertain if he was determined to seek out her constant companionship or desperate never to meet her again. Winifred had meant to do no more than cut an intellectual dash and prove herself to be the equal of her cultivated host. But she had succeeded, by the intensity of her manner and the intimacy of her questions, in binding them together. They were no longer casual acquaintances. It was clearly time to return to the drawing room.

Mary and Martha were told that it was no longer necessary for them to stare at the flowering cactus, and they were led toward the sound of Mrs. Spooner's unmistakable drone and the consumption of the scones which she had personally baked to mark the occasion, her scones being regarded as the best in South Yorkshire even though she said so herself. She was, at the moment of her son's reappearance, entertaining her guests with simultaneous accounts of her late husband's virtues and the men of greater wealth and superior social status who had asked her to marry them. She was just moving on to the revelation that, even at her age, there were still "gentlemen who hoped," when she saw her son out of the corner of her eye. Without completing her sentence, she assumed a coy smile and observed, to the general discomfiture of all but Winifred, "We thought that we'd lost you. What have you been talking about?"

Without a moment's hesitation, Winifred told her, "Your son says that he was at London University at the same time as Dante Gabriel Rossetti. Imagine that."

Thomas reached for a cup of tea with a shaking hand.

CHAPTER SIX

PRIMARY EDUCATION

Winifred Banks left Riverdale Grange convinced that she had embarked on what would become a rewarding friendship. All she wanted or expected was the chance to talk about subjects which were prohibited at Frederick Hattersley's table. As the carriage crunched down the long gravel drive she had no doubt that she could cultivate her new acquaintance without compromising her independence. But she was less certain about the obstacles that would be put in her path. Would Mrs. Spooner be friend or enemy?

At first it was friend. Thomas's mother encouraged, even promoted, the friendship. Indeed, no sooner had Winifred left the house on the day of their first meeting than Mrs. Spooner began to make plans for future visits. She had convinced herself that Dante Gabriel Rossetti was a mutual acquaintance who had recently moved from London to South Yorkshire, and she suggested that the old friends should be reunited at a dinner party over which she would preside. Thomas made ineffectual attempts to explain that neither he nor Winifred had either met or was likely to meet the poet and painter. But the correction was brushed aside as his usual denigration of his mother and a snobbish reluctance to allow her to meet his London friends for fear that they would regard her as a northern bumpkin.

"It may surprise you, but Miss Banks actually enjoys my company. I could tell that at once. I shall invite her here, with or without your permission. I cannot imagine why you should wish to deny me such little pleasures—unless you want to keep me away from anyone who likes and admires me!"

Thomas mumbled and capitulated. So for weeks—while he thought of Winifred Banks with a mixture of awe and terror, bewilderment and admiration—Mrs. Spooner entertained her to lunch, insisted on her company on expeditions to the spas of Buxton and Matlock and subjected her, over coffee in the mornings and tea in the afternoons, to lectures on topics about which the lecturer knew nothing. At first Thomas simply waited for his mother's mood to change. For there had been many previous protégées and always, after a month or two, they became objects of unqualified hatred as they were adjudged guilty of betrayal or neglect.

Whenever Winifred visited Riverdale Grange, Thomas always sidled into the drawing room with deep apprehension. For he felt unable to survive a second experience as emotionally intense as his five minutes with Winifred in the conservatory. But gradually—first to his relief and then to his pleasure—he discovered that the young woman with golden hair that hung to below her waist did not always assail and assault him as she had done on that first afternoon. In the conservatory he had felt that an emotional undercurrent flowed between them. But he decided that the eddies and ripples had only flowed one way and that if the waves were ignored they would soon cease to break. He walked with her in the arboretum at his mother's bidding and found it a tolerable experience, and he introduced her to the works of Darwin and Huxley without feeling more than passing resentment that she read the texts at a speed to which he could not aspire. He invited her to study the stars through his telescope— though imperfectly, since propriety prevented her from observing the heavens while lying on her back—and he attempted to persuade her that painting had not begun with Millais and Holman Hunt. In fact, he became her tutor, as she had decided that he would months before as she listened to Frederick Hattersley's interminable complaints about his interest in the frivolities which fascinated her. She was determined to learn and he was flattered to teach. Superficially, it was a wholly satisfactory relationship.

Mrs. Spooner gave a fair imitation of welcoming the friendship. For years she had affected a desire to see her son settle down before his mother went to join the husband whose absence grew more unbearable each day. Sometimes, after Winifred had left, she was explicit about her anxieties.

"You ought not to be surprised that I worry about you. I'm your mother. I think about you in this big house without anyone to look after you and everybody taking advantage of your good nature."

Thomas listened to his mother's protestations with undisguised irritation. He had no doubt that her enthusiasm for Winifred would pass. But he knew that, at the moment, the young woman fitted exactly into her plans. Her existence allowed the relationship between mother and son to be elevated to previously unanticipated emotional heights. It enabled her to joke about his attractions and to humiliate him with mock protestations that he should do the right thing by the young innocent. At more solemn moments, she reassured him with absolute sincerity that, whatever other people might say, she herself would never reproach him for abandoning his mother in sickness and old age.

As the friendship between Mrs. Spooner and Winifred Banks survived through summer into autumn and winter, Thomas came to realize that the young woman possessed one virtue which, above all her other admirable qualities, sustained the esteem in which his mother held her. Nobody who knew her could possibly believe that a woman of such spirit would ever consent to become Mrs. Thomas Spooner.

Thomas's mother was absolutely sure of it. Perhaps years ago, Winifred had hoped for a love match. But now she was visibly, and too often audibly, proud of her independence. With a little money of her own and the fierce conviction that women should not devote their lives to men, it seemed inconceivable that she would sacrifice her independence for the dubious pleasures of marriage. Mrs. Spooner could encourage Winifred's friendship with her son without worrying about his being snatched from his mother's loving care. And her enthusiasm for Winifred was demonstrated by the convulsions of self-congratulation which always greeted the young woman's arrival at Riverdale Grange. Every excursion into the kitchen was followed by the announcement of a culinary triumph. Needlework was favorably compared with the work of both Mortlake and Bayeux. Portraits, painted in the years before Thomas's birth, were adjudged to do their subject less than justice and to demonstrate that the sitter had grown more beautiful with the years. All of the compliments contained a grain of truth. Mrs. Spooner's tragedy was that she congratulated herself so often that she built up in others a stubborn resistance to repeat the high opinions which she had herself expressed. Winifred's triumph was that she was able to rise above the barrier of self-congratulation which separated Mrs. Spooner from the rest of the world.

Witnessing the calm composure which allowed Winifred to parry all of his mother's thrusts, Thomas felt certain that the serenity could not last. But it lasted for almost a year. It even survived the refusal of invitations issued at times and in ways which were intended to force Mrs. Spooner's latest closest friend to make artificial and arbitrary choices between personal convenience and demonstrations of affection. On their receipt, notes conveying regrets were described as proof of selfish ingratitude. Messages explaining that prior arrangements left no choice but to decline with thanks were regarded as calculated insults. Thomas was invariably required to assuage his mother's feelings of rejection first by assuring her that no slight was intended and then by denouncing the ingrate who had slighted her. But next day other invitations were dispatched, and the moment that one was accepted with gratitude Winifred Banks again became a paragon of virtue.

Even after almost a year of observing Winifred's strange influence over his mother, Thomas remained astonished by its success. It even extended into the area of her life where every nerve end was exposed and every emotion, false and genuine, was kept on public view—the unique relationship which she had enjoyed with the late Mr. Spooner and her inconsolable regret that he was no longer by her side. Every demonstration of Winifred's charm began with Thomas expecting an orgy of self-pity and recrimination and ended with his bewildered gratitude. Incredibly, she was even able to reconcile Mrs. Spooner to her son's enthusiasm for the Liberal Party.

Admittedly, the reconciliation was built around the emollient figure of Anthony John Mundella, the new Liberal Member of Parliament. Mr. Mundella's radicalism was not in doubt. He supported the universal education of the laboring classes, the right of working men to combine in unions and improvements in the Poor Law. But he thought of himself, and described himself, as "the Parliamentary Agent for the Corporation of Sheffield and to the Sheffield Chamber of Commerce." On the day of his election, his defeated opponent had predicted that he would be "a nobody in the House," and he had replied with the promise that he would become "somebody in Shef-field." For the next two years, there was no bill affecting tariffs, patents or government contracts on which he did not speak—always advocating Sheffield's cause. At first, Thomas Spooner had gone—furtively —to the meeting in Robert Leader's house in Moor End at which Mr. Mundella had been asked to contest the 1867 election in the Liberal cause. When he felt able to tell his mother that he proposed to attend Mr. Mundella's lecture on primary education, he was so confident of her approval that he invited her to accompany him to the Temperance Hall. She accepted and announced (without feeling it necessary to consult her favorite companion of the moment) that Winifred Banks would also wish for a ticket.

Winifred, as always, arrived in good time and began at once to compliment Mrs. Spooner on her dress. The crisis arose twenty minutes before the Mayor was due to lead Mr. Mundella onto the Temperance Hall platform, when Thomas gently suggested that he might get his mother's hat and coat.

"I'm not coming. I thought you knew."

"I'd no idea," said Thomas. "But if you're not well, we'll stay at home too. It really isn't a very important lecture."

"I wouldn't hear of it. The last thing you want is to be housebound because of me. I shall be perfectly all right on my own."

Winifred joined in the protestations. "We'd much rather stay. We wouldn't enjoy it without you."

"Nonsense. You're far too sensible to allow the thought of a sad and lonely old woman to spoil your pleasure." Then she turned to Thomas and asked him an unexpected question. "What happened fourteen years ago, fourteen years ago today?"

Thomas confessed that he did not know and his mother burst into tears at the revelation of his ignorance.

"He doesn't know. He doesn't remember the day on which his father had his first heart attack."

It had taken seven heart attacks to kill Mr. Spooner, and his son was about to observe that he could hardly be expected to commemorate every one, when Winifred took charge.

"Perhaps he does not remember the date, Mrs. Spooner. But that does not mean that he did not love his father. It only means that his love was different from yours. And that you would expect."

To Thomas's amazement, his mother stood for a moment in silence and then—instead of announcing her refusal to be told the nature of the relationship which she enjoyed with her late husband—she kissed her son on the cheek and expressed the apparently genuine hope that he would enjoy the lecture. Her wish was not granted—he barely heard a word throughout the whole evening. He was haunted by the debilitating suspicion that he had witnessed some sort of necromancy. The lion was lying down at the lamb's instruction. Meanwhile, the young woman who had been the agent of the magical event clapped at every suggestion of compulsory education. When the Established Church was denounced for its stubborn refusal to relinquish its hegemony over the nation's schools, she applauded even more loudly. And at the mention of Mr. Foster and the bill he proposed to introduce into the House of Commons, she rose in uninhibited rapture.

The final applause being almost finished, Winifred, who could never wait to leave a hall once the entertainment was over, stood up. To her consternation, she felt Thomas take her hand in his and gently pull her back into her seat. A few enthusiasts continued to applaud, but most of the audience were busily buttoning up coats against the cool night air, pulling on gloves and ensuring that hats were at exactly correct angles. As the activity bustled on around them Thomas turned in his seat to face Winifred, not knowing or not caring that he blocked the path of a whole family who were anxious to squeeze past him into the aisle.

"If I do not say it this minute, I shall never say it. So I must say it now."

Winifred was about to ask what idea needed such urgent expression that a whole row of Liberals must be inconvenienced while the words were spoken, when Thomas, who could recognize the sign of burgeoning bon mots, laid a restraining hand on her arm.

"Just for once, no interruptions. No comments. No corrections. No intelligent questions. Just listen until I finish."

Winifred began to fear that they had become a spectacle, for the hall was almost empty. Even the family which had hoped to squeeze past them had escaped by turning in the opposite direction and edging their way along almost a whole row of red velvet seats. She hoped that whatever Thomas wished to say would be said quickly.

"You remember one day in the arboretum you told me that you had wanted us to be friends from the moment that Frederick told you about me?"

"I remember it well." Thomas, she decided, had inherited his mother's insecurity. Her duty was quickly to calm his fears of rejection before he created a scene. "And I flatter myself that I am your friend."

She stood up in a way which made clear that further restraints would not be tolerated. In consequence, frightened that the moment would pass, Thomas was forced to speak in a voice so loud that Winifred feared it would be heard on the other side of the hall.

"I want us to be married friends."

Winifred's progress toward the door continued at an accelerated pace. Thomas followed half a step behind. In a minute they were out on the pavement in Pinstone Street, looking—like the other middle-aged and middle-class couples—for the carriage which had arranged to meet them.

They walked for some minutes without speaking. Never until that moment had Winifred even contemplated the idea of becoming Mrs. Spooner. At the age of twenty-nine she took it for granted that, having reached such an advanced age, she would remain a spinster. But although she was reconciled to a permanently passionless existence, she still retained the romantic notions that she and Emily had first developed during whispered conversations in their darkened bedroom all those years ago in Doncaster. Marriage could not possibly be built from a relationship which had already lasted a year without a single mention of love. In the old days she had looked forward to being a wife, not a married friend. According to her usual role of frankness, she told Thomas so, as soon as they were in the carriage.

"I have always believed that there should be something more to marriage than simple friendship."

"I do assure you that . . . I did not mean for a moment . . ."

"Neither did I. I meant that I wanted to be in love and that I wanted the man I married to be in love with me." Her mind was filled with Pre-Raphaelite images of Abélard and Héloïse, Dante and Beatrice, Lancelot and Guinevere. "Have you ever been in love, blindly, recklessly, unthinkingly?" She was genuinely curious again.

It seemed to Thomas that at such a moment he had a duty to answer the question honestly.

"Once upon a time," he said, for he felt that he was beginning a fairy tale, "there was a girl in London. I was twenty-one."

The story was told in brief, unconnected sentences.

"She lived in St. George's Square. One day, when I went to call, she ran to meet me as I climbed the stairs to the drawing room. I saw her looking down over the banisters. I did not believe that she could be as pleased to see me as she seemed. Then I realized that I made her look like that—happy, satisfied, victorious. I thought that if there is a heaven, for me it will be this moment made to last for eternity. I suppose that I was in love then."

"But you do not think that now . . . that heaven is an eternity of this carriage ride?"

"I no longer believe in heaven."

"Or love?"

"I believe in happiness. I believe in something more certain and more dependable than a moment that is built into a lifetime. I believe in the pleasure that we shall find in each other's company, in what both of us will learn and each of us will teach. I believe that I am happier and more contented when you are with me than I am when you are far away. And the way to have you with me all the time is to marry you . . ." Thomas paused, overwhelmed by the eloquence of his own argument. Then he added what he also felt in his heart. "And I believe in the honesty of my proposal."

Disconcertingly, Winifred smiled the serene private smile that so unnerved Mrs. Spooner, the smile which implied that she knew secrets that were revealed to no one else.

"I don't envy you the job of breaking the news to your mother. But then I don't envy you the job of asking Frederick for his permission. But I suppose you've got to do it. He's the nearest thing there is to the head of the family. He'll give me away."

It was not until the carriage pulled up outside Frederick Hattersley's house that Thomas fully realized that his proposal had been accepted and that he had failed to warn her that she was marrying a man with a weak heart.

Thomas Spooner did not look forward to the conversation that courtesy required him to have with Frederick Hattersley. He recalled the day when the elegant Horace Hardwick had turned up at Riverdale Grange to ask for the hand of Victoria Spencer, a distant orphan cousin. Thomas's father had taken his duties *in loco parentis* so seriously that he had kept the suitor waiting until it was certain that the young man's nerve had completely broken. Mr. Hardwick had dropped his top hat and gloves several times while he waited in the reception hall, and when Victoria's uncle finally came out to lead him into the study, he had stood up so quickly that the silver-topped cane which he was holding elegantly between his knees fell to the tiled floor with a deafening clatter. Then he began to ask for Victoria's hand before her uncle had sat down in one of his high-backed leather chairs. Having realized his error, he had been completely incapable of beginning his carefully prepared speech again. Thomas did not propose to allow anything like that to happen to him.

So he sent his partner a note, composed in careful but not original language. Much of it was copied from the letter which Frederick himself had written in preparation for the meeting that changed the company's name.

Recent developments make it essential for us to meet and talk at an early date. Since the matters in question are pressing, I shall presume to call at Alderson Road tomorrow evening. I regret that I can reveal no more in writing.

The letter, having been read and reread several times with increasing satisfaction, was marked "Strictly Private and Highly Confidential" and posted to the Heather Works. Thomas calculated that it would be in the cutler's shop by the time Frederick arrived on the following morning, and would, he hoped, ensure that a whole day's work was disturbed by anxieties about the urgent matters that made an early meeting necessary.

The journey to Alderson Road was carefully planned and exactly timed, for he was determined to avoid the indignity of arriving first and he had no doubt that Frederick would remain at the works until half past six no matter how concerned he was about the meaning of the cryptic note. The maid who opened the door delighted him with what was supposed to be a reproof: "The master's been waiting on you for half an hour or more."

Thomas strode into the living room and, determined to maintain his ascendancy, declined to sink into the vast chesterfield to which he had been directed and sat instead upright on the edge of a hard-backed chair. He cleared his throat, stared straight at Frederick— who stood, arms folded, in front of the fire—and began his prepared speech.

"I have come to tell you that Winifred—your sister-in-law Winifred, that is—and I are going to be married."

"I expected something of the sort. Anyone with eyes to see knew that it were coming. Emily will be very pleased. She feared that her sister would die an old maid."

Thomas, deflated to the point of humiliation, asked if Frederick would be pleased as well.

"I'm pleased enough to walk her down the aisle on my arm and pleased enough to pay for the wedding breakfast—pay for everything, that is, except strong drink. If you want alcohol you must pay for it yourself. I'll be pleased for my two little girls to be the bridesmaids and I'm pleased you've come to tell me rather than pretend that you're asking my permission. She's got a mind of her own, that one, and if she's set on marrying you nothing will stop her. Her own father couldn't stop her. So I'm glad you've been straight about telling me instead of playacting about me being t'head of family."

"I think that Winifred would like you to approve."

"I do approve. To be honest, I'm glad that she's going."

"You'll forgive my saying so, but that is hardly a gracious reaction to my news."

"I mean no offense. She's good company is your Winifred and I like her well enough. Having her here these last three years has been a blessing for Emily. Taken her out of herself. Kept her company. Winifred and me have enjoyed many a good argument. I've taken more chi-iking from her than I've taken from any other woman, and from most men, and enjoyed it. But now I've got two boys it's all different."

"She is devoted to your sons."

"I know that. And I know something else. She is certainly a radical and probably an atheist. And I don't want either Joseph or Herbert to grow up with such a person in the house. What's more, she's all painting and poetry. And I don't want those lads to grow up with that, neither. I want them to grow up serious. I couldn't turn her out. But I'm glad she's going. In any case, we won't have the space when we move into the smaller house."

"Space?"

Thomas thought he must have misheard. For a moment it had seemed that Frederick had spoken of moving into a smaller house.

"I need the capital. I've meant to tell you for months, but I've not had the chance. That's why I made the effort to see you this afternoon. Left the works early to be sure that I got here first. I've bought a place, the old Empress Works in Eldon Street. I'm setting up a new company, a company of my own. Hattersley and Sons, Cutlers. Or perhaps Hattersley and Sons, Scissor Makers and Medical Instrument Manufacturers, or Hattersley and Sons, Scissor, Shear and Medical Instrument Makers."

Frederick paused to allow each one of the possible names to reverberate inside his head.

"I've not quite decided the name, but the company will mostly make scissors. So I need the capital. It was want of capital that made me fail before. I'm not going to make that mistake again."

"And what about the Heather Works?"

Thomas realized that he had suddenly become a supplicant. But he needed to know the answer to his question and could not think of anything else to say.

"I shall take Jack Foster with me. But you'll be glad of that. The cutler's shop and the cutler have cost you money and brought you no benefit. You did it for me and I'm grateful. Now I'll take him off your hands. I'll pay half of the value of the wheels and the hearth. I've had them all priced. I'll register a new maker's mark at t'Cutlers' Hall. I've wrote to t'Company already." Frederick almost smiled. "To tell all, I've applied for membership."

"You seem to have got it all worked out."

"I had to ponder it all, didn't I? I've got responsibilities now."

"And the Heather Works? What about your responsibilities there? Are you dissolving the partnership?"

Thomas could no longer maintain the tone of contemptuous disapproval which he hoped had made Frederick realize that no gentleman would have behaved in such a way. His next question sounded as if it was prompted more by panic than by disdain.

"Couldn't you make your scissors at Hattersley and Spooner?" He quickly corrected himself. "Hattersley, Sons and Spooner."

"I want the scissors factories to be just Hattersleys, me and my sons. I respect spades and spades have done well by me. But spades and hoes and pitchforks are not a trade like scissors—not even good spades like them we've made together. I want Joseph and Herbert to be craftsmen, craftsmen cutlers like their father, and I want them to inherit a cutlers' business."

"So you'll leave the Heather Works?"

"I'll leave if that is what you want. But I'd rather stay and take a quarter instead of a half of the profits. That'll more than pay the wages of a good manager. Add what you save on the cutler's shop to what you save on me, you'll be well in hand."

95

Thomas decided that it was the time for a little quiet dignity. He held out his hand.

"I can see that nothing I say will change your mind. And I hope that we will remain friends as well as partners—partners of a sort."

Frederick crushed Thomas's knuckles in his huge fist and, in what was as near as he ever got to a show of public emotion, responded to the appeal to his better nature which few people believed him to possess.

"That we will, Thomas. That we will. Friends and partners, partners and friends."

He had never used Thomas's Christian name before and, moved by the unexpected intimacy, the new friend and partner thought an emotional response would be appropriate.

"We'll be more than friends, we'll be relations."

For a moment Frederick looked puzzled. Then he understood. "So we will. So we will. In the excitement of talking about t'scissors factory, I forgot all about that."

There and then, Thomas decided that he would wait until the next day to break the news to his mother.

CHAPTER SEVEN

BUILDING BRIDGES

Thomas Spooner's instinct was to tell his mother of his intended marriage with his chosen bride sitting by his side. He believed that Winifred's presence would stem the tide of false emotion which might, were he on his own, drown him in a sea of resentment and regret. His fiancée—as he could still barely believe her to be— insisted that he face the ordeal alone.

"She is entitled to her moment of private grief. With an outsider there, she'd feel that she had to pretend to be pleased. After tomorrow she'll certainly be saying what a catch you've made. And in front of me she'll pretend to be delighted. But it's better to let her get her real feelings out of her system right away."

"But she always liked you."

"She will not like me now. I am taking her only son. You've chosen me, instead of her. That's what she'll think. You ought to give her the chance to say it."

Predictably, what Mrs. Spooner said was an exact reflection of Winifred's prophecy. But it reflected a distorted image of her true opinion.

"Don't say that, Thomas. Don't say that."

She was sobbing.

"But, Mother." Thomas struggled to be reasonable. "You have always said how much you want me to settle down and how much you admire Winifred. I really thought that you had picked her out for me."

"It's not me I'm thinking about. You should know that. It's your father. What would he say?"

Thomas calculated that his father would be mildly incommoded by the necessity to shake his son by the hand, moderately anxious to avoid discussion of romantic or emotional matters and desperately determined not to allow either the wedding or the preparation for the wedding to disturb the normal pattern of his life. That, he decided, was not the answer which his mother wanted. So he compromised between following Winifred's example by telling the simple truth and proceeding according to his own instincts by avoiding a head-on collision.

"I really don't think he'd object. He'd quite like Winifred, and he'd hope that everything turned out well. I'm not sure that he'd be very glad, but I don't think he'd be sorry."

"How can you say such a thing? You haven't thought about his wishes at all. It breaks my heart to think that you have forgotten all about him. He is always with me, every minute of the day. I wouldn't do anything without thinking how he would feel about it."

Thomas wanted to say that he knew what she said was true and that he hoped that his mother wanted him to enjoy an equally devoted marriage. But he did no more than wait while his mother changed course.

"And what is to happen to the house and the factory? What will happen to the farms and the pit and the quarry?"

"The quarry was sold ten years ago."

"That doesn't matter. What will happen to the factory, to the farms and to this house? Who will have it when you're dead and gone?"

"Who would have it if I remained a bachelor?"

"I've thought about these things even if you haven't. When I die, everything is yours. Then one day, everything will go to those awful Hattersley children. I know their sort. Take everything and give nothing in return. They will live in this house—the house your father built for him and me—after you're dead from a heart attack."

"Mother." Thomas was becoming desperate with exasperation. "All I plan to do is marry Winifred. This is all fantasy."

"Marry! Marry a woman ten years younger than you! What sort of a marriage will that be? There'll be no children. She'll see to that.

Then after you're dead and gone, the Hattersleys will move in. I can see it. But I can't bear to think about it."

Thomas was about to speak, when his mother detected a twitching of his lips and, suspecting his intention to take part in the conversation, decided to preempt him.

"Children! Don't tell me that you're thinking about children. I couldn't bear it. Your father, your father . . ."

Mrs. Spooner sank down onto a sofa, and Thomas, in one of the few brave moments in their entire relationship, decided to explain in simple language.

"I hope we shall have children. And you should hope so too. I'd like a son. But that's as may be. With or without children, I want Winifred."

His mother chose not to understand her only son's real emotions.

"As always, you'll do what you like. But remember, while I am alive those Hattersley children won't get a penny of the money, and while I'm alive I am Mrs. Thomas Spooner."

It was agreed that the wedding should be on June 12. For months Winifred worked to ingratiate herself with her future mother-in-law. She applied herself to the task with a single-minded determination which her fiancé found both frightening and flattering. Her technique was to escort Mrs. Spooner to all the cultural occasions which the old lady wished to attend.

Winifred regarded attendance at meetings of the Rotherham Literary and Social Society as the supreme sacrifice. Mrs. Spooner expressed particular enthusiasm for attending a *conversazione* at which Charles Grice, the manager of the Effingham Iron Works, had arranged a display of furniture in the style of James I. So Winifred overcame her natural reluctance to endure a soirée over which Mrs. Evelyn Linley presided at the piano, and accepted the invitation. Thomas was encouraged to accompany the two ladies by the prospect of seeing the photographic pictures of the Rocky Mountains which Lord Milton had sent to grace the occasion. At first, Mrs. Spooner had believed that Lord Milton would be there in person. But Thomas consulted the advertisement in the *Sheffield and Rotherham Independent* and confirmed that she would be neither overawed nor elated. The pictures were to be sent in the care of an underfootman. To Winifred they all looked the same. Thomas was about to explain the geological significance of one particular mezzotint when a waiter offered him a glass of claret cup. He refused with an intense determination and, leading Winifred to the buffet—glass of lemonade in hand—confessed the errors of his youth.

"I should have told you sooner. I used to drink too much."

"I know," said Winifred. "Your mother told me."

"Did she tell you how much?"

"She said you drank a great deal, that you got in with a fast set and that you've broken the habit."

"Did she tell you about my heart?"

"She said it was weak but that having given up drinking had added years to your life."

"I'm not a very good risk."

"I'll take it. I only wish you'd told me yourself. You should have trusted me."

"I thought you might change your mind, not take the chance."

"I'm marrying you and we'll take the rest as it comes. I'll risk you, if you'll risk me. To prove it, from now on I shall call you Tot. Isn't that what your London friends used to call you—for reasons we'll not go into?"

They took the rest as it came for almost ten uneventful years. The winds of change, which blew outside the lives of Hattersleys, Spooners and Bankses, only occasionally fluttered the curtains at Riverdale Grange or rattled the windows of the smaller house at 16 Asline Road into which Frederick Hattersley had moved to raise capital for the new cutlery business that he had set up at the Empress Works in Eldon Street.

The war of 1870 between France and Germany had been a boon to the Sheffield cutlery trade. Although created to promote trade and industry, the German Zollverein, temporarily occupied in defeating Napoleon III, had little time and less resources to devote to the manufacture and export of table knives and fish forks. The demand for spades, which fainthearts had feared would fall off with the ending of slavery in America, had grown with the opening up of Africa. Before the victory of the Union, the Heather Works had done regular business with the Confederacy and had sold to the Southern states gross after gross of specially ordered spades with blades that bore the insignia of the great plantations. Ten years later, the company was doing ten times as much business south of the Sahara. The new blade plates were stamped with the coats of arms of the Africa charter companies. Hattersley, Sons and Spooner prospered. But it prospered slowly. Thomas Spooner instructed his new general manager to take the advice of Frederick Hattersley. And Frederick Hattersley, with a quarter interest in the firm which he maintained as refuge and insurance, instructed the new general manager to act with caution. Meanwhile, Hattersley and Sons, Scissors and Tailors' Shears Maker, grew so rapidly that the premises within the Empress Works in Eldon Street could barely accommodate the extra men and new machinery.

At seventy-five, old Mrs. Spooner looked much the same as she had looked at sixty. She was a little more wizened. But she was no less straight, and her hair—which had turned white overnight with the news of her husband's death—shone as it had shone in all its colors since she was a girl of sixteen. Age had not brought her either the gift of wisdom or the blessing of charity toward others.

Emily Hattersley, having done her duty by her husband and produced him two boys, showed no further sign of increasing her family or of being interested in anything outside it. She sat in the parlor at Asline Road, mending and darning (despite her husband's insistence that the work should be done by servants), and listened to accounts of Frederick's increasing success. Frederick himself, who seemed to have grown in height as well as weight, retained all his old interests and habits. His world was made up of chapel, choir and work, and the greatest of these was work. But work had taken on a new dimension. He had become a member of the Cutlers Company, and more important, he was working for something. Little Joseph and Herbert were paraded in front of him each night like exhibits in the display case of a cutler's workshop.

Thomas Spooner was hardly working at all. He had begun to write a great political work, extolling the virtues of the working classes. His enthusiasm had moved from natural science to moral philosophy and he almost regretted the years he had spent as a follower of Charles Darwin rather than of Matthew Arnold. However, he never produced a first chapter which was sufficiently satisfying to enable him to move on to the second. Winifred devoted herself with unremitting enthusiasm to all the obligations of a wife—except the job she most wanted to do. Old Mrs. Spooner's prediction that she would not bear children came true. But the prophecy that Winifred would be childless by choice was proved wrong every time that her daughter-in-law visited another doctor in the search for fertility. At the age of thirty-five, she despaired of having children of her own. So she turned her maternal instincts toward her nephews and her nieces.

The girls, Mary and Martha, who grew up to look like their aunt but act like their mother, retained Winifred's affection but not her interest. The boys fascinated her, and the older they grew, the more fascinated she became. Certainly her enthusiasm for Joe and Herbert grew as a by-product of her declining hope of having sons herself. But her interest also grew because her nephews grew more interesting.

Joseph was clever. He would stand in front of his father in the drawing room reading carefully selected extracts from the *Sheffield Independent*. The selection was made each morning against two criteria. First, the passage had to be more difficult than it was reasonable for a boy of his age to read on sight. Second, it must not contain the smallest item of news or comment by which Joseph could be corrupted. As the years passed the selected paragraphs grew more difficult to comprehend—or so Frederick felt as he made sure, during the day, that he could understand every word. But not once—between his fifth birthday, when he read about Mr. Gladstone's resignation, and his eleventh, when he recited "The Epithets of Movement in Homer"—was Joseph allowed to look upon "Woman Assaulted in Attercliffe Bath House" or "Soliciting in Pond Street. Three Fined."

Herbert, only one year younger, had to be forced to read—often with the encouragement of his father's belt. But he would straighten up from the punishment smiling, so as to make clear that he bore no malice. Frederick sometimes wondered if his second son ever felt the leather hit his hide. For within a moment of the punishment being complete, he would be humming a merry tune or telling his father of the adventures he had enjoyed during the day. He possessed a quality that Winifred Spooner described as "charm." Charm was a quality of which Frederick deeply disapproved. Affronted that his sister-in-law should accuse his son of possessing such a characteristic, he increased his resolve to save both his boys from Winifred's undesirable influence. There was no way in which he could prevent aunt and nephews from meeting. Their mother took them to tea at Riverdale Grange and twice weekly, while Herbert rushed out into the garden to explore the secret land by the rhododendron bushes, Joseph sat in the drawing room listening with undivided attention as Winifred told him the story of the Holy Grail or showed him the colored maps in an atlas from her husband's study. They visited the Spooners every Saturday afternoon and while Winifred and Thomas taught Joseph about perspective, iambic pentameter and the Duke of Marlborough's campaigns in the Low Countries, Herbert rushed into the garden and practiced gymnastics on the close-cut lawns. Distressed that his nephew-by-marriage concerned himself exclusively with physical things, Thomas Spooner nevertheless bought a set of Indian clubs and told the budding athlete that if he learned to twirl them with Corinthian skill, an épée would be purchased and fencing lessons arranged. Herbert smiled his winning smile and wondered if he could bring his football to Riverdale Grange. Permission was, of course, granted. But Aunt Winifred's garden was not, as he had originally believed, as big as Bramall Lane, to which Jack Foster had taken him to see the Sheffield Club play a team of soldiers from Hillsborough Barracks. So each Saturday afternoon (to his real regret) he broke a rosebush, flattened a herbaceous border or disturbed the careful pattern of a bed of hardy annuals. Although he was always sorry to cause such damage, he never thought of giving up his football. When Herbert came into the drawing room—obviously repentant and carrying a crushed plant or prematurely pruned bush—his uncle always exhibited both distress and anger. But the boy told his aunt that he was sorry, and she—for all the rationality in which she took such pride— always said that he had made a pretty apology and accepted his promise that he really would be more careful in future.

Frederick Hattersley believed that the weekly exposure to such indulgence would undermine Herbert's character, and he attempted to repair the damage each Saturday evening by reimposing the discipline that aunt and mother had abandoned on Saturday afternoon. So as soon as his father got home from work, Herbert was required to stand before him and respond to a catechism about his conduct. At some point during the cross-examination, the son would say—and almost mean—that if only his father came to Riverdale Grange on Saturday afternoons, all the problems would be solved. The defendant was either acquitted or simply warned as to his future conduct.

Joe's Saturday caused a different sort of concern. His father feared that he might develop an interest in impractical things which would drive all common sense out of his head. But he took a badly concealed delight in the reports that he received about his elder son's intellectual promise. After Herbert had confessed to the damage that he had done to plants and bushes, Joseph was obliged to recite the lessons that he had learned. His father always pretended that his only concern was to make sure that his son's mind had not been contaminated by talk of evolution, Lord Byron or anything creditable to France or Germany. But his intention was to bask in the reflected glory of Joseph's inherited genius. It was the responsibility of his son and heir to fulfill all his father's dreams—Councillor Hattersley, Justice of the Peace, Mayor and Master Cutler, and, if he had held office in the right year, eventually Alderman and Knight. Joseph was not perfectly equipped for the task. But properly prepared, he would carry it out. The dreams of Councillor Frederick Hattersley JP might have to make way for the reality of Councillor Joseph Hattersley JP. But the family would have been vindicated.

It was not the only idea that Frederick Hattersley revised. Anthony John Mundella displayed such a devotion to Sheffield and its industry that he became the object of veneration to the spade master, cutler and potential dynast. Frederick actually joined the Liberal Party and, having paid more than his dues, adorned Liberal platforms all over the town. He was always the first to rise from his seat, applauding when Mundella sat down. He found politics increasingly exciting. So he looked forward with particular pleasure to a great gathering which was held in Paradise Square. It was in that square, he told Emily, that Charles Wesley had preached in 1775. And in that same square in 1878 Frederick Thorpe Mappin—the greatest and most benevolent of all Sheffield's steel masters—presided at the meeting with Frederick Hattersley, Scissors and Tailors' Shears Maker, sitting at his right hand.

The meeting began at seven o'clock and Mr. Mundella began to address an enraptured audience on the subject of tariff reform. He was still speaking at half past eight, when the Tories began to arrive. They came in drays like members of workingmen's clubs on their way to a bank-holiday picnic—noisy, aggressive and drunk. First they pulled up behind the massed ranks of Liberal supporters, trying to look as if they had no interest in what was going on in the rest of the square. Then, rising from the wooden benches which ran along the carts' sides, they began to hurl insults at the Member of Parliament just as he reached the passage of his speech which called for a compact with the German Zollverein.

Alderman Mappin was outraged. For he saw, sitting shamefaced amongst the drunken mob, some of Sheffield's most illustrious steelmakers. Stopping Mr. Mundella in midperoration, he addressed the hecklers.

"You are," he said, "in breach of the peace. Unless you leave this square at once, I shall name those—masters and magistrates amongst you—whom I recognize. And shame upon you."

The noise continued and Alderman Mappin rose in his seat.

"I name as breaching the peace: Samuel Osborn, Jonathan Steele, Augustus Cammell, William Stephenson, William Thorpe, Arthur Roberts, William Hadfield . . ."

Slowly the noise subsided and the drays of drunken hecklers began to pull out of the square. The Liberals cheered and Mr. Mundella pronounced his benediction on the meeting.

"It was," said Frederick Hattersley, "the finest thing I ever saw."

"And," replied Frederick Thorpe Mappin, "the most difficult thing I ever did. They are, or were, my friends."

Back at 16 Asline Road, Frederick first told Emily of his admiration for Mr. Mappin's reckless disregard of his own commercial interest, but then added that he could not express unqualified admiration. "It was easy enough for him, with all his money. It's the little men like me that they'll take it out on. And he'll forget all about us."

It was, therefore, with real astonishment that six months later he received an invitation to attend the opening of Firth College by Prince Leopold. The note accompanying the invitation said that Alderman Mappin had caused his name to be added to the list and that after the ceremony his benefactor hoped that he would join Mr. Mundella's party for light refreshment. His pleasure was only slightly diminished by the discovery that Thomas and Winifred Spooner had received a similar invitation. He worked off his annoyance by denouncing his sister-in-law for her insistence that Mr. John Ruskin's attendance at the ceremony was far more important than the presence at the occasion of a prince of the blood royal.

CHAPTER EIGHT

THE END OF INNOCENCE

Prince Leopold's visit was a great disappointment to both the Hattersleys and the Spooners. Indeed Frederick Hattersley, who saw no more of Queen Victoria's son than the top of his hat bobbing above the enthusiastic crowd, said (in far too loud a voice) that he could not be anything other than a disappointment to anyone except Mr. Mark Firth. The Prince visited the Firth Works, walked in Firth Park (which his brother the Prince of Wales had opened the year before), talked to the pensioners in the Firth Almshouses and then performed the opening ceremony at Firth College. The Prince spoke in the most complimentary terms about Mr. Firth's philanthropy, benevolence and public spirit and remained so long in his company that he was too late to make his promised visit to the works of Messrs. Dixon and Sons, Filemakers.

When the formalities were over at Mr. Mundella's reception, Frederick complained bitterly of the slight to local industry, and his anger was not in any way assuaged by the discovery that an industrial visit was planned for the following day, when the Prince was to witness the casting of a gun barrel at the works of Mr. Thomas Firth. His most bitter remarks were fortunately drowned by the noise of the band of the Royal Engineers giving three cheers for the Prince Leopold—

which they followed by three cheers for Mr. Mark Firth. Winifred and Frederick looked at each other in mutual disgust.

Winifred's disappointment had a different cause. Mr. Ruskin attended neither the opening of Firth College nor any of the receptions which followed it. He was in Sheffield. Indeed, he had been sighted by the local newspaper paying a courtesy call on the Prince at Oakbrook House. And it was rumored that the royal itinerary was to be altered in order to accommodate a visit to Mr. Ruskin's museum in Walkley. But it seemed unlikely that Winifred would be able, as she had hoped, to meet her greatest hero. She was about to say that the whole day had been a complete waste of time, when Frederick Hattersley took her husband aside and, much to Thomas's surprise, began to ask his advice about the education of Joseph and Herbert. Thomas brushed aside Frederick's apology for troubling him with such matters.

"I'm flattered to be asked. Do you want them to board or be day boys?"

"Stay at home."

"Then I suppose that it ought to be Wesley College."

"Would I get 'em in?"

"You would if I spoke to the headmaster."

Frederick Hattersley dissembled badly. "I saw your name on the list of proprietors and I hoped that you'd put in a word."

It was Thomas Spooner's instinct to apologize, even when he suspected that he was being exploited in some way. "I fear that I know very little about the school. My father bought shares when it was founded. Really as an act of charity. I have kept them and they make me a few shillings a year. I know Mr. Shera from the Bach Society. I'll gladly write to him. But I know really very little about his school."

"I know everything about it. I've read the brochure. And I'll tell you what I want."

Frederick took from his pocket a carefully folded piece of foolscap paper and, smoothing out the creases, set out his requirements as if he were ordering nails from the local ironmongery. Holding the sheet of paper in front of him like music at a choir practice, he began to quote the passages from the prospectus which he had laboriously copied out.

"Neat penmanship, ciphering, bookkeeping, land surveying, mental arithmetic and the principles of a sound English education under the supervision of the headmaster."

"I'm sure all the boys get that."

Frederick consulted his paper again. "That's where you're wrong."

Thomas was disconcerted to discover that Frederick knew more about the Wesley College than he did.

"All the boys get 'discipline enforced by uniting firmness and kindness.' What I read out, and what I want, is just for the Commercial Division."

Thomas realized that he was not being consulted but exploited. "I will write to Mr. Shera about places in the Commercial Division."

"And there's summat else. I want both of them to get the entire education quick. I suppose if Herbert starts now, he might go on for a bit longer. He'll need to. But I want 'em both finished before their fourteenth birthdays."

"My dear Frederick, education just isn't like that. You can't buy it by the yard."

"That's as may be. But you know as well as me that at fourteen they'll have to finish."

"But why?"

"Because they'll have to sign their indentures and start apprenticeships. I want them both to have a good grounding. All the things that nobody ever learned me about business. But they've got to know the trade. If they can't work with the tools, they'll never build a business. They're going to be cutlers, and cutlers need to serve their time."

Thomas Spooner was growing impatient and he spoke with an irritation that was unusual in such a self-effacing man.

"You knew nothing about spade making when I took you on. You hadn't done your time as a spade maker. Why shouldn't Joseph be able to do what you did?"

"Spades is one thing, Mr. Spooner, but scissors is quite another. I want those boys to make scissors like their grandfather did, and they can't do that unless they know the trade." The formality of address was intended to indicate disapproval of his partner's tone.

Thomas decided to ask the question which he knew Frederick would think both impertinent and irrelevant. "But do they want to make scissors?"

"Herbert does, young as he is. He'd rather be with Jack Foster in the cutler's shop than eating his dinner. And if Joseph hadn't been given so many airs and graces by them who ought to know better, he'd want to be a cutler as well. Any road up, it's none of their concern. They were born to a scissor maker, and scissor makers they are going to be. In the meantime, I want them to get an education at Wesley College. Perhaps I'd better write to this Mr. Shera myself."

"I will write with pleasure," said Thomas. "I will write tomorrow."

Frederick Hattersley insisted on taking the boys to Foster's in Fargate himself. Emily, who had been the victim of his bad temper when he learned the full cost of the complete Wesley College outfit, feared that he would buy knickerbockers which were not made from one hundred percent new wool and boots with thick soles and steel cleats to protect the heels and toes from wear and tear. But she did not think it her place to advise him about his purchases. Her concern proved misplaced. He returned home cursing the cost of education, but weighed down with every item listed in the College brochure. No distinction had been made between essential, desirable and optional —with one exception. The recommended set of geometrical instruments was adjudged inadequate. Instead of buying the standard plywood box complete with tin-set square and protractor and steel compasses and dividers, he insisted on visiting Wilkinson and Wilkins (Instrument Makers) Ltd. of West Street, where he purchased two velvet-lined mahogany caskets. Within them—secure in specially constructed niches—where innumerable instruments made of gleaming brass.

When, on the Monday which followed the Christmas holiday, the brothers were dispatched, eager but apprehensive, to their first morning at Wesley College, the boxes of geometrical instruments featured prominently in their father's advice about facing the new world of learning. They stood before him in the drawing room. Herbert—although the younger, a good inch taller than Joseph—shifted his weight from foot to foot in impatience to begin the great adventure. Joseph stared earnestly at his father, apparently attempting to memorize every uplifting word.

"Be a credit to your mother and me. Think of us, at home, hoping and praying for your success. Work hard. Only hard work brings owt worth 'aving. Never use foul language and have nothing to do with them that does. Foul language is the sign of a weak mind as well as filthy imaginings. Respect your teachers. They're gentlemen with far more learning than you and I will ever get. They've never made anything. But don't despise 'em for that. Somebody has to do their work. Remember to be proud—proud of your name and your reputation. You have the best sets of protractors and compasses in the school, and don't forget it. Every other boy will be envious of those instruments. Whatever you do, don't lose 'em. They cost three and ninepence a set."

To Emily's surprise, Frederick was home from Eldon Street by five o'clock. At first she feared that he was ill. Then she remembered her husband's proudest boast that he had never suffered a day's illness in his life. As he peered anxiously out of the window she realized that he was waiting for the boys' return. For the first time in their whole life together, he began to exhibit signs of nerves.

"The tram down to Snig Hill ought not to take more than twenty minutes. Let's say ten minutes' wait and then another twenty minutes up here. If they left prompt, they ought to have been here more than half an hour since."

Emily was required to confirm his calculation and share his concern. At a quarter to six, when the boys had still not appeared at the end of the path, she was genuinely and desperately worried. Frederick was worried too. He disguised it by denouncing the irresponsibility that had caused Joseph and Herbert to delay their return by some unworthy diversion, and promising to celebrate their return by "thrashing them within an inch of their lives." When he heard the gate creak open, he strode out to the front door in order to begin his confrontation at the first possible moment. Herbert looked as though he had already been thrashed to within an inch of his life.

"Bert had a fight." Joseph meant to do nothing more malicious than report the sensational news. "He had a fight with four boys at once, I saw it all. I was very frightened. But," he added virtuously, "I didn't run away."

Emily cooed and tutted as she examined the lump on Herbert's temple, the grazes on his knees, his split lip and the nail marks that ran in three parallel and bloody lines across his cheek. Frederick was outraged that his younger son had been so brutally beaten and that his older boy had not gone to the help of his brother. But most of all, he was concerned by the possibility that he might have been wrong to send his boys to Wesley College. His fear had been that exposure to the sons of the professional middle classes might blunt the cutting edge of their character. Now he wondered if Wesley College was one of the public schools which the penny dreadfuls wrote about—institutions in which new boys were tortured and, worse still, prefects drank cider and flirted with chambermaids.

When Emily reported "very sore, poor lamb, but nothing broken," and sent the maid for a bowl of hot water and a flannel, Frederick opened the inquest after calling for tea, his sovereign remedy for all emergencies.

"...and some cakes and sandwiches. We'll have it together in here, not in t'kitchen. But keep the girls away. It's none of their concern and we don't want them gossiping and giggling about it all up and down the road."

Herbert winced as the compress was transferred straight from the bowl of boiling water to his brow. His father, ignoring his pain, invited him to tell his adventure story.

"It was the compasses. The compasses out of the instrument box. First they took Joseph's and then they took mine. They said that they were poison darts taken from the pygmies of the jungle in Heeley and they threw them at trees. Sometimes they stuck in and sometimes they fell out. I told them to stop and they wouldn't."

"Why did they do that?"

Frederick's reverence for property made him incapable of comprehending why even twelve-year-old boys might risk doing damage which reduced an object's value.

"Because they were different," said Joseph from behind a piece of fruitcake.

"Who were different?" his mother asked. "Were they bigger than you or Church of England or what?"

"Not the boys," Joseph explained, "the compasses were—"

His father corrected him.

"Better you mean. Better. That's why they wanted to smash 'em. Better than anything that they had, better than anything at that school. I shall see that Mr. Shera tomorrow and I shall tell him what's what."

Emily, painting iodine on Herbert's knee, added, "You won't go to school tomorrow. You won't go until your father makes sure that everything is all right."

"I want to go tomorrow," said Herbert, "but I don't want to take that compass set. And I don't want Joe to take his either. He won't fight if they steal them. I'll have to fight for him again."

"He beat them all," said Joseph proudly. "There were four and he beat them all. I was frightened but he fought them all."

Frederick Hattersley took his younger Herbert by the hand.

"I'm very proud of you, son. Fighting is bad, but sometimes you have to fight for what's yours by right. And you have to stick up for what's yours and what's right. Those instruments are yours. My gift to you. I shall see Mr. Shera and I shall make sure that next time you go to Wesley College nobody will take them from you. You won't have to fight again."

"I don't mind fighting," said Herbert. "It's the instruments I mind. Joe likes them because he thinks they'll help him to be clever. I hate them because they're different from everybody else's."

His father was too disturbed to interrupt with the correction that they were not different but better.

"I don't want to be different. I want to be ordinary. I'm happier ordinary."

When, the following day, Emily recounted the conversation to her sister, Winifred marveled at the wisdom of her nephew. It was not a philosophy which she shared. But it was a philosophy. And it had come from the boy who was regarded as the dullard of the family.

"What did his father say?"

"He didn't know what to say," Emily confessed.

"He disappoints me. I would have expected 'Out of the mouths of babes . . .' (Psalms, verse eight, chapter two)."

The advantages of being ordinary were not recognized by the whole Hattersley family. Mary and Martha—who had grown into young women of exceptional beauty—stood before their mirrors for hours each day in grateful recognition of their extraordinary appearance. When Mary was elected Whitsuntide Queen of the Calver Street Chapel Sunday School, she listened to the minister describing the virtuous character and noble disposition which had made her the elders' choice. But she knew that really she had been chosen because of her long golden hair, her sapphire-blue eyes and her straight nose. The noble disposition of which the Reverend Horace Beardsley spoke so eloquently prevented even a moment's speculation on the relationship between her success and the unusually large subscription to the organ fund which her father had made shortly before the elders began their annual deliberations.

Martha assumed that she was heir apparent and, sure enough, the following year—shortly after Frederick Hattersley had contributed generously toward the cost of repairing the chapel roof—she succeeded to the crown. On Whit Monday morning, as she waited for the arrival of the hired horse and carriage which would carry her to the start of the Whitsuntide Procession, she sat nervously by the living-room door while her mother pinned the crown of May blossom into her thick yellow hair (which seemed to shine almost as much as Mary's had shone the year before) and her father offered a few words of uplifting advice about the duties and responsibilities which the year of office would impose on her.

"The hawthorn blossom is to remind you of the Crown of Thorns. Even today, sitting up there in your pride and glory, you are to remember Him and His suffering to redeem mankind. You are to remember and be humble. That's what the crown—"

"That's not what Aunt Winifred says."

Joseph was reading in the corner of the living room, forgotten.

"Joseph! Your father knows about the Whitsun Procession. You mustn't contradict him."

Emily did not want her husband's righteous indignation to disturb her thoughts about the day when Martha, looking as much as she looked that morning, would walk into the Calver Street Chapel as a bride. But Joseph persisted.

"She says that the Whitsun Sing isn't anything to do with Christianity. She says it's pagan and calls it the Old Religion. Martha is getting married to the earth, either that or being made a sacrifice. She's going to water the earth with blood and make sure the corn grows." Joseph was clearly eager to add further details.

"Out. Out and stand in the hall till you hear Herbert call that the carriage's come."

Emily, who faked shock at the thought of what her daughter was about to undergo, repeated her husband's instruction.

"What nonsense Winifred does talk."

"It's worse than nonsense. And that one sits every Saturday afternoon drinking it all in. If only he went out into the garden and kicked a ball like his brother, I'd be happier about it altogether. He's like an old man before he's been a boy."

Joseph, listening mortified in the hall, heard the carriage pull up outside the front door. His first instinct was to beat Herbert in the race to tell his father that it had arrived. Then he decided that his brother would bound out of the drawing room and brush him aside. Since he was certain to lose, he chose not to compete. Herbert did not, however, appear through the drawing-room door. Joseph was about to take advantage of his brother's negligence, when he heard his father's voice. The sound of carriage wheels on the drive had reached the drawing room—though the lookout had not reported the arrival. Joseph found the attack on Herbert immensely reassuring.

"I told him to stand in that window and tell us when it got here. I never heard him go out, did you, Mother. He'll be at the back kicking that football. If he's too mucky to go to church, I'll have the hide off his back."

"There won't be time," said Emily, while Martha, her glacial calm unmoved, primped at her fringe, and Mary, who had appeared from her bedroom, looked bored as was only appropriate in someone who had gone through it all before.

Frederick warmed to his subject. "That lad gets dafter as he gets older. You'd think he'd take a leaf out of Joseph's book and try to behave like a man. I'd trust Joseph to do anything I telt him. But Herbert, I sometimes think he's soft in t'head."

Joseph, the wounds of the previous minute instantly healed, glowed to hear the flattering comparison. So his father did love him after all and did love him best. It was then that Frederick expressed to Emily a thought which increasingly obsessed him, a thought which reverberated through his mind whenever Herbert seemed especially stupid or Joseph appeared particularly timid.

"If little Frederick had lived, he'd been worth both of 'em put together. Twice both of 'em put together. I could tell that morning when I saw him lying in your bed that he were a real Hattersley."

Emily dabbed her eyes and Martha awoke from her dreams to ask who Frederick was.

"He was my firstborn son. He should have been your brother."

"Please, Frederick. The carriage is waiting and we'll all be late and upset."

There was no stopping the full flow of his maudlin insensitivity. "Your mother had difficulties. And he died. Died the moment that he was born."

When Herbert returned from the garden—almost clean enough to go at once to the Whitsuntide Sing—Joseph whispered the strange intelligence to him.

"We had a brother once. Did you know? Dad loves him more than he loves us because he looked like him."

"What happened to him?" Herbert sounded uncharacteristically anxious.

"He died, before we were born."

Neither boy was completely reassured or wholly comforted by the knowledge that the son whom their father loved best was dead. Joseph worried that his father did not love him more than he loved

114

anyone else in the world. Herbert worried that his father did not love him at all, and he went on worrying about it all the way to Norfolk Park. He could not remember ever having worried for so long, and he was desperately anxious to ask Joseph what he ought to do to win his way back into his father's affection.

Herbert's anxiety was increased by the circumstances of the journey. Martha and her mother sat on the back seat. Emily had buried herself in one corner in the belief that it was better for her to be crushed than for the Whitsun Queen's dress to suffer a similar fate. Frederick, sitting uncomfortably with his back to the driver, occupied more than half of the front seat. His sons, squashed into the other half, were unable to discuss the subject which interested and worried them most. Forced to think rather than to talk about the little boy whom their father loved best, they grew increasingly certain that their places at Wesley College were the preliminary to exile in an orphanage.

Frederick and Emily had obtained seats in a rickety wooden stand which had been specially constructed for distinguished visitors. Herbert and Joseph were left to stand by a roped-off enclosure in which the scrubbed coal wagons and the hosed-down grocers' drays were being formed up into the procession. As soon as the brothers were sure that their parents had gone beyond earshot, they began to discuss the morning's extraordinary revelation.

"I don't believe it," said Herbert. "We'd have heard about it before."

"It's true. I know it's true. I could tell by the way he spoke."

"Then what ought we to do?" The straw at which he clutched having been snatched away, Herbert looked to his brother for wisdom.

"All he wants," Joseph told him, "is for us to be good at something. That's all he cares about. Being good at things. I'm going to get cleverer and cleverer and know more and more. Then he'll like me more and more."

"That's no good for me." Herbert recognized his own limitations.

"You're good at things. You're good at football and good at singing."

"My voice will break next year."

"Well, you're good at football anyway."

"Do you think football will do?"

"Football and something else. You think of something as well."

And so the great competition for Frederick Hattersley's affection began. Since the participants were twelve and thirteen years old, they did not understand that there was only one way in which they could win their father's affection. They had to be like him as he believed that little Frederick, dead in his first hour of life, would have been like him. They were in competition not with each other, but with their father's fantasy. There was no way in which they could win the unequal contest.

CHAPTER NINE

EXCEPTIONAL ABILITY

Thomas Spooner had not intended to accompany his wife to the Whitsun gathering in Norfolk Park. She had tried to persuade him first that he would enjoy the singing, second that he would be amused by the parade of Methodist respectability and third that he had a duty to family and friends which required him to spend one uncongenial morning offended by the sound of simple hymn tunes and annoyed by platitudes which passed for conversation between pious Nonconformists. She advanced her last desperate argument with a conviction which she had been unable even to simulate for her previous proposition. Winifred was very strong on duty—duty and pride. Her pride demanded that she spoke only of Thomas's obligation to his distant relations by marriage. The debts which he owed to his wife were not a subject on which an emancipated woman could express an opinion. At breakfast on Whit Monday, all pretense of potential pleasure abandoned, she made a last desperate plea, looking furtively over her shoulder in the hope that her last appeal would not be interrupted by her mother-in-law.

"James Montgomery's silly hymns are no more attractive to me than they are to you. But I do know what's right. We went last year

117

when Mary was Calver Street Queen and Emily will never forgive us if we don't see Martha's moment of glory."

Thomas was both pleased and surprised that he had stood out so long and successfully. "It's no use, my love. I am not going to Norfolk Park."

He returned to his kipper, smiling with satisfaction at his bravery.

"There isn't a cloud in the sky. You needn't worry about the weather."

The Marquess of Queensberry's rules being abandoned, Winifred pressed home the advantage she always enjoyed in a verbal rough-and-tumble. "I know why you won't go. You're worried about three years ago when you got soaked and had to spend ten days in bed with a chill. You're worried about your chest."

Putting on the voice he employed to emphasize his natural dignity, Thomas corrected every detail. "It was four years ago and I was in bed for less than a week. You know perfectly well that my reasons have nothing to do with my chest. I am staying at home because I have my book to write and because the voices of three thousand untrained and underrehearsed children will not be pleasing to me. The weather has nothing to do with it."

Winifred was still deciding whether to call him a prig or end the argument before something was said that one of them really regretted, when Doris, the new parlormaid, came in with fresh coffee. It was Doris who told them the news—spluttering it out in little excited sentences. The story was too dramatic to keep to herself, but she knew that it was not her place to speak until she was spoken to. She had heard it on the early-morning tramcar as she traveled in from Darnal, and she knew it to be true because it came from one of the parade marshals who worked at Crossley's drapers in Spital Hill and had once walked out with her sister Alice. Mr. Thomas Miles, for twenty years the conductor of the Whitsun gathering, had died in the night.

"Are you quite sure?" Winifred, being a radical, had little confidence in the working classes.

"Positive, mum. Jimmy Pleasance—that's him from Crossley's—had been got out of bed early. They're gonna put black crêpe on the Sunday school banners and t'band's going t'park early to practice a funeral march to start off singing wi'."

"Poor old Mr. Miles. Bet you really envy him, Tot. He'll escape

'Command Thou Blessing from Above' without having to put up with his wife's reproaches."

Thomas was about to grasp the olive branch, when it was snatched away from him.

"You better come after all. If you ask nicely, they might let you conduct. You'd come for that, wouldn't you?"

"I'll come anyway."

Thomas did not enjoy being in anything except complete harmony with his wife. And he was made to feel all the more insecure by the suggestion of sudden death from a heart attack. Thomas made light of his angina pectoris. But when he pondered his future he was mortally afraid. His fear made him anxious to enjoy every minute. He had learned that the sure way to achieve the comfort of married bliss was to accept Winifred's judgment. Wherever possible, he did it with a minimum sacrifice of face.

"It will be a sad and dreary day now, whatever happens, and we must make the best of it for Martha. I shall take her an orchid from the conservatory." He added a wistful afterthought: "The replacement conductor will certainly be my old friend Dr. Henry Coward, a real musician."

Thomas Spooner was astonished by how pleased he suddenly felt at the prospect of a morning on the brown, trampled grass of Norfolk Park. And Winifred, equally relieved to find herself at peace with her husband, did not even tell him that the gift of an orchid would be entirely inappropriate. Against every impulse, she held her tongue and hoped that he would simply forget the idea. But she was disappointed.

"I'd better cut the orchid straightaway. Doris, find some black silk for armbands; your mistress will sew them on." Suddenly his enthusiasm was boundless. "I shall be ready in ten minutes. We need to leave in twenty-five."

Winifred's reserves of emollience were not inexhaustible. "Stuff and nonsense. We don't need to leave for over an hour. Why do you need to make everything seem urgent?"

At that moment old Mrs. Spooner appeared in the doorway. She was wearing a coat, but her bonnet was in her hand. Disheveled hair suggested that she was not about to put the hat on but had only recently removed it.

"I think that I shall stay at home, dear. It looks like rain. I'm glad that Thomas isn't going. I don't want him to get a chill like he did last year. Not with his weak chest."

Naturally enough, Mrs. Spooner attributed Winifred's fit of giggles to a calculated and continual desire to insult and humiliate her mother-in-law. Thomas, who had suffered more than enough tension for one breakfast time, pretended that he had not heard the announcement of changed plans and reiterated his earlier concern to the room at large.

"We really do need to leave very soon. There may be a crush."

Mrs. Spooner—unsure of what was happening but certain that it was all planned for her discomfiture—swept out, bonnet in hand, muttering, "Of course there won't be a crush. You don't have to invent stories to keep me away."

There was a crush. Somehow, the news of Thomas Miles's death had spread through the parishes of the Sunday School Union, and hundreds of men and women who had sung James Montgomery's hymns when they were children had converged on Norfolk Park to pay tribute to the conductor under whose baton they had once harmonized. By the time the Spooners arrived within sight of the park, the road which led to its wrought-iron gates was jammed with jostling families, who—once inside—sweated without a glass of ginger beer or lemonade to slake their thirst. The hawkers, who had set up their stalls early in the morning, had sold out more than an hour before and had left the park in search of new supplies to be sold at twice the usual price to the collapsing Sunday scholars and their exhausted parents. They knew that after two hours of continuous hymn singing had parched their throats beyond endurance, they would hardly calculate the cost.

With mutual reluctance, having instructed the driver of their hired carriage not to move from the spot on which he set them down, Thomas and Winifred walked the last half-mile. It was almost half an hour before they reached even the foot of the hill which acted as an amphitheater. So the proceedings were about to begin when they arrived at the back of the huge semicircle of carefully arranged children which bent around the hay cart from which Dr. Coward was to conduct. The curve of children had taken hours to form into proper shape. Early in the morning Jimmy Pleasance and his fellow stewards had marked out a giant arc. Thirty feet in width, it stretched for almost two hundred yards from end to end. Posts and flags marked its furthest boundaries. And between them the crescent had been divided by pegs and tape into thirty-seven segments. Each one was identified by a number displayed on a pole which, on that dolorous day, was draped in black. The numbers had been allocated to Sunday schools by the wholly un-Wesleyan process of drawing lots. By the time the Spooners arrived, each Sunday school had formed up in its apportioned and appointed station. At one end of the semicircle Darnal Reform and Darnal Independent stood side by side, temporarily joined in Whitsun unity. At the other extreme, Philadelphia Primitive Methodists and Mount Zion were shoulder to shoulder. In between were the other Sunday schools of the Sheffield Union.

Parents and friends, standing on the gentle slope of the hill, behind the ministers and elders who sat on rickety collapsible seats, had mysteriously sifted themselves into a fair representation of the social classes. At the front of the crowd the men wore top hats and the women were engulfed in tulle decorated with artificial flowers and fruit. Behind them stood men in bowlers and women in modest straw and unpretentious felt. At the very back, hardly able to hear the softer notes of the sadder hymns, the crowd wore flat caps or had their heads tied in shawls.

At the moment when the Spooners arrived, Dr. Henry Coward—splendid in immaculate tailcoat and high collar—climbed in absolute silence onto his temporary dais and indicated his wish that the band should rise. Standing, as if to play the national anthem, the musicians struck up "The Dead March in Saul."

The Spooners gave up all hope of finding the Hattersleys and reconciled themselves to a position behind three thousand sweating children at the edge of the crowd. They spent a restless two hours waiting for the program of hymn and prayers to end. Their one consolation was that they were so near to the exit that they were within a few yards of the refreshment marquee, to which Winifred insisted they must have been invited—since they were close family of one of the Sunday school queens. The last note of "A Home in Heaven" had hardly died away before they were inhaling the familiar smell of damp canvas and reviving themselves with ginger beer.

Amongst the other relatives who rushed toward the long trestle table with unashamed haste were Joseph and Herbert Hattersley, who had bounded ahead of their more inhibited parents. Herbert whooped at the sight of Aunt Winifred and rushed to hold her hand. Together with Joseph, he stood in her care while Thomas went off to look for the adults in the hope that he might cross paths with Dr.

121

Coward and take the opportunity of congratulating him on the singing. The boys were becoming restless, when Winifred was approached by a middle-aged gentleman who wore a well-pressed but ancient frock coat and a tie fastened in an unfashionable bow. He spoke with exaggerated courtesy.

"Forgive me, dear lady, for this intrusion. My name is Shera. I am the headmaster of Wesley College."

Winifred began to assure him that her husband had often spoken of him and that the meeting was a great pleasure. But Mr. Shera was not in a mood to be interrupted.

"My excuse for accosting you without the privilege of an introduction is my desire to congratulate you on the performance of this young man." Mr. Shera grasped Joseph by the shoulder. "He is a scholar of quite exceptional ability. I am proud to have him in my school, though I sometimes think that he deserves a place in a more illustrious institution than mine. You must be very proud of him."

"I am very proud of them both." Winifred squeezed Herbert's hand.

"Forgive me, madam. I am most remiss. I was quite carried away with my desire to tell you of your older boy's prowess." Mr. Shera smiled a sickly smile. "I do understand the pride that a mother feels in all her children."

It was with immense pleasure that Winifred observed the profound embarrassment which followed her explanation that she was aunt, not mother. Her victim was still wincing with pain and cringing with shame when a triumphant Thomas Spooner appeared, arm in arm with a slightly bewildered Dr. Coward. The conductor knew that somewhere he had previously met the enthusiastic admirer who insisted that his wife was waiting to meet the hero of the day. But he could not remember where and when. As Thomas led him from end to end of the crowded tent Dr. Coward was subjected to detailed cross-examination about the technique of conducting oratorio. It was with relief that the maestro reached what he hoped to be the safe haven of Winifred and the two boys. To his distress, Winifred's conversation was no less animated. He tried to concentrate his mind on memories of more tranquil occasions, and waited for a gap in the flow of words and a chance to slip away. Just as the moment of escape seemed near, Dr. Coward's attention was diverted from the dash for freedom by an unmistakable sound. One of the two little boys, who stood ignored at the side of the strange couple by whom he had been abducted, was softly humming "The Dead March in Saul."

122

Dr. Coward—a musician and a music teacher above all else—turned and looked down at the young soloist. He noticed an Eton collar which had turned limp and grubby in the June sunshine, and a mop of fair hair which was already beginning to fall naturally into the fashionable quiff which dandies of the day carefully cultivated across their foreheads. But it was the smile that made him take an interest in the boy. Another lad—apparently the singer's companion—shifted his weight restlessly from foot to foot. But if the singer felt bored and anxious to leave, he showed no sign of his impatience. He was singing to himself and for himself and he was clearly enjoying the performance.

"Do you have piano lessons?"

Herbert showed no sign of being irritated by the interruption.

"No, sir. Mary and Martha do. But not me and Joseph."

"Violin then?"

"No. None of us has a violin."

"Singing lessons then?"

Winifred, who had not spoken for several minutes, thought it her duty to interrupt. "He's a great singer. He's worrying about his voice breaking and having to leave the choir."

Thomas, anxious to establish his musical credentials, did not want Dr. Coward to think that he took Herbert's talents too seriously. "It's just the chapel choir and the choir at Wesley College."

Dr. Coward turned toward Herbert to make clear that it was to him that all further questions were directed. "What was that song you were singing?"

"I don't know. I only heard it today."

"Where, today?"

"It was the tune the band played at the beginning. They played it very slow. It was what they played when the conductor told them to stand up." Herbert was amazed by the ignorance of the questions.

Dr. Coward stared Thomas accusingly in the eye. "This boy ought to be given music lessons. Anyone who can carry a piece like that in his head after a single hearing possesses considerable talent. I suspect that he is blessed with an exceptional ability to read and retain a score."

"That," said Winifred, "is the second time I have heard about exceptional ability today."

Dr. Coward—as if in reproof—bowed stiffly to Winifred, nodded curtly in Thomas's general direction. Then, turning on his heel, he advanced with extended hand toward Mr. John Truswell, whose "homemade specialties of potted meat, pressed brisket" had been both advertised in the brochure that had been printed for the occasion and inserted in the sandwiches prepared for consumption by Ministers, Elders and Honored Guests.

"A sad day, Mr. Truswell. A sad day."

"A sad day, indeed."

The sentiment was echoed by William Walker, who had set up an outpost of his bookshop in the corner of the tent, under the sign "Agent for the British and Foreign Bible Society." He noted, to his satisfaction, that the sale of black-edged mourning cards was going particularly well.

"I have a slight pain in my chest," Thomas said, tugging at his tight collar and making his way to the door of the tent.

"We'll go home at once," replied Winifred. "When we get into the carriage, Tot, say exceptional ability to me. I've got a wonderful idea."

"Exceptional ability?"

Thomas found the prospect of another wonderful idea unnerving.

"Yes, exceptional ability! Everybody seems to be talking about it today."

The Spooners did not discuss exceptional ability on the way home, for their neighbor in Ranmoor, old Mr. Dixon, could not find his carriage and drove home with them through the hot afternoon. Even Winifred's exuberance was inhibited by the combination of a reluctance to talk about family matters in front of strangers and an inability to talk about anything at all while her mouth was full of the Doncaster butterscotch which Mr. Dixon made at his Britannia Works. Tea was an immovable family feast at Riverdale Grange. So it was not until the early evening, when old Mrs. Spooner was in her room changing for dinner, that Winifred was able to tell her husband of the afternoon meeting with Mr. Shera. She ended her account of the conversation with a passionate assertion.

"We have to do something for them. If we don't, those talents will all be wasted."

"What can we do?" Thomas had memories of the offer of medical help that he had once made to Frederick Hattersley.

"We can't let them go off to apprenticeships when they're thirteen or fourteen."

"I don't know whether their father means to take them away from school or not. But I do know that if that is what he intends, nothing and nobody will change his mind."

"I shall try to change his mind," said Winifred.

"How on earth do you suppose you can do that?"

"I shall start by finding out what is possible, whether or not we can get proper music lessons for Herbert and what school Joseph should be sent to if he is to be given the chance to go to university. Then, when I know what can be done, I shall think of how we can persuade Frederick to do it."

"He could go to university if he stayed at Wesley College."

"If he stays at Wesley College he'll stay on that dreadful commercial course. Mr. Shera himself said that he deserved a better school."

Thomas Spooner knew that he ought to dispose of the idea there and then. But first he had to visit the bathroom and break, under his nose, a vial of the solution which brought relief to the pain in his chest. Then, when the medication had done its work and he felt capable of a confrontation, supper was served and common courtesy required him to eat and make the conventional small talk with which cultivated families passed their mealtimes. As soon as supper was over and his mother had left the dining room, he cleared his throat in preparation for a carefully worded explanation as to why the fate of Joseph and Herbert must be left in their father's hands. But before he could begin, his mother reappeared at the door. When her son and daughter-in-law did not immediately abandon their conversation in order to compliment her upon her appearance, she made one of her sudden preemptive raids on the conversation.

"Is Mr. Gladstone really going to repeal the malt tax?"

"I think so, Mother."

Thomas was sure that the Grand Old Man had announced exactly that intention, but single-word answers never satisfied Mrs. Spooner.

"How can you go on supporting that dreadful monster? Now he's just pandering to the brewers."

Thomas had no wish to embark on a major political argument with his mother. So he gave a noncommittal grunt. But Mrs. Spooner was not to be denied.

"You agree with me, don't you, Winifred?"

"I think I do," said Winifred, who usually had definite ideas about everything. "I think I do, but I'm not sure."

"How can you say that? You can't agree with making drink cheaper. I know that you've both lost your faith, but I hope that you haven't lost your principles. Have you, Thomas?"

Her son grunted again. The same question was repeated to Winifred, who made the mistake of giving a considered answer.

"If Gladstone does do it, he'll be trying to help the farmers, not the brewers. The chapels aren't complaining. The temperance associations want a bigger tax on beer, that's all."

A cause for offense having been created, Mrs. Spooner was able to enjoy a carefully controlled spasm of righteous outrage.

"I shall not be patronized in my own house. Even though I am so ignorant, I do have some pride. I shall leave you to the sort of conversation which is beyond my limited intelligence. Perhaps, when you have a minute, you will ask Mrs. Tasker to bring a cup of tea to my little room."

"I can't put up with this much longer," said Winifred

Thomas drew a deep breath and retired to bed in silence. The pain in his chest was getting worse.

Downstairs at 16 Asline Road, the evening of Whit Monday passed in what appeared to be tranquillity. Mary and Martha, despite their father's disapproval, were allowed to wear their hair in a complicated arrangement of curls, plaits and ringlets which they had discovered by chance in a picture taken by the London Stereoscopic Co. and displayed at an exhibition of photographs which they had been forced to attend. Mary, as the heroine of the hour, had been permitted to invite a friend to supper and, the meal being finished, the three girls sat in the bay window of the drawing room playing solitaire and Halma—card games being prohibited. Emily embroidered, as she embroidered every evening, while Frederick Hattersley turned the pages of an ironmonger's catalog in order to keep a careful eye on what was being sold by his rivals. He snuffled and sneezed into a huge red handkerchief, for pollen was still in the air and the hay fever which had plagued him all day had persisted into the evening. In the attic bedroom at the top of the house, Herbert snuffled and sneezed in proper family tradition. In between the dabbing of his inflamed nostrils he carried on a furtive conversation with Joseph, who lay half-asleep in the bed beside him. Both boys knew that if the maid of all work, in her box room across the attic landing, heard them talking

126

she would rush in and order them to sleep or, worse still, tell their father the following morning.

"Tell me again what Mr. Shera said."

Herbert had asked the question ten times.

"Nothing. I've told you, nothing. Nothing much."

"He did, he said something about you. I heard him."

"He said that I'm clever. Now go to sleep."

"Did he say anything about me?"

"He might have done, but I didn't hear him."

"That other man said that I would be a great musician."

"No he didn't. He said you could sing. That's different."

"You told me that if I became a good singer our father would like me."

"I told you that if you became good at anything he would be pleased. That's different too. Shut up and go to sleep."

Joseph turned toward the wall. The wallpaper was rough and cold, but he pushed himself against it in the hope that he would be so far away from Herbert that his sleep would not be disturbed by his brother's itching and twitching. He was almost asleep when the first of a fusillade of sneezes struck the back of his nightshirt with a force which penetrated the thick flannel. He knew that Herbert's sneezes came not singly but in battalions. The seventh eruption having reverberated around the bedroom without its last echo being accompanied by a new explosion, Joseph closed his eyes.

"Tell me about tomorrow," Herbert demanded.

"I don't know." Joseph's only interest was in sleep.

"Yes you do. You were there when Father told us about it."

"You were there as well."

"But I didn't understand it all. I want you to tell me. I want you to tell me now."

Joseph paused for a moment in order to decide whether the best way of silencing his brother was to answer the question or to ignore it. Herbert shook him by the shoulder and hissed into the side of his face, "Tell me! Tell me!"

Convinced that there was no escape from some sort of explanation, Joseph hoped that a single answer would suffice.

"We're to go to the works with father and see the new things."

"What new things?"

"The German new things."

127

"What German new things?"

Joseph decided that he would make one last desperate attempt to satisfy his brother's insecurity. "They're machines for making scissors. The Germans don't make them like we do. They have big machines that squeeze pieces of steel into the right shape. Do you understand that?"

" 'Course I do," said Herbert, taking reckless advantage of his brother's indulgence. "But what else?"

"We've got one."

"Got what?"

"Got a German machine, stupid. And we are going to see it tomorrow."

"One day," said Herbert, revealing that he had always understood the purpose of the next day's visit to the Empress Works, "we shall have a hundred German machines. I heard our father say so."

"Ten."

Joseph's respect for accuracy had suddenly put him on the defensive.

"In my works," Herbert insisted, "there will be a thousand German machines."

With a deep sigh the younger brother closed his eyes, rolled over onto his back and, since hay fever made it impossible for him to breathe through his nose, began to snore with a rasping rhythm which prevented Joseph contemplating sleep.

There was, Joseph decided, no point in waking Herbert. There would be anguished cries of anger and surprise. Then he would collapse again into his snoring sleep. Joseph decided to let the gale blow itself out.

With meticulous caution he first sat up and then stood up on the bed. Having steadied himself on the bedroom wall, he carefully stepped over his sleeping brother, silently lowered himself onto the floor and tiptoed toward the only chair in the room. It stood in front of the dresser. Sitting on it, Joseph looked past the ewer and bowl, beyond the oval mirror in its oak stand, through the gap in the hastily drawn curtains and out of the window which opened onto a part of Sheffield he had never visited and did not know. He could see the lights blinking in one of the hills on which the town was built. One light shone particularly brightly and Joseph decided—for no better reason than the romantic attraction of the invention—that it was Mr. Shera who lived beyond or below that incandescent star and made all the other inhabitants of the galaxy seem dim and dull. For Joseph had heard and understood every word that Mr. Shera had said to his Aunt Winifred that afternoon. Mr. Shera had called him "a boy of exceptional ability."

It was at that moment, with the lights of Sheffield sparkling like stars in the summer sky and Herbert's snores reverberating in the room like the grunts of a contented pig, that Joseph decided on his destiny. Herbert could run the German machines and stamp out the scissor blanks to be filled, sharpened and polished. He was going to get an education. At the age of fourteen, he was wise enough to add (with a sigh that demonstrated regret as well as apprehension), "whatever my father wants."

CHAPTER TEN

DESTINY

The new German machine puffed out steam and stamped out scissor blanks with greater success than even Frederick Hattersley had anticipated. Jack Foster, elevated in a week from foreman to manager, supervised the mass production of the crudely fashioned scissor bowls with mixed feelings. It had taken him seven years to learn how to tap them out on the little pointed anvil that now stood neglected on his bench. But the machines would make them all prosperous.

After six days of confirmation that the steam presses really worked, the Mester went out and found new orders and, the new customers having signed the order forms, two extra grinders were hired to smooth the rough work into the quality expected from Frederick Hattersley and Sons. That was the way that the Mester worked—no new orders until he was sure that he could meet the old orders and no extra workers until the new orders were won. The Mester was steady. But although he would never make a fortune, he would never go out of business. That was a great consolation. It allowed Jack to enjoy his football and his family without worrying about the future. The only cloud in his sky was the prospect of an expansion so rapid that he would be required to work on Saturday afternoons. Saturday afternoons were sacred.

As soon as work finished on Saturday morning, Jack Foster hurried out of the Empress Works gate and greeted the round and rosy Mrs. Foster, the round and rosy infant in the battered perambulator and the round and rosy Jack junior, clinging to his mother with one hand and holding a bottle of ginger beer in the other, as if they had been separated for a year rather than four hours. Mother and child then spent the afternoon in undisguised admiration while Jack justified their awe and esteem by playing admirably at cricket or football according to season. It was in order to make those Saturday afternoons possible that Jack Foster went to work with such enthusiasm. He knew that they could not last forever. But he worried in case success might bring his happiness to a premature end.

Winifred Spooner—in her house high above the smoke and grime of industrial Sheffield and higher even than the public parks where the workmen spent their salubrious Saturday afternoons—also endured a week of worry. According to Emily, both Joseph and Herbert had thoroughly enjoyed their day at the Empress Works. Joseph had appeared to be making a careful mental note of everything he saw, and his father had come home full of praise for the intelligent questions his son had asked. To Herbert, Jack Foster was already a sporting hero. And he followed the new manager from stamping machine to grinder's hulls with an admiration which Frederick Hattersley did not realize was more related to ability to bat and keep goal than to skill at forging a scissor bowl out of a rod of metal or the talent for supervising the working of the machine which could do the work of ten scissor forgers.

Emily described her sons' enthusiasm to her sister with relief as well as with pride. Had the boys not lived up to their father's expectations, their character defects would certainly have been blamed on her. Winifred, on the other hand, heard the stories of their successful day only with apprehension. The idea that her nephews might want to be cutlers had never occurred to her. And since she had not worked out how to arrange for Joseph's superior education, she was fearful that the new and unexpected enthusiasm might take permanent hold before he could be presented with the prospect of a better life.

The plans for Herbert were already laid. All that the younger boy

131

could reasonably expect was the music lessons which fitted his talents and ought to satisfy his ambitions. More important, two nights a week of instruction under a local teacher would leave him free to complete his apprenticeship as a scissor maker, which would qualify him to assume control of Frederick Hattersley and Sons. His ultimate artistic destiny—chapel organist, choirmaster or conductor of a temperance society band—would allow him all the time he needed to supervise the Empress Works when his father grew too old to manage the family business. With Joseph away—first at school, then at university and eventually adorning one of the professions—someone would have to stay in Sheffield. And Herbert, whose abilities were musical rather than intellectual, seemed preordained to play the support role. It was, Winifred assured herself, exactly what he would want to do.

"I want to do something for Herbert," she told her sister.

"It's his birthday next month."

"I've bought him a present for that. But I want to do something else. I want to pay for music lessons."

"Are you still on about that talk you had with Dr. Coward? I've told you, I think you've made far too much of it. It was just a chance remark."

Winifred was sometimes astonished by her sister's presumption. Emily had not been present to hear Dr. Coward's encomium. More important, her comment implied that she possessed an understanding of human nature which, since her life was centered in a kitchen, was clearly beyond her comprehension.

"You're wrong, Emily. He really meant it. It would be wicked not to give him a chance. Dr. Coward said so."

"He said that, 'wicked'?"

Winifred began to feel impatient. "He said that Herbert should have music lessons."

"I'd like him to concentrate on his studies. Making him do school-work is hard enough as it is."

"Music lessons will give him an interest."

"I'll speak to his father."

"I've said I'll do it."

"Sometimes, Winifred, you really are silly. Why cause me unnecessary trouble? Frederick will want to do it himself, if it's to be done at all. Try to be sensible."

"Very well, if you want to be huffy about it. Can I tell you the name of a teacher that I've found, or is that testing Frederick's patience too?"

"You can tell me that. But please don't be silly about it. It only causes trouble."

"Patrick Ignatius Martin. He lives in Sharrow. Don't worry about the name. He's given up Rome in favor of Salzburg and Vienna. He only worships Mozart now."

Joseph's future was more difficult to arrange. For Winifred had decided that Joseph was very special indeed—so special in fact that none of the schools about which she knew were suitable to his prodigious talent. Thomas had been a boarder at Scarborough, and the stories which he had told of his time in that seaside establishment had convinced her that the east coast college was as inadequate to the needs of her nephews as it had been unworthy of her husband's talents. Harrogate she believed to be filled with the hearty sons of wool merchants whose heads she assumed to be as thick as their accents. St. Peter's in York had the distinction of antiquity. Guy Fawkes had been a pupil there. But who had ever read about St. Peter's in the *Strand Magazine* or the *Illustrated London News*? Winifred—without any evidence to support the conclusion except her casual conversation with Mr. Shera—had come to the firm conclusion that Joseph's genius demanded his enrollment in one of the great public schools. And she was not the woman to abandon a dream just because every sensible person would realize that it could not come true. Her preference was for Eton, the place where Mr. Gladstone had enjoyed his spiritual and intellectual friendships with Arthur Hallam. But if Eton was not possible, Harrow would do. Lord Byron went to Harrow. To Rugby she was positively opposed. She knew of no poet who had been educated at Rugby except Matthew Arnold, the latest object of her husband's veneration. She was deeply impressed by *Culture and Anarchy*. But Winifred's plans for Joseph were the product of the high romantic, not the intellectual part of her character. That side of her brain could not even contemplate her protégé following in the footsteps of a school inspector. She would like it to be Eton or Harrow. But she conceded in her more practical moments that she would agree to any of the ancient public schools. However, she had no idea how entry into one of these great institutions could be arranged. They did not advertise. She had little doubt that an unsolicited application from a Sheffield matron would be dismissed with amused contempt. She dared not confide in Thomas and ask for his help, for she could not risk bombardment with his irrefutable logic and invincible common sense.

The discovery that Joseph and Herbert might become contented scissor makers filled her with renewed despair. After the depressing lunch with Emily at which she had learned how much the boys had enjoyed their days at the works, she sat silent in the small drawing room at Riverdale Grange pretending to sketch the bunch of daffodils that stood on the triple-tiered circular table. Thomas described her as being preoccupied with her own thoughts. She denied it. Just before dinner he inquired if he had offended her in some way. She assured him that he had not. After an almost totally silent meal, he expressed the fear that his wife might be unwell. His wife insisted that she had never been in better health.

Back in the small drawing room, Thomas found the continued silence unbearable. So he began an attempt to amuse his wife with readings from the *Sheffield Independent*. After reporting several items of local news, he turned to an item concerning the previous month's appointment of Mr. Anthony Mundella as Vice President of the Board of Education.

He added an editorial note of his own. "Quite splendid. And what a blessing that we were wise enough to choose him instead of that bumptious Joseph Chamberlain. I saw Mr. Mundella deal with a deputation of Anglo-Catholic bigots who wanted to keep their stranglehold on our schools. He took the wind right out of their sails. Do you know what he said to the Dean of York?"

Winifred—noting that Thomas had begun to acquire his mother's annoying habit of asking questions which could have no answer—admitted that she did not.

"He looked him straight in the eye and said, 'It is not Christian to deny a boy of unusual ability the right to develop his God-given talents.' I hope the Dean knew that he was being given a lesson in theology by an Italian!"

But Winifred had stopped listening. She turned to her husband as if she had not heard a word of what he had said to her. To his surprise, she made an admission. "I fear, my love, that you were right before supper. I do not feel very well. I should have admitted it sooner."

As always, in matters affecting his wife, Thomas's reaction was both genuine and extreme. "I will send Lizzie down to Broomhill for Dr. McPharlane."

"You will do no such thing. I shall be as right as rain in the morning. An early night will set me up like new. I shall go at once."

"At once?"

"At once. I shall sleep in the landing bedroom."

Winifred was gone before Thomas could repeat his increased anxiety and renewed belief that the doctor should be called. In his concern, he did not notice that she left the room at a speed which must have increased her debility.

She undressed in the bedroom which she and Thomas shared. As always in her usual anxiety to get on to the next part of her life, she tossed her clothes across the backs of chairs, onto the tops of mirrors and over the rail of the brass bedfoot. Impatiently, she buttoned up the high collar of her nightdress and struggled into her dressing gown. Then she sat down at the dressing table. But instead of pulling the pins out of her hair and enjoying both the sight and the feeling of it falling over her shoulders, she opened one of the little drawers that flanked the dressing table mirrors and took out four sheets of writing paper, an envelope and a little traveling pen. She reached to the back of the drawer and pulled out a tiny black bottle. Where cork met glass there was a brown line of encrusted ink. Winifred smiled. Ten years must have passed since last she wrote a secret letter.

At the sound of a familiar footfall on the landing, she pushed paper, pen and ink inside the wide lapels of her dressing gown before she picked up the silver-backed hairbrush that Emily had given her on her twenty-first birthday. Thomas knocked, paused, called, paused and entered, insistent on seeing his wife into bed. She took his arm as they crossed the landing, pulling the dressing gown across her chest and complaining of the cold. All suggestions that she should return to the warmth of the master bedroom were dismissed peremptorily.

"What I don't want tonight is fuss. I shall wear my dressing gown in bed."

"In bed?"

"Where else?"

Thomas, still worrying, decided that his wife would only be agitated by further unwanted offers of help.

As soon as he was gone and the door closed, Winifred emptied her contraband onto the lace counterpane. There was no desk in the landing bedroom. Methodically, she removed the china trinket bowl and pin trays, the glass flower vases and the porcelain milkmaids, flower sellers and shepherdesses from the dressing table. Then she began to write. She was uncertain whether to begin with "My dear Mr. Mundella" or with a more formal salutation. So a space was left at the top of the page and the first paragraph boldly begun:

> You will, I hope, forgive me for writing to you with this request for advice and assistance. But my husband has told me of your concern that boys of humble means . . .

Even as she read her words, she realized that they would not do. They would produce, in the Member of Parliament's mind, a picture of Poor Law children, ragged and barefoot. Twice more she began and twice more was dissatisfied. She decided to draft out her letter on the back of one of the spoilt sheets. It took over an hour of writing and crossing out before she was satisfied. Then, first making sure that there was no ink on her fingers, she began to make the fair copy. It was after midnight when she wrote the final essential sentence.

> We are not without means and we will gladly pay whatever fees and boarding costs are involved. Our request is for advice, *not* charity.

Then all that was left was for the letter to be topped and tailed. It was too late for careful consideration of etiquette and propriety, so she decided on a compromise. She began with what she feared was the overfamiliar "Dear Mr. Mundella" and ended with what she knew to be the overformal "Mrs. Thomas Spooner." Then she opened the linen chest and put pen, ink and paper under a pile of carefully folded towels. She had written secret letters before.

Nine hours later, she was woken by the song of a thrush which Thomas (reading *The Times* on the bedroom sofa) later described as "inconsiderately fortissimo." He came across and kissed her on the forehead. His manner suggested more indulgence than reproach.

"You should have told me. I really do admire your poetry. When you're ready I hope that you will let me see it."

Winifred tried not to look bewildered as she sat up in bed. Smoothing down her nightdress, she suddenly noticed the brown stain on her left breast. The rim of dried ink around the lid of the bottle had been warmed by her body heat as she smuggled the materials of her plot from bedroom to bedroom. To Thomas's alarm, she reached up and, putting both hands behind his head, pulled his face down toward her. As she kissed him she had only one thought. Fortune favors the brave.

A week passed without a reply from Mr. Mundella. Winifred confirmed, from *The Times,* that the House of Commons had reassembled after its Whitsuntide recess, and began to search the *Sheffield Independent* for clues about the Member of Parliament's whereabouts. There was nothing in its pages to suggest that he was out of the country or that he was in any way indisposed. Had he, she wondered, been offended by her request or affronted by her manner?

Each morning, over breakfast, she stared at her husband with undisguised envy. Suddenly all his letters seemed full of interest. Every envelope intrigued her, and, too proud to admit her curiosity, she tried to imagine the sort of person who wrote them by an examination of the writing with which they were addressed. One or two actually had the names of the correspondent printed on the back. Suddenly, bills from London booksellers and appeals from local charities were objects of mystery and excitement. When she read "Walter Clegg, Solicitor and Commissioner for Oaths," she could hardly restrain herself. For Walter Clegg was the lawyer who had defended Charles Peace, Sheffield's most notorious criminal. She felt sure that Thomas would eventually tell her about the contents of the long letter which he read, read a second time and then read carefully again. Then, after several minutes spent staring into space over his wife's shoulder, through the window and apparently beyond the garden, he spoke to her.

"What in God's name have you done?"

She knew at once that the letter from Walter Clegg was somehow connected with the favor which she had asked of Mr. Mundella. Was it, she wondered for a moment, illegal to write to a Member of Parliament asking for help? Had she libeled Mr. Shera and Wesley College? Without a word she held out her hand for the letter, and without a word Thomas handed it to her. Behind her she could hear her mother-in-law demanding an explanation of what was happening.

"What's the matter? Is everything all right? You've turned white as a ghost. Thomas, just tell me nothing's the matter. I just sit here with nobody to talk to, worrying about you. I don't want to interfere in your business. Put me out of my misery. Tell me what it is . . ."

But the voice gradually faded. Winifred was vaguely conscious that her mother-in-law's pleas and entreaties were growing more insistent. But neither old Mrs. Spooner's growing hysteria nor Thomas's blank, bewildered stare was capable of distracting her from the letter.

We represent Frederick Hattersley, scissor and tailor's shears manufacturer of Asline Road, Highfields, and Empress Works, Eldon Street.

We are informed by our client that you, or your agent or persons representing you and acting with your knowledge and approval, have attempted to induce my client's sons, Joseph and Herbert Hattersley, to act in a way which is against the wishes of their father and, in their father's judgment, against their best interests.

We are instructed to inform you that, Joseph and Herbert Hattersley being minors, your attempt to alienate them from their father is unlawful as well as improper and we are instructed to ask you for immediate written assurances that you will desist from such behavior forthwith. Failing receipt of suitable assurances, it is my client's intention to obtain an injunction in the High Court, forbidding you or your agent to approach his sons either verbally or in writing.

We are further instructed to inform you that Joseph and Herbert Hattersley have been indentured as apprentices and bound to journeymen and that attempts to persuade them to break their indentures would be a further offense. It is Mr. Hattersley's intention that his sons should leave school immediately and concentrate on their apprenticeships exclusively.

I am finally instructed to advise you that my client proposes to dispose of his interest in the company of Hattersley, Sons and Spooner and to dissolve the partnership by which that company is controlled. He will communicate with you shortly to end his association with that company.

Winifred laid the letter down by her teacup. Calmly, she turned to her mother-in-law.

"You are responsible for this. I don't know how you did it. But I know that this is your work."

Mrs. Spooner whimpered, and Thomas looked hopelessly first at one woman and then the other.

"Ask her what she has done." Winifred was no longer calm as she began to realize the consequences of the letter which she had just read. She was shouting. "Ask her what she has done. She is a wicked old woman. Jealous, mean and greedy."

"I have done nothing. How dare you accuse me in my own house. I don't even know what you're talking about. You won't tell me. It's shameful. Stop her, Thomas."

But Thomas was coughing too violently to hear his mother's plea, and Winifred was so caught up in her hatred that she did not even notice.

"I know it's you. You are a liar as well. Somehow, you've done all this."

Thomas coughed on, his napkin to his lips. He pushed his fingers inside his collar and tried to loosen it.

"What I did I did for the best," said Mrs. Spooner, still unaware of her son's distress. "I did it to save you and Thomas from your own foolishness. I understand those people. You don't."

"So you did do it, you wicked old woman. You did do it." Winifred was screaming.

"It was a mistake. I didn't plan to do it when I opened the letter, I thought it was for me. It was addressed to Mrs. Thomas Spooner. That is me and nobody else. I read it before I realized."

Suddenly, Winifred was calm again, contemptuous instead of frightened. Her hatred had not diminished but it was the hatred of a composed woman, not of a girl who has been found out and who is awaiting punishment.

"Which is it then? Which story describes the way that you've ruined your son's business and ruined the lives of two innocent little boys? Which is it? Did you not do it, or did you do it by mistake, or were you right to do it? Which is it? We know why you did it. You acted out of envy and jealousy. But which excuse?"

The question was never answered. For suddenly there was a crash from the other side of the table. Thomas, having failed to attract his family's attention by coughing, spluttering and choking, had adopted the final expedient. He had fallen dead amongst the breakfast pots and cutlery.

In the weeks which followed, Winifred was constantly astounded by the kindness with which she was treated. Her mother-in-law, having explained that she had opened the letter addressed to Mrs. Spooner —since that after all was her name—gave up attempts to justify sending the letter on to Frederick Hattersley and offered instead a

139

small annuity. It was too small to make any significant difference to Winifred's income but far too large to be accepted with dignity.

Frederick himself spoke to her as if she were a man.

"It was me," she told him, "not Thomas. You must blame me."

"I know that," said Frederick, "I know that. But he should've kept control of you. That's a husband's job. Especially a husband with a young and headstrong wife. But that's all forgotten."

"Are the boys . . . ?"

"The boys are doing very nicely. That's why it can be forgotten. I were probably wrong to send them to t'Wesley's College in t'first place. Now it's all straightened out I can afford to forget it. You do the same."

When Mr. Shera called round to offer his condolences, Winifred almost told him about the great injustice that had been done to Joseph. But she did not trust herself to tell part of the story without revealing the full truth about Thomas's death—a truth which had united the family in a determination to ensure that it would never be revealed. So she did not raise the subject of the boy's wasted talent. But as he left Riverdale Grange the headmaster asked Winifred about her nephews' future.

"Make them work hard," he said. "Little boys need to be driven, not led."

"Their father will do all that is needed in that direction. He will drive them."

"And they will work in his business."

"They are bound apprentices, and having learned the trade, they will inherit the company."

"Perhaps that is all for the best. They were willing boys. But neither of them was a genius."

Winifred could not disguise her astonishment. "You told me that Joseph possessed 'exceptional ability.' "

"Dear me. It is, I fear, a phrase which I use too lightly. I like to please parents and to encourage the boys."

"I . . . we had great hopes for him."

"I trust, my dear Mrs. Spooner, that I did not encourage such hopes. One of the boys, I think Joseph, was an above-average pupil. But nothing more. He will make a great success of running his father's foundry. Just the thing he is cut out for."

And before Winifred could correct him about Joseph's destiny, Mr. Shera had bowed his way out of Riverdale Grange.

CHAPTER ELEVEN

THE RESOURCES OF CIVILIZATION

At first, it seemed that Mr. Shera was right. Joseph and Herbert left Wesley College without audible complaint or visible disappointment. Neither of the boys had liked school—Joseph because he wanted to read rather than to follow the technical disciplines of the commercial course, and Herbert because he wanted to do neither. Frederick Hattersley was able to convince himself that they left school without regret but not that they took up their apprenticeships with enthusiasm. They rose early, washed quickly and left punctually for work each morning. They willingly performed the menial tasks which were supposed to build the character of apprentices. Neither possessed the driving ambition which Frederick Hattersley hoped they had inherited from him. But they worked hard.

They left home together at half past six on each working day, traveling by foot and by tramcar the route which their father would follow an hour later. Within moments of their arrival at the Empress Works, Jack Foster began to build their characters by requiring them to clean out blocked drains, oil rusty machinery and sharpen blunt tools. Being the master's sons, they were required to work longer as well as harder than apprentices from outside the family. They were never allowed to leave for home until Frederick Hattersley's horse and trap had clattered out of the yard. And since their father never left for home until half past six, Joseph and Herbert worked a regular twelve-hour day. Once home, they ceased to be bound apprentices and became again Hattersley sons—a role which carried a higher status but no less onerous obligations.

Within ten minutes of arriving home, they were required to be washed and changed into the knickerbocker suits that they had worn at Wesley College. Fortunately, their father had made prudent purchases, and even after a year of natural growth and increased muscular activity, the jackets did no more than strain across expanding chests and, after Emily had worked on the turnups, the trousers hovered at about the proper height above insteps. The school suits were judged exactly right for family supper, an occasion of some solemnity but not one sufficiently elevated to justify the exposure of Sunday best to the risk of gravy stains.

The table—and the family which sat around it—was always arranged in the same way. Emily sat at the end of the table nearest to the door which linked dining room to kitchen. Although the maid of all work was employed to serve at meals—as well as scrub floors, clean windows, black-lead grates, make fires, wash pots and sweep carpets—the mistress of the house did not trust her to have the vegetables on the sideboard at exactly the moment when her husband had carved the joint. In consequence Emily was constantly performing a maneuver which she described as "nipping out"—a description which annoyed her husband almost as much as he was irritated by the activity itself. Mary and Martha—on each side of their father at the one end of the table while their brothers flanked Emily at the other—sat erect and silent. Occasionally, they communicated with each other by the exchange of glances. Their secret messages were usually provoked by a comment of their father's which, in some mysterious way, reminded them of a conversation held in the privacy of their bedroom. Occasionally, Mary would adjust a ringlet or Martha would straighten a ribbon or tighten a bow. But most of their energies were concentrated on sitting erect with spines pressed hard against the backs of chairs. Good posture, they had no doubt, was one of the social graces which they must perfect before they could be certain of ensnaring rich and handsome husbands.

The talking was done by Frederick, who boomed out unsolicited opinions about his limited range of interests, and examined his sons' knowledge of the same subjects. Cutlery, God's will and choral music combined with his new enthusiasm for Liberal politics to dominate each supper's conversation. He hated to be interrupted. But his family could never concentrate for the length of a whole diatribe.

"Where are you going now?"

Emily had risen from the table and had turned toward the kitchen door.

"I'm just nipping out to make sure of the custard."

"Lizzie'll do that. What do you think we pay her for? Five shillings a week and can't be trusted to make the custard! Sit yourself down— unless you're not interested in last night."

The whole family was interested in last night. For Frederick had traveled to Leeds with his new political friends to celebrate the election of a Liberal government. Herbert Gladstone, the Prime Minister's son, was Member of Parliament for that town, and his father, the Grand Old Man himself, had spoken at the banquet in the Cloth Hall Yard. How could anyone be anything but excited at the prospect of hearing what would undoubtedly be a detailed description of the whole event? But Emily knew that duty required her to maintain the inflexible order of her priorities.

"She'll make it lumpy. She always does. And it will spoil the apple pie I baked this morning. You'll still be telling us about Leeds when I get back. It went on long enough. You didn't get back till after two o'clock."

Frederick Hattersley wondered—as he wondered, on average, twice a month—if his wife meant to poke fun at him. He decided, with relief, that she was not sufficiently intelligent to behave in so impertinent a fashion. As he awaited her return, and the reassembly of his full audience, he filled the time with a sudden catechism of Joseph and Herbert.

"The trademark on the knives was a fish. Who made them?"

"George Fisher and Company," said Herbert with an impressive certainty.

"Wrong. You're supposed to have learned your marks. Do you know, Joseph?"

"John Herring and Sons."

"Why didn't you shout out like Herbert, if you knew?"

Joseph shrugged his shoulders and stared past his father and out of the window into the autumn dusk.

"Don't be so rude," said Emily, suddenly reappearing with a cut-glass jug of steaming custard. "Answer your father properly when he speaks to you."

"Quite right."

Frederick believed that manners maketh man—manners and a thorough understanding of the cutlery industry.

"What's George Fisher's mark?"

There was absolute silence.

"What is it, Herbert?"

"Don't know."

"Joseph?"

"A fisherman with a net in one hand and a fish in the other."

"If you knew, why didn't you say?"

His exasperation with what he believed to be Joseph's absentmindedness gave way to pride as he began to describe the great occasion in which he had taken part. Pulling a menu card from an inside pocket, he read with increasing difficulty from the vast bill of fare. Clear Game Soup he negotiated easily enough and he advanced on Fillets of Sole à la Tartare and Mayonnaise of Lobster with commendable courage. Filets de Volaille en Chaud Froid and Noix de Veau he avoided altogether, moving on to the safer ground of Venison Cutlets, Veal and Ham Pie, Roast Mutton, Turkeys, Beef à la Mode, Tongues, Chicken, Roast Beef, Hams, Galantine of Pheasant, Grouse, Partridge, Roast Pheasants and Game Pies. He was just deciding whether or not he had the courage to attempt the puddings (which ranged from Crêmes Bavaroises through Tartlettes à la Parisienne to Charlotte Russe au Café) when Herbert interrupted him.

"Did you eat all that?" He was clearly impressed by his father's capacity.

"I had a bit of most things."

Frederick meant to make his reply sound like the modest admission of an extraordinary appetite.

"And Mr. Gladstone," said Emily, "did he eat all that?"

"He ate nothing. He didn't even come in until the eating was done. His son was there all along, tucking in with the rest of us—Lord Frederick Cavendish, the Right Honorable Mr. Childers, Sir Matthew Wilson . . ." He left the end of the list unfinished as if there were more aristocrats and Privy Councillors than he had time to mention. "But Mr. Gladstone himself came in when we'd done. You wouldn't expect the Prime Minister to eat all that. I'm sorry though that he missed the music. Who wrote 'The Lost Chord'?"

"Arthur Sullivan," said Herbert.

"And *Carmen?* They played 'Selection: *Carmen.*'"

"Bizet." Herbert had no doubt.

"After 'God Save the Queen,' we had the speeches. Joseph, run into the kitchen and get the *Independent.*"

Emily tutted at the idea of anyone leaving the table before they had finished the apple pie, and Mary and Martha giggled in unison for no reason that was apparent to their parents. But Joseph, knowing what was in his father's mind, scurried eagerly away. When he returned, Frederick searched the paper for the account of the banquet and, having found the page and column, instructed his son to read the passage of the Prime Minister's speech, which it quoted word for word. "Stand up and speak clear."

Joseph showed enthusiasm for the first time that night.

"If it shall appear that there is still to be fought a final conflict in Ireland between law on one side and sheer lawlessness upon the other, if the law purged from defect and from any taint of injustice is still to be repelled and refused and the first condition of a political society is to remain unfulfilled, then I say, gentlemen, without hesitation, the resources of civilization against its enemies are not yet exhausted."

Frederick clapped almost as heartily as he had applauded on the previous night, and both Emily and Herbert joined in. Mary and Martha sat unmoved, while the young orator sat down in exhausted silence.

"What's it about?" asked Herbert.

"It's about Ireland and that murdering Fenianist Parnell," his father told him. "He wants to take Ireland away from us."

"Mr. Martin is Irish."

Herbert was anxious to force himself into the conversation. Frederick ignored him. It was catechism time again.

"How did they all know—everybody there—that I was a Sheffielder, a Sheffielder cutler? No, no. Not *you*, Mother." Frederick stopped Emily answering just in time. "I know you know the answer. Herbert, how did they know that I was a cutler?"

"You looked at the makers' marks."

"No, I didn't. Well, not so that they could notice. I didn't pick the knives up and study them. Do you know, Joseph?"

145

"You took your steel out of your waistcoat pocket and sharpened your knife before every course."

"If you knew, why didn't you say without prompting?"

Joseph gave an ingratiating, self-deprecatory smile in the hope that his mother would find it more acceptable than a shrug of his shoulders. He did not know why he had not answered the question.

When the children had gone to bed, Frederick Hattersley began to address his wife, ducking and weaving from side to side so as to watch her reaction to his diatribe without his view being obstructed by Lizzie as she cleared the table.

"I don't understand him, I don't understand him at all. He works hard, does as he's telt and learns quick. Jack Foster says he can shape a bowl as quick as a man who's been at it for ten years. He does nothing wrong. But he's just not interested. What do you reckon he really wants?"

"He just wants to read books."

"But reading's nowt. Reading is what you do as well as summat else. It's not a job. Reading won't earn his living. Reading is laking, not working." As in all moments of anguish, Frederick Hattersley's accent thickened.

"I don't know what to say. He's very strange," said the strange boy's mother. "You'd hardly believe that Herbert is his brother. Herbert seems to enjoy everything."

"Herbert enjoys everything and understands nowt." At once, Frederick Hattersley felt ashamed that he had spoken so severely about his second son and began to retract his libel with what passed, in him, for grace. "He tries to do too much. Choir three times a week. Football on Saturdays. Dashing about and laughing. He sings at work."

"Jack Foster told me that they were both good boys."

"Herbert'll make a fair craftsman. That's what Jack meant. But I can't see him running the company."

"Joseph will do that."

"He will. He will that. He'll do it if I have to break his neck to make him. Somehow I'm going to put a barrel of gunpowder under him."

The sentence trailed off into a long silence which was only broken by the triple chime of the grandfather clock in the drawing room proclaiming that it was ten o'clock and bedtime.

"Come, Mother," said Frederick, "it's bed for us."

Emily put her hand on his arm. "What were you thinking about?"

"I were thinking about that little fella that died years sin'. He'd have been a real son to me. He looked like me. I thought that as I saw him lying there on the pillow that first day. He'd have run the company."

"Frederick, it's not right to think about him so much. It's not right for you and it's not right for Joseph and Herbert." Emily paused only a moment to think if it was right for her. "They know you'll never be satisfied with them, even though they don't know why. They're good lads, both of them."

"They could both be better." Frederick Hattersley had no wish to be consoled.

"They do well enough, Frederick. Don't make them think that you're always disappointed."

"If it keeps them up to t'mark."

"I'm not so sure, Frederick. Sometimes never satisfying makes people give up trying to satisfy. In the end they don't bother anymore because they've no hope of pleasing, whatever they do."

They did well enough for the next four years. No apprentices ever spoilt less work or broke fewer tools. Joseph's conduct equaled his craftsmanship. He was never late, insolent or disobedient. Indeed, he rarely questioned either instructions or advice. If Jack Foster worried about him at all, it was because he showed occasional signs of being "goody-goody." But goody-goodies did not work as hard as Joseph, or pay so little heed to the cuts and burns which were the unavoidable consequence of the forger's working day. Goody-goodies were elaborately polite to their fathers and fawned on their employers, they went to church on working days, condemned drink, complained about rough conduct and expressed surprise that anyone found horse racing interesting. Joseph was guilty of none of those sins. He simply never did anything wrong. Jack was driven into the last refuge of the bewildered adult.

"He's a deep one, that Joseph," he used to tell his cronies in the Barracks Hotel on Langsett Road.

He never said it when Herbert was there, and Herbert was there almost every Saturday dinnertime. For the Barracks Hotel had a football team and that team was trained by Jack Foster, who—as his status had improved and his physique deteriorated—had made the reluctant transition from player to coach. It was Jack who had persuaded Herbert to leave the chapel team at Calver Street and play in the northern parks and on recreation grounds with the Barracks

Hotel. For the Barracks was—according to the trainer—"a man's team, not a bunch of lads." Herbert arrived at the public house each Saturday filled with the apprehension of the young enthusiast. He was frightened that if he played he would play badly. But he was even more afraid that he would not play at all. He competed for a place in the side with the soldiers stationed in the garrison from which the hotel took its name—grown men of the York and Lancaster Regiment with sideburns, waxed mustaches and arms adorned with tattoos which commemorated long-forgotten triumphs over distant warlike tribes and local friendly girls.

On Saturdays, at half past one, Herbert enjoyed a glass of light ale while the soldiers—with whom he would soon take the field of athletic endeavor—finished their fourth or fifth pint of the day. He would have gladly drunk more. But he always feared that the effects of a full pint would remain with him throughout the afternoon and that he would return home with the smell of beer still on his breath. Brave halfback though he was, the thought of his father finding out the truth about his Saturday excursions filled him with dread.

The full name of the team for which he played was kept from Frederick. As far as his family was concerned, Herbert played for the Barracks, a team built around patriotic infantrymen who were so concerned with their fitness to defend goal and empire that they shunned alcohol as they had once shunned cholera-infected water in India.

Jack Foster had worked out in detail how he would react if his part in the conspiracy were ever to be discovered. He knew that the deception would be regarded as far more serious than the drink. If confronted, he would blandly insist that he had no idea that Frederick Hattersley was being deceived. Having confirmed by implication that Herbert was guilty of the more serious crime, he would then defend him on the lesser charge of enjoying the occasional drink—at the same time adding conviction to his own claim of total innocence. He had rehearsed his defense time after time.

"You know what young apprentices are like, Mr. Hattersley." Jack could hear himself speaking. "He's very well behaved by comparison with some we've seen, your Bert. Never thought you didn't know and never thought you'd mind."

Jack Foster realized that his employer did not know and that if he were ever to find out, he would mind very much. But he did not regard the potential concern as proof that Frederick was a good father. Jack was a family man of the sort that matched tolerance with affection. So, insomuch as he allowed himself to judge his master's conduct, he dispproved of Frederick Hattersley as a father almost as much as he admired him as a cutler.

There was no doubt that Herbert was difficult. But anyone with half an eye could see that the more his father demanded of him, the more difficult he could become. He was just a young lad, with a young lad's feelings and a young lad's hopes. Jack Foster was not a man to ponder the need to love or be loved. For he took love for granted. And he thought of the love of father for son as indistinguishable from pride in the son's behavior. He could not understand why Frederick Hattersley wanted to make his sons into different men. But he knew that the willful decision to ignore his younger son's existence—except when reproof or punishment proved necessary—was foolish as well as cruel. He could not accommodate his employer's perversity. They had both been apprentices and they both ought to know how apprentices behaved.

So Herbert's Saturday afternoon half-pint came as no surprise to Jack Foster, and he could not imagine how Frederick Hattersley could possibly believe that his son played serious football without setting foot in a public house. Sheffield Wednesday themselves had their offices in the Cambridge Hotel, and their dressing room, for home games at Olive Grove, was the Earl of Arundel and Surrey. Football and licensed premises went together. It was only natural—as it was natural that after choir practice on Tuesday and Friday evenings, Herbert would meet a girl at the vestry door and meander with her hand in hand into the darkness behind the chapel. Jack did not, however, know that after his Monday evening music lesson with Mr. Patrick Ignatius Martin, Herbert was offered, and accepted, first a drop of whiskey to drink his teacher's health, then a bottle of stout to relax his vocal cords and finally another drop of whiskey to celebrate his God-given voice. So he did not realize that the young left half was becoming a heavy drinker.

For a year, Herbert's partiality remained a secret. There was never any alcohol at 16 Asline Road, and Herbert made a careful point of never drinking even half a pint of ale or stout within an hour of returning home. The addiction might have steadily grown without the family ever knowing had not Mary suddenly acted out of character. For the first time in her life, she developed a genuine enthusiasm, and when the object of her sudden ardor—Vernon Tomlinson, a corn merchant's son from Conisborough—proposed marriage, she displayed a decisiveness of which her parents did not think her capable. She accepted at once and, within minutes, began to stipulate the sort of wedding, house, housekeeping allowance and family she expected her husband to provide. Mr. Tomlinson, enjoying both a sudden infatuation and a guaranteed income, agreed to everything. Frederick Hattersley, having consulted his wife about what was best for her daughter, agreed to the match, and the marriage date was fixed. After a wedding breakfast at which everyone agreed that Martha would soon follow her sister down the aisle, the happy couple left for a honeymoon in Buxton, and the younger guests congregated in the drawing room at Asline Road. Frederick and Emily sat uncomfortably in the dining room.

At first they quite enjoyed the sounds of genteel pleasure. They knew that it was Martha who entertained on the piano because of the unimaginative choice of pieces and the eccentric selection of notes. And Herbert's voice was as unmistakable as it was persistent. His repertoire embraced a wide range of tenor and baritone solos, from the "Kashmiri Love Song" to "The Old Superb." As he moved on to humorous music hall numbers his mother began to feel nervous; but, surprisingly, Frederick retained his good temper until the supper had been served and cleared away, when there was almost complete silence in the drawing room and Emily was emboldened to wonder if she should take them in some more pie and cakes. Her husband, who had been half-asleep in his chair at the head of the table, came to complete consciousness with a start and a change of mood.

"Certainly not! I can't imagine what you're thinking of, Mother. They should have been gone an hour ago."

He was about to stride into the drawing room and bid them abuse his hospitality no more, when movement in the hall gave Emily the hope that the unwelcome guests were leaving without being told to go.

"We'd better remember our manners. Let's go and say good night; it will stop them from hanging about in the hall."

Inevitably, Frederick led the way out of the dining room. He was therefore the first to see Herbert, leaning against the banister and gently vomiting onto the bottom stair. In his hand was an empty sherry bottle. Together with its original contents it had been smuggled out of the wedding breakfast.

"Where's Joseph?"

"He went to his room as soon as the music started," said a youth with a brocade waistcoat who had clearly shared the stolen sherry. "I think he took a book."

"He should have been here, keeping an eye on things. Fetch him down, Martha."

His daughter, still clutching her sister's bouquet, daintily picked her way over her brother's vomit to carry out her father's bidding.

Three or four of the young people had begun to collect their coats and edge nervously toward the door. One young lady actually said that her father must be outside in his horse and trap by now, and that when he had agreed that she should come, there had been a reciprocal promise that she would not keep him waiting. She held out her hand to Emily.

"No you don't," said Frederick. "I've got something to say."

Joseph, in threadbare dressing gown, stood at the top of the stairs. The young revelers tried hard to focus a steady gaze on various pieces of wallpaper rather than look at Emily, who was weeping, Herbert, who was sitting on the stairs with his head between his knees, or Frederick, who it was assumed was about to do or say something violent. The assumption proved correct. Taking hold of his son's hair, he pulled the miscreant to his feet. Then he slapped him, first on the right cheek, then on the left. The girls began to cry and Emily spoke with a firmness which would have surprised those who did not understand her.

"No more!"

Martha, on the landing, screamed. Joseph began to descend the stairs for no particular reason. Frederick did not hit his son again.

"If you behave like an animal, you shall live like an animal. When you've cleaned up your mess, you can spend the night in the washhouse. The rest of you"—he turned theatrically on the recent revelers —"are never to set foot in this house again. Never. None of you."

There was a rush for the door, but he had not finished.

"Both of my sons have disgraced themselves tonight—Herbert because of what he did and Joseph because of what he did not do. I am ashamed of them both."

Before the front door had finally slammed closed and the bolts had been slid into place, the family had begun to argue. Emily could not believe that he meant it. Martha asked him if he knew how cold it was out there, and Joseph, in case his father did not know the answer to the question, estimated that it was about thirty degrees Fahrenheit. But Frederick was immovable. Herbert, his cuffs wet from mopping the stairs and his feet wet from washing his shoes, was bundled out into the yard.

"He'll freeze," warned Emily.

Joseph hoped that he would have enough sense to light the gas under the boiler, and Martha wept to think that she would never see her brother alive again.

"Don't be so daft," said Frederick. "He'll wrap himself in those potato sacks and he'll be outside at seven in the morning waiting for somebody to cook his breakfast."

He fell asleep as soon as his head hit the pillow and began rhythmically to snore.

Emily crept out of bed at four o'clock, fearful that if she woke her husband he would complain about her "fussing" over Herbert. Frederick had woken at three and lain awake—pretending sleep—in the hope that his wife would creep downstairs and see if his son was safe in the washhouse. When, at last, she made her reconnaissance, she was horrified to discover that Herbert was not there. She could find no evidence to suggest that the washhouse had been occupied during the night. The old potato sacks were still in a neat pile in the corner. The broken-down leather chair in which Frederick had assumed his son would sleep was still on its side. No attempt had been made to light the gas jets under the boiler. She described the scene when, an hour later, Frederick admitted that he was awake. He feigned composure.

"You can be sure he'll be back when he's hungry."

Frederick made the prophecy with apparent confidence. But he agreed to Emily missing morning service so that she could stay at home and look anxiously out of the window. And when, after lunch, Joseph announced that he was going for a walk, his father did not ask him what route he proposed to take. For, although he would not admit it, he hoped that brother was going in search of brother. Martha whimpered in a corner of the drawing room and, when Joseph returned with no information, announced her conviction that Herbert was dead in the canal.

"Don't be stupid," her father told her. "Last night he couldn't have found his way to the canal. He'll be back before bedtime."

Frederick spoke with absolute conviction, but when at nine o'clock there was an urgent knock at the front door, he smiled in a way which suggested more relief than triumph. He soon composed himself and set out the family in preparation for the prodigal son's return. Emily was installed in her armchair on the right-hand side of the fire. Joseph and Martha were placed side by side on the horsehair sofa. The way in which the head of the household stood, feet apart, in front of the mantelshelf did not suggest that the fatted calf was to be killed. To everyone's surprise, it was Lizzie who, having fumbled for agonizing minutes with the front-door bolts and chains, knocked and entered the drawing room.

"There's a lady to see you, Mr. Hattersley. She says that she's come about Mr. Herbert."

CHAPTER TWELVE

MISS ANNIE ELLIS
TELLS A STORY

The lady was large, no longer young but, in her distinctive way, undeniably attractive. She was not the sort of lady with whom either Frederick or Emily Hattersley was used to entering into conversation. The seam of her claret-colored coat was split where it stretched over her ample bosom and there was a stain on her deckled lapel. Her hair was pinned up, but a good deal of it eluded the pins and fell down onto her shoulders. At her throat there was a complicated, but not very clean, bow which reminded Joseph of Dog Toby. He wondered if his father would act the part of Punch, Judy, the policeman or the crocodile. When the cross-examination began, he decided that it was the policeman.

"And who might you be, my good woman?"

"I'm the barmaid at the Barracks—the Barracks Hotel. My name's Annie Ellis. Miss Annie Ellis."

Emily gave a little gasp of horror.

"And what, may I ask, have you to say about my son?"

"I know where he is. And you've got to get him back. The army's not the life for Bert."

Emily's gasp turned into a scream. Frederick was too astounded to resent being given instructions by a woman of dubious age and character about which there could be little doubt.

"Are you telling me he's joined the army?"

"I am."

"And how, may I ask, do you happen to know?"

"He was with me the night before he left."

Emily and her daughter each suppressed a scream.

"Which night?"

"Last night."

"Where?"

"In the Barracks. I have a room at the top of the house. He came there when you turned him out."

"Has he been there before?"

"Have you turned him out before?"

Frederick Hattersley lost his judicial calm. "If you speak like that to me I shall send for the police."

"And charge me with what? I've done nothing wrong."

"Abducting a minor. My son is not yet of age and you are at least thirty."

"Twenty-five. And you can be as rude as you like. You let yourself down, not me. I'm just here to help because I can't bear thinking about Bert, cold and miserable in them barracks. He's not cut out for it."

Emily resented the suggestion that this person with painted cheeks and dirty shoes visible below the torn hem of her skirt should presume to care about Herbert's welfare.

"Don't you dare tell my husband that he's rude. And don't you dare tell us about our duty . . ."

Boldness being Miss Ellis's stock-in-trade, she was about to tell Mrs. Hattersley that she had never mentioned duty, and that if anybody in that room had a guilty conscience she was sorry, but there was nothing that she could do about it, when Frederick took over the conversation.

"You leave this to me, Mother. You shouldn't be bandying words with a person of this sort—"

"Of what sort?" screamed Annie Ellis. "Of what bloody sort?"

Martha turned bright red and Emily, apparently forgetting that it was her husband who had told her to be quiet, asked if Frederick was prepared to allow her to be ordered about in her own drawing room. Frederick reassumed command.

155

"Off to bed, you two." He jabbed a hand in the direction of his gawping children. "Mother, I have something else to say to this person, if you will excuse us for a minute."

None of them moved except Joseph. As Joseph moved his father changed his mind.

"No, you stay here, Joseph. I want a witness to all this. It's about time you began to accept your responsibilities. You can come with me to Hillsborough Barracks when we have finished our bit of business with this . . . er . . . young lady."

"Tonight?"

Joseph was not sure that even the prospects of Herbert's release justified turning out in such weather.

"Tonight," said Frederick. "Have you no concern for your mother's feelings? The longer he stays in, the more it costs to buy him out."

"A lot of good it will do you." Annie Ellis was giggling. It seemed to Frederick like a moment for biting sarcasm.

"It may be, my good woman, that you know more about the army off duty than I do. That would not surprise me at all. But I do happen to know a little about the law of the land. There will be a price to pay. And I shall pay it. But my son will be bought out and he will be bought out tonight."

"Not from Hillsborough Barracks he won't. Because he's not there." Annie Ellis smiled with triumph. "He's gone to York to join the Hussars."

Emily responded with proper maternal loyalty. "I don't believe you." She found something particularly shocking about the Hussars.

"I ought to know, love."

Emily shuddered at the woman-to-woman familiarity.

"I bought his ticket, seeing as how you keep him so short he couldn't afford it himself."

Her mother's ire being roused, Emily turned on the philanthropist. "And you claim to worry about him now. Without your money he would never have gone to York at all. He would be here, safe and sound in bed."

Annie giggled. "Oh no he wouldn't. If I hadn't have given him two shillings, he would have walked all the bleeding way. Talked about it last night. Sat up in bed and sang songs, even when he was sober, about being a cavalryman. 'M'Old Shako' and 'The Trumpeter,' the songs he sings down in the taproom for the boys. There was no stopping him going to York. He needed half a day mucking out them stables to get sense into his head. But I'll tell you, he'll want to be out now. You know that. You know him as well as me."

Almost everything about Annie Ellis had begun to affront Emily. The day before, she would not have believed that she would ever meet such a disreputable person. Yet this woman stood in her own drawing room and not only spoke of her son's behavior in bed but presumed to equate his parents' understanding of his character with her own. Emily swept out into the hall.

"Get your coat," said Frederick Hattersley to his son, "and go down to Heeley Bottom and get a cab."

"We're not going to York tonight?" Joseph spoke less in hope than in despair.

"That we're not. I'm going somewhere else tonight."

Frederick wrinkled his forehead and pursed his lips so as to leave no doubt that his mysterious destination could not be revealed to the sweating Annie Ellis, on whom he turned his pale blue eyes.

"I take it you came here for money."

He examined the contents of his purse and pulled out a half-sovereign.

"I did not. I came here because I care for Bert."

"No doubt you'll take the money nevertheless."

Frederick Hattersley, his judgment of human nature proved correct, ushered his unwelcome visitor out. When his wife heard the door bolts slam, she turned to her husband, hoping for a word of comfort and concern about the ordeal which she had suffered.

"I'd get back to bed if I was you. It's an early morning tomorrow. First train to York for me."

Emily held her husband's greatcoat as he pulled it on in impatient anticipation of Joseph's return with the hansom cab.

Only once before had Frederick Hattersley called at the Foster house. Jack recalled the awful occasion with a terrible clarity. But it was not an evening to which he gladly referred in conversation. Frederick, who remembered the evening equally clearly, had no inhibitions about recalling that terrible night.

"Long time since I was here, Jack."

"More than twenty years, Mr. Hattersley."

"Seems like yesterday in some ways. You looked like death. I remember thinking you were as white as a corpse."

"What can I do for you tonight?"

It seemed late for reminiscence, and Jack had no wish to talk about Frederick Hattersley's previous visit at any time of the day.

"It's something similar."

Jack looked incredulous. Twenty years before, he had endured the visitation of an avenging angel. Frederick Hattersley had stood on his doorstep and told him to make a choice. If he mended his ways, his job was safe and his debts would be paid. If he persisted in his sinful habits, he would be discharged from the works and the bailiffs would be round in the morning. Jack suggested that the offer was best discussed inside the house. But Frederick had declined to enter the house of an admitted adulterer. After two decades of scrupulous propriety, Jack had not expected to be knocked up by nemesis again. He kept his nerve.

"Similar? In what way, Mr. Hattersley?"

"The flesh, Jack. Sins of the flesh. It's our Herbert this time."

"How can I help?" Jack was careful not to ask for the details of the offense.

"I shan't be at work tomorrow. The young fool's joined the army. I'm going to buy him out."

Even a lifetime's experience of Frederick Hattersley's megalomania was not enough to convince Jack Foster that he had been knocked up after midnight in order to be warned of his master's absence from work the next day. So he waited to hear the real reason for the late-night visit, believing—as a result of his experience of Frederick Hattersley's character—that he knew the reason for the delay. Frederick had come to ask him a favor. And he was finding it acutely painful to make his request. Jack repeated his offer.

"Anything I can do, I will. You know that, Mr. Hattersley."

"You could start by saying what a young fool he's been. You could start by sounding as if you're on my side."

"That goes without saying, Mr. Hattersley. You know that."

"There is one thing I'd like you to do."

"You've only to ask."

"I want you to go to Campo Lane tomorrow morning and see Mr. William Walker at number forty-five."

"And what am I to say to him?"

"He is the agent for Mr. Mundella."

"Yes?" It was cold as well as late. Jack could not disguise his impatience."

"I can't tell you more but Mr. Mundella, or at least those associated with him, have been asking me about various business matters."

Thinking that he still had learned very little about the following day's mission, Jack tried again.

"I'm still not sure that I know what that's got to do with me."

"It's got nowt to do with you. But Mr. Mundella has interests in a medical-instrument factory—something and Ross. I want Herbert to finish his apprenticeship there. I want them to take his indentures."

Jack rarely argued with his master. "Shouldn't you go yourself, Mr. Hattersley? He's more likely to take notice of you."

"It needs to be sorted out tomorrow and I'm in York bringing that young fool back. He'll do it if you tell him that taking on Herbert will help with the other matter. Say I'll be indebted to him."

"Will he know what the other matter is?"

"He will. But you won't. You'll know soon enough. For the moment it's none of your business."

"I still think you should go yourself."

"You've got to go. There's no choice. I want it sorted out tomorrow by the time I get home. I don't want him hanging around about here. I want him off."

"If that's what you want."

"It is. And I want you to have a word with him when he gets back. He'll take notice of you, especially if you tell him that you've had a bit of similar trouble."

"How do you mean?"

"I mean trouble with a woman. And I mean trouble with me when I found out. I'm not sure he understands that I'm serious. If he crosses me, I'll finish with him. You know that, Jack. Tell him that you've been through it."

"It won't be so easy with Herbert. He's not broken like I was. He'll not forgive you if you ride him hard."

"Do you hold it against me now?"

"No, I'm grateful. It was the right thing for me. Probably not for her. But for me."

"There you are then."

"Here I am."

"I'm glad you realize when you're well done by."

"I'll do it to the best of my ability, Mr. Hattersley."

"You don't sound as if you look forward to it."

"I don't. But I'll do it."

"You look right bad again. As bad as on that night. Are you all right?"

"Of course I'm all right, I'm always all right."

It was his invariable answer to all serious questions about his welfare. And very often it was the truth. But when he was sad or disappointed, lonely or afraid, he would still say the same. To preserve the fiction of his emotional invulnerability, he was willing to hide all sorts of instincts which might have been counted to his credit. Rude man, Jack Foster. Hard man, Jack Foster. Selfish man, Jack Foster. He was none of those things. But he was prepared to sacrifice recognition of his virtues in return for ignorance of his weaknesses.

Jack Foster knew that he ought to tell Frederick Hattersley that love was sometimes more potent than fear and that forgiveness and understanding could work miracles which were beyond the power of threats and punishment. But that would have required him to acknowledge—at least by implication—that he was not invariably and invincibly all right. He could not admit that vulnerability—even though he realized that, by failing to argue for gentleness, he was betraying Herbert.

Frederick climbed into the hansom cab.

"You don't have to worry, Jack."

Jack looked skeptical.

"You can keep the indenture fee. I'm not sure you should have got it in the first place, since you pay him nowt. But I gave it to you out of softness and you can keep it."

CHAPTER THIRTEEN

MARCHING ORDERS

The first train of the day left Sheffield for York at six o'clock. Frederick Hattersley arrived at the Midland Station just before half past five and, having bought himself a second-class ticket, stood, cold and irritable, under the snow-covered roof of platform number four. He longed to sit in the comforting warmth of the waiting room. But he feared that a cutler of his acquaintance might be sitting in front of the roaring fire, and he had no intention of being drawn into conversation about the purpose of his journey.

For the first two miles of the journey the sky was as gray as the stone walls of the railway cuttings through which they traveled. At Wath and Mexborough the gray heaps of slag were topped with an icing of snow, and at Pontefract the whole world was gleaming white under the feeble winter sunlight. It was, by Frederick's calculation, exactly seventeen minutes before the train was supposed to arrive at York when it began to snow again, adding to the great drifts which already engulfed the hedgerows. As he climbed down from the train under the roof of George Hudson's station he marveled at the cast-iron pillars on which the great arches were built. There were bigger pillars in the Crystal Palace—taller and greater in circumference. Frederick knew that full well. But they were not topped with Corinthian capitals like the columns in a Roman temple. He determined to look for the marker's cast mark when he returned to the station, after the day's stern work was done. Beyond the ticket barrier, the cab rank was empty. An obliging porter brought him the bad news.

"They're not coming out this morning, boss. Horses can't keep their feet. A big bay broke its leg in Petergate yesterday morning."

Frederick Hattersley looked at the gray sky and the falling snow that joined it to the icy pavement.

"How far to the barracks?"

"Which barracks? There's barracks out at Clifton and barracks on the Fulford Road."

"I want the Hussars."

"Cavalry's out on t'Fulford Road. Tha's lucky. It's nearer than t'other."

"How far?"

"Two miles, around by t'wall."

The porter was given a threepenny bit and asked, as politely as Frederick Hattersley could manage, for more precise instructions.

"First of all, follow t'wall." The porter waved airily at a pile of frozen rubble which seemed to run along the top of a high bank, opposite the station entrance. "Keep going. Keep going past Micklegate. When tha gets over t'Skeldersgate Bridge, turn right. Then across Castle Mill Bridge down Castle Gate, and keep going until you see t'barracks."

"Another threepence if you'll take me."

The porter looked at the sky and shook his head.

"Sixpence."

"I'll find you a lad for sixpence. Fourpence for him and twopence for me."

"Fourpence for him. A penny for you. And another penny for him if he takes me all the way without stopping and keeps up with me from start to finish."

"What about coming back?"

"We'll find our own way back, my son and me."

And so the deal was struck and Frederick Hattersley strode out. At his side was a little engine cleaner with a broken hand who could not follow his calling. Together they strode off into the snow, down Baggots Street and Prices Lane, across the Ouse and the marshes on its eastern bank and out into the open countryside. Frederick Hattersley declined every suggestion that they might get a good warm inside one of the numerous public houses which lined their route. They ignored the Windmill, the Punch Bowl, the Trafalgar Bay, the Cygnet, the Victoria, the Moat House, the Swan and the Old Ebor.

They walked together for almost an hour. Frederick Hattersley did not at first realize that the great gray edifice that appeared out of the snow was the citadel which he had come to storm. He expected barracks to have tessellated towers, turrets and gatehouses protected by either drawbridge or portcullis. The Fulford Road Barracks looked like a Poor Law institution, a workhouse for the indigent and homeless. Frederick Hattersley looked suspiciously through the wrought-iron gate. The guardhouse convinced him that it was some sort of military establishment.

A soldier stood under cover of its veranda. The soldier was on foot. Frederick Hattersley had taken it for granted that the Cavalry Barracks would be guarded by a troop of mounted hussars. So his immediate fear was that the boy had brought him to the wrong place.

Before he paid his appointed fee, he shouted through the gate, "Who are you?"

The soldier, his coat stretching almost to the ground, turned his pillbox-topped head, tapped his whip against his riding boot without condescending to answer.

"I'm looking for the Hussars."

"The Third Hussars are barracked here."

Reluctantly, the trooper came out from the cover of the veranda and peered through the gate. The visitor appeared respectable. He pulled the heavy iron gate open just enough for Frederick Hattersley to squeeze through. The trooper could feel the snow on the back of his neck.

"On the veranda, quick."

To his annoyance, the unexpected visitor paused while he opened his greatcoat, removed his purse from his trouser pocket and carefully counted out five pennies for the urchin who accompanied him. The boy took the coins and began to argue.

"You can give me a penny for the porter. I'll give it to 'im."

"I've given it you. Fourpence for you, a penny for the porter."

"You said fivepence for me."

"I said fourpence and another penny if you kept up and caused no bother. You kept stopping and nagging me to go into public houses. Be grateful that you've got anything. And remember to give a penny to the porter."

The trooper, recognizing the voice of authority, echoed it, as he had heard corporals and sergeants echo the orders of officers. ". . . to the porter."

The boy continued to argue. "I never. I kept up all the way 'cept just once when my cap blew off. And I only asked if you wanted to call in a pub."

"Don't you dare question my word." Frederick Hattersley was counting out five pennies.

". . . question my word," repeated the trooper.

Then he pulled his visitor inside the gate and slammed it shut as if he feared that the barracks would be stormed and overrun by tired, cold and resentful thirteen-year-old boys. He had recognized Frederick Hattersley's greatcoat as being made of high-quality worsted, and, assuming that the working boots were worn only as protection against the snow, he treated the man inside the expensive clothes like an officer and a gentleman.

The object of his respect had hoped to be invited at least inside the guardhouse. But he was escorted only as far as the veranda before he was asked his business.

"I want to see the officer, the officer in charge."

"The Colonel, sir? I don't think that will be possible, sir. Not the Colonel."

The absurdity of the question had unnerved him.

"I'll get the orderly sergeant, sir."

The trooper disappeared, still bewildered by the civilian's presumption. Just before the guardhouse door was pulled shut, Frederick Hattersley saw a cast-iron stove and smelled a strange mixture of coke fumes and frying bacon. The raucous sounds of military camaraderie floated out on the cold air. They made him fear that Herbert might be attracted by the company.

"Please, God, don't let him like it," he prayed. "Make him have the sense to come home."

The orderly sergeant, having been told that a gentleman awaited him, hurried out with his greatcoat lapels turned down in conformity with Queen's Regulations rather than buttoned up in protection against the weather. The top band of gold frogging shone from the front of his tunic. Frederick was impressed by the brocade and reassured by the busby and white hackle. He would have preferred a burnished bronze helmet. But he had far more faith in a busby than he could possibly feel in a pillbox hat. When the orderly sergeant

164

lifted his swagger stick to touch his cap in an almost military salute, Frederick noticed that the royal ciphers on the cuffs of his greatcoat were so large that the hind legs of lion and unicorn brushed against the buttons on the back of the sleeve.

But it was the orderly sergeant's whiskers which impressed most. They spread down the sides of his face in a profusion of bright brindle curls and joined with his fearsomely aggressive mustache. It was, Frederick Hattersley decided, the face of a fighting man. The exaggerated courtesy with which he spoke emphasized his status as the epitome of chivalry.

"What service may it be my pleasure to perform for you, sir?"

Frederick Hattersley recognized the South Yorkshire accent and decided to take advantage of the knight-errant's undoubted local pride. Fumbling inside his topcoat, he withdrew his business card. It was a card to be proud of—stiff white pasteboard with gilt edges, and printed in the classic italic script, *"Frederick Hattersley and Sons, Cutler."* Below the name was the proud description, *"Scissors and Tailors' Shears Maker."* In the bottom left-hand corner was added, *"The Empress Works, Sheffield."* The printer had told him that the definite article added distinction.

Surprisingly, the warrant officer took almost a minute to comprehend the card's message. Then, having read it once and looked up toward its owner, he read it again.

"We don't buy stores here, sir. That's all done by the Quartermaster General in London. If you write to him at the War Office, he'll no doubt attend to you. Though I doubt we need many tailors' shears."

The trooper, standing one pace behind him, sniggered.

"That is not the nature of my business."

"May I then have the privilege of knowing what your business is?" The exaggerated courtesy had turned to sarcasm.

"That I shall tell to an officer."

"Then I fear you will have to wait. You'll see no officer here until two o'clock."

"I demand to see an officer now. I am a taxpayer and I know the law. I demand to see an officer—"

"The only officer who can do what you want done is the Adjutant. And he won't be back in barracks until two o'clock. No use arguing with me. I'm only carrying out my orders."

Frederick Hattersley responded with matching calm.

"Why must I wait for the Adjutant? Why can't—"

"Because the Adjutant is the only officer authorized to allow recruits to be bought out. That's why, sir."

Confounded, Frederick Hattersley simply asked, "How did you know?"

"I can tell, sir. I can tell from looking at you. Worried father written all over your face. Not angry father. That's something quite different. Worried father. And we've had six young gentlemen take the shilling in the last week. You'll have to wait for the Adjutant, sir. He's the only one."

"Can I wait inside?"

"Afraid not, sir. War Office property. No civilians in there, sir." The trooper sniggered again. "If you take my advice, you'll get yourself a bite to eat and be back by two o'clock. You've got well over two hours to wait. It's a long time for a gentleman like yourself to stand out in the street, snow or no snow."

Too proud to ask for directions to a cheap hotel, Frederick Hattersley squeezed out of the gates, which the sniggering trooper had obligingly opened just wide enough to allow an undignified exit, and headed for York. George Hudson's Railway Hotel was, he decided, likely to be too expensive for his liking. So he made straight for the city center through what, in the half-light of the falling snow, looked like the gateway into a fairy castle. He hurried through the narrow streets, searching without success for a coffeehouse or tea shop, peering down the side streets and hurrying at the approach of each corner, in the hope that warmth and comfort was only a curve of the pavement away. After a mile of disappointing turnings, the three great towers of the Minster suddenly appeared in front of him like an ecclesiastical mirage.

At first he thought that he must be the victim of some sort of optical illusion. No building in the world could be so big. Calver Street Methodist Church, St. Mary's, the Cutlers' Hall and Joseph Rodgers's Pond Street factory could all have been fitted inside twice over and still left room for the Castle Brewery. Inside, wonder turned to awe. Down the nave, arch followed arch up to and beyond the sculptured rood screen. And when he looked to heaven and the ceiling, arch stood upon arch into the vaulted roof. The stained-glass windows glowed with light, even though the sun was hidden by clouds and snow. Frederick, who believed that he lived in the first age of real enlightenment, marveled at the workmanship. What sort of men, he wondered, had carved the delicate columns and held the keystones in place? Then Great Peter began to strike noon, each clear note reverberating around the Minster like a thunderclap.

Frederick Hattersley was a modern Christian of the scientific school, and he knew that when God spoke to men, he sent his messages through the sights and sounds of everyday living. The sea did not part and water did not turn into wine. Messages, like miracles, seemed no more than luck and coincidence to the godless. When God spoke, only the Elect could understand. And when God spoke, the Anointed must listen and the Chosen Few must heed the word. Frederick Hattersley sank to his knees on the flagstones and, in the silent, empty cathedral, prayed.

"O God, give him some sense. If I get him out of this mess— which, as You know, is his own fault—make him start to use his head. Make him think before he acts. And give him the brains to understand that he does not need anybody else to love him—besides his mother, that is—because I love him and will make sure that he does what is best for him. Send him the sense to do as he's told."

The anxious father was back at the barracks by half past one. A different trooper stood on casual guard. He challenged the snow-covered civilian without moving from his sheltered place against the guardhouse wall. The explanation that the visitor was expected and that a meeting with an officer had been arranged brought on a bout of giggling. It seemed to Frederick Hattersley that hysteria was endemic in the 3rd Hussars.

"Adjutant's been and gone. Came at one o'clock because of the snow—that and the prisoner. Won't be back till five."

As the trooper spoke—insolently and clearly enjoying his insolence—Frederick Hattersley began to feel a pulse beating inside his right ear. Suddenly he was warm for the first time since he had left home in the early hours of the morning.

"Get that sergeant out here and get him quick."

The trooper responded with a gratifying change in attitude.

"Sergeant's not here, sir. Corporal Smart is guard commander till three."

"Then get him. Get him out here this minute."

Frederick Hattersley noticed, to his relief, that the hammering behind his ear had stopped. His father had been delivered from his grinder's asthma by a sudden seizure, when driven to rage by a neighbor's dog. Frederick lived in constant fear that, having avoided inheriting the feckless character and bronchial collapse, he might have acquired whatever physical condition had widowed his mother and begun the agonizing poverty of his youth.

The corporal—emaciated and clean-shaven apart from a straggling sandy mustache—appeared at the guardroom door and attempted to seize the initiative.

"Look here—"

The pounding in Frederick Hattersley's ear started again.

"No, you look here! And first of all, tell that young man of yorn to open these gates. I'm not doing business through two ton of wrought iron."

Without waiting for the corporal's order, the trooper clanged back the bolt and pulled the gate open on its creaking hinges. Frederick Hattersley (the drumming in his ear having again subsided) strode uninvited onto the guardhouse veranda and pulled an envelope from inside his coat. He held it under the corporal's nose.

"Can you read?" He did not wait for an answer. "Well, read this address."

The careful copperplate script was augmented by a detailed explanation.

"Do you see? Mr. Mundella. Mr. Mundella, MP. Mr. Mundella, Privy Councillor. Mr. Mundella, President of the Board of Trade. Mr. Mundella is an acquaintance of mine. This letter concerns a mutual business interest. If I do not have my rights—if I don't see an officer within the hour—I shall add a postscript to this letter. And rest assured that Mr. Mundella will speak at once to the Secretary of State for War."

The corporal was visibly shaken. But he was far from ready to surrender. He had faced Pathans and Fuzzy-Wuzzies, Afghans and Matabeles, and he was not going to retreat in confusion before a scissor maker with reinforcements in Parliament.

"You cannot come inside the guardhouse, sir. You are welcome to wait under cover. But I can't tell you how long that wait will be. I shall send a galloper to the mess. But I can no more order an officer to come here than you can order me to send for one."

The tone, though firm, was satisfyingly respectful. Indeed, it contained a touch of deference. Frederick Hattersley decided to patronize the corporal.

"Very well, my good man. You seem to be doing your best. I shall

168

not report you—at least for another sixty minutes. I give you, and the Hussars, an hour. No more!"

As the galloper emerged from the guardhouse door Frederick Hattersley pulled his watch from inside his coat. To Frederick Hattersley's disappointment, he disappeared into the snow on foot. Within ten minutes he was back, panting from his exertions and cursing the weather.

"Is he coming? Have you got the officer?"

"That's not for me to say. I take messages. I know nowt."

An anxious hour followed, during which Frederick Hattersley pulled out his pocket watch a dozen times and wondered at every inspection what he would do when his bluff was called. He was actually opening the front of the silver half-hunter when a distant figure, approaching from the direction of the main building, provoked the suddenly vigilant trooper at the gate to rush to the guardroom door, beat on it with his fists and scream at the top of his voice in falsetto, "Stand-to the guard!"

Frederick Hattersley looked up, expecting a martial figure resplendent in the uniform of the Queen. Walking toward him was a man barely older than Joseph. He wore a green tweed ulster and deerstalker cap. Where there should have been black leather boots and spurs there were thick woolen stockings and brown boots. Ensign Worsley had spent the weekend at home at Hoveringham. He was the first officer to finish lunch, and the Adjutant had asked him to "slip across to the front gate and deal with the nonsense going on out there."

The orderly sergeant puffed along a couple of paces behind. He thought of the main gate as the personal property of the senior NCOs, and he was not prepared for an ensign to make decisions about its supervision and control. When warrant officer and second lieutenant were within ten paces of the guardhouse, the sentry sprang to attention and cried out again in apparent hysteria, "Call out the guard!"

Four troopers tumbled out onto the guardroom veranda. Ensign Worsley touched the peak of his deerstalker and turned to the cause of the trouble. "Good God, man, how long have you been out here? You'll freeze to death. Come into the guardhouse."

"Begging your pardon, sir . . ." The orderly sergeant leaned forward from his position two paces behind the ensign. "Begging your pardon. But with the prisoner being held in there, taking in a civilian would be against Queen's Regulations." He paused for several seconds and then added an emphatic "Sir!"

"Stuff and nonsense. It's against my regulations to stand out here in the snow. In you go, sergeant."

With obvious reluctance, the warrant officer turned the door handle, pushed and stood back to allow the ensign proper precedence. Frederick Hattersley followed. The coke fumes made him cough and his eyes began to sting. So it was a few moments before he looked in the direction of the wooden bench which ran along the far back wall. On it sat Herbert. He was still wearing his best suit and the white shirt which he had put on clean for his sister's wedding two days before.

It was several seconds before Frederick Hattersley noticed that his son was handcuffed to the arm of the bench.

"My God, what have you done?"

Even at that moment of emotional extremis, Herbert was astounded to hear his father use such a profanity. He was not, however, at all surprised that his guilt was taken for granted.

"Nothing, Father, nothing. You ask 'em. I've done nowt."

Frederick, wholly unconvinced of his son's innocence, walked toward him. Herbert turned his head away, expecting a blow. But the orderly sergeant seemed to fear that father was somehow trying to effect the son's escape. He leaped at the clearly overwrought civilian, grasped him by the arm and twisted it up into an agonizing half-nelson. He turned to Ensign Worsley.

"Begging your pardon again, sir. But this is what I feared. I've seen such things before. Better if we go outside to do your business, sir. It's the sight of the boy. Better go outside."

He began to frog-march his second prisoner of the day toward the door.

"For heaven's sake, ser'eant, take your hands off him. I don't think he's going to burn the barracks down. Are you all right?"

"Just tell me what he's done. We'll stand by him, me and his mother, whatever it is. We'll get him a lawyer. Is it too serious for bail?"

The four troopers standing uneasily and embarrassed around the guardroom began to snigger again. Even Ensign Worsley smiled. "There'll be no need for any of that. He tried to run away last night. That's all. He wanted to go home."

The orderly sergeant, disagreeing with the ensign's judgment about the seriousness of the offense, added a footnote. "Twenty minutes after taking the shilling. That's all. Twenty minutes after taking the shilling."

"We'll not argue about it, ser'eant."

Ensign Worsley was both young and progressive. But he was not prepared to dispute military laws with a noncommissioned officer in front of a middle-aged civilian.

"There's been enough fuss about this young man already. He should have been off the premises within half an hour of his father getting here."

Frederick Hattersley could not remember for what he had prayed in York Minster. But he knew that the prayer that he ought to have said had been answered. Free from the orderly sergeant's grip, he went over to his son and pulled Herbert's bowed and unusually tousled head toward him, not worrying that the remnants of Saturday's brilliantine might stain his precious topcoat.

"What are we to do?"

Herbert, suffocating against the wet wool, marveled at both his father's humility and his apparent willingness to associate himself with the prodigal son.

"The Adjutant set a price of five guineas. Five guineas to buy him out. And of course . . . you'll have to repay the shilling. You should have been told all this this morning. I'm sorry. We could have got it over with. "

"Do I pay you now?"

"Pay the ser'eant."

Frederick Hattersley took out his purse and fiddled inside it until he found five sovereigns and three florins. He handed it over without even asking for a receipt. He hardly heard Ensign Worsley wish him well and was barely conscious of the handcuffs being unlocked from Herbert's wrist.

Father and son walked out of the barracks together. They walked arm in arm like a courting couple, an unusual intimacy which allowed them both to be covered by Frederick's topcoat. Neither man trusted himself to speak. Herbert wept, and the cold tears almost froze as they ran down his unwashed cheek. Frederick trembled, frightened, not by what the orderly sergeant had done but by the feeling that he had been totally in his power. Ashamed of his weakness, he hoped that the feeling that he might collapse was really the result of a day without food. So they stopped just before the station, and bought bread and cheese. There was an hour to pass before the next Sheffield train, and the two men sat together in front of the waiting-room fire, at first eating silently and then, as their bodies grew warm and their spirits revived, making little single-sentence attempts to bridge the gap that the day's events had opened up between them.

"I'll never do owt like that again."

"Your mother'll be worried to death."

"I don't know how I could ever have been so daft."

"Are you all right now?"

"My arm hurts a little bit . . ."

"How did you hurt it?"

"It were locked to the bench all day."

Frederick established that his son had not been ill-treated, and expressed his genuine relief. Herbert confirmed that he had not meant to cause anxiety, but cut short his account of the anguish which drove him to enlist when he was told that the events of that awful night were best not spoken about.

"I would never have done it if you hadn't locked me out. I'd've just slept it off and been ready for chapel in t'morning."

Combined with the vomit stain, which still disfigured the toe of Herbert's shoe, the suggestion that he was in some way responsible for his son's behavior hardened Frederick Hattersley's heart. He stared grimly at the stained patent leather. Herbert did not have the sense to stay silent.

"I'm happy enough at home. I never really wanted to join t'army. I were just daft for a bit and showing off in front of her. I would never have even gone to see her if you hadn't kicked me out. I'm not one to give up a warm bed and me comforts. I'll be happy as Larry when I'm back 'ome."

Any residual doubts that Frederick had about his obligation to be kind by cruelty were dispelled by his son's continued attempts to rehabilitate himself.

"I'll never run away again, whatever happens. Never. I'll be up for breakfast at six o'clock sharp tomorrow and ready for work. And every day till I'm out of my time."

"Not at the Empress Works you won't nor from Asline Road."

Herbert stopped crying and stared into the fire. For some reason his recovered composure touched his father.

"Back there in that barracks, I thought I couldn't do it. I thought that I'd take you home and we'd start all over again. But that would be no good, no good for you. I'm getting you out of the road of that trollop who came round to our house."

"What trollop?"

It was as near as Herbert could get to defending the lady's honor. Frederick paused to consider the possibility that there were several.

"That woman from the Barracks Hotel. How else do you think I knew you were here? You're too daft to look after yourself. You'll be back at that public house with them drunken louts you play football with. I'm getting you away. You've got to go. You'll go on Monday and you'll stay away. I've arranged for you to go to Nottingham."

"There'll be nowt for me to do in Nottingham."

"You'll finish your apprenticeship."

"Not in Nottingham, Father. There's no decent cutlers in Nottingham. I'm going to be a Sheffield scissorsmith. I'll not go."

Frederick Hattersley knew that he should not accept such impudence. Had Herbert said such a thing at home, he would have been denounced and punished. But it was a doleful day and his son's pride in the Sheffield's name was a redeeming grace.

"I know that it's not Sheffield. But it's all for the best for you, which is all that me and your mother want. You're to finish your time with a firm of medical-instrument makers. There's them that say it's a superior trade to scissor making. Mr. Mundella owns the factory there. I sent a message to his agent late last night."

"They might not take me on."

"They'll take you on all right. Mr. Mundella and I are going to come to an agreement about a bit of business. They'll take you on."

"Where will I live?"

"We'll find you something."

"Mr. Martin comes from Nottingham."

"There'll be none of that. Put that right out of your head. You're not going to live with Irish singers. You'll live where I tell you to live."

On the journey home, Frederick Hattersley snored in the corner seat of the second-class carriage while Herbert, too tired to sleep, thought of the new excitement that awaited him. He was to leave home, to live on his own, to learn a new trade and to see a new town. Perhaps enlisting had not been the disaster he feared when, early that morning, he had tried to climb the barracks wall and, having been caught, was told that he would be tied to a gun carriage and shot as a deserter. By the time he reached Sheffield he was happy again.

CHAPTER FOURTEEN

BETWEEN FRIENDS

John Gunn was the most popular local preacher in all of the Nottingham circuit. Members of his Sunday morning congregation always stood about after the service telling each other how moved they had been by his sermon. They were, however, never able exactly to describe what it was about either the style or the content which so moved them. Ebenezer Becket of Arnold preached more powerfully and Charles Blake of Beeston was more persuasive. William Chambers from Woollaton was famous for his displays of emotion and Arthur Grigg of West Bridgeford for his conspicuous erudition. But none of them could create the feeling of well-being and contentment which sent John Gunn's Methodists home to a satisfying Sunday dinner. His secret was a great capacity for happiness. There was so much happiness in John Gunn that it spilt out and washed over those around him.

His popularity was undoubtedly assisted by his appearance and by his status as an eligible but confirmed widower of thirty-six. His determination not to marry made him the object of particular interest to Nonconformist matrons who expressed constant anxiety about the loneliness of his life, the neglect of regular meals and the state of his socks. They told each other how happy they would be were he to find a second soul mate. About that, they were less than completely honest. Part of John Gunn's attraction was his lonely devotion to the memory of his wife.

"After Mary there'll be nobody else for me."

Whenever he said it (and he said it whenever an elder's wife expressed the hope that he would "one day . . ."), there were always tears. Of course, the tears were never his. John Gunn, master baker, was far too manly a figure to permit such self-indulgence. But the ladies always wept with admiration for the love and loyalty which prompted his gentle reproof. When they apologized "for even mentioning the subject," John Gunn would put his hand gently on the miscreant's arm and say, "I know that it's Christian kindness that prompts you."

"It is, Mr. Gunn. It is."

"It's not that I'm ungrateful: it's just that after Mary . . ."

Other men speaking so uninhibitedly about their emotion might have embarrassed their listeners. But John Gunn's affection for the wife who had died in childbirth was so obviously sincere that it was impossible for even the most sternly masculine member of his congregation to feel any sense of disapproval at his lack of proper reticence. Sometimes the old preachers considered his character and wondered if he possessed shortcomings which the charitable congregation (who booked his services six months in advance) overlooked. But their discussions always ended with descriptions of his virtues.

"He's very genuine," said Ebenezer Becket of Arnold.

"And very hardworking," added Charles Blake from Beeston.

"He'll do anything for anyone," Woollaton's William Chambers said, recalling many acts of kindness.

"Indeed he will," echoed Arthur Grigg of West Bridgeford.

John Gunn's willingness to oblige was wholly spontaneous. He took it for granted that the world was populated by his friends. So he simply behaved toward the world as was appropriate to such an affectionate relationship. And he was happy in whatever he did. So when he was suddenly asked to stand in for an absent colleague, he found just as much pleasure in deputizing for the sick Sunday school teacher as in spending the afternoon on his original intention of sitting in his garden or reading.

It was because of John Gunn's well-known willingness to be exploited that the Superintendent of Nottingham's Albert Hall called round to see him with a "totally unreasonable request."

"I'm sure it isn't unreasonable, Superintendent. Otherwise you wouldn't ask me. You know I'll help if I can."

"You'd better wait to hear what it is before you agree."

"I talk too much, Superintendent. I'll be quiet while you tell me what awful burden you want to heap upon me."

"A young man is coming to Nottingham next Sunday. I have been charged with finding him suitable lodgings—lodgings in which a friendly guardian will keep an eye on him. I know that I could not impose him on you for long, but if you would take him for a week or two—just until we find him something more permanent—we would both be very grateful. Mr. Mundella and I, that is."

The mention of Mr. Mundella (whose name was still revered in Nottingham despite his departure to Sheffield) was intended to leave John Gunn in no doubt about where either his duty or his self-interest lay. The stratagem was wholly unnecessary. Had the Superintendent told the truth—that the manager of Mr. Mundella's small medical-instrument factory had asked him to find lodgings for the young man —John Gunn would have been just as willing to help. He had barely finished the sentence before his suggestion was enthusiastically accepted.

"I would be delighted to help. Anyway, I need some company. I've lived here on my own for too long. A bit of noise around the house will do me the world of good. When did you say he was coming?"

"Next Saturday. But you'd better know the whole story."

"I assume that the lad is or has been in some sort of trouble. I'll keep a friendly eye on him."

"He ran away to join the army."

"Is that all? I thought that it was at least the sin of Cain. I'll try to stop him doing it again."

The Superintendent, grave in his duty, was made graver still by John Gunn's flippancy. "He ran away because of his father."

"His father is a bad man?" For a moment John Gunn was grave too.

"He is an excessively good man, as far as I can make out. Obsessed by virtue. He has driven his son very hard."

"I shall not drive him at all. I shall be less virtuous. I shall provide him with a respite from morality."

"I doubt it. But this is my warning. You will have the father to deal with. Letters, visits, instructions, injunctions . . . Mr. Mundella would understand if you felt unable to help."

176

"You know that I'll do it, Superintendent. I shall probably do it badly—row with the father, neglect the son, offend Mr. Mundella and alienate half of the circuit's preachers. But I shall do it. Tell me when they are to arrive and I shall meet them at the station. Mrs. Watkins will come in on Saturday for once and prepare them a huge tea."

John Gunn began to feel genuinely enthusiastic about a task which he had originally agreed to perform for no better reason than the desire to do his duty.

Frederick Hattersley instructed his sons to be ready to leave the works at one o'clock sharp. For the first time, they traveled home with their father in the trap. The whole family was to have a proper dinner before he and Herbert set out on their great adventure. Herbert, anxious to begin his odyssey, denounced his father's greed to brother Joseph.

"You'd think that he could have managed on a pie at the station, just once."

"Don't be stupid!"

Joe had little sympathy for his father's sentimental wish to keep his family around him until the last possible moment, but he was openly contemptuous of his brother's failure to recognize the real reason why the departure was being postponed. "It's not the food. It's the last rites, the sons around the family table for the last time. You'll see him blowing in his handkerchief and pretending that it's hay fever."

The nose blowing began during the consumption of Brown Windsor soup and rose to a noisy crescendo just as the roast beef was being brought to the table. The ritual of knife sharpening being interrupted, the joint was sent back to the kitchen to be kept hot while an edge was put on the blade. No sooner had the first slice been cut, and placed (with unusual disregard for precedence) on Herbert's plate, than the sniffing began again. The huge spotted handkerchief was pulled out of the inside pocket once more and the sirloin was returned for a second time to the oven in the kitchen.

The lunch dragged on for so long that Herbert began to worry about missing the ten-to-five train. But just after three, both the snuffling and the dinner were over and there were twenty minutes to wait before the cab arrived. Herbert and Frederick Hattersley sat silently in the drawing room, longing to hear the sound of horses' hooves on the road outside. Emily began to say that it was nice to have the twenty minutes' extra time together. Then, looking around the room

177

at the glum faces, she realized that, for the others, it was not nice at all. She, too, began to feel that the delay extended rather than postponed the parting.

To Herbert's surprise and relief, the train journey itself was almost as silent as the last moments in Asline Road. His father told a couple of already well-known anecdotes about life in the Sheffield knife grinders' hulls during his apprenticeship. Just as the train began to pull into Nottingham Station, Frederick leaned forward in his seat, and grasped his son's knee.

"Your mother'll worry about you, if we don't hear. Send us a card every weekend."

He took out of his pocket half a dozen picture postcards of the new Sheffield Town Hall. Each one had a stamp already stuck in its top right-hand corner.

Herbert opened the carriage door long before the train rocked to a halt. He was the first passenger to climb down from carriage to platform. His father was almost the last. Frederick was weighed down by his greatcoat (unscathed from its exposure to a full day of York snow), and his mobility was impaired by his Sunday top hat and the button boots which were never seen at the Empress Works. He carried a box which—since it obviously contained tools—was an incongruous accessory to the best uniform of the provincial lower-middle class. Herbert beside him was, at least physically, a miniature edition of the older man—shorter, thinner and younger, but obviously cast from the same mold. He carried a leather suitcase in one hand and a carpetbag in the other. Under his left arm he held, with some difficulty, a brown-paper parcel. It was the present which his mother had given him at the moment of parting. Recognizing his gift as a Bible, he had not bothered to open it on the train.

Lodger met landlord at the ticket barrier. The greetings were stiff and formal. John Gunn seized the toolbox from Frederick, the suitcase from Herbert and then, with some difficulty, the carpetbag as well. There were no hansom cabs outside the station, for Saturday travelers did not usually avail themselves of such luxuries. So the bags were left in the care of their owners while John Gunn sprinted to the Welbeck Street cab rank. On his return, he climbed down from the seat next to the driver and loaded the luggage onto the roof while the Hattersleys looked on, Frederick in the manner of a master supervising a servant and Herbert in a way that betrayed his bewilderment at the way in which his world was changing. The journey to

Huntingdon Street took fifteen minutes. John Gunn pointed out the sights of Nottingham from the cab window. When they arrived at number 117, Frederick Hattersley spoke for the first time since he left the station.

"Nice little house. His mother and I are very grateful for this, Mr. Gunn. Very grateful indeed. So is he."

Herbert himself registered neither opinion nor emotion. Mrs. Watkins was waiting and suggested they have tea at once. In the middle of ham and pickles, Frederick turned and stared at his host.

"You'll forgive me if I speak while eating. But there's a lot to be decided. You know nowt about us and we know nowt about you. We'd better both find summat out before the last train goes back to Sheffield."

The new landlord offered a brief account of his life and work. But instead of his guests reciprocating with the story of their lives, Frederick Hattersley began an interrogation. At first, John Gunn simply answered the questions, confirming that Herbert would make his own breakfast and bed and that a hot meal would always be waiting for him on his return from work. The suggestion that, after tea, Frederick should inspect his son's bedroom was accepted in good part. But there were some instructions about the young man's welfare to which the new landlord could not, in all conscience, agree.

"He'll go with you to chapel on Sunday."

"I'm a local preacher, Mr. Hattersley. I'm at a different place each Sunday."

"Can't he go with you?"

"I certainly don't mind. But I fear I would make the young man a laughingstock. In any case, if he's to stay in Nottingham, he needs to have a chapel of his own, where he can find friends."

"But you'll make sure he goes, and tell me if he doesn't."

"I'm going to be his landlord, Mr. Hattersley, not his jailer. He's a grown man—or very nearly. If he is to live here, we have to be friends."

"At any rate, you'll keep him away from drink?"

John Gunn did not reply.

"You don't keep strong drink in this house?"

"A bottle of sherry. A couple of pints of Bass. I'm not a total abstainer."

"He is. He is from now on. He's to go nowhere where alcohol is either sold or drunk."

"All the sports clubs in this town have their headquarters in public houses. And I heard that he was a sportsman. I meant to take him to Meadow Lane next Saturday to see Notts County play—"

"He's given up football, because of the drinking."

"What do you expect him to do to pass the time?"

"Work. Work and study. He can join the Mechanics' Institute. He can read. And he can go to chapel. I take it that even in Nottingham they do not have strong drink at the chapels."

"I think," said John Gunn, "that you and I had better have a look at the bedroom."

Frederick Hattersley put his face close to the bedroom window to make sure that his son would not be subject to any lethal draft and, satisfied, looked under the bed to confirm the presence of a chamber pot.

"You'll not let him lie here all hours on Sunday. Up by seven. An extra hour is all he's to get."

John Gunn sighed. "It won't work, you know. I'm not the landlord you're looking for. I'd like to oblige, but it will only cause trouble and I like to avoid trouble. I'll take him for a bit. But you'll have to find somewhere else for his permanent lodgings."

Frederick Hattersley did not argue. "How long can he stay?"

"A month."

"A month it is, then. What am I to pay?"

"You're to pay nothing. He's my guest."

"I can't accept that. We've got to be businesslike. I didn't ask for charity."

"Nor are you getting it."

"If I don't pay, he doesn't stay."

"Put five pounds in the chapel poor box, when he leaves."

"Five pounds for a month! It won't cost you that."

"I didn't say it would. But five pounds is the price. And for that I see that he goes to service at the Albert Hall every Sunday whilst he's here. Starting tomorrow."

Self-consciously they shook hands and descended to the living room. Herbert was finishing off the game pie.

When it was time for Frederick Hattersley to go, father and son walked out together into the cold January night. They crossed Huntingdon Street and leaned on the wall which was built where, in any normal road, another row of houses would have been. They stared into the blank void which lay on the other side of the coping stones,

180

wondering what their future would be but pretending to wonder why below and beyond the wall there was only darkness.

"I hope for your mother's sake you'll behave yourself. You know that she worries about you."

Herbert was about to answer, when suddenly, beneath their feet, an express train roared into the valley which, forty years before, an army of railway navvies had cut into the Nottingham rock beyond Huntingdon Street. The smoke and steam engulfed them and, for the first time that day, Frederick was overcome by a genuine fit of coughing and sneezing. He staggered back from the wall, searching for his handkerchief. Herbert led him, temporarily blinded, back toward the house. John Gunn left them in peace. God, he decided, had ordained that, as they parted, father should be dependent upon son.

The Methodists of Nottingham chose the site for their Albert Hall with meticulous malice. It stood on the south corner of Derby Road and North Circus Street. Facing it on the north corner, the Catholic Cathedral of St. Barnabas—brazenly designed by one Augustus Pugin in a style which denied that the Reformation had even happened—pointed its sharp Gothic arches toward a blatantly papist heaven. For thirty years, the cathedral was a reproof and a reproach to any Nottingham citizen who believed in the Thirty-nine Articles. It seemed to confirm John Henry Newman's impertinent assertion that "the English Church is born again. It is the coming of the second spring." But then, after the careful collection of five thousand pounds, the Albert Hall was built. What it lacked in originality of name it made up for in solidity and simplicity of design. Nonconformity was vindicated.

It was to the Albert Hall that Mrs. Watkins and her grocer husband took Herbert on the first Sunday of his life in Nottingham.

John briefed them about his lodger when they called to collect him at half past ten.

"He's a perfectly good lad who will come to no harm if his father lets him be."

Mrs. Watkins looked skeptical.

"I've not pressed him to tell me the details. But I know the basic facts. Ran away to join the army. There's nothing wrong in wanting a bit of adventure."

"What about the drink? I heard his father say something about drink."

"He's a good footballer, Mrs. W. All the clubs meet at public houses."

"Charity will be the death of you, Mr. Gunn."

Because she did not suffer from the same weakness, Mrs. Watkins kept a close eye on Herbert throughout the service. When it was over, Herbert stood on the pavement in North Circus Street, stamping his feet on the cold stones and waiting for Mrs. Watkins to finish her gossip with her friends from the Ladies' Sewing Guild. He had heard the impious bells of St. Barnabas ring out several minutes before he left the chapel. As he waited impatiently to walk home the Catholic congregation began to spill out onto the pavement. To his surprise and delight, amongst them was Patrick Ignatius Martin, LRCM, whose music lessons he had been forced to terminate when his father discovered that they always ended with a libation to St. Cecilia.

Herbert was about to run across the road to greet him, when he noticed, to his astonishment, that a second Patrick Ignatius Martin had appeared around the corner of the cathedral. On his arm was the most beautiful girl that Herbert had ever seen. She was tall—taller than either of the Patrick Ignatius Martins—and black hair fell in curls from under her fur hat. The shape of her face reminded him, not altogether romantically, of the ace of spades. And even from the wrong side of the street he could see her green eyes, shining at the Patrick Ignatius Martin who was escorting her to the tram stop at the pavement's edge. That moment marked the birth of chivalry in Herbert Hattersley. How could such a creature—the fur at the hem of her coat swinging with her lilting walk—be expected to travel by tramcar? For a moment he was filled with panic that she would clang out of his life forever. Then one of the Patrick Ignatius Martins saw him and bellowed across the road in his thick Irish brogue, "Herbert! Herbert Hattersley! God be praised! Is it you? I knew you'd been exiled to Nottingham for your sins but I didn't think to see you outside the mass. Come across here and sing us a note or two. I'd thought we'd never meet again." Herbert's response, though fast, was not fast enough. "Are you coming or are you not? I've m'brother here I'd like you to meet. And his daughter. Hurry yourself, for the tram will be along any minute."

Herbert hurried himself and discovered that the second Mr. Martin was in fact called Robert. The first—Patrick Ignatius—waved in the general direction of his beautiful niece. "I'm here because of her father. M'brother's a lace designer. Very distinguished man. Artist like me." The tramcar rattled into view. "Will you come to see us? I go back to Sheffield on Tuesday."

Herbert promised with complete sincerity that he would call at the first opportunity.

"Please do," added Robert as he climbed aboard. "Come this evening. Five Cavendish Street. Half past six." From the tramcar's platform, Patrick, his twin brother, shouted the final and totally unnecessary inducement. "We'll have a great sing!"

Meanwhile Venus, finding that the inside of the tram was full, had climbed to the open top deck, apparently unaware of the havoc she was wreaking in the road below.

To Herbert's relief, John Gunn raised no objection to his paying a visit to "an old Sheffield friend I met outside the Albert Hall this morning." He did, however, ask a question which paralyzed his infatuated lodger with fear.

"Which Cavendish Street?"

"*Which* Cavendish Street?"

"There are at least three."

Herbert sank back into his chair with a groan.

"Why didn't you ask them?"

"I had no chance. They were on the tram."

"Going which way?"

"Up the Derby Road."

"Then we know which Cavendish Street. Cavendish Street, Lenton. Easy."

From that moment on, Herbert was John Gunn's bondsman, tied to him forever by a debt of gratitude too strong ever to be broken. At first, it was the gratitude of a drowning man for the lifeguard who had rescued him from the sea. For he took it for granted that if he were denied the hope of ever seeing Mr. Martin's niece again, he would decline and die. But in the years that followed that fateful Sunday, he began to understand that it was also the gratitude of a man who, having been snatched from the waves, realizes that a world in which one man jumps to the rescue of another is full of hope and promise.

John Gunn had become his first friend—not because he had provided him with information which had saved his life and sanity but because he had helped him for no other reason than that he wanted to be helpful. He had not tried to influence his decision, even less dictate the course of his life. John Gunn had been happy to let him decide for himself how he wanted to spend his evening. He determined there and then that the next day he would beg John Gunn to let him stay a tenant at Huntingdon Street forever.

The idea was carried in his mind only for a second. There was no time for more consideration of his domestic future. He had only three and a half hours to wash, change his shirt, polish his shoes and make the twenty-minute journey to Cavendish Street, Lenton.

He arrived at the end of the road before six o'clock and hung about, anxious and conspicuous, until twenty minutes past the hour. Then, unable to wait a moment longer, he marched to the front door of number 5 and pulled on the rusty bell. Nothing happened. Swallowing his panic, he lifted the equally corroded knocker and beat it on the door. To his relief, after much grinding of bolts, turning of keys and rattling of chairs, the door opened.

"Sorry to keep you waiting. We usually keep this door locked," said the Mr. Martin who stood in the dark hall.

Herbert noticed the picture of the Sacred Heart on the wall and felt the tribal fear of a Nonconformist about to enter into a Catholic household. That, as much as his uncertainty about the welcome he would receive from Mr. Martin, made him stammer his greeting.

"Is . . . it Mr. Martin? Is . . . it . . . you . . . Patrick?"

"I'm Robert. We know it's confusing but we can't help it. Twins run in our family. Our mother was a twin. I've got twin daughters. You saw one this morning, after mass."

Herbert leaned against the hall wall, incapable of fully comprehending what he had been told. The discovery of one Celtic goddess had turned his life into turmoil. The idea that there were two such creatures, identical in every exquisite detail, made it difficult for him to stand erect.

"Come and meet them," said Robert Martin.

The door at the far end of the hall opened to reveal Patrick Martin, violin in hand, peering into the dusk.

"Are you going to stand there all night?" he asked. "Come and join the ceilidh."

The ceilidh was taking place in Robert Martin's studio, a room which—despite a great bay window which stretched along its front wall—was, on the January evening of Herbert's visit, so dark that it was difficult to make out the figures who congregated around the piano. The two gas mantles above the fireplace were turned down to little more than an orange glow and, although there were candles in both the brass holders on the front of the piano, only one was lit. Its

184

little pool of light barely lit the musical stand, but it spread back across the top of the piano and illuminated a silver-framed picture of two little girls wearing what Herbert took to be bridesmaids' dresses. A string of breads hung over the complicated pattern of leaves and flowers which decorated one corner of the frame. On the far side of the room, Herbert could just make out a sloping drawing board standing at shoulder height. Two of the walls were decorated with framed lace samples, patterns which Robert Martin had designed and submitted (with an invariable lack of success) to various expositions.

Behind the piano an almost unrecognizable male figure stood ready to turn the pages of sheet music for a pianist whose outline could barely be distinguished in the flickering candlelight. The woman playing the piano was, he supposed, the paragon's sister. But he had no doubt that the girl who leaned elegantly against it was the divinity whom he had seen outside St. Barnabas's Cathedral and with whom he had fallen immediately in love. Despite the gloom, she was incandescently recognizable.

Patrick Martin was anxious to make the formal introductions. "For God's sake, Robert, can't we turn the gas up, and light the other candles? I can barely see m'self sing. And I certainly can't see the young Herbert's handsome face."

"You know very well that we can't. If you want light, come through into the living room. There's light enough there."

As they filed through into the living room Herbert's curiosity overcame even his impatience to meet the woman of his dreams.

"Is it the lace?" he asked Patrick Martin. "Is that why the gas is turned down? So as not to fade it?"

"It is not."

"Then why is it?"

"Better not ask."

They filed out into the living room. Herbert banged into the doorjamb in his anxiety to show proper precedence to Miss Martin. The introductions began.

"This," said Robert Martin, "is my little girl, Clare. She's home just for a week and then off again."

Herbert tried to behave courteously. But he could not look Clare Martin in the face without shading his eyes as if he were staring into the sun. He feared that the object of his veneration would regard such behavior as eccentric or, worse still, uncouth. So he focused his gaze on her feet. Even the sight of the patent-leather boots made him feel dizzy. But at least he was not blinded by the radiance of her countenance. He just managed to stutter "How do you do?" before she turned her gaze from him and asked her father, "Where's Augusta?"

"She's coming. She's just putting the music away."

Herbert braced himself for a second supernatural experience. He endured no more than a mild shock. For the girl who bustled into the room, although undoubtedly Clare's sister, was not a pea out of the same pod. She had the same shining black hair and piercing green eyes. But she was at least four inches shorter and a stone heavier in weight.

"... and my other little girl, Mr. Hattersley, Augusta. She's Clare's twin. But not identical. Patrick and me are identical in looks but different in ways. The girls, like my sainted mother and her sister, look different but act the same."

"We do not," said Augusta.

"Why, you do," contradicted her Uncle Patrick. "You're both great artists."

"Gussie's the artist. I'm just an actress."

"Clare's a professional. I've never earned a penny from the piano —except by teaching little girls scales. I've never performed."

The idea that Clare Martin was a professional actress took Herbert's breath away for the fourth time that day. That anyone so beautiful should also live a life which was so exciting and enjoy prospects so romantic was an idea too unreasonable for immediate comprehension. He managed to stutter, "Where do you act?"

The star half turned and condescended to notice his existence for a second time. "I am with Mr. Wilson Barratt. This week we perform Mr. G. R. Sims's *The Lights o' London* at the Theatre Royal."

"She's a flower girl," her uncle explained. "A flower girl in the Strand in London. She sings a line of one of the old street cries."

Her father rushed to rescue her reputation. "But she's back in the last act as a debutante out for the night with a masher. The masher has a red-lined cloak."

"White," said Clare. Clare liked things to be exact.

"We're all going to see her tomorrow night." Augusta seemed genuinely excited.

"And on Wednesday." The artist's father seemed more excited still. "Would you like to come?"

"Which night?" Herbert hoped that the answer might be both.

"Either," said Robert Martin.

Herbert chose Monday—Monday being the sooner. Then he asked, "Can Mr. Gunn come?"

Clare showed a sudden interest in the conversation. "Is Mr. Gunn the cricketer?"

"I don't think so. He's my friend."

"I'm forgetting m'manners," said Robert, leading into the living room the man who had stood by the piano. "This is Tom Cross. He comes here courting. Though with what success I do not know. He's too shy to speak until he's spoken to. I would never have won and wed their sainted mother if I'd have behaved like that."

Herbert Hattersley contemplated suicide. The idea that anyone—least of all the gaunt figure who now held out a bony hand—might have already laid claim to Clare Martin's affection had never entered his head. The object of his fear and hatred spoke.

"I think that I know Mr. Gunn," said Tom Cross. "Is he the preacher? I think I've heard of him at chapel."

Patrick Martin, who enjoyed causing trouble, turned on Tom. "You see, he's a heathen like you, Herbert. It's probably a sin to let him in the house. If he ever gets up the nerve to propose to Gussie, heaven knows what we'll do."

Propose to Gussie! Herbert's life was saved. For a moment he was in ecstasy, noticing neither Augusta's anger nor the statue of the Virgin Mary on the table behind him. Twitching with relief, he touched it with his elbow. It rocked. But Augusta caught it before it fell, and her anger turned to laughter. Everybody joined in. Even Herbert forgot his humiliation. There was general agreement that the time had come to return to the gloomy room and the music.

"Herbert's a great singer." Patrick Martin tapped his violin bow in the lid of the piano as he praised his pupil. "A great voice Herbert's got. Let him see the music over your shoulder, Clare. He can sight-read, too. We'll think about a tenor part in a minute. Let's just have a good sing all together to begin with."

Trembling at the thought of standing so close to Clare that their bodies might touch, Herbert prayed that his sight-reading would survive the ordeal. There was still one more hurdle to be overcome before the blessed moment of proximity could be experienced. Robert Martin had enjoyed enough music for one evening, but he would not leave the chorus and orchestra to perform in his studio until they had made solemn promises about the gas and candles.

"I rely on you, Gussie. Patrick can't be trusted. You look after things."

Augusta thought that an explanation was needed. "Father's an artist, not a musician."

"But what about the gas?"

"I'll show you," she promised him.

While her uncle tuned up his violin she pointed to the wall which was furthest away from the light. On it was what Herbert took to be another framed lace sample. But he could not be sure. For it was shrouded in sheet, blanket and counterpane—each one hanging down like the covers of a badly made bed.

"Augusta, how could you?" Clare hissed.

Her sister giggled.

"Don't talk about it anymore," pleaded Clare. "For God's sake, don't mention it again."

CHAPTER FIFTEEN

A FREE MAN

I t was a difficult first day. Herbert Hattersley had never believed that he had much to learn from the surgical-instrument makers who worked for Hudson and Ross. For he took it for granted that a Sheffield apprentice, within a year of completing his indentured service, must know at least as much as any time-served journeyman from another town. His father had warned him that his new work would be "more delicate." But the warning had done nothing to undermine his confidence. He knew that, despite his lack of brains, he could grind and set a scissor blade as well as any craftsman twice his age. And he could not believe that scissors designed to cut through human tissue were fundamentally different from scissors forged to cut paper and cloth. His problem on his first Monday in Nottingham was a total inability to concentrate on the work in front of him on the bench.

At Hudson and Ross—where surgeons' scissors were made by the dozen—they still forged by hand. Herbert, who already had the prejudices of a craftsman, felt no inclination to brag about the stamping machines that hissed steam back home at Frederick Hattersley and Sons and spewed out hundreds of scissor blanks each hour. He simply wanted to prove that he could bore a rivet hole to exactly the shape and size to allow two blades to open and shut firmly and smoothly as they swung across each other. But as soon as he began to concentrate on the intricate filing, Clare Martin's face shone out at him from the polished steel, and the sound of her voice—which he had only heard speak half a dozen sentences—rang in his ears above the noise of the scissor maker's hull. There was no clock in the factory, and Herbert did not boast a pocket watch. So he could only guess how much of the day had passed. When, at last, the whistle blew for six o'clock, young Mr. Hudson (the seventy-year-old son of the company's Scottish founder) came over to welcome the new apprentice. He looked down at the scissor blade which Herbert had left on the bench.

"It's very good work," he said, "but it's not done."

Herbert was already knotting his muffler.

"At this company we finish the piece before we go home."

Herbert was more anxious to demonstrate his independence than to display his capacity for clear thinking. "So do we in Sheffield."

"Well then, you'd better finish this one."

It took Herbert twenty minutes to finish the filing. By quarter to seven he was washing and having his second shave of the day. Despite his haste and the dull razor, when he washed off the remnants of the lather there was not even the smallest nick or cut to deface the pink smoothness of his cheek. As he stood on the pavement in Huntingdon Street it was, he decided, his lucky day.

There was a moment's concern when the first pedestrian to whom he spoke could not provide directions to Woollaton Road. But just as he was about to approach a second passerby, he saw the great white colonnade of the Theatre Royal. John Gunn, who had made his way straight from the bakery, was already there. Herbert insisted that they at once take up their agreed position, "near to the left-hand pillar, facing the road," even though it was twenty minutes before the appointed meeting time. As the excited theatergoers surged up the steps and jostled each other in their anxiety to squeeze through the doors, Herbert decided that he was at the start of the happiest night of his life.

The performance itself—the first by a professional company which Herbert had ever seen—was all that he had hoped it would be. He recognized Clare the moment she sauntered on past the cardboard Savoy Hotel. He watched entranced as she stood, front stage left, while the other characters of the capital—fish porter, policeman, Pearly King, Beefeater, Grenadier Guard and housemaid—took up their positions in the tableau. As soon as she had disappeared behind the canvas St. Bride's Church, his attention began to wander to the scarlet and gold decorations of the baroque auditorium and to the audience who sat in front of him. As Clare Martin climbed the social ladder from hawker to socialite, he became an expert on the rear view of the English bourgeoisie on a night out. For ladies it was an age of high-piled hair and bare shoulders. The study of chignon and bare flesh was so absorbing that he had to be invited to leave his seat when the curtain came down on the first act. Throughout the interval he was in such a daze that, without thinking, he complied with John Gunn's suggestion that he should decline whiskey and ginger and accept Apollinaris water. When the performance ended with the announcement that Clare and the whole company would live happily ever after, Herbert felt sure that the same prospect awaited him.

Clare, still wearing her exaggerated stage makeup, arrived breathless from the stage door. She touched her rouged cheek and explained that she had not wanted to keep them waiting. Tom Cross, allowing his instinct for respectability to overcome both natural diffidence and carefully cultivated chivalry, blurted out that it would be all right, as they were taking a cab home—and then blushed as red as Clare's paint. Clare stared at him coldly over a great bouquet of roses which she held with difficulty in the crook of her arm, half balanced on her wasp waist.

"Who sent you those?"

Herbert felt that Augusta's question was as much a reproach as a simple request for information. Clare heaved up the bouquet. A card was attached to it by the white ribbon which held the stems together beneath a huge bow. She read the name but not the message.

"Alexander Markham."

Robert Martin was filled with awe.

"Do you think it's one of the real Markhams?"

"I've no idea."

"Don't you know him?" asked Patrick.

" 'Course not. He just sent them as a sign of respect."

Augusta giggled.

Even John Gunn was impressed. "Does this happen after every performance, Miss Martin?"

"Sometimes two or three. Sometimes they send them. Sometimes they bring them."

Supper at Cavendish Street was purgatory for Herbert. He had always known that, without some act of reckless daring, he would not see Clare Martin again for three months. For, the next time that he was invited to spend an afternoon with her father and sister, she would be in another town, performing at another theater. Earlier in the day, he had constructed complicated fantasies about how, on the following Sunday, he would travel with her to Leicester, Leeds or Manchester and receive, as reward for his devotion, the promise of regular correspondence. He knew that, as the parting drew nearer, the dream would fade and he would be left to wait for her return to Nottingham at Easter. But he had not thought of the life for which she would leave him. The discovery that it would be filled with unknown men who sent her bunches of flowers was beyond endurance —particularly when he thought of the sort of rival with whom he had to compete.

"Who are the Markhams?" Herbert whispered to John Gunn as the two dozen roses were crushed into the largest vase that the Martins possessed.

"They own half the coal mines in Nottingham." Seeing the young man's pain, John added a note of comfort. "But we're not sure he's one of—" He stopped in midsentence. It was thoughtless to demonstrate that he recognized the cause of Herbert's anguish.

At midnight, Patrick Martin suggested a sing. Clare declined with disdain. John Gunn agreed that it was time to say good night.

"We get up before six," he explained. Clare gave a little gasp at the thought of anything so uncivilized.

As lodger and landlord walked home together, John Gunn apologized again. "I never thought I'd make a mess of it so quickly."

"Make a mess of what?"

"Looking after you, that's what. When you got here on Saturday, do you think that your father thought that you'd be out until all hours on your first working day, or that you'd be going to the theater with a family of papists?"

He might have added, "Or that you'd fall in love with an actress." But he contented himself with a more feeble conclusion. "He wouldn't be best pleased."

"I want to stop," said Herbert.

John Gunn was not familiar with the South Yorkshire patois.

"We're only five minutes away from home."

"I want to stop there. I want to stop with you. I want to stop permanent."

"It wouldn't be like it's been these last couple of days."

"I know it wouldn't. I know what I've got to do now—work hard, get up early and keep m'self to m'self."

"What would your father say?"

"He'd be glad. I know he would. If you'll have me, he'll let me stop."

"We'll see how things work out for a week or two."

"Until Easter. Let me stay until Easter."

John Gunn grinned under cover of the pitch-black January night. "What happens then?"

"I have to go home the week before. Joe finishes his apprenticeship and we're all to celebrate."

John Gunn was impressed by the ingenuity of Herbert's reply. But he did not mean to allow him to escape with one quick-witted answer. "So you'll not be here for the Easter weekend, whatever happens?"

"Yes, I will. If you will have me." Believing that he could risk telling John the truth, he confessed. 'That's why I want to stay. If I have to find new digs, I'll be in Sheffield till Easter Tuesday and then m'father will come back with me."

"So now we have it. Your great desire to live with me amounts to no more than an insurance policy to make sure that you're here in Nottingham when that young woman comes back."

"I want to live with you anyway. At least I think I do. I've only lived at your house for two days."

"I set great store by that 'anyway,'" said John Gunn. "Honesty is the best policy and shall be rewarded. Till Easter then. You'll lodge with me until Easter. I'll write to your father tomorrow. It's tomorrow already. I'll write today . . ."

The lodger whooped a cry of triumph and bounded down the road in a great leap of joy. So he barely heard his landlord complete his offer.

"If you're going to be here for a bit, we'd better have those nice Martins round for tea next Sunday. Pity the other daughter won't be back until Easter."

But when Herbert did realize what John Gunn said, he whooped and leaped again.

Only once during the long three months of waiting did Herbert visit Cavendish Street. A month after his first visit (and one week after the Martins had been to tea with John Gunn), a little note arrived announcing that Patrick was making another brief visit to Nottingham and hoped that his old pupil would join him for a sing on his first evening in town. When Herbert arrived, only Patrick Martin was in the house.

"There's only me here," he explained. "Robert's in Lyons looking at lace and Gussie's gone to Birmingham to see Clare in *The Silver King*. They couldn't leave the house empty. Not with . . ."

Herbert was about to ask about the new play and Clare's health when his host—disappointed at his failure to create an air of mystery—answered the question which he wished he had been asked.

"It's the painting. Bob thinks it's by Raphael. He swears it's worth a fortune. He bought it for a pound in a Paris back street during the Great Exposition. He's paid people to come from London to see it and they say there's nothing to it. But I'm here guarding it as if it were the bones of Saint Patrick."

They each drank a bottle of Bass, and they sang together some of the songs from the new Gilbert and Sullivan operetta which was popular in London.

"God, I enjoyed that," said Patrick Martin.

His eyelids had begun to droop and his head was beginning to loll back onto the antimacassar. He had one more comment to make before he fell asleep.

"Call round when I come back on Easter Sunday and we'll have another sing."

Nineteen years of unremitting Methodism had left their mark. Herbert prayed in silent gratitude. The promise he had made to John Gunn would be kept in full measure. Until Easter he would live the life of a perfect apprentice and lodger.

He never arrived late at Hudson and Ross and never left in the evening without finishing the piece of work which he had begun. At Huntingdon Street he struggled each evening with an improving book or educational magazine before he insisted on performing various domestic duties which were the proper concern of Mrs. Watkins. He watched Notts County—or Notts County Reserves—play football every Saturday afternoon without even suggesting that he might take his boots to one of the public houses which were the headquarters of local teams. He saved three shillings a week out of his meager wages by spending nothing except the few coppers that he needed for stamps and postcards, after his father's supplies were exhausted, and to pay his bus and tram fares on trips of historical interest. He visited Mortimer's Hole in the Castle Rock and climbed up to the castle itself to visit the museum within its recently rebuilt walls. He stood on the spot where Charles I had raised his standard at the start of the Great Civil War and, most significant of all, spent an early evening staring at the front of the Trip to Jerusalem without going inside the inn from which Nottingham pilgrims had set out for the Holy Land. He joined the Albert Hall Choir and, instead of going home between work and practice, stayed at his bench and studied the score of the oratorio which he was about to rehearse. John Gunn marveled at what love would do.

"It's magic," he told Mrs. Watkins, when she expressed delighted surprise that the yard had been swept and swilled down. "It's just as much magic as if the elves and pixies had come from Sherwood Forest to do it for you. May I be forgiven for the blasphemy! It's not magic—it's a miracle!"

"I can't make him out, Mr. Gunn. In some ways he's like a little lad and in others he's like a man twice his age."

"I can't make him out either, Mrs. W, and I'm not going to try. I'm going to rejoice that the sight of that young woman has made him pull his socks up. And lo, a blade for a knight's emprise, filled up the fine empty sheath of man."

"Is that from the Bible, Mr. Gunn?"

"It's a poem by Robert Browning. My Mary gave me a little book called *Men and Women* when we were courting. Browning was a great believer in the power of love."

"It's made him grow that terrible mustache."

Mrs. Watkins referred to Herbert, not Browning, with whose features she was not familiar."

"It's a small price to pay, Mrs. W."

She was obviously not convinced.

Early on the morning of his return to Sheffield, the mustache was removed—expertly amputated by the barber who prepared Herbert for the reunion by cutting his hair unfashionably short. Thus improved, he boarded the nine o'clock train. When it arrived on time, he felt an inexplicable reluctance to arrive at the Empress Works before the beginning of the ceremony which marked the end of Joseph's apprenticeship. So he walked the two miles to Eldon Street —working out the complicated calculations which had, for three months, so absorbed him. It was two days since he had been to chapel, and his last visit to the Albert Hall did not seem very long ago. Multiply that time by two and a half, and he would be with Clare again. He arrived at the factory exactly at noon. His father was standing at the gate waiting to greet him.

"I thought tha'd let us down again. I thought you weren't coming."

"I said I'd come. I wrote and said."

"We checked t'timetable yesterday. Train should have got in best part of an hour sin'. Was it late, or are you?"

Herbert dropped his carpetbag on the pavement. He had not expected a fatted calf to be slaughtered. But he had hoped for some expression of pleasure at his arrival. He was about to say that he had meant no harm, when Frederick Hattersley strode off into the works, shouting back over his shoulder, "Now you're here, get into t'press shop without wasting any more time. T'men have been standing idle for an hour without a stroke being done."

"Can I get a drink of water first? I'm parched with the walking."

They were the first words that he had spoken to his father in three months.

"Tha'll get a drink of water in t'press shop. We're wasting time."

The men (who had been standing idle for ten minutes) loitered in uneasy little groups, uncertain of whether or not they were expected to talk to each other. A barrel of beer, which stood in one corner, was to become the focal point of the day's events, in front of which the ancient ritual would be performed. When the ceremony was over, the men would form up into a straggling line as they waited for the new journeyman to knock out the bung and offer each man a pint in which to drink his health. Breaching the barrel was essential to the tradition. Without it, nobody would believe that the apprenticeship had been completed. So it was allowed even in factories owned by Sheffield's most bigoted total abstainers—although the teetotal masters always ostentatiously drank the toast in water from a glass which was placed, for their pious convenience, on top of the barrel. At the Empress Works, the barrel bore a jug of water and two glasses—one for Frederick Hattersley and one for his younger son.

Frederick Hattersley picked up the mallet with which the barrel was to be breached and, using it like a gavel, tapped the barrel rim. It was an entirely unnecessary preliminary. For the men had stood in total silence from the moment when the three Hattersleys formed up in their family tableau—the elder son to the father's left and the younger to the right. A cough suggested that the Master of the Empress Works was about to make a speech. But instead he waved imperiously toward the back of the shop and Jack Foster appeared, carrying the two parts of the contract by which Joseph had been bound apprentice. Seven years before, on the day when it was signed, it had been cut in two—cut with indenture shears which left the severed edges jagged. Jack Foster handed one half to the apprentice and one to his master, and, with suitable theatricality, they matched the edges of the parchment. Not surprisingly, the serrations fitted each other exactly. Jack Foster, acting as witness, confirmed in appropriately solemn voice that they were indeed constituent parts of the same document, and thought of the trouble that he would have been in had he brought half of another indenture down from the office safe.

"On this day and by this act," said Frederick Hattersley, handing both parts of the indenture to his son, "you become a free man and a journeyman cutler. Well done, thou good and faithful servant (St. Mark, chapter twenty-five, verse twenty-one)."

As the biblical addition had not been expected, the assembled workmen began to applaud before it was finished. It was not the most rousing of ovations, for every man carried a pot mug or pewter tankard brought for the occasion from home and it was difficult, so impeded, to clap with uninhibited enthusiasm. But they had shown willing, so the new journeyman knocked out the bung of the barrel and Jack Foster slipped a wooden tap into the hole with the speed and dexterity of a man familiar with the licensed trade. The mugs and tankards were filled to overflowing, and when Herbert and Frederick had charged their glasses with water, the company's youngest employee was pushed to the front of his workmates. He was a fourteen-year-old laborer from the grinders' shop. Apart from a patch of white flesh around his nose and mouth which had been protected from the dust by the newfangled paraphernalia required by Factory Acts, he was covered from head to toe in a sticky mixture of steel and grindstone particles bound together by oil and water. His sole duty was to clean away such swarf from the grinding wheels. He stood tongue-tied in front of his employer. The men encouraged him to perform his part.

"Go on, say it, Jimmy."

"Say it."

"Tha knows what to say. Get on wi' it."

"Say it, Jimmy."

"Say it," said Frederick Hattersley, as if the alternative to speech were death.

"And God bless the new journeyman," piped Jimmy Shepherd.

Protected by the repeated prayer and the click of pot on pewter, Joseph whispered to Herbert, "And God help him when his father finds out."

"What you done?" Herbert feared that his question could be heard above the noise.

"It's not what I've done. It's what I'm going to do."

"What you going to do, then?"

The answer did nothing to relieve Herbert's anxiety. "I'll tell you in bed tonight. Really, I suppose it's God help you, not God help me."

Herbert had the rest of the day to brood. He tried to get a moment alone with Joseph as the new journeyman changed back into his working clothes, but no sooner had he asked his urgent question than Jack Foster came into the storeroom to replace his best suit with the well-worn tweeds which were the working clothes of a manager. For the rest of the day, Joseph made sure that there was no opportunity for a private cross-examination. As they rode home side by side in their father's carriage, Joseph smiled at the thought of his secret, and Herbert frowned as he tried to guess what the secret might be.

The house at Asline Road was filled with all the family that Frederick Hattersley possessed. Mary, a buxom three months' pregnant, was there with her overfelicitous corn-merchant husband. Martha— living up to all she had been taught about the origins of her name— was carrying cold cuts and collations from kitchen to dining room. Aunt Winifred was waiting in the hall. To Herbert she looked not a day older than when he had played in her garden in the great house in Ranmoor. But even when she was barely thirty, to him she had seemed as ancient as Methuselah, so he treated her as he had always done, with the concern appropriate to a sprightly octogenarian. When the two boys squeezed, shoulder to shoulder, through the parlor door, their mother bustled out of the kitchen to greet them. Herbert expected that her first words would be for Joseph, for the day of triumph was his. But she grasped her younger son, hands in hands, and— leaning back as if to get the vision into proper perspective—announced that he had not changed a bit.

"I've only been gone three months."

"It was your first time away," she replied, as if he should have aged with homesickness.

"He must be feeding you well, this Mr. Gunn. You're growing a paunch," said Mary, absentmindedly stroking her own swollen stomach.

"Disgusting," said Martha, grinning at them from the dining-room doorway.

Joseph stood patient and ignored, his great day forgotten as his family celebrated Herbert's return. While his brother was led into the parlor he tiptoed upstairs to bathe and prepare for supper before Herbert was able to corner him again in the privacy of bedroom or bathroom. He was back down in the parlor by the time Martha said that dinner was ready.

"Any mucky pup who hasn't had a wash better get one quick."

"We can't begin until Mr. and Mrs. Foster get here. It wouldn't be manners."

Herbert was astounded by his mother's reproof. In thirteen weeks' absence, he had not forgotten her preoccupation with polite behavior. But the idea that Jack Foster and his still round and pink wife were to join them was barely credible. At Asline Road, family gatherings were kept strictly to the family. It was not until supper was over that Herbert began to understand why the Fosters had been afforded the unusual privilege of being treated like Hattersleys. Inevitably, after Frederick Hattersley had finished his second helping of apple pie, he began to reminisce about the way in which the end of apprenticeships had been celebrated in the old days.

"It was barbarous," he reported, smiling at the memory. "Lads had their trousers taken down and things were done to them I wouldn't mention in front of ladies. Swarf, oil, all sorts."

"Father, please!"

Martha was scandalized. Mary blushed and examined the pie she had left on her plate.

"Just think of how lucky you are, my lad. Count your blessings and" —Frederick Hattersley reached into his pocket—"remember your mother and me whenever you take a look at this."

He pulled out a long silver chain and the silver half-hunter which was attached to it. Holding it in front of Joseph's face and looking more as though he intended to hypnotize his son than to give him a present, he swung the watch like a pendulum.

"It's not new. It's better than new. It's the one thing that my father left me. The only thing that he had to leave. My mother took it out of his waistcoat pocket on the day that he died, and kept it under her mattress for fifteen years. She worked her fingers to the bone, washing and scrubbing at chapels and churches, not just houses—chapels and churches on Monday mornings after hundreds of muddy feet had tramped through 'em the day before. But she never sold this watch. Never sold it and never pawned it. She gave it to me on the day I finished my apprenticeship. Now it's yours."

Joseph said, "Thank you," and stared at it as if the hypnosis had been successful.

Jack Foster suggested a speech from the "son and heir," but Frederick Hattersley had not finished.

"I've summat else to tell you. Jack knows already. That's why he's here. We're going to open a new place and Jack's going to be boss, at least until Joseph is ready to take over. I've been hearing about Nottingham, hearing about it from Mr. Mundella's agent who did me a favor after Christmas. Dozens of new businesses are setting up all over the town. Last week in the House of Commons, Mr. Mundella called it 'a new cradle of enterprise.' I've bought a little business, with a workshop behind. We'll sell our scissors and shears and we'll buy in knives, the best knives, Sheffield knives. And we'll set and sharpen scissors in the back and make a few specialist items—felt shears and medical instruments. We'll start to cut into Hudson and Ross's medical-instrument trade. In a year or two, Herbert will come into the business. Jack will come back here then. He's going to live in digs for a bit. Then it will be the two of you. One in Nottingham and one here."

Herbert's heart leaped to think of life lived for the foreseeable future in Nottingham.

Frederick would have gone on for another five minutes had Joseph not interrupted him.

"It won't work."

"Why won't it work?" Frederick Hattersley was too astonished to be angry.

"Because it's going to be big business in the future. Big business and mass production. I thought you knew that. I thought that was why you bought the German presses. Handwork is finished. Even for surgical instruments."

"You don't know everything just because you're out of your indentures today. Mr. Mundella would not have recommended it if it wasn't a good investment."

"Mr. Mundella didn't. At least not according to what you just said.

200

It was his agent—who lives in Sheffield and knows nowt about cutlery."

Herbert was astonished by how bold Joseph had become.

"The discussion's over. The decision's taken. The shop opens on May first, the cutlers' shop a month after."

"Not with me it doesn't," said Joseph.

There was a moment of silence before Frederick Hattersley spoke. "What did you say?"

Father Hattersley was frightened more by his brother's calm than by his father's anger.

"I'm not working for you in Nottingham or anywhere else. I meant to tell you when Jack and his missus had gone home. But I'd better tell you now. I'm leaving—leaving the factory, leaving Sheffield and leaving England. I'm leaving for good."

Please, God, prayed Herbert. Don't let this stop me going back to Nottingham tomorrow.

CHAPTER SIXTEEN

ENTERPRISE

The description of Nottingham as "a new cradle of enterprise" was not solely the produce of hustings hyperbole. A series of remarkable industrial events had transformed the town's commercial reputation in a single decade. John Player opened a factory for the mass production of "ready-rolled" cigarettes. Dr. Francis Bowden made his fortune and opened up the countryside to the industrial poor by mass-producing the safety bicycle. His company took its name from Raleigh Street, in which it was founded. William Gunn (the cricketer who, for a moment, Clare Martin had hoped was Herbert Hattersley's landlord) and J. T. Moore set up a cricket bat manufactory in Haslam Street off Lenton Boulevard. As Mr. Mundella had predicted, by the end of the century each concern led the world "in the production of the goods which it had chosen to make and sell." Gunn and Moore, speaking on their own behalf, were more modest. They claimed no more than that they made "the best cricket bats in Christendom."

Yet, during that decade of progress and production, it was a fourth company which began to print the name of Nottingham indelibly on the industrial history of modern England. For years, John Boot's herbalist store at 10 Goose Gate had been famous for "selling all things cheaply, not one or two like other trades do" but all of the "2,000 items in stock." Even when the proprietor was (according to the *Local Preachers' Magazine*) "taken ill repeatedly and could no longer be employed in the vineyard," the business continued to expand, under his wife's management. A second shop was opened in Alfreton Road. Then, suddenly, the British public turned away from herbal remedies and toward patent medicines. Boot's family store would have gone bankrupt if John Boot's son, Jesse, had not turned with them.

When Frederick first heard the stories of Jesse Boot's success, he was profoundly contemptuous of both the man and his enterprise. Making patent medicines was not real manufacturing. And Boot had created and expanded his business by methods which Frederick regarded as little short of disreputable. Frederick believed in quality— quality which spoke for itself. Jesse Boot filled page after page of the *Nottingham Daily Express* with advertisements for his "one hundred and twenty-eight proprietary remedies," each one of which "retailed at wholesale prices." Allen's Hair Restorer sold at only half its usual price. Woodhouse's Rheumatic Elixir, Clarke's Blood Mixture, Widow Welch's Pills, Roche's Embrocation and Roper's Royal Bath Plasters were all on sale at prices lower than those recommended by the Society of Chemists and Druggists of the Town of Nottingham. And "exclusive items"—Boot's Patent Lobelia Pills "for asthma, indigestion and spasms," Boot's No Name Ointment, Boot's Celebrated Bronchial Lozenges and Boot's Aromatic Composition Powder—were all priced more cheaply than the equivalent products at Boot's competitors. Having failed at herbal remedies, the company flourished with patent medicines.

Although Frederick Hattersley disapproved of both Boot's product and the method by which it was promoted, he was deeply impressed by the way in which it was financed. The money to finance both mass production and the more expensive "Health for a Shilling" advertising campaign had been borrowed largely on the strength of Jesse Boot's Methodist connection. Three principal investors—Jelland, Armitage and Hind—had cast their bread upon the waters. When the tide came in at the end of a year, their talents had multiplied tenfold. It was Hind who put the idea of Nottingham as "a new cradle of enterprise" into the head of his old friend Alfred Mundella, when the Minister returned to Nottingham in support of the local Liberal candidates. At the same time, he mentioned to Mr. Mundella's agent that he was always ready to help suitable new ventures. It was Jesse Hind's money that the agent offered to Frederick Hattersley.

Jesse Boot's story was the sort of romance which brought a tear to Frederick Hattersley's sentimental eye—heroic mother struggling to survive in the hard world of men, determined son rebuilding the family business and vindicating his father's faith in the family and twenty percent return on invested capital. But, as with all genuine sentimentalists, the moment of emotion soon passed. He knew (without the benefit of Joseph's wisdom) that the idea suggested to him by Jesse Hind was commercially absurd. Hind believed in shops—particularly shops which sold their proprietor's product. The future of scissors lay in mass production, with the output sold by ironmongers who distributed their overheads between paraffin and nails, candles and pickaxes. Yet, when Frederick was asked about a little medical-instrument maker's workshop and a shop which bore the name of "Frederick Hattersley and Sons of Sheffield," he described himself as "very interested."

It was an honest enough description. For, increasingly, his ambitions pointed him toward the world outside the Empress Works. The new shop, were he to buy it, would make a loss. But, contemptuous of shopkeepers, Frederick Hattersley believed that, thanks to his superior abilities, he could keep the loss down to a manageable level. It would be a price which was well worth paying. For it would bring him into contact with men of wealth and influence, men who could help him attain the goals for which he had struggled during the last hard twenty years. The company, the bank balance, the factory and the reputation for quality were the approach march. The real battle was for position—position which came from, and encouraged, respect.

So he instructed Hind, Hind and Seagrove to acquire on his behalf an empty shop in Alfreton Road. He did not waste a moment's thought about the disruption that his plans would cause to the life of Jack Foster and his family. The idea that Joseph might stand in the way of his plans would have struck him as absurd. Frederick was unable to absorb even the fact of his son's defiance.

"I don't follow you. What are you on about?"

"I'm leaving, I said. I'm leaving England. We'd better talk about it later. Just you and me."

"We'll talk about it here and we'll talk about it now. You tell me, bold as brass, that you're off—leaving home, leaving the family, leaving the country—and then you tell me to mind my own business. You must think I've gone soft in the head."

"I didn't tell you to mind your own business. It is your business—yours and mine and nobody else's."

"It's family business. It affects everybody around this table."

Jack Foster stood up, and tapped his wife on the shoulder in case she did not realize that she should stand up too. "Anyway, it's none of our business, Mr. Hattersley. We'd best be off and leave it to t'family. You better tell me what you want of me at the works in t'morning."

"Sit down, Jack. It affects you as well."

Frederick Hattersley was not going to allow events in his own dining room to take on a life of their own.

Jack Foster sat down. But Joseph stood up. "All I wanted was to sort this out without a big row. I should have known that we couldn't do that in this family."

His mother spoke for the first time. "Don't be so stupid. How could you expect it to happen without a row? You can't announce that you're leaving home and expect us to behave as if you're going out for a walk."

Once Emily Hattersley had spoken, all the other women felt able to speak in their turn. Aunt Winifred put her hand on Joseph's arm. "Sit down, just for the moment. Sit down, for me."

Mary held her stomach and told her anxious husband that she was not supposed to get upset. Martha, sobbing, turned on Joseph.

"It's always like this at this house. Everything always turns into trouble and rowing. Other families aren't like this. Herbert caused all that trouble at Mary's wedding."

Herbert was appalled to be so badly treated. "Come on, Martha. This is nowt to do wi' me. That's not fair."

Joseph had moved to the door. "I'm going for a walk. Like Mother said."

"I said no such thing."

"I'm going anyway. We can all do with cooling down."

He left as calmly as if he had been allowed to leave Sunday dinner early in order to supervise the little ones at Bible class. His father bustled after him. First he hit his knee on the table leg, spilling the contents of every jug and gravy boat all over the tablecloth. Then he caught his foot in the rug and stumbled against the sideboard, rattling the ornaments and vases which filled its shelves, niches and brackets. Winifred shouted after him, "It's best to leave him alone for a bit."

"Hush, Winifred. You'll only make things worse," her sister warned.

Frederick, striding after his son, added the women's vaporings to the other intolerable events of the evening. As he hurried down the path and out onto Asline Road, a passing workman touched his battered cap.

"Pleasant evening, your honor."

The pale spring sun shone low out of an almost cloudless sky and the warm, still air carried no sound except the noise of the workman's wooden clogs on the paving stones. Frederick Hattersley could not bring himself to reply.

When father caught up with son, he was greeted in the casual manner of one chance acquaintance passing another in the High Street. Frederick had expected the passionate argument to be renewed with complaints about being followed. He fell in step beside Joseph and waited for the assault. To his surprise, they walked together in silence for half an hour.

Joseph did not wander like a man with time to kill or undesirable companions to avoid but in the manner of a traveler certain of his destination. He walked down London Road and, turning past St. Mary's Church, he climbed up the hill that led to Norfolk Park. Before he reached its great wrought-iron gates, he turned toward the square of almshouses which the good Duke in his charity had built for the Sheffield poor. At first, Frederick thought that his son was going to visit one of the paupers. But, to his relief, they walked on past the row of neat front gates into a little garden. It ran along a ridge of rock that overlooked Sheffield town center to the north. In the middle of the garden there was a carved obelisk. It was a monument to the men and women who had died—many of them in the Pond Street slums, five hundred feet below—during the great cholera epidemic.

"What have you come here for?"

It was inevitable that Frederick would ask the first question.

"Have you noticed?" Joseph asked him. "The point on the top of the monument isn't a proper pyramid? It slopes in more from one side than the other. Do you think it's a mistake, or did the mason mean it to be like that."

"I asked you what you came here for." Frederick, fighting to keep a grip on events, had no time for aesthetics.

Joseph chose to answer a difficult question. "I often come here. I come here most days. You get a good view."

"A good view of what?"

Father and son looked out over Sheffield. In the valley below them, Pond Street slums, relics of a time when it was legal to build terraces of workmen's houses back-to-back against a common wall, huddled together. The bricks, which had once been red, were so caked in grime that they were indistinguishable from the gray slates above them. One roof gleamed a white message to the city and to the world. Joseph Rodgers's factory, elegant cheek by squalid jowl with its workmen's houses, proclaimed its name and trademark, gable to gable: "King of Knifemakers and Knifemaker to Kings." Beyond it, on the other side of the valley, a gentle slope rose up toward the center of the old town. Father and son could see the spire of the parish church and beside it the curved roof of the old town hall, the tower of St. Paul's Church and the greater tower of the new town hall which overshadowed it. Beyond the buildings and above the spires and towers, faint and distant below the horizon, were the moors where Yorkshire and Derbyshire met. Joseph felt no sadness at the thought of never seeing that landscape again, just astonishment that, at last, the dream of escape had come true. Again it was Frederick who broke the silence.

"What do you come here to look at?"

"I come here to think."

Joseph's defense was breached. The temptation to recriminate had grown too strong to resist.

"I suppose this is where you thought about leaving home."

"I've thought about that everywhere. I've thought about it more than most things."

"It's time you told me what you've decided. It's more than time. I need to know and I'm entitled to know."

If Joseph had not been so certain about his father's unyielding character, he would have believed—just for a second—that Frederick was asking for help and not demanding obedience.

"Canada. I'm going to Canada. I've worked it all out. It's Canada that's got a future. It's the Empire. I've taken notice of your Mr. Chamberlain and I'm off."

"He's not *my* Mr. Chamberlain!"

"He is, even if you've stayed with the other lot. He stands for the same as you—England, the Empire and master manufacturers, like him. Men who make things, not lords or dukes like Hartington and Harcourt. I almost decided to go to South Africa. But I decided on Canada. I'm off Monday."

"Monday! Less than a week. How can you be? Where's the money coming from?" Frederick had not quite given up hope. "I hope you're not expecting owt from me?"

"I wouldn't take it. I'm working my passage on the SS *Endeavour,* sailing out of Liverpool on Tuesday. I've saved a few pound for when I get there. And today's been worth a bob or two."

If there had been a suggestion of conciliation in Frederick's manner, the mood had changed.

"You're going to sell the watch, you Judas. You've been planning to sell the watch ever sin' I told you that I'd give it to you."

"I've done no such thing. I shan't sell the watch. I got five pound from Auntie Winifred—"

"I might have known she'd be behind it."

"She knew nowt. Nowt until I told you today. It were a present for finishing my time. Don't blame her. She knew nowt."

"Don't expect me to be grateful for that. It's a disgrace that I were told at the same time as her—no real relation. You've been planning this for weeks, you conniving little bugger."

Joseph had never heard his father swear before. He was as stunned as if he had been slapped across the face—too stunned to answer.

"We fed you and kept you and paid you all these years, and what reward do we get?"

Joseph's confidence was revived by anger. "You've had your money's worth out of me."

"How can you say such a thing?"

The mood had changed again. Joseph was not sure if the sudden display of righteous indignation was genuine or counterfeited to give his father the moral ascendancy.

"Your mother and me will never think of what we've done for you in pounds, shillings and pence. We're family."

It was time to tell the truth. "You've not had your money's worth and I know that better than most. You never have and you never will. That's why I'm going. That's the real reason. I can't stand being such a disappointment every minute of the day. I've never measured up to your hopes. I can't."

208

"You could have done if you'd tried. You're clever enough. You're just not interested."

"You're doing it now. Just what I can't stand any longer. I measure up already. But you don't believe it and never will. You're pining for a son who doesn't exist and I get measured every bloody day against something which is just in your imagination. I'll have it no longer. Herbert can run the business. He can do it if you give him a chance."

Joseph walked out of the garden and down the road toward Norfolk Park. The light was beginning to fade and, down in Pond Street, candles were flickering behind the grimy windows.

"Your mother will be worried to death."

"We'll be home in half an hour."

"Worried after you've gone, if you really go."

"I'm going, Father. I'm really going."

"Will you make scissors?"

"I'll make whatever they want. I'll make anything."

"But you won't sell the watch?"

"No."

"Nor pawn it neither?"

"I won't sell it and I won't pawn it. That's a promise."

They walked home together in silence.

Joseph's departure was the first thing Herbert thought about when he woke up at five o'clock on the following morning. Joseph himself slept serenely on, but his brother stared, desolate, at the ceiling and wondered why life was so unfair. He was at the beginning of what he had expected to be the happiest week of his life. But now the dream was shattered. When first he heard of Joseph's plan, he had been filled with a fear that he would not be allowed to return to Nottingham. Then the return itself had filled him with awful dread. He longed to see Clare Martin but could not bear the thought of parting from Joe forever. His confusion was increased by his inability to understand the turmoil by which he was surrounded.

"Don't you feel sad, leaving us and Sheffield forever?"

"I've hated it. Hated it since I was made to go to the works, hated Jack Foster . . . Would you feel sad at going, if you hated it all?"

"I'd feel sad because I like the works. And I like Jack Foster a lot. I thought you did. Anyway, I'd feel sad at doing anything for the last time, whether I liked doing it or not."

Lying awake, waiting for the alarm clock to rattle, Herbert considered whether, in the new and terrible circumstances, he wanted to go or stay. He made the decision which, whenever he was faced with difficult choices, he was to make for the rest of his life. He did not want to stay in Sheffield any more than he wanted Joe to go to Canada. The idea of not seeing Clare next Tuesday seemed almost as intolerable as never seeing Joseph again. It was unreasonable of fate to force him into such a choice. So fate, having asked the unfair question, would be left to provide the answer. He would let events take their course.

Fate, acting through Frederick Hattersley, accepted the responsibility and Herbert was hurried off back to Nottingham on the first available train. There were a few words of sentimental farewell. His mother said that soon he would be the only son she had, but did not specify whether she was predicting disaster at sea or legal disinheritance. His father was more explicit.

"I hope you understand."

"Understand what?"

"Your new responsibilities. You'll have to run the company now, run it when I'm dead and gone."

"You'll live forever, Father," said Joseph, who was waiting to walk with Herbert to the station. "You'll see us all off."

"It's nowt to do wi' thee," his father told him. "You left Frederick Hattersley and Sons last night. I'm having the letterhead changed."

"It was never right anyway. We were nowt to do with the company really."

"Not now. No more rowing. Not at the very last minute," said Emily. "At least let's part in peace."

They parted in peace of a sort and, for Herbert, the day grew more peaceful as Sheffield faded further and further into the distance.

The fear that Joe had gone forever ached dully at the back of his mind. But at the front of his thoughts were the sharp pangs of pleasure which transfixed him every time he remembered his plans for Easter Saturday afternoon. They had been laid by John Gunn, who had invited all the Martins to a concert in the Albert Hall. It was assumed that Tom Cross would come, for it was taken for granted that he followed wherever Augusta led. So John had bought seven tickets in all. Herbert calculated that even without any pushing or jostling, the odds of his sitting next to Clare were almost two to one. And he took it as a racing certainty that one of the families would invite the other home to tea. Indeed, he had noticed that in anticipation of the surprise invitation, John Gunn had brought home from the bakery a large pork pie, a Dundee cake and a dozen Nelson squares.

The program consisted entirely of sacred music, as was only fitting for the day between the Crucifixion and the Resurrection. But if the whole afternoon had been devoted to Gregorian chant, Herbert would have looked forward to the outing with almost uncontainable excitement. Waiting outside the hall, he stared nervously up Derby Road. He could not bear even to contemplate the idea that Clare would not come. But he could not quite believe in the miracle of her arrival. His skepticism was wholly justified.

At almost ten minutes to three, John Gunn had to work hard to keep his friend and lodger calm.

"They'll be on this one," he said, waving his hand in the direction of the noise which was approaching them down the Derby Road.

When the clanging bell and rattling trolley turned into a tangible tramcar, they could still not be sure. For the juggernaut obscured their view of the pavement to which the light of Herbert's life would descend. When it swayed off toward the town center, it revealed only four figures standing in front of Butt's grocer's shop and waiting to cross the road. Clare Martin was not amongst them.

It was Robert Martin who explained her absence. "I'm afraid my little girl's not very well."

John Gunn at least maintained the courtesies and expressed the hope that she had not contracted anything serious. Clare's father, with an apparent lack of concern which Herbert thought scandalous, assured him that it was nothing much and showed every sign of being more worried about getting into the hall before the concert started than about his daughter's condition. The three healthy Martins seemed to enjoy themselves immensely. Tom Cross signified polite appreciation and John Gunn exhibited enormous pride at the display of virtuosity which the chapel provided. Herbert suffered enough for them all—torn between the fear that Clare was mortally ill and the hope that she was at least ill enough to justify her absence. Had it been an evening of unqualified joy, he would not even have thought of Joseph. But gloom bred gloom and he began to think of Clare out to dinner with one of her rich admirers and his brother lost at sea.

The Martins—invited to Huntingdon Street on the assumption that they could not come—accepted the invitation with obvious pleasure.

211

Herbert's worst fears were confirmed. Knowing the terrible truth seemed infinitely preferable to the uncertainty of fearing that he had been betrayed.

"How is Clare?" he asked Tom Cross, having cornered him in the kitchen. "How is she really?"

The answer was as bad as he had feared: "Fit as a fiddle and twice as bigoted."

Herbert did not understand.

"Bigoted," Tom repeated. "Bigoted like all bloody papists. At the very last minute, with everybody dressed up and ready, she announced that it would be wrong of her to come. 'It's a religious service,' she says. 'At least my conscience tells *me* that it is.' With which she offs her hat and coat and asks who'd moved her rosary from the mantelpiece."

Even in his moment of extremis, Herbert was impressed at the quality of Tom's imitation.

"I thought they were all Catholics."

"They are. But you'll learn, my lad, that there are Catholics and Catholics. Mr. Martin himself doesn't seem to believe a thing. Augusta has to persuade him to go to church on Sundays. His brother's just the same. But Clare's a fanatic. She goes to church every morning. I knew she wouldn't go to the Albert Hall. She'd burn it down, she would."

"But how can she be so religious if she's an actress?"

"It doesn't work like that for Catholics. They can do what they like as long as they confess afterward. It's only us who have to live good lives. They can be as bad as they like, if they go to confession."

"I don't think Clare's bad." Herbert was asking for reassurance.

"Not bad," said Tom. "Haughty. She thinks she's better than the rest of us."

"Perhaps she is."

"You'll never find out, old lad; she's off tomorrow for another year. She's not even coming home for Christmas. She's got a part in a new play. It's about sin and retribution and she says that's why she's been called to act in it. I heard her tell her father that if he wants to see her at Christmas, he'll have to go to London. If you're so keen to see her, you'll have to do the same."

Tom's suggestion was not meant to be taken seriously. And in order to convince Herbert of the deep irony with which he spoke, he gave a long, and intentionally hollow laugh to underline the impossibility of the suggested journey ever taking place. The subtlety was lost on Herbert.

"I'll go to London in a week or two. Perhaps not to see her. But I shall go. I shall go in t'summer."

"It'll cost pounds. Where will you get the money?"

The answer, though Herbert did not know it at the time, was to be provided by Patrick Ignatius Martin.

There were several possible explanations for Patrick Ignatius Martin's decision to move to Nottingham. The one which he preferred was fraternal affection. Only his niece Augusta was skeptical about the notion that he was motivated solely by concern for his brother's welfare.

Robert Martin's increasing eccentricity was too obvious to be a matter of dispute. But he was afflicted by a gentle lunacy with which his daughter was able to deal without either danger or distress. His madness was focused on his painting—the priceless Old Master which he had bought for a few francs in a Paris back street and which the art world, for reasons of spite and malice, refused to recognize as the genuine Raphael which he knew it to be. His mornings were spent writing to whichever painter was mentioned in the daily paper. Whistler never replied. Ruskin's secretary sent formal notes of acknowledgment. Mrs. Holman-Hunt threatened legal action if persistent annoyance of her husband continued. Robert Martin moved on to priests and politicians—some of whom could not distinguish between a Fra Angelico and a Fragonard. The priests were sympathetic and the politicians dismissive. Occasionally, total strangers were accosted in the street and invited to verify the authenticity of the Martin Annunciation. Augusta lived in a state of constant, if mild, concern for his welfare and safety. But her serious concern was financial. The few savings which had been accumulated during the years of lace design would not last forever. She could not imagine how Uncle Patrick could help rid her father of his obsession. But she knew exactly the effect that his arrival would have on the dwindling bank balance.

When Patrick Martin arrived, carrying no more than his fiddle and a wicker basket filled with threadbare clothes, he told his niece that he had sold his books and furniture as his only way of raising the ready cash which allowed a man of his ferocious pride to pay his own way.

Augusta, being of a practical turn of mind, asked him for an immediate contribution toward the upkeep of the house. He gave her a sovereign. Two weeks later, she asked again and he replied almost truthfully that he had no more to give.

"Can you not earn something?"

"Where would I be earning money, tell me that?"

"You could take pupils again. We've got a good piano."

"Where would I find pupils? There's nobody in your parish who can afford shoe leather. They won't pay for singing lessons."

"Tom will ask around at his chapel. And so will Herbert Hattersley. He'll do anything we ask him. He's sweet on Clare, that one. He'll do anything."

"I wouldn't mind seeing young Herbert again," said the virtuoso. "We had many a good sing together."

Having conceded his willingness to look for work—at least to Augusta's satisfaction—he left for the Robin Hood, to see if his credit was good for half a pint of stout.

Herbert responded to the invitation to visit the Martins with all the pathetic eagerness which Augusta had anticipated. When he was told that it was Patrick Martin who had suggested the urgent meeting, disappointment competed with curiosity. Patrick Martin himself was both pleased and surprised to see the young man but, when reminded that he had been invited to talk about work, tried hard to recall the exact aspect of that unpleasant subject which Augusta had wanted him to discuss. All he could remember was a suggestion made to him on the previous Saturday night by the potman of the Robin Hood. The discovery that the new customer was Licentiate of the College of Music had provoked an appealing suggestion. There was always a great demand for new entertainers to perform at smoking concerts in the upstairs room. For the price of a pint, an introduction to the master of ceremonies could be arranged. Herbert's arrival at Cavendish Street inspired Patrick Martin with an idea for making a living without having to endure an intolerable amount of exertion.

"How about earning a bob or two?" he asked.

Herbert was speechless with gratitude.

"You'll have to get tails and a white waistcoat. That is, if you haven't got them already."

Herbert confessed with shame that he did not possess such garments.

"No matter, we'll hire them for a shilling from the pawnshop. What we need next is a repertoire. Tell me what you sing these days."

Herbert offered the various oratorios which he had rehearsed so assiduously at the Albert Hall and, noticing that the recital was not being well received, added the martial songs which had been such a success at the Barracks Hotel. "M'Old Shako" was accepted with particular pleasure.

"We need a three-part program. Gilbert and Sullivan to begin with. They're great favorites these days. Then a few patriotic songs. 'M'Old Shako' will fit in very well. Not too many, mind you. We don't want it to get too boisterous. I can't abide stamping and clapping while I'm playing. We send them home sentimental. 'Danny Boy,' 'In the Gloaming,' 'I Hear You Calling Me' . . ."

Patrick Martin had meant to continue his list, but he was so moved by the memory of his favorite requiem that he burst into song.

> *"Though years have spread their weary lengths between*
> *And, on your gr-a-a-ave, the mossy grass is green. . . ."*

"Am I to sing tenor?"

"Tenor or baritone, it doesn't matter. You've got a fine voice, Herbert. You can sing anything. They'll love you."

"I don't know who they are."

"The Buffaloes. It's their smoking concert, next Saturday night."

"The Buffaloes!" A vestige of respectability combined in Herbert's mind with the memory of one of his historical visits. "They're the men who burned the castle down."

"That was the Bulls. Anti-Catholics who didn't want the likes of me getting the vote. We're talking about a different sort of cow altogether —the Antediluvian Order of Buffaloes."

"What are they for?"

It seemed a sensible enough question.

"They're for nothing. They're a Friendly Society and they save up for Christmas and funerals and that sort of thing. But really they're for nothing except singing. . . . We'll have to start rehearsing now. Three nights ought to be enough."

Herbert needed no more prompting. It was going to be a sing like the sings he had loved in the Barracks Hotel, and he was going to be paid for it. John Gunn would have to be told that he was performing

215

in front of a more exalted and abstemious audience. But the deception of his friend was a small sacrifice to make in comparison with the reward. Two shillings would go into his London fund, two shillings, paid in recompense for enjoying himself in the upstairs room of the Robin Hood. Glancing in the Martins' kitchen mirror, he noticed with much satisfaction that his mustache was clearly visible again. He decided to grow whiskers.

The tailed coat and white waistcoat fitted Herbert perfectly. Unfortunately, Patrick Martin had neglected to ask the pawnshop for patent-leather shoes, so the impression of harmonic sophistication was slightly diminished by the heavy boots which he wore.

"Stand behind one of the piano legs."

The impresario and accompanist was himself resplendent in a claret-colored smoking jacket (several sizes too large for him) and a huge cravat which had once been white but had, with the years, turned as khaki as the new camouflage uniforms which the War Office was trying to impose on the army.

Their entry was greeted with heartening applause, and the friendly disposition of the audience was emphasized by the two pint glasses of beer which were standing on the piano lid, awaiting the arrival of the artistes. Patrick Martin drank his down without pausing for breath, wiped his mouth with the back of his hand and announced that his drink was stout. A pint of stout was immediately provided. As if in gratitude he played a couple of unrecognizable chords. The whole room fell silent.

"My young associate will begin," said Patrick, speaking in a voice which he believed conveyed breeding and culture, "with a selection from the works of Gilbert and Sullivan."

"My object all sublime . . ." sang Herbert.

He had steadfastly refused to become a tenor, and as the applause mounted, he decided that his integrity had been rewarded. His reception was ecstatic.

"And now *HMS Pinafore*," said Patrick.

"When I was a boy, I served my term . . ."

The audience was convulsed with ecstasy again.

When Patrick responded to calls for an encore to what he described as "The Savoy Selection," tankards of beer and stout were passed up onto the platform without solicitation. Herbert still had to finish his first glass, so Patrick, anxious, as he explained, not to offend so friendly an audience, drank both pints. The patriotic songs were an even greater success than the "Musical Moments with Gilbert and Sullivan"—an additional description of part one of the program which Patrick invented when, as he put it, he was inspired by the warmth of the reception. "Tom Bowling" was a particular triumph and formed a happy bridge between tunes of glory and songs of sentiment. The bridge could not, however, be crossed until additional liquid compliments had been consumed. But once Patrick had waded across, the audience began to clamor to be saddened. They were in no condition to make a critical judgment of Herbert's "On with the Motley" but simply stood and applauded, only interrupting their demonstration of enthusiasm to wipe away the tears that ran down their rough cheeks. Patrick Martin agreed to drink their health. And as he toasted "an audience of taste and discernment" coins—some of them silver—began to land on the stage. Herbert thought that he was already in heaven.

It was a long walk back to Cavendish Street. For much of it Patrick had to be supported, and he persisted in disturbing Herbert's progress and euphoria by constantly pausing to make speeches about the meaning of life, the prospect of salvation and the importance of ending every performance with a sentimental ballad. Occasionally he introduced an autobiographical note.

"I wasn't always like this, you know. There were times ... There were times ... I could play the piano as well as any man in Dublin. I wasn't always as you see me now. I might have been a second Chopin. Or the Abbey Liszt. Chopin or Liszt. I could have been both ... either."

"I know you could," agreed Herbert, dragging him on toward home.

"I might have been a second Liszt or the Abbey Chopin," continued Patrick, staggering off down a side street. "But I have fallen low."

He was still mourning the death of his murdered talent when they arrived in Cavendish Street. Both Augusta and her father were woken up by the renewed assertion that he could have been a second Chopin.

Robert Martin came downstairs carrying a heavy brass candlestick, ready to defend with his life the Raphael which, he assumed, art thieves had come to steal. Augusta—who boasted no dressing gown —was wrapped in an old topcoat. As always, she took command.

"Just lie him on the sofa in the studio. He's a dead weight. We'll never get the old fool upstairs." Then she added a friendly afterthought. "There's a tin of peppermints on the shelf in the kitchen. If I were you, I'd suck one."

Herbert took her advice. As he pulled the older man's feet clear of the studio floor coppers began to fall out of the pockets of his tattered smoking jacket.

"I reckon we made the best part of a quid tonight."

"Good," said Augusta. "We could do with it."

She had meant to dampen his enthusiasm. But seeing him so anxious to please and be admired, she allowed herself to voice an opinion which, despite its sincerity, she had first believed best left unexpressed.

"You do look nice, Herbert. Apart from the boots, that is." A further qualification was inevitable. "Pity it's not in a better cause."

CHAPTER SEVENTEEN

LESSONS IN FAITH
AND MORALS

The musical partnership which Herbert founded with Patrick Ignatius Martin faced only the problems of instant success. But the branch of Frederick Hattersley and Sons, which was to be established in Alfreton Road, Nottingham, enjoyed no such good future. Indeed it did not open for business until the early winter of that year. For a month after Joseph's departure, the Nottingham venture was mentioned only once at the Empress Works, and then by Jack Foster. His inquiry about his own future was answered with the menacing promise that he would find out soon enough.

Then, just as Frederick Hattersley's spirits improved enough to allow him to contemplate the future, Jesse Hind wrote to say, "The recent absence of instructions has made it impossible to complete the transaction within the time period previously specified." The assumption, in Sheffield, was that the solicitor had lost all enthusiasm for the complicated conveyancing that would earn him a fee of half a guinea. But Frederick decided that it was best to keep his peace and bide his time. So he confirmed that he did intend to install machinery in the room over the shop and that the ground landlord should be so notified. When Jesse Hind's clerk wrote back and told him that the deeds would not change hands until November, he accepted the delay philosophically. Meanwhile, Herbert's only difficulty was his inability to fulfill the number of engagements which the potman at the Robin Hood was able to put in his way.

The demand for artistes of taste and talent was insatiable. The Buffaloes boasted of their discovery to the Foresters. So Herbert and Patrick were invited to perform at the Antediluvian Order's Ladies Night in the Royal Marine Hotel, Alfreton Road. Then the Foresters boasted to the Oddfellows. So when the Provincial Grand Master of the Manchester Unity visited Nottingham, Herbert and Patrick provided the entertainment at the end of the evening. Two days later, they took the place of a sick tenor who should have sung at the concert which followed the special meeting of Lodge 224 of the Ancient Order of Druids at the Langham Hotel. Amongst the audience was Wiliam Pollard, landlord of the Midland Hotel, Woollaton Road. He invited them to sing in his public house on the next night and promised them a weekly place in one of the concerts which were held there on Thursday, Friday and Saturday. Patrick Martin's only problem was persuading entertainments secretaries, who wanted a performance next week, that they must wait at least a month.

Herbert wrestled with a more intractable dilemma. He did not find it easy to deceive John Gunn. But he found it absolutely impossible to tell him that he spent one or two evenings a week singing in public houses. The problems of constant deception became almost unbearable when John began to take a friendly interest in his lodger's new activity. After the second engagement—for which Herbert had borrowed his Sunday shoes—John asked, in the most affable of manners, when he could join the audience at one of the recitals of sacred songs for which his young friend prepared so assiduously. Herbert suggested that the most suitable occasion would be a special Advent performance of the *Messiah* planned for the first week in December. The tangled web grew tighter around him.

On the morning after the Druids' special meeting, Patrick was told by the pawnbroker that the pledge on the tailcoat and white tie had been neither renewed nor redeemed. A customer had offered to buy it outright for five shillings, but he would give it to Herbert in return for the promise of a free performance at the Annual Christmas Dinner of the Credit Agents' Association. Herbert wanted to turn the offer down, for he had no idea how he would explain that the evening suit —which he had claimed to John Gunn had been lent to him by a church organist temporarily incapacitated with rheumatism—had suddenly become his property. But when the pawnbroker agreed to throw in a pair of buckled shoes (one with its buckle still attached), Patrick would not even contemplate a refusal. Herbert returned home from one of the Midland Hotel's musical evenings with sad news.

"Mr. Sullivan, the man who lent me this suit, died yesterday. His wife wants me to keep it in memory of him."

"Died of rheumatism?"

"I think it was rheumatism."

"Hope it wasn't rheumatic fever. That's catching. Do I know this Mr. Sullivan? Perhaps I should write a note of condolence to his wife."

Herbert was not to be deterred by thoughts of infection. He was, however, terrified by the suggestion that John might know his benefactor.

"You don't know him. He had only been in Nottingham a bit."

"But what about the infection? Should you be wearing the suit? It might have microbes in it."

"It's all right. He hasn't worn it for ten years. His wife said so."

John's smile was wholly inappropriate for a conversation concerned with death and disease. But Herbert was simply grateful that he pursued the question no further.

. The hurdle of the evening suit having been successfully surmounted, the next barrier to Herbert's peace of mind was the business card. One evening Patrick Martin showed him a design—agreed with A. Hindley, Mourning Card Specialist of Milton Street—which he proposed should be printed on one gross of gilt-edged pasteboard.

"We can't do it, Patrick. We can't do it that regular. John Gunn will find out and I'll be done for."

Patrick Martin was not in any mood to be deflected from his purpose. Ignoring Herbert's protests, he began to read aloud the proposed inscriptions. On one side, in italic script as severe as the engraving on a coffin plate, he intended to have printed the words *"Patrick Ignatius Martin L.C.M."* and, below it (in only slightly smaller letters), *"Herbert Hattersley, baritone."* On the other side was a description of what the Licentiate thought was on offer: *"Ballads and arias from Mr. Hattersley and pianoforte recitals by Dr. Martin."*

"Dr. Martin! Dr. Bloody Martin! Who's Dr. Martin when he's at home?"

"I'm entitled. It's honorary, but I'm entitled. Every L.C.M. is. If I'd sat the fellows' examination, you would have had to call me professor."

"You'd have had to pass the exam as well as take it."

"Not too smart, young fellow-me-lad. I'd have passed with flying colors if I hadn't missed it altogether. Everybody said so."

"Why did you miss it?"

"That's none of your business. Be quiet for a moment and let me tell you the good news."

"If it's more engagements, it's no use telling me. I daren't do it. I can't spend night after night in pubs."

"This one isn't in a pub. This one's the Mechanics' Hall."

Herbert looked skeptical.

"It's the Robin Hoods' Banquet. Well, it's the Noncommissioned Officers' Banquet anyway. It's their celebration of the Queen's Jubilee. The Mayor and Sheriff are going to be there and Lord Somebody-or-other from St. Albans. The announcement says that 'the musical entertainment is likely to be of an elaborate kind,' and we can be part of it."

"I don't believe you."

"Well, it's true. I swear on my mother's grave, God rest her sweet soul. Somebody dropped out and a corporal who heard us in the Midland Hotel came round to see me. You tell John Gunn that you are to sing for Alderman Turney and Alderman Dennett, and let's see what he has to say about that."

What John Gunn said about it left Herbert as near to speechless as his temperament allowed.

"I'm glad you've told me. I was going to ask. I should have asked you before. But, to my shame, I put it off—as I fear is often my habit with unpleasant duties. I gave myself until Friday, first of the month. Then I was going to ask you. But it's better this way."

Herbert tried, unsuccessfully, to look bewildered.

"You've got to tell your father."

"I will, I'll write today. I expect that he'll be singing somewhere as part of the Jubilee. I meant to write anyway and tell him about the electric light that they're going to put on top of the castle. I bet they're not having an electric light in Sheffield."

"You've got to tell him about the other singing. If you don't, I will."

"What other singing?"

"You know perfectly well what other singing. Singing in public houses. I knew about it almost from the start."

Herbert, too afraid to inquire how John Gunn had found out, stopped the pretense. "If I tell Father, he'll stop me."

"Only if it's public houses. There are dozens of other places where you and Patrick Martin can sing. I know that out at Selston they are looking for entertainment for their Jubilee Tea. They would be delighted to have you."

"They don't pay."

"Is pay important? Why do you need money?"

Herbert stared stubbornly at his feet, unable to spare any energy for arguing about money. His strength was all employed in worrying about how he could continue his musical career.

"M'father wouldn't mind some of them."

"I said that. He wouldn't mind the Robin Hoods' Banquet even though it is in a public house. He'd think that respectable enough. Can't you just sing at respectable functions? It's really the Midland Hotel that he'd take exception to, and the Buffaloes."

"I'll think about it," said Herbert.

John, having come during the six months of their acquaintance to understand his lodger, knew what "think about it" meant. Herbert would do nothing until Patrick Martin presented him with the date for their next engagement. Then, if it was in a public house, he would tell his partner of the risk he ran of his father finding out. Martin would urge him to pretend that he was going somewhere else, and Herbert, anxious not to deceive but desperate to sing, would not make up his mind about whether to follow instinct or conscience until the very last minute. What he eventually decided would depend upon Patrick Martin's eloquence, the chance of a successful deception and the way he felt, at the moment of decision, about Patrick, John, his father and life. John Gunn, who often preached sermons on the text "Helmsman, steer a steady course," decided to offer an incentive to responsible navigation.

"Think about it, by all means. If nothing else happens that he would mind about, I shan't tell your father. I *should* tell him, I know that. One of us should tell him anyway. But I won't. What's more, I'll help you to get decent engagements, engagements of which we can all be proud. The Cooperative Bakers' Society is having an anniversary supper out in Colston Bassett in August. I know that they are looking for entertainers. I'll put a word in for you."

Herbert smiled, as if life was beginning to become worth living again.

"But don't forget," John reminded him. "The next pub night and one of us will tell your father. Think about it."

Herbert thought about it and he discussed it with Patrick Martin. It was agreed that the Midland Hotel would be told that the duo was not available for any of its concerts, but Patrick added, without consulting his partner, "until the autumn." They would concentrate on "respectable functions." The Cooperative Bakers' Society was a success of sorts. Herbert introduced a new item into his repertoire—"The Death of Nelson"—and it was warmly received. However, the occasion lacked the conviviality of an evening in a bar or taproom. John Gunn was as good as his word and—noticing an advertisement in the *Nottingham Daily Express*—drafted a letter tendering for the supply of musical entertainment for the Nottinghamshire Agricultural Show, to be held at Newark-upon-Trent. Herbert and Patrick were delighted to receive a piece of paper which bore all the marks of a legal contract and, when show day dawned, traveled hopefully north. At two o'clock it began to drizzle. By four it was raining hard. At six Mr. James Barron, the Secretary, paid the performers off and sent them home. Despite the immense consolation of fifteen sixpences rattling in Patrick Martin's pocket, Herbert was desolate. He was still disconsolate at the end of the ninety-minute journey home, a personal record for sustained misery. John Gunn concluded, with both satisfaction and relief, that Herbert sang more for pleasure than for profit, and comforted him with the splendid news that the Master Bakers themselves wanted "Martin and Hattersley" at their Christmas prize giving. The invitation had not been easy to arrange. But John was certain that the only way to avoid catastrophe was to organize prestigious bookings which made Patrick Martin's public houses seem unattractive. He believed implicitly in man's instinct for improvement.

The crisis in Herbert's singing career came with an invitation from the Black Boy Hotel. John Gunn had constructed guidelines to influence Herbert's judgment about the acceptability of individual engagements—telling him that he must make each decision for himself but that they would be made more easily if they were based on an established principle. What the landlord of the Black Boy proposed was clearly well outside the rules. The concert was to be held on Sunday night. And it had no special purpose. On the evidence of the letter, it was to be held in the hotel for no better purpose than the encouragement of drinking. Herbert knew that he should not go, but Patrick was sure that a convincing and successful alibi could be constructed.

The invitation had come at a difficult time in their professional relationship. They had argued throughout the previous week even about accepting engagements within the guidelines.

"We've got nothing for September."

"We should take t'Masons."

Patrick Martin had turned down the Lace Market Lodge of the Masons out of hand and without consultation. It was, he explained when Herbert found out about his perfidy, a matter of conscience.

"I didn't argue about the Society of St. Vincent whatsit. I don't like Catholics any more than you like Methodists. But I agreed to do it."

"Masons aren't Methodists. It's different altogether."

"If Lord Salisbury's a Mason, why isn't it respectable?"

"Because they hate Catholics. They're an anti-Catholic secret society and they worship graven images. They murder priests and take blasphemous oaths."

"Lord Salisbury doesn't do any of those things."

Confounded, Patrick Martin changed tack. "I don't claim to be a pious man, but there are some things that I just won't do. Anyway, it wouldn't be anything like the Black Boy. They're making a presentation to a celebrity. They want all G and S. I shall play a couple of overtures. You can sing 'A Wandering...'"

"I'm not going to sing tenor. I've told you."

"You're a silly boy with a lot to learn, but no matter. Do 'Bow! Bow! Ye Lower-Middle Classes' and I shall bob up and down on the piano stool. That will get a big laugh."

When Herbert did not protest, Patrick Martin moved on to his plans for the deception.

The evening went wonderfully well. The sermon was short. So Herbert was able to change into his tailcoat without undue hurry. At first, Patrick and Herbert were unnerved by the size and nature of the all-male audience. It packed the best room at the Black Boy from wall to wall and it radiated prosperity from the quality of the bowler hats, which half of the men were wearing, to the highly polished boots that stuck out from under tables weighed down by beer and whiskey. Patrick cracked his knuckles as he obsessively checked the sheets of his music, and asked Herbert, time after time, "How do you feel?" His manner implied that he expected the answer "Hysterical." Herbert felt fine. And his confidence increased as he listened to what the master of ceremonies called "the turns" which preceded "The Magic of the Savoyards."

A thin tenor sang "Irish Traditional Airs." Only Patrick Martin wept. A distinguished elderly gentleman, with flowing white hair, played a selection of Paganini's Variations on what he claimed to be a Stradivarius. A large lady with a feather boa and scarlet sash announced "The quality of mercy is not strained," and went on to justify that assertion. Shakespeare received only polite applause. Tennyson's "Charge of the Light Brigade" was greeted with a standing ovation.

"I thought for a minute," Patrick whispered to Herbert, "that she was one of those low lady comediennes. I should have known better, posh audience like this."

Herbert whispered back, "Where's the celebrity?"

"Couldn't recognize him. He's a footballer or cricketer. Nothing important."

There was a brief interval, during which Herbert drank lemonade, and then the master of ceremonies announced "Selections from Gilbert and Sullivan." Herbert smoothed down his mustache and confirmed that his new kiss-curl was in exactly the right position on his forehead. Patrick's amusement at the thought that he might forget to slick it back before he went home was lost in the need to concentrate on the overture to *The Gondoliers*.

There followed the usual twenty minutes' triumph only interrupted by a gentleman at the back who—when Herbert sang "either a little Liberal or else a little Conservative"—cried out, "Or Joseph Chamberlain!" The heckler was shushed from all sides, and after Herbert's song was over, the master of ceremonies offered a profuse apology and the assurance that the hooligan was a foreigner from Heanor. He then crashed his gavel down with unusual force.

"Gentlemen, your best respects and attention, please, for Mr. James Warwick of Messrs. Richard Warwick and Sons, Brewers of Newark-upon-Trent—and our guests of honor."

To much cheering and stamping of feet, three figures approached the platform. One was of medium height but of a width and girth greater than anything that Herbert had ever seen before. Behind him came a pale, gaunt giant. Following the incongruous pair came a dapper little man whom Herbert judged to be approaching forty and, on the evidence of his nut-brown complexion, a countryman. He wore a brown bowler hat. The fat man spoke. "We are here to make a presentation..."

The landlord staggered onto the stage carrying a table on which two silver goblets were already standing. The audience drew in its breath in gratifying unison.

"... to the two greatest batsmen in all England." The fat man ignored the murmurs of confirmation and continued. "In particular we celebrate the third-wicket record in East Melbourne, Australia, last winter for the Nonsmokers against the Smokers—even though, as a brewer, I think they were on the wrong side."

Mr. Warwick paused for laughter, which did not materialize, and Patrick turned to Herbert. "If you really mean that you have to be home by eleven, we have to go here and now."

"Who are they? Who are they?"

"Nobody. Just cricketeers. If you don't come now, you're going to spoil everything. Y'll never get out again. Besides, I've something to tell you when we get back to Cavendish Street."

Herbert was so intrigued that for a moment he forgot his feelings of disappointment—disappointment that he would not see more of the two obviously famous figures but, most of all, disappointment that, because the evening was a guilty secret, he would not be able to tell John Gunn of all that had happened to him.

Herbert changed back into his Sunday suit in Robert Martin's studio while Patrick drank a bottle of stout.

"I do believe they thought that I was teetotal as well. I've never had a night in a pub with so few drinks."

"It would do you a power of good."

"Don't deny me the one little pleasure I have. Anyway, I need a bit of Dutch courage before I tell you what you must be told."

The revelation was interrupted by Robert Martin, who came into the kitchen while Herbert was still struggling with his back stud. He was reading aloud from a dog-eared book. "The geometer bending down with the brass dividers is almost certainly Euclid." He gripped Herbert by the elbow. "You see. The man in the corner of my Raphael has a pair of compasses. Euclid again. Euclid proves it."

Herbert was still not convinced of the painting's authenticity. He took advantage of Augusta's arrival to make his exit. "I'd better be on my way."

"Uncle's got something to tell you first. It's about Christmas and the Master Bakers."

"What about Christmas?"

The Master Bakers were to be Herbert's passport to permanent musical respectability, the magic words which he intoned whenever his father questioned the sort of audiences in front of which he performed.

"I wish I knew. I wish I knew myself," said Patrick.

It was obvious, even to Herbert, that Patrick was lying. Augusta lost patience.

"There's no need to keep it secret. Just tell him."

"It's not certain that I'm going yet. You said I couldn't go."

"You're talking nonsense, Uncle Pat, and you know it. Nobody said you couldn't come. I only said that you should pay your own fare."

"You know I can't pay my fare. You might as well come straight out with it and say that you don't want me in Dublin."

"All I said was that making all this money, more than a pound a week, you ought to be able to pay something toward it."

"More than a pound a week! You told me it was no more than ten bob." Herbert, outraged, was trying to work out how much he should have been paid if the total weekly income was his five shillings and Patrick's pound.

"I don't get a pound a week, nothing like it. That's why I can't pay my fare to Dublin."

"For heaven's sake, Uncle! You know perfectly well that somebody will buy you a ticket. Tell Herbert what's happening. He needs to know. He has to tell Mr. Gunn. He can't let the Bakers down at the last minute."

"I suppose *I* can. I suppose *my* reputation for reliability doesn't matter."

"You don't have a reputation for anything except singing and drinking, and you don't lodge with Mr. Gunn."

"You've got a cruel tongue, Gussie—a cruel tongue and a hard heart."

Augusta, convinced that her uncle would not put Herbert out of his misery, decided to perform the coupe de grâce herself.

"We're going to Dublin in December. Our other sister, Kathleen, is taking her final vows and we're all going to—"

Patrick Martin was not satisfied that his niece's explanation did justice to the drama of the occasion. "She'll be wed to the Holy Mother Church. Ring on her finger and promises to love, honor and obey—"

Augusta completed the story. "It's the great moment of her life. So we're all off to Dublin. That's the excuse, anyway."

"Do we have to miss the Bakers?"

"We might." Patrick could not bring himself to confirm the disastrous news. "We might just—"

"We *will*," interrupted Augusta. "We definitely *will*. The vows are on the same day."

Patrick Martin turned to his brother, who was sitting at the kitchen table, oblivious of the turmoil with which he was surrounded as he read and reread the commentary on Raphael's *School of Athens* that he had read a thousand times before.

"I swear your daughter *enjoys* giving bad news. She delights in it."

Robert had followed none of the conversation. "Which daughter?"

"I meant Gussie. But it's the same with Clare. Hard as nails, Clare. Don't know where either of them gets it from. Not our side of the family. We're all soft as butter, thank God."

Suddenly a terrible thought entered Herbert's head. "Is Clare going to Dublin?"

"Of course," answered Augusta dismissively. "It was her idea. She wouldn't miss it for a hundred pounds. She ought to become a sister herself."

"She'll pay my fare." Patrick Martin smiled for the first time that evening. "She'd never become a nun," he added maliciously. "Loves the world too much to renounce its wickedness. The World, the Flesh, the Devil."

He repeated the names of the three Great Temptations as if they had some relevance to what he was saying.

"Don't you be so sure," said the father of the possible novice. "She talked about it all the time when she was a little girl."

"It's not worth talking about now."

Augusta was anxious to go to bed. She edged Herbert toward the door. "All we know for certain is that she's going to be in Dublin for Christmas."

"Not coming home at all?" Herbert heard himself ask the question as if his voice belonged to someone else.

"Not until Whitsun," Augusta told him.

As he walked home the air seemed particularly cold for September.

It was Herbert's habit to engulf John Gunn in a daily avalanche of autobiographical trivia. No piece of badly tempered metal was delivered to Hudson and Ross without its tensile strength being analyzed in Huntingdon Street. And every new oratorio which was introduced into the repertoire of the Albert Hall Choral Society was examined, not in terms of its musical potential but in the light of the ease or difficulty with which one baritone member of the chorus was able to master its intricate score. Only on the subject of Clare Martin did Herbert observe the rule of rectitude which, in his boyhood, Jack Foster had urged upon both Hattersley boys. "The more it hurt, the more you keep it to yourself." Joseph had applied Jack's rule to all of his life. Herbert could manage to live by the precept only in relation to the pain that Clare Martin caused him. And even then, his silence on the subject was based more on a proud reluctance to admit he was rejected than on any general theory about reticence and discretion. On every other aspect of his life, he needed to obtain John Gunn's advice, support and approval. The necessity to remain silent about his evening at the Black Boy was so painful that it could barely be borne. He needed John to rejoice with him at the rapture with which his performance had been received, and he needed John's sympathy and support to help in the formidable task of recovering from the terrible discovery that Clare would not be in Nottingham at Christmas.

As he trudged back to Huntingdon Street it was the desire to burst through the door and describe the applause that had greeted his second encore which was most difficult to suppress. A life kept secret from friends is not a life at all, for it does not exist in the world of common memory and comfortable conversation. When, on the day after the performance at the Black Boy, he discovered the identity of the two guests whom Patrick Martin had dismissed as "nobody important," he found the idea of keeping silent about his privileged encounter absolutely intolerable. He had shaken hands with William Gunn and Arthur Shrewsbury—the two greatest batsmen in English cricket. It was impossible for him not to boast about it to John Gunn.

He kept the story to himself for almost two days—filling the small intervals between thinking about Clare's betrayal with plans about how he could brag about the meeting without confessing to the circumstances in which it had taken place. His eventual scheme seemed plausible, at least to him. He would say Gunn and Shrewsbury had been fêted at Hudson and Ross and presented with canteens of cutlery to mark their epic innings in Australia. As soon as he got home he launched into the story.

"William Gunn had a handshake like a five-pound vise. M'knuckles ached for an hour. But Arthur Shrewsbury was a funny little chap. Not a bit like an athlete. Never took his bowler hat off from start to finish."

Long passages of invented conversation were spilled out over John Gunn before the attempt was made to pretend that it had all happened in a cutlery and surgical-instrument factory. He was about to launch into the lie when he felt a restraining hand on his arm.

"I don't know what to do about you. I thought I knew this morning. This morning I was going to write to your father. But now, now that you're making a clean breast of it, I'm not sure."

The description of the Hudson and Ross workmen applauding in the factory yard faded in Herbert's mind.

"You deceived me. There's no doubt about that. But I hate treating you like a baby. If I hadn't promised your father in a moment of weakness, I wouldn't have dreamed of acting like a policeman to a man your age. The daft thing is, you needn't have done it." John Gunn tried hard not to smile. "Changing clothes at the Martins and then changing back again after the concert! I doubt if your father would have minded. He would have thought a presentation to Mr. Gunn and Mr. Shrewsbury very respectable."

"So you won't tell him?"

"I ought to tell him about the deceit."

"But you won't?"

"Not this time, because I'm soft. But I'm not so soft that I won't tell him if it happens again. Don't rely on that."

"How did you know?"

"I read about it in yesterday's paper."

The *Nottingham Daily Express* was folded back to the Local Events page, and a circle had been drawn in ink around one particular item. Herbert was anxious to read his first mention in print. But he had to wait to hear a little homily.

"Lies are wrong, Herbert, wrong in themselves. But what's more, you've got to be clever to get away with them. It's easier to be honest and open, easier as well as right. You're not clever enough to be a rogue. If you ever fall for real temptation you'll be ruined. You're not the sort of man who gets away with things. You're the sort that gets caught."

After a moment's suitable silence to allow the moral to sink in, John handed Herbert the paper. It described the occasion in minute detail and, after reporting verbatim the speeches of both the host and his guests of honor, it listed the artistes who had "contributed to a splendid evening." Amongst them were "Professor Patrick Martin L.C.M. on the pianoforte, assisted by a young Sheffield baritone."

CHAPTER EIGHTEEN

TWO MEDALS

V ery much to his own surprise, Herbert survived until the following spring. He survived the breakup of his musical partnership with Patrick Martin, his father's visits to Nottingham to supervise the development of the new business, Christmas at home in Sheffield without Joseph and the last tedious weeks of his apprenticeship. He even survived the anguish of separation from Clare. As autumn turned to winter and winter gave way to spring the pain of her absence changed from the continual gnawing ache of desolation into the occasional agony of imagined rejection. By the time Christmas was past he was struck by the pangs of unrequited love only when something happened to remind him that his heart was broken. Then—when her name was mentioned or he read a particularly sentimental line from the libretto of an operetta or musical comedy—emotion built on emotion and he wallowed in romantic grief. But he did not remain desolate for long. He was helped out of each trauma by his age, his temperament and John Gunn.

Herbert's musical career foundered in October, wrecked by his fear of performing in public houses, and the discovery that Patrick Martin had cheated him out of five pounds, seven shillings and sixpence. At first, Herbert believed that Augusta had been wrong to accuse her uncle of earning more than a pound a week. But gradually suspicion began to build up in his usually wholly unsuspicious mind. Patrick blamed it on Augusta.

"She's poisoned your mind against me with her tittle-tattle. Has she been telling you things behind m'back?"

"She told me nothing. I want you to tell me and to show me. I want to see the money handed over and I want to split it fifty-fifty."

The senior partner prevaricated for weeks. Then, one Friday evening, at the end of a performance given to employees of the Nottingham Omnibus Company, all doubt was removed. Patrick had disappeared—an increasingly frequent feature of his evening's performance. The organizer, anxious to walk home a young lady from the accounts office, refused to wait for his return and thrust four half-crowns and a sixpence into Herbert's hand. When Patrick returned—still buttoning his fly—he was greeted with the innocent message that the hour's work had yielded more than either of them could have expected. Patrick might have bluffed it through by inviting Herbert to join him in a celebration of the unexpected half-guinea. But, fuddled with drink and fearful that he had been found out, he blustered, "After all I have done for you . . . I earn every penny we get. Without me . . ."

Things were then said which no two human beings should say to each other—things which, having been said, made a continuing relationship impossible. "Thief" and "liar" were among Herbert's milder descriptions of his erstwhile partner, and neither description wounded Patrick as much as the allegation that whatever little talent he had ever possessed had been destroyed by age and alcohol.

"Without me you wouldn't get any bookings at all. Nottingham's full of old drunks who play the piano for half-pints. Why should they pay you good money?"

"Come, come, gentlemen," said the master of ceremonies. "We don't want a scene."

"We've got a scene," said an unrepentant Herbert.

Patrick cared for nothing except his musical reputation. "We've got a scene, because he thinks he can sing. I taught him everything. Everything I learned at the Dublin Conservatoire. Without me he'll never sing in public again."

"If you go on like this, neither of you will ever sing in public again."

Suddenly aware of the spectacle they were creating, Herbert turned on his heel and strode silently away. That young man, thought the master of ceremonies, possesses an instinct for dignity. Patrick Martin enjoyed no such blessing. As the pianist slunk out of the room he aimed a great hay-making blow in what he thought was the general direction of his erstwhile partner's disappearing figure. It missed by several feet. Herbert, halfway out of the door, knew that he should not look back. But the temptation was irresistible. Behind him, on the floor, lay Patrick Martin, his smoking jacket over his head and his trousers split open along the seam of their threadbare seat. Herbert had only one wish—never to see or hear of Patrick Martin again.

In November the contract for the premises in Alfreton Road was signed, and for weeks the new owner fumed and fretted about the cost of the work that was needed to convert the first floor into a cutlers' workshop.

"I told you, Mr. Hattersley." Jack Foster decided that it was better to be abused for impertinence than blamed for the cost of reinforcing the floor and cutting the hole in the wall through which the grind-stones were to be lifted in.

"You told me that t'steam engines couldn't be geared down, and you were wrong. What you didn't tell me was that you'd employed embezzlers as builders."

"I never employed t'builders. You found them."

At such moments Frederick always found solace either in an-nouncing that he would walk over to Hudson's "to see how our Herbert's getting on" or in examining the shop window. The great pane of glass was to him a constant consolation. For it was decorated with a curve of enamel letters which proclaimed the owner's name and occupation: "Frederick Hattersley and Sons, Cutlers." It was the additional information, spelt out in a straight line that stretched across the arc's diameter, which gave him particular pleasure. It read "of Sheffield." Origins were very important to Frederick Hattersley.

Christmas proved more congenial than Herbert had thought pos-sible. Mary and her husband came to dinner, bringing the new baby whom they had prudently christened Frederika. Martha brought a new young man who—being pious, respectful and rich—was natu-rally much more acceptable to Frederick as a would-be son-in-law than her previous beau, whose only qualifications were kindness and affection. Aunt Winifred's decision to spend the festive season in genuinely festive company removed one source of potential friction.

There was one maudlin moment when Frederick Hattersley, hav-ing allowed each guest a single glass of sweet sherry, proposed the toast of "Absent Friends." Mary sniffed and Martha snuffled. But the mother of the absent friend whom Frederick had in mind cut short the dolorous episode by bustling into the kitchen in the pretense that the maid, who was anxious to be off to Christmas celebrations of her own, could not be trusted to lift the plum pudding out of the steamer. Emily muttered as the kitchen door banged shut behind her, "Who'd have credited it? Not even at Christmas. Not a word."

Frederick, who took life literally, imagined that she was complaining about the maid. "I've told you before, if she's impertinent, sack her. Dumb insolence is just as bad. We pay her enough. There's plenty more looking for jobs. You should be sitting there and being served, not working in your own kitchen."

Herbert found some comfort in the discovery that nothing had changed at Asline Road. The last four months of indentured apprenticeship, with the routine barely changed from the previous year, had been almost unendurable. Rightly convinced that he had learned all that Hudson and Ross could teach him, he had suggested that he should start early on journeymen's work for apprentice's wages. Young Mr. Hudson was not the man to abandon the conventions which had dominated the seventy years of his working life. So Herbert, although near perfect, continued to practice. Test pieces were reproduced over and over again right until the last day.

The despair created by each vicissitude was terrible but brief, and it was always followed by the surprising discovery that life would go on despite the moment of boredom or disappointment. But he learned nothing from experience. Every new disappointment convinced Herbert that he would never smile again. So the return to optimism and happiness always came as a surprise—even though it was the predictable result of a pathological inability to remain miserable for very long. John's reaction to the moments of anguish was just as misguided and equally egocentric. He thought that only he could revive his lodger's flagging spirits. So, insisting that he had no wish to be a snob, he explained why Herbert should rejoice that the smoking concerts were over.

"It's not the sort of thing you really should be doing, public houses or anywhere else. You are, after all, going to be the owner of your own company one day."

Herbert smiled as the thought of his own future status temporarily obliterated the memory of his lost singing career. John Gunn's capacity for encouraging happiness was almost as great as Herbert's inability to remain miserable.

"In a month or two you'll have finished with Hudson and Ross. And then you'll be your own man, working for journeyman's wages in Alfreton Road."

The thought of an increased income and greater freedom changed the smile to a broad grin.

Clare was rarely mentioned at Huntingdon Street. Herbert recalled his passion increasingly infrequently, and when it did come to mind the thought of it embarrassed him. John Gunn, being a romantic, occasionally wondered if, after two brief meetings, something that might be properly described as love had been born. But he always dismissed the notion as absurd. Herbert was not quite twenty-one and as foolishly susceptible as most young men of his age. John was anxious that Herbert should not be hurt—and was determined not to rejoice at anything which caused him pain. So he tried not to take comfort from the obvious truth that the disastrous union would always be prevented by Clare's own thoughts on the subject—if she even thought about it at all. John's attempts to keep his mind off the subject altogether were helped by Herbert's estrangement from Patrick Martin. For months the family's name was never mentioned in Huntingdon Street.

Herbert had refused the offer of a party to celebrate the end of his apprenticeship. Every suggestion—from supper for parents to buffet for friends—had been rejected. On his first day at the Alfreton Road shop, Jack Foster predicted how his father would react, and sure enough, the anticipated letter arrived. The envelope was marked "Private and Confidential" in the carefully formed script which Herbert instantly recognized.

"I can tell you what it says before you open it."

Herbert grinned. "Go on then, tell me."

"Bet me a bob I can't guess and I'll give it to you, word for word as near as damn it is to swearing."

"No bet."

If Herbert had taken the bet, he would have lost. For the letter was exactly what Jack expected it to be, a combination of magisterial reproof and agonized rebuke.

For my own part, I do not mind the slight. It was on your mother's behalf that I felt hurt and angry. I assume that you have not been unwell or in some way incapacitated for the last three weeks. Otherwise John Gunn would surely have written to tell us. Gentlemen have a duty to respect ladies' feelings. Hurting your mother was unforgivable. Please accept my congratulations on completing your apprenticeship.

Inevitably, Herbert reported the letter—and its contents—to John Gunn and, almost as inevitably, was surprised by John's reaction.

"I hope you've written. You shouldn't have needed telling."

"Come on, John, I'm a man now. Twenty-one."

"Then behave like a man and act responsibly."

Herbert blushed like a little boy. "I have written."

"Have you posted it?"

Assuming the silence to be an admission of guilt, John made what he hoped was a helpful suggestion. "Add a note on the back of the envelope inviting your mother over to Nottingham when next your father comes to the shop. She'd like to see where you lodge. Invite her here for tea."

Encouraged by the belief that his invitation would be declined, Herbert agreed. To his surprise, his mother accepted. To his astonishment, she announced that, since his father would not be in Nottingham for more than a month, she proposed to make the journey without him on the following Saturday. To his horror, she added that, as she could not travel alone, Aunt Winifred would accompany her.

"But I'm playing cricket on Saturday."

Inspired by his meeting with William Gunn and Arthur Shrewsbury, Herbert had become a dashing, though generally unsuccessful, batsman in the second eleven of the Arnold Cricket Club. It marked a renewed interest in healthy exercise which John Gunn was anxious to encourage.

"Invite them. I'll join you. If it's a nice day, we'll take a picnic."

John was thinking of the varieties of bread which he could bring home for Mrs. Watkins to convert into sandwiches. It would be an opportunity for retaliation. Bakers have their pride and he had spent months listening to stories which were designed to demonstrate the moral superiority of men who bend and shape hot metal.

Herbert agreed with reluctance, and his forebodings were more than confirmed when, on the village green in Gotham, he was clean bowled before he had scored. To add to his shame, his mother comforted him with the news that he looked particularly handsome in his cream shirt and flannels. Aunt Winifred rhapsodized about the perfect English summer day, and John told, in excruciating detail, the fable of the Gotham fools who, seeing the moon reflected in the lake, attempted to catch it in a net. He also talked about the bread and cakes. Winifred was affecting interest in the mass production of bridge rolls when John began to fear that he was making himself ridiculous.

"You will have noticed, Mrs. Spooner, that I am an enthusiast for my trade."

"I notice and I applaud. I admire enthusiasm."

"Even in bakers?"

"Even in bakers."

Winifred blushed, fearing that she had endorsed the disparaging implication of John Gunn's question. The baker reacted with the disarming frankness that elderly ladies in his congregation found simultaneously disturbing and attractive.

"No need to be embarrassed, Mrs. Spooner. Bakers are intrinsically ridiculous." Winifred did not have time to argue before John warmed to his subject. "Life is particularly hard for bakers who are local preachers. A Sunday never passes without somebody telling me not to live by bread alone or asking me if I have cast anything upon the waters recently."

"Or"—Winifred joined enthusiastically in the game—"if you give your customers stones when they ask . . ."

"Exactly." John was vindicated. "The Bible's full of bread and the Methodist Church is full of people who know the Bible from start to finish."

"And make feeble jokes."

Winifred feared that she again sounded rude, rather than sympathetic as she had intended. She decided to prove that she was not above another bread quotation. "Neither did we eat any man's bread for nought, but wrought with labor and travail night and day."

John Gunn prided himself on his knowledge of both Testaments. "That's not from the Bible."

"It's painted on a picture, a picture by Ford Madox Brown."

"I'm afraid that I know nothing about painting."

Winifred's enthusiasm for exaggeration had not faded with the years. "Ford Madox Brown is perhaps the greatest painter since Raphael."

Herbert laughed, a deep spontaneous guffaw. And Winifred, who began to fear that the laughter was directed toward her, turned on him out of self-protection.

"I take it that you've become an art critic since you left Sheffield?"

John Gunn was an instinctive peacemaker. "He meant no offense, Mrs. Spooner. It's sort of a family joke. We know, or used to know, a man who thought he owned a Raphael."

"Perhaps it is a Raphael."

"He bought it in France for a franc."

To John Gunn there was nothing more to be said on the subject. Herbert had an even more convincing argument with which to demonstrate that the Raphael was a fake.

"You know the man, Auntie. At least, you know his brother. Do you remember Patrick Martin?"

"The music teacher? The Irishman your father thought was a Fenianist?"

Herbert seized the opportunity to blacken the hated name. "Yes, that Irishman, liar, drunk, swindler and probable Fenianist."

"And his brother's got a Raphael."

Had anyone but Emily made the comment, it would have been regarded as ironic.

Winifred was not in the mood to allow the authenticity to be questioned. "I must see it."

Herbert was unusually stern. "We never see them now."

Winifred was not to be denied. "But they do still live in Nottingham, don't they? Emily and I would love to see it. Can you arrange it for us, Mr. Gunn? If Herbert won't, will *you* ask them?"

The inclusion of Emily in the request was intended to spread the blame and make the request irresistible.

"Of course I can, Mrs. Spooner, if that's what you really want. When?"

Emily, incriminated, decided to become party to the conspiracy to make Herbert wish that he were dead. "My husband's coming to the shop, two weeks on Monday. I didn't know that when we arranged to come today. I'm glad I didn't or we might not have come. Thank you very much, Mr. Gunn. Thank you for a most enjoyable picnic. It will be lovely to come again."

Winifred had, as usual, got her way. "A fortnight on Monday then if that's what suits Emily. Is that all right with you, Mr. Gunn?"

"Of course," said John, astounded that his well-known fund of human charity was enough to prevent him from telling the extraordinary Mrs. Winifred Spooner that a fortnight on Monday was not all right at all.

Frederick Hattersley arrived at Alfreton Road shortly after eight o'clock, determined to show the shop to Emily and Winifred before they set out on their voyage of artistic discovery. He noticed, much to his satisfaction, that the steam engine was already throbbing with the steady beat which signified that the fire under its boiler had been lit a good hour before. The inscription on the window glowed white and gold in the morning sunlight, and behind the gratifying words, brass and mahogany .gleamed out of the shadowy showroom. A heavy counter ran across the width of the shop, and behind it, on the far wall, were glass-fronted cupboards displaying examples of the finest cutlery to be made anywhere in the world. At one time Frederick had thought of exhibiting the maker's name and mark above each sample, with Joseph Rodgers's famous Maltese cross in the place of honor next to his own name. But he decided not to share the glory even with the King of Knifemakers and Knifemaker to Kings. So the only name on view was Hattersley. In front of the counter stood four cabinets—made in the same mahogany and brass as the other fittings. They would soon be filled with surgical instruments, made by his own son. Jack had suggested that until Herbert had worked his way through the full range of scissors, clamps, forceps and bone shears, samples could be bought from Hudson and Ross or, better still, from W. and H. Hutchinson of Matilda Street, Sheffield. But Frederick had dismissed the notion. Instruments, in which the shop was to specialize, would be made by Hattersleys and sold by Hattersleys.

The brass and mahogany fittings gave him particular pleasure. Jack had said that they made the whole establishment look like a cross between a saloon bar and a mortuary, but he did not understand their particular significance. He thought they were there just to signify quality—heavy, expensive, tailor-made and durable. In fact, they were a symbol of Frederick Hattersley's progress. Over twenty years earlier, he had seen cabinets almost identical to those which would soon hold the medical instruments, in Thomas Spooner's study. Then they had contained fossils which Spooner had believed were the evidence of evolution. There and then, Frederick had decided that one day he would possess such pieces of furniture and put them to some use which was worthy of their splendor. He stared at them through the window with almost parental pride, until, at twenty minutes past eight, the proper object of that emotion appeared behind the counter, ducked through the door which connected the two halves of the shop and, without realizing what awaited him, opened the door for business.

The greetings between father and son were brief.

"God Almighty!"

"That's a fine way to begin the day. You'll be good enough not to blaspheme in my presence, whatever you do with your friends." Remembering that his wife and her sister stood behind him, Frederick Hattersley added an afterthought. "Show a little respect for the ladies."

It was not only his son's language of which Frederick disapproved. Herbert was dressed in what he regarded as the height of summer fashion and his father recognized as the depth of decadence. His suit was made of oatmeal-colored tweed, the single-breasted jacket cut high at the front and decorated with cuffs and an edging of white brocade. Beneath the jacket, the waistcoat was double-breasted, cut square across the trouser top and made in a material which, while of a different texture, was of almost identical color. The shirt collar was so stiff and so high that Herbert's chin was held permanently in the air above a white cravat, which was kept in place with a tiepin that (though it had cost only sixpence) looked remarkably like a pearl. The whole ensemble had been bought with the smoking concert earnings. Frederick Hattersley rightly suspected that, somewhere at the back of the shop, there was a straw boater with a colored silk band.

"Is this what you wear for work? Is this what you put on to forge scissors?"

"I'm not forging scissors today, worse luck. I'm taking Mam and Aunt Winifred to see this Raphael."

Raphael was no more than an archangel to Frederick. "I thought they were going to see a painting. Any road, I thought Mr. Gunn was going with them."

"He was, but he's busy."

"And you're not, I suppose."

"Jack said you'd expect me to go."

"So I do." Frederick had again forgotten the ladies standing behind him.

"That's why I put m'best suit on."

"I think you look very nice, Herbert."

It was the first time that his mother had spoken. She stepped forward and kissed him.

It took Frederick half an hour to inspect the showroom and to describe the quality of the fittings to Emily and Winifred. Herbert assumed that the workshop visitation would take place after he had left for Huntingdon Street, but his father insisted that they climb the stairs together. With the ladies in the showroom drinking tea out of Jack Foster's mustache cup and Herbert's Jubilee mug, the two men surveyed the single grinder's hull and bench at which the instruments were to be forged.

"Just like the old days." Frederick had accepted mass production but had never pretended to like it. The sight of the sort of bench on which he had learned his trade warmed and softened his heart. "Where's old Jack? I've a little ceremony to perform but I don't want to start without old Jack."

"He's not been too good for the last week. His breath's very short. Takes a bit to get him going in the morning."

"Can't be helped."

Herbert, who had hoped that Jack's absence would result in the abandonment of all the feared formalities, noticed with profound regret that his father had assumed the pose which he always struck in preparation for the expression of solemn or profound opinions. He put his hand into his jacket pocket and took out a pocket watch. It was new, but it was a near replica of the heirloom that he had given to Joseph.

"We . . . your mother, that is . . . would have liked to have given it to you on the day. Your mother was very hurt."

Herbert hung his head. His father pressed the watch into his hand and then extracted from his trouser pocket a chamois-leather bag. It contained seven sovereigns—one for each year of his apprenticeship. Herbert mumbled his gratitude.

"And this."

Frederick felt in his left-hand waistcoat pocket and extracted a coin. It was big—bigger than a florin—and made from copper like a penny piece. It was, Herbert decided, low-grade metal—a lower grade than the alloy used in coins of the realm, for it seemed that the image on its face was almost worn away. It was the figure of a woman, but it was not Britannia. She stood erect, holding scales in one hand and a branch of some sort in the other. Engraved around her were

243

the words "Sheffield Penny Token." Herbert took the coin and examined it more closely. On the back, a house, with identical windows in a row from end to end, was surrounded by letters so worn that Herbert could barely read them, though the date—1813—was clearly visible. He held the coin between finger and thumb, rotating it so as to catch the light in the hope of making out what it said. He was playing for time while he decided what to say by way of a reply.

"Thanks. Thanks for the watch and the money. Thanks very much . . . for this."

His father took the coin out of his hand. "It says 'Overseers of the Poor.' It's a Poor Law token, outdoor relief from the workhouse. You could only spend it on bread and potatoes. Couldn't buy beer with those."

"Where did you get it?"

"I found it in the bottom of y'granddad's toolbox after he died. He couldn't have known it was there, or he'd have spent it, somehow."

Herbert was still not sure how to react.

"I wanted you to have something of his. And I wanted you to remember. You're two generations away from the workhouse. Make sure this family's not back there in another two."

While Herbert was drawing breath in preparation for saying thanks again, his father pointed to the stairs.

"Get along with you. Your mother and aunt are waiting. I'll keep an eye on things till Jack gets here—if he's good enough to come today. And I'll thank you to be back here by ten o'clock, wearing proper clothes."

The Martins' house was almost exactly as Herbert had expected it to be. Patrick showed no sign of malice or remorse, but greeted his ex-pupil and late partner as if no disobliging word had ever passed between them. Robert unveiled his picture with due ceremony and Emily Hattersley adjudged it to be very nice. Winifred told Mr. Martin that she knew exactly why it might be thought a Raphael, but, when he asked her what she meant, offered no convincing explanation. Augusta tutted, shook her head and handed out tea and buttered barm-cake. After several periods of bewildered silence she made a suggestion. "Why don't you consider it, Mrs. Spooner, and discuss it with other experts, and then write to my father with your opinion?"

"A gem," said Winifred under her breath. "She's a gem, this one."

Herbert, pensively examining his Poor Law penny, was thinking of Clare, and longing to get back to his cutler's bench, when Augusta disturbed his reverie. Having solved Winifred Spooner's immediate problem, she turned her attention to the task of diverting the young man's attention from what she feared were sad thoughts of her sister.

"What's that, a medal?" Herbert handed it over without comment. Augusta inspected it, first with bogus pleasure and then with genuine interest. "We've got a medal made out of the same stuff."

She reached up onto the studio mantelshelf and lifted down a pewter mug. From inside it she drew out a magnificent bronze medallion, almost twice as big as Herbert's token, and made of metal so hard that the embossed portrait, which stood out from its face, was as clear and sharp as on the day when it had been cast. Herbert turned the medal over and read the message on its back. "Crystal Palace, Handel Festival, June 1857."

"Look." Augusta took the medal out of his hand and showed him the name engraved on its rim: "W. G. Martin, Performer."

She rubbed it against the bib of her apron to remove the remnants of brass polish that clung to the letters. "That was my granddad. He was a singer like you. He was a baritone too. They sang *Acis and Galatea*. My dad says it's our most precious possession—after the Raphael, of course. It proves what a singer Granddad was. Where did your medal come from?"

"It belonged to my granddad."

Herbert was only half listening.

"You see," said Augusta, smiling. "We've got more in common than you think."

CHAPTER NINETEEN

LOVED HER NOT LESS

John Gunn—ever concerned for the welfare of his friend and lodger—looked forward to Whitsuntide with profound apprehension. He was sure that Herbert still harbored unreasonable hopes of gaining Clare Martin's affection. And he feared that foolishness and frustration would drive the young man into a declaration of devotion which would be painfully, though understandably, rebuffed. His anxiety was not justified. He had forgotten how easily young hearts are mended, as well as broken. So although he expected a Sunday of catastrophe and a Monday of despair, Whitsuntide was no more than a weekend of continual anticlimax.

Clare Martin arrived in Nottingham on Sunday morning and, having pronounced herself indisposed, retired at once to bed. On Monday morning, she rose early, wore her mysterious black lace mantilla to six o'clock mass and was back in her room before the rest of the family was awake.

Herbert had spent several days working out a strategy which would both ensure a meeting and maintain the dignity appropriate to his mustache and carefully cut hair. It involved a Sunday afternoon walk down Cavendish Street, and the affectation of the airs suitable to a young man doing no more than taking a stroll. The rain, which swept across Nottingham from early in the morning, made the pretense difficult to sustain. Nevertheless, he set out exactly as planned and sauntered, nonchalant though soaking wet, toward the Martins' front door. Augusta would, he knew, leave home at about three o'clock for Toll House Hill and the Convent of Mercy, where she played the piano for the Sunday school. He was equally certain that when she saw him, there would be an immediate invitation to step inside. As he laid his plans Herbert visualized her bustling him up the steps and insisting that she could make him a cup of tea and still be at the convent in time to play the first hymn. He felt no resentment at the thought of the way in which she would take command of the occasion. Indeed, he positively looked forward to seeing her plump figure emerge from the front door. To his distress, when—after he had walked up and down the road twice—the door opened, the figure which appeared on the top step was not Augusta but her uncle, Patrick.

As he laid his careful plan, Herbert had realized that a meeting with his erstwhile patron and partner would probably be unavoidable. But his experience on the day when the Raphael was on view had convinced him that as long as it took place in the company of the other Martins, Patrick's inept attempts at apology or recrimination would be at least inhibited. And he felt sure that if the old trouper did explode into either anger or remorse, Augusta would (as always) say or do something that restored the climate of mindless congeniality in which Herbert thrived. The idea of facing Patrick Martin in single combat so terrified him that, for a moment, his instinct was to turn and run. But during the seconds of indecision, he was recognized— recognized and greeted like a prodigal son who, having returned, turned grief into instant joy.

"Bertie, Bertie, Bertie!" Nobody had ever called Herbert that before. "M'dear boy. Right glad I am to see you."

Before Herbert had opened his mouth, he was inside the front door, and Patrick's brown bowler hat was back on the antlers that hung in the hall and acted as a hat stand.

"Gussie! Gussie!" Patrick was in the mood for affectionate diminutives. "Look who's come to see us."

"I doubt that it's us he's come to see." Augusta hurried out of the kitchen, wiping her wet hands on the skirts of her apron.

They passed into the studio, where Robert Martin was examining his picture through a magnifying glass. Too preoccupied to be either sensitive or discreet, he did not think to dissemble about the real reasons for Herbert's visit.

"She's not well. She's been in bed all day."

Herbert blushed and stared at his feet. Patrick Martin screwed up his purple face into a hideously coy smile and Augusta went into a complicated mime. Pointing upstairs, she rubbed her stomach, to suggest cramps, and turned up her nose to imply that the real illness was a bad attack of superiority. Patrick offered Herbert a glass of Irish whiskey. Augusta said that the tea was mashed. Robert proposed a detailed examination of the halo around the head of his Madonna. Herbert declined all offers. He was, he insisted, on his way to visit a friend who awaited his company with growing impatience. He bade a courteous, if stilted, farewell to each member of the family and walked briskly back down the garden path. As he made his way home he was surprised by how little disappointment he felt. In a way, he was relieved. He could barely remember what Clare looked like and he could not imagine what they would have said to each other had they met.

For the next year Herbert thought of Clare Martin only on the increasingly rare occasions when her name was mentioned. He was young and possessed a steady job, two fashionable suits and black hair that shone like polished ebony beneath its brilliantine. He played cricket with passion and football with skill, sang to anyone who could be persuaded to listen and flirted with girls from the local lace factories on every piece of open ground in Nottingham. He also walked home from chapel and choir practice with all the unattached and personable young ladies in the parish. But he preferred the company of the factory girls. With them there was fun of every sort and no nonsense about the hope of settling down one day in a nice little house in Lenton.

John Gunn discussed Herbert's evenings in the parks and recreation grounds as if they were spent in studying the flora rather than the fauna. But Jack Foster always began the working day with banter about the previous evening's amorous adventures. Herbert usually willingly joined in the fun and boasted about the affection in which he was held by the Valenciennes scallopers, drawers-back, seamers, dressers, frillers and ginnyers who paraded arm in arm in the haunts where he and his friends hunted. Jack thought the names of the trades at which they worked particularly amusing. He had been brought up in the world of foggers, buffers and hafters. Too often for Herbert's liking, the banter turned into serious conversation based on the belief that the girls from the lace factories were not the ideal companions for the future master of Frederick Hattersley and Sons. The bawdy jokes were used as introduction to the good advice which Jack Foster believed he had a duty to dispense.

"Out scalloping again last night?"

Herbert's grin encouraged Jack to go through the whole litany of well-worn jokes.

"Bit of drawing back, I shouldn't wonder."

"Aye, and ginnying."

Herbert entered into the spirit of the thing as he always did. Although Jack's tone always changed from humor to menace, Herbert was never prepared when the change came.

"Do you know how much scallopers make a week?"

Interested though Herbert was in factory girls, he was not familiar with the evidence about their wages which Lady Assistant Commissioner May E. Abraham was preparing for submission to the Royal Commission on the Labour and Employment of Women. He made no response.

"Twelve bob a week. Twelve bob a week for six days."

Herbert nodded absentmindedly, remembering little Ginny Hawksley, who had gone with him into the deserted bandstand without mentioning a word about her wages.

"And they're going to get less. They're all going to be turned out of the factories and made to work at home. Then they'll not make half as much. Gives you pause. Six days for six bob. Makes you think."

It did not make Herbert think at all. But, anxious to oblige, he halfheartedly signified interest in the conditions of the lace industry. The conversation was traveling by a tortuous route to the destination which Jack intended.

"It makes you think that it must be a rough sort of lass—a lass from a pretty poor sort of family—who's prepared to work that long for that money. Still, I suppose there's nowt wrong in you having your bit of fun as long as. . ."

At last Herbert's interest was aroused. "As long as what?"

"As long as one of 'em doesn't get her claws into you."

"Don't worry about that, old lad." Herbert tried to assume the air of a man of the world. "Safety in numbers. That's what we always say. Love 'em and leave 'em."

He was searching about for a third cliché with which to demonstrate his sophistication, when the point was pressed home.

"What happens if one of 'em gets in the family way?"

Herbert was scandalized. "You dirty old bugger! Nowt like that ever happens. Nowt at all. None of us does owt like that. Bit of a kiss and a cuddle, that's all. You've got a filthy bloody mind."

"Nobody caught me in bed with the barmaid from the Barracks Hotel."

Herbert was scandalized again. "You're the only one as ever mentions that. . . . Everybody else . . ."

"Nobody's forgot it. Not your mother or your father. Not your sisters. I'm the only one with the nous to worry about summat like it happening again, and the guts to talk to you about it. Your father puts his faith in God. I'd rather put mine in a word to the wise. You've got a good life ahead of you, as long as you do nowt daft."

"I'll be all right. That's what you used to tell me to say, isn't it?"

"I used to tell you to say you were all right when you were feeling bad. That's different. I'd rather you keep out of trouble than learn to grin and bear it. If one of them lasses is having your baby, I'd tell you to pretend you were glad. But making the best of a bad job's not the same as looking for trouble."

"I'll be all right, I tell you."

"I doubt it. Some has it in 'em to be all right and some not. With you I doubt it. I only hope you have the sense to ask for help when you need it."

"And who do you expect me to ask?"

"When I was in trouble, I went to your father."

"I'll not go to him."

"He helped me. He helped me all he could."

"Perhaps. But I'll not go to him. If I need it—and I won't—I'll go to John Gunn."

"From what I hear, Mr. Gunn has woman problems of his own."

Herbert mistook jealousy for malice. "I should never have told you. Get on with t'bloody work and stop clacking."

It was too late. The story had been told. Herbert regretted it. But he recognized that, reticence and discretion not numbering amongst his virtues, it was inevitable that the outcome of the morning spent inspecting the Raphael should have been reported to Jack, and that the drama which began that day should have been described in daily detail as it unfolded. The inspection had been an artistic disaster but a social triumph . Winifred had taken to Augusta as, in the past, she had taken to so many people whom she designated as being in special need of her care and protection. Miss Martin, she had decided, deserved something better than the domestic slavery which seemed to be her lot. So—no longer able either to decide her husband's destiny or to guide the fortunes of her two nephews—she took up a new protégée.

Each month, Winifred visited Nottingham and, having taken Augusta to lunch at the Midland Hotel, took her latest acquisition on a voyage of female discovery. Together they watched a matinée at the Theatre Royal (when the play was suitable), wandered through the arboretum (when the weather was fine) or, in the absence of any preferable alternative, discussed the books which they had read since their last meeting. The discussion of literature was not a great success, for Augusta could not keep up the pace which her mentor set, and Winifred veered wildly between irritation at being three chapters ahead and determination not to give away those parts of the plot which would be best revealed in the original words of Sir Walter Scott or William Makepeace Thackeray. To the astonishment of everyone who knew her, the independent-minded Augusta accepted the patronage and allowed herself to be patronized.

When the educational activity was over, Winifred always visited her nephew. It was, she believed, her duty to express his mother's hope that he was well, and to pass on what information about the family seemed necessary to Herbert's happiness. The news that her own mother-in-law had died at the age of ninety, leaving the entire Spooner fortune to a distant relative in Wales, was mentioned one evening in passing.

"You must be very hurt," said John Gunn.

"No," Winifred replied. "I wanted nothing to do with it or her."

It was exactly the answer which she had given to Frederick Hattersley when he advised that the will should be contested in court.

Herbert Hattersley hated his aunt's monthly visits to Huntingdon Street. Because of his need to be loved and his hope of being admired, he never considered the possibility of being out when she arrived. It was his duty to greet her with a kiss on the cheek and to remain drinking tea, eating Dundee cake and listening to conversation which bored him, until it was time to escort her to the station. Halfway through the evening Winifred always told him that a handsome young man should have something better to do with his time than dance attendance on an old woman. Herbert was invariably on the point of agreeing, when John answered that neither of them had anything to do which was more important than looking after their guest. When the time came for Winifred to leave, her nephew hustled her into her coat with a vigor which would have been more appropriate to the eviction of an unlawful tenant than to the departure of a favorite aunt.

The worst evenings were those on which Winifred arrived with Augusta. For then John would take the older woman to the railway station while Herbert walked the younger to the Derby Road tram stop. Herbert could not prevent the feeling of panic which engulfed him at the thought of being seen with so profoundly unfashionable a figure. But he knew that his terror was unworthy of the gentleman he hoped to be. So he struggled to remember that he had been seen with so many wasp-waisted daughters of shopkeepers that no one doubted the sort of conquests of which he was capable, and he performed his courteous duty with polite resignation.

There were other reasons why the prospect of walking Augusta to the tram stop unnerved him. In company she was jolly, reassuring and generous. When the two of them were alone she treated him like a joke, bombarding him with questions about his character and conduct which might have been either serious or satirical.

"You do smell nice," she said one evening. Herbert smirked with pride and pleasure. "Is it the brilliantine?"

Herbert confirmed that it was.

"M'dad mentioned it. He thought it was lovely. It reminded him of a girl he once knew in Lyons."

They walked on in silence, Herbert unsure if he had been flattered or insulted.

John Gunn, on the other hand, seemed positively to enjoy the women's company. Indeed, having observed the way in which preparations were made for their calls. Herbert began to suspect that the time which the ladies spent at Huntingdon Street was the highlight of his landlord's month. John spoke to them in a way which his loyal congregations would not have believed possible. There was one conversation which Herbert had regarded as dangerously gallant—at least by the standards of gallantry expected from a middle-aged Nonconformist baker. It included one passage of banter by which he was particularly perturbed. Foolishly, he had reported it to Jack Foster as an episode in the long saga.

"Tell me more," John had demanded, "about the picture with the quotation about bread painted on its frame. Is it yours?"

Winifred smiled condescendingly. "Alas, no. I could not afford it. Anyway, it would not be right to keep it in a private house. It needs to be admired."

"Has it told you so?"

Winifred chose to take the slight joke seriously. "Pictures don't have emotions, Mr. Gunn. They inspire them."

John was not crushed. "Not only paintings, Mrs. Spooner." Herbert stared at the lay preacher, unable quite to believe what he was hearing. "How do you know so much about paintings, Mrs. Spooner?"

"My husband, my late husband, taught me. I'd known about the Pre-Raphaelite Brotherhood for years. But he taught me what they really meant."

"Did you enjoy learning?"

"From him I did."

"And would you enjoy teaching someone who knows nothing but would dearly love to learn?"

Herbert gave thanks that, for once, Augusta was not there. All the way to the tram stop she would have mocked him about his earnest and eager landlord.

"If you were really interested you would have learned before."

"I never had hope of such a teacher before."

Listening to their conversation, Herbert was so unnerved that his knife rattled on his plate. If he spoke like that to a girl from one of the lace factories, she would dig him in the ribs and tell him not to be so silly. And were he to address one of his friends' sisters in that tone, they would have assumed that a proposal of marriage was soon to follow. As the chain of thought raced through his head he rashly decided that he must consult Jack Foster about how to protect John Gunn from his own foolishness.

"He's like a sixteen-year-old. All cow-eyed."

"I'm not surprised. She's a handsome figure of a woman, that aunt of yours. And he's been on his own for ten years or more."

"But he's too old for all that. He's more than forty and I reckon that she's older. He may not feel daft talking like that but I feel daft listening to him."

"Well, you shouldn't. Forty's young. Youngish, anyway. It's certainly young enough to lose your head over a woman. I've known it happen to men of seventy."

253

The discretion which comes with maturity having failed to prevent John Gunn from making himself look ridiculous, Herbert was easily convinced that the torpor which accompanies senility would not protect him from turning brief folly into lasting shame. The thought of so elderly a pair striking up a permanent relationship was so embarrassing that he was lost for words. Jack Foster struggled to find a way to console him.

"Maybe nowt will come of it. He took a long time to get over his wife by all accounts. Perhaps he's not over her yet. That's another thing that you'll learn. Sometimes feelings last—even when . . . even when she's gone."

Herbert was briefly reminded that his own heart was broken. "Are there people who never get over it, never get over a woman who they've lost?"

"There are. But usually they're more than twenty-one when the sad event occurs. I don't think it's likely to happen to you."

"Nobody was talking about me. I was asking about John."

Jack felt ashamed to have caused the lad such unnecessary anguish. He tried to make amends. "I reckon that your Mr. Gunn is the type that doesn't change. He won't want a new wife. Give him a couple of months and he'll make it clear that there's nothing doing. Mark my words, it will all be over by October."

Jack Foster's hopes for October were not realized. Indeed, it was during that month that Winifred invited John Gunn to visit Sheffield. The invitation depressed Herbert profoundly. Its acceptance turned depression into despair. It was clear that, in his relationship with Winifred Spooner, John Gunn no longer behaved rationally.

The Sheffield trip was ostensibly designed to further Augusta's education—a process which had, for several months, ranged widely over art, literature and science. Those subjects being exhausted, teacher and pupil moved on to political philosophy. Seminars on that topic, when conducted by Winifred Spooner, always turned into descriptions of the policies currently espoused by the Liberal Party. Augusta listened in silence.

Augusta Martin knew virtually nothing about politics. But the one issue about which she felt real passion was at the center of the Liberal program. Like Mr. Gladstone—whom she hated and feared as a wild, rather than grand, old man—she believed in Home Rule. For although a Conservative by instinct, she was Irish by upbringing, devoted to Ireland and all things Irish by a special passion which came from having made only a brief visit to that most distressful country. So, when Winifred suggested a visit to Sheffield during the annual meeting of the Liberal Assembly, she piously agreed in the hope of hearing something to the advantage of the Old Country. She also liked the idea of a day out of Nottingham.

Augusta's surprise at the discovery that John Gunn was to join them on the second day of the outing was too great to be disguised. "You'll tell me next that young Herbert is coming as well."

She was almost a year young Herbert's senior. The nickname illustrated the nature of the relationship rather than the difference in age.

"I asked him." Winifred put on her severe look. "But the silly boy refused. He wants to play football and flash his smile at the girls in Castle Boulevard. We spoilt him when he was a little boy because he used to flash that smile of his at us." The severe look disappeared with the memory. "He was born smiling, poor lad."

"Why poor lad?"

"Because he'll have to find out that life is a serious business, and it will come as a great shock to him when he can't smile his way out of all his trouble. However, he's not coming to Sheffield and that's that. He's got a new friend, didn't you know?"

Augusta could not disguise her nervousness. She asked the question far too quickly for Winifred to have any doubt about the nature of her anxiety. "What new friend? I've not heard."

"It's a man"—Winifred tried not to pause—"called Abraham Wilkinson. A real fast one. Goes to horse races and wears flashy clothes. Says he's related to the Morleys."

"How has Herbert come to meet a man like that?"

"He works for Morley's. Herbert sold him shears. Anyway, he's a bad influence. Herbert's daft enough to try to keep up with him. And from what I hear, this Mr. Wilkinson will encourage him."

Augusta rallied to Herbert's defense. "Be fair. He's only young. He wants a good time. He's a musician and a craftsman. And a sportsman. He's never pretended to be interested in much else. I don't blame him for not coming to Sheffield."

The two women talked about politics all year, with Winifred telling Augusta the story of Charles Stewart Parnell as if it were a romance published in a weekly magazine. She set out the drama, episode by episode, beginning with the allegation that the Irish leader had supported the Fenians who had murdered the Lord Lieutenant of Ireland in Phoenix Park. Then she demonstrated the perfidy of Parnell's enemies with a copy of *The Times* in which was printed the counterfeit letter by which they had sought to implicate and destroy him. Great emphasis was put on the haughty disdain with which Parnell had initially refused even to comment on the accusation. Then the eventual decision to prosecute for libel was described with obvious relief. Augusta, entering thoroughly into the spirit of the adventure, could scarcely resist cheering when she heard that a brilliant young barrister called Herbert Henry Asquith had forced the editor of *The Times* to admit his doubts about the letter's authenticity. The arrival in the witness box of Richard Piggott and the accusation that he had forged the letter left her in intolerable suspense. The news that Piggott had fled the country and shot himself in a cheap Madrid hotel was like the happy ending to a novelette. Together, Winifred and Augusta rejoiced. And together they rejoiced even more to think of Parnell, vindicated by a Parliamentary Commission, not even condescending to respond to the House of Commons' apologetic ovation.

Politics, Winifred explained, was the most exciting pastime in the world—an occupation which was far too important to leave in the hands of men. It was disgraceful that women couldn't take part in the Liberal Assembly. But at least they could observe. Thanks to her radical connections, she had been able to obtain tickets for the visitors' gallery. Morning would be spent in the formal sessions. Then, after an afternoon of rest and recuperation, they would push and jostle their way into one of the great public meetings and hear the Liberal Party leaders address their faithful followers.

"Will Mr. Gladstone be there?" asked Augusta, half-fearful of being in the piercing gaze of the Grand and Terrible Old Man.

"He never comes. I don't know why. But he never comes."

"But Parnell, he'll be there?"

"No, he won't. He's not even a Liberal. At least, he'll not be there in the flesh. In spirit he'll be everywhere. Honored now as he should have been honored years ago."

Winifred tingled with unusual excitement as she looked forward to the third week in November. She had, of course, no way of knowing that, five days before the Liberal Assembly was due to begin, Charles Stewart Parnell would be accused of committing adultery with the wife of his friend and colleague Captain William O'Shea, and that he would offer no defense, since the charge was "in all particulars correct."

On the morning when Winifred read the awful news in the *Morning Post,* her first instinct was to telegraph Augusta canceling the visit to the Liberal Assembly. With Parnell disgraced, and probably destroyed, there could be no joy in the meeting for her, and she naïvely believed that the whole proceedings would be shrouded in the gloom of hopes dashed and promises unfulfilled. She was deciding on the wording of the telegram when the post arrived. It contained a letter from Herbert—written in a hand which strangely combined the shape of his father's careful characters with an irregularity which showed how great the effort of writing had been. Its contents convinced her that it was an aunt's duty to put aside her distress and continue with the original plan.

> Mr. Abraham Wilkinson, who is a buyer at I. and R. Morley's, has asked us to tender for ten gross of shears. He wants to visit father at the Empress Works. He wants to go next Friday so that he can see the Liberals. I have told him that Father can get tickets so as to impress him. Can we go with Augusta, you and John? It is very important for you to say yes.

For a moment, Winifred stared at the letter's single paragraph, wondering what special need her nephew had of a widowed aunt's assistance. Then she noticed a postscript which explained it all.

> It is very important for you to say yes. Mr. Wilkinson has a sister named Charlotte who hopes to come too. I have told her that my party includes ladies and that she will be most welcome.

Winifred put down the pad on which she had meant to write the telegram. She feared that her renewed enthusiasm for attending the Assembly was more the product of hope that at last Herbert had developed a genuine interest in the family business than the result of the pleasure which she felt at the prospect of spending an evening with her wayward nephew.

The first day of the Assembly was a huge disappointment to the two women. Winifred enjoyed moments of brief pleasure as she identified the great names of the Liberal party sitting on the platform or mingling with the delegates, and she took great pride in pointing them out to a suitably impressed Augusta. Gradually she sank back in her seat with relief as she realized that Parnell's character and conduct would not be excoriated in every debate.

In public, Parnell was never mentioned at all. The topic of the morning was the Eight-Hour Bill. Its merits were debated with a passion that the two visitors were unable to share beyond the first ninety minutes of righteous indignation. Nor did the afternoon discussion about variations in the level of annual subscriptions contain the political thunder and lightning which Winifred had expected, and promised to Augusta. Thursday evening, spent at Asline Road, was even less enjoyable. Frederick had failed to obtain a ticket for the dinner to be held that night at the Sheffield Reform Club, and although he fought against the temptation to work off his resentment on his wife, his sister-in-law and his sister-in-law's friend, he often lost the battle.

At one point during the evening, he managed to legitimize his temporary hatred with the complaint that attempts to debate the state of the Irish Party and the turpitude of Parnell, its leader, had been stifled. "They won't get away with it. Not here in Sheffield. Liberals and Methodists are t'same here. Down in London they may not mind what Parnell's up to. But we mind up here. A letter came t'works today. We're all going to sign it and send it to Mr. Gladstone."

For a moment Winifred forgot that her brother-in-law was one of nature's Pharisees. "You've never signed it? Ireland's done without him."

"I never was for Home Rule. Lord Hartington and Joe Chamberlain were right about that. And I'm even stronger against adultery."

His wife blushed and lowered her eyes at the sound of the awful word, and Winifred, out of respect for her sister, changed the subject. She assumed command of the complicated plans for the following night.

"John," she said, "gets into Sheffield at two o'clock. He'll come into the last session of the Assembly."

Emily noted with pleasure as well as surprise that first names were in order.

"I'll get there late," said Frederick, who was enjoying the martyrdom of a thoroughly unsuccessful two days. "Herbert's bringing a buyer from Nottingham and I'll be with him till six. I shall send Herbert down with the man's sister. She's coming especially for the meeting. Though what it's to do with a woman beats me."

Frederick looked at Winifred to see if she was suitably offended.

"Don't worry about the buyer's sister," said Winifred, as if Frederick were incapable of such an emotion. "Emily and I will look after her. We'll all meet outside the Drill Hall at half past six."

Half past six was not a moment too early. The doors had already been open for an hour, and so many people had streamed into the Drill Hall that Winifred worried that Augusta would not get a good view of the platform and John Gunn feared that Winifred would be crushed to death. He peered anxiously over and between the ranks of enthusiastic Liberals who were hurrying eagerly into the Hall. Just at the moment when he had decided to suggest that Herbert and his charge should be abandoned, shining black hair was sighted above the crowd. When, for a moment, the crush parted, he thought that a small blond soldier was hanging on to his lodger's arm.

Abraham Wilkinson's sister wore a scarlet pillbox hat on top of her golden ringlets, but she wore it at an angle that defied both Queen's Regulations and gravity. A double-breasted jacket, of the same color, was decorated with gold frogging designed in the military manner to emphasize width of shoulder and narrowness of waist. The martial illusion was heightened by two huge gold epaulets and by the red stripe which ran down each side of her black hobble skirt. As Herbert and his companion approached, Winifred drew in her breath in aston-ishment and Augusta began to giggle. There was time for only the most perfunctory introductions, during which Herbert appeared to have forgotten the names of his aunt and landlord.

"Let's get in," said John Gunn, suddenly pleased that they were short of time.

A platform had been erected in the center of the Drill Hall. On it were a dozen seats, arranged in a circle so that their eventual occu-pants would face different sections of the audience which surrounded the platform on every side. Winifred calculated that the principal speakers would face the great window at the far end of the hall, and wanted to push through the crowd—which already stood shoulder to shoulder—in order to stand facing them. John Gunn forbade it, so she proposed that they climb to the gallery and secure a vantage point there. Augusta suggested that since the standing room in the body of the hall was already full, the seats in the gallery would certainly be taken. Winifred was still arguing when the stewards began to clear a passage for the platform party.

Each dignitary was instantly recognized and immediately applauded. Joseph Arch represented agriculture and labor, and was cheered for that. Charles Bradlaugh was cheered as the representative of radical dissent. John Morley was cheered as Gladstone's representative on earth, and Sir William Harcourt was cheered for being second in the Party only to Mr. Gladstone himself. Mr. Mundella was cheered for being Mr. Mundella, and Miss Mundella was cheered (almost as loudly) for being Mr. Mundella's daughter. When Dr. Spence Walsh—the President of the Assembly and chairman of the meeting—took his place on the platform, an even greater cheer went up for the whole assembled galaxy. Dr. Walsh motioned in the direction of the single cornet player. Instantly and in perfect unison the whole Drill Hall burst into song.

> *"Give Two Ringing Cheers for Gladstone,*
> *Grand Old Chieftain of Our Clan."*

Five verses having been accomplished, an attempt was made to sing the national anthem. To the consternation of Privy Councillors present, the majority of the gathering insisted on singing not the usual words but "God Save the Grand Old Man." The reporter from the *Sheffield Independent* (who was required to protect his paper's good name by always showing the Liberal Party in the best possible light) wrote in his notebook, "They loved her not less, but Gladstone more," as the defense for the enthusiasts' conduct which he would recommend to his editor. When Sir William Harcourt began his address with the moving, though slightly spurious, greeting "Fellow Yorkshiremen . . ." a great roar of enthusiasm thundered around the Drill Hall. Winifred remained in ecstasy until the meeting was over, and then she stood outside with Augusta, waiting at the agreed spot to meet Frederick Hattersley and Abraham Wilkinson.

They waited for about half an hour and neither man appeared. Then, with the Drill Hall almost empty, two dispirited figures appeared not from inside the building but from the far end of the road by which it was approached.

"Is everything all right?" asked Emily.

"It is not." Frederick addressed not his wife but the world. "We got here ten minutes before the meeting started and they wouldn't let us in. I showed 'em the tickets. Told them who I was. But no. They said it was full. Sent us off to an overflow meeting in the Albert Hall."

John Gunn decided to attempt a diversion from denunciation. He had invited the whole party to dinner at the Victoria Hotel, where he was staying for propriety's sake. And he suggested that they should begin to make their way. Frederick was not ready. He had questions to ask about the meeting which he had missed.

"What did they say about Parnell?"

"Nothing," Winifred told him with great satisfaction.

"Well, they did at the Albert Hall. Lord Compton said that he has committed a most serious social sin and should resign."

Winifred was about to express her horror at the official recognition of so primitive a view, when Frederick began to make it clear that he regarded Lord Compton's condemnation as inadequate.

"Serious social sin! Is that how he describes it? Some of us think different." He took out of his pocket a piece of paper and waved it in the night air. "This letter will appear in the *Independent* tomorrow. This is what it says about Mr. Charles Stewart Parnell. 'I know of many Liberals who, like myself, are strongly opposed to a man leading a political party who has sacrificed his character and blighted the lives of others....' George Pepper wrote this. You listen. He's put it just right. Listen. 'Is the sin of adultery less heinous than the sin of robbery? I think not. Then why should the latter be punished, when the former goes unpunished?' That's what's wanted from the party, a moral lead. But we haven't got it."

John Gunn's embarrassment was turning into apprehension—apprehension that Frederick Hattersley would die of a sudden seizure or, worse still, demand the declaration of a holy war against all adulterers and fornicators. He made another attempt to move the little gathering of family and friends toward the Victoria Hotel and supper.

"We really must be on our way. We'll exchange accounts of the meeting over supper."

Determined to avoid another denunciation of adultery, Winifred contributed to the diversion. "Have you met Mr. Wilkinson's sister?"

Abraham Wilkinson, who was beginning to think that he had bought ten gross of tailors' shears from an Old Testament prophet, took up the theme. "Mr. Hattersley, may I present my sister Charlotte..."

Frederick, as always impatient of the social graces, leaned forward in what was almost a bow and offered his hand. "Miss Wilkinson . . ."

The small, blond, martial figure who was hanging on Herbert's arm turned her adoring gaze from son to father.

"Not Miss Wilkinson, Mr. Hattersley. Mrs. Gregory. Wilkinson was my maiden name."

CHAPTER TWENTY

DOING WHAT'S RIGHT

The Victoria Hotel had carried out John Gunn's instructions in every detail. When the party arrived, the candles on the table were already lit and the modest supper, which had been ordered earlier in the day, was served with the dispatch required of a meal which began after ten o'clock at night. The soup was hot and the lamb chops were tender. After prolonged examination, which involved Frederick shaking a knife close to his ear and Herbert pressing the prongs of a fork on the table, the cutlery was declared to be of adequate quality. John Gunn wondered if he ought to demonstrate a similar pride in his own trade by inspecting the bread rolls. But he could think of no other test than actually eating them, and he was not sure how he could carry it out in a way which demonstrated that he was doing something more technical than bolting his food. In any case, he had other things to worry about.

Frederick Hattersley showed every sign of enjoying the evening. He denounced, in ascending order of outrage, the sins of the flesh, the pusillanimity of the Liberal Party's national leadership and the incompetence of its local managers. Denunciation had become one of Frederick's favorite occupations, competing for his enthusiasm with singing, praying, making scissors and being impatient with his wife. John Gunn—who had arranged the event in order to ingratiate himself with Winifred's family—would have been delighted with the success of his enterprise had it not been for one shadow which fell across the immaculate tablecloth. It was the shadow of Charlotte Gregory.

Mrs. Gregory sat—as befitted the sister of a prospective customer—at Frederick Hattersley's right hand, nodding in agreement with his condemnation of lechery and flashing knowing smiles at Herbert. John's concern was not only with the moral conduct of the young man for whom he felt an increasingly paternal obligation. He was terrified by the likely reaction of the real father were that pillar of society to notice, as John feared he must, that Herbert held Mrs. Gregory's hand under the cover of the table, relaxing his grip from time to time in order to squeeze her knee. At midnight, when Emily announced that she could not keep her eyes open a moment longer, John was forced to the thankful conclusion that Frederick had not seen the amorous adventure going on by his side. Upstairs in the Victoria Hotel, as John began to undress in his unheated bedroom, he felt the sweat run cold down his back.

He spent much of the restless night trying to decide where his duty lay. Herbert, he kept reminding himself, was an adult. But the local preacher's conscience kept adding that the young man was his adult lodger and his adult friend. Moral indecision was not a new experience, but it woke him at six o'clock the following morning and converted his usual pleasure at the thought of eggs and bacon into nausea. At the railway station, Winifred—who had brought Augusta for delivery into his safekeeping during the journey home—looked so serene that it was difficult to believe that she had noticed her favorite nephew's conduct on the previous night. Perhaps, thought John, she was so pure that she never noticed corruption. It was difficult to believe that Frederick was afflicted by moral myopia. John wondered why he had been the only one to realize what was going on, and began to feel guilty. Was there something especially prurient about his character which made him notice evil that more innocent men and women did not even see?

Augusta settled herself in the corner of the carriage and methodically adjusted herself, and the whole compartment, for the seventy-minute journey which lay ahead. She swung her wicker suitcase onto the rack before John could even make the courteous offer. Then—true to her philosophy that "hands wash, leather doesn't"—she took off her gloves before she pulled up the window. While John apologized for his failure to do his gentlemanly duty she wriggled herself down into the seat cushion, smoothed out her skirt, made sure that her hat brim was exactly horizontal across her brow and turned her steady gaze on John Gunn.

"What about Herbert, then?"

He did not reply. He was too shocked to answer. The silence was filled with an unnecessary explanation of what Augusta had meant.

"Herbert and that woman. What about that, then?"

"I don't think that it's any of our business." John spoke with no conviction.

"Do you think that anyone will tell his father?"

For a second John Gunn was affronted. "I shan't, if that's what you're suggesting. Rest assured of that. If I say anything at all it will be to him. Herbert himself."

"It's a miracle that Mr. Hattersley didn't see for himself. The man must be stupid."

"Perhaps he could not imagine that such wickedness was happening before his eyes."

"I don't mean Mr. Hattersley. I mean Herbert. He's not wicked, just stupid. All that it can do is cause him trouble. Trouble for nothing."

Augusta's emphatic defense of Herbert's morals, if not his intellect, had given her the initiative.

"What ought we to do?" John genuinely sought advice.

"We should do nothing. She'll get fed up with him. She's lonely. Her husband's left her, more or less. She needs something to do with her time. But she'll get bored with him. It'll all blow over."

"Where's her husband now?"

"He's gone to France to work in Lyons. His dad was French. I think that he came over to work at Hollingsworth's when they put that new machinery in and then the family stayed here. After they'd been married six months, Charlotte left him and he got a job back in France."

John Gunn had been horrified enough at the thought of sheltering an adulterer of any sort under his roof. The discovery that the woman in the case was married to a man who might not even be British added an extra dimension of scandal to the sordid affair. It was the lay preacher, not the friend, who passed judgment.

"It is a very wicked thing that he is doing."

"Not all that wicked, Mr. Gunn. Not as wicked as the dirty-minded will expect." Augusta realized the implication of what she had said. "I didn't mean you, Mr. Gunn. I really didn't mean you."

John Gunn smiled in the way which made the ladies in his congregation catch their breath. "I know you didn't. The idea never struck me." He spoke with absolute sincerity. Augusta's composure was restored.

"All that goes on is a drink now and then in the best bar of the Adelphi and a bit of a kiss on the way home. I know Herbert and I know Charlotte Gregory."

"How do you know a woman like that?"

"I know both of them. Both her and her brother. Tom Cross works at Morley's with Abraham. And Charlotte Gregory came over to our church for instruction. She's not called Gregory really. At least, she doesn't spell it like we do. She spells it in French. But she changed it back to the English when her husband went home."

"She's a Catholic?"

Although John Gunn had heard talk of the Whore of Rome, he had always assumed that the Catholic vice was drunkenness, not lechery. Sexual promiscuity he associated with the aristocratic members of the Established Church. He was partly reassured in his convictions by Augusta's reply.

"A convert. Her husband's a real Catholic and she was baptized before they were married. I went to her first communion with Tom Cross and her brother."

"But you acted like strangers."

"I doubt if she remembered me. It was two years ago and I'm not the sort that a woman like that remembers. I remembered her, though I thought it best to keep me mouth shut last night."

"I'll find it very difficult to do the same when I see Herbert."

"You'd best leave him be, Mr. Gunn. Really. You've got your own life to worry about. It's about time you proposed to Winifred. She's been waiting for months."

Having said what she would have described as "her piece"—the opinions she had left home determined to express—Augusta recomposed herself in the corner of the carriage. In the opposite seat, John Gunn began to fidget silently. He fidgeted for the rest of the journey.

It took John Gunn six months to accept Augusta's advice, and Winifred took almost as long to confirm the prediction that it was expected and would be welcomed. Even then—after the official announcement of their engagement—there was no rush to the altar.

"We are not children," said Winifred, "and we have both been married before."

Winifred did not believe that age and enthusiasm were incompatible and that nobody who had already experienced the honorable state would be impatient to enjoy it again. She would gladly have married John on the following day. But she thought that he would expect her to be reticently reluctant. So she argued for delay. John—who would willingly have taken out a special license—thought that her reluctance was genuine. So he pretended to agree that they must both exhibit the calm composure appropriate to middle age. Between them, they lost three months of their lives.

John knew that the wives of chapel elders who expressed public delight would also express private surprise. Had he not told them a hundred times that "after Mary there could be no one else for me"? Yet devotion to his dead wife had been replaced by an obvious infatuation with a woman whose attributes included a number of qualities of which Methodist lady chapelgoers deeply disapproved. She dressed fashionably. She was highly intelligent. She was very self-confident. Indeed, the second Mrs. Gunn showed disturbing signs of being a modern woman. They could jut imagine inviting her home to tea. But they could not think what they would talk about over the buttered scones. When the date was set, they began at once to collect for a wedding present. They decided upon a silver teapot—"something really nice and durable, something we can have engraved." It was generally agreed that only an expensive present could adequately reflect their joy that John had at last found happiness again.

The date was fixed for December, for John and Winifred wanted to be together in their own home by Christmas. There was much planning to be done and many hard decisions to be taken. The hardest decision concerned Herbert. Neither of them wanted him to stay at Huntingdon Street. Both felt profoundly guilty at the thought of asking him to leave.

The idea that a recently married couple might not want to start their life together with a lodger sharing their parlor, bathroom and breakfast table did not come spontaneously into Herbert's mind. Jack Foster raised the subject with him as they sat, in the early evening, behind the closed door of the Alfreton Road shop. They were going

267

together to the Goose Fair and as they awaited the arrival of the teenage Foster children, on whose behalf the excursion had been arranged, Jack raised the subject of "the future." Herbert's thoughts were on the night ahead and his hope that Jack would leave for home before the time when Charlotte Gregory and her brother were to meet him outside the Mechanics' Hall, where Messrs. Livermore Brothers, Court Minstrels, were to perform. He found Jack's homilies hard enough to bear even in the middle of the dullest day. When his mind was on an evening of pleasure, they were beyond endurance. The preamble concerning serious talks about something unpleasant was so unwelcome that he was unable to follow the drift of the conversation.

"Have you thought what you're going to do?"

"What?"

"What you're going to do. Have you thought about it?"

"Do when?"

"When your Aunt Winifred marries John Gunn."

Herbert remained puzzled. "What should I do? What do you mean?"

"Are you going to go on living there?"

"I suppose so. I've never thought about it."

"Well, you need to. The time's come for a change. More changes than one if t'truth were known."

Herbert was jolted into concentration. The subject of Charlotte Gregory was, he felt sure, about to be raised. He prepared himself for moral execution. The reprieve was not unconditional.

"Time's come to talk to your father about what you're going to do. It's time you were back in Sheffield doing a real job."

"I'm doing a real job here."

"You know very well you're not. Neither of us is. It's a miracle to me that your father has kept t'shop going this long losing money and gaining no credit. How much do you think we sold last week?"

"My instruments sell."

"Them instruments of yours don't make money. Half t'bills have been paid from Sheffield this year. I tell you, he won't go on with it much longer. You want to get back home and do a proper job. You'll be running that works soon. It's time to find out about it."

"Joe will do that."

"Joe's not coming back. If he hasn't written in years, he's not going to turn up one day and ask for a job."

"Half is his. Half of t'Empress, whatever he's doing."

"That's as may be. It wouldn't surprise me if your father left the whole bloody lot to the Temperance Union. Any road up, somebody needs to be there now, helping your father. He's getting on for sixty. Go home and tell him that you want a decent job—helping him. He'll be very pleased."

"I want to stay in Nottingham."

"No doubt you do. No doubt you do. But think on. Time has come for you to be back there. For his sake as well as your own."

"Won't you come back to Sheffield if he closes down here?"

"I might. But I shan't work at t'Empress. Not for long anyhow."

"Why not?"

"I'll tell you soon enough. You think about what I told you."

Herbert was about to promise that he would, when the front door was rattled impatiently. The Foster family was anxious to be on its way to the Goose Fair.

The great days of the Goose Fair were gone. The steam engines and the barrel organs, the helter-skelter and the big-wheel which had once spread themselves from Wheeler's Gate to South Parade had been crushed and crowded into the Market Place itself. Not even the arrival of electricity—which was to illuminate the fair for the first time on the day the twentieth century began—would fully compensate for the passing of the time when, for more than a week, the Goose Fair occupied Nottingham like a victorious invading army.

But the young Fosters had not known the Goose Fair in its glory days. To them—despite their father's constant insistence that there was something bigger and better in Yorkshire—it was still a fairyland of noise and excitement. Inevitably, there were great arguments about how their time, and pocket money, should be spent. Lizzie Foster, aged fourteen, demanded to see "the only clairvoyant in the world who appeared, by special desire, before the Prince and Princess of Wales, also Members of both Houses of Parliament, of the medical profession and all learned bodies." Young Jack, aged ten, first insisted upon visiting "Captain Rowley and Hanibal and Prince, his two African lions." But a sign advertising "the Prairie Wonder, the dead shot of Texas and his beautiful sister Lallow," caused him to switch enthusiasm from continent to continent. Willie Foster, fifteen the previous month, and determined to enjoy a grown-up experience, announced his intention of visiting the waxworks which advertised life-size representations of Ally Sloper, Jack the Ripper, Mrs. Maybrick and Charles Peace at their horrible trade. At the mention of murder, Lizzie and young Jack both abandoned previous interests and insisted that they accompany the elder brother to the Chamber of Horrors. Jack Foster tried, feebly, to persuade them that there were other sideshows with greater attraction.

"If that's Jack the Ripper," asked Lizzie, "why has he got that big medal and that red sash across his chest? It makes him look like a lord."

"He was a lord, silly," Willie told her. "It was the Duke of Clarence, Queen Victoria's son. He was the one that slit those women open."

Jack Foster was about to ruin the evening by forbidding any of the children to enter the waxworks, when Lizzie provided a merciful distraction.

"Charlie Peace, he came from Sheffield like us."

"That," said Herbert, "is why we are not going in. We're all too ashamed." Laughing, they moved on to the next pool of light which beckoned from beyond the darkness—within it was a shooting gallery.

The proprietor stood in front of his elaborately decorated stall, a magnificent figure against the background of a shoddy canvas which (since it had been originally intended for a theatrical performance of *The Arabian Nights*) was displayed under the title "The Afghan Campaign." But the show was not all fake. The voice which advertised the gallery's delights had once rung out across parade ground and barrack square. However, the brass helmet from beneath which the extraordinary voice emanated had once been the property of the Nottingham Volunteer Fire Brigade. To Willie, the helmet seemed as genuine as the hussar's scarlet tunic stretched tight across the showman's chest and stomach and the four campaign medals stuck on his chest.

"Let me have a shoot," cried Willie, pulling at his father's arm. "Let me have a shoot." He redirected his entreaties toward Herbert.

Jack Foster—momentarily incapacitated by one of the sudden stabs of pain which were becoming an increasing hazard in his life— was happy to let Herbert deal with his son's pleas. He turned in the direction of the military figure, who had, for a moment, laid down his megaphone in order to refresh himself from a pint bottle of stout. The face which the rusty horn had obscured was as military as the yellow facing on the scarlet tunic. The whiskers—grayer now than in the days of service to the Queen—were in desperate need of a good barber. But they clearly revealed how ferocious they had appeared in the days when they bristled against England's enemies. The nose was crisscrossed with purple veins, a memorial to twenty years spent in public houses of garrison towns.

"How much for a go?"

The showman stood his ground in front of the rough wooden counter on which the words "Firing Step" had been crudely painted. Fastened to the counter by long iron chains were six elderly rifles. Twenty yards away, across a patch of ground on which a light sprinkling of sawdust had been scattered, were the targets—six martial profiles (each one remarkable for its aquiline resemblance to the Duke of Wellington) topped by exotic examples of military headgear.

"Knock four of 'em over," promised the hussar, "and win a lovely prize. Six shots a penny."

Herbert gave the hussar a threepenny bit.

"I like a sport," said the showman. "You look like a sport. It's an honor to watch you try your luck."

"It's not my luck we're trying," Herbert told him, picking up a rifle and handing it to Willie.

"Come, come, sir." The showman's voice was husky with reproach. "This isn't a weapon for a child. This 'ere is a real rifle. It could dislocate his shoulder from the recoil. Not to mention what might 'appen if he swung around. The law'd be down on me if I let a child shoot."

Willie began to snivel. His father, coughing into his handkerchief, seemed to have lost all interest in the evening. Herbert rose to the occasion.

"I'll shoot for him. I'll shoot for all three."

The threepence being saved, it was possible to be magnanimous.

"I knew that I could recognize a sport."

Herbert picked up the first rifle, took exaggerated aim and, after an agonizing pause, pulled the trigger. A shako rattled, quivered and fell back. The hussar handed him the second rifle. He fired quickly and a bearskin toppled over. With his third shot he hit, but did not move, a kepi. His fourth sent a busby flying from the top of the rampart.

"Do you want the other two?"

Herbert missed with his last two shots.

"Nothing to play for."

The showman smiled with pleasure at the thought that the first

271

penny victory had been a stroke of luck. Willie chose a bottle of cheap but highly colored sweets as his prize, and Lizzie Foster waited nervously as her champion prepared to fire six shots in her name. He missed the first but hit with the next four, and Lizzie proudly pinned on a brooch which, from a distance of twenty yards, might have been mistaken for a ruby. The showman reloaded his rifles and waited for the natural order of things—which was success for one marksman in an evening—to be restored. Herbert shot a third time. He missed, hit, missed and hit and hit again. The last shot was followed by a squeal of delight from Lizzie and a roar of triumph from young Jack, who picked up the tiepin which matched his sister's brooch.

The showman believed that the secret of life was to build success out of failure.

"Come on, who's next? Who's next to win a valuable prize? This sportsman won three out of three. Who wants to do the same?"

As his next customer took aim he turned to Herbert.

"Where the bleeding 'ell did you learn to shoot like that?"

"In the army."

"Thought so. Could tell at once. Invalided out, were you? Couldn't have served long."

Herbert did not answer. He was busy straightening his tie.

"What was you in?"

"Hussars."

"Where did you serve?"

"Here and there."

Herbert assumed an air of mysterious modesty and began to saunter toward the next booth, followed by the three beneficiaries of his prodigious marksmanship.

Jack Foster, still coughing, was several paces behind. Suddenly he felt a tug on his coattails.

"He's not a deserter, is he?"

"No," wheezed Jack, dabbing his eyes as well as his mouth, "he's not a deserter."

As soon as he was out of the circle of light which illuminated the rough ground in front of the rifle range, Herbert stopped and told the children to wait for their father. When Jack caught up with them, he was unable to speak for several seconds. Then when the coughing subsided, he turned to Herbert with incredulous admiration.

"In the army? You learned to shoot in the bloody army! I've never

272

known such a bleeding nerve. How long were you in, a day? Did you even see a bloody gun? In the army? Cor Blimey Charlie!"

Herbert grinned. "Shouldn't have asked so many questions. It was none of his business."

"Where *did* you learn, anyway?"

"We shot rats in t'stockyard at home. And I've been rabbiting with Abraham Wilkinson. I've not shot much, but I've got a good eye. You know that, Jack."

"You mean you were lucky."

"That as well. But I always am."

"Why didn't you just say that to him?"

"He reminded me of someone I used to know. Someone who did me a disservice, a long time ago. The sight of him gave me a right shock. Made me want to . . . Made me want to sound big."

"We've done nothing yet." Lizzie made the complaint to her brothers, but she hoped that Herbert and her father would hear.

"I'm whacked," said Jack. "Can you manage another half-hour, Herbert?"

Herbert consulted his pocket watch. Whenever he looked at it, he thought of Joe—somewhere in Canada and, no doubt, still telling the time of day by the real half-hunter, the heirloom of which his was a modern replica. Herbert thought of Canada as one vast, rolling prairie and he found great difficulty in imagining Joe making scissors in the great outdoors. But he felt sure—since such a feeling was convenient —that his brother was happy. It was his habit to think about Joe for about half a second every time he saw the watch. Then when the watch was returned to his pocket, he went back to the real world of Nottingham and Frederick Hattersley and Sons.

"I've got an hour. We can see everything in an hour."

Jack Foster sat on the steps of the roundabout called the Flying Swans while Herbert and the children toured the fair. In an hour, they saw almost everything and did enough for the young Fosters to talk about at school for the next month. But Lizzie was not quite satisfied. When she was delivered safely back to her father, she expressed sorrow, not gratitude.

"We've not been on the helter-skelter."

"Would you mind?" asked Jack, feeling in his pocket for the necessary sixpence. Herbert looked reluctant. "Somebody has to go so that some great brute doesn't come rushing down behind them and

273

smash his boots into their backs. They won't think that they've been t'fair if they haven't gone down t'helter-skelter."

It was not the fear of hobnails hitting his kidneys which made Herbert reluctant to climb the helter-skelter steps. He was terrified of creasing his carefully pressed trousers on the coconut mat which would carry him, like a toboggan, on his descent into the sacks of straw at the bottom of the slide. But he saw the three anxious faces and agreed.

"Put that away. It's my treat."

Lizzie and Willie screamed all the way down.

"Time to go," Jack Foster told them, and, tired but fulfilled, they dragged their feet back home.

Herbert, feeling immensely satisfied by the good deeds he had done that evening, took up his position outside the Mechanics' Hall. It was ten minutes to ten and the second performance of the minstrel show was just reaching its glorious climax. Even outside in the street, he could hear the joyous spirituals promising salvation and eternal life and he could imagine the great eyes rolling in the blackened faces and the white gloved hands clapping in time to the music of heaven. Ten minutes and he would be buying three tickets for the third performance, and within half an hour, he would be sitting next to Charlotte.

He adjusted the knot of his tie a dozen times, and pulled down the points of his waistcoat almost as often. By ten past ten he started fiddling with his watch chain—more to relieve his anxiety than to make sure that the two loops hung down in identical curves. When, at twenty past ten, the minstrels' banjos struck up the overture, he thought of walking toward the Corn Exchange in the hope of meeting Abraham and Charlotte hurrying in his direction. Then he feared he might miss them in the crowd. So he waited as the minstrels moved into the next item of their repertoire.

Herbert waited for another half-hour, sometimes fearing that Charlotte was dead and sometimes fearing that she was not. For although her death would have left him inconsolable, he would have preferred it to desertion. Several times he thought of buying a single ticket and going in alone. That, at least, would have shown his independence of mind. But then he feared that he would look ridiculous, sitting alone and rejected, in a suit clearly designed for a night's entertainment with the lady of his choice. At a quarter to eleven he decided to go home, wondering if there was any hope that a catastrophe would provide an explanation which would make his life worth living again. He looked once more into the late-night crowd, hoping against hope that he would see Charlotte Gregory and her brother pushing their way through the drunken revelers. He saw Abraham, looking unusually disheveled, hurrying toward him.

He did not think for a moment that a catastrophe had overtaken Charlotte. Indeed, he had no doubt of the message which Abraham was carrying. Suddenly it was all clear to him. Charlotte's husband was back in Nottingham. He walked toward his friend—not sure if he could accept the news with dignity, and wholly uncertain how he would behave tomorrow and the next day when he thought of Monsieur and Madame Grégoire together in the big front bedroom of the Wilkinsons' house at Beeston. Abraham's first words confirmed his fears.

"It's Charles Gregory . . ."

Abraham Wilkinson paused, afraid to finish his sentence.

"It's Charles Gregory. He's dead. We got a letter from France this morning. He died a week or more since. As far as we can make out, it was pneumonia, but they call it something else out there. One thing's certain. He's died without a penny to his name. No more money's coming from Lyons. She's a widow now, without a penny." The phrase seemed to appeal to Abraham Wilkinson. "Without a penny. Just as I was beginning to make my way. Without a penny."

Herbert could not think what to say. Abraham had another message to bring. "She's only got you now, Herbert. You'll do right by her, won't you? You won't let her down."

CHAPTER TWENTY-ONE

HERBERT HATTERSLEY
FACES UP TO HIS
RESPONSIBILITIES

H erbert had never thought of Charlotte Gregory as imposing duties upon him. Charlotte was for pleasure—to be treated with respect, thought of with affection and protected from hurt and harm to the full extent that the irregular relationship allowed. But the idea that he might assume resonsibility for her future happiness had been kept out of his head by the acceptance that one day their little idyll would have to end. He was not the man to hide the bewilderment in which the news of André Grégoire's death had left him. Indeed, he exuded perplexity. Abraham Wilkinson walked home wondering if his sudden announcement and anguished plea had provoked hope or despair in his friend. Herbert himself could not have answered the question. He had not prepared for such a turn of fate and it took him several hours even to grasp that life was simultaneously freeing Charlotte and trapping him. To his surprise, as he began to absorb the implications of Abraham's news, the idea of spending his life with Charlotte Gregory grew increasingly attractive. The following evening he hurried to the Midland Hotel, where he knew that, despite the recent bereavement, Abraham would take an early evening glass of whiskey and Apollinaris.

Abraham Wilkinson had already taken for granted that the illicit relationship would, in the new circumstances, be turned into a lawful union. Instead of feeling resentment at the presumption, Herbert was flattered by the implication that he was a suitable brother-in-law. Pleasure quickly turned to irritation as Abraham began to set out the demands of propriety. His code of honor—which had not prevented him from arranging secret assignations between his married sister and her lover—required Herbert and Charlotte to be kept apart during the period of mourning. All he would allow was a formal note of condolence to the widow and the promise that, when the body had been brought to Nottingham and buried, a decorous (and suitably chaperoned) supper could be arranged. In the three weeks which it took for the coffin to travel from Lyons, Herbert made regular visits to the best bar of the Midland Hotel in search of reassurance. Abraham always provided it.

"It's all I can do to stop her coming," Abraham complained on the night before the funeral. "Can't wait to see you. But she takes my advice. She knows that none of us—making our way in the world— have anything to gain from a scandal." He tapped Herbert condescendingly on the shoulder. "I'll be inviting you round next week. Don't worry, old man."

At the funeral, Herbert occupied the role of family acquaintance. He was, therefore, neither invited back to the house for refreshments nor required to wear a black suit. He stood at the back of the knot of mourners which clustered around the grave, straightening the crêpe bandage around his arm and staring at the Widow Gregory leaning on the arm of a wizened man in a coat with a fur collar, whom Herbert took to be her French father-in-law. She dabbed her eyes as the first handful of earth was thrown onto the coffin.

Herbert felt affronted by the sight of Charlotte mourning her dead husband and terrified that her grief might be genuine. He knew that Abraham would disapprove of him looking agitated and anxious. But that was what he felt, and he had never been able to disguise his feelings. He could ony have appeared calm and composed if he had been calm and composed, and at the graveside he feared that he would never enjoy such comfortable emotions again.

Four days after the funeral, the anxiously awaited invitation arrived. It was written on the bottom of a black-bordered printed card. The formal message expressed the gratitude of Mrs. Charlotte Grégoire for the many condolences which she had received. Herbert resented the reminder of Charlotte's previous married state but rejoiced at the thought that she was Mrs. André Grégoire no longer. The handwritten postscript was limited to the bare essentials of the invitation. "Tuesday. Ten o'clock. Here."

Herbert was uncertain about whether or not he had been invited to supper. So, working on his belief that it was better to risk eating two meals than face the possibility of consuming none, he sat down with John Gunn in the kitchen in Huntingdon Street and, unthinkingly, subjected himself to the concerned inquiries about his health and happiness which John Gunn regarded as a landlord's obligation under life's tenancy agreement. The news that Herbert was to visit Abraham Wilkinson and his sister tempted John to ask for reassurance about his lodger's understanding of the dangers which lay ahead.

But he was not quite sure that Herbert's private life was any of his business. And he was absolutely certain that to ask questions on the subject was to cause certain friction and possible conflict. He hit upon a formula for salving his conscience and, simultaneously, preserving the peace.

"If you're in tomorrow night, I'd welcome a bit of a talk."

John Gunn congratulated himself on his ingenuity. If, after careful thought, he decided that it was his duty to speak to Herbert about the future, he had prepared the way. If, on the other hand, he decided to mind his own business, he would use the opportunity to discuss the consequences for Herbert of his impending marriage to Winifred. He found the idea of discussing either subject deeply distasteful. So he felt particularly virtuous in forcing himself to face up to one or other of the unpalatable topics. He decided that moral duty required no more than a general caution.

"Be careful tonight."

As Herbert left, John Gunn regretted saying even that. He hoped that his message would be interpreted as a warning about the danger of crossing the increasingly busy Derby Road.

Supper at Huntingdon Street proved a wise investment. Abraham Wilkinson answered his own front door and announced, conspiratorially, that the maid had been sent away for the night. He shook Herbert's hand with the heavy enthusiasm of a man congratulating the winner of a sporting event and led his guest into the dining room. In the middle of the table there was a silver tray on which stood a whiskey decanter, a soda siphon and two cut-glass tumblers. Herbert noticed the silver collar around the decanter's neck and the silver coaster on which the decanter stood. It was the possession of what Herbert's mother would have called "nice things" which accounted for much of Wilkinson's attraction. Herbert was not the man to argue with the owner of such high-quality property. So when, without speaking, Abraham poured out a large measure of whiskey and held the soda siphon at an inquiring angle, Herbert simply nodded— despite his detestation of all spirits. It did not seem the right moment at which to ask for a bottle of pale ale.

"Charlotte's in the drawing room. She'll be in directly. I thought that we ought to have a talk first—man to man."

Herbert nodded, as he had nodded his reluctant agreement to whiskey. Abraham did not waste time.

"If I were to agree to marriage, I'd need to know that you could provide . . . You understand, old man, I've got to ask these questions. I'm the only family she has, now . . ."

Even Abraham Wilkinson realized the mistake he had made by adding the last word. He was, however, not too contrite to continue in the same tone.

"Don't like doing it. Pretty shaming. But has to be done. Hope you understand."

Herbert nodded again.

"Well, could you . . . ?" Abraham paused theatrically and then gabbled in the pretense of shame. "Could you keep her?"

Herbert was as near as he ever came to being offended. He made a point of not nodding. Abraham correctly surmised that his immobility, far from signifying a negative answer to his question, was a sign of resentment at its being asked.

"I guessed from meeting your father that you were not short of a penny. I helped him on with his topcoat. Weighed a ton. Must have cost five pounds. Saw his boots, too. Looked like they were workingmen's boots, but weren't. When I saw the boots and felt the coat, I got his number: rich and careful." Abraham laughed without humor.

Herbert was uncertain how to react. He felt genuinely superior to a pen pusher with no qualification except two years at a private school and a distant relationship to the owners of the company which employed him. But Abraham was the brother of the woman whom he hoped to marry. And he had in his possession innumerable items of desirable property—cuff links, hip flasks, cigar cutters, cigarette cases, signet rings and walking sticks topped in silver. They were the symbols of the good life to which Herbert aspired. Making a mental inventory, Herbert decided to forgive Abraham his impertinence.

"The company's half mine, or will be. Half mine and half my brother Joseph's. He's in Canada. So I'll manage it when my father goes."

Abraham would have pressed for more precise details. But Charlotte, tired of waiting to occupy the center of the stage, made her entrance before being invited into the dining room by her brother in the way which he had insisted propriety required. Her widow's weeds were of lilac and primrose and were notable for the huge leg-of-mutton sleeves which billowed out above the elbow and clung tightly to the forearm. She walked two paces toward Herbert and, inclining her head, waited for him to advance and kiss her on the cheek.

"My dear . . ." Herbert had never heard her say anything solemn before. She sounded strangely old.

"Are you all right? Has it been awful?"

Herbert was not inquiring about grief and sorrow, for he had convinced himself that Charlotte felt neither. His concern was the anguish which she must have been caused by their month's separation. The generous part of his nature made Herbert hope that there had been moments of gaiety and pleasure. But his insecurity made him need her to say that she had survived a month of bitter loneliness. Charlotte did not answer his question but, taking him by the hand, led him around the table and sat him down—brother and sister on the other side, separated from Herbert by the siphon and decanter. Charlotte took command.

"I know that you will not want to be discreet. But my brother, who understands such things, is certain that a period of discretion is necessary—necessary for my sake. For six months no one will know. We shall see each other. I could not live, otherwise. But only with my brother to chaperon us. That is my brother's advice and we would not get better from the Prince of Wales."

A more inquiring mind than Herbert's might have wondered why the Prince of Wales was regarded as the arbiter of matrimonial etiquette, but Herbert merely resumed his nodding.

"For the time being there can be no ring. We can, however, exchange tokens."

The mention of rings made Herbert panic. There was no proposal, no betrothal, no formal engagement. If he was to retreat, this was the moment for withdrawal. But he did not want to withdraw. He wanted to marry Charlotte and join her in bed every night without being afraid of dirty-minded neighbors. Above all, rather than crawling out from between the warm covers at midnight, he wanted to still be in her bed in the morning. So he nodded again.

There was a brief, unnerving silence and Herbert heard himself saying, "It all fits very well. In a week or two, I shall go back to Sheffield to take over running the factory." Charlotte and Abraham were about to be impressed by the authority of his manner, when Herbert spoiled the effect by adding, nervously, "I'll see you at week-ends, though, won't I?"

"Once each month." It was Abraham who replied.

"Once each month," echoed Charlotte, "until the announcement."

Abraham and Charlotte stood up in unison. Herbert, not realizing that they expected him to leave, prepared to follow them into the drawing room.

"Before you go . . ." Charlotte did not understand that their coded message had not been translated and thought that she was postponing Herbert's departure. "Before you go, I have a gift for you."

Herbert opened the small leather box. Inside it was a tiepin.

"It's gold, like the ring which . . ."

Tiepins, Herbert knew, came in a variety of shapes and sizes. Those with which he was most familiar were single steel spikes, topped by a piece of colored glass, masquerading as a ruby or emerald. But Charlotte's gift was of a different class. It was a simple bar of gold, designed to be fastened horizontally across the tie by a pin that stretched its full length from hinge to safety catch. Herbert thought of it as his first nice thing and attempted at once to fasten it to his tie with a crude stab which bent the nine-carat pin on the thick silk. Charlotte took it from him, straightened the pin and worked it into the cloth. Herbert was overcome by her touch, by the sight of her gift and, above all, by the thought of the trouble to which she must have gone to find the perfect present.

"I shall wear it every day—every day of my life."

The late Monsieur André Grégoire had used exactly the same words when Charlotte gave it to him on their wedding night.

Charlotte Gregory's sudden conversion to impeccable propriety had exactly the effect which she had intended. Herbert began to think of her as a virgin goddess to be wooed in the temple of respectability and won at the shrine of middle-class morality. The sign and symbol of his new determination to settle down and straighten out his life was the tiepin. It took some time to fasten it across his tie to his complete satisfaction. And at first the suitable angle was achieved only after several unsuccessful attempts, some of which were accomplished only by grazing his stomach with the point of his pin. On the first full day of its use, he actually stabbed himself in the navel. But the risks were worth the reward. The pin being successfully secured in place, he buttoned his waistcoat over his precious secret. The purity of his feelings for Charlotte required him to avoid the slightest risk of revealing to the world that she was anything other than a grieving widow. As he walked to work he put his hand inside his jacket to ensure that the amulet was still in its proper place near to his heart.

As he expected, the workshop and showroom in Alfreton Road were locked and empty. Jack Foster, once the most reliable of workmen, now rarely arrived at his place of employment until an hour or more after the premises were officially open to the public. Herbert, who was always behind his bench before seven o'clock, calculated the state of Jack's health by the time that he first heard the jingle of the bell above the showroom door. Few customers called at any one time during the day. None came before noon. So any early sign or sound of life, below the workshop stairs, marked the beginning of Jack's slow ascent. On mornings when Herbert felt a particularly urgent need to talk, Jack's health seemed always at its worst. When on such mornings Jack eventually arrived, Herbert was too anxious to begin his story even to preface his monologue with an inquiry about his colleague's health. After a few minutes of anecdote and rhetorical questions, he would feel a moment's guilt about not having asked Jack how he was. But the shame did not last for long. The answer to his question should have been obvious. Although Herbert did not notice it, Jack was dying.

"I'm taking your advice. I'm going home to see m'father. I want a proper job, a job in t'factory."

"A job running the factory." Jack was leaning with both arms on the bench.

"Nothing wrong wi' that, is there? It's my right."

"I hope Mr. Hattersley will think so."

"I thought you wanted me to go back there and have a proper job."

"So I do. So I do. I'm just out of sorts this morning."

"You do think it's time, don't you, Jack? Time to do a right job."

"I do that. But for the right bloody reasons, not to impress them Wilkinsons."

Jack was looking at the gold pin which was just visible above the top of Herbert's calico apron. Herbert noticed and grinned. He then unfastened the pin and, with some difficulty, reattached it to his tie and shirt well below the top of the apron's bib. He had failed to keep its existence secret. But he was determined to protect its perfect patina from the sparks that flew from the little anvil on which the surgeons' knives were forged. Having, with much concentrated effort, fixed the pin in an acceptable position, Herbert felt able to defend himself against Jack's implied rebuke.

"What's a good reason, then?"

"A good reason is wanting to be a cutler, not a bleeding shopkeeper."

"I never wanted to come here. He sent me here."

"He sent you here for your own good."

"He wanted to get rid of me."

"If you telt him that you wanted to go back, he'd jump at it. All I hope is that it's for a good reason, not just to cut a dash with that there Mrs. Gregory or whatever her name is."

"That's none of your business, Jack. What goes on between that lady and me is nowt to do wi' thee."

"I'm glad to hear that she's a lady. There's them that thinks different."

"You bastard." Herbert, having recovered enough composure to speak, could think of nothing else to say.

"I didn't ought to have said that and I'm sure that she's a very nice woman. It's just that I've known you since you were a nipper and I want you to be careful."

"I've told you, Jack. It's none of your business."

The apology had been difficult to make. Its rejection hardened Jack's heart. "That is where you are wrong. It's summat to do wi' me because it makes things awkward between Mr. Hattersley and me. I ought to tell him what's going on. But I don't tell him, do I? I've never told him, not half the things he ought to know about. But I don't like lying to him. When he says, 'How's Herbert shaping?' I don't like lying to him."

"You don't lie. You just keep your mouth shut."

"I may deceive your father, but I don't deceive m'sen. I lie to him.

But I suppose I'll go on hushing things up, so there's no more to be said."

"Only that you're like a bloody lapdog. I'm surprised that you don't sit up and beg when he comes in t'room."

"It's better than lifting m'leg and pissing on his boots like you do when tha gets a chance. Shit on him. That's what tha does."

"Sit up and beg, little lapdog."

"When I needed help, he gave it me, without any beggin'. Without even askin' even."

Herbert suddenly feared that his tiepin had become loose and, fearful that he would lose it, he groped under his apron with both hands. It took him several minutes of hard effort to fasten it securely.

"Another thing," said Jack Foster. "I'm supposed to look after your health."

"What if you are?"

"Never use that tiepin to fasten down your collar. You'll cut your bloody throat and, as usual, I'll get the blame."

Herbert did not even smile, but Jack laughed until he was so weak that he had to sit down on the grinder's stool. When he had recovered his wind, he looked up at Herbert, still grinning.

"Deceit becomes a habit and I'm well practiced. Before you speak to y'father, work out what you're going to say. Tell him you want a proper job. Tell him you want to help run t'Empress Works. Nowt else. He'll be right pleased. I've telt thee, he'll welcome thee wi' open arms."

Herbert took Jack Foster's advice. He could not see his father until the weekend, for traveling to Sheffield before Saturday was unthinkable. So he used the three days of waiting to prepare a speech. Some sentences—concerning the pride he felt at being a time-served cutler and specialist medical-instrument maker—were committed, word for word, to memory. He could not make up his mind if the announcement of the hope of doubling the size of the company in ten years would be regarded as admirable ambition or if it implied an unwarranted criticism. But he knew that it was important to say something about the family rallying round without implying that his father was in need of help. By the time he set out, he was totally convinced of the sincerity of his purpose. In preparation for convincing his father, he had convinced himself that his only interest was in playing a full and honorable part in the company which bore his name.

Some of Frederick Hattersley's belief in duty and destiny had rubbed off on his younger son, creating in Herbert a real passion to be part of Frederick Hattersley and Sons. So Jack Foster's fears that the move to Sheffield was meant to do no more than impress Charlotte Gregory was, at least in part, unfounded. However, Herbert had to admit, to himself, that for some reason which he could not quite understand, he was desperate to convince Charlotte's brother that Frederick Hattersley's mantle would fall on him. But if Charlotte and Abraham were in any way responsible for his new enthusiasm, they could be credited with doing no more than awakening his slumbering instincts. After three days' careful thought, Herbert felt ready to speak to his father with genuine conviction. But before the meeting, he had personal matters which needed his careful attention.

He concentrated on those preliminary tasks with such dogged determination that, as he traveled to Sheffield to discuss his fate and future, he felt his right-hand pocket every ten minutes to make sure that its essential contents—an envelope containing a lock of his own hair and a purse—were safe. The hair had been picked up from the floor of a barber's shop the previous day and could, if the worst had come to the worst, be replaced. In the purse, there was three pounds, seven shillings and sixpence—his week's wages and the ready cash kept hidden under the newspaper that lined the drawer holding his underwear, in case of emergencies such as the sudden sight of an irresistible tie in a haberdasher's window. The money, he calculated, represented about a quarter of his total assets. Satisfied that the purse and envelope were safe, Herbert made his determined way to Church Street and the studio of the Sheffield Photographic Company.

Herbert put himself in the hands of the photographer, who chose an Arcadian backdrop and then invited the subject of the portrait to lean nonchalantly against a high-backed chair, before he disappeared under his black cloth. The sodium flare exploded just as Herbert was adjusting the angle of his head and, despite the assurance that the new high-speed shutter would produce a perfect result, Herbert insisted on a second photograph, "just to make sure." The cost of two portrait sittings was three shillings. An extra fourpence was required to pay the cost of the finished "vignette" being sent by express post to Nottingham.

Having reassured himself that his purse—and the three pounds, four shillings and twopence which it contained—was safe, Herbert walked back to Fargate, where, at number 20, C. R. Pleasance, the "art jeweler," offered "solid gold at good prices." Herbert wanted silver—not because of the price but because, as a cutler, he felt a natural affinity with the silversmith's trade. He knew exactly the gift that he was to buy and, once inside the shop, he described it with the precision of a craftsman. The shop assistant, whose salesman's instincts were offended by the idea of a customer making a purchase without examining the full range of merchandise, offered to open cabinets, withdraw velvet-lined trays and "see what we have in the back." But Herbert insisted on repeating his detailed requirements.

"An oval locket, inch and three quarters top to bottom and inch and a half across, plain back, front engraved with French curves and buckled belt shaped as in a letter Q."

The assistant accepted defeat and produced a locket of exactly the sort specified. Herbert went on to describe the chain with which the locket should be complemented—". . . flat links, engraved, front fastening, on a spring-loaded ring."

It was the sort of locket which his Aunt Winifred wore, and was therefore certain, in Herbert's estimation, to be a perfect gift for a lady. The shop assistant folded the locket in tissue paper before putting it inside its box. It was not until the final brown-paper wrapping had been tied in place that Herbert asked the total price. It cost two pounds, five shillings and sixpence. He was left with barely enough in his purse to pay his rent. But he had prepared for such an eventuality. All would be well if he could get to Leopold Street before noon when the banks closed.

He arrived at the Leopold Street branch of the Sheffield and Hallamshire Savings Bank at two minutes to twelve. Only one bank clerk was still behind the counter. He greeted Herbert with an ingratiating familiarity.

"What a pleasure. What a pleasure, after all this time. I thought that you'd forgotten us."

Herbert remembered him only too well. For years, during his apprenticeship at the Empress Works, he had been sent to the bank on Friday mornings to draw out the week's wages. The same bank clerk who now reached over the counter to shake his hand had always counted out the money. As the coins clinked he had preached little sermons about Herbert's good fortune in being born into the Hattersley family and the importance of his emulating his father in all that he did.

"Come to make a big deposit, Mr. Herbert?"

"I'm taking some out." Herbert already felt ashamed.

"How much, Mr. Herbert?"

"How much have I got in?"

"Don't you know? Your father will know how much he's got in, down to the last farthing. You can be certain of that."

"I'm just making sure."

The bank clerk disappeared to consult the ledger while an office boy (it being past noon) locked the front door and stood on guard ready to release Herbert when his business was done. The clerk reappeared with a piece of paper which he handed to Herbert to make sure that the secret was kept from the office boy. On it was written "£3 19s 11½d." Herbert's reaction confounded the idea that he had even the roughest notion of what his account contained. He had hoped to draw out four pounds and leave as much in.

"How much will it be, Mr. Herbert?"

"All of it."

"Not all of it, surely, sir? I hope you'll keep a few coppers in, just to keep your account with us. We'd hate to lose you." He turned to the office boy. "This is Mr. Herbert Hattersley. Mr. Frederick Hattersley's son."

The office boy seemed unimpressed.

"Three pound fifteen," said Herbert.

The bank clerk began to count the money out of the drawer and, having found three clean pound notes, paused and turned to his young assistant. "I'll lock up. Leave me the keys and get along with you."

The office boy was around behind the counter and on his way home before the six half-crowns were out of the till.

"I'm very glad you've popped in, Mr. Herbert. These days, I hardly ever see your father, Mr. Frederick Hattersley."

I know who my father is, thought Herbert, anxious to get the money in his purse and be on his way.

"Is your father well?"

"Very."

"And Mrs. Hattersley?"

"Very well."

"And Mr. Joseph?"

"Fine."

"We send letters to Mr. Joseph, but he never replies. That's what worries us. We thought something might have happened to him, out in Canada."

Herbert was incapable of hiding his feelings. "Where do you send them?"

It was not the question of a man anxious that the bank should not make an error but the inquiry of a brother who hoped for news.

"To the Empress Works, like your father instructed. Isn't that right?"

"Quite right. We send them on."

"Well"—the bank clerk smiled unpleasantly—when you next write, ask him to reply. I wouldn't ask, but it's really quite important."

"There isn't any trouble, is there?"

"It's not for me to say."

There was no attempt to disguise the pleasure which the moment of power provided.

"Suit yourself," said Herbert, unable immediately to think how he might persuade the clerk to end his anxiety.

"It's bank rules. I can't say anything."

Herbert—who could not bear uncertainty—decided to use the one weapon that he had at his disposal. "If he is in some sort of trouble, my father would expect you to tell us."

The mention of the magic name cast the anticipated spell. The reply was full of reproach.

"You know very well that it's not trouble, Mr. Herbert. Quite on the contrary. It's the money that gets paid into his account every month. It's mounting up. The manager said to me only the other day, 'That money ought to be earning more than it's earning here.' And I said to him, 'He may not know how it's piling up, being in Canada.' Your father would want the money to be earning. Keeps his fingers on everything, does your father. Mr. Frederick Hattersley."

"Is there a lot?"

"Now, Mr. Herbert, you know better than to ask me that."

The bank clerk slowly closed one eye in a hideously coy wink.

CHAPTER TWENTY-TWO

FOR RICHER, FOR POORER

M ost evenings Emily Hattersley, sitting opposite her husband in the parlor at Asline Road, fell asleep over her embroidery and remained happily unconscious until her husband shook her awake and announced that it was time for bed. But on the night when Herbert came home, she remained conscious and alert until well after ten o'clock.

"Are you tired, Mam?" her son asked her with unusual concern for her health and welfare. "I'd be off upstairs if I were you."

Emily looked up from her stitching, looked at her husband and concluded that since he was apparently content to remain in front of the fire, there was no reason why she should not do the same.

Another hour passed, and although Emily began to feel drowsy and her head began to nod, her husband remained immovable in his chair, staring at the Bible in which he was searching for a text. He still preached the occasional sermon and he still took his inspiration from Proverbs. For much of the evening, he had wrestled with a difficult choice between "Go to the ant, thou sluggard; consider her ways and be wise" and "The path of the just is as the shining light," as the appropriate moral to offer the Bible class on the following Sunday. But having been inspired by the sight of Herbert fidgeting in the corner of the room, Frederick decided that a sign had been sent from heaven to guide him to a new text. "He that begetteth a fool doeth it to his sorrow."

The decision being made, he could have gone to bed at his usual time. But he suspected that Herbert wanted to talk with him, and he wanted the talk to be private. His wife, he knew, would never even consider joining in the discussion. Indeed, had she even thought that the men wanted to talk amongst themselves, she would have gone to bed at once. But the discovery that a conversation of secret significance was about to begin would have alarmed her. She would have decided that the serious subjects which had been discussed concerned either Herbert's future or Joseph's whereabouts. She would restrain herself until morning; then Frederick would be subjected to anxious questions about her sons' future. The prospect of Emily's neurotic concern was so unattractive to him that Frederick was prepared to lose an hour's sleep in order to avoid it. But his wife would not go to bed. It was one of those occasions when she almost seemed to be frustrating his will not by stupidity but by malice.

Just after midnight, Frederick's nerve snapped.

"Why don't you go on up, Mother? I'll be with you in ten minutes."

Emily having left, Frederick returned to his examination of Proverbs.

Ten minutes of silence followed; then, "Father."

"Yes."

Herbert had hoped for a more encouraging response.

"I've something I want to say."

"I didn't think that you'd come all this way for the pleasure of my company."

During the silence which followed, Herbert told himself that his whole future hung on the next few sentences, that he knew exactly what to say and that the worst that could happen would be disinheritance. He launched into his opening line.

"I know that I've behaved like a fool . . . in the past, that is."

The qualification concerning the past was necessary to avoid even the briefest suspicion that he had come home to confess some recent misdemeanor. He had convinced himself that, after the opening sentence, the words would flow from his lips with the fluency of a chapel superintendent. Unfortunately, despite the hours of practice and preparation, the conversation did not follow the course which Herbert had planned.

The opening statement—describing pride in trade and gratitude to family—went well enough. So did the bold assertion which followed —the calm and confident insistence that he was capable of assuming far greater responsibilities than those which he had discharged in Nottingham. But although he had learned the whole speech by heart, his mind kept wandering from the words which he had committed to memory. A vision of Joseph constantly pushed its way into his brain —not Joseph cold and hungry in the Rocky Mountains, as he had once feared, but Joseph sleek and prosperous on the lush prairies of modern Canada and sending money back to Sheffield. Herbert was genuinely relieved to think that his brother was prospering. But he did not want him to prosper in Sheffield, and on the evidence obtained in the Leopold Street branch of the Sheffield and Hallamshire Savings Bank, Joseph's clear intention was to return home. Why else, Herbert kept asking himself, should Joseph be making regular monthly payments into his Sheffield account—the only interpretation of the bank clerk's news which seemed remotely plausible? In an attempt to exorcise the specter of his brother's return destroying all his hopes and plans, Herbert improvised a few words at the end of his carefully constructed passage about the inheritance of his father's instinct for business.

"I know Joseph's got his rights. And I don't want to push him out. I mean . . . we both have . . . It's between us . . . both of us . . . Isn't it?"

There was no opportunity to curse himself for sounding more interested in the inheritance than in the opportunity before his father spoke for the first time. "Don't you worry about Joseph. I'll deal with him. He'll get what he deserves, what's his by right. No more, no less."

Herbert was relieved by the interruption, for he thought of his father as unable to listen in silence to anything except a Sunday sermon, and would have been unnerved if his speech had been shown anything approaching respect. But it was his father's only interjection. And as he continued to plead his cause he grew increasingly unnerved by the careful concentration on what he had to say. He waited to be interrupted again, but no real interruption came. In consequence, the confrontation took on a surreal quality, and by the time he began his peroration—the sanctity of hard work and the rewards of determination—his nerve had completely snapped. He stammered out the last few words and sank back in his chair. There was an interminable silence before Frederick Hattersley spoke. His question could hardly have been less helpful.

"So what do you want?"

Herbert, bewildered by his father's apparent continued incomprehension, could only tell the simple truth.

"I want to come home."

"I guessed it. Jack Foster told me as much." Before Herbert could fully develop his feelings of betrayal, Jack Foster was exonerated. "He told me weeks ago. Told me that you were ready to do a proper job. He's a good friend to you, is Jack."

"Then can I come back to t'Empress?"

"All in good time you can. Come at turn of t'year."

The turn of the year suited Herbert very well. But before he had time to express a word of gratitude, his father began to berate him as if he had complained of the delay.

"I'm going to do my duty by Jack, and you should want to do the same. As long as he wants to drag himself to that shop, it's going to be there for him. I would have closed it three months since except for him."

"What do you mean, except for him?"

"Except I don't intend to shut while he's able to work."

"Able to work?" Herbert had risen to new heights of incomprehension.

"Jack's dying. You must be blind not to have seen it."

While Herbert was trying to comprehend what his father had told him the conversation moved on.

"I was influenced by them Liberals. That shop never made a penny. Anyway, I'll be influenced by them no more."

"Poor old Jack."

"Next time I shall vote Unionist. That conference finished me off. I've never been a Home Ruler and they were Home Rulers from start to finish. Next time I'm with Mr. Chamberlain."

"So am I! Poor old Jack's a Chamberlain man."

Herbert admired Chamberlain's dashing appearance and devil-may-care style. He had no idea about Jack's allegiance. It just seemed right to keep him in the conversation.

"Tha knows nowt about it. Any road, if tha comes back here, tha'll be too busy for politics, too busy for anything except t'works."

Herbert glowed with gratitude and pride.

"We'll keep shop till Christmas at least. Don't make any more scalpels that we won't sell. Find out about keeping books. Pick up things from Jack. Help him all you can. You'd do better living with him than with that John Gunn. Jack could do wi' t'rent money and you could give him a hand with those lads of his. It's not going to be an easy month or two."

"What shall I say to John? He'll not want me to go."

"Sometimes I think you're not quite all there. He won't want you in his house when his new wife gets there. He's too frightened to tell you to get out, and your Aunt Winifred's too softhearted. But neither of 'em want you there. You should know these things without telling. It won't be long before you're thinking about settling down yourself."

Herbert was desperately afraid that his father would want to talk to him about the importance of a sensible marriage. To his relief, the conversation moved on to doom and death.

"I'll tell you now, Jack won't be in that shop after Christmas." Frederick Hattersley seemed triumphant in his certainty. "But we won't put t'shop on market till after Christmas either. We'll not sell it till he finishes."

"What will he live on after he finishes with us?"

"What do you think? He'll live on me till he goes. Then his wife and his children will live on me till those boys start earning. It'll be a great burden, but it's my duty and I shall do it."

"It might not be that bad. He came to work yesterday." Herbert sounded as if he wanted to comfort his father with the thought that the expensive duty might yet be avoided.

"He'll die all right. It's cancer." Frederick pronounced the dreaded word as if it were the name of the God of vengeance and hate. "When you get cancer, you don't get better. You can rely on that. Cancer eats you up, rots you away. Jack's as good as lying in his grave tonight."

The thought of Jack Foster—once so bold and brave—lying in his grave filled Herbert with fear—fear for Jack and fear for himself. As he thought of Jack, in coffin and shroud, the pallid face became his own. He had seen funeral processions making their slow progress toward the graveyard and he had heard his mother whisper, "He's gone," about some elderly neighbor. But death, until that minute, had been none of his business. He had gone home to Sheffield to consider his future and, for the first time in his life, he had come face to face with mortality.

The realization that one day he, too, would be the passenger in a slow hearse, and that the local matrons would tell each other, "He's gone," filled Herbert with more emotions than he could control. He felt a desperate need to tell his father that he loved him, and that he would never again do anything which hurt or offended his parents. But at the same time as he longed to atone for the errors of the past, the determination to build a happy future grew increasingly strong. He could not wait to return to Nottingham, hold Charlotte Gregory in his arms and hear her say that they would never be apart again. As he sat opposite his father his stronger feeling was the fear of being on his own, of lying in the bed which he had once shared with Joe and staring up into the darkness above him, as he would one day stare, sightless, up into the lid of his own coffin. He was desperate to engage his father in artificially animated conversation about scissor manufacturing, Irish Home Rule, association football, choral music or anything. But his father picked up the Bible.

"No doubt you'll want to get upstairs. I hear you're off first thing. Any road, I've got a sermon to write for tomorrow evening."

The vignette arrived in Nottingham by the first post on Monday morning. It took Herbert only a few seconds to cut it down into a shape and size which enabled him to fit it into one side of the locket—a task which he accomplished almost as quickly. The lock of hair was trapped behind the glass on the other side with the same skill. But it took almost fifteen minutes to pack his gift into a presentable parcel and over an hour to compose the message which went with it. The package was sent to Charlotte Gregory by registered post.

He received no note of thanks or acknowledgment but, assuming that Charlotte was waiting to express her pleasure during a visit he had planned for Thursday evening, looked forward with confidence to the reunion. As always, it was Abraham Wilkinson who greeted him at the door and with whom he was expected to make desultory conversation while Charlotte made her last-minute preparation for the audience that she would give him. Abraham assumed his usual manner. It was a disturbing combination of diffidence and familiarity.

"You'll forgive me mentioning it, old boy, but Charlotte's a bit disappointed. I don't like saying it, but only fair to let you know what's up. If she pouts a bit, it's nothing to worry about, just the locket."

"What was wrong with the locket?" Herbert felt all the confidence that came from absolute faith in Aunt Winifred's good taste.

"It's very nice. Of course it is. But Charlotte set her heart on gold. She's got this silly idea that wedding tokens—like wedding rings— ought to be gold. That's why she bought you the tiepin." Abraham Wilkinson waved his hand in the direction of Herbert's navel. "She thinks that sending silver shows that you don't really care. Silly I know, but . . ."

Abraham Wilkinson would have said, "You know women," but his explanation of Charlotte's disappointment had gone on for so long that Herbert had thought of a response. He was certain about the quality of his gift but less confident about its suitability for the occasion which it marked, for he could not be sure who had given his aunt her locket or what event it was bought to commemorate.

"It's not the wedding token," he said. "It's just a gift. The wedding gift is gold. You should have known that, Abraham. It's ordered and it will be here next week."

"Charlotte will be delighted."

As always, Charlotte arrived exactly at the moment that ensured the greatest impact. With the endearing self-obsession of a child of five she demanded to know, "What gift?"

Herbert had already exhausted his reserves of ingenuity. So, instead of insisting that it was a surprise, he cast about in his mind for a piece of gold jewelry that he had seen his Aunt Winifred wear. He could think of only one.

"It's a brooch set in gold. The picture's ivory, but the surround is gold."

He could hear himself apologizing, but no apology was necessary. To his relieved surprise, ivory set in gold was judged to be quite acceptable.

"A cameo," cried Charlotte, clapping her hands in childish delight. She hugged her brother, kissed Herbert lightly on the cheek and did a little pirouette between sideboard and sofa.

Herbert's satisfaction at the success of his stratagem was short-lived. For the more Charlotte enthused about the gift, the more concerned he grew about his almost certain inability to provide it. He had no idea how or where he might find a brooch of the sort that his Aunt Winifred wore. And were one to be found, there was no hope that he would be able to buy it. After the financial transactions of the weekend, he had returned to Nottingham with three pounds, thirteen shillings and sixpence. Thirty shillings had been paid at once to John Gunn—the rent which should have been left on the kitchen mantel-shelf before he left for Sheffield on Saturday morning. Two shillings and elevenpence had been spent without the transactions being noticed or recorded. On the following day, he would be paid his weekly wages. His mind digressed to the pleasant thought that because of his new responsibilities he would be paying the wages to himself. But for the moment, putting aside the coppers which were left in the Leopold Street Bank, he possessed two pounds and sevenpence in all the world. The kind of gold and ivory brooch which his Aunt Winifred wore could not be bought for that sort of money.

It was not Herbert's habit to stay gloomy for long, particularly when the future was illuminated by a watery shaft of light which could be interpreted, no matter how implausibly, as blazing sunlight. Dawn broke out of the classified advertisement columns of the *Nottingham Evening Post*. J. Smith, jeweler, of Park Street was pleased to announce that he had opened a new branch at 9 Chapel Bar. For a week, every item in the shop was on offer at ten percent below the usual price. Cameo brooches were specified as being amongst the special bargains.

Given the chance, Herbert Hattersley always respected the disciplines of his trade. So, anxious as he was to visit Chapel Bar, he waited for Jack Foster to arrive rather than leave the shop unattended and, instead of paying his own wages during the morning, he obeyed his father's rule that pay packets were distributed at noon on Fridays. He left for the jeweler's with four pounds in his purse. To his delighted astonishment, five minutes later he found a brooch almost identical to the one which his Aunt Winifred always wore. It was slightly longer and the gold around the cameo was more ornate. The picture, cut into ivory, was not the head of Aphrodite but a scene from Arcadia with kneeling shepherd paying court to sitting shepherdess. It was not the brooch which he had described to Charlotte, but there was no reason why it should not become the brooch which Charlotte expected. It cost two guineas.

Had the jeweler given Herbert time to think, the brooch would have changed hands there and then. But, noticing his customer's interest in the price, he feared that the sale would be lost unless he made some sort of helpful offer.

"You could pay a pound now and the balance over the next three months." Before Herbert had a chance to accept, the point was pressed home. "More and more people are paying this way these days. Very many respectable people. Some of the best families in Nottingham have bought goods from me in this way."

Herbert needed no convincing. He signed an agreement to pay three and sixpence a week for the next three months and danced back to work. He believed that he was humming under his breath. As he jostled his way along the pavements people turned to get a second sight of the tall, handsome young man with carefully clipped mustache and immaculately brilliantined black hair who was singing in perfect pitch and tune "Brightly Dawns Our Wedding Day."

The joy with which his gift was received, and the ease with which he paid off the balance of the price, made Herbert Hattersley a regular customer of J. Smith, jeweler, and a regular patron of the "easy payments scheme" which the enterprising businessman offered to a small selection of trusted customers. Charlotte Gregory's birthday, which fell inconveniently in November, was celebrated with a gold muff chain. Her Christmas present was a fob watch. In between birthday and Christmas he gave her, for no particular reason, a heavy chain bracelet with a lock in the shape of a heart. Each item involved him in a weekly expenditure of only a few shillings. So it was not until early in the New Year—when he called in at Park Street to collect the ornate clock which he had bought Winifred Spooner and John Gunn as a wedding present—that he realized that he was behind with his payments.

The jeweler was perfectly pleasant about the unexpectedly increasing debt. He calculated the outstanding weekly repayments on the back of an envelope, added in the outstanding balance on both the clock and the amethyst earrings which Herbert had bought Charlotte in anticipation of her emergence from purdah and gave assurances about his continued availability at all times. Herbert felt absolutely confident about his ability to clear his debt without having to make an unacceptable reduction in his standard of living and unpleasant changes in his style of life. Confidence led to complacency, and complacency combined with the hectic pace at which he lived the next few weeks to push the thought of his debts to the back of his mind. Several times he meant to travel to Park Street in order to make the regular payment which he had promised. But on each occasion more pressing business intervened. He was moving lodgings to Jack Foster's terraced house in Southwell Street and he was learning how both to manage the finances of a small business and to share a table with a man who knew there were only a few dozen meals between him and eternity. He was helping John Gunn with odd jobs of decoration and furniture moving—to prepare his house in Huntingdon Street to receive his new bride. And an increasing part of his interest and energy was concentrated on the day when Charlotte would feel herself able to make a public announcement of her intention. It was not surprising that he overlooked a small matter like his legal debts. But on the eve of John Gunn's wedding to Winifred Spooner, when Herbert was trying on his new suit and wishing that Charlotte could see him in his splendor, he was rudely reminded of the penalty for his forgetfulness.

Little Jack, who had grown as his father shrank, answered Jack Foster's front door and came back into the living room saying that Herbert had a caller who would not move from the hall. Herbert descended the stairs from his bedroom, splendid in double-breasted waistcoat, high collar and broad bow tie. The smell of raw leather, blown in from J. Wragg's boot works, hung in the air, and Herbert made his usual joke.

"You get a good tanning here."

The visitor, who had not removed his hat, did not smile. Herbert asked his guest to sit down. His visitor declined without thanks.

"You Mr. Hattersley?"

"That's me."

"Mr. Herbert Hattersley?"

"Right again."

"Normally resident at 117 Huntingdon Street?"

"That's where I used to live, yes. I've moved here."

The visitor took a paper from his pocket and Herbert at last sensed impending doom.

"Has something happened to Mr. Gunn?"

He would have assumed that Jack Foster had died in the street, but he could hear him coughing in the living room.

"Mr. Gunn was well when I left him half an hour ago."

"What is it then?"

"Debts, Mr. Hattersley, debts."

The man in the bowler hat unfolded his piece of paper.

"Debts amounting to twelve pounds, fourteen shillings and sixpence. All of it owed to Mr. J. Smith, jeweler."

"Is it as much as that?"

Herbert began to whisper in the hope that the man in the bowler hat would do the same. His wish was not granted.

"It is. The question is, when are you going to pay it off?"

"I pay bit by bit. We arranged that."

"That was all very well while you kept up the payments. That agreement's done for because you didn't pay. You owe the lot now. That was the deal."

298

"I can't pay that."

Herbert found it difficult to believe that the man in the bowler had not enough sense to realize it for himself.

"I hope that's not so, Mr. Hattersley. I really do. For if you don't have the money, we'll have to have the goods."

"I've given them away."

"I don't doubt it, seeing the nature of the items. That's why I ask where they are now. Where's the brooch—cameo, ivory surrounded by nine-carat gold, Birmingham 1890? That's the one you've owed for the longest."

Herbert was speechless. The man in the bowler hat had to prompt him.

"Can you not pay anything off?"

"Two pounds."

"Two pounds now?"

Silence was assumed to mean consent, so the man in the bowler hat tried to build on the offer.

"How much tomorrow?"

"Tomorrow? For God's sake!"

"Yes, tomorrow."

It was so long a time since Herbert had done business with a pawnbroker that he knew that his calculation would be unreliable. He added topcoat to best boots, cuff links to blue serge suit. After some hesitation, he added the watch which his father had given him on the day that he completed his indentures.

"Four pounds."

"Including that new suit?"

"Not including this new suit. It's for a wedding, tomorrow."

"That's not my concern. My concern is the money you owe."

"Not the suit. Not until after the wedding."

"I shouldn't, but I will. I feel sorry for you. What a way to start married life. It'll get me into trouble, but I'll do it out of kindness. Two pounds now, four pounds tomorrow. In the shop by five."

"I'll be there." Herbert, having been reprieved for twenty-four hours, was smiling again.

"And the rest, six pounds, fourteen shillings and sixpence to be exact—we'll want within a week."

Herbert stopped smiling. It was, he thought, all desperately unfair —unfair that he had to lose his watch for several weeks, unfair that his enjoyment of the wedding would be spoilt, unfair that he would have to pay it back, and it was particularly unfair that his attention should be distracted from thinking about his future wife, and the pleasure she would have derived from seeing him in his new suit.

Winifred Spooner, on the eve of her wedding, was not thinking of her future with John Gunn, as Emily, who sat with her in the bedroom, assumed. Winifred rarely listened with great attention to what her sister had to say. But she was by nature usually kind and invariably courteous, so she normally responded with an absentminded "Really" or "Well, well" to her sister's anecdotes about domestic life in a Sheffield suburb. But on the eve of her wedding Winifred said not a word. Instead, she sat on the side of her bed, stared at the suitably unostentatious wedding dress and allowed Emily's prattle to bubble around her and wash over her head. Emily did not mind. She thought it natural enough for Winifred to have thoughts only for her new home, her new husband and her new life.

Winifred was not thinking about the future but of the past. She had not the slightest doubt about her love for John Gunn or of her desire to be his wife. If she felt any regret it was for the wasted years when they had known each other but had not known that they were in love, and the wasted months which followed when they had understood their feelings but hesitated to express them. Winifred was over forty and John Gunn was ten years older. They would not have many years together, and Winifred could not wait for those best years of her life to begin. But the joy with which she looked forward to the time ahead did not prevent her from remembering the times which lay behind her. A chapter of her life was drawing to an end, and she would have betrayed her past had she not spent that last evening thinking about absent friends.

A full decade after his death, the thought of Thomas still made her feel protective. She had always been impressed with his knowledge and his scholarship. But she had also always felt sorry for him. He had never disappointed her, but he had always disappointed himself. She still wanted to tell him not to worry about the books which he had not read, the galaxies which he could not identify through his telescope or the music which he could not play on his violin. She knew that, if he had lived for another ten years, she would never have seen him as confident as he was kind and he would never have believed that he could be admired for his gentleness as other men in his world were admired for their strength. Winifred blamed it all—

the uncertainty, the insecurity, the anguish—on Thomas's mother and she wondered what life would have been like as his wife without old Mrs. Spooner sharing their table and snoring in her room across the landing. Perhaps, at least, she would have persuaded Thomas that he was not on trial and that all he needed to prove he had proved to her already.

"You'll not be sorry to see me married, Emily, widowed sister hanging about all the time. The house will be yours at last. No sudden visitors."

"How can you say such a thing? I shall hate it."

"Then why doesn't Herbert come to live with you? I think it's stupid to put him in lodgings. You could persuade Frederick to let him come if you tried."

"I can't persuade Frederick of anything these days. Anyway, Herbert doesn't want to live here."

"Of course he does. He's just pretending he's independent. Ask him and he'll be here like a shot."

"You're wrong, Winifred. He doesn't want to come here. There's some sort of mystery. I thought he might be getting serious with a girl."

Winifred looked at her feet. "I don't think that he'll be marrying for some time, if that's what you mean, Emily."

"Praise be. I saw that friend of yours, Augusta Martin, looking at him and I thought, if she gets her claws into him she'll not let go. I know the sort."

"He could do a lot worse than Augusta."

"How can you say that, Winifred? She's a Catholic."

"She'd be just right for Herbert, steady him down."

"I hope you've not been trying to bring them together. You've always wanted to run other people's lives."

"And never run my own very well."

Emily walked across to the dressing table. She had noticed a tiny fingerprint on the top left-hand corner of the center mirror. She breathed on it and polished the glass clear with her handkerchief.

"Leave well alone, Winifred. That's what I always say. At least when things go wrong you don't get the blame."

"We'll see. Anyway, I'm really beginning to feel young again. I've been old for too long. I haven't been blamed for anything really bad for years."

. . .

Frederick Hattersley gave Winifred away for the second time, and for the second time paid for the modest and abstemious wedding breakfast. His wife—who had looked forward to a good cry—did not feel really happy until the couple had left for their honeymoon in Scotland and the guests had begun to drift away. For it was not until then that she felt absolutely certain, from careful observation, that Herbert had not the slightest interest in Augusta Martin. To his mother's delight, he hardly spoke to her all afternoon. Indeed, he hardly spoke to anyone. He seemed so deeply preoccupied that she convinced herself that he was in love with someone else.

"I hope," she said to Frederick, "that she's a good Methodist."

Her husband had no idea what she meant and did not feel sufficient interest in her opinions to ask.

Herbert struggled to put his financial crisis out of his mind. For it was not, as his mother would have put it, "in his nature to brood." But when the joviality was over and the last guest had gone, he sat amongst the crumpled wrapping paper and empty present boxes and tried to concentrate on the problem of raising six pounds, fourteen shillings and sixpence during the next six days.

In normal circumstances he would have thrown himself on the mercy of his Aunt Winifred. But she was on her way to an unknown destination in Scotland, and sitting next to her in the railway train was John Gunn, the friend to whom he would have turned if his aunt failed him. Jack Foster lay in a haze of pain and laudanum on the bed which Herbert had carried down into the living room in Southwell Street, and no man of sentimental disposition would even contemplate postponing the payment of rent to a friend in such a state of health. Abraham Wilkinson, Herbert felt sure, carried three times as much in his back pocket. But he could not possibly be asked for help a few weeks before his sister's wedding. He might even suspect that the whole marriage was being arranged in the hope of financial gain. His mother, he knew, would tell his father, and his father would want to know why the money was so desperately needed. The problem seemed so intractable that he put it out of mind until after the weekend.

It was a dismal Monday morning. Mrs. Foster had not expected her husband to last out the night and Herbert had sat with her in the living room, mopping the sweat from Jack's forehead and chest and giving him little sips of water whenever he said that his mouth was hot and dry. There had been a hemorrhage just before dawn. And as

Herbert had struggled to swallow down his nausea and helped to wash Jack and change his bedclothes he had felt sure that he was witnessing the final horror. But Jack was still alive at eight o'clock, and by nine, when his well-trained wife was telling Herbert that he would be late for work, the patient was having weak and tepid tea held to his lips in the hope that it would slake the fire in his throat.

There were bills to be paid at the shop, so, instead of going straight to his bench and losing himself in the work which he enjoyed, Herbert opened the cashbox to see if he could clear the accounts without writing to his father and waiting for the carefully addressed registered envelope which would be delivered by return of post. He counted out twelve pounds, five florins and half a crown and he smiled. He struggled to remember part of a poem which he had learned at school— "water, water everywhere and not a drop to drink."

When Herbert added up the bills, the total came to twelve pounds and thirteen shillings. It was not, he decided, worth writing to Sheffield for a few coppers. He would lend the cashbox sixpence until, at the end of the week, the regular registered letter arrived with the wages and a new cash float. There was, he thought, no point in a man who was in desperate need of six pounds worrying about sixpence— especially if looking after the pennies required him to go through the tedious business of setting out on paper a detailed statement of income and expenditure. It was the application of a principle which was to dominate his life.

There was only one big bill to pay. Hallam and Hill of Greyfriars Gate advertised their terms as "net cash on delivery." But Mr. Hallam was an enthusiastic Liberal, and when Frederick Hattersley was first introduced to him, the coal merchant had offered whatever assistance was necessary to help the scissor maker establish his Nottingham shop. Frederick Hattersley had accepted with gratitude what he interpreted as quarterly credit. Surprise combined with the hope that he had found a potential major customer to persuade Mr. Hallam to break the rule of a business lifetime. The coal merchant regretted his decision from the moment at which it was made and attempted to rectify his irresponsibility by supplying Messrs. Hattersley and Sons with a twelve-weekly account. It concluded with the item "Total Outstanding," and the promise that Mr. Hallam himself would be around to collect his debt within seven days. Herbert, who did not want the tedium of the coal merchant's company to last a moment longer than was necessary, counted out what Hallam was due before he arrived.

Even with the best hard coal at thirteen shillings a ton, eight pounds, one shilling and sixpence seemed a big bill. But it was winter, and if Jack had ordered a couple of hundredweight to take home, it was not the morning to complain.

Mr. Hallam bustled in and asked anxiously if the bill had arrived. Herbert allayed his worst fears and pushed eight pounds and a florin across the counter. The coal merchant examined his payment with his usual care.

"What's this?"

Herbert was not in a jovial mood. "It's your money. I'd have thought that you'd have recognized it. You looked hard enough."

"You've given me—"

"I know what I've given you."

"Do you know you've given me five pounds too much? Money must be easy to come by in this shop."

Herbert snatched at the bill. But Mr. Hallam pulled it away and held it in front of his customer as if it were a notice.

"What does it say?"

"Eight pounds."

"I don't think you can read. It's a good job I'm honest. That's a three."

Hallam pointed to the faded figure, written by some idle clerk with a pen which should have been dipped into the ink before the bill was made out. He slid five back across the counter and left the shop muttering, with obvious regret, "Good job I'm honest."

Herbert picked up the money and looked at it as if he couldn't quite believe what had almost happened. He had almost given away five pounds of his father's money.

His first reaction was fear. If his father found out, there would be hell to pay. His second thought was that with any luck his father would never have known about it. His third was that even without luck his mistake could have been kept from his father for several months. From then on, the train of thought moved irresistibly onward. He had been prepared to lend the company sixpence. Why should the company not lend him five pounds? After all, he was underpaid. And everything in the firm's bank account would be his one day. In any case, he was only borrowing the money. Gradually he would pay it back. He locked the front door of the shop and hurried around to Chapel Bar before he changed his mind or lost his nerve.

For the next seven days, Jack Foster's condition did not change.

Indeed, Herbert began to wonder if his father had been right to tell him to start selling up. At the rate the scissors were selling, the shop would be empty in a fortnight and Jack's coffin would pass by a property with a "For Sale" sign outside. He took nine pounds in six days, put seven in the cashbox and paid the rest to the jeweler. The letter of instruction which accompanied the usual cash float told him that, since Jack could not last another week, there was no reason why he should not advertise the emptying showcases in the classified columns of the *Evening Post*. Frederick Hattersley specified an asking price of slightly more than they had cost and drafted out the notice, combining the minimum of words with a maximum of exaggeration. "Superb, almost new, mahogany showcases..." Herbert was sure they would not sell. They went in two days. Since Jack Foster could not possibly last another week, it seemed entirely reasonable to avoid Frederick Hattersley's anguish by redeeming the pocket watch from the pawnbroker before he came over for the funeral. So part of the proceeds from the showcases was used to recover all the pledged property, though the larger part of the income was sent to his father together with a note which reported the sale.

"You'd think the lad could make plain figures," Frederick Hattersley said to his wife. "I can't make out if this is a five or an eight."

Jack Foster hung on to life for another three weeks, during which time Herbert was able to justify using his father's money to provide Charlotte Gregory with a silver buckle and the Foster family with various expensive items of food which none of them wanted and Mrs. Foster rightly said she was sure her lodger could not afford. When Jack died, kicking and struggling so hard that Herbert could barely hold him down on the bed, more than fifteen pounds had been stolen from the cashbox. Herbert believed that he had borrowed rather more, but had no doubt of his ability to pay it back before his father noticed.

CHAPTER TWENTY-THREE

CHANGING PARTNERS

Herbert did not expect his father to go straight to the shop as soon as Jack Foster's funeral was over. Frederick Hattersley went back with the other mourners to the Foster house in Southwell Street, for respect required the dead man's employer, oldest friend and greatest benefactor at least to break bread with his widow. But his anxiety to leave was clear from the moment he arrived. When he apologized to Mrs. Foster and told her why he had to go, the widow began to cry for the first time since Jack died.

"I want to get his tools. They ought to be kept bright and they ought to go to someone who deserves 'em."

Herbert looked hurt.

"You've got a set, just as good. You don't want two. When I get a real good apprentice, I'll promise them to him when he finishes his indentures. We'll pay for them, of course. Herbert will give you the money out of the cashbox."

Adding unexpected generosity to his characteristic sentimentality, Frederick quoted a price more than twice the actual value. With Herbert one pace behind him he swept out of the funeral tea.

The shop was almost bare and looked twice as big as when it had been filled with showcases. Frederick Hattersley counted ostentatiously, pointing to the marks on the floor which showed where the showcases once stood.

"How many did we have?"

"I can't remember."

"You can't remember! How much do you think they're worth? I suppose you can't remember that, either."

Herbert did not answer.

"I couldn't make out your figures on the bill of sale. Was it eight or five?"

"Eight, we've sold all eight."

The marks on the floor allowed no other reply.

"There was only money for five."

"Yes, that's right, five."

"From t'marks on the floor it looks like eight's gone."

"Perhaps it was eight, I'm not sure."

Herbert was rescued from further cross-examination about the showcases by his father's interest in the cashbox. Frederick tipped the small change onto the counter and unfolded the bills of sale and receipts which were kept under the lead weight.

"How much coal did we buy last quarter?"

Herbert could not remember. But he read the bottom of the bill and answered in pounds sterling rather than tons.

"Eight pounds' worth. Eight pounds, one shilling—"

"—and sixpence." His father finished the answer. "Eight, not five? Old Hallam can't write either."

"No, eight. Definitely eight."

"You must be eating it. Let's look at your little book."

Frederick opened the counter drawer, pulled out the account book and began to turn its almost empty pages.

The silence unnerved Herbert. "It's not quite up to date. I'm sorry. It's been Jack's illness and all that."

Frederick Hattersley stood up, holding the account book between finger and thumb as if he were afraid of its infecting him. He dropped it into the still-open drawer and began, silently, to climb the stairs into the workshop. Herbert followed and watched as his father began to examine Jack's tools. When one showed a speck of rust, he made disapproving noises at the back of his throat.

"You should have looked after them. You really should."

Herbert did not realize when the subject changed back from neglected tools to incomplete accounts.

"He that is slow to anger is better than the mighty and he that ruleth his spirit than he that taketh the city (Proverbs, chapter twenty-six, verse thirty-two)."

Despite his craftsman's pride, Herbert was surprised that even his father was making so much of his failure to keep Jack Foster's tools clean and bright. He was, as a result, totally unprepared for the next question.

"How much did you take?"

"How much what?"

"Do not provoke me. You know full well what I mean."

"No, I don't." Herbert sounded absolutely sincere, even though he was beginning to understand the full horror of his father's question.

"I'm not playing games. You stole upwards of twenty pounds."

"I didn't. I swear I didn't."

"Then how much did you steal?"

Herbert could not look his father in the eye.

"Ten. No more than ten. And I only borrowed it. I always meant to pay it back."

"I'm not going to argue with you. The money doesn't matter. Keep it. It's the last penny you'll get from me. All I want now is you out of this shop, out of the Empress Works and out of my sight."

"Just for borrowing a few quid?"

"You're a liar as well as a thief. It wasn't borrowed. You never meant to pay it back. You stole from your own father."

Herbert was bewildered by fear and by the conviction that his father's behavior was too unreasonable to be genuine. Not even his father could take ten pounds so seriously.

"You don't mean it. You couldn't disown me for a few quid."

"You keep saying 'a few quid.' Families live on a few quid for months. And the sons don't lie to the fathers. Not real sons."

"I'll pay it back—every penny. Just give me the chance."

He was still sure that his father would relent in a week or two—and that he could talk his way back into his father's affection and with his repayments buy himself a future at the Empress Works. But if his father persisted in a show of authority, during the few weeks of ostracism he would have to explain to Charlotte and—what was worse—her brother why he was exiled from his own family. The horror of being engulfed in such an avalanche of recrimination paralyzed him. He waited, without moving or speaking, to hear his father's next denunciation.

"We're done. Done forever. I'd stand everything except lying. I forgave your brother for walking out."

Herbert was shocked into contradiction. "You never have. You—"

"Don't be so daft. Why do you think I put money in his bank every month? I do it to prove that he's forgiven. I've paid money in every month so that, one day, he'll know that I've forgiven him. He'll know that, however long he waits before he comes back. But I won't forgive thieving."

"You'd forgive him anything. But not me. It's one law for him and another for me. You'll drive me away, like you did him."

"Not to Canada, I won't. You can't afford the fare unless you've stole more than I think."

"What will me mam think?"

"She'll bide by what I say. She won't like not seeing you—"

"Not seeing me?"

"I don't want you in Asline Road again. I'm not having a thief under my roof."

"I'm not a bloody thief. You don't even think I am. You just want to see the worst in me. You hate me for not being that bloody baby that died before I was born. And you want me to be like Joseph. Well, I can't be like either of them, whatever you want. I just can't do it."

"That's all rubbish. It's the dishonesty I won't forgive. I wanted you to be honest, that's all. I'd have forgiven you anything else like I forgive Joseph. I forgave your fornication."

It was then that Herbert, for all his simplicity, knew that it was all over. He was from that moment finished—finished with the family and finished with the firm. Father did not remind son of the shadow across their past—the farce of his leaving home, the shame of his night with the barmaid whose name he could no longer remember and the humiliation of his rescue from the Hussars in York—because he still carried the scar on his memory. He wanted to demonstrate the depth of his contempt—to show how much he despised Herbert, what shame he felt to admit that he was father to such a son. Herbert turned and walked toward the stairs without speaking. But his father had not finished.

"Another thing. You'll have to find new lodgings."

Herbert paused without looking back. He knew his father well enough to suspect that he had carefully planned a new assault. He waited for the blow to fall.

"From now on, I shall be keeping the Fosters. I'm glad to do it. But they're not going to use my money to buy your groceries. I shall write to Mrs. Foster tomorrow. If you're not gone by Friday, the money will stop."

As Herbert left the shop he heard his father's heavy boots kick Jack Foster's hitherto highly respected bag of tools from one side of the workshop to the other.

Herbert stepped out from under the protection of the shop doorway into the rough weather of the world outside. He was halfway along Alfreton Road before he realized that he had left his topcoat in the workshop. The rain, which had fallen only lightly on Jack's grave, had set in for the night. But Herbert had too little nerve and too much pride to go back.

"Let him sell it and get some of his money back," he said to himself. "Let him have it and enjoy me getting wet."

He turned up the collar of his jacket and thought of Charlotte Gregory. Normally, he had only to picture her in his mind in order for his spirits to rise. But on that afternoon, instead of the idea of Charlotte filling him with hope, it deepened his dejection. He had failed her. What was worse, she would soon find out that he had failed her. He no longer hoped that his estrangement from his father would be only temporary. He no longer even wanted a reconciliation. But somehow he had to justify his reduced circumstances to Charlotte and her brother.

Normally, he would have asked both John Gunn and Jack Foster to advise him and would then have agonized about which one to believe. But, walking on in the rain, he thought only of what Jack Foster would have told him to do. It was a mark of the pain which he felt at Jack's death. But it was also the result of the fear that John Gunn might give him advice he could not accept—advice to tell the truth. Jack's reaction—which he could invent for himself—would be more palatable. Herbert knew that Jack would have told him, "Don't let the bastard know it hurts." He would not have used that exact language, for he would have been unable to treat Frederick Hattersley with the open hostility which he felt for his enemies and the enemies of his friends. But after the ritual statements of admiration, and the essential call for proper filial respect, he would have told Herbert not even to let his father see the pain. Herbert would have promised not to whinge or whine and gone on to wonder what advice of value Jack would add to the usual cliché of strength and courage.

310

As he walked toward the Corn Market all he could think of was the moral which Jack had drawn from his triumph at the Goose Fair shooting gallery, when Herbert had shot three times and won three prizes. The proprietor of the gallery had not even attempted to disguise his annoyance at Herbert's success. But, having recovered from the shock of having to give away three tawdry prizes, he did his best to build success out of adversity by turning to the gawping crowd and urging them to follow Herbert's inspiring example.

"See this young man. Three prizes out of three. No reason why another sportsman shouldn't do the same. Who's going to do the same? Penny for three shots."

Jack, he decided, would have drawn the same moral from the tragedy which had engulfed him. He would have told him to resist all temptation to complain about the shoals and rapids, and ride the swift current down to the open sea. As Herbert walked mechanically into the saloon of the Black Boy Hotel he thought (as he had thought so often in the past) that Jack's advice was tailor-made for a man of courage and determination—a man like Jack himself. It was, however, of no value to a man like Herbert.

Herbert chose the saloon bar because, wet and bedraggled as he was, he was anxious not to run into any of his own friends, and he felt—sitting there without a coat surrounded by other men without coats—that he had already come down in the world. There was sawdust instead of carpet on the floor and it stuck to the toes of his waterlogged shoes. When he sat down on the bare wooden bench, his sodden trousers flapped against the back of his legs. To his surprise, the pint of bitter tasted no different from the pints of ale he had drunk in more salubrious surroundings. Indeed, it tasted so good that he bought and drank a second and then a third. It was while he was on his way through the fourth that he decided what to do.

Charlotte was now his family. Instead of worrying about how he could keep his troubles from her, he would allow her to help him bear them. He was not, however, even after four pints of best bitter, prepared to tell her the true reason for his reduced circumstances. All she needed to know was that she must protect him from the wickedness of the world—protect him by welcoming him into her house at once and marrying him as soon as possible. There was no reason why she should be told—or ever find out—the real circumstances which required the early assumption of her marital duties.

311

Some explanation would be necessary. But it did not have to be the truth. Jack would be proud of him. He was taking advantage of adversity.

The development of the idea was swift and inevitable. If a reason had to be invented, it was only sensible to think of something which was to his credit. After his fifth pint, he began a slow and uncertain walk to his now temporary lodging with the Fosters, so preoccupied with working out his plan that he did not even turn up the collar of his jacket against the rain. The living room was deserted and Herbert went over to the sideboard and pulled out one of the exercise books in which Jack had amused himself by designing presentation scissors. He turned page after page until he found a sheet of graph paper on which there was drawn neither coat of arms nor allegorical animal. Tearing it out, he began to write with an indelible pencil. Spots of moisture fell on the paper from his hand and arms, turning some of the words purple, as if they were meant to be emphasized with particular passion. A letter, he had decided, was essential. For he could not tell his story to Charlotte face-to-face. He wrote with remarkable speed and fluency.

> . . . how he found out does not matter. He would have behaved just the same, even if I had told him. He would never agree to me marrying an R.C., no matter what. He said straight out, either give her up or leave the firm . . .

Originally, he had meant to build the whole letter around a line he had heard in a melodrama at the Nottingham Playhouse—"Now you are my only wealth and I shall treasure you forever." But he could not be sure that Charlotte had not seen the play. So he simply ended the note with the dramatic promise "I shall come to you tonight."

When Willie Foster came home after tidying the flowers on his father's grave, Herbert gave him twopence to take the letter around to Charlotte Gregory and, having climbed the stairs with some difficulty, removed his shoes and jacket and fell asleep on his unmade bed. When he woke up two hours later, his collar and shirt were almost dry and his trousers smelled of damp, warm wool.

As he spluttered awake he struggled to remember why he felt so afraid. As his thoughts fell into shape he recalled how his life had changed. He had got up that morning saddened by the death of his friend and apprehensive about the day of mourning which lay ahead.

But he had been full of hope for the future. Now, as for the second time that day he swung his feet off the bed, he felt a moment's despair. He had been disinherited and dispossessed. Were it not for Charlotte he would be absolutely desolate. He must go to her at once and enjoy the comfort of her love and support. Gradually he began to feel again the hope which had flooded over him in the Black Boy. Charlotte would realize that, whatever the usual proprieties, she must now marry him without delay and provide the warmth and comfort which his own flesh and blood denied him. Some good would come out of unjust treatment.

He pulled off the crumpled trousers of his dark funeral suit and kicked off his mud-stained shoes without untying the laces. He piled them in a heap in the corner of his room and, having torn off the starched collar which still flapped from its back stud, he pulled his shirt over his head and threw it on top of the other discarded clothes. It took him only a moment to dress in his second best suit and the least frayed shirt that he could find. He could not wait to get to Charlotte and her reassuring embrace. He ran to her house.

He had to try the bell twice before he heard any movement in the darkened hall. Then Abraham Wilkinson opened the door. His hair was disheveled and his eyes red. He, too, had been drinking. But, unlike Herbert, he had not slept it off.

"I am surprised to see you."

"Didn't he bring my letter? I'll skin him alive when I get back." It seemed impossible that Charlotte had not told her brother that the love of her life was on his way to claim his bride.

"Charlotte showed me the letter."

"I said I'd come."

"I know. But we thought you wouldn't."

Herbert was bewildered by Abraham's perverse reaction to his message and irritated by his failure to lead the way into the drawing room. After a couple of silent moments on the steps, he asked resentfully, "Well, are you going to keep me talking on the steps?"

"Perhaps you better come in."

Abraham made clear from his tone of voice that the suggestion was made with great reluctance. Herbert settled in an armchair without invitation.

"Where's Charlotte?"

"She's up in her room."

"Well, tell her I'm here."

"She knows you're here. She saw you through the bedroom window. It's no good waiting. She won't come down."

Herbert could tell from Abraham's manner that Charlotte stayed in her room out of choice rather than incapacity. He waited for an explanation, as always hating the agony of uncertainty more than he would have hated the agony of knowing the worst. Abraham poured himself a glass of whiskey without offering one to Herbert, and drank it down in one gulp. Then he poured out a second measure and pushed the decanter toward his guest. He was sweating and the corner of his left eye had begun to twitch.

"She thinks you've let her down, old man. Truth to tell, so do I. We thought you'd realize when you'd thought about it for a bit. That's why we didn't expect you."

"Realize what?"

"That Charlotte can't possibly marry you now."

"Now what?"

"Now that you have no prospects."

"But I've given it all up for her."

"That's as may be. But it doesn't alter the position. You haven't got a penny to your name. Yesterday, you were going to inherit a business. Today, you own no more than the suit you stand up in. You don't even have a place to live. I wouldn't let her marry you now. You couldn't keep her."

"I want her to tell me. I want her to say that she's leaving me because I'm poor."

"Look here, old chap, it really is time for you to behave like a gentleman. Charlotte feels pretty badly let down. She won't see you. She's locked in her room sobbing her heart out, poor child. It's like a breach of promise. She's looked forward to it for weeks—a quiet wedding and then slipping away to Sheffield where nobody knew about the previous little mistake. And she's looked forward to being the wife of a factory owner and never having to worry about where the next penny is coming from. You've snatched all that away from her and very nearly broken her heart."

Abraham Wilkinson was astonished by the force of his own eloquence. Righteous indignation was a new and enjoyable experience. He decided to add outrage to indignation.

"I'm surprised you've come, Herbert. I really am. I thought better of you. A gentleman . . ."

"But I did it all for her . . ."

The choice between love and inheritance was no longer a fantasy. The decision which he had been forced to make that morning had become a fact of Herbert's life. Having invented the fairy tale, he had become part of it, and the feeling of outrage at being penalized for his romantic altruism was made even stronger by the thought that the punishment was being meted out by the woman for whom the sacrifice had been made.

"I did it all for her, don't you realize that?"

Herbert pushed past Abraham Wilkinson and began to climb the stairs, calling out, "Charlotte!" and adding forlornly, "It's me, Herbert."

Abraham hurried ponderously after him, blustering. "Look here, old man. This is not the way to behave. Go on like this and I'll send for a policeman to turn you out. You can't intrude on a lady like this. I really will send for a policeman."

Herbert had got as far as the first landing, when Charlotte appeared at the top of the stairs wearing the same wasp-waisted yellow dress which had enthralled him on the night when they had first talked of marriage.

"Do not dare to come a step further!"

Herbert froze, four feet below her.

"You have betrayed me, Herbert, and I shall never forgive you. Never! Can you not imagine the anguish that I have suffered today— suffered because of you? Leave this house. Leave it now!"

Before the echo of slamming doors had faded behind her, Abraham Wilkinson, sitting on the stairs with his head at the level of Herbert's knees, offered an idea which he had planned to suggest at the beginning of the confrontation.

"Look here, old chap. I don't think that everything's lost. Why don't you go back to your father and apologize? You can tell him that Charlotte's not a real Roman. Only took it up when she thought she might marry a papist. Tell him she's given it all up now and she'll walk down the aisle a Wesleyan or whatever chapel like a shot. She does want to marry you, old chap. But she's got to think of her future. Hope you savvy."

Herbert left the house and walked slowly back to the Market Place. By the time he arrived it was raining again. So he took shelter in the Black Boy Hotel. The men who had drunk with him in the middle of the day still sat on the wooden benches, and as he ordered his pint of bitter they greeted him like an old friend. It was warm in the taproom and there were pickled eggs and cold sausages for sale. As Herbert was drinking his third pint the barman unlocked the lid of a battered upright piano which stood in a corner by the fire, and an ancient on crutches hobbled across to the stool and began to thump out martial melodies. Several of the regulars performed solos and Herbert, abandoning all thought about building a fortune and reclaiming his bride, volunteered first "The Old Superb" and then "M'Old Shako." The reception was as rapturous as it had been during his evenings of fame. When he sat down again to consider how he could rebuild his life, he felt a new confidence about the future. All he had to do was think of a way of placing his foot on the bottom rung of the ladder, and his natural talent would propel him toward the heights. With a few shillings in his pocket, he would be able to make the first stride.

His overconfidence was interrupted in mid-optimism by the sight of a page from the *Evening Post* which had apparently been left in the hearth by the potboy who made the fire. It looked as if it had been held up in front of the grate in order to encourage the reluctant coals to catch fire, for a hole which had been burned in the center of the sheet was surrounded by brown scorch marks. Only a small part of the column of classified advertisements was readable.

The Ancient and Antediluvian Order of Buffaloes announce their intention of forming a Lodge at Mapperley. The inaugural meeting will be held at the Duke of Devonshire Hotel and will be followed by a smoking concert.

It was not an evening on which Herbert would have readily acknowledged the characteristics which he had inherited from his father. Nor did he feel particularly sympathetic toward the Noncomformist conscience which Frederick Hattersley had displayed to such devastating effect earlier in the day. But the years of weekly sermons and the evenings of unremitting Bible study had not been wholly in vain. Herbert had been sent a sign. He knew what to do.

Life had also changed for the Martin family. Robert Martin's discovery of yet more proof of the Raphael's authenticity had impressed his brother and daughter less than it had impressed the *Nottingham Evening Post*. But they had both been deeply affected by his belated admission that failing eyesight and advancing years had finally combined to force his retirement from the business of lace design. He had not earned fees of more than a few shillings a week. So the reduction in income was not a tragedy. The interest on his small savings, augmented by Augusta's occasional earnings from piano lessons, was enough to eke out a modest existence now that Patrick Ignatius Martin had moved into a home for ancient Irishmen. Uncle Pat still came round on a Sunday for a good meal, but he no longer took money out of the teapot on the mantelpiece and spent it on drink. Times were hard in Cavendish Street. But, for a year, they were also peaceful and Augusta enjoyed the peace.

However, when the tranquillity of her daily life was suddenly shattered, she accepted her fate with fortitude. Then, as was her nature, she began to prepare with methodical care for the changes which it was her duty to accept with good grace. The changes to which she had to reconcile herself were substantial. Clare and Kathleen were coming home.

Kathleen's decision to return to the town of her birth was not prompted by a sudden desire to be united with her family. Since entering the order of the Sisters of Mercy, she had become a child of the Church with no parents except those with which she had been supplied on the day of her admission to the order. But it was the will of her superiors that she should retrace her steps to Nottingham, there to teach at the new boys' school at number 25, 26 and 27 Derby Road, which had been opened as an annex to St. Mary's when St. Joseph's Elementary in Kent Street had been demolished to make way for the new Victoria Station. Kathleen wrote home to say that she would soon be in residence in the convent behind St. Barnabas's Cathedral. She ended her note with a message which Augusta read with some relief. Sister Maria Assumpta, as Kathleen was known in the order, would only be able to visit Cavendish Street rarely and briefly. Recognizing the advantages of a well-ordered existence, she suggested a regular arrangement. She would call at six o'clock on each Tuesday evening and remain until seven.

Sister Maria Assumpta arrived in Nottingham within a week of the letter announcing her return. Clare gave more than a year's notice of her intention. But the news of reunion filled Augusta with immediate foreboding. It could, she decided, lead to nothing but trouble all around.

Clare's return was arranged at the suggestion and under the pa-

317

tronage of Edward Gilpin Bagshaw, Bishop of Nottingham and, by convention, Hypaepa. Bishop Bagshaw was an unconventional prelate who possessed a strong opinion on every subject. Each one caused outrage in some members of his flock. Added together, the sum of his opinions and prejudices offended the whole diocese. He was a radical who claimed to have espoused progressive views on the conditions of the working class long before, in 1891, Pope Leo XIII published *Rerum Novarum*. Indeed, he had subsequently written a pastoral letter, *Mercy, Justice and the Poor,* which clarified, extended and corrected the Holy Father's views in a way which the pious regarded as certainly impertinent and probably blasphemous. Bishop Bagshaw was opposed to both laissez-faire and monopoly, both of which systems he believed to exploit the laboring masses. In their place he proposed nationalization. He was particularly enthusiastic about the public ownership of water. He denounced the Primrose League from his episcopal pulpit.

But as well as being a social radical, Bishop Bagshaw was also a theological reactionary, who forbade Catholics to enter the new Nottingham University College on pain of excommunication. Yet while he believed that the real fall from grace took place not in the Garden of Eden but outside the cathedral in Wittenberg, he was progressive to the point of perversity about liturgy and music. He played Mozart and Haydn during the sung mass and, to do justice to their music, he recruited women into the cathedral choir. When the Carl Rosa or the Moody Manvers Operatic Company came to town, he invited Catholic members of the company to perform from the sanctuary steps. Clare he actually discovered during one of her rare visits home. On the Saturday evening, one of the young priests told him that Robert Martin's daughter, the actress, was up from London. The Bishop was not a man to distinguish between performing arts. He invited her to sing Gounod's "Ave Maria" from in front of the marble altar rail with which, in a moment of madness, he had replaced the wrought-iron gates of Pugin's rood screen. Clare declined, explaining modestly that such a performance was beyond her talents. But looking at her most pious under her black lace mantilla, she announced that it was her wish to serve the Church in whatever way the Bishop chose.

Clare was travel-weary. She had lived for almost ten years in hotel bedrooms, waiting in vain to be cast in big parts. She longed to think of a good reason to return to Nottingham and sit by the fireside every night instead of strutting onto the stage and supporting a leading lady without half her talents and looks. Bishop Bagshaw provided an excuse. It was her duty to give up the life of bright lights and luxury and return to her native diocese. There were a thousand jobs—none of them specified and all of them unpaid—that she might do about the cathedral. Bishop Bagshaw felt certain that she had been called to glorify God and gratify the Bishop's interest in the theater simultaneously. She could also comfort her father in his declining years. After a long and increasingly dramatic correspondence, it was agreed that Clare would devote her life and talent to God—but not for another year. For Clare Martin felt it her duty to sail with Mr. Wilson Barratt to the United States of America, where they were to perform *The Sign of the Cross*. She would make her last bow at the end of the triumphant three months' American run which, it was confidently predicted, the company would be afforded by a discerning public.

Augusta began to prepare for Clare's return more than a year before the reunion was due. She was whitewashing the ceiling of what was to become her sister's bedroom when Herbert Hattersley made his unexpected call. She went to the door, believing that it was her father who was knocking, and intending to complain that, thanks to his carelessness in once more forgetting his keys, she had first to descend and then to reclimb thirty-seven stairs. The sight of Herbert on the doorstep filled her with simultaneous pleasure and embarrassment. She was delighted to see him, but ashamed that he should see her with her head tied up in a kerchief.

The sight of Augusta, sleeves rolled up and arms speckled with whitewash, had a strange effect on Herbert. He had meant to tell her exactly the story which he had told Charlotte Gregory—the choice which he had been forced to make between love and fortune, with special emphasis on his father's anti-Catholicism. But seeing her standing at the front door, round and practical, he found it impossible to tell an outright lie. So he compromised between invention and truth. Money had been lost. His father blamed him. They were temporarily estranged. He could only live during the period of reconciliation by re-creating his musical partnership with Patrick Martin. Augusta cross-examined him about the practical consequences of his unhappy condition.

"Have you talked to John and Winifred?"

"No. Nor will I."

319

"Why on earth not?"

"Winifred would tell my mam, and she would tell my father. I'm not having him think that I'm begging for help. I'll manage on m'own."

"Where are you living?"

"I'm still with Mrs. Foster. But I'm getting chucked out. I've got to find somewhere."

"Have you got any money?"

"Three pounds ten. I've pawned everything again and paid me father ten pounds. I'm not going to be beholden to him. I've kept three pound ten to see me through a couple of weeks."

"Thirteen ten. You must have pawned a lot."

"Everything I've got. Watch, best suit, best shoes, my tools. I've even pawned my tiepin. The one nice thing that I've ever had."

That was the moment when Augusta decided to take on the management of Herbert's life.

"Herbert, I don't know what we'll do with you. You'd better come here for a bit, until you can find somewhere better. There'll be nobody in Clare's room till next year. Mind, you'll have to help and I won't have you sitting about the house all day. You can keep an eye on Dad."

Augusta noticed that Herbert was trying not to grin. She hoped that he would fail to hide his feelings. He possessed an inexhaustible capacity for happiness, and it was that quality above all others which had made Augusta love him. She did not need him to be penitent and solemn. The object of her existence was to make him smile without letting him know that she was the cause of his pleasure. She walked over to the mantelpiece and picked up the teapot which stood between the candlesticks.

"You can't have your tools in pawn. You'll never get another job without them. A craftsman can't be without his tools. We'll get your watch out too, and your best suit. That tiepin can stay where it is."

CHAPTER TWENTY-FOUR

MYSTERIOUS WAYS

Finding Herbert Hattersley another job proved more difficult than Augusta Martin had anticipated. British industry was at the beginning of its long decline. Even in Sheffield, German scissors and spoons, forks and knives, which had so impressed the Sheffield manufacturers when they visited the Great Exhibition of 1851, had begun to appear on the shelves of ironmongers' shops. For in the Cutlers' Hall of that town, the grudging admission of the high quality and low price of the Zollverein's product had not been matched by any new ideas about how the new competition might be defeated. And as demand fell, more and more of what was made was spilled out of the machines which hissed steam and flashed sparks where time-served forgemen once tapped out their handmade pride. The sun had begun to set on the day of the craftsman. Finding a cutler's job in Sheffield would have been difficult. In Nottingham, it was impossible.

Much to Herbert's relief, Augusta, who took command of his life within twenty-four hours of his bag being unpacked in Cavendish Street, agreed that it would be futile to apply to any Sheffield company. For Herbert had left his previous employment in circumstances which he was unable, or unwilling, to describe, and in his home town questions about why Frederick Hattersley's lad had been sent down the road by his own father would have been unavoidable in that closed community. She did suggest that he look around in Nottingham, starting with the company at which he had finished his apprenticeship. Obediently he strolled past the gates of Hudson and Ross to see if a notice advertising vacancies had been hung from one of its wrought-iron spikes. There was no notice, but a razor grinder of Herbert's acquaintance was lounging on the pavement.

"Got the push, then?" he said amiably.

"Setting up on my own," Herbert told him and hurried on.

Augusta did locate a job sharpening and mending at I. and R. Morley's. But that, Herbert explained with impressive conviction, was not employment that could be accepted by a Sheffield tradesman. After a couple of months he was arguing that there was no hurry. He was again making a fair living in the clubs and at the smoking concerts.

In the patois of the area and time, fair living meant a better than living wage. But as a description of Herbert's earnings from his evening recitals, it had an additional meaning. Patrick Martin no longer acted as manager and accountant. Herbert made the bookings, agreed the payments and distributed the takings in a ratio of two to one in his own favor. Patrick, no longer capable of performing complicated piano pieces, had been relegated to the role of accompanist, expressly forbidden by Augusta to drink more than two pints in any one evening, collect the takings or call himself "Professor." All in all, it was a very satisfactory arrangement. However, much to the regret of the baritone soloist and impresario, Masonic dinners were still excluded from the list of possible engagements. Patrick Martin was too senile to exercise a Catholic veto, but Augusta acted as his moral proxy.

"It's like the baptism of desire," Kathleen explained during one of her brief weekly visits. "He would refuse to visit those idol worshipers if he knew what was going on."

As time passed, Herbert's work increasingly became his pleasure. During the long days of inactivity, he looked forward to the evenings with growing impatience. Augusta told him to "keep from under my feet while I'm clearing up," and Robert Martin talked with growing obsession and decreasing sense about the "Old Master" which changed with alarming frequency from a Raphael to a Rembrandt and back again to a Raphael. But after eight o'clock, life was all admiration and applause. He usually got back to his lodging after

Augusta and her father had gone to bed. But no matter how late his return, he would be up for breakfast, dipping his bread in the bacon fat and describing the previous night's triumph. Augusta decided that he was enjoying himself far too much, and made a special journey to see John Gunn and Winifred in order to enlist their assistance in persuading Herbert to return to gainful employment and the boredom which was the lot of the working classes.

John had already made feeble attempts to advise and console his young friend. And Winifred had caused much offense by offering him money. But it had been decided between them—much against the instincts of even a Winifred—that there was nothing to be gained by "nagging the lad."

"He's not a lad," Winifred replied. "He's nearer thirty than twenty."

"All the more reason for minding our own business." John was delighted to have made a rare riposte. But he added, "It's important to be there to help if we're asked." He hoped that the request would never come.

So, for months, aunt and friend contented themselves with inviting Herbert and Augusta and her father to Sunday dinner and asking anxious little questions about everything being "all right." Herbert observed the rules of life which had been laid down for him by Jack Foster. So, even when uncertainty about his future gnawed at his solar plexus or Charlotte Gregory's failure to reply to his notes made him doubt—for a brief moment—that life was worth living, he always gave the same reply. "I'm all right, always am."

He continued to be all right into the summer and John Gunn always accepted his assurances with visible relief. Winifred, on the other hand, was irritated by what she regarded as a perverse refusal to open his heart. She knew exactly the remedy for all his troubles. But she could not arrange the cure until he admitted the illness. Augusta, who had discovered from daily observation that Herbert was a more complex character than she had once believed, spent the months wondering if he could really possess a capacity for happiness so infinite that he could never feel the emotions that come with experience of life's pains. It made him in her eyes a saintly figure, capable of rising above the tribulations of this world. And it was in those terms that she described to both the Gunns his apparent willingness to spend the rest of his life singing for small groups of half-intoxicated men.

"He doesn't realize what trouble he's storing up for himself. He thinks that he can float along from day to day without worrying about anything. He's like a big good-tempered dog. Kids can pull him about. He can be locked out in the yard or get a thorn in his foot, but give him a good meal and a warm fire and he'll go to sleep smiling."

"Do dogs smile?" John Gunn asked, not so much to tease Augusta as to deflect the subject from the dangerous road which it was taking toward the need for someone to speak to Herbert "in a fatherly sort of way." The pause which his question produced gave him false hope that he might change the whole conversation from a discussion of Herbert's future to an examination of one or two eternal truths. "They say that animals can't smile because they have no souls."

"You know very well what she means, John." Winifred was so irritated by the obvious attempt to deflect the conversation from the subject of the duty that she almost added that Augusta could hardly have pursued her canine metaphor by describing Herbert as jumping up and licking her face or rubbing himself against her leg. She resisted the temptation. Nor did she mention that what in dogs is sentimentally described as smiling is the result of flatulence. Instead, she seized the opportunity which Augusta's expression of concern provided. "She means that he hasn't enough sense to see the trouble he's in. We always said that if we were asked to help we would."

John was about to say that what they had meant was that they would help when Herbert himself requested their aid, and Augusta was on the point of insisting that she had never said that Herbert had no sense. But Winifred was in full spate. The flood was irresistible.

"You have to talk to him, John, man to man. Heavens, you claim to be his friend. It's what friendship is for, telling each other what to do."

"And what do I tell Herbert?"

"You tell him to get things straightened out."

"They're sorted out already. He paid back all the money his father says he stole, even though he only lost it. And his father sent him a receipt as if he'd paid a bill for scissors."

"Exactly." Winifred was in a mood to regard every criticism as approval, and every refutation as evidence that she was right.

"You see, John, we're halfway there already. Tell him to go to his father and ask for his forgiveness. I know Frederick Hattersley. He wants to be loved, the same as the rest of us. And he particularly wants Herbert to love him."

"I'm not sure. Mr. Hattersley's a hard man."

"You're just saying that as an excuse, an excuse to avoid having to talk to Herbert—man to man. Man to man!" Winifred snorted offensively.

It was John Gunn's habit not to be provoked by his wife. "I shall talk to him. But I shall make sure that I say the right thing: something that helps. Suggestions welcomed."

Winifred was past being either calmed or humored. "If you want a suggestion, I'll give you one. Tell him that all his father wants is a loving son and respectable grandchildren. Tell him to go home to Sheffield and say that he's sorry. Tell him that he has to put that awful woman out of his head and he was a fool to think that his father wouldn't find out."

"There was nothing to find out." Augusta was disturbed by the direction Winifred's mind was moving.

"Well, perhaps not. Just tell Herbert to see sense and settle down with Augusta here."

John had more courage than Winifred realized. "I say it with no pleasure, for a husband should never have to speak to a wife in this way. But sometimes you shame me, Winifred. I do not understand how a clever woman can be so foolish and so cruel. Let's change the subject before we upset Augusta any more."

"That's all right," said Augusta. "What Winifred says is true."

Herbert passed his summer days at Trent Bridge cricket ground, hurrying off just before the close of play at half past six to change into the appropriate clothes for his evening performance. His real pleasure was not watching the match but telling whoever happened to be within earshot how the match should be played. No ball was ever bowled without Herbert explaining that it should have been of a fuller length or on a different line. Each stroke was followed by comments about the batsman's failure to move his feet or apparent inability to hold his head steady right up to the moment of impact.

After moments of undeniable success or indisputable brilliance, he prefaced his criticism with judgment: "Lucky, very lucky." No one who heard him could doubt that he was remarkably knowledgeable about the game. But most people who listened to his persistent comments wished that he would be knowledgeable more quietly.

Between overs, he always explained to his Nottingham cronies how a Yorkshire bowler would have shattered the wickets and how a Yorkshire batsman would have driven every ball to the boundary.

Next year, he promised, Yorkshire visitors would show them how the game should be played. He had believed since childhood—with, it must be said, some justification—that the Sheffield cutler was the best in the world. During the summer of 1894, he developed the conviction that Yorkshire cricketers enjoyed a similar distinction. The view was reinforced by Yorkshire's absence from Trent Bridge that year.

It was to Trent Bridge that John Gunn was sent by Winifred after she had chosen to interpret one of his constant prevarications as the promise of immediate action. Late one Friday night, after he had been challenged for the thousandth time to say whether or not he intended to do his duty, he answered, "I suppose so." It was fatigue rather than sudden determination which made him abandon his usual habit of reciting the difficulties of treating a man of twenty-six as if he were a child of five. But Winifred accepted his reply as a sacred promise given by husband to wife. On the morning after the thoughtless comment was made, she laid out her plan over breakfast. She happened to know that Herbert would spend the day watching cricket. It would be an ideal opportunity for John to discharge his responsibilities—a view which, like Herbert's judgments about Yorkshire cricket, was reinforced by ignorance. Having never been to Trent Bridge herself, Winifred believed it to be a larger version of the village green on which she had once seen Herbert play. She had a romantic vision of the two men pacing the long grass beyond the boundary and thinking their profound thoughts about duty and destiny to the sound of birds singing in the branches of heavily laden apple trees. John Gunn simply found the moral pressure too great to resist.

He arrived at the ground at lunchtime and made his way to the Trent Bridge Hotel, in which he assumed Herbert would spend the forty minutes' break in play. The air in the long bar was thick with smoke, and the smell of beer was so strong that John feared that he would be choked by the alcoholic fog. He pushed his way between the groups of men, looking with distaste at their tankards and glasses but envying the camaraderie of their intense conversation. He disapproved of Herbert being amongst them almost as much as he hated being there himself. But the young man had to be found. So he jostled his way through the crowd, pausing only to stare at the faces which were half turned away from him. John Gunn was a methodical man.

By the time he got to the far end of the bar, he had looked into the face of every drinker. Herbert was not there.

Nor was he in the tearoom, which smelled of stale bread and overripe tomatoes, nor in the lavatories, which smelled of the urine which had spilled out of the clogged vitreous enamel stalls and spread across the brick floor. Herbert was, he decided, not at Trent Bridge at all but engaged on some disreputable pursuit which he had chosen to keep from Augusta Martin by pretending that he was spending an innocent day watching cricket. It was a relief to step out into the autumn sunlight and take deep breaths of the clean air. John Gunn tried to calm himself by thinking of next Sunday's sermon and wondering if he could contrast the man-made squalor of the Trent Bridge Hotel with the God-given purity of the atmosphere outside. He was trying to make up his mind whether or not he could admit to having been in the long bar when he reached Parr's Tree—the great elm which grew inside the boundary and was dedicated to the memory of the only man to have hit a six over its spreading branches. In its shade, several families were playing their own scratch games of cricket with battered bats and balls which were no longer round. Amongst them was Herbert Hattersley with Willie and Jack Foster.

Herbert greeted John with genuine pleasure. "It's right good to see you. I never thought she'd let you out." He laughed hugely at his own joke. "First time this year and t'season's nearly over."

Willie Foster—whose turn to bat had only just begun—began to complain. "It's not fair. It's my innings and nobody's bowling."

Jack tried to pull the ball from Herbert's hand. Herbert hung on, and said reproachfully, "Let's give Mr. Gunn a bowl. That's polite."

"I've really come to have a word with you."

Herbert turned and bowled Willie a fast yorker. It passed over a pile of coats which were acting as a wicket.

"Out!" cried Jack. "It's my turn again."

"I wasn't ready," Willie complained.

"Herbert appointed himself umpire and held up a finger. "I've got to talk to Mr. Gunn for a bit. Practice catching. We'll be back before the umpires come out."

The two men sat down on the grass by the boundary rope.

"I suppose Aunt Winifred sent you."

"Why do you say that?"

"Because I've known her longer than you have. And I know you

327

an' all. I've never seen a man look so hangdog. You've come to say something that you don't want to say. And she's sent you."

"I've come to say something for your own good."

"Then get on wi' it."

"First of all, stop talking like that. You only become a Yorkshire tyke when you want to show how tough you are. You don't have—"

"I am a Yorkshire tyke and I'm not ashamed of it."

"All right, but just talk to me in a way I can understand."

Herbert grinned and pulled blades of grass out of the ground. His defenses were down. "I suppose you want to talk about jobs."

"I want to help you to find one."

"Have you suddenly bought a cutler's company or is Mr. Joseph Tyzak a friend of yours?"

To Herbert's disappointment, John did not ask who Joseph Tyzak was. So he was unable to exhibit the contempt which he felt for anyone who did not recognize the name of Sheffield's most famous scissor maker.

"Does it have to be cutlery, Herbert? There are a lot of other things you could do."

"I didn't learn much from my father. He didn't try to teach me and I was no scholar. But he did teach me one thing. Be proud of your trade. When our Joe went off to Canada, Father made him promise not to sell his watch and to stay a cutler. Self-respect, John. You and Jack Foster used to tell me that self-respect was the most important thing. I keep mine by being a cutler in work or out."

"But you earn your living singing."

"But that's not work. I'm an unemployed cutler, a time-served scissor maker who can't get a job. I'd rather be that than a baker."

"I wasn't offering you a job in the bakery."

"I wouldn't take it if you did."

There was a long pause while Herbert thought of apologizing and John considered telling him not to be so rude. The pavilion bell broke their silence.

"We'd better go and sit down," said Herbert.

"I'll come with you."

"You won't like the kids. They don't sit with their hands folded like we used to do in Sunday school."

"I'll risk it."

"Do I get more advice, or have you done enough to stop Aunt Winifred from nagging at you?"

"I shall tell her I tried. But I shall know that I didn't try very hard. She'll try herself next time."

"Answer will be t'same. It's pride, John. If she doesn't understand that, she doesn't understand much."

"She'll understand. And she'll be pleased to see you with Jack Foster's lads."

"No doubt she will. But she'd be happier to see me with Augusta Martin."

"She's a matchmaker, Herbert. Middle-aged women are. You mustn't mind."

"Well, I do. It makes me feel so soft. It's not just because . . ." He could not quite bring himself to mention Charlotte Gregory's name. "It's because Augusta's my pal. We get on fine. We have jokes and I takes things from her that I wouldn't take from most people. But I'd no sooner think of her like . . . like . . . like . . . like that than I'd . . ."

The invention of a suitable comparison was too much for him. So he subsided from incoherence to silence and applauded grudgingly as the Nottingham batsmen strode out to the wicket. The Foster boys whooped their way back to the bench, demanding lemonade, and Herbert threw Jack a threepenny bit. As the two men walked back toward the pavilion Herbert began to complain about the field that the Sussex captain had set and his choice of bowlers. It would, he announced to the crowd in general, be quite different May next year when Yorkshire came to Trent Bridge. Then they would see how cricket should be played. Was there, John Gunn wondered, ever a time when Herbert sat in Sunday school with his arms folded in front of him?

Together they watched the cricket until tea. Then they trailed behind the young Fosters as the two boys made a desperate dash to the open space under Parr's Tree. By the time the men caught up with them, coats had already been piled up to make a wicket and young Jack was taking strike against Willie's bowling. A dozen other scratch games went on around them on wickets which were pitched so close together that one batsman jostled another, and bowlers, running in to deliver thunderbolts, collided with fielders from other games, desperate to save a snick or drive from reaching an imaginary boundary. John Gunn did not enter the maelstrom of leaping, shouting, pushing, falling, fighting little boys. But Herbert stepped majestically into their midst, towering above them. He remained serene as first one urchin fell over his feet and then another cannoned into him and bounced off again like a train hitting the buffers. Willie was about to begin an absurdly long run in preparation for delivering a ludicrously slow ball, when Herbert held up a regal hand in the manner of umpire Fred Coward, who had been the star of the Notts versus Gloucester match the previous week. Herbert's intervention was too sudden to allow a dignified deceleration or a controlled halt. Willie simply fell to the ground. Young Jack shouldered his bat in a fair imitation of Arthur Shrewsbury waiting for the sight screen to be moved, as Herbert approached him.

"Nay, nay. You know better than that. Shoulder pointing down the wicket. If I've told you once, I've told you a hundred times, you've got to be sideways on."

Herbert took the ancient bat out of Jack's hand and composed himself into an almost perfect stance: bat behind right foot, weight distributed equally between the feet, left shoulder pointing directly toward the bowler.

John Gunn watched and felt ashamed that he had first gone to look for Herbert in a public house. Then he remembered that when he had not found him there, he had assumed that his talk of a day at Trent Bridge had been no more than a subterfuge. He tried not to think of where he had suspected Herbert was or what he had suspected Herbert was doing. Before him was the endearing truth. Herbert, his smoking-concert mustache clipped to perfection and his hair slicked down with enough brilliantine to grease the axles of every train on the Midland Railway, was playing with the sons of his dead friend. His trousers were creased at front and back in the style favored by the Prince of Wales. His waistcoat was double-breasted and had too many buttons to be really respectable. But he was spending his Saturday afternoon teaching two little boys how to play cricket. John's first instinct was to run home, rejoicing, and tell Winifred of a sinner saved. Then he realized what her reaction would be. She would take his story as proof positive that Herbert ought to settle down with Augusta and raise cricketers of his own.

For Herbert, the autumn was a theatrical triumph with more engagements offered than he could accept. But it was also a time of personal tragedy. Patrick Martin remained sober and accepted the role of accompanist. A note from Charlotte Gregory asked solicitously for news of his health and, more significantly, the health of his father. At first the letter stirred up all the old longings. Then, realizing that he could

330

never be reconciled with her until he was reconciled with the master of the Empress Works, Herbert plunged into black despair. But, having carried the letter in his pocket for more than a week, he then came to a conclusion which allowed him to tear it up without regret. Charlotte still wanted him. And that made him feel happy. But she wanted the works as well. The works were not in his gift. Without consulting John Gunn or imagining what Jack Foster would have said, he decided that Charlotte had been a high romantic episode which was over. Soon, somebody just as beautiful, just as fashionable and just as passionate would come into his life. And she would be single. In the meantime, he would sing every night of the week, be applauded at the end of his performance and receive furtive smiles from the married women in the audience. He had again experienced that sort of sadness that makes young men happy.

Augusta continued her determined attempts to find him employment suitable to her standards of dignity. Sometimes, while sitting by the fire, she would read out sections from the situations-vacant columns in the *Evening News* as if she believed the advertisements for blacksmiths' strikers and wages clerks were of general interest to the family. Herbert, knowing that they were intended for him, would reject them either because they needed neither skill nor qualification or because they required skills and qualifications which he did not possess. Augusta's alternative strategy was to break his addiction to applause and cries of encore by preventing him from singing six nights a week. It was equally unsuccessful, but she never gave up. She worked particularly hard during the half-dozen days each year when Herbert—true to the traditions of his family—saw the world through watering eyes and sneezed down an increasingly sore and swollen nose. Augusta's invariable remedy was a week at home in the even temperature of the Martins' living room.

Herbert always rejected the idea out of hand, as he rejected the various patent medicines which had been bought on his behalf at Boot's Family Chemists after recommendation by a shop assistant who could barely read the labels. Her hopes of bread poultices (front and back to relieve the congestions) and her dreams of mustard baths (to sweat it out) abandoned, Augusta concentrated her energies on what she believed to be persuasion.

"It's just stupid. You'll just get worse."

"I'm all right."

"I don't know how you'll manage to sing."

"He has a double whiskey ten minutes before he starts. It clears his throat a treat." Patrick Martin was trying to be helpful. His only reward was a stony stare from Augusta and a look of absolute hatred from Herbert, who began to sneeze.

"That's better, much better. It's loosening, loosening on your chest. A couple of days in bed . . ."

Between sneezes Herbert told her, "I've got bookings."

"Bookings can be canceled, can't they, Uncle?"

It was Herbert who replied. "Not mine. I'm not letting 'em down."

"I could get Horace Healey. He'd be glad to stand in for a couple of nights. He's got the sack from the Robin Hood for fighting with the cellarman. But his voice isn't bad."

"Horace Healey won't sing in place of me."

Patrick Martin totally misunderstood the cause of Herbert's annoyance, and attempted to recover his position by ingratiation. "Not as good as you, Herbert. Not as good as you. Leastways, not when your throat's not sore."

Augusta was about to seize on the admission when Herbert cut her off.

"I'm going. There's no more to be said."

"It's not as if you need the money." It was Augusta's last throw.

"How do you know I don't need the money? You don't know that."

"You spend nothing."

"Well, I need the money."

"Are you up to something, Herbert?"

It was Augusta's accusation that prompted Patrick Martin to be helpful for the third time.

"He gives too much away. Pounds. He gives Mrs. Foster seven and six a week. He's too generous. Buys too many rounds. I've told him so."

"For Christ's sake . . ."

There was a moment of shocked silence as the sound of blasphemy and the fear of profligacy echoed around the room. It was broken by the entrance of Robert Martin, who walked into the room reading out loud from the *Evening Post*. As always, he was only fully aware of the small part of the world which revolved around his Old Master.

" 'Mr. Robert Martin, a retired lace designer of 5 Cavendish Street, Woollaton, Nottingham, has at last found evidence to prove that a painting he brought back from France, twenty years ago, is a genuine

Raphael. Mr. Martin told a *Post* reporter that he had recognized the picture as soon as he saw it in a Paris furniture shop. But it was not until he got a letter from the British Museum—' "

Augusta had seen the letter from London weeks before. "Father, we're talking. Talking seriously."

Robert Martin was not in a mood to be silenced. " '—last week that he knew it was worth one thousand pounds.' "

His brother shook him by the hand.

"You know it's all rubbish, Uncle Pat. You shouldn't encourage him."

"Why shouldn't I now? Everybody needs a bit of magic in their lives. The Old Master is his. Let him have his dream. It does no harm."

Robert, unaware of the philosophical dispute which he had caused, proudly read the headline—" 'Nottingham Man's Fortune Find' "— and disappeared into the studio to gloat over his treasure. Herbert took advantage of the diversion to begin his escape toward the stairs.

"If you're back before midnight, I'll come down and make a pot of tea." Augusta knew it was only a small incentive to an early night, but it was better than nothing.

There was a moment when she thought that, either by chance or by choice, Herbert had swallowed her bait. For she heard what she first thought was the sound of footsteps in the hall downstairs before she had even fallen asleep. She lay absolutely still, straining to hear a second sound which would confirm that Herbert had returned. But all that broke the silence was the clock striking eleven. Herbert was never home so early. The sound of footsteps was, she decided, the product of hope and imagination. Pulling the blankets over her head for comfort, she fell sadly to sleep.

The crash that awoke her twenty minutes later seemed to come from the garden, and after a few seconds of startled confusion Augusta decided that it was the sound of breaking glass. When she heard what she took to be a whimper of pain, a clear picture formed in her mind. Herbert, drunk, had fallen through the kitchen window as he lurched toward the back door. Anger was quickly overlaid by fear. Perhaps he lay on the kitchen floor or in the yard, bleeding to death. So great was her anxiety that Augusta rushed for the bedroom door without covering her nightdress with the old coat which passed for a dressing gown. Before she reached the landing, a second crash—this time the certain sound of splintering wood—reverberated around the house. It was followed by a rattling of pots and pans and the dull thud of a heavy object hitting the floor. Halfway down the stairs, Augusta heard the most frightening sound of all.

"Then put it down, you bastard."

The voice was not Herbert's.

By the time Augusta reached the hall, four men were huddled in the kitchen door. One of them—an unshaven youth in his late teens —was kneeling on the floor, holding his head in his hands. Blood was running between his fingers. A second man had his right arm locked around Herbert's neck, and as he pulled the still-immaculate head further and further back he punched at whatever part of the struggling body his left fist could reach. Herbert himself was brandishing a bloodstained poker in the direction of an elderly man in moleskin trousers who, determined not to risk the fate which had befallen his kneeling confederate, skillfully kept out of reach and made up for his reluctance to join battle by encouraging the others.

"Break his back, Sean, if the bastard won't drop it."

Suddenly the youth on the floor lunged forward. Herbert kicked him in the ribs, and he fell back again, cursing. But the man in the moleskin trousers recognized that his victim was off balance and, catching the poker in both his hands, he wrenched it out of Herbert's grasp. Herbert turned toward him and Augusta saw first the blood running from his nose and mouth and then the object which he held under his arm. It was a roll of dirty canvas and, to Augusta's horror, she recognized it as the Old Master. For most of her life she had felt nothing but loathing for the painting. It had exerted a consistently disruptive influence on her life. But the discovery that it had been cut out of its frame scandalized her. It was her father's icon and it was being defiled.

There was only a second in which to worry about the picture. The man in the moleskin trousers swung at Herbert with the poker—first hitting him on the forearm and then, when his guard was down, smashing it into his ribs.

"Drop it, you bastard!" he cried again.

Augusta echoed his sentiment.

"Let them have it, Herbert. It's worth nothing. Give it them. It's not worth getting killed for."

"For God's sake, listen to her. Holy Mary Mother of God."

For the first time, Augusta noticed that Patrick Martin was cowering in a dark corner, crossing himself and calling on the army of

334

saints and martyrs to protect him. Augusta ran at the man with the poker and caught it as he swung it at Herbert's head. He pulled it out of her grasp and she noticed, through her fear, the soot on the palms of her hands. Herbert, a forearm across his windpipe and his lip split, was barely audible.

"Get out of the way. They'll kill us both."

Augusta grabbed the poker again. "Drop it, Herbert. Give it to them."

"For God's sake, Gussie."

He had never called her that before.

"I can't look after you and the bloody picture." The disheveled youth rose to his hands and knees and Herbert kicked him in the ribs again. "Get back upstairs."

The man who had Herbert's neck in an armlock loosened his grip for a moment. Herbert elbowed him in the face.

"Give it them, Herbert. It's worth nothing."

"It's ours and we're keeping it."

The disheveled youth rose for the third time and for the third time was kicked to the ground.

It was not until the next day that Augusta thought about Herbert describing the picture as "ours," for at the moment that he claimed part possession, the man in the moleskin trousers raised the poker above his head and held it there in both hands like an executioner taking careful aim at the neck on his block.

"Let him hit me," prayed Augusta. "In God's name, let him hit me."

He hit Herbert on the shoulder and Augusta heard something break. It was then that Robert Martin called down from the landing. His voice was filled with rage.

"I shall kill anyone who touches that painting."

"Christ, the house is full of men." The arm suddenly disappeared from around Herbert's throat.

"He's got a gun." The unshaven youth dived through the battered front door.

Robert Martin appeared at the bottom of the stairs holding in his hand a round ebony six-inch ruler. The man in the moleskin trousers walked warily backward holding the poker defensively in front of him as he made a tactical retreat. Robert, hardly able to speak for anxiety, darted across to Herbert, who was leaning against the wall.

"Is there any blood on the picture? If you've got blood on the picture . . ."

The thought was too terrible to be sustained.

. . .

Herbert, with a reckless disregard for his recently acquired reputation for bravery, yelped like a whipped puppy every time the doctor touched him. After almost an hour of poking and shouting, the diagnosis was complete. The right collarbone was broken. So was a bone in the left forearm. Two ribs were fractured and two more were probably cracked. The split lip, having been stitched, would heal completely and leave no impediment to his speech. There would however be a scar. He suggested that the mustache be allowed to grow to a length which hid the disfigurement. Rest was essential. A bed should be brought downstairs. To avoid "complications," Herbert should remain in it for at least six weeks.

When Sister Assumpta called next day for her weekly visit, the house had already been transformed into a sanatorium. Augusta's single bed had been put up in the studio, and Herbert—looking and feeling infinitely pathetic—lay in it, his bandages hidden by the best Martin counterpane. His face was bruised and swollen both from the blows and from the stitches. Augusta was preparing beef tea, which she hoped the patient would drink through a straw.

"It's God's will," said the Sister of Mercy. "And God's punishment. It's punishment for Dad worshiping that picture. It was a graven image."

"It's a bit unreasonable to break Herbert's bones because our father worships false gods."

"Herbert's been punished for his dissolute life. You're the one who's been treated unfairly. You're..." Sister Assumpta bit her tongue to avoid further bad feeling and then tried to put her point more tactfully. "I do feel sorry for you, Augusta, waiting hand and foot on a perfect stranger for months. And a man at that."

To the nun's surprise, her sister was smiling.

"God works in mysterious ways."

CHAPTER TWENTY-FIVE

IN SICKNESS AND IN HEALTH

At first, the agony was almost unbearable. The weak mixture of laudanum and water which Augusta allowed Herbert to sip made his head spin without even numbing the nerves which sent messages to his brain from his broken arm and collarbone. For a fortnight, he lay on his back, itching under the bandages which held his broken ribs together and trying to convince himself that he would feel better tomorrow. Those early weeks were, according to the doctor, a great test of his physical strength and moral courage. Herbert passed both —the first thanks to the years of football and cricket which had not been quite washed away by the evenings of ale and stout, and the second because of his unquenchable optimism. The belief that everything would turn out for the best never deserted him—despite much evidence to the contrary. When he examined, in his shaving mirror, the fast-healing cut on his top lip, he even looked forward to wearing a bushy mustache which would be needed to cover the scar.

Augusta allowed him few visitors. John Gunn came round, morning and night, to perform the intimate tasks which she could not decently carry out. Winifred called in each evening to make sure that "everything was all right." But for the first fourteen days, apart from them and the older Foster boy, the only person allowed into the studio was Emily Hattersley. Robert Martin, his Old Master safe though cut from the frame, was content to spend his days guarding the picture in his bedroom. His brother Patrick was so afraid of the signs of mortality that he gladly accepted his exclusion from the sickroom.

Even Emily's visits were unwelcome. Winifred Gunn insisted on writing to tell her sister of Herbert's injuries, although Augusta predicted that no good would come of it. Augusta was wrong. The immediate result was a reply containing a five-pound note. It ended with a message of concern and good wishes from Herbert's "loving father" —a message of which Frederick Hattersley was totally unaware. No mention was made of a possible excursion to Nottingham. But the five-pound note had barely been put inside the teapot on the mantelpiece when there was the sound of a hansom cab outside the door and Emily was rattling the rusty knocker. Mother had to be restrained from embracing bruised and battered son, and she broke down in tears when, the curtains being drawn, she saw the great wound on his lips. She gave Augusta another five-pound note before leaving. Winifred and John passed an intriguing evening at home, discussing whether Emily had told Frederick that she was visiting her son or had pretended that she planned to pass the day with her daughter in Doncaster.

"Did she mention his father?" Winifred asked Augusta next day. "It's not natural him writing Herbert off like this."

"Not in my hearing. And she made a point of saying that the five pounds was from her pin money."

"Let me know if you need any more."

One of Winifred's favorite sayings was that a little help is worth a lot of pity.

When the sharp pain of fractures turned into the dull ache of healing, Herbert began to enjoy himself. He complained a lot, but they were the complaints of a man who had decided to make the most of his condition. When he complained about the length of his hair, Augusta offered to cut it and her offer was angrily rejected. When his back became sore from the days of immobility, Augusta offered to rub it with methylated spirit and was told to send for young Jack Foster. When his face began to itch under three weeks' stubble, Augusta offered to shave him and was told to balance the shaving mug and mirror on the bed.

"When I think of the things I did for you that first day, you might at least let me hold the mirror."

Herbert turned bright red. "Don't you dare say anything like that again. To me or to anybody. Anyway, it's easy enough."

Without stropping his razor (a task which he could not have performed half lying down), he began to shave under his chin. He cut himself along the line of his jawbone and immediately a drop of blood fell onto the sheet.

"See what you've done..." The reproof lasted for only a second. "It'll wash. Don't bother about it."

Herbert did not bother about it, or about much else, and during the days of recovery and the weeks of convalescence he bothered about less and less as Augusta bothered about more and more. As a result, they began to develop what the fast-improving patient regarded as the right relationship. He was doing Augusta a favor by allowing her to look after him. And Augusta was showing appropriate gratitude. It was therfore with surprise (though not resentment, for that was not in his nature) that after the doctor had pronounced him fit for normal life, Herbert found that Augusta made additional demands upon his time and good nature.

"Will you do something for me, Herbert?"

"Depends what it is." Herbert's grin created a tingling sensation in the small of Augusta's back. It also convinced her that, after the necessary amount of banter, he would agree.

"Promise. Promise before I tell you."

"Tell me first. Then I'll say if I'll do it."

"Tom Cross would do it. I'd only have to ask him. He'd do it like a shot."

She wondered if she had gone too far. To her relief, Herbert's grin only got wider. "Then you'd better ask him. He's sweet on you. He'd do owt you wanted. He's soft in t'head."

For Augusta the joke was over. "You shouldn't speak of him like that. He's been a good friend to you. Only yesterday..."

"Only yesterday what?" Herbert was not sure if he could manage two mysteries at the same time.

"He's heard of a job. He asked me if I thought you'd take it."

"Not a job in the packing shop at Morley's, I won't."

"It's not. It's in your trade."

The moment she said it, Augusta knew that what she said was

339

untrue—untrue, at least, by the strict definition of craftsmanship which Herbert used. She knew too the hopes which she had reawakened in him. He was grinning again. But it was not the grin of a young man who enjoyed gently teasing a young woman. It was the grin of a time-served cutler who hoped soon to be back forging scissor blades. Augusta had built up those hopes. And since they were false, they would be dashed. It was not Augusta's way to cover up the unpleasant things of life.

"Well, nearly in your trade. It's looking after Morley's scissors and shears. Tom says that there's hundreds of them. And you'd lend a hand with the sewing machines. They sharpen the needles every day. The scissors are nearly all from your works. That's why Tom thought—"

"I know where they come from. I sold most of 'em to Abraham Wilkinson. I made some of the crimping shears myself. It's not much different from t'old job you found for me before." Self-pity was not amongst Herbert's vices, and he meant his response to be no more than a statement of fact. He tried to explain. "It's not my trade, Augusta. Setting and grinding is a job for a gypsy with a handcart."

"You'll not do it, then? She knew that it was cruel to ask him directly but also knew that she must ask.

"Was that the favor? To talk to Tom about the job?"

"The favor was something different?"

The chance to change the subject being offered, Herbert clutched at it with desperate gratitude. "Tell me what it was, then."

"It's only a little thing."

"Ask me, Gussie. For God's sake, ask me."

"I want to go to London in March. It's Clare's last play. I want to see it. But I need someone to go with."

Herbert did not respond. He was worrying about where he would live when Clare came home in May. For six months he had pushed the thought to the back of his mind, and he did not thank Augusta for reminding him of troubles ahead.

"I'll pay your fare . . ."

There was still no response.

"You wouldn't have to carry the bags. We'd get a porter to save your shoulder."

"I did plan to go to London once."

"Then you'll come. Please say you will. I can't go on my own."

340

Herbert could keep up the pretense no longer. The smile spread so quickly across his face that he felt the stitch marks across the scar under his newly grown mustache.

"We'll both go to the play, won't we?"

"'Course we will. I wouldn't go without you."

In Sheffield, the end of the financial year had brought its usual anxiety to Emily Hattersley. She had only a hazy idea of why the early days of March were always marked by bills and account books being spread all over the dining-room table or why Frederick, usually so punctilious about leaving for the Empress Works no later than half past seven, stayed at home until noon day after day. Emily liked life to be as tidy as her drawing room. And her husband's presence in Asline Road during the day was, in itself, as disconcerting as a fall of soot onto the carpet or a threadbare patch appearing on the arm of an easy chair. What was worse, Frederick did not stay in the drawing room as in the other domestic catastrophies with which she equated his mornings at home. He banged the table and called for tea, complained that the fire made the room too hot and that the draft under the door made it too cold. If he had to leave his labors for a moment, the maid was summoned and required to swear—on pain of instant dismissal—that she would not touch any of the papers on which he was working, and when he returned she was called back to explain why she had disobeyed his orders and disturbed the invoices, which lay exactly as he had left them. Worst of all, when the morning's bookkeeping was done, Frederick would stay at home for his dinner. Throughout the week in which he prepared his accounts, he sat down in the kitchen exactly at noon and set to work on the ham and pickles which were his staple midday meal. Emily, sitting opposite, watched him and listened to his complaints about the government, the local council and his workmen—who were usually denounced as lazy, often condemned as dishonest and sometimes excoriated as both.

"It's never been t'same since Jack went to Nottingham."

Emily nodded, neither knowing nor caring what it was that Jack Foster's departure had changed.

"I was a fool to do it, a fool to myself. It cost hundreds of pounds setting Herbert up in that little business, and see how it turned out."

His wife vaguely recalled that at the time when the Nottingham enterprise was mooted, other reasons—reasons to do with establishing the company and its master as forces to be reckoned with—had been advanced for buying the shop in Alfreton Road. But she thought it best not to jog her husband's memory.

"And now he's turned his back on me."

Frederick seemed genuinely to believe that he had been deserted by his ungrateful son. For a moment Emily thought she saw a tear in his eye. It was, she felt, the moment to be helpful.

"He does want to see you, Frederick. On that very first day—the day after he was attacked—he asked if you were coming to see him. When I write to Winifred at the weekend, I'll tell him that he's welcome to come home on Sunday."

Frederick seemed barely to hear her. He was submerged in a morass of self-pity.

"You can't bring Joe back. Joe's gone forever. He ought to be taking over, running the works. I'm at an age when I need the support of a son. Somehow, Emily, I must have sinned greatly, and God is punishing me. Whatever it was, I am being made to pay a thousand-fold—Joseph, Herbert and before them little Frederick. He's the one I really need, the one I really miss."

For a moment Emily feared that she was about to be asked to kneel in prayer. She consoled herself with the thought that a conversation directly with God would at least divert Frederick from continuing his statement of grief about the death of his first son.

The thought of little Frederick, lying dead by her side almost thirty years before, no longer caused her pain. She had borne and brought up four other children, and the sorrow which she now felt was for the two living sons whom for years she never even saw. But the infant's death had come to represent the failure of her whole existence. When her husband did not ask her to clasp her hands, she offered up a prayer of her own: Please God, do not let him go on about little Frederick. The name had become a symbol of her husband's despair. The child had never even been christened. Indeed, it had not even come to life. But it was spoken of, almost every day, as if it had once been the center of the family. Her prayer was not answered.

"If you could only know how I feel. A father deprived of the love of a son."

"You had two other sons, Frederick." For a moment she feared that he would notice the tone of reproach in her voice. But he was too maudlin to recognize any emotions except his own.

"Women don't understand these things. He'd be manager of the

342

works by now and we'd have something to build for. We'd be bigger next year than this. And we've done pretty well in t'last twelve months if them invoices are anything to go on. I've got nothing to look forward to. No reason to go on working my fingers to the bone."

"You've got the girls and the granddaughters. You'll leave them all very well provided for. When you think how you started, that's a great thing, Frederick—something to be proud of and give thanks for."

"Give thanks for! You don't understand. Daughters are nowt. Daughters won't run that factory or work them presses. I wouldn't 'ave minded about any of the rest—Cutlers Company, chapel, Liberals. They could all have slighted me and I wouldn't have cared, if there was a son to hand it on to."

He pulled his red spotted handkerchief out of his pocket and began a virtuoso performance of noisy nose blowing.

"They haven't slighted you, Frederick. You left the Liberals because of Ireland, and it's only the big men who get made bailiffs of the Cutlers."

Frederick was not in a mood to be consoled. "What about the chapel?"

"You were always so hard on them and so demanding with the minister. He didn't like you correcting him all the time."

"He didn't know his Bible. Still doesn't, if I'm any judge. Though they probably won't mind in Birmingham. Won't even notice, I shouldn't wonder."

"I know you were right, Frederick. But that made it worse. After that Good Friday when he prayed, 'Forgive them their disbeliefs,' and you shouted out, 'Forgive *thou* their disbeliefs,' he told Ernest Shaw that he would never speak to you again, never."

"Oh dear me!" Frederick's attempts at irony were never a success. "Oh dear me! That's a very Christian reaction, I must say, a very Christian reaction from a man of God. When I was a boy, ministers respected the Word of the Lord. If I'm a martyr because I know the scriptures, I am a martyr for my faith. And I'm proud of it."

For the first time in her life, Emily attempted to use the Bible as she had seen her husband use it a thousand times.

"What about the Prodigal Son, the one that was lost and then found? If Herbert came here, would you run down Asline Road to meet him or whatever it is the Bible says you should do?"

"I can give you ten quotations to match that one. There's the parable of the Talents and there's the Foolish Virgin ..." Frederick was distracted by the thought that the second example was not altogether appropriate to his younger son.

"Would you do it? Would you welcome him back?"

"When the Prodigal Son returned, he admitted that he had sinned. Will Herbert say that he no longer feels worthy to be called my son? Will he beg to work like one of the hired men?" Frederick snorted in triumph. "All that's part of the parable as well. If you start quoting the Bible you'd better get it right."

"I'll ask him," said Emily.

"Ask him what? I don't follow you." The fey disregard for continuous thought which had once seemed so attractive had become Frederick's greatest domestic trial. "You're not making any sense. I'd better be on m'way."

Emily was suitably humble. "I just meant that I would do what you want. I'll ask Herbert if he'll come home like the Prodigal Son and ask your forgiveness, and I'll tell him that you'll kill the fatted calf if he does."

At the moment of his mother's unexpected triumph, Herbert, her second surviving son, was traveling down the Euston Road on the top of an omnibus. Had he been borne toward Camden Town on a fiery chariot, the feeling of triumph could not have been greater. He was in London.

Augusta, sitting next to her sister on the other side of the gangway, made her way to Clare's theatrical lodgings with greater apprehension. The sun, behind her back and low on the rooftops of Bloomsbury, glowed a dull orange, and Clare pointed out, with animated gestures, the landmarks of the capital which would have been visible had it not been for the intervening buildings. But Augusta neither saw nor heard. All her energy was devoted to worrying about the luggage. The promised porter had not been employed, since neither she nor Herbert had possessed sufficient nerve to request assistance from one of the burly men who lounged near the barrier. Despite Herbert's shoulder, the bags had been carried easily enough to the bus stop. But when Clare had thoughtlessly insisted on climbing to the top deck, the cases had been left under the stairs. Everything of value which Augusta possessed was therefore out of sight. She had no hope of seeing her belongings again.

Herbert was preoccupied by a distant spire which he had identified at the moment he saw it as the Houses of Parliament. As the bus

344

made the brief darts and sudden stops which marked its eastward progress he realized that it was not the tower of Big Ben which he saw pointing to heaven.

"Is that Westminster Abbey?"

"Is what Westminster Abbey?"

"That spire, or tower, or whatever?"

"That's another railway station. That's St. Pancras."

The intonation was intended to demonstrate metropolitan sophistication. But Herbert was in no way abashed. All he could think of was Gilbert Scott's Gothic fantasy, outlined against the sky with the dark silhouette dotted by particles of light from the window of the hotel behind the arches and pillars of its façade. Its pinnacles and minarets reminded Herbert of the palaces in the picture books of his childhood. If London had railway stations which looked like fairy castles, it must have cathedrals which were fit to grace heaven itself.

"Bloody hell," he said as the bus pulled up under the artificial cliff on which the celestial station was built. "Bloody hell."

"Herbert!" Clare was scandalized.

There was six hours to spend between their arrival in Camden Town and their departure for the Lyric Theatre. Herbert wanted to mount an immediate sight-seeing expedition. But the sisters, who had not seen each other for more than a year, persuaded him that he needed to rest—as a way of finding time to exchange reminiscences. Herbert expected to hear Augusta tell the epic story of his battle to save the Old Master. Instead, Clare talked exclusively about her tour of America. Baltimore, Pittsburgh, Philadelphia and Washington were all described in detail, with special emphasis on Washington, which, as well as being the capital of the Union, was the city in which Miss Maud Jeffries had fallen ill with laryngitis and thus provided an opportunity for her understudy to play the leading part for six consecutive performances.

"Were you frightened?" Augusta asked.

"Every night. But I wanted to go on doing it."

"If you were a leading lady instead of... instead of..." Herbert had no tact. "Would you want to go on acting?"

"If I'd been a success, you mean? I don't know. I wasn't, so I don't know. As it is, I want to go home and settle down."

Herbert, who thought of settling down as being married, wondered if Clare had become engaged.

"Do you know that I'm twenty-seven and I don't own a stick of furniture?"

"It'll be lovely to have you at home." Augusta sounded as if she were offering consolation.

"Two old maids under one roof. Never out at night later than nine o'clock. But remember, when you see Mercia on stage tonight, that I've spoken all those lines. I've played Mercia for six evenings and two matinées. I've converted half of Rome to Christianity and then died in the Coliseum. When I'm selling gloves in Swears and Wells, remember that."

Herbert knew that he was expected to say something gallant. But he found it impossible to speak the words. After the years of infatuation and disappointment, she had become mortal. He could not even imagine her onstage, kneeling before the cross and crying across the footlights. But four hours later, there she was, barely recognizable in her stage makeup as she listened attentively to the leading lady's insistence on martyrdom.

"What He calleth me to do, that I will do. Let the task be what it may. I have put my hand to the plow and I will not turn back."

At first all that Herbert could think of was Maud Jeffries—Maud Jeffries of the big brown eyes and oval face. Then Maud Jeffries existed no more. Mercia lived and she cast a spell over the whole audience, just as she bewitched the noble Marcus, the patrician Roman sent by Nero to exterminate the Christians of the capital.

"What this Christianity is I know not. But this I know. If it made many such women as Mercia, Rome—nay, the whole world—would be the purer for it."

Mercia perished just before the final curtain came down, taking Marcus with her to everlasting life.

"Thus, hand in hand, we go to our bridal. Christianity hath triumphed. The light hath come. Come, my bride. Come to the light beyond."

Clare was a Vestal Virgin in the first act and attended on Nero in his imperial box at the Coliseum. In the second, she was one of the Christian maidens who were fed to the lions as hors d'oeuvre, immediately before the leading man and the leading lady provided the main meal of the day.

"You'll have noticed," she said on the bus during the journey back to Camden Town, "that I play a spinster in both acts. It's called type-casting in the theater."

Herbert and Augusta both spent restless nights. Augusta worried about how bitter her sister had become, and Herbert tried to work out why Clare's comments about settling down had so affected him. As he lay, anxious and half-asleep, he could hear his mother explaining the importance of possessing "nice things"—nice things which built a home, planted roots, held the family together and made the family respectable. As always, she was interrupted by her husband. In Herbert's dreams his father's insistent voice boomed the virtue of property and possession and emphasized the importance of goods and chattels as a sign of success.

"I had nowt when I finished my apprenticeship, nowt except the clothes I stood up in and an old set of tools that nobody would work with in those days. Ten years later I was my own mester."

The bankruptcy and years of failure had been blotted out from the family memory with such success that Herbert did not even think of them. He thought, instead, of his own condition—the son of a cutler who had lost his inheritance and, like Clare, had reached the age of twenty-seven without ever owning a single stick of furniture. He longed to settle down.

The desperate desire to get home to Nottingham, find a job, rent a house of his own and live in guiltless respectability spoilt his morning in London. Augusta would not join him on his brief sight-seeing tour. So he journeyed alone to Trafalgar Square, walked disconsolate down Whitehall to the Houses of Parliament and trudged desolate across St. James's Park to Buckingham Palace. To the sisters' surprise, he arrived back at the Camden Town lodgings three hours earlier than he had promised. Instead of worrying about missing the train, they were disconcerted by the male presence in the corner of Clare's single room who turned the pages of an old copy of the *Strand Magazine* in an unsuccessfull attempt to prove that he was not listening to their conversation.

The conversation was almost entirely domestic, and because it concerned the number of sheets which Clare would bring with her to Nottingham and the furniture which could be put in her bedroom, it filled Herbert with despair. Clare discussed her plans to "settle down" as if they were intended to be a reproach to the feckless and foot-loose. And as the conversation continued it became clear to Herbert that the new, more respectable and responsible life which she was planning was to be conducted from the room in Cavendish Street which he occupied. The gloom persisted throughout the journey to

347

the station. After Clare had bidden her sister a sad—but temporary —farewell, Augusta at last felt the waves of insecurity which were radiating from Herbert with increasing frequency.

"Did you enjoy yourself?"

"Yes, I did."

Herbert turned to look out the window as if to hide his sorrow. To his annoyance, Augusta still seemed not to realize that he was putting a brave face on his misery.

"I'm ever so glad. Herbert, Tom Cross wanted to come but he's such a nuisance."

Herbert barely heard her. He was thinking of his comfortable room, his regular three meals a day, his darned socks, washed shirts and starched collars. And he was wondering if it was all soon to come to an end. Augusta persisted.

"I think Tom gets dafter."

"He used to be sweet on you."

"Still is. That's what he's daft about. I can't talk to him without him going on about settling down."

The idea was haunting Herbert. "Why don't you say yes? He's got a good job and that little house he inherited. You can't go on looking after your dad forever. You're not getting any younger, are you? Why don't you marry him?"

"Because I want to marry you."

Herbert prayed that the train would enter a tunnel. It rattled on, leaving Augusta looking straight into his eyes and showing not the slightest sense of shame as she repeated. "I want to marry *you,* not him. I want to settle down with you and look after you. I've always wanted somebody to look after. Somebody sensible, not like m'dad. Somebody you can look after properly because they want to be looked after. And you're the one, Herbert."

"How do you know I want to be looked after?"

Augusta knew that there was no fight left in him. "You do, don't you, Herbert? You want to settle down and stop rattling about. You're all but thirty. It's daft behaving like a kid. You want to stop behaving daft, don't you?"

"I do," said Herbert.

Augusta was emboldened by the sound of the words. "You'll have to take that job at Morley's."

"All right," said Herbert.

CHAPTER TWENTY-SIX

BY ANY OTHER NAME

Everyone except Frederick Hattersley was delighted by the news that Herbert and Augusta were to marry. And even Frederick, although horrified by the thought of being related to a Catholic, permitted himself to hope that "she'll steady him down." Robert Martin, during one of his lucid moments, expressed more relief than proper respect for his daughter would have allowed. Herbert was hardly a good catch. But with Augusta approaching her thirtieth birthday, her father was grateful to see any fish dangling from the end of her line. Winifred Gunn believed that Augusta would be "the making of him," and did not even think about what effect Herbert would have on her. Tom Cross, who had been expected at least to sulk, offered what appeared to be genuine congratulations and suggested that since the house next door to his in Grove Road had been empty for six months, the landlord would offer it cheap to any tenant who was prepared to take it on at once.

Emily regarded the marriage as the opportunity to achieve the great family reconciliation which had become the object of her existence. She was not a scheming woman, but she had worked out in her mind how her obsession should be pursued. She calculated that, within a year, Augusta (who showed every sign of robust health) would become a mother. The baby might well be a boy. If Herbert produced his father's first grandson, all bitterness and resentment would be submerged in Frederick's dynastic ambitions. Emily could imagine herself saying, "They want to name him after you. If you'll agree."

Frederick, unwilling to "set foot inside a Catholic church," refused to attend the wedding. But he agreed that his wife—whose soul was either less precious or more robust than his own—could risk exposure to the sights, sounds and smells of Rome. He warned her— relying on his special study of papal blasphemy—that there would be lighted candles on the altar, that bells would be rung during the service and that incense would be heavy in the air.

Father Payne, the young priest who had taught Herbert all that Rome required him to know about the duties and responsibilities of a Catholic marriage, explained that there would be no lighted candles or ringing of bells and the censers would remain unlit. There could, of course, be no Nuptial Mass. The whole ceremony would be held in the porch rather than in front of the altar. No flowers or organ music would accompany the ceremony. It was a great pity to cause the Catholic party such distress, but it could not be helped. The young priest added that the Church holds out its arms, ready to welcome and embrace the world.

Herbert thanked him politely and stepped into the sunlight of Derby Road to continue his contemplation of the Mystery which had occupied his interest throughout the day's instruction. He could not understand how the cutters of I. and R. Morley and Company Limited had managed, in so short a time, to do so much damage to the scissors and shears which had been expertly forged, ground and set, only five years earlier, by Frederick Hattersley and Sons, Cutlers of Sheffield.

The first baby took longer to arrive than Emily had anticipated. For several years her daughter-in-law traveled across Nottingham and spent her mornings giving piano lessons to the girls of St. Catherine's (Higher Grade) Elementary School. Her technique—striking the knuckles of errant pupils with a heavy ebony ruler—lacked sophistication. But it pleased the Sisters of Mercy who supervised the school. During the same two years, her husband became an expert sharpener of sewing-machine needles. He proved himself capable of fulfilling all the extra duties which Morley's imposed upon him as the sharpening took less and less of his time and the scissors and shears were brought up to a condition which required only brief and routine maintenance. He gladly worked all the overtime which he was offered and restricted his spending money to the price of a single pint each night. He was an enthusiastic member of Morley's Sports and Social Club and played for the company at cricket and football. But he never went on the outings to Southwell or Newark, and Augusta never suggested that they should go together. The ambition of their life was to buy easy chairs for their unfurnished parlor and linoleum for the two bedrooms in which the floorboards were still bare. They were determined to do it without the added income that only smoking concerts could provide. Herbert had found respectability and he liked it.

The news that the long-anticipated baby was at last on its way stimulated even further the instinct for propriety which had slept in him for so long. There was talk about another shop—but a shop which, being a general ironmonger's, both prospered and fulfilled his need to be surrounded by cutlery. When Augusta gave birth to a boy, all the feelings of family that had been born in him—but which had been suppressed by the years of his father's tyranny—burst out in joyous expression. He talked incessantly about moving back to Sheffield. Having been born in Nottingham, the baby did not qualify to play cricket for Yorkshire. But Herbert was determined that it should not be denied life's second great privilege: an apprenticeship served under the supervision of the Cutlers Company of Hallamshire. While he planned the grand design of his son's life Augusta dealt with the details which did not warrant the father's attention.

"Kathleen will organize the christening." She still could not bring herself to call her sister "Sister Assumpta." "She's really looking forward to it."

Herbert nodded. He was wondering if his still-unnamed son should spend a few years at Wesley College. He had not enjoyed his own time there. But brother Joe—who knew so much more about life than he did—had always said that a good education was essential to getting on in the world.

Through the miasma of hopes and ambitions—wholly undisturbed by any thought of how his paternal aspirations would be financed—he heard his wife ask him, "Can we have it a week on Sunday?"

"What a week on Sunday?"

"The christening, silly."

"That's very quick. Will everybody be able to come at such short notice?"

He had a hazy idea of placing a small notice in the classified columns of Canada's equivalent of the *Nottingham Evening Post*. He felt sure that if Joseph saw it, he would be on the first clipper home.

"It's got to be quick. That's what the Church says."

"Sunday week seems too quick to me."

"It's what the Church says. If he dies before he's been christened he doesn't go to heaven. He goes into limbo."

The thought of the tiny infant, who was sleeping peacefully beside its mother, dying during the next nine days brought both immediate tears to its father's eyes and instant agreement to whatever suggestions were made to safeguard its welfare. Augusta took advantage of the temporary lump in her husband's throat.

"Shall we have Clare and Kathleen as godparents?"

Herbert swallowed hard and spoke up for his son. "He needs a godfather. He needs a man. Let's ask Tom. Tom's been very good to us. Without Tom we wouldn't have this house."

"It can't be Tom. He's not a Catholic. It's got to be a Catholic. We could have my dad."

The thought of the crazy old man having at least a theoretical influence over his son's future almost overcame Herbert's male prejudice. But not quite.

"All right. Let your father do it. What are we to do about mine?"

"You must invite him. You must write and invite him."

"He'll expect to be asked to be godfather."

Augusta could have expressed her genuine incredulity that, after the years of rejection and estrangement, Frederick Hattersley should even contemplate being offered such an honor. But instead, she repeated the suggestion that Emily Hattersley had first made to Winifred Gunn and Winifred had passed on to the expectant mother.

"Let's call him Frederick. Your dad would like that."

"I thought he'd be called Herbert. I thought you'd want to call him after me. I thought that's what you'd like."

"I'd like to make it up with your father. I'd like to have you back at the Empress Works, your works. And I'd like him"—she inclined her head in the direction of the sleeping baby"—"to work there one day. I'd like you and your dad and him all to be a real family again. That's what I'd like." Augusta ignored Herbert's jutting lower lip—the sure sign of hurt and disappointment. "Let's call the next one Herbert. Let's call this one after his granddad. I can see us now, taking him to visit your mum in Sheffield and you taking him down to the works. Shall I write a letter telling your dad?"

As Augusta anticipated, the proposal was irresistible. But Herbert, being the master of the house, insisted on writing to his father himself. The decision to call the baby Frederick had, after all, been his and his alone. Augusta got the pen and ink from the cupboard in the kitchen and, since there was no suitable paper in the house, cut the flyleaf out of the Bible that her father had given her to mark her First Communion. She thought about drawing faint pencil lines along the blank sheet as a guide to Herbert's faltering longhand. But she decided that her helpful assistance might be misinterpreted as lack of confidence. She offered no advice about the wording of the letter. And even when her husband asked whether he should begin with the announcement of their choice of name or with the invitation to attend the baptism, Augusta prefaced her opinion with the humble concession that it was for Herbert alone to decide.

"It's up to you. But I'd begin by asking for permission to call the baby Frederick."

"Ask him! He's not got a patent on it."

"It'll sound nicer. He'd like it. I'd say, 'It is our hope that you will agree that our first son should be named Frederick after you.' That's what I'd say."

Herbert licked his pen nib, dipped it in the ink bottle and began to write.

" '. . . should be named . . .' "

" '. . . Frederick after you . . .' " Augusta prompted.

It was necessary for Herbert to argue. "Why not put 'named after his grandfather'? That makes it sound really like family."

"He might think that we meant my dad."

"He'd never think that." Herbert dismissed the idea with a contempt which made clear that such a notion could never enter a sensible head.

Augusta capitulated. "Your idea is best. Say '. . . called Frederick after his grandfather . . .' That sounds just right."

Herbert, who had never doubted the superiority of his own wording, slowly wrote down Augusta's words. After an hour's intense concentration, the letter was completed and Herbert, who had found the effort of taking unconscious dictation exhausting, sank back onto the bed next to his wife. His exertions were to prove well worthwhile. For its reception at Asline Road was more enthusiastic than Emily had dared to hope. With his head moving from side to side as he followed the words along the line, Frederick Hattersley began to smile. He then began to "agitate"—a description of his behavior which his wife often used when talking to her sister but never when talking to him. Agitation, although debilitating to experience, was really a sign of Frederick's excitement. It was caused by the fear that an anticipated pleasure might, in the end, not materialize.

Was it, he asked Emily with real interest in her maternal experience, wise for so young an infant to be taken out of the house within ten days of its birth? Why, he demanded with the authority of a concerned grandfather, was there such an unholy hurry to get the christening over? How long would it take to get a proper inscription engraved on a silver loving cup? Was there a Sheffield firm which made spoons and pushers, or would he have to take the awful expedient of buying Birmingham made? Did the bank have brand-new guineas in stock, or would they have to be ordered? He did not fully regain his calm until he was on his way to Nottingham—two hours earlier than was necessary for arrival at the time which his son had suggested.

Father and son greeted each other as if the five years of separation had never happened. Frederick behaved as if the prodigal had not left home, and Herbert—shabbily elegant in the suit which had seen him through his own and John Gunn's wedding—acted as though there were no question of his being denied entry into the Promised Land. The only sign of the estrangement was the father's patronizing inspection of his son's house. Frederick climbed to the attic and checked that the skylights locked securely, turned on the kitchen tap to confirm that it produced a stream of clean water and rattled the poker up the chimney to make sure that there was no loose soot to obstruct the free flow of smoke.

"It's bigger than it looks," he said. "But jerry-built. Too many drafts for a young baby."

"I think it's a lovely house," said Emily.

"When they've got it all furnished . . ." Winifred, as always, meant well. She was tactless by nature. Frederick offended by callous intention.

"You'll need some carpet instead of that oilcloth. You can't have that baby crawling about on cold oilcloth."

Frederick reached into the depth of his inside pocket and pulled out his wallet. He gave Augusta a five-pound note.

"You buy a carpet. Axminster is best. And get a little runner for the hall."

Augusta was about to make a token protest, but there was a sound of wheels and hooves on the road outside and a familiar knock on the front door. John Gunn, having preached his morning sermon, had arrived in his horse and trap.

"You're not going to take that little baby in that." Frederick was scandalized. "He'll get his death of cold."

"A hansom cab's coming," Augusta assured him. "That's just for John and Winifred and Tom Cross from next door."

At that moment, as if to remove any residual doubt that might exist about the care which was being lavished on the youngest of the Hattersleys, the cab arrived. The grandfather took instant command. Pushing past the other members of the family, he strode down the narrow passage which connected living room to front door without even noticing that one shoulder brushed against the clock, and stopped it, while the other brushed against a cheap reproduction of *The Light of the World*. Holman Hunt's masterpiece was left swinging against the wall.

Frederick called back from the pavement, "I'll look after this. Where am I to tell him we're going, Albert Hall?"

Clare, primping her hair, answered him. "St. Barnabas's."

"St. Barnabas's! What sort of place is that?"

It was Augusta's turn to explain. "It's a cathedral, Granddad. Your grandson is going to be baptized by a bishop. In a Cathedral."

"Not a Catholic bishop, in a Catholic cathedral!"

"Of course it is, Granddad. You know I'm a Catholic."

"He's not. Herbert's not." Frederick turned on his son. "Have you agreed to this, Herbert?"

Herbert could not bring himself to answer. Augusta answered for him.

"It was all agreed before the wedding. Herbert agreed. He saw Father Payne and he agreed to it all."

"Well, *I* didn't agree. I didn't agree to anything. I didn't agree then and I won't agree now."

"Come on, Frederick. You can't argue about it now. We're on our way to the church." Winifred prided herself that she could say anything to her brother-in-law without him taking offense. If he had struck her, she would not have been more shocked by his response.

"Mind your own business. You interfere too often in matters which are not your concern. It's about time somebody told you what's what. You can make an idiot out of your husband, but you'll not make a fool out of me."

John Gunn knew that he ought to defend his wife, but he decided that it would be best to turn away Frederick's wrath with a soft word. "It's up to them, isn't it, Mr. Hattersley? That's only reasonable. They're the parents. I'm sure you agree that—"

"I'm the grandparent. And I won't see my grandson baptized in a Catholic church by a papist priest who calls himself a bishop."

Pulling his wife behind him, Frederick Hattersley walked out into Grove Road and—gallantly, as he thought, leaving the hansom cab for the christening party—strode off in what he wrongly believed to be the direction of the railway station.

Twenty minutes later, in the vestry of St. Barnabas's Cathedral, Father Payne—who was a cautious man—checked the details of the baptism at which Bishop Bagshaw was about to officiate.

"The godparents: Miss Clare Martin and Sister Assumpta, Kathleen Martin, and Mr. Robert O'Connell Martin?"

The baby's father nodded.

"And the child is to be named Frederick?"

"Herbert," said the father. "Herbert after me."

Father Payne felt sick at the thought that the Bishop might have intoned the wrong name. He could not imagine how he had made such an error. Being a humble as well as a careful man, he accepted all the responsibility. "I'm so sorry. Somebody has made a silly mistake. Please forgive me."

"There was a silly mistake," said Herbert. "But I made it."

To nobody's surprise, it was Clare who suffered most visibly from the catastrophe which preceded the christening. The whole family returned to Grove Road, dispirited and depressed. But the less sensitive members of the family assumed brave faces. Augusta busied herself with the baby. Winifred made tea and cut sandwiches. Patrick Martin produced a half-bottle of Irish whiskey and shared it with his brother Robert. Clare sat on a hard chair in the corner of the room staring into the middle distance. Tom Cross, filled with pain of his own, was delighted when Clare acknowledged his existence.

"Will you walk down the road with me? I need a breath of air."

Tom obliged with unreasonable alacrity. Halfway down the road, she confessed her pious concern.

"It wasn't a proper christening. You can't call a child Herbert. It isn't a proper name. Have you ever heard of a St. Herbert?"

"Isn't he the one with the stag, the stag with the cross instead of antlers?"

"That's St. Hubert. I tell you, he's not been properly christened. Somebody's got to tell Augusta."

"That's your job, not mine. I'm just a Methodist called Tom. Is there a saint called Tom?"

"I can't face her yet. Will you walk with me for a little?"

It had begun to rain and Tom, having been to a christening, was wearing his best suit. "Let's pop into my house for a minute."

He found it difficult to get his key into the lock and bumped into Clare as he pushed the door open. In his front room he was not sure what to say. After a moment of silence, Clare began to cry. Tom was bewildered.

"It can't be that important. I don't understand about you Catholics, but it can't be that important."

"That's not why I'm crying. I'm crying for me, not them."

"Crying for you?"

"I'm crying because I'm thirty-two and a buyer at Swears and Wells. I'm crying because I go home to a single bed and I'm crying because Augusta has a baby and I don't."

"You must have had dozens of chances."

"Hundreds . . ." Clare laughed bitterly.

"Why did you never say yes?"

"Because I always had something better to do. And I was always waiting for somebody better to come along. Now it's too late."

"No, it's not. There must be—"

"Yes, it is. You're a kind man. But it is too late. It's too late for me, whether anybody else ever asks me or not. I'm on my own now and can't change, whoever asks me. Not that anybody will ask me now."

"I'll ask you."

Tom Cross had waited ten years for the moment to tell Clare that he loved her. At last the moment had come.

"Don't be silly. You were always Augusta's young man. I'm not

357

stupid. It's not very flattering to turn to me because Herbert Hattersley beat you to it."

"I never wanted Augusta. It was always you. I courted her so that I could see you. I hardly dared speak to you. You looked at me as if I was dirt."

"Augusta told Herbert you proposed to her."

"I never did any such thing."

Clare had no doubt that he was speaking the truth. She had begun to enjoy the afternoon, and she waited for Tom to make it even better.

"I always loved you and hoped that one day . . ."

"One day you'd save me from a dragon."

Tom had tears in his eyes. Clare touched his face.

"And this is the day, is it? Today, you save me from the Dragon Despair."

Clare Martin leaned toward him and, holding his hand in both her hands, kissed him as he had never been kissed before. The use of his tongue having returned, he began to stutter.

"Do you mean . . . ? Do you want . . . ? I do . . . Will you . . . ? That's what I want."

"That was not a proposal. We are not engaged to be married, nor likely to be. Put all that out of your mind."

She kissed him again.

Robert and Patrick Martin went home without Clare, explaining—what Augusta already knew—that she was a strange girl whose moods were beyond their comprehension. Herbert was bitterly sorry that his father's behavior had so embarrassed Tom that his friend and neighbor had slunk off to his house without saying good night. The new parents were in bed by ten o'clock and asleep within the hour. It was their first good night's rest since the birth of their son.

Little Herbert woke at six and began to cry, but his father slept on. His mother changed his wet clothes, fed him and, holding him against her breast, walked up and down the bedroom in the hope that he would fall back to sleep to the sound of her regular heartbeat. After she had paced to and fro for five or ten minutes, she thought that she had heard a sound in the street below. Pulling back the curtain, she was astonished to see her sister Clare making a stealthy exit from Tom Cross's front door.

The five years which followed were marked for the Hattersleys, the Gunns and the brothers Martin by no more than the routine events of family life. Tom Cross and Clare Martin continued their great adventure. But the golden moments were brief and secret. Most of their days were as humdrum as the days spent by their friends and neighbors. In the great world beyond Nottingham, Queen Victoria died and was succeeded by the dissolute Prince whose waistcoats and watch chains Herbert had once admired and whose trousers (pressed front and back, rather than down the sides) he had imitated despite the express instructions of his father. The Boer War was fought and won, but nobody was quite sure which side had been victorious. A new Catholic Bishop of Nottingham, who had served as a chaplain at Khartoum and Tel-el-Kebir, preached his sermons on the subject of the just war. On the Methodist circuit, John Gunn, like most of the local preachers, avoided mentioning the battles but rejoiced at the peace. When the relief of Mafeking was announced, the Hattersleys, the Martins, the Gunns and Tom Cross were all safe asleep in their beds.

On the night when the old century ended and the new one began, a party of sorts was held in Cavendish Street. Herbert sang a couple of songs, Augusta played "The Blue Danube" on the untuned grand piano, Patrick Martin was restrained (with considerable difficulty) from playing his fiddle and his brother Robert proposed a toast "to the future." Clare cried when she heard the word spoken and Tom Cross comforted her with an obvious intimacy that, in the emotion of the moment, he did not attempt to hide. John Gunn added a few words of his own about growing old gracefully and his wife giggled like a young girl. The celebration broke up before one o'clock on the first morning of the new century.

A month later, Augusta gave birth to a second son. It was agreed for no particular reason that the baby should be called Leslie. But on Clare's insistence, a genuine Christian name was registered on its baptismal certificate. Karl was chosen because his mother liked the sound of the word and the father did not realize that it had German origins. In 1902, the two boys acquired a sister. She was christened Augusta after her mother, and her name was immediately reduced to Gus by her father. Diminutives were his style. From the day of their births his sons had been called Bert and Les.

When, a year later, Augusta told her sister that she was pregnant again, Clare determined to find the child a name which was consistent with the dignity appropriate to her nephews and nieces. Winifred persuaded Augusta that if the baby were a boy, he should be called

John after his great-uncle by marriage. Clare gave her reluctant agreement, on the understanding that, since John would undoubtedly become Johnny, a second, irreducible name was necessary for general use. She suggested Roy, in memory (though she did not admit it) of an actor of that name with whom she had enjoyed a brief liaison. The idea was rejected by her sister.

"I hope," said John Gunn loyally, "that if it's a girl, they'll call her Winifred."

"Not a hope. They'll be too worried about it turning into Winnie or Win. In any case, the problem is not what it will be called but how it will be fed. What he makes at Morley's won't keep five of them."

"What worries me," her husband replied, "is the idea of him starting singing again. It must be a temptation."

"I'd rather he sang than starved. It's all so stupid. He should be in Sheffield working for his father. I'm going to talk to Frederick myself."

"Not if you've got any sense. You'll only get your head bitten off. Neither of them will thank you for it."

"I'll see what Emily says."

Emily was full of apprehensions. Herbert, she knew, was needed at home. His father had completed his allotted span, and although he remained physically robust, his sudden fits of depression suggested that (as in every other particular) the Bible was to be taken literally when it promised no more than three score years and ten. He still left for the Empress Works at half past seven each morning. But if he talked at all in the evenings his conversation consisted almost entirely of a catalog of catastrophes—orders lost, men laid off and machinery sold for scrap. Sometimes he blamed his decline on cheap foreign imports and faithless British customers. But most of his time at home was spent in silent contemplation of failure—the wife who had failed to understand him, the sons who had failed to respect him, the chapel which had failed to acknowledge his service and his fellow cutlers who had failed to recognize the quality of his scissors and the contribution which he might have made to the industry. There were occasional moments of concern for Emily which almost turned into tenderness.

"At least we've got that bit in the bank. It'll keep you when I'm gone. I give thanks at least for that."

Before Emily had time to insist that she would go first, that he had the constitution of an ox and that she would not want to be left without him, the old bitterness returned.

"You can be sure if I don't look after you nobody else will. Herbert can't, and those girls won't. Far too interested in their own affairs. After all these years, we're still looking after ourselves. After all we've done to look after other people. Have I told you where all the papers are?"

"Yes, Frederick. They are in the tin box in the top left-hand drawer of your desk."

"And the key?"

"There's one on your chain, the big chain that all your keys are on. And there's another in the little wooden box under the sheets in the spare-room blanket chest."

"Nobody ever touches those sheets, do they?"

"Nobody ever comes here now, Frederick. We never open it."

Frederick looked so content that Emily wondered if the moment was right to return to the subject of a reunion with Herbert. The moment seemed so propitious that it was only indecision about the best way to argue the case which prevented her from making an immediate plea for either Christian charity or self-interest. While she was considering whether to beg that Herbert be forgiven or to suggest that help was needed at the Empress Works, Frederick fell into a deep sleep. An hour later, when he woke up, Emily had lost her nerve. Her courage was partly revived by the benevolent smile with which he announced that it was getting late. The phrase was familiar enough. Frederick used it every night of his life to signify that he would be pleased to drink his last cup of tea. Emily scurried off to the kitchen, hoping that his good humor would last and she would be brave enough to do her duty.

When she got back, to her surprise Frederick was standing by the fireplace, holding his hand over his right eye as if he were trying to focus his sight on some indistinct object.

"I've got a funny headache," he complained. "A sort of stabbing in here."

He removed his hand and bent down so that she could examine his eye. After forty years, she still marveled that it was so blue.

"Can you see anything? Is it bloodshot?"

Before Emily had time to reply, Frederick was so violently sick that the nausea which his wife felt at being drenched by his vomit was almost pushed out of her mind by amazement at the quantity of half-digested food and drink with which he sprayed her dress, the tea tray and the rug in front of the fire. As she cowered back Frederick grabbed at her for support. His weight was too much for her to bear and, still holding the tea tray, she crashed into the fire guard. For a moment, she lay half-conscious in the hearth. Then gradually, as her senses returned, she felt the ache in the side of her head where it had hit the brass fender and the heat in her arm where it had been scalded by the hot tea. Both pains were forgotten when she saw, out of the corner of her eye, Frederick's hand, hideously burned. He had held it out before him to break his fall and had plunged it into the fire before rolling over onto the parlor floor. Whimpering like a puppy, she crawled out of the parlor and down the hall and—with supreme effort—opened the front door. She shouted, feebly, into the night for ten minutes or more. Then Mr. Yeardley from next door came out to make his nightly inspection of his shuttered windows.

It was morning when she woke up in the spare bedroom. The new maid was standing in the door, with Dr. MacDonald hovering behind her. Emily vaguely heard the doctor ask, "What time is the sister expected?"

"Don't know," said the maid. "A daughter was supposed to be here at nine."

Emily could only just make out the doctor against the sharp landing light. But she had no doubt who he was and why he was there.

"He's dead, isn't he? He's dead."

Dr. MacDonald pushed his way past the maid, who stood blocking the doorway, awkward and afraid.

"No, he's not. He's had a stroke and he's got a badly burned hand. But he's still alive. You can see him later on."

Emily sat up. For modesty's sake she began to pull the counterpane around her. Suddenly she felt the pain in her scalded arm and winced. "He's going to die though, isn't he? I saw him lying there. He's going to die."

"It all depends."

"Depends on what?"

"Whether or not he has another stroke. It wasn't a very bad stroke."

"If he does? If he does have another one?"

"If he has another stroke today, he might die. He'll certainly be bedridden."

"I knew it."

The memory of her husband lying unconscious across the hearth was too strong to allow Emily even to hope for his recovery.

"If he gets through the day, he might be all right. The longer he hangs on, the better his chances of getting really better. He might live twenty years. We must hope and pray."

"Amen." The maid, still standing in the doorway, had been schooled in her master's ways.

The doctor, who was a forthright man, feared that he had given Emily too much hope. He decided to extinguish it. "I doubt if he'll walk again. His left side's paralyzed and I don't think we'll get that leg working. He might be blind in his right eye and his speech may be a bit—"

Emily, too frightened to listen any longer to the litany of disability, tried to push herself up on her good arm. "Give me that."

She waved the maid in the direction of her dressing gown. Dr. MacDonald sat on the bed beside her and, as he helped her pull it on, held a restraining hand on her shoulder.

"You've got a lump on the side of your head as big as a pigeon's egg and I gave you something to make you sleep less than eight hours ago. You'd better take it easy. You're not as young as you were."

"I want to see him."

For the first time in her life, Emily felt completely in command of her own destiny and she did not intend to allow a Scottish doctor to tell her what to do. As she walked out of the bedroom she was making plans. Herbert would come home to run the factory. She would use her own savings to buy him a little house in Ranmoor. Frederick's affliction was God's will for her as well as for him. She would buy a nice wicker bath chair, nurse him herself, and every day that he was alive would be the penance she had to pay for her years of silent resentment.

Herbert, having received his mother's letter and forgetting the lesson that his last hope of inheritance should have taught him, did not hesitate. He called briefly at I. and R. Morley's and handed in his notice. His letter consisted of a single triumphal sentence on which Augusta had not been consulted—"I am leaving forthwith to take up a position of manager of a company of scissor makers in Sheffield." Remembering the advice which his father had given him to augment his managerial training on the commercial course at Wesley College, he ended, "and oblige."

The machine shop manager did not respond in the spirit of Herbert's salutation.

"You've been here five years and you leave on five minutes' notice."

363

"I've no choice," said Herbert. "I need to be in Sheffield by dinner-time."

"You'll not get last week's wages."

"I don't need them."

"Whose firm is this, then?"

"It's my father's . . . and mine."

"I should have guessed. Just as well. You'll never get another job here, whether you make a go of being a manager or not."

"I shall make a go of it. Don't fret yourself about that."

Herbert waved a cheery goodbye to the girls in the cutting room on the other side of the wire mesh which hemmed in his workshop. At the station, he bought a first-class ticket.

He resisted the temptation to go straight to the Empress Works and took a hansom cab to Asline Road. The sight of his father, lying like a corpse in the great family bed, filled him with terror. Frederick Hattersley was barely recognizable. His once florid face was as white as the pillowcase beneath his head and he seemed to have shrunk to half his normal size. His bandaged hand lay on the counterpane and Herbert retched at the sight of the brown stain on the gauze. Strangest, and most frightening of all, was the two-day growth of stubble which covered the lolling jaw. It was piebald, black and white, and, because it looked so confused and unkempt, seemed to typify his father's condition. Herbert had never seen those cheekbones anything except immaculately shaved. It was as if the moths and dust, about which he had heard so much in chapel, had already begun their corrupting work.

"Does he just lie there?"

"He tried to say something this morning, when we fed him. The doctor says that he's improving."

"Fed him?"

"We pour a little beef tea down him. When Martha came over she brought a special cup. Like a little teapot with a spout. We've got to keep his strength up. He's as strong as a bull. That's what's kept him alive."

The mention of his sister reminded Herbert of the message that Augusta had told him to bring.

"If you need any more help . . ."

"Winifred will stay until my arm gets better. Then I'll be all right. I'd rather look after him myself. . . . You can feed him now if you like."

She made the offer as if she were making a personal sacrifice in order to perform a favor to her son. Herbert shuddered.

"I'd better get down to the works. Nobody's been in charge for two days. They'll all be sitting on their backsides."

His mother did not seem even to notice his vulgarism.

He did not get back from the works until after ten o'clock. Emily was in bed and Mary, who had made a brief visit—"queening it," as her mother said—had long returned to the calm waters and lush pastures of Doncaster. Winifred sat in the parlor reading a Fabian tract. Years afterward, Herbert still remembered its title—*Twentieth-Century Politics* by Sidney Webb. As always, Winifred spoke first.

"He recognized your mother clearly enough this afternoon. He's made up his mind to get better. We've not seen the last of that one. Not by a long way."

She tried to sound more confident than she felt. Herbert sat in his father's own chair, not claiming possession like a man who had entered into his kingdom but sinking back like an exhausted traveler.

"I'm glad to see you here, Herbert. It's right. It's the one good thing to come out of this tragedy." Herbert still did not speak. Winifred hated silence. "You'll make such a job of the works. I know you will."

Herbert laughed. "The works are finished. They've not got enough orders to last a fortnight. They're trying to sell the scrap in the yard. Two presses haven't worked all year and nothing's been done to keep them in proper fettle. The foreman left a month since . . ." He broke into his own catalog of disaster. "He's been selling it off, bit by bit, for years because he was too old to run it himself and too proud and too stupid to get somebody who would."

"Herbert. You're talking about your father. He's lying upstairs on his deathbed."

"He's as strong as an ox. You said so yourself. And he's as stubborn as a mule. If he hadn't had his seizure, he'd have had to close down t'works within a couple of months without a word to you or anybody else."

The radical spirit of inquiry was still not dead in Winifred. "If he sold it off, bit by bit, what did he do with the money? I'll ask Emily."

When they took the tea into the side room, Winifred repeated the question. Her sister was not sure of the answer. "He told me last week that we had enough to live on until we died—just about enough, he said. I think he's given something to charity. But I'm not certain."

365

Herbert had no doubts.

"He sold it cheap out of spite. And closed bits down because he got so bitter and twisted. Losing it was better than leaving it to me. He wants the works finished. And I'll stay and finish it. It's a son's duty. But don't expect me ever to forgive him, living or dead."

CHAPTER TWENTY-SEVEN

SERVICE AND SACRIFICE

Herbert traveled home to Nottingham third-class and walked home from the station. As he turned the corner out of Castle Boulevard into Grove Road he was vaguely conscious that workmen were pulling down the houses at the end of his street. But he was so preoccupied with the problem of telling the bad news to Augusta that he did not even wonder if, at last, the land was being cleared for the new public house which, rumor had suggested, was soon to be built by the Newark Brewery Company.

Uncharacteristically, he had decided to face the ordeal at once, and he was still rehearsing his opening sentence as he pushed open the kitchen door. Hanging on the peg behind it was the navy-blue cloak of a Sister of Mercy. Normally, the prospect of an hour's polite and pointless conversation with Sister Assumpta filled him with gloom. But the sight of her pallium revived his instinct for procrastination. He seized on the excuse to postpone his gloomy announcement. Throwing his hat into a chair, he walked through into the parlor as if he had craved his sister-in-law's company all week. The room was empty and silent. Herbert shouted, "Anybody at home?" and the unmistakably elevated voice of Clare answered from the bedroom. Her tone was even more imperious than usual.

"Is that you, Herbert? Come up. Come upstairs, straightaway."

Herbert's mind was filled with thoughts of illness and injury. So he assumed, with consternation, that Augusta, eight months pregnant, had been struck down like his father. He leaped back into the little passage which connected kitchen to front room and began to climb up the steep stairs three at a time. The bedroom door was ajar and he banged it wide open with the palm of his outstretched hands. For the second time that week, the shock waves ran up the back of his legs and tingled in his fingertips. Before him was a scene which his father-in-law, Robert Martin, would have instantly recognized as the inspiration of a Florentine or Umbrian Old Master. Its title would have been Madonna and Child with Attendant Angels.

Augusta sat up in bed, cradling in her arms their new baby, which had been born—premature but healthy—in the early hours of the morning. On her left, poised elegantly on the edge of the mattress, was Clare, magnificent in a fair imitation of Queen Alexandra's pearl choker. She had obviously come straight from Swears and Wells. On the new mother's right, balancing the tableau exactly, was Sister Assumpta. Wisps of hair fell from under her wimple and lines of exhaustion creased her carbolic red face. The mother was serene—more serene than her husband had ever seen her. Indeed, to Herbert's surprise, she radiated so much happiness that she looked almost beautiful.

"Look," said Augusta, waving her hand in the vague direction of the baby's head.

"What is it?" Herbert asked, quite defeated by the emotional challenge. "Is it a boy?"

"Can't you tell? Can't you see?"

"I think it's a boy."

Herbert's knees were still like jelly and his head still spun. He felt a desperate desire to throw Clare and Kathleen downstairs so that he could touch his wife's hand and cry at the thought of being a father again.

"Of course he's a boy, silly. But can't you tell anything else about him?"

Suddenly the memories of sickness and death surged back into Herbert's head. In a panic, he asked, "Is there something the matter with him?"

Augusta addressed the sleeping child in her lap. "Isn't Daddy an old silly. Of course there's nothing wrong with you. He's special, that's what he is."

Herbert looked at the creased, purple face, the tight eyes, the tuft of tawny hair and the clenched fists. He had seen them all, three times, before. But if Augusta chose to think of the child as special, she was well within her rights as a mother. He waited for more postnatal nonsense.

"He's going to be a priest," said Augusta. "I could tell that, the moment that I saw him."

"So could I," echoed Clare.

Assumpta nodded, and added in a tone so doubtful that it was almost sacrilegious, "I do hope so."

Although he knew that both his sisters-in-law would disapprove, Herbert sat on the bed. The idea of his new son becoming a priest was obviously no more than a dream. But he was unnerved by his wife's sudden flirtation with fantasy. Augusta was the practical one, and his flights of imagination could, in consequence, sweep through the family sky secure in the certainty that his down-to-earth wife would hold him back from ascending to the most dangerous heights. Had he thought that there was the slightest risk of his sleeping son taking the vows of Rome, Herbert would have been immobilized with despair. The thought of having to talk about it until Augusta and her sisters accepted the impossibility of their hope made him desperate at least to postpone the discussion of how the absurd aspiration might be realized.

"Let's have him. Let's hold him for a minute."

He leaned toward his wife. In response, his wife moved affectionately in his direction.

"Careful. Don't drop little Father Hattersley."

Augusta's new skittishness almost produced exactly the result which she had sought to avoid. Herbert cursed under his breath. Like all good Nonconformists, he had been brought up amid stories of priest-ridden Catholic families who sacrificed food and clothing to afford the cost of sending a son to a seminary. How was it, he wondered, that—having avoided all this rubbish in the irrational aftermath of Herbert's and Leslie's births—the nonsensical notion had suddenly added an extra complication to his already chaotic life?

Above all, he wanted to be left alone with his wife. Without her sisters looking at him as if he had committed some terrible offense, he would be able to enjoy the pleasures of new fatherhood free from all thought of clerical ambition.

"Are you all right?" he asked Augusta.

It was intended as a prelude to telling the sisters that he could manage on his own and that, after the labors of the day, they deserved an early night.

"Of course I'm all right. It was a bit of a shock when he started to come this morning. But I'm fine. And when I saw him, Herbert, I felt so proud. What a week it's been. I think that he came early because of all the excitement. You haven't told me anything about Sheffield."

Mercifully, the baby belched. Augusta leaned forward to take him and Herbert handed his son back to her in panic.

"I think you'd better leave us for a minute or two," said Clare, sounding as if she would like to retreat herself.

Sister Assumpta added her usual postscript. "Let Herbert go downstairs and have a bite to eat while you have a little sleep. You can talk about Sheffield later."

Clare began to help Augusta slide down the bed while Sister Assumpta carried the baby toward the basin on the washstand.

"Off you go." Clare dismissed Herbert. "I'll be down in a minute. Put the kettle on."

"We've talked about names," Augusta shouted after him. "I think it ought to be Frederick now."

"Frederick Roy," added Clare, determined to combat the horrors of Fred or Freddie with an irreducible single-syllable second name. Her second attempt to immortalize an old love was successful.

"If that's what you want."

The agreement was grudging, but Clare was satisfied.

Sister Assumpta returned to the Convent of Mercy as soon as little Bert and the babies had been brought home from the neighbors, washed, fed and put to bed. Clare stayed to make her brother-in-law's supper and to see Augusta safely off to sleep. The supper was, as Herbert had expected, barely edible. Clare's cooking reflected her hatred of food and her contempt for people who enjoyed it. Herbert attempted to swallow the half-fried liver without chewing it. When his fork had first sunk into the still-pink offal, blood had seeped out onto the plate. In consequence, the idea of biting the warm intestine was too horrible to contemplate. But he gulped it down because he feared to do anything that might provoke conversation. If Clare were allowed to talk she would undoubtedly ask him about his visit to Sheffield. The one benefit which had resulted from his unnerving exchange with his wife was the postponement of the awful moment when he had to tell her that, far from being the new master of the Empress Works, he was unemployed.

Clare timed her exit with the precision expected of a professional actress. She pulled the back door shut just as Tom Cross, in the next yard, pulled his silently open. Stepping inside without a sound and without a word, she took off her hat and coat. It was essential to both of them that such evenings began with a brief imitation of married life. Usually cocoa was made and desultory comments were exchanged about the experiences of the day. Even on an evening when Clare bore the momentous news of the new nephew's arrival, only the usual half-hour was spent on preliminaries. By half past nine they were in bed and by ten o'clock they were ready to talk again. Like all unmarried lovers, Tom thought less of the joy of meeting than the pain of parting.

"How long can you stay?"

"All night."

Tom wished that Clare could have given him the glad tidings with rejoicing in her voice. But the fact of her staying was more than enough to compensate for her apparent lack of enthusiasm.

"How'll you manage that?"

"I told Herbert that I'd be back in time to get Augusta up. Father will think that I've spent the night next door."

Tom said nothing. It was Clare's turn to be depressed. Tom's silence always signified disapproval.

"Do you think it's very wicked, Tom, the scheming and the lying?"

"It's all wicked, Clare. We both know that."

"But you still do it. And nobody makes you. If you don't want me to come around anymore, you only have to tell me so."

"You know that's not it. I'd just rather . . ."

Clare reached out in the dark and, with remarkable accuracy, clamped her hand over his mouth. "You promised that you wouldn't talk about marriage again, or about wickedness."

"Don't you think that it's wicked?"

"It's wicked enough to go to hell for."

"Then why don't you—"

371

She reached out again but, missing his mouth, struck him a glancing, but irritating, blow on the nose. Tom sniffed before continuing his inquiries.

"Do you tell them at confession?"

"I did, after the first time."

"And what did the priest say?"

"He said that the important thing was to promise not to do it again and to mean it."

Tom could hardly bear to ask the obvious question.

"And did you?"

"At the time I did. I meant it all at the time. I cried all night, because I thought I'd never do it again. If I hadn't meant it, I wouldn't have got absolution—at least not from God. He would have known and, whatever the priest might have said, I'd have been damned at the next communion."

Tom concentrated hard, trying to follow the theological implications of Clare's explanation. The complications of her story increased as the narrative continued.

"But next day I knew that I couldn't keep the promise. And I knew that at the next confession I might make the promise, but I wouldn't mean it—not for a moment. So I don't tell the priest now. Anyway, I couldn't tell them every week. What would they think of me?"

"Why do you still go?"

"Because I'm a pious Catholic."

Tom—whose upbringing had been based on prejudices identical to those which Herbert Hattersley held—understood that Rome built its temples on a combination of conjuring tricks and conundrums.

"It's all right for you Romans. You make your penance and go off to heaven."

"I shall not confess. I shall not do penance, and if there is a heaven, I very much doubt if I shall ever get there."

"Then you can't be a pious Catholic." He was about to add, "And there's no reason why you should not marry me." But he realized that to do so was to break his promise again and to risk another glancing blow on the nose.

"There are a lot of different sorts of Catholic, laddie. Father, Uncle Pat and, I suppose, Augusta are one sort. They believe. They don't always like it. Sometimes they hate it. But they believe in everything: stigmata, body and blood of Christ, everything. The day after the Pope announced that he was infallible, they all believed it. I couldn't and I didn't. I don't believe in anything. But I love it all. I love the white vestments on holy days and the green vestments on ordinary days. I love the idea of mysteries which I can't understand and shouldn't try to understand."

"But—"

"I love the way we genuflect in front of the altar, kiss the Bishop's ring, cross ourselves, bless ourselves with holy water in the porch . . . I love the theater of the Church. I'm absolutely faithful to the statues of Our Lady and true to the painted Stations of the Cross. Do you understand?"

"No, I don't. Not a bit."

Tom thought it best to lie. He could have admitted that he had always known that Romans worshiped false gods and bowed down before graven images. But Clare, apparently excited by the statement of her credo, had reached out to him once more. When they were lying quietly again, she felt a sudden desire to convince him that her sort of Catholicism brought a special blessing.

"When I went next door this morning, Augusta was really down in the dumps and she couldn't understand why the baby had come early. She wanted Herbert. I cheered her up by telling her that I thought the baby would make a priest. She bucked up straightaway. I couldn't have said that about him being a local preacher."

Tom was already asleep. He did not wake until the light had begun to stream through the uncurtained windows and Clare had started to get dressed.

"Go back to sleep," she said. "I'm tiptoeing next door."

"Come back tonight."

All thought of faith and morals was forgotten.

"I can't. I'll come tomorrow. Same time."

Tom leaned out of bed and caught Clare by the hand. "Tonight. Tonight, please."

"I tell you I can't! I'm going with Kathleen to make the arrangements for the christening. It's my turn to be godmother again. Father Payne and me."

"Why Father Payne?"

"I told you. Frederick Roy is to become a priest."

"Get away!"

"I told you in the night and you didn't believe me. Well, it's true."

Tom remained incredulous.

"God works in mysterious ways," said Clare.

"I thought you said last night—"

"I did and I said that I'd see you tomorrow."

Before Tom could reply, the latch on the back door had been silently lifted and had silently fallen back into place.

Augusta took the bad news from Sheffield with her usual equanimity. Within five minutes of being told that the Empress Works was finished, she was persuading her husband to see if his old job back at I. and R. Morley's was still available. The vacancy had been filled and the foreman told him so with obvious pleasure.

"Sorted out next day. Never expected to see you again. I thought that you were going off to manage your father's works."

"I did. But—"

"We took you at your word. You said you were going to better yourself. Never thought you'd be back after all you said about being a time-served cutler. Never thought you'd polish needles again."

"Well, I will. How can you have filled it after three bloody days? I don't believe you."

"I tell you, we've got somebody. Anyway, after the way you spoke to me, it's a matter of principle. You're not welcome here. You're too good for us."

The foreman did not add that the principle was reinforced by his daughter's insistence that he find a job for the young man she was courting.

"I'll bet you a bloody quid that he can't do the job like me. You'll be throwing money away."

The foreman felt unable to argue against Herbert's point with suitable conviction. He took refuge in abuse. "Just shove off. Perhaps your friend Mr. Cross will get you a job in the packing department. We've heard enough about him. They've always got laborers' jobs going there."

Herbert recognized the calculated insult and, pulling in his stomach and holding his head erect to prevent any suggestion of a double chin, he made a dignified exit, telling himself that whatever the extremity of his family's predicament he would never work as an unskilled laborer. His resolution lasted for a couple of hours. When he got home to Grove Road, Aunt Winifred was visiting and she could talk of nothing except the building work which was going on at the end of the street.

"There was a painting I was fond of when I was young," she said.

"It was called *Work*. At the front, men are digging a great hole. I haven't thought of that picture for years. It's just like that down the road—two men carrying bricks in hods and a notice advertising for men to sign on."

Herbert cursed under his breath.

"Did you get your job back?" Augusta asked, discreetly feeding the baby under her shawl.

"It's gone, gone already."

As always, Winifred was wonderfully helpful. "They still want men down the road."

He was trapped. "I'll go down later on and see if they'll take me on there."

The clerk of works asked him where he had dug foundations before.

"I haven't. I'm a cutler, a time-served cutler. I make scissors and medical instruments."

"Well, you won't be able to dig foundations with them. Have you got a spade?"

"My father used to make spades—ten gross a day at best times."

"All you need is one. Come back with one tomorrow and we'll set you on and see. I doubt if you'll last very long. It'll be too like hard work for your taste."

Herbert proved him wrong. His back ached and his hands blistered. But with the spade—bought after he had pawned his real tools—he dug for nine hours a day for six days a week for almost six months. There were times when he thought that he could not carry on and that Augusta would have to choose between starvation and her husband's return to the clubs, pubs and smoking concerts which she hated and despised. But he carried on. He carried on for little Bert. For he had begun to develop feelings about his eldest son which Frederick Hattersley would have recognized as part of the family inheritance.

It was Augusta who read the advertisement for polishers at the Raleigh Bicycle Company. Herbert knew that two years before, he would have rejected the idea with offended contempt. At the Raleigh works, polishers did work which, in Sheffield, was done by women. But, to Herbert, the indignity of becoming a "buffer girl" had to be weighed against the pain in his back, the blood on his palms and the pay, which was a penny an hour more than the wage of a building laborer, and the obligations of fatherhood. He redeemed his tools from the pawnshop and turned up at the Raleigh works the best-equipped polisher in the history of black enameled cycle frames and chromium-plated handlebars. With his irresistible optimism, he was convinced that he had taken the first step toward becoming a scissor maker again and a credit to his son. He had not lost hope by the time of little Bert's First Communion.

All the family and most of their friends agreed to attend the great event. After some persuasion by Clare, Tom Cross agreed to go in order to support the Nonconformist friend and father, and Winifred said she positively looked forward to watching her scrubbed and combed great-nephew paying his respects to God and Bishop Brindle. John Gunn—by coincidence preaching across Wellington Place in the Albert Hall—could not be at the service. But he emphasized how much he looked forward to joining the parents after the ceremony and referred mysteriously to the present he had bought to mark the occasion. Clare insisted that Tom meet her in Wellington Place almost an hour before the service began and took him on a detailed tour of Pugin's Victorian Gothic cathedral.

Tom was horrified. And the more Clare explained to him, the more horrified he became. Clare knew nothing of Pugin's medieval philosophy—of his refusal to attend the consecration of his own church in Derby because women sang in its choir or his attempt to turn Cardinal Wiseman out of the Nottingham cathedral because he had allowed women to enter the sanctuary behind the rood screen. She simply loved the elegance of the lancet windows, the passion of his stone St. Barnabas at the entrance to the sacristy, the pathos of the Paschal Lamb in the rose of glass above the altar and the medieval splendor of his painted walls. Tom seemed hypnotized by the great crucifix which dominated the nave. When Clare managed to distract his attention from the tortured figure which hung on a cross of traditional Nottingham pattern, she led him into a side chapel. Offended by the sensuous greens, reds and blues of its walls, he looked upward past the pillars and windows and past the angels bearing the shields of the Blessed Sacrament which gave the chapel its name. The ceiling was deep blue and illuminated with clusters of gold stars. It was difficult to believe that such a place could be used for Christian prayer. Tom made his unsteady way to the pew which Clare had told him was his appointed place, and he braced himself for the pagan ritual which was to come.

Gradually, the young communicants and their parents filed into the cathedral, genuflected before the altar and sat in reverential silence. The boys were dressed properly enough—knickerbockers and Eton collars for the sons of well-to-do families, sailor suits for the unconventional and adventurous and extra darning and mending for the offspring of the pious poor. But the girls wore what Tom could only describe as wedding dresses. He drew a deep breath and waited for the entry of the clergy, comforted by the knowledge that he sat between Herbert Hattersley and Winifred Gunn—the son of a chapel elder and the wife of a man who, that very minute, was preparing to preach a Methodist sermon. Until the procession of choir and clergy entered the church, he had real hope that God would forgive and understand.

Tom thought that the smell of incense would choke him, and as the altar boy who carried the censer swung it in his direction he ducked as if to avoid a blow. When Bishop Brindle, vested in alb, stole and cope, reached the altar steps and sprinkled holy water on the purple cloth and its gold candlesticks, he wondered if he could endure the full service.

"Asperges me, Domine, hyssopo et mundabor."

"Sprinkle me with water, Lord, and I shall be clean," translated Clare from two places along in the pew.

Then the officiating priest turned around and Tom felt that he could stand no more. He was used to sober suits and dark ties or, when the chapel was at its most formal, black cassocks topped with clerical collars on bands. Before him was Bishop Brindle in both the peculiar finery of his calling and the particular relics of his military past. Pinned to his episcopal purple and gleaming more brightly than his pectoral cross were his decorations—awards for gallantry, distinctions bestowed by foreign potentates and campaign medals bearing the unmistakable profile of the young Victoria. In the place of honor just above his heart was the Distinguished Service Order on its white and maroon ribbon. It had been won in the campaign which began at Akabar, led on to the victory at Omdurman and ended with Kitchener's recapture of Khartoum. Then came the British War Medal for Egypt 1882, its ribbon decorated with three oak-leaf clasps to mark the Bishop's mentions in dispatches. It was followed by the Turkish Orders of the Medjidih and Osmaneih. The Egyptian War Medal, 1896–98, also bore three oak-leaf clasps. The Khedivae Bronze Star was embellished with three gold clusters.

"In Nomine Patris, et filii, et spiritus sancti."

Tom clasped his stomach—partly because of genuine nausea and partly because he wanted to convey the impression of sudden and irresistible indisposition. Pulling what he hoped was an apologetic face, he pushed past Winifred and hurried out down the side aisle. Despite the clatter, Clare's gaze never shifted from the altar. Herbert thought of following his friend out into the Derby Road, but decided that his duty lay with little Bert, who—hair slicked down in imitation of his father's—was waiting to witness his first transubstantiation.

"Introibo ad altare Dei."

"Ad Deum qui laetificat juventutem meam."

Herbert tried hard to concentrate upon the ritual which was going on around him, watching Augusta carefully so as to kneel, sit or rise only a fraction after she took up the proper position. As he did not know that Tom—his stomach now back to normal—was regaining his composure in the back row of the Albert Hall, a nagging worry about his friend's welfare buzzed at the back of his head. But the sight of his son taking the eucharist, Eton collar still immaculate and socks pulled properly up to his knees, filled him with too much paternal pride for much serious thought about anything else.

"Per omnia saecula saeculorum."

Bishop Brindle slowly climbed the pulpit steps. The congregation knelt. There was more mumbling. The congregation stood and then sank back into their pews.

"My text is taken from the first Epistle to the Corinthians. 'If the trumpet gives an uncertain sound, who shall prepare himself for the battle?' "

To Herbert's surprise, the congregation began to fidget and Winifred wondered if it was usual for the smell of incense to change from the sickly odor of sanctity to something reminiscent of burning wood. She would have whispered her thoughts to Herbert, but she knew that he could smell nothing and the rest of the congregation had begun to settle down. Roy slept in his mother's lap and Les and Gus dozed so peacefully on each side of her that it seemed a shame to do anything which might disturb them.

"It is for that reason that the Church has always called on its faithful sons and daughters to reject all idea of compromise with those of other faiths. For that reason we have been unable—"

A priest walked toward the pulpit and handed the Bishop a piece of paper. Herbert watched with interest to see the climax of the next ritual. Bishop Brindle opened the paper, read the message which it contained, coughed, read it again, coughed again and addressed his throng in a voice quite different from the one which he used for his sermon.

"My friends. There is a fire at the Albert Hall. I understand that most of the . . . er . . . Methodists have left the building safely. But the fire has caught hold. I ask you to remain here calmly and pray with me that the Lord delivers us from all harm, either the falling tower of the chapel or a spark which might ignite our holy house."

By the end of the announcement, the Bishop was again speaking in his sermon voice and half the congregation was on its knees. One or two men, in defiance of his request, stood up as if to leave. The smell of smoke was so strong that even Herbert noticed it.

"My friends. As your bishop, I tell you that your duty is to stay here and pray."

"Not mine." Herbert's stage whisper made the two rows of pews in front of him turn around. Clare made a hissing noise, intended to quiet him. Augusta had a mother's preoccupation.

"Don't be silly, Herbert. We've got all the children."

"You stay. I'm going to see what's going on. John might be in there."

Winifred had already picked up her gloves and was making her way down the center aisle. Herbert began to cough. The idea of smoke had begun to constrict his chest.

Les and Gus had woken up. Augusta, still clutching Roy tight to her bosom, leaned sideways.

"You stay still and keep quiet. God is watching. If you fidget, God will be angry and so will I."

In the cathedral there was only a suggestion of smoke in the air and, for most of the congregation, it did no more than catch the backs of their throats. But as soon as the heavy iron-clad north door was pulled open, little gray clouds began to swirl into the porch and Herbert started to fight for breath.

"Go back inside. I'll find John."

Winifred was concerned for her nephew but more anxious that her search for her husband should not be handicapped by an asthmatic liability. Herbert had no wind to spare for an argument. He ran through the swirls of smoke around the corner from Derby Road into Wellington Place and did not stop until the crowd of people staring at the Albert Hall prevented him from running any further. They were staring at the windows which, one by one, burst out in an explosion of shattered glass and then spat gobbets of flame into the cold night air. There was a great gasp of horror and astonishment at the first signs of fire inside the tower, then a great crash as the chapel roof fell in and the sky was lit up by an orange glow from the burning pews below. A policeman was trying to make way for the fire engine, which warned of its approach by clanging its bell. Herbert grasped him by the shoulder and half turned him around.

"My husband's in there." He thought of himself as speaking for Winifred, who had panted up behind him.

The policeman neither noticed the mistake nor appeared to resent the assault.

"Everybody's out. There's nothing to worry about except the building. Just keep clear and let the engine through."

Winifred tugged at Herbert's sleeve, anxious for him to repeat the policeman's reassuring message. Tom Cross, who had seen it all from the back of the chapel, was a step behind her.

"He says they're all out. Everybody's safe," Tom shouted above the noise of the crowd's continual astonishment as another ball of fire fell from the tower and more flames billowed from under the charred eaves.

"Is anybody injured?" Winifred was asking Tom, but a man with greasy black stains across his face answered.

"Everybody's all right except the preacher. He was at the wrong end of the chapel. Got out last. They've sent for the ambulance."

"Where is he?" Winifred sounded completely calm.

The man with the soot-stained face was not sure. But a woman holding a brown jug of milk pulled out her free hand from under a tattered shawl and pointed in the direction of the garden in the middle of Wellington Circus.

Herbert, who knew that he should have waited for Winifred and Tom, made off toward the mound of grass, in giant strides. He ran in a straight line, pushing out of his way the gawping men and staring women who blocked his path. He leaped over the low wrought-iron fence which bounded the garden and, gasping for breath, fell to his knees beside a group of men and women who were themselves kneeling on the grass. They were all looking at John Gunn. His face was blackened by fumes and his hair matted by sweat and soot.

He was alive. His chest heaved in silent convulsions. That in itself unnerved Herbert, for he was used to diseases of the throat and lungs producing sounds like the priming of a steam engine or the swinging of a gate on rusty hinges. Suddenly, the heaving stopped and the men, kneeling in an almost reverential group, stopped complaining about the time it was taking for an ambulance to arrive.

"I don't like the look of him. I don't like it at all," said one.

"Neither do I. Not a bit," said another.

Herbert leaned down to put his head against the motionless chest to listen for the sound of a beating heart. John's mouth opened and closed in what seemed to be the formation of a single word. Herbert saw Winifred's shoes on the grass in front of him.

"It's me, John. It's Herbert."

John, eyes still closed, tried to speak again and Herbert bent down until their faces touched. Twice more John tried to speak and failed. Then, as Winifred fell onto the grass beside her husband and took his hand in hers, John tried again and—by supreme effort of will—succeeded. In a voice so low that only Herbert heard and understood, he spoke one word.

"Mary."

CHAPTER TWENTY-EIGHT

WOMEN'S RIGHTS

John Gunn's death had the same effect on Methodist and Catholic. The Hattersleys and Martins felt suddenly mortal and began to think about mortality. Only Tom Cross philosophized aloud about the message and meaning of life.

"It just shows. You can never be sure. Never. It makes you think."

Clare Martin, who had already learned that lesson, was uncertain about what conclusion she was expected to draw from Tom's discovery. She asked him to explain himself and he gladly did.

"I want to make the best of things while we've got the chance."

"So do we all, Tom. Nobody wants to be unhappy. Nobody chooses to be sad."

"Then we've got to make the best of things."

Clare was determined not to understand. "Not showing when it hurts. What did that man Jack Foster used to say? 'Don't give them the satisfaction.' I'll remember not to tell you when I'm miserable."

"That's not what I mean. What I mean is making the best of the time that we've got. Enjoying life."

"And how do you suggest we do that?" Clare, knowing what the answer would be, was already impatient.

"By you and me getting married."

Clare gave him her hard stare. It was supposed to freeze water and turn men into stone. But Tom was less afraid of her contempt than of missing his chance of marrying her.

"I've thought about it," he began, "and I've decided. I'll—"

"Oh, you've decided, have you? You've decided."

"Yes, I have. I've decided that I'll do anything. I'll become a Catholic if you want me to."

"The last time you were in a church, the smell of incense made you feel sick."

"That's different. This time I'll know what to expect."

"Tom, love. It isn't that. I keep telling you. Marrying you—marrying anybody—just isn't what I want."

"How can you say that? Every woman—"

"No, not every woman. Not me. I want to be free to send you home on those nights when I can't stand the sight of you for a bit."

"What if I don't come back one day?"

"That's a risk I've got to take. Being on my own is what I want and I'm going to do what I want. Don't forget, Augusta's my twin. We're both peas from the same pod."

"Don't tell me she does what she wants. She must be as miserable as sin. They haven't got two pennies to rub together."

"Well, you'd know. You courted her for years. You'd know what she wants."

"I never did! You know I never did."

"I know no such thing. But I know that she meant to get Herbert from the moment she saw him, meant to marry him and mother him. And she did it. She's doing what she wanted."

"Herbert doesn't do what he wants. She bosses him something terrible."

"You are a baby, Tom. The thing about Herbert is that he wants and enjoys bossing. He really enjoys it as long as she doesn't go too far and he can pretend that he doesn't notice. When he's at work, hating that bit of a job and thinking that he ought to be a boss in Sheffield, he says to himself, 'Never mind, by half past six I'll be back at home, being bossed by Augusta.' Then he's happy again."

Clare's philosophizing was not quite over.

"It's Winifred who worries me. She's been disappointed all her life and now she's all on her own with nothing to do."

"How can you say such a thing? She was happily married to John Gunn for years and before that . . . Anyway, she's old. Sixty. She'll just

... just ... go and live with her sister in Sheffield. From what I hear, she could do with the help."

"A dollar she doesn't."

Clare had learned a number of vulgarisms during her years on the stage. From time to time they slipped out.

If Tom had taken the bet, he would have lost his five shillings. Winifred Gunn, who felt so young that she would never reveal her age, knew exactly what she would do. For a moment she did think of living in Sheffield and helping nurse her crippled but tenacious brother-in-law—thought of it as a theoretical possibility. For she knew that there would be those who believed that it was her duty to devote the rest of her life to the widow's traditional task of sacrificing herself for other members of the family. She felt a moral obligation to consider the course of action which she knew some of the chapel elders would expect at least. But having considered it, she dismissed it as impracticable. She decided, without much agonizing doubt, that she had obligations to fulfill in Nottingham.

The obligations were both public and private. There were more nephews to guide and encourage, and her experience with the first Herbert and his brother, Joseph, had in no way discouraged her from playing a great-aunt's part with the second Herbert and his brothers, Leslie and Roy. Indeed, when she conceded (even to herself) that mistakes had been made, they were classified as valuable experience which would enable her to help the young Hattersley boys in a way which had not been possible with their father. About their sister, Gus, she did not concern herself. She saw no paradox in her assumption that a little girl's future was not worth bothering about and the second enthusiasm to which she determined to devote her time and energy —the suffrage movement.

Little Roy was too young to excite her interest. She had never felt any enthusiasm for making clucking noises at babies incapable of being influenced by her uplifting advice and example. Leslie had not quite reached the age at which he might reasonably be expected to produce a rewarding reaction to atlases, spelling books, educational games and conversation carefully modulated to improve his diction. Winifred was not a woman to waste time on a child who was not yet able to benefit from her wisdom and experience. So she was left with little Herbert as the potential Galatea to her Pygmalion.

Winifred was even less successful in her attempts to educate Bert than she had been during her similar endeavors with his father. He failed to open any of the books which she bought him and showed no interest in pressing flowers or identifying the birds of the East Midlands. Fortunately, his great-aunt had a second interest with which to occupy her widowhood.

In the ten years since her husband had forbidden her to work for the election of women to the School Board, her enthusiasm for politics had grown. Winifred had long believed herself to be a socialist, though at chapel and home she admitted only to advanced liberalism. With time on her hands, and a small annuity, she decided to devote herself to the women's cause. She proposed to enlist in the monstrous regiment by abandoning the Albert Hall and worshiping instead at the High Pavement Unitarian Chapel. The elders' ladies would tell each other that memories were too painful for her to make a regular Sunday visit to the place in which her husband died. A few bigots might express polite surprise that she had suddenly come to the view that Jesus Christ was not the son of God. But others would understand that belief in the Trinity was less important than support for the belief that women should be allowed to take their full place in society.

The Unitarian Chapel in High Pavement was the center of the suffrage movement. Winifred felt sure that if she sat in its pews for a couple of consecutive Sundays, she would be invited to a gathering of desperate and determined women. She was right. As she left the chapel after her second visit she was handed a pamphlet edged with purple and green. Headed "Votes for Women," it advertised a public meeting to be held in the Large Hall of the Mechanics' Institute. The meeting was to be addressed by "Miss Pankhurst and her Friends."

It was not Winifred's habit to do things silently or on her own. So she hurried around to Grove Road and invited Augusta Hattersley to join her at the meeting. Augusta declined—claiming to be too busy but demonstrating by her demeanor that absence of interest as much as lack of time prompted refusal. Winifred's second choice was Clare Martin, who, as a woman of spirit, ought to have supported the suffragists' cause. Clare accepted the invitation and regretted her decision the moment that it had been made.

There were several times as they walked together to the Mechanics' Hall that Clare thought of abandoning Winifred and the meeting. The older woman talked incessantly of other memorable gatherings which she had attended, and prophesied with depressing certainty that the evening's event would not compare with the historic rally which followed the Liberals' Sheffield Assembly. Clare knew nothing of political behavior and might well have benefited from Winifred's instruction. But the two women—one childishly eager to show off her knowledge and the other determined not to be patronized—were mutually antipathetic. Had they not been swallowed up in the crowd milling outside the door, Clare would have turned on her heel when —for the fifth time—Winifred told her, "Stay close to me and you'll be all right."

The hall itself was only half-full. A few dozen eager women— sporting the purple and green favors of the suffrage movement—sat in the front rows. Behind them the audience was mixed, half men and half women. At the back of the hall the chairs were filled with men. In the gallery what places had been taken were occupied by youths, some of whom (to Clare's surprise and Winifred's consternation) were equipped with rattles, penny trumpets and homemade gongs. When Sylvia Pankhurst appeared—magnificent and daring in a loose, light blue, short-sleeved gown—there was cheering from the front of the hall, polite clapping from the middle, silence from the back and a cacophony of noise from the gallery. Mrs. Pethick-Lawrence and Miss Una Dugdale, who followed Miss Pankhurst onto the platform, emulated the manners of the principal speaker, acknowledging the audience's existence with neither wave nor smile. Clare was impressed. Miss Pankhurst spoke first.

"Ladies and gentlemen. This meeting has been called to demand—"

Anyone in the hall who had not come to the rally already apprised of its purpose would not have discovered the object of Miss Pankhurst's visit to Nottingham. The pandemonium was instant and deafening.

"What we claim is—"

The amateur orchestra in the gallery gave forth again and the men at the back cheered the instrumentalists, not the speaker.

"At the present time, men who are householders and pay their rates and taxes—"

The men at the back of the hall broke into a spontaneous chorus of "For He's a Jolly Good Fellow," in tribute to the respectable middle classes of whom Miss Pankhurst spoke.

For almost a quarter of an hour, Miss Pankhurst continued the unequal struggle, and Winifred muttered, "Shameful, shameful, shameful!" under her breath. Clare sat watching the scene, her eyes glowing with excitement. When Alderman J. H. Green and the Reverend J. Lloyd Thomas mounted the platform to call for order and respect, she almost joined in the ironic cheers.

It was several minutes before the Alderman was heard. Then, after an artificial silence had fallen on the hall, he urged the "good people" assembled in the "temple of democracy" to show that the citizens of Nottingham respected free speech. He lifted his eyes up to the gallery. "Now, my young friends up yonder. Do let us show that you know how to behave."

Out of gratitude for his confidence, his young friends blew their penny trumpets, twirled their rattles and beat their homemade gongs. Another chorus of "For He's a Jolly Good Fellow" was dedicated to the Alderman. It was followed by a selection of popular songs. The line "My wife won't let me," which concluded a music hall ballad entitled "Waiting at the Church," was sung with particular vigor.

It was then that a dozen men from the back of the hall rushed the platform. Bravely Alderman Green and the Reverend Thomas tried to bar their way. But they were brushed aside. Winifred cried out and Clare watched with fascination, half hoping that the evening of drama would be ended with some sort of violence. But the men meekly took seats on the platform and for a few minutes, although the whole hall was tense with anticipation, they sat like a chorus waiting to support the soloists in front of them. It was the first time that Miss Pankhurst had been allowed to complete an audible sentence.

"Don't you think we are capable of using the vote wisely? I dare say that we can teach some men a lesson."

It was then that the men on the platform took the mice out of their pockets and sent them scurrying in the direction of the speakers.

The pandemonium which followed was not of Miss Pankhurst's making. Her only concern seemed to be for the welfare of the mice. One, which was cowering in terror, she picked up and handed to a reporter who had climbed onto the platform in order to obtain a better view. Having dealt with the frightened rodent as compassion required, she offered the floor to Miss Dugdale, who, having been shouted down, invited Mrs. Lawrence to attempt the impossible. Mrs. Lawrence shouted at the top of her voice. Each of the noisy hooligans could shout louder.

"Enough is enough," said the Reverend Thomas to Alderman Green and a message was sent to the policemen in the Secretary's office.

The four officers who appeared in the gallery proved even more popular than the Alderman and the minister. The singing of "For He's a Jolly Good Fellow" was renewed with vigor and, as if in tribute to the smart uniforms and military bearing, was followed by "Soldiers of the Queen." Miss Pankhurst tried again.

"Our tactics have succeeded. Otherwise, we should not have received so much kind attention."

Provoked by her contempt, the youths in the gallery and the men at the back of the hall began to stamp their feet in unison. The policemen tapped one or two politely on the shoulder and requested that seats be resumed. The requests were ignored. A chair was thrown in the general direction of the platform. It was intended to do no harm, but it unnerved Mr. Walter Bryant, the Secretary of the Institute, who feared that one of the suffragists would be killed or, worse still, that his windows would be broken. Arms waving, he approached the platform. There was no chorus of "For He's a Jolly Good Fellow" for him, for the rowdies sensed that their evening's fun was over.

"The meeting is closed," he shouted.

Miss Pankhurst repeated the message. "The meeting is now closed, friends."

There was sporadic booing and a great cheer as a strong force of policemen moved in to clear the hall. Clare and Winifred waited with the suffragists in the front row—partly for safety's sake and partly because, as the evening went on, they more and more identified with their cause. Miss Pankhurst and her colleagues sat calmly for fifteen minutes until all but a hard core of barrackers had left. Then, as the women's leader rose to leave the platform, the huddle of men at the back began to cry out what they believed to be witticisms.

"Give us a kiss."

"Meet you behind the gasworks."

"Who's doing your old man's washing?"

Winifred, affronted by the ribaldry, turned her head away from the awful sight of the leering men. Clare, anxious to miss nothing, stared at them with unashamed interest. In the middle of the grinning, giggling group she saw the unmistakable black, brilliantined head of Herbert Hattersley.

Herbert had not, at the beginning of the evening, meant to attend the suffragists' meeting in the Mechanics' Hall. He had done no more than make his usual visit to the Grove Hotel to drink his usual single pint of beer. But to his surprise—for it was only half past six—a pianist of little talent but immense enthusiasm was thumping away. Gradually men whom Herbert did not know drifted into the saloon bar and stood around the piano as if they were waiting for their evening to begin. Herbert Hattersley ignored them until the pianist struck up "Absentminded Beggar." Then, drumming his fingers on the cast-iron table, he first began to hum, then to sing. At first he sang softly to himself. Then he began to boom out Rudyard Kipling's injunction to "pass the hat for your credit's sake and pay, pay pay!"

"That's a good voice you've got there," said the man at the next table. "Sung professional, have you?"

"A bit. You know. Just a bit." Herbert glowed with modesty.

"Give it up during the war, did you?"

"About that time."

The pianist had started the chorus again.

"Come on," said the man at the next table. "Duke's son—cook's son, son of a hundred kings. Fifty thousand horse and foot going to Table Bay."

After they had reached "pay, pay, pay!" again, he turned to Herbert, one old soldier to another.

"I was at Colenso. Sixty-sixth Battery, Royal Field Artillery."

The man at the next table repeated the battle honor. "Colenso."

"Wounded twice. What was you in?"

"Cavalry," said Herbert. "Hussars."

The man at the next table leaned across and shook Herbert's hand. "And see where it's got us. Two South Africa men, and if I'm any judge, you're as hard up as me."

Herbert grinned, nodded and accepted the offer of another pint.

"And see what they're doing to this bloody country . . ."

One thing led to another and each pint led to the next. By eight o'clock Herbert had drunk more than he had consumed in a single evening since he was married, and sung more songs than it was reasonable for him to remember. He had also agreed with the man at the next table that England was going to the dogs and that women were the cause of the decline. Through the haze, he shook hands with the wounded gunner's friends as they arrived and introduced themselves by rank and regiment. Each time, Herbert replied, "Herbert Hattersley. Third Hussars."

" 'Ere," said Corporal Hyde of the 60th Rifles. "Why don't we 'ave a bit of fun? Them suffragists are holding forth at the Mechanics' to-night. What do you say to a forced march down there and a bit of fun?"

"What about the Old Comrades?" the man from Colenso asked.

"The Old Comrades can wait a bit."

The corporal attempted to form his irregulars into a column and began to sing. "Boots, boots, boots, boots movin' up and down again."

"There's no discharge in the war!" came back the reply.

Herbert got them into tune but could not bring himself to use the words with which Corporal Hyde parodied the ballad of time-extended regular soldiers.

"There's no discharge from . . ."

There was much discussion about having one more pint to prepare the raiding party for the rigors ahead. It ended with almost unani-mous agreement that such a precaution was essential. Only Herbert dissented. He explained that before he set out on his punitive expe-dition against the uprising of presumptuous women, he had to run down the road and warn his wife that he would be late home.

"You're late now," Augusta told him.

"I'm going to a political meeting," he explained as if he believed it and as if what he was about to do was an adequate excuse for what he had failed to do already.

"Not one of those smokers at the Unionists?"

"No, a real meeting. I heard about it in the Grove. I thought that I ought to start taking an interest."

"Don't be too late," his wife said. "I've got something to tell you."

Herbert did not enjoy the meeting. As the effect of the alcohol wore off he felt increasingly guilty about the company which he was keeping, profoundly ashamed of the exhibition of brutish ill manners to which he had been party and more and more anxious about the secret which Augusta was waiting to reveal to him. He did not notice his Aunt Winifred in the audience, and when he saw a figure which looked like Clare Martin, he assumed that fear of exposure had made him imagine that his sister-in-law had witnessed his shameful con-duct. He decided not to accompany his new cronies to the White Hart and the Old Comrades meeting but marched home at light-infantry pace, regretting everything about his evening except the songs which he had sung in the Grove Hotel. By the time he arrived at the corner of Grove Road and Lenton Boulevard, he was sober enough to realize that the songs were, in part, the cause of his deplorable behavior. But he could not bring himself to regret having sung them. Even as he worried about what it was that Augusta had to tell him, he looked forward to another night and another sing.

Clare was sitting in the living room. She had little Roy on her knee. Augusta sat by the table, turning the handle of a cast-iron mincing machine which spewed long worms of suet into a bowl already half-filled with fragments of raisins and sultanas. She was making mince-meat in preparation for Christmas.

"You're late." It was Clare who broke the silence.

"I've been to a political meeting. I told Augusta I was going."

"What a coincidence. I've been to a political meeting."

Herbert gave a silent prayer of thanks that his sister-in-law had not seen him at the back of the Mechanics' Institute Hall. He was so relieved by his escape that he almost allowed himself to ask if she was on her way next door. Augusta turned the handle of the mincing machine with a methodical determination.

"He's asleep again now, Clare. You can take him back upstairs."

"I like nursing him. I really do. Funny, isn't it?"

"I'd rather have him back in bed. It doesn't do him any good picking him up every time he cries."

Her husband suspected from her tone that Augusta was not what she called "best pleased." The way in which she began to dismantle the mincing machine confirmed his fear. She unscrewed the wing nut which held its spindle in place and banged onto the table, with undisguised aggression, each of the moving parts which she extracted from inside its drum. She unscrewed the second wing nut, pulled the handle clear and started to unfasten the body of the machine from the table edge. Without turning around, she spoke as if she were addressing one of the table legs.

"I've been to the doctor."

Herbert had not anticipated another baby so soon. But he liked babies and he liked the idea of babies even more. He reached out toward his wife, hoping to touch her hand. She pushed the chassis of the mincing machine in his direction.

"Put that to soak in the kitchen. I don't want the suet to dry on it."

"When did the doctor say to expect it?"

"I'm not pregnant. At least, if I am, I don't know about it."

"She's ill, Herbert."

The tone of reproach in Clare's voice was a clear implication that Herbert should have recognized her condition without needing a doctor to tell him about it.

"What is it?"

"Dropsy," said Augusta, and waited for the sound of the word to reverberate around the living room.

"Does it make you feel bad?"

"It's made me feel bad since Roy came."

"You should have told me."

"I thought you'd see."

"How could I see?"

Clare told him. "You could have seen her legs swell at night. Her legs swell to twice their proper size and her feet get so big that she can't get her shoes on. You should have seen that, for God's sake."

"I did. She said it was called 'white leg' and that it would go away after a bit."

"Well, it didn't."

"Is it bad? I mean . . ." Herbert stood behind Augusta with his hands on her shoulders, looking hopeless. "I'm sorry, love. I just didn't think. Tell me what I've got to do."

"It's not as bad as Clare makes out."

"Well, how bad is it? What did the doctor say?"

Clare was merciless. "She's not going to die, if that's what you mean. At least not yet, not if she's properly looked after. But you've got to change your ways."

Herbert felt genuinely aggrieved. He had been mildly drunk once in five years and had walked home and walked it off. Yet he was being accused of causing an illness from which his wife had suffered for several months. He spluttered. Clare leaped on him.

"If you want to know about it, I'll tell you. If you want to go back to the pub, you'd better be on your way and let me help Augusta clear up."

"I'll tell him," said Augusta. "Leave it to us. We can work it all out."

"No, you can't. You'll tell him not to worry and tuck him up in bed in case the shock has strained his heart."

"Perhaps I will. But that's my business. You can't just call in here on your way to heaven knows where and start telling us how to behave. This is for husband and wife. Herbert will look after me. I know that."

Herbert smiled, convinced that his wife's confidence was entirely justified. Clare snorted and began to pull her coat on.

"Do you feel all right? You look very flushed." Augusta was clearly worried about her husband's appearance. Before he could answer, Clare snorted a second time with such dramatic effect that even Herbert understood her message.

"Can I get you some supper?" He spoke without moving from his chair.

"No, it's quicker for me. I waited for you. It's no bother."

Clare, on the point of lifting the latch, snorted yet again.

Herbert responded. "Sit yourself down." He stood up and took a single step in the direction of the kitchen.

"Thanks, love."

Clare was sure that Augusta was agreeing to inconvenience her husband simply to impress her sister.

"There's no tea in the tin." Herbert, in the kitchen at last, sounded desperate.

"I'll come and do it."

"No. Sit there. Where's the new packet?"

"In the top cupboard. A red packet behind the treacle."

"Got it."

There was a rattle of crockery. Augusta pushed herself out of the chair. "What's happened? What's smashed?"

"Nothing. I was just getting the cups out."

"Be careful with the milk. There isn't much left. Just half fill the jug. I'd better come and do it."

Clare snorted again as Augusta hobbled toward the kitchen, snorted her way out of the back door and snorted across the yard toward Tom Cross's lighted kitchen window.

CHAPTER TWENTY-NINE

RESPONSIBILITY

Augusta found no difficulty in describing the causes and symptoms of her illness.

"It's really thrombosis. The veins in my legs got blocked while Herbert was on the way. So I made the extra water and it all ran to my ankles. It went after a bit. But then—after Gussie and Leslie came —it started again. That's why my legs swell at night. It's the water, back again. Only worse."

Herbert could feel his feet beginning to bulge as the water, built up during his most recent pregnancy, dripped in his imagination down inside his thighs and calves. Augusta put her left heel on the coal bucket in the hearth and pulled up her long skirt.

"Heavens, I'm like an elephant tonight."

Her husband knew that he must look. But he had to brace himself before he dared to turn his head in the direction of the bulging foot. The hairs bristled on the back of his neck as he struggled to say something suitable to the occasion.

"Is it white leg... what you said before?"

"It's worse now. It's dropsy. I can't remember the posh name."

To Herbert's horror, she placed her right foot on the coal bucket, next to her left, and displayed a second ankle which was almost twice its proper size.

"It'll go down in an hour, if I keep my feet up."

Perversely, she immediately put both feet back on the carpet and, leaning forward, took the blackened kettle off its hob and stood it on the fire. The little water left from the last tea making boiled at once.

"Pass me my handbag, love."

Herbert did as he was told, fearing that he was about to witness some awful medical ritual. Augusta took an envelope out of her bag and, to her husband's consternation, held it in front of the boiling kettle and steamed it open. For Herbert, watching his wife steam open a letter was almost as painful as witnessing an awful proof of her illness or injury. To steam open a letter was to flout authority, a practice with which he did not hold. Augusta noticed Herbert's distress but she did not acknowledge even his interest until she had carefully extracted the half-sheet of writing paper and laboriously deciphered the spidery longhand writing. Then she told Herbert what he had already guessed.

"It's from the doctor to the infirmary."

"What if they find out that you've opened it?"

"They won't if I'm careful. Anyway, I need to know what it says. If I'm going to die, I need to know about it. I'd have to make plans for the children, and for you. But that doctor wouldn't tell me. Neither would you."

It was only then that Herbert asked her what the letter said. She handed it to him, and his lips moved silently as he tried to form the words which were sprawled out across the top of the note. "Edema due to glomerulonephritis."

"Is that what you've got . . . that . . . due to . . . that? It sounds terrible."

"Read all the letter. Read to the end."

"It's all medical, all of it except the dates."

"They're birthdays. Les's birthday, Gussie's and Roy's. That's one of the things. No more babies. Not for a bit anyway. And I've got to take things steady."

Herbert leaned over his wife and kissed her on the graying hair on the nape of ner neck. She tossed her hair like an irritated horse. But she was smiling. Herbert had tears in his eyes. He rose to the level of sentimentality expected of him.

"No more babies. Four's enough for me."

"And I'll have to give up the piano lessons. I can't trail across to St. Mary's every morning."

"You should have given it up years ago. You should have given it up when you had Bert."

"You say that, Herbert, but how would we have managed? How will we manage now?"

"We'll manage."

"It's no good saying that without thinking about it. It won't be as easy as you pretend."

Augusta was anxious to pursue the subject of balancing the household budget.

"It won't be easy without my bit coming in."

"We'll manage, I tell you."

"How?"

Herbert, as always, had no enthusiasm for answering hard questions. "We will. Getting you better is all that matters."

Augusta put her feet back on the coal scuttle.

"Wouldn't you feel better on the sofa?"

Herbert smoothed out the rug that covered the hole in the arm through which the horsehair showed, and picked up the cushion which had fallen onto the carpet. Augusta hobbled across the room and sank down in the place which he had prepared for her. As she stretched out, her feet—grotesquely misshapen—emerged from under her dress.

"They'll be right by bedtime. But I don't think your wife is going to show much ankle in future—whatever the fashion."

"What about doctors and medicine?"

"That's what I am going to the infirmary to find out."

"But the doctor must have told you . . ."

"He said medicine. Camomile is what he said. And if it gets really bad, I have to have it drained."

The pain in Herbert's ankles returned. It was twice as bad as before. "Drained. That sounds terrible. God Almighty. Do you really think . . . ? What do they . . . ?"

Augusta ignored the incomplete question, leaving in Herbert's mind the clear impression that she knew the answer but thought it best to spare his feelings by keeping the details secret.

"I hope I can start on the medicine next week, after the infirmary. That's if we can afford it." The conversation had returned, as Augusta intended, to the subject of money. "It'll cost the best part of three shillings a week."

"Then we can. That's barely the cost of a daily pint. We can do without that."

Ignoring the underestimation, Augusta sighed audibly. "That's a wonderful thing to say. I'm a lucky woman. But it isn't necessary. There's a better way. I've had an idea."

Herbert—delighted that his act of sacrifice had been properly appreciated—waited for the lucky woman to explain her plan.

"You could do a little job in the evening."

Herbert's response was predictably enthusiastic. The dream of singing—respectably and with his wife's approval—seemed about to come true.

"I've been thinking about that—thinking about it myself."

"That's wonderful, Herbert. I heard of a little job the other day."

Disappointment and alarm spread across Herbert's face and Augusta tried to calculate the depth of each emotion. She decided that his reaction was not as antagonistic as she had feared it would be. Relieved that his response was so restrained, she pressed on with her plan.

"It's a little grinding job. Sharpening and grinding."

Augusta knew that describing the job was the moment of greatest risk—risk of hurting her husband so badly that going ahead with her scheme would be almost as painful to her as it was to him. For he had told her that sharpening was work for gypsy peddlers who traveled the country hawking their wares, as if putting an edge on a knife was no more difficult than selling herbs or telling fortunes. Herbert had told her the tale of the hawker who, being given a saw to set, had tried to grind it on his emery wheel. For reasons which she could not understand, he had roared with contemptuous laughter at the story. Nervously, she added another detail.

"It's five hours a week."

Herbert was still not ready to agree. "How did you find out about it?"

Instead of answering that question, Augusta told him. "They want Saturday afternoon. Saturday afternoons in particular."

Herbert thought, I'll miss the match, and Augusta could tell by the way in which his lower lip trembled that he was beginning to feel sorry for himself. But he said, "Saturday afternoon it is then, if you're sure the job's still going."

For a moment Augusta felt real pride. She believed in the sanctity of self-sacrifice and she knew how great a sacrifice her husband was making. As Herbert's waist had expanded and his breath shortened, he had abandoned playing football and become an enthusiastic spectator at Meadow Lane. He had not become a supporter of Notts County, for he remained faithful to Sheffield United and much of his pleasure was derived from making unfavorable comparisons between the team of his real affection and the eleven incompetents whose antics he witnessed every other Saturday afternoon. Watching County —as he bored the men around him on the terraces with stories of United—gave him a rare feeling of indisputable superiority. And there was a second reason why he looked forward to a lifetime of Saturday afternoons at Meadow Lane. Soon Bert would be old enough to go with him—to be lifted over the turnstile and shepherded down to the front of the terrace where he could watch the game with other little boys.

"That's my lad," Herbert would say, when the great day came— nudging the man next to him and pointing to the rows of identical close-cropped heads twenty yards in front of them.

"That's him, the one without a cap. He's a great footballer. They say he'll be a professional one day. They say he'll be on United's books when he's sixteen."

Herbert could think of nothing else except that fading dream. However, he repeated, "Saturday afternoon it is. No bother. I hope it's not gone. You should have told me straightaway. It might have gone." There was only the faintest sound of hope in his voice.

"No, it hasn't gone. He said he'd keep it. Said that you'd have first refusal."

It was then that Herbert became curious about how Augusta had found out about the sharpening job. So he asked her for a second time and, for a second time, she answered a different question.

"I wouldn't even have told you about it if it hadn't been for the dropsy."

"I don't mind. It'll be nice to work with the tools again. Where is it?"

"Alfreton Road. It's the old shop." Augusta decided to risk everything. The time had come to reveal all the details. "Willie Foster's come into a bit of money. It's hard to credit, he's been working for years. The shop's been empty all these years and he's rented it to make it an ironmonger's. He wants to repair knives and scissors and he went and asked Winifred if she thought you'd do it and she came and asked me."

"You don't repair knives and scissors. You sharpen 'em. You set 'em and you grind 'em. But you don't repair 'em." It was all that Herbert could think of to say. So he said it again. "You don't repair knives and scissors."

He might have asked Augusta if she understood the anguish which he would feel spending each Saturday afternoon doing the work of a gypsy peddler in the shop where he had once made medical instruments. He could have told her of the humiliation of laboring for Willie Foster at the bench where he had once dreamed of becoming master of the Empress Works. Or he could have described the shame of returning to the scene of the silly little crime that had brought him so low. But Willie Foster's father had convinced him that when it hurt it was important for the pain not to show.

Herbert had so often been complimented on his cheerful disposition that he had begun to believe that nothing made him unhappy for very long. He would, he was certain, feel better in the morning.

"I'll go and see him tomorrow. A real chip off the old block, Willie is. I liked him when he was a lad."

"You were very kind to him, Herbert. I remember you taking him to cricket matches. He's repaying your kindness. It just shows."

When, next night, Herbert Hattersley called at the Fosters' house, Jack's widow—no longer pink and round but wizened and gray—told him that her son had walked around to the shop to clean the window. Herbert followed and found the new ironmonger preparing to open for business on the following Monday. Working by the light of the gas lamp which stood outside on the pavement, he was prizing from the plate glass the enamel letters which the old owner used to read with such unreasonable pride—"Frederick Hattersley and Sons, Cutlers and Scissor Makers of Sheffield." Herbert consoled himself with the thought that, as well as doing his duty by Augusta, he was doing his best for his son. At ten, Bert was very little like his father had been at the same age. But that did nothing to dampen the hope that he would become the man which Herbert had once hoped to be.

Herbert had not inherited Frederick's belief in dynasty and family destiny. But he had a clear view of his son's obligation. Bert had a duty to be a superior version of his father—avoiding Herbert's occasional mistakes and achieving the success which Herbert had been so unfairly denied. Frederick's obsession with the firstborn had almost been forgotten. But the idea that the eldest son was special was in Herbert's blood. His only ambitions for Bert were modest, perhaps even trivial, by comparison with the Sheffield dreams of a great cutlery empire. But he wanted Bert to follow in his footsteps by doing the things which he believed that he had done well himself. And he wanted his son to live the good life which had always eluded him. He hoped to live again through Bert and, thanks to him, enjoy the second chance that life will not provide. Little Bert was a diminutive Herbert. When Bert laughed his father was happy. When Bert cried his father was sad. Herbert would humiliate himself in the old shop on behalf of his son.

Herbert struggled to do all that was necessary to safeguard Augusta's health and protect her welfare, and when his determination or spirits flagged he always thought of Bert who, when he grew up, would redeem all his father's failures and make the indignities worthwhile. He did the work of a gypsy peddler for six, rather than five, hours every week. But he came to an arrangement with Willie Foster that allowed him to mind the shop when Notts County was playing away and Willie was watching Nottingham Forest. The rest of the grinding and setting he did on weekday evenings after cycling straight from the Raleigh on the heavy upright "All-Steel Bicycle" which the company had sold him at cost price.

The income lost to the family when his wife stopped giving music lessons having been almost made up, Herbert continued to make nightly visits to the Grove Hotel. At first he simply called in after his hour's work in Alfreton Road was over and drank a single pint in the public bar. Then he adopted a scheme which, he convinced himself, provided more security and comfort for his sick wife than his delayed return home. Having finished his hour's sharpening and setting, he made his way home to Grove Road and, on entering at the back door, always asked with real concern, "How do you feel, love?"

"I feel fine." The reply never changed. "I'm fine. I don't know why you worry about me so much."

Reassured, Herbert sat down at the kitchen table and ate the meal which his sick wife had prepared for him. Then, having finished his meal, he washed in the basin of hot water which she had filled in the kitchen and changed into the clean—or nearly clean—shirt which she had warmed in front of the fire, and pulled into place the collar which she had starched and ironed. Uxorious duty done, he walked down to the Grove Hotel where—since he had changed into his suit —he was able to drink in the lounge rather than in the public bar. He was always home before ten o'clock.

His singing, which had caused Augusta such distress when done in public or for money, was confined to one hotel and his own living room—where it caused Augusta unqualified delight. Each morning he got up early and cleared out the ashes in the grate and laid a new fire. On Monday mornings he got up particularly early and filled and lit the boiler in the washhouse. When the sheets and towels were thoroughly soaked, he rotated the wooden dolly-peg in the zinc wash-tub with such manic vigor that his wife feared for the safety of the threadbare bedclothes. On Sundays he swept the yard, cleaned the windows and peeled the potatoes. But for one particular, he did everything possible to ensure his wife's complete recovery. Unfortunately, with Augusta's happy complicity, he failed in the area where success was most important.

First there was little Muriel. Then, within a year of Muriel's birth, Augusta was pregnant again. After the miscarriage, she was confined to bed for six weeks. When, after another twelve months, she was pregnant once more, the doctor told her not to put a foot to the floor for two months. She stayed in bed with better grace than before. But it did not save the baby.

Winifred asked Clare if she should offer a word of advice about how, in the future, such dangers could be avoided. Clare warned strongly against such an initiative.

"Even when Catholics do such things, they don't thank you for reminding them of it. Anyway, Augusta doesn't and wouldn't dream of it. It is called faith. The Church tells her that she exists to bear children. She believes it. Faith, Winifred, faith. It will see her through dropsy and a lot more.

With some reluctance Winifred agreed to concentrate her time and energy on helping to care for the patient and her children. Clare insisted that she would continue to keep an eye on them overnight.

Augusta loved all her children, but she loved them in different ways. In the early years of her illness she realized that she would come to rely on her daughters more and more. So she loved them with antic-ipated gratitude. Les was kind and sensible and he received a kind and sensible love in return. Bert she thought of as what he was, his father's boy. Roy was treated with a respect which amounted to reverence. For Roy was going to be a priest.

Winifred, who would not accept that Bert was exclusively his father's property, spent her days trying to love him and, with even less success, trying to make him love her. Bert showed every sign of growing up into a perfectly normal boy. And normal boys do not crave the company of elderly great-aunts. Winifred believed in presents and would certainly stoop to buy affection. But she only believed in presents of an improving nature. Bert showed no sign of wishing to be improved.

It was Bert's attitude to work which finally turned Winifred toward his brothers. Bert had agreed, with neither enthusiasm nor resentment, to stay at school until he was fourteen. Then, having taken part with his father in a great deal of pointless whimsy about becoming a cutler, he announced that Tom Cross had got him a job in the packing department at I. and R. Morley's. Winifred, who still had a little influence at the bakery which John had once owned, tried to convince him that he ought to learn a trade. Bert was not ungrateful, but he did not see his future mixing dough and icing wedding cakes. He signed on at Morley's and the baker's apprenticeship was marked out for Les.

On Les's first day at the bakery, Winifred acquired a new great-nephew to worry about. The boy to whom Augusta gave birth after six childless years was christened William George in the front bedroom of 59 Grove Road, since the proud mother was too ill to leave her bed. The father, agonized by the spreading of the dropsy to his wife's neck and shoulders, was fascinated by his new son, who had been born complete with a head of hair which emerged into the world looking as though it had been slicked down with brilliantine. While Augusta was what the neighbors described as "at death's door" Bert took advantage of his mother's incapacity and joined the Boy Scouts, an organization which Augusta had proscribed as being identified with the Church of England. Disloyally, Winifred encouraged the treachery. She bought him hat, neckerchief, lanyard and belt, promising the full uniform as soon as he passed his tenderfoot test. She thought of Scouts as his last chance to prove that he was interested in more than swimming in the canal and fishing in the river Trent.

As always, she was disappointed. Bert's fascination for tying knots, following tracks and identifying edible roots was only temporary. He remained a Scout for little more than a year, finally confessing that he had never felt any enthusiasm for being prepared or doing his duty to God and the King, but had hoped that, one day, he might go to camp in Sherwood Forest. The uniform was passed on to Roy just as Augusta's attention was diverted by the birth of Charles Sydney—"definitely the last," as Herbert told the doctor who fought to save the mother's life.

Roy became a Boy Scout of the intellectual variety. During his first week in uniform, he read *Scouting for Boys* from start to finish. Then he persuaded his Great-Aunt Winifred to buy him books on the wildlife, the plants and the topography of the East Midlands. He worked through them all methodically.

Augusta boasted to her sister Clare, "He can read as well as I can."

The paragon's father added as a footnote, "He reads too much. He ought to get out like Bert."

The two women defended Roy in different ways.

"Bert didn't do much scouting either, as I recall," said Clare. "No more than Roy does."

"Poor lad," said Augusta. "Roy does try to do all those things. He tries very hard. But the glasses don't help."

"They certainly don't go with the uniform. He's more an altar boy than a Scout." Clare hoped that her faith in Roy's clerical instinct was justified.

Augusta had no doubt that what her sister said was true. "You know he got a prize? He brought it home yesterday." She pulled open the top drawer of the sideboard and felt behind the knives, forks and spoons which lay side by side in their separate compartments. When she withdrew her hand, she was holding a bronze medal. "I never got one of these, did you, Clare?"

Clare took the medal and tried to translate the Latin message which surrounded the tableau of Virgin Mary and infant Jesus flanked by kneeling children.

"I certainly did not. *'Mater Admirabilis Monstra' . . .*"

"It's in English on the other side," said Herbert.

"No, it's not," his wife corrected him. "Read the other side, Clare. Read it."

" 'Reward for Good Conduct and Advance in Learning from the Catholic School Committee.' "

Herbert stretched and turned to his wife. "I thought, love—I thought last night when you showed it me—that I had a medal like that one, only it was from the Poor Law. Do you remember? You had one as well, your granddad's Handel Medal from Crystal Palace. I wonder what's happened to them?"

Augusta reached into the drawer again and, from behind the knives, forks and spoons, pulled out the two medallions which, so long ago, she had used to prove how much she had in common with her husband.

"Good," said Herbert. "I'm glad they're not lost."

He returned to his paper and began again to search for the news which increasingly obsessed him. Thanks to the other old soldiers with whom he occasionally drank at the Grove Hotel, he had made a wonderful discovery. He had found out who was responsible for the failures which had dogged him for twenty years.

Herbert Hattersley declared war on Germany long before Herbert Asquith followed his example on August 4, 1914. The official casus belli were well known in 59 Grove Road. For as soon as Herbert Hattersley finished reading the sports pages of the *Nottingham Post* or *Evening Mail* and glanced at the headlines of foreign news, Germany's multiple iniquities were explained to the family in language which grew so familiar that the older children taught their younger brothers and sisters to chant their father's unchanging complaints as if they were part of Church liturgy.

"Who supported the Boers against our army?"

"The Germans."

"Whose battleships were built because they were jealous of our navy?"

"The Germans."

Some of the complaints were too complicated for translation into children's games. Herbert's contempt for the little German Emperor —posturing in his preposterous boots and eagle-crested helmet— was an adult passion based on resentment that the dwarf behind the waxed mustache should believe himself the equal of the Britannic Majesty to whom he was lucky enough to be related. But it was not the principal cause of Herbert Hattersley's anger. The underlying reason for the undying hostility was never mentioned across the breakfast table or in the late evenings when the newspapers were taken from under the cushion of the best armchair and used again to prove the invincibility of Sheffield sportsmen and the perfidy of the government in Berlin. The betrayal which caused most anger and indignation was German industry's willful disregard for the legitimate interests of Herbert Hattersley and his family.

Had it not been for the Germans, Herbert Hattersley would have been able to continue his proper trade of medical-instrument maker and the family business, which was rightfully his, would be prospering under his direction. In winter, when the gas lamp outside the shop was lit, he could see the outline of the boast with which it had once been decorated: "Frederick Hattersley and Sons, Cutlers and Scissor Makers of Sheffield." As he tied on his calico apron and gave the grinding wheel a few speculative turns he cursed the nation which— by selling cheap cutlery to undiscerning customers—had caused his downfall.

He had not the slightest doubt about the cause of his destruction. The confusion over the accounts and the subsequent disagreement with his father were blocked out of his mind. So was Frederick Hattersley's obstinate refusal to move the Empress Works with the times. All that Herbert remembered was the cheap Soligen knives in Nottingham shop windows—knives with blades which bent, handles which came away from shafts when put in hot water, but knives which sold for half the price of knives made in Sheffield. The Hattersley children, instead of being taught the virtues of prudence, punctuality and parsimony in the family tradition, were encouraged to look under pots and pans for the trademark of the Zollverein and to translate DRGG as "Dirty Rotten German Goods."

Germany was also convicted of causing his minor irritations. He did not blame the Hohenzollern for Augusta's dropsy, but he did hold them responsible for circumstances which aggravated her condition. As the swelling got worse Augusta spent more and more time resting in bed. And most of that time was employed in worrying about her children. She worried about the girls because too much of their young lives was spent on housework. She worried about Les because she feared that the world would not properly reward his special sort of reticent virtue, and she worried about Bert because Herbert hoped for so much and she did not want his father to be disappointed again. She worried about Syd and George because they were so young and did not receive the care and attention which an able-bodied mother could have given them. But most of all she worried about Roy.

Roy grew increasingly priestly with every day that passed—doing the things which teenage boys do but doing them in a priestly way.

He looked out on the world through rimless glasses, parted his hair almost in the middle and adapted his inherited enthusiasm for football and cricket into a passion for scores, records and statistics. To Augusta the vocation had become obvious. Yet it was a vocation which she increasingly feared would be denied her son because she was married to a polisher at the Raleigh Bicycle Company.

Augusta never put her sadness into words. But several evenings each week—as her husband was putting on his clean collar—he caught sight of her in the mirror, brooding about the denial of God's will and her ambition. It was an ambition which Herbert did not share. All his thoughts for the future concerned Bert and he had neither hope nor wish to see his third son a priest. But the constant reminder that his wife's great hope would be frustrated by his failure was a burden which bore down on him so heavily that often the feeling of shame and guilt troubled him all the way to the Grove Hotel.

Sometimes to comfort their sister, Clare and Sister Assumpta talked about France and Spain where poor boys from families which could barely feed and clothe them were sent to seminaries by the Church itself. But Herbert did not believe that such things happened in England, and the idea of his son becoming a pauper priest, relying on the charity of Rome, seemed doubly wrong. He wanted to afford whatever his wife chose for Roy and he wanted—relying on the status provided by his prosperity—to forbid his wealth being spent on making his son an agent of the Pope. It was thanks to Germany that he was so far away from living the life of his choice. He dreamed of the whole British Empire taking vengeance on the architects of his humiliation and of the Hattersleys of 59 Grove Road taking part in the act of retribution. Yet when the day of atonement dawned, he did not even realize that the family was preparing to strike back and that his son would be the champion who fought in the family name.

CHAPTER THIRTY

FOR KING AND FILEY

On the morning of April 24, 1914, Bert hurried down the passage which separated 59 Grove Road from the shop next door. But he hurried with care. He had grown from a wiry child into a tall, muscular youth. The khaki kit bag which he carried on his shoulder was so huge that he swayed slightly as he walked, and he was anxious not to graze his bare forearm or, far worse, scuff the dirty canvas against the crumbling brickwork of the passage wall. As always, the gate at the end of the passage was ajar and, as always, Bert kicked it wide open. He lifted the kitchen-door latch with his left hand and, leaning forward, used the kit bag as a gentle battering ram to swing it back on its hinges. Inside the kitchen, he let the kit bag fall onto the pegged rug which his mother repaired each Sunday morning by replacing the tufts of old cloth that the flying sparks and spluttering coal had burned. His father stood with his nose close against the sideboard mirror, far too engrossed in the task of trimming his mustache to notice what was happening in the room behind him. But he did hear the thud of the falling kit bag. Turning with a start which almost destroyed the careful balance of hair on his upper lip, he uttered his sternest rebuke.

"Eh up, steady on," he said, and returned to his preparations.

When he next turned around, his son was piling what appeared to be secondhand clothes onto the kitchen table. Herbert Hattersley watched with apprehension as a pair of heavy boots was removed from the kit bag, fearing that the heap of flannel shirts and heavy trousers might, in some way, be related to angling—a pastime which, much to his father's distress, Bert preferred to more physical sports. His second reaction was more considered but equally characteristic.

"You better move 'em before your mother comes downstairs; there'll be hell on. What are they anyway?"

Without waiting for an answer, he began to rub brilliantine onto his hair. Upstairs, Augusta Hattersley heard the noise of the kit bag hitting the kitchen floor as she began what was known in 59 Grove Road as a "lie-down." The noise convinced her that Syd or George had suffered some awful catastrophe, a conviction intensified by the knowledge that her husband had promised to keep an eye on them through the kitchen window as they played in the yard. She had no doubt that she was urgently needed downstairs to prevent her husband from good-naturedly compounding a fracture or increasing the bleeding which he was attempting to stanch. She moved as quickly as she could, pulling battered old shoes onto her grotesquely swollen feet and holding her breath as she struggled to refasten the hooks and eyes of her loosened corset through the wool of her dress. By the time she got downstairs, Bert had explained to his father the significance of the kit bag and its contents and Herbert Hattersley had become an expert in the uniforms of the Territorial Army.

Augusta Hattersley was only an expert in bringing up children and humoring their father, and she had made a point, throughout her marriage, of knowing nothing in order that her husband should enjoy the pleasure of remedying her ignorance. She did, however, recognize a soldier's uniform when she saw one. Such a uniform was laid across the best and only comfortable chair in the kitchen, like a scarecrow that had lost its stuffing. Her husband—sitting on the edge of the table and attempting to wind large strips of cloth around the bottoms of his trouser legs—was too busy playing soldiers to concentrate on the consequences of what their son had done. Augusta felt a deep resentment that her husband, who doted on Bert, had neither the sense nor the energy to save him from disaster. It was Herbert's job. But Herbert showed no sign of doing it. Augusta, as always, took over.

"Have you signed the papers yet?"

It seemed the obvious question, the test by which she could judge what hope remained of her putting things right as she had put things right so many times before. She was appalled that her son answered so calmly.

"Tonight, straight after work. We all did it tonight. Ten of us."

Augusta had always been responsible for family discipline, while Herbert concentrated on sentiment and indulgence. Bert often argued with his mother—usually by employing the same unsuccessful tactic. What he had done, or what he had wanted to do, was—he would claim—no more than normal behavior. When, at the age of five, he had wanted to play on the land at the other side of the railway line, he had insisted that Ed Berry, Johnny Paice and Jack Burton were all allowed to play there. Five years later, after he was caught smoking, his defense was that Ed, Johnny and Jack were inveterate smokers. His mother was never impressed. For she believed that, in all of Nottingham, hers were the only children who were properly brought up. The announcement that half the neighborhood had taken the King's shilling only left her in despair, particularly if, as she suspected, the lead had been taken by Jack Burton, Bert's hero and the object of her concentrated disapproval.

"Don't suppose you know if we can get you out—buy you out like your father was. Having been through it, Herbert, you'd think you'd realize. I'll go tomorrow and find out how much it will be."

Herbert did not resent, in the slightest, the reference to his single day's service with the cavalry. He told his wife, "Don't worry, love. It'll be all right. He's only a Territorial. Not a regular like I was."

Augusta was not satisfied by Herbert's assurances. She wanted a more certain solution to the crisis. "Have you got time to change your mind, or do I have to buy you out?"

"I don't want to be bought out, Mam," Bert told her. "I won't change my mind."

"You will," Augusta Hattersley insisted, "when you are on a boat going to Egypt or South Africa."

"It's only the Territorials, Mam, it's only evenings."

As Bert attempted to extend his explanation his father interrupted him with what he believed would be the crucial comforting fact. Beaming with pride, he explained, "He keeps his rifle in Derby Road Drill Hall."

There then followed an extended presentation of all the facts about the Territorials which Herbert Hattersley knew—three in all. Lord

Haldane (although a Liberal) deserved much credit for inventing them. The name was based on the notion of the "Territorial Commitment" to serve within Great Britain, not abroad. Young men could join immediately after their sixteenth birthday. Herbert was wrong about the minimum age for enlistment, for he simply repeated the lie which Bert had told in anticipation of his mother's questions. Augusta, confounded by the unusual experience of being wrong, accepted the details—real and invented—with no more than a repeated request for reassurance.

"Only at nights?"

At last, Bert was able to add the information with which he had longed to astonish his family since he got home.

"And Filey. A week at Filey. Every summer we go to camp at Filey. First week in August."

His mother's response was numbingly predictable. Had it been designed to dampen Bert's spirits, it would have been no different. In fact, it was intended to be nothing except cautious.

"What about Morley's? They won't let you go."

"Morley's is OK. They want us to join. They put a notice on the board. Jack Stanley, Walter Howell, Bert Godfrey, Harry Hart and Ed Berry. Six of us was from Morley's. We all joined at the same time. We all took notes from Mr. Cross. Nip round and ask him, if you don't believe me."

"He ought to have had more sense. And more decency than to do it without mentioning a word. I'll go round there in a minute and ask him what he thinks he's up to. Does your Auntie Clare know about this?" Fearing that even the question might compromise Bert's innocence, his mother added, "There's not much goes on around here that she doesn't know about. There'll be a real to-do if she knew but didn't tell me."

"You really won't go next door will you, Mam?"

Augusta did not reply. She would not shame her son, but she was not yet ready to sound conciliatory.

It was the camp in Filey—"Fascinating Filey," according to the recruiting poster—which had persuaded Bert to enlist. He was sixteen and by every test (including his own esteem) he was a man. He shaved twice a week. Each Friday night he bought three Woodbines and three matches from the corner shop. On Lenton Recreation Ground or the wasteland at the other side of the railway line, he shouted and whistled at passing girls. But he slept in the same bed as his little brother Roy. And their bed was pushed against the sloping wall of the attic so that there was room for Leslie's bed to be squashed against the opposite wall. He had never been on holiday. And he had never seen the sea. The idea of skirmishing in the sand during the day and chasing the local girls along the promenade at night was irresistible. When the history of the Territorials was written, the noble voices which called men to the colors were described in patriotic detail. But the motives of 2042 Private Hattersley Herbert, D Company, 1st/7th (Robin Hood) Battalion, Sherwood Foresters (Notts and Derby Regiment), were never adequately described. He volunteered for King, Country and a week at Fascinating Filey.

Of course, his father saw his enlistment differently. Herbert Hattersley's imagination was incapable of visualizing anything which might permanently disturb the even tenor of his ways. He did not think of Bert pinned down by machine-gun fire, impaled on a bayonet or hit by shrapnel. He saw his son, smart as paint in a neatly fitting uniform, mounting guard at some great ceremonial. On the night of enlistment he walked home from the Grove Hotel fantasizing about the glories yet to come. The scene formed in his brain, like an extract from a play with a happy ending. "Was that your Bert that the Lord Lieutenant spoke to on the parade ground?" "It was." "What'd he say?" "It took me hours to get it out of him. Even then he wouldn't tell the whole story. Something about him being a smart soldier and a credit to the regiment. Bert said it was bred in him."

Herbert Hattersley unlatched the kitchen door, hoping that although he was unusually late home, the young soldier would not yet have gone to bed. He found the living room empty. But he was still not ready to end his military reverie. As always the gas was left burning. He turned it up and raked over the embers of the day's fire. But instead of sitting in front of it with the *Nottingham Post,* he began furtively to unpack the kit bag which was still standing in the corner of the room, occasionally fortifying himself from a pint bottle of light ale which he had providentially brought home from the Grove Hotel. The trousers he simply laid on the horsehair sofa. A puttee fell out of his hand and rolled across the kitchen floor. The tunic was hung on the doorknob while he removed his jacket and carefully put it over the back of a chair. Nervously listening for signs of movement in the bedroom above, he slowly pulled the tunic on. He reached down unsteadily into the kit bag and pulled out the webbing belt. He was about to fasten it around his waist when he noticed with disgust that the steel clasp which covered the buckle, instead of shining like silver, was as dark and dull as the kettle on the hearth. If Augusta had black-leaded it every morning along with the kitchen grate and the oven, it would not have been very different.

Herbert held the unpleasant object between finger and thumb, and examined it with the practiced eye of a failed cutler. The clasp was, he decided, some sort of test of Bert's guts and determination. It would take weeks of spit and polish just to make it look clean. Meanwhile, each Friday night, a drill corporal with a red sash across his chest would stand so close to Bert that the recruit would feel drops of spittle hit his face as he was abused about the disgraceful state of his equipment. Herbert decided to give his son's military career a flying start.

He draped the belt around his neck like a prizefighter's towel and, with both hands thus kept free, turned off the gaslight and felt his way out of the darkened living room. He closed the back door without a sound and, taking hold of his bicycle with the tight grip of fear, wheeled it gently out of the yard and down the passage, carefully avoiding stones and potholes which might rattle loose mudguards and cause the rusty saddle springs to squeak. He perched himself unsteadily on the cracked leather saddle and pedaled off toward the old shop.

The combination of the last bottle of light ale and the night air had an immediate effect. It took him some time to get his key into the lock and he had to make several attempts at fitting a new mantle before he was able to light the gas. As he struggled to pull the gossamer hood over the copper jet he bitterly remembered the days when, from that very shop, he had sold gas mantles by the gross, each box labeled with the advice: "The longest day has passed away, prepare for the longest night."

The single jet cast only a half-light on the bench at the back of the shop. But somehow Herbert Hattersley managed to unscrew the bolt which held the grinding wheel to its spindle. Fastening the buffing wheel in its place was even more difficult. But he did it. Then, holding the clasp against the soft fiber at the wheel's rotating edge, he worked away for an hour, only stopping to blow the dust from the clasp's improving surface so as to convince himself that it was gradually beginning to shine. When the work was done, he was sober, exhausted and covered from eyebrows to chin in fine gray dust. And the

412

clasp was fit to be stamped "Made in Sheffield." So he blew out the gas, locked the shop and cycled off into the cold clear night, singing the songs of a man who was satisfied with his labors. As he approached Grove Road the night watchman at Gunn and Moore's cricket-bat manufactory could hear his fine baritone voice praising the achievements of the British private soldier. "And when they say we've always won, and when they ask us how we've done, we'll proudly point to . . ."

Next morning, as always, he was the first of the family to descend the steep stairs into the kitchen. He raked out the cinders from the black grate and replaced them with a pyramid of rolled-up newspaper and kindling wood. He took great pride in keeping the edifice symmetrical and ensuring that when he covered it with half-burned coals it did not collapse. As soon as the fire was lit, he put the kettle on the hob so that it would be halfway to boiling—and half-ready to make the tea—by the time he returned from the yard with his full bucket of coal. He was about to open the kitchen door when he heard footsteps at the top of the stairs. Quickly he took the webbing belt with its gleaming clasp from under the cushion in the best armchair and laid it along the table so that the clasp hung down over the edge like a silver medal on a khaki ribbon. As he filled the coal bucket he grinned like a child in anticipation of sharing Bert's joy. He could vaguely see his son's figure through the window, and the moment it moved in the belt's direction he burst into the kitchen. Bert had his back to his father, but Herbert Hattersley could see that he held the bet in his outstretched hands, like a snake which he was about to dedicate to some pagan god before sacrificing it on the altar of the kitchen table.

"What about that then?"

Herbert, thinking of the pride with which the belt would be worn on that evening's parade, waited to be engulfed in a deluge of praise and gratitude.

Bert turned around. Despite the three Woodbines bought and smoked each weekend, the frequent shaving and the girls who were lusted after and shouted at from a safe distance, he was crying.

"You bloody old fool. We're the Light Infantry. The bloody thing's supposed to be black. They'll kill me tonight. You've done for me, you soft old bugger."

Herbert was speechless with humiliation. He had proved himself a fool to the son on whom he doted. But, at the bottom of the stairs,

Augusta, who had arrived unnoticed, was in no way incapacitated by the horror of the scene which she had witnessed. She hit 2042 Private Hattersley Herbert across the side of the head with the flat of her hand. It was a blow of such force that he dropped the belt. Before he could pick it up, he was addressed in a tone which demanded his undivided attention.

"Never let me hear you speak to your father like that again. While you live under this roof you will treat him with respect. Or, big as you are, I shall give you the hiding of your life."

Lady Middleton, along the road in Woollaton Hall, could not have been more imperious. Augusta was speaking in memory of the young man with sleek black hair, the Herbert Hattersley with whom she had fallen in love, cheerful, confident and everybody's friend. Above all, she was fighting to retain respect for her own past.

"Do you understand?"

To her husband she gave an order as irresistible as anything likely to be shouted across the parade ground behind the Derby Road Drill Hall.

"Take it to the Raleigh and get it blacked in the paint shop."

That night, Bert arrived at Derby Road Drill Hall with a belt clasp of regulation black. The drill corporals wore the red sashes which his father had talked about. But they did not stand so close to him that their spittle splattered his face when they barked their orders. They did, however, expect more from the men they drilled than the recruiting officer had led the volunteers to expect. Ordinary territorials got by on one night of training each week—a couple of hours on the parade ground, followed by a few minutes in which they dismantled and reassembled their rifles, naming the individual parts as they did so. But Bert had joined the 1st/7th, the Robin Hoods, the City Battalion of the Sherwood Foresters, which boasted a laurel wreath around its cap badge to prove that it was no ordinary territorial regiment. The 1st/7th Battalion marched on Tuesdays, performed what they quaintly called "musketry" on Fridays and, on Sundays, paraded again at ten o'clock for a purpose about which Bert was not altogether clear.

Sunday dinner at 59 Grove Road was Augusta Hattersley's one social event of the week. Sister Assumpta came round from the convent. Clare brought Tom Cross from next door and, since the service at High Pavement ended at eleven o'clock, Winifred arrived far earlier than was convenient to her hosts. Herbert got back from the Grove

Hotel shortly after one o'clock and gave token assistance with the final preparations—"showing willing," as his wife described the ten minutes of activity. He pulled the table from against the wall, set the chairs around it, piled cushions in the easy chairs so that the guests who sat on them could reach the table, and spread out the best cutlery across the white cloth. The cutlery was the only property of value which the Hattersleys possessed. Herbert polished every blade and spoon bowl in memory of the days when he made scissors and scalpels of equal quality. Then, when the weekly joint of beef was almost cooked, he sharpened the carving knife with operatic bravado, holding the steel upright in front of him and pulling the cutting edge up and down its full length with a dramatic speed which the children (who were always called in to witness the performance) greeted with the gasps of wonder and shrieks of delight that they knew their father expected. He went on sharpening until his wife decided that the joint was cooked and had stood long enough to be carved. Then it was placed before him on the table. But instead of carving it himself, he handed Augusta the knife as if it were a sword prepared for some mystic rite.

In neighboring households, the men could barely strop a razor, yet they were allowed to carve the one joint of the week. But at 59 Grove Road, it was the woman's task. Augusta had no doubt that were Herbert to perform the ritual, he would cut the slices so thick that even if there was enough to go around on Sunday, there would be nothing left cold for Monday, for Tuesday's meat and potato pie and for the mince on Wednesday. All she asked of him was that the knife was ready when the meat was cooked. The Sunday joint could not be allowed to wait.

It waited on the morning of Bert's first parade. It waited until half past two and then the impossible was first contemplated and eventually accepted as unavoidable. The family sat down to dinner without one of its members present. They had just taken their uneasy places when Bert appeared, hot and sweating, in the doorway.

"Upstairs and put your suit on. Quick," his mother told him.

"Aw, Mother," he replied, collapsing into his chair.

"I said, go upstairs and put your suit on. Quick."

Augusta paused in the distribution of roast potatoes. Everyone else around the table stopped talking and waited to be embarrassed as Bert slunk away, humbled in front of his family. But Bert sat tight, entirely unmoved. He was too exhausted to feel the usual fear of his mother. Augusta stood up, a Rodgers of Sheffield tablespoon in her hand.

"Upstairs. Now!"

Herbert Hattersley decided to reason with his son. Gently he took hold of the damp arm of the soggy tunic and led its occupant into the yard.

"You know your mother'll make you do it. It'll only take five minutes."

"Dad," his son replied, "I'm fucked."

Herbert Hattersley's fear left no room for any other emotion. But as soon as the sustained silence from the kitchen confirmed that his wife had not heard his son pronounce the awful word, shame began to mix with the panic. No one at the Raleigh would ever say such a thing. Were such an expression to be used in the Grove Hotel, the culprit would be removed from the bar at once and told never to return. Yet his son, after three parades with the local territorials, seemed to use such language as if it were normal conversation. Herbert found it difficult to express his shocked amazement.

"What's happened to you up there?"

Since, at that moment, his wife appeared in the doorway like an avenging angel, Herbert Hattersley was, at first, relieved that his son gave a literal answer to his question.

"I got there at nine and we drilled for nigh on two hours. Then we marched to St. Mary's. That took twenty minutes. Then, after the service, we marched back and the Adjutant said we were a disgrace to the regiment and that we had to drill till two, and Sergeant Willis drilled us until half past. It'll be the same next Sunday. We have to do it every week. I feel terrible."

Even Herbert realized, from Augusta Hattersley's reaction, the full significance of the confession. His son had attended a church parade and had, in consequence, taken part in a service conducted according to the rites of the Church of England.

"May God forgive you." If Augusta had any hope of divine mercy, it was based on her belief in the redemption of the invincibly ignorant. "Did you know what you were doing? Did you think about it? Roy, young as he is, would never have done it."

Bert knew exactly what he had been required to do. The church parade, far from being an act of genuine worship, was simply an excuse to drill on the Day of Rest. He could not answer any of her questions about the form of service or the extent of his participation.

He did dimly recall that the Lord's Prayer went on slightly longer than was usual at the cathedral and that the priest was shabbily dressed. The rest was a haze, driven into the back of his mind by exhaustion. He could, however, distinctly feel the ache in his shoulder where his rifle had so often thudded against his collarbone, and he knew that the skin on the tops of his toes was worn away by the constant friction of knuckle against leather. But after ten minutes of amateur inquisition, he had not given a single sensible answer to one of the questions about his apostasy.

Sunday dinner was ruined. The Yorkshire pudding had collapsed. The gravy had coagulated. The meat, like the vegetables and potatoes, was cold. Bert himself was, after all, allowed to sit at the table in uniform. For his mother regarded him as more the victim than the culprit. His father—incapacitated by the horror of a disturbed Sunday afternoon and terrified that he might be required to exercise discipline or exert authority—retreated into his own thoughts on the subject. All the other adults had an opinion to express.

Sister Assumpta, ever kind and comforting, assured Bert, "Everything will be all right as long as you go to confession and promise that, now you know it's wrong, you won't do it again."

Her brother-in-law assumed that she meant all right in heaven, for he knew, from his own limited experience, that if Bert promised never to go to church parade again, it would certainly not be all right with the Sherwood Foresters.

Clare took an impious interest in the form of the service. "Were the regimental colors on parade? Did you carry them down to the altar?"

Bert was about to reply with the literal answer that he did not but somebody else did, when his mother told his aunt, "It's not a moment for such questions. You should know that, Clare."

Winifred and Tom Cross looked at each other in bewilderment. Catholicism—even after twenty years of close friendship with Catholics—still simultaneously astonished and terrified them both. Sister Assumpta was overwhelmed by the unpleasantness of it all. But she did make the one practical suggestion of the day.

"We ought to talk to a priest."

Augusta built on the idea. "We ought to talk to Father Payne. He christened him."

There was the implication in her tone that the job had been done inadequately and that Bert's apostasy was the result of the mistake.

With Bert still comatose in the wicker chair, his mother put on her only coat and set off for the cathedral, thinking that at least the crisis had struck while she was actually wearing her best dress. She did not, therefore, need to go through the arduous business of changing her clothes before she sought solace, consolation and advice. As he gradually recovered Bert worried not about his immortal soul but about the awful risk of missing his week at Filey.

Father Payne saw her at once, although he was weeding the small patch of garden behind the cathedral on which he lavished his affection. For he had the arrangement of altar flowers and the mending of surplices to consider. He listened impatiently and unsympathetically to Augusta's account of her son's sin, which he decided to classify, at least in his mind, as venial rather than mortal. But his conclusion came as a great relief to Augusta.

"The boy is not to blame," he said, rubbing his hands together to remove some of the soil. "The blame lies heavily on those adults who tempted him. I shall see them tomorrow. Rest assured it will be stopped."

Early on Monday morning Father Payne, having inspected his roses and trodden on a couple of slugs, set out for the Drill Hall. The only soldier available for theological disputation was Corporal Timmins, a Boer War veteran who was employed as little more than a uniformed caretaker. Father Payne was not a man to do business with other ranks. So he simply told the corporal that he wanted to discuss a personal matter concerning a new recruit called Hattersley. Corporal Timmins was immediately sympathetic, assuming that the lad had either got a local girl into the family way or contracted some unmentionable disease.

"Captain Wakefield, sir, the Adjutant, sir, will be here in five minutes, sir."

Corporal Timmins made a mental note to identify this young Hattersley and treat him with special respect.

The Adjutant was not the whiskered warrior whom Father Payne had expected. Pale, clean-shaven and in his late thirties, he hurried into the Quartermaster's office, bracing himself for the tiresome conversation for which he had been wrongly prepared.

"I'm told there is a problem about one of my soldiers."

"Indeed there is." The priest was wearing his portentous look.

"I'll do what I can. But you understand he is still a civilian. It may not be a matter for me."

"But it is, Captain, I assure you." The drama had to be heightened.

Captain Wakefield was a man of action, not words. He could not think of anything else to say, so he sat silently waiting for the flood of disgust and recrimination which he expected to follow the description of the ruined girl. The discovery that the young man had committed no more serious an offense than attending church parade against the wishes of his mother came as a great relief. Father Payne wondered if the boy should leave the battalion. The Adjutant's relief was not so great that he was prepared to sacrifice battalion numbers. He played for time.

"What does the young man think about all this?"

Father Payne was scandalized by the thought that the young man might even have been consulted. He ignored the question. Matters of faith and dogma were not subjects on which he would ask the opinion of adult parishioners. The idea that a sixteen-year-old boy might be allowed to comment on such topics was offensive to him. Captain Wakefield had hoped that the priest would reply at some length, for he had already thought of a solution to the problem but was finding difficulty in choosing the right words in which to express it. When he spoke, he began badly but rapidly improved.

"Is not some sort of compromise possible . . . compromise, of course, by the battalion, the regiment, the army . . . not by you or the cathedral? Could not the young man march with the battalion to the door of St. Mary's and then remain outside, assigned to some special duty? I hesitate even to comment on a subject about which you are an expert and I am an ignoramus. But certainly the army has a procedure for such things. If he does not wish to take part in the service, we will certainly not try to persuade him to do so."

Captain Wakefield leaned back in his chair, well satisfied with his performance. His satisfaction was wholly justified. Father Payne was impressed by the idea, impressed by the authority with which it was advanced, impressed by the Adjutant's respect for Rome and, above all, impressed by the prospect of explaining, in 59 Grove Road, how his own ingenuity had averted a family crisis. He accepted the suggestion.

"I will tell the young man tonight what he must do."

"I think you had better ask him if he will do it." The Adjutant's suggestion was meant to be proper and helpful. Matters of faith were one of the few areas of personal choice left to private soldiers. And it is an adjutant's job to understand the strange psychology of young men. "He may not want to behave differently from his comrades. But if he does, tell him to make himself known to his company commander on Friday night. I fear that he may not want to do it. Eighteen-year-old recruits are always afraid of looking foolish, of seeming to stand out from the others, of being laughed at."

"*Sixteen*-year-old." Father Payne could not resist the correction. "Sixteen."

It seemed strange to the priest that Captain Wakefield should insist on arguing with him. "Eighteen. I do assure you."

Unused to contradiction, the priest persisted. "I know the family well. I baptized the boy myself. The week that Mr. Gladstone died. It was 1898. He is sixteen."

There was nothing left to be said. Captain Wakefield walked Father Payne out of the Quartermaster's office and across the parade ground. At the gate on Derby Road, he gave the priest the professional officer's farewell, the salute performed by touching the peak of his service cap with his swagger stick.

"Goodbye, Father, and remember, eighteen."

Father Payne was too pleased with himself to report or even remember the Adjutant's strange behavior. Bert was sent for and told what he must do. He accepted his orders without argument. He had no intention of behaving in the way which the priest proposed. Like his father, he was devoted to avoiding trouble for himself and pain for others. So he happily made the promise, knowing that when he broke it he would do so in a good cause. For several weeks, Captain Bailey, commanding D Company, waited for a Catholic private soldier, whose name he could not remember, to identify himself. But even when volunteers to guard the rifles were asked to step forward, Bert stood fast. Once, he came home from St. Mary's humming "Onward Christian Soldiers" as he changed into his suit. Roy, watching admiringly from the bed which they shared, asked him what the song was called.

"It's our quick march," he was told. " 'To Be a Farmer's Boy.' "

So, every Sunday between the last week in April and the last week in July, Bert Hattersley committed his little heresy. Whatever punishment was imposed upon him for the deception of his family and the denial of his faith, he was robbed neither of the talent necessary to become a good soldier nor of his enthusiasm to spend a week at Fascinating Filey.

CHAPTER THIRTY-ONE

DUTY DONE

At first, Winifred Gunn shared Augusta Martin's horror at the thought of young Bert serving in the Territorials. But she was horrified for reasons which were quite different from those which had caused the rifleman's mother to oppose his enlistment. Winifred's concern was not for the young soldier's safety, for she had visited the public library and discovered—slightly to her surprise—that Herbert had been right to insist that the "Territorial Commitment" required only service in defense of hearth and home. But, although she did not worry about the risk of death and mutilation, she was deeply concerned about the principle of accepting the King's shilling. While he was guarding railway stations and reservoirs from the threat of an imaginary invasion Bert would be releasing a regular infantryman for service overseas and thus making a war in Europe more likely. Winifred had become a pacifist—following the lead of the Labour Party, of which she had become a member, and the suffragist movement, to which she was devoted.

It was in their cause that she paraded outside the Nottingham Guildhall at the beginning of July 1914. Inside, Irene Casey was reappearing before the Nottingham magistrates, charged with loitering with intent to commit a felony and willfully damaging six panes of

421

glass. Miss Casey, it was claimed, had committed those acts on the day before King George was due to visit Nottingham.

Neither Winifred nor any of the other Nottingham suffragists was allowed into the court. So Winifred did not hear Detective Constable Smith describe the contents of the parcel which Miss Casey had been carrying when she broke the six panes of glass. They included a twenty-foot fuse, a detonator and three quarters of a pound of geddite.

In fact, Winifred knew nothing about the prisoner in the dock—except that she was a member of the Women's Social and Political Union and that while in custody she had been forcibly fed, according to her statement, one hundred and seventy times. Winifred was, in consequence, unequivocally on Miss Casey's side. After she had been refused admission to the court, she called at Grove Road—ostensibly to make one of her routine inquiries about the family's health and welfare but, in reality, to find another audience on which to shower her righteous indignation.

"I don't know anything about such matters," said Augusta.

"You can't say that, Augusta. You can't just say that you don't know anything about what's being done in your name."

Herbert sat in front of the fire, saying nothing, fearful that if he spoke, his aunt would remind him of his previous inglorious involvement in a suffragist meeting. Winifred launched into an assault on Major Ashworth and the other Nottingham magistrates. Augusta felt that she must say something but was not sure what it might be.

It was at that minute that Bert burst into the room, carrying a copy of the *Evening News*.

"Have you heard about this woman with a bomb? They reckon she was going to blow up the King. She was charged in the Guildhall, this afternoon."

He handed the paper to his father as Winifred rose to Miss Casey's defense. "She was charged with loitering and breaking a window, not murder."

"It says here . . ." Herbert paused dramatically before he read from the paper, " 'At the conclusion of D.C. Smith's evidence the Chief Constable (Mr. T. Clarke) remarked to the magistrates, "I am bound to ask for a further charge against her under the Explosives Acts. I am in touch with the Attorney General with a view to more serious charges." ' " Herbert took obvious pleasure in his aunt's discomfiture.

He turned to his son with obvious relish. "Your aunt was there, at the court today. She was demonstrating for Miss Casey."

"Get away!"

"I was there to support that poor innocent woman."

Bert had snatched the paper back from his father and was frantically reading the paragraph, which was headed, "A Bold Move." His mother was concerned by his obvious agitation.

"What's bothering you? You look frightened to death."

"I want to see if her name's in the paper. It says that the suffragists stormed the court. I'll get it in the neck at tomorrow's parade if they find out that my aunt was one of them."

"Don't worry." Winifred was more amused than angry. "Even your territorials aren't clever enough to work out that you're related to old Mrs. Gunn—unless you've been talking about me."

During the months which followed, Bert rarely talked about anything except the Territorials, and Winifred spoke about the suffragettes less and less. Irene Casey—finally on trial at the end of July—confessed that she had intended to assassinate King George. It was not the death blow to Winifred's radicalism. But it reminded her—as she had been reminded on average about once in each year during the two previous decades—that she often leaped before she was sure that there was a safe footing on the far bank. She remained certain that Bert should not have joined the Territorials and took refuge in a heresy of which, ten years before, she would have thought herself incapable. Let's hope he's like his father, she said to herself. Let's hope the enthusiasm will wear off after a month or two.

Afraid that Bert might lack his father's infirmity of purpose, Winifred comforted herself with the delusion from which the whole nation suffered. She consoled herself that there was not going to be a war.

The Hattersleys of 59 Grove Road read in the *Nottingham Guardian* that a Habsburg princeling had been assassinated in a Serbian town which they could not find on the map by two men whose names they could not pronounce. But the idea that England might, as a result, soon be at war never entered their heads. It would be unreasonable to blame them for their ignorance. Better-informed families continued their summer routines as if the map of Europe were not about to be rearranged. The Kaiser went on his usual yachting holiday in the

Norwegian fjords. Marshal von Moltke, Commander-in-Chief of the German army, continued to take the waters in his favorite spa. On the evening of Friday, July 31, 1914, while Bert was packing his kit bag in preparation for annual camp, the British Cabinet was meeting in emergency session to discuss the possibility of war in Ireland, not war with Germany. Filey still seemed like a holiday. Herbert Hattersley walked with his son to the Derby Road Drill Hall so that Bert could push the complicated bundles of khaki canvas and blancoed webbing on his bike rather than carry them on his back. Ten yards from the Drill Hall, Bert fastened on his equipment, and his father pedaled home thinking that the lad had become an old soldier.

Bert had feared that he would not sleep on his first day away from home. But he was snoring on the Drill Hall floor by half past nine and had to be shaken conscious at five o'clock the following morning. It was not a day on which a shave was necessary. Nevertheless, he shaved in his billycan of cold water. The march to the Victoria Station took almost an hour. Nobody in Bert's carriage had ever been on a railway journey before or traveled outside Nottingham. Their first expedition ended not in Filey, as they had expected, but in Hunmanby, three miles to the south.

The disappointment they felt and the hopes they harbored of an evening visit to the resort were worked off by an afternoon of hard labor—pitching the great bell-tents, securing the Quartermaster's stores and building the field kitchens out of turf. Once or twice they caught brief sight of the sea over the sand dunes which separated the beach from the mown wheat fields in which they built camp.

Bert knew that there would be no pleasure on Sunday. But on Sunday, they worked harder than even the most cynical squaddie had anticipated. There was drill before and after breakfast. Instead of the usual church parade, the chaplain conducted a "drumhead service." The whole battalion was drawn up on the crushed stubble which had become the parade ground, and the padre, just visible behind a pyramid of steel and pigskin, spoke of fighting the good fight, living a pure life, fearing God, honoring the King, respecting women and remembering their mothers. Then, after bacon and fried potatoes, they drilled again, practiced the construction of temporary shelters by slinging blankets between pairs of rifles and, after bayoneting sacks of straw, were told to clean their equipment in preparation for the evening's big event. It turned out to be inspection by the Officer Commanding the East Midlands Division, Major-General the Honorable E. J. Montagu-Stuart-Wortley. He addressed the battalion on all the subjects covered earlier in the day by the padre and added a few words on the Boer War and the Sudanese Campaign, in which he had played a distinguished part.

It was not until Monday afternoon that Bert prepared to sample the long-awaited pleasures of sea and sand. The battalion formed fours and marched to the beach. On the word of command, tunics, shirts, trousers, socks, boots (and any item of underclothing that overfastidious soldiers happened to be wearing) were removed and placed in neatly folded piles in front of the naked bathers. Bert, as a child, had always been bathed with his brothers and, as a boy, he had often spent hot summer evenings splashing about in the canal. But he had never seen a naked adult man. He could not avoid a guilty adolescent need to make comparisons and was fascinated with the different patterns and colors of body hair. But when he thought of the other soldiers looking at him, he felt a desperate need to cover his embarrassment with the North Sea that was gently breaking on the sand ten yards away. They stood for what seemed like an hour waiting for the order to run into the sea.

For a moment, the great commotion behind the ranks encouraged the belief that bathing was about to begin. Then a noncommissioned officer ran along shouting, "Clothes back on!" As the company commanders called their men to attention Jack Burton asked, in a stage whisper, if there were sharks in the sea.

"None of your business, lad," said Company Sergeant-Major Bright. "Just get those bloody boots tied up quick and leave thinking to them that is capable of doing it."

What had happened was the business of every man there. A telegram had arrived from Division Headquarters. It was a message from the Division Commander himself. Captain Wakefield had assumed that it was a message of congratulations on the smart turnout at the previous day's parade and almost left it untouched on his desk until the afternoon's bathing was finished. But his adjutant's instinct for good order prevailed and he tore the envelope open. The battalion was to return at once to Nottingham, there to await further instructions.

It took the territorials two hours to strike their tents, pack their personal belongings and secure the Quartermaster's stores. By nine o'clock they were back at Victoria Station. Before they could file off the platform into Shakespeare Street, the police had to clear a path

425

through the crowd which stood shoulder to shoulder outside the station. The special edition of the *Nottingham Guardian* which had heralded the Robin Hoods' return was still on sale: "War with Germany Imminent," "Territorials Return for Mobilization." Bert Hattersley had, at last, seen the sea and felt the strange holiday sensation of sand between his toes. But there had been no promenade, no funfair, no end-of-the-pier concert party. He had got no nearer to Fascinating Filey than four acres of grass three miles south of that promised land. His reward for the months of sweat behind him and the years of blood and toil to come was two days in a field at Hunmanby.

Captain Horace Wakefield's only consolation was the certainty that his whole life was organized with the military precision appropriate to a professional soldier. During the years of optimism and ambition, when he had hoped for a glittering military career, he had planned his days by the minute. As a young subaltern in South Africa, he faced the Boers with boots which were cleaned, cheeks which were shaved and bowels which were opened at exactly the same time each day. And, as the tunes of glory began to fade, his enthusiasm for the well-ordered life became a retreat and a refuge. When his once high hopes ended with the appointment as Adjutant to a Territorial battalion, he determined to remain true to his own demanding standards. Captain Wakefield was reliable.

On the morning of August 4, 1914, he woke earlier than usual. At first, he assumed that the sun was disobeying orders. Then, when the clock at his bedside table convinced him that it really was only half past five, he lay wondering why his metabolism had betrayed him. After a few moments' hard thought, he concluded that his adjutant's instinct had woken him in case of an early emergency. He decided to make his way immediately to the Drill Hall.

A workman leaned against the green, cast-iron Drill Hall railings, contemplating the flat tire of a bicycle which he had neatly balanced on one pedal against the pavement edge. Captain Wakefield noticed that the early-morning sun shone on the workman's brilliantined hair.

The feeling of camaraderie which unites all classes at the time of the breaking of nations welled up inside the Adjutant's tunic. "Mornin'. Punctured?"

He sounded genuinely concerned. Herbert Hattersley confirmed the Adjutant's perceptive diagnosis with a presumptuous nod and grasped the opportunity further to postpone what had become a walk to work.

"Don't often see you here this early."

Captain Wakefield remained benign. "Big day today. Back from camp last night. 'Spect mobilization this mornin'."

"I know. My lad's a Robin. He's not gone to work today. He's waiting to hear. A very smart soldier, my lad. You'll know him— Hattersley, Herbert Hattersley like me. He's called after me."

The proud father was about to mention that he was himself an old cavalryman, when Captain Wakefield decided to cut short a conversation which was clearly getting out of hand.

"I only meet soldiers who have been very good or very bad . . ." His false smile was intended to signal that the conversation was over.

"You'll know him all right. He's the one who doesn't go to church parades. He's RC, like his mother. I'm Methodist but she's strong RC. He's the one that stays outside St. Mary's." He smiled at the thought of his son's notorious conduct and repeated, proudly, "You'll know him all right."

Captain Wakefield knew him all right. Indeed, he had thought a great deal about the Catholic recruit who had, so far, failed to identify himself to his Company Commander. Ever since his strange meeting with the gaunt priest in the soil- and grass-stained cassock, the Adjutant had feared that the ambiguity about the soldier's age would result in some sort of difficulty for the regiment. After twenty years in the army, Captain Wakefield had no scruples about allowing boys to fight as if they were men. Poverty, paternity and the police—the three Ps to which the recruiting sergeants drank each night—encouraged dozens of likely lads to lie about their age. But once they had taken the King's shilling, the lie became the official truth. This young man —Captain Wakefield's adjutant instinct warned him—would, one day, be encouraged by his priest to tell the truth. He felt a deep distaste for anyone who would inconvenience the army over such a trivial matter. He decided that the boil ought to be lanced.

"I'm glad we've met, Hattersley. I've wanted to talk to you for some time, but never been sure how it could be arranged. Weeks ago, a priest came to see me about your son. Suggested he was underage. Don't think he is. But don't want any trouble. Talk to him tonight. Find out what's goin' on."

Captain Wakefield turned on his well-polished heel and disappeared into the Drill Hall, leaving Herbert Hattersley slowly to work out the implications of his confused inquiry. By midday, Herbert was suspicious and by half past five he was sure. Bert was too young to be a territorial. Augusta would arrange for his release. He hurried home.

When he got to Grove Road, his wife was having one of her lie-downs. Clare, who had made the family's tea, was emphatically in charge.

"She's really very poorly. I've sent Gus to the chemist's."

"Where's Bert?"

Clare was scandalized by Herbert's apparent, and uncharacteristic, lack of interest in his wife's health.

"Herbert, she really is very ill. I've sent Roy and George out be-cause they were making so much noise. Syd's gone with Bert. I hope Muriel is still asleep."

"Where's Bert gone?"

"To get a paper to see the news."

Clare still had only one thought. "Are you going upstairs to see Augusta?"

What hope she had of her wish being gratified was totally destroyed by the appearance of Bert, little Syd on his shoulder, in the kitchen door. Herbert Hattersley could have procrastinated in the hope that Augusta would recover in time to confront her son about his age before he was called to the colors. But he decided, as an old soldier, to act. He would talk to his son, man to man, in a conversation so serious that it justified the use of the front room. Then, when Gus got back with the chemist's patent remedy, it would be taken to her upstairs by a good father and responsible husband. He would tell his wife that—in her absence—he had solved a family crisis. Bert was not leaving home to serve in God knows what distant part of Britain. Tomorrow, the boy would be spending his usual day stamping the trademark on I. and R. Morley's stockings.

It was at that moment that Eddie Berry and Jack Burton marched into the yard at light-infantry pace with Jack, playing the part of sergeant-major, screaming exaggerated abuse. Clare was outraged and demanded a little consideration for the sick woman upstairs. The three abandoned their drill with unconvincing apologies and began to talk to each other in the exclusive language of an elite brotherhood. As Herbert listened to their boasts about distances marched and speed of rounds fired he grew increasingly apprehensive about chal-

428

lenging Bert's membership in the charmed circle. When he forced himself into their conversation, it was the failed cutler and the frustrated baritone who asked the question. It was not the inquiry which the good father and the responsible husband had intended.

"Bert, Bert . . . Bert." It took some time for Herbert to gain his son's attention. "We were having an argument at the Raleigh. We were arguing about territorials, what you do . . . where you serve . . . that sort of thing . . . I bet a bob that you have to stay in England."

Jack Burton, smart as always, told him, "We might go to Scotland."

Eddie Berry, naturally respectful and therefore solemn, offered a serious answer. "If there's trouble we'll go to Ireland so the regulars can go to France."

"But *you* can't go to France."

Bert sensed that, for once, his father was in earnest. "Not likely."

"We'll only get to fight Germans if they come up the Trent," said Jack. "By then your Bert will have got his marksman's badge and I shall be a general."

Captain Horace Wakefield spent most of the following day engaged in the tasks which were essential to a Territorial battalion's preparations for war. Obliging local printers produced leaflets calling the men to the colors. "Embodiment Notices" were published in local papers. The Quartermaster produced an inventory of portable stores and the Regimental Sergeant-Major confirmed that the armory's register was up to date and accurate. The anticipated telegram arrived at seven o'clock in the evening. It was addressed to "Lieutenant Colonel C. W. Birkin, Officer Commanding," but—as was his right and duty—the Adjutant opened it. Its message was a single word. "Mobilize."

Throughout the night, men reported to the Drill Hall and were told to muster at first light. The roll was called at nine o'clock. From a battalion of almost eight hundred men only seven were missing and even they arrived before the Robin Hoods marched off to temporary billets in the Victoria Hall at ten. Sleeping-out passes were issued to those who wanted them. But Bert, Eddie, Johnny and Jack elected to remain in barracks, dividing their evenings between the Mechanics' Institute, which had become the Other Ranks' Mess, and the streets of Nottingham, where their uniform proved irresistible to local girls. When, after almost a week of cottage pie and admiration, they formed up in the Great Market Place to receive the Mayor's farewell message, their thoughts were almost equally divided between the young women of their recent acquaintance who wept at the edge of the crowd and the prospect of new conquests in Derby.

Herbert and Augusta Hattersley were in the Market Place with Syd, George, Roy, Gus and little Muriel. Leslie could not miss a morning's work at the bakery, but he bought Syd a penny paper Union Jack and made Muriel promise to blow a kiss for him.

When the Mayor rose to speak, Roy recognized him at once. "It's Mr. Ball from 32 Lenton Boulevard. He has *The Times* every morning." Having reached the age of eleven, Roy delivered newspapers.

"Every man may rest assured that no dependent left behind, whether wife, children, father or mother, will suffer want. You are nobly doing your duty to us. We shall do our duty by you."

As the Lord Lieutenant called for "three cheers for the Robin Hoods" Herbert Hattersley nudged his wife and confided in her a secret which she, like everyone else in Nottingham, already knew. "The Mayor's son's a Robin."

Thanks to his training in the Officer Cadet Corps at Trent College, Albert Ball had been commissioned subaltern that day. Herbert sounded proud that Bert was to serve side by side with the son of an alderman. On that day, he was proud about everything.

"What are you going to do?" Johnny Paice asked Jack Burton.

"Think about it for a bit."

Johnny was not satisfied. "What do you think now?"

Jack lit a Woodbine and took cover behind its smoke, folding the letter back into the packet. It had been given to him, as it had been given to every soldier in the battalion, with the six shiny new shilling pieces which the privates received on their weekly pay parade. It had been written with methodical care by Captain Wakefield, and it announced that every territorial was offered the chance to volunteer for active service overseas "forthwith." It ended with a paragraph which the Adjutant regarded as a model of impartiality.

The choice is yours and yours alone. You must decide whether to volunteer to fight for King and Country alongside your friends and comrades or to remain at home performing whatever tasks the War Office think suitable for men who will not go to the front. Think hard and choose carefully. Your reputation and that of your family depends upon your choice.

430

Perhaps Privates Paice, Burton, Hattersley and Berry thought as hard, in preparation for their careful choice, as their age and temperaments allowed. But nothing in their conversation suggested that they were weighing moral duty against legal obligation, contrasting risk with reward or comparing pleasures with penalties. For most of the time, they simply asked each other variations on the same question —the question that not even Jack was able to answer.

"Have you no idea, Jack?" Johnny persisted.

Suddenly Bert came to life. "I'm going. I'm going to volunteer."

Johnny was incredulous. "What the bloody hell for?"

Bert had no answer. "Perhaps I won't. I don't know, do I?"

Eddie offered comfort of a sort. "We've got till Sunday."

Eddie had been amongst the hundred Robin Hoods who had initially refused to submit to an enteric fever injection. The medical officer, fearing mutiny, had decided to reassure rather than bully the frightened soldiers. So he told them stories about rotting corpses, carnivorous rats and water drunk from stagnant pools. It had done nothing to improve general morale. But most of the soldiers agreed to roll their left sleeves above their elbows and turn their heads to the right. Eddie was sure that at some time during his exhortations, Captain J. W. Scott had mentioned that next Sunday's church parade was the moment of decision.

"That's it then," said Jack, reassuming command.

"We'll decide next Saturday night and we'll forget it till then."

There were murmurs of agreement prompted by relief that the decision could be postponed for five days.

"And we'll all do the same," Bert added anxiously.

Johnny Paice asked again, "What do you think you'll do on Saturday, Jack?"

Next morning, the battalion paraded as usual at six o'clock. All men being reported as present and correct or accounted for, the second-in-command gave an order which, for all its simple clarity, left Bert bewildered.

"Volunteers for active service overseas, stand fast. Men not volunteering, one pace forward, march!"

Out of the corner of his eye, Bert could see Johnny staring into the middle distance, his pinched white face even more pinched and white than usual. Jack, who was supposed to tell him what to do, stood behind him in the third rank. The back of Eddie's neck, immediately ahead, gave no hint of its owner's intention. For a second, Bert hated them all—Jack, Johnny, Eddie, his mother, Father Payne, even Mr. Lawton, his old teacher at St. Mary's School. The people who were supposed to help him and tell him what to do had deserted him when he needed them most. Then he heard the crunch of hobnail boots on gravel and realized that he had made up his mind. He had stood fast while others had stepped forward. Eddie and Johnny had, he could see, done the same. But what about Jack? Suddenly, he was terrified of going to fight without his hero and best friend.

"Volunteers," shouted the second-in-command. "Right turn. March 'em off, S'geant-Major."

As they turned, Bert could see Jack smiling as he, too, marched off toward breakfast and active service.

Eddie Berry left his bacon and eggs untouched. "We've fucked it," he said, his head in his hands. "We've all got to go to fucking France."

"It was you who said we could decide on bleeding Saturday."

Eddie was scandalized by Johnny's allegation that somehow he was responsible for the horrors which lay ahead.

"Was it bloody hell? I told you what the MO said. It was clever Mr. bleeding Burton who told us to make up our minds on Saturday. Christ Almighty. What'll we do now?"

"Go to France," said Jack, "and, if we've got any sense, keep quiet before the corporal hears your whining and puts us all on a mutiny charge."

"How many of them neshed it?" Bert suddenly began to imitate both his father's braggadocio and the Yorkshire patois in which it was expressed.

"Half the bloody regiment," said Johnny, looking around the mess hall.

But he was wrong. As they filed out after the double ration of eggs and bacon which was their reward they saw the men who had not stood fast, still at rigid attention on the square. They remained dotted about the parade ground in the uneven pattern that they had created by stepping forward—the second-in-command having decided that justice required that they be given a chance to change their minds. On the far right, ten men from A Company stood shoulder to shoulder. To the left, a dozen D Company privates were scattered like pawns at the end of a chess game. Where C Company had been, not a man remained.

"Crackers," said Jack, "we're all bloody crackers."

CHAPTER THIRTY-TWO

THE FAMILY GOES TO WAR

The news that Bert had volunteered did not reach 59 Grove Road for over a week and even then not from Bert himself. Augusta Hattersley was out in the yard, hanging out her weekly washing, when Mrs. Paice from number 32 bustled down the passage between the houses with a letter in her hand. Mrs. Paice was constantly "neighboring," a sin of which Augusta particularly disapproved, for gossiping was not respectable. Augusta objected, in principle, both to borrowing and to lending and she would never even have contemplated leaving her children in another family's care. She prepared to rebuff her visitor. Mrs. Paice would not be denied.

"Why didn't you tell me?" Mrs. Paice was too angry to show her usual respect.

"I'm sure that I don't know what you mean." Augusta intended to sound distant. She took cover behind a wet shirt which flapped, patched and pathetic, in the summer wind.

"I mean our Johnny volunteering to fight, as you well know."

Augusta realized at once the implication of the angry allegation. "Of course I knew. I didn't think that I needed to tell you. I thought your Johnny would have had the decency to tell you himself."

"I found out just now. Nearly ten days after. He might be in France. Gussie, you should have told me."

"As you know, I keep myself to myself, Mrs. Paice."

Augusta meant both the form and content of her reply to be a rebuke. Nobody called her Gussie to her face. "Did he say anything about Bert?"

"You know very well he did." Mrs. Paice was weeping. "They all decided together one Saturday night. They'd been out drinking if you ask me."

"Not our Bert," said Augusta, picking up her clothes basket to signify that there was nothing more to be said.

In the Hattersley household, it was always Augusta who raised the serious subjects. Usually she waited to raise them until supper was eaten and cleared away. So when Herbert saw her sitting at the unlaid table—clearly waiting to talk to him—he assumed that the news was particularly momentous. Fearing that she was ill again, he sank down, agonized, beside her.

"Bert's volunteered to go overseas."

Herbert felt part relieved, part horrified and totally bewildered. He looked at his silent and hopeless wife.

"What are you going to do?"

The question seemed wholly unreasonable to Herbert. Augusta knew perfectly well that it was her job to answer serious questions, not to ask them.

"There must be something that we can do," she went on. "He's so young."

It was then that Herbert had one of the few moments of inspiration that illuminated his whole life. It was matched by a moment of parallel and almost equally rare bravery.

"He's too young. He always was. He shouldn't have signed on at his age."

Having admitted that he knew that Bert should not be in the army, Herbert was at once afraid again. He was afraid of Augusta's anger. But he was even more afraid of what might happen to his son. So he persisted.

"He was too young to join and he's too young to go to France. But I'm damned if I know how to get him out."

To Herbert's astonishment, there was no explosion of anger. For his wife regarded his explanation as a message of hope, not an admission of his complicity. Bert could be saved from the horrors into which Jack Burton had led him. Father Payne would know what to do and he would do it, if she was ever to darn a cassock or polish an altar rail again. Out of a respect for the priest's cloth she washed, carefully arranged her hair, put on her best coat and struggled painfully into her shoes before she set off for the cathedral presbytery.

Father Payne spoke to her in the garden where he was lifting potatoes. He did not pretend that he had not known from the beginning.

"The boy had reached the age of reason. He took the decision of his own free will. What he has done is a glorious thing. We must not discourage his instinct for service and sacrifice." He plunged his fork into the damp soil and leaned on the handle as he made sure that he was not outflanked. "There is nothing to be done. I have no doubt that Bishop Brindle would agree. He says that his years with the army were his greatest service to Our Lord. Let us go inside and pray together that, although alone and far from home, he will lead a good life."

For the first time, Augusta Hattersley declined a priest's invitation to prayer. Father Payne offered her a cabbage. Like the invitation to prayer, it was rejected.

On her way home, she began to worry about her pride and presumption. She believed that she could and must do what Father Payne had told her was impossible and wrong. And she was determined to do what he had told her was wrong. To reject the advice was deeply painful to her. But she had no doubt that she must fight on. By the time she got back to 59 Grove Road, she knew exactly what was to be done. She would write to her Member of Parliament. It was against the law for Bert to be a soldier and it was the Member of Parliament's job to see that the law was kept. Herbert would tell her where she had to write. He used to sing at Conservative and Unionist smokers. Indeed, he was a vociferous—if inactive—Conservative and Unionist himself. Herbert knew about these things.

"The man for this job," Augusta was assured, "is Lord Henry Cavendish-Bentinck." Herbert Hattersley, gratified in equal measure by the hope of his son's return and the request for his advice, pronounced each syllable of the name with exaggerated care.

"I thought our man was called Yoxall."

"Our man is," Herbert explained, "but he's a Liberal." The chance to remedy his wife's ignorance was not to be missed. "He won't do at

435

all. He used to be a schoolmaster. Lord Henry Cavendish-Bentinck is the man for this job. He's been a soldier himself."

Augusta did not bother to question the logic which led her husband to believe that a retired professional soldier would be an ideal ally in her battle to rescue their son from the army. There was, however, the usual argument about who should write the letter and it ended with the usual arrangement. Augusta gave her husband a little advice about its composition but gave it in such a way that, without his realizing it, the letter was written by her. On his own initiative, Herbert added a postscript of his own invention. It respectfully promised His Lordship the humble respects and continued support of his humble and obedient servant. The concluding words were "and oblige."

At the House of Commons, a clerk opened the carefully constructed letter and read the simple facts which it set out. It was not, the clerk decided, necessary to show it to Lord Henry. So he sent it, with compliments and a request for the favor of a reply, to Major-General the Honorable E. J. Montagu-Stuart-Wortley, Officer Commanding the East Midlands Division. At Divisional Headquarters, the orderly sergeant passed it on with more compliments to Brigadier-General C. T. Shipley, Commanding Officer the Sherwood Foresters Brigade. Eventually, and inevitably, it landed on the desk of Captain Horace Wakefield, Adjutant 1st/7th Battalion.

When Captain Wakefield read the letter which Brigade had sent him, he was outraged. He had always feared that this Hattersley would cause trouble. Now the battalion was embroiled in the indignity of a Member of Parliament's letter. Division would suspect that morale was low in the Robin Hoods and Brigade would hold him responsible. Captain Wakefield felt no resentment, only guilt. His adjutant's instinct should have warned him that the lad was trouble, and he should have taken appropriate action. But he still had no idea what appropriate action he could take. So he consulted the padre. The Reverend Henry Hayman—Friar Tuck to his friends and to the soldiers when he was out of earshot—lived up to his jovial reputation. He offered the Adjutant a drink and assured him that there was nothing to worry about. He would compose a response to battalion's letter which would bring the whole unhappy incident to a close. The following day, after dinner in the mess, he poured Captain Wakefield another brandy and offered him a draft which he regarded as a credit to his Oxford education and a tribute to his cloth. Every word was true.

This is not the first occasion on which doubts have been raised about this soldier's age. A Catholic priest (indeed, Father Payne, on the staff of the Catholic Bishop of Nottingham) discussed it with me some months ago. After our conversation he took no further action. I took an opportunity to tell Hattersley's father of our concern about his son's age. He did not avail himself of the chance to give me definitive information about his son's date of birth. There is no doubt that Hattersley is now into his eighteenth year ...

Captain Wakefield's reply was passed up along the route down which the original inquiry had descended. At each stage the recipient made the minimum alterations necessary to suggest that it was an original composition. Eventually, the version to which Major-General Montagu-Stuart-Wortley claimed authorship lay on the House of Commons desk of Henry Cavendish-Bentinck. His clerk made the few changes which were necessary for it to be transferred to House of Commons paper. The final draft explained that after the most thorough examination, the Member of Parliament had concluded that there was no possibility of immediate discharge. The clerk concluded with Lord Henry's thanks for the promise of continual support, signed it himself and (without troubling his master) posted it to his Lordship's humble and obedient servant.

Bert stayed in England for five more months. During the first winter of the war the Robins were twice put under orders to sail for France, and twice the orders were canceled. On each occasion, embarkation leave was promised, and when the plans to embark were abandoned, the leave was abandoned too. When the family was first warned that Bert was on his way to France, Gus—aged thirteen—opened her money box and spread its contents across the kitchen table. There was, she calculated, enough to buy twenty Woodbines as a parting gift and still have something left over for Christmas and Bert's birthday.

When the second embarkation was canceled, the family decided that the presents they had bought to speed Bert on his way would be parceled up and posted. Everybody was sending cigarettes—Mam, Dad, Leslie, the men from Morley's. Gus wanted to be different. So when she opened her money box again, she took out every one of her eighteen penny pieces and bought a shilling imitation-leather wallet and a twopenny notebook to fasten in it. She wrote on the first page of the notebook in her best St. Mary's copperplate, "Good Luck and Safe Return." Then she added, "To my dear brother Bert for September 1915."

"It's for his eighteenth birthday," she explained to her proud father, who watched in admiration as she formed the careful letters.

"You'll see him before then."

Despite the experience of the years, Herbert could still not distinguish between hope and reality.

When the third order to prepare to sail was posted, there was no promise of embarkation leave. Eddie Berry cursed and said that he knew for a fact that the Robin Hoods were the only battalion in Britain to be sent to France without a single day at home. Bert just carried out the next order, dazzled and dazed by the great adventure which he decided to record, in indelible pencil, on the pages of Gus's notebook.

Feb 24. Started from Bocking to Southampton. 114 miles. Embarked for France at 6:30. Steamed 3 miles out.

It was another false start.

Feb 26. Stayed in Harbor. Taken off at 3:30 for rest camp. Dangerous to move on account of German submarines.

On February 27, he "embarked at 2 o'clock on the Trafford Hall for Havre, France." And on February 27, they did not turn back. After an hour in the Channel, Bert was violently sick. Jack Burton, suddenly much older and far wiser, held his head when he vomited over the side, gave him a drink of water and held his head when he vomited again.

For the next eight months, Bert laconically recorded the great events of the Robin Hoods' campaign.

March 5th. Went to trenches with 1st Hampshires. Relieved after 24 hours duty. C. V. Shepherd killed by accident.

March 7th. Fatigue duty in Plugstreet Wood.

Two days later, he had mastered the proper spelling of the clump of trees which was to appear in so many dispatches and on so many citations for gallantry.

March 9th. March from Ploegsteert to Merris. 14 miles.

While official dispatches recorded that the battle for Ploegsteert Wood "was not crowned with the success hoped for" and that it proved "a murderous encounter," Private Hattersley 2042 noted the miles that he had to march between each engagement. Fourteen on March 11. Twelve more on the thirteenth, eight on the fifteenth, twelve on the sixteenth and twelve more on the following morning. The daily entries lasted six weeks. After that, only the great and terrible events were recorded.

September 3rd. Relieved the 8th Battalion near St. Elves. In the trenches where Sgt. O'Leary won the V.C.

Thursday Sept 29. Germans exploded two of our mines and then shelled us with 3 different kinds of shells.
    Lieutenant Cordeaux killed same night besides 20 other men wounded and killed.

October 4th. Went up to trenches in motor buses, went to place where big advance was made, hundreds of dead lying on the ground.

Bert was sick again—sick with nausea and sick with fear. And once again, Jack Burton, older and wiser, held his head. Then they went with the rest of C Company to help bury the putrefying dead. It was Jack's last act of friendship, his last chance to behave in a way which—had she ever come to know it—might have begun to change Augusta Hattersley's judgment of his conduct and character. After October 13 it was too late.

Our Division made an attack upon the Hohenzollern Redoubt. Jack Burton was killed on the same day, we were relieved from the trenches on the 4th day, then we went for a rest.

Jack and Bert had been born in the same year in the same road. They had played together on its pavements, chased each other down the passages between its houses and smoked their first cigarette together on the wasteland in which it ended. Bert knew that four lines was not much of an epitaph. When the battle was over, he tried again.

439

Jack was killed on 13–15, he was killed in a bayonet charge, I think that he was hit in the head by a piece of shell. Jack was eighteen and he was 17½ when he first came to France. The trench where we were attacking was called the Hohenzollern Redoubt and it was a very strong German position. Pt. H. Timson was killed at the same time trying to bury Jack.

It was the last entry. For almost a year, Bert had struggled with numbed fingers, damp pages and an indelible pencil that left blue blotches between the lines. After October 13, the diary did not matter.

When the news of Jack's death reached Grove Road, all the old animosities were forgotten. Augusta Hattersley told the sorrowing parents how much she had always admired their son, and Mrs. Paice went from house to house swearing that the elderly couple would die of grief. None of the neighbors even attempted to counterfeit the spirit of careless bravado which the *Nottingham Daily Express* encouraged its readers to believe they ought to share with "the lads at the front." According to the newspaper reports, the Robin Hoods—having twice captured the Hohenzollern Redoubt and twice been driven out by the Germans—leaped over the parapet for a third time singing a popular music hall song of the period: "Here we are, here we are, here we are again."

When Herbert first read the story, his heart swelled with patriotism. Then he thought of the Burtons across the road. Had they heard young Jack sing that song in their backyard? And did they think of him singing it when he fell?

Augusta reacted to the story in exactly the way she reacted to every story from France. Bert was still barely eighteen, and he had soldiered without a break for eighteen months. For a year, he had lived, slept, eaten and fought in the mud at Loos. Somehow he must be got home and it was her husband's duty to ensure his return. She did not blame Herbert for the enlistment. But she held him responsible for Bert's continued service. Herbert had failed to obtain his son's discharge. Indeed, he had not even attempted to arrange it. Augusta grew to hate her husband's sentimental assertions of love and pride. She decided that it was time for action and she knew that the action must come from her. So she took the initiatives which she knew to be appropriate to Bert's father. Letters were written to the King, the Prime Minister and even the Archbishop of Canterbury—though little faith was placed in the likelihood of help from the Primate of All

England. Any notable—local or national—whose picture appeared in the paper was asked for help. Most replied. A few tried. None succeeded. Month after month Augusta remained undaunted.

Early one May morning in 1916, little Roy returned from his paper round anxious as usual for his breakfast and unusually willing to talk about his experiences amongst the big houses on Lenton Boulevard. Normally, the delivery was uneventful. He trapped his fingers in ornate iron letter boxes, avoided vicious dogs and longed for an end to the fast which early-morning mass required and the paper round prolonged. But on that morning, he had met a war hero whose picture had appeared in papers he delivered.

Alderman Ball was, as usual, taking the air. As always, he gave the paperboy a cheery greeting. Then his son appeared through the front door of 32 Lenton Boulevard. When he got home, Roy pointed excitedly at the paper which his father was attempting to read.

"That's him," he said. "He was in the garden with Alderman Ball."

It was Lieutenant Albert Ball, lately of the 1st/7th Sherwood Foresters but recently transferred to the Royal Flying Corps. The caption beneath the picture was an encomium:

In seven weeks, Lieutenant Ball flew seventeen operational sorties and had many skirmishes with German aircraft. After his leave is over, he is being posted to No. 11 Squadron on the Somme.

Herbert Hattersley began to ask his son questions about the Lieutenant's appearance. They seemed to be based on the hope that the hero of a dozen dogfights ate his breakfast in jodhpurs, leather helmet and goggles. Augusta interrupted him. She had only one thought. If Lieutenant Albert Ball had leave, Private Hattersley should have leave too. While the bacon fat was still congealing on the plates she decided that, next day, she would accompany Roy on his paper round. If the Alderman was not in his garden, she would ring the bell.

Roy was horrified to hear of his mother's intention. To his knowledge, no paperboy in all of Nottingham had ever been accompanied on his round by a mother. But, at the age of twelve, he had learned that it was useless to argue with the full force of Augusta's will. The following morning they set off together, the son making no attempt to cover his reluctance. The mother, no less anxious than the son, was absolutely determined to do her duty.

Alderman Ball was, as usual, pacing his drive. He was only momentarily startled to see his paperboy accompanied toward his front door by a portly lady in her mid-forties. As Town Alderman and Chairman of the Gas Company he was often asked for assistance by both the deserving and the undeserving poor. He invited his panting visitor into the hall. Augusta thanked him but began to tell her story from the top step.

"I hope you will forgive me presuming, but I saw the picture in the paper. My son joined the Robin Hoods on the same day as yours. And he's not had a single day's leave. It's wrong for a lad of eighteen to be in the trenches for more than a year..."

"How old did you say?"

"Eighteen."

"So how old was he when he went to France?"

"Just seventeen."

He needed the age repeated before he believed it.

"Yes, sir, just seventeen."

"And not a day's leave?"

"Not a day's leave, sir."

Alderman Ball took his visitor's elbow and led her into his hall and sat her down on a chair next to the hat stand. Roy stood outside on the steps beyond the front door, nervously trying to make out his mother's shape through the stained glass. Augusta was given a cup of coffee, which she drank but did not enjoy, while all the details were taken down in Alderman Ball's pocket book.

"I will, I promise you," he told her, "do all that I can. It may not be much. The man I knew best in the battalion, Captain Wakefield, is back home in England. He had a nervous breakdown. But at least I'll try."

Augusta told herself that it was important not to hope for too much. When she got home, she wrote at once to Bert. But she did not mention the meeting with Alderman Ball. Bert had been disappointed too often.

Just a few lines to tell you we are all right at home and glad to hear you are all right. I got your welcome letter on Saturday.... Tom Cross has sent me these cigarettes for you from the men at Morleys. ... Mr. Lawton told your Dad on Saturday you were to be sure and go in to see him when you come home. They paid a bonus last week and most people think that they are keeping it in hand for their old boys. Good night and God bless you, may He send you safely home . . . will write again on Wednesday. . . . I am thankful you sound so cheerful.

Twelve-year-old Roy added a philosophic note:

Just a line wishing you in the best of health. Mother posted the fags she told you about tonight but they won't be sent out till tomorrow owing to an alteration in the collection. . . . I expect you are sorry you haven't had leave before now but your turn will come before long.

Gus, aged fifteen, included her own letter in the same envelope:

Dad has received your letter and has written to you. . . . We had quite a little party last Sunday night. All Tidy's and Florrie Smith and her husband and Alice Smith and the Swanns. Mr. Swann is a terror. You just ought to have heard them (I mean Mr. Swann and our dad) telling the tale. What one couldn't say the other could. Roy kept saying to me that Leslie was giving Alice Smith the glad eye. . . . Well dear laddie, I hope you will get leave before long. . . .

Bert read the letters sitting in his billet at Sus-St.-Léger. He had arrived in that shell-shattered town for what battalion orders called "rest and recreation." But he had spent his days in the weary tedium of mock attacks: always leaping the same parapet, always charging the same trench and always bayoneting the same straw-stuffed German. After he had killed the scarecrow a score of times, the plan of battle was clearly fixed in his mind. An artillery bombardment would demolish the enemy barbed wire, collapse the enemy trenches and destroy the enemy's morale. Then the Robin Hoods would advance under cover of smoke, dispatch the few surviving Germans and await the arrival of reserves, reinforcements and the rations. He marched back to the front line certain that, having survived the Hohenzollern Redoubt and Gommecourt Wood, the next battle would be no more than a Sunday picnic on the banks of the Trent.

For ten days it rained. Communication trenches collapsed under the deluge. Ammunition dumps disappeared beneath avalanches of slurry. Dugouts were washed away by sudden waterfalls of brown slime. The Robins dug to rebuild what the rain had destroyed. Occasionally, artillery salvos disturbed the digging. But for most of each day the German Second Guard Reserve worked like the Sherwood Foresters to rebuild its trenches faster than the rain could sweep them away. Then the deluge stopped and, from both sides of the line, the guns continued the work which rain had abandoned. Each morning the Sherwood Foresters marched to the front line and, during lulls in the bombardment, piled new sandbags on old and dug away at the crumbling trench walls. Each night they marched back through the mud of the supply trenches to their billets, there to sleep soaked to the skin on sodden mattresses until a sudden artillery bombardment sent them rushing, half-dressed and half-asleep, into waterlogged dugouts.

After almost two weeks of drudgery, the battalion was told to form up in "parade-ground fashion."

Eddie Berry looked for the silver lining. "At least it can't be the big push. We've not got the strength to hold our fucking rifles, and they know it."

Johnny Paice's years in France had made him suspicious of authority. "Then why the bloody hell are they handing out live rounds?"

Bert was too tired to answer. That morning, wringing water out of the socks which he had worn for a week and was going to wear again that day, he thought that he would gladly be shot in return for a dry hospital bed. The idea of a "Blighty Package" lifted his spirits. He fancied a small piece of shrapnel in his right arm and a stretcher-bearer close at hand.

As the battalion was stood at ease he feared that he would fall asleep on parade. He could hear the distant voice of the padre intoning a prayer which he had never said at home in St. Barnabas's Cathedral: "O God of battle . . ." Bert replied to every line as if it were a real prayer and demanded real responses. "I will not go to sleep. I will not go to sleep on parade."

He did not go to sleep even during the long journey through the knee-deep mud of the support trenches. The battalion shuffled forward a few yards at a time. Then they waited until the soldiers who blocked the trenches further up the line were, in their turn, able to shuffle a few paces forward. Whenever they stopped, they had to pull their feet free of the mud that sucked them in. The Robin Hoods squeezed into their appointed place after midnight. They had begun to edge down the mile of support trench at two o'clock in the afternoon.

"I haven't been so bleeding squashed since Forest played Villa in the Cup." Eddie was squirming from side to side, trying to rest both elbows on the sandbagged parapet, but the line of men was packed so close that he had to turn half sideways toward Bert.

"I'll sleep standing sideways or standing on my head."

But Bert was wrong. He did not sleep through the night of endless artillery bombardment broken only by the cries of wounded men, jammed so tight between their comrades that the stretcher-bearers could not reach them. When, at six o'clock, the familiar whistle began to blow, Bert was watching the stars gradually fade behind the German lines.

Eddie Berry spat over the parapet. "Where the bloody hell's the tea and rum? The Salvation Army complain that the officers get us blind drunk before an attack, and we stand here shivering in the bleeding cold without a smell of the bleeding stuff."

The first Very light of the morning cast a green glow over the trenches. Johnny Paice, leaning against Eddie Berry, looked like the genie Bert had seen escape from a bottle in the pantomime at the old Lyceum Theatre. When the order "Fix bayonets!" echoed down the trenches, Eddie was just sufficiently awake to disentangle his arm from the mass of rotting sandbag where it had spent the night. It was numb with cramp. He managed to withdraw his bayonet from its sheath, but before he could fasten it to his rifle he had lost all feeling and the bayonet fell on the water duckboards. He turned to Bert as he would have turned to his mother.

"My hand's gone to sleep."

Smoke canisters began to plop reassuringly into no-man's-land, exactly on time and exactly on target. The smoke was thicker than Bert had expected, and it was because of the coughing that hacked up and down the line that he did not hear the order to advance. The line moved forward and, moving with them, he was over the parapet and in the mud between the British trenches and the British barbed wire before he realized that the attack had begun. Automatically, he advanced as he had been taught to advance: walking until he heard the order to run, leaning slightly forward, looking for the marked gaps in his own barbed wire and determined to form up again into an orderly line once he was through them and out into open ground. He was barely through the British wire when the whistles began to blow and C Company broke into a run, cheering as they had been taught to cheer. Bert ran on, half-surprised that the smoke was still so thick but too tired to worry about anything except keeping up with the rest of the platoon.

It was exhaustion which made him fall. The patch of mud on which he skidded and fell was no different from the patches of mud behind him on which he had skidded but run on. He lay for a moment, spitting the bitter slime out of his mouth and screwing up his eyes to clear his vision. Then, still lying half-buried, he looked up. The smoke had begun to clear. Two hundred yards ahead was the German wire. Wire in loose coils. Wire stretched taut between posts. Wire crissed and crossed from pole to pole. Wire which the British bombardment had left intact and impenetrable. C Company of the 1st/7th Sherwood Foresters—apart from Private Hattersley Herbert 2042—was running toward it, like fish hypnotized by a net.

As Bert looked up the sudden specks of light which he had been taught to recognize as machine-gun fire began to sparkle on the German parapet. Their rattle was lost in the noise of battle which deafened the twenty-mile salient. But Bert recognized the flashes and knew why the Robin Hoods had begun to fall. He was used to the noise, accustomed to the mud, familiar with the sight of men dying around him. But never before had he witnessed such things alone.

When he looked up at the German wire and saw the flash of their machine guns, he was afraid. Instinctively, he said a prayer. It was a real prayer which began not "O God of battle . . ." but "Mary Mother of Grace . . ." Then he pulled himself out of the mud and did what the months of training—from the field at Hunmanby Gap to the first trench at Loos—had taught him to do. Thinking, Don't hold that rifle too tight . . . look where you're bleeding going . . . keep your wits about you, lad, he stumbled on toward the enemy.

CHAPTER THIRTY-THREE

DUTY BY THE DEAD

At 59 Grove Road, Herbert and Augusta Hattersley were much encouraged by the dispatches from the front which appeared in the *Nottingham Express.* "Heavy Fighting to Our Advantage" lifted their patriotic spirits. But the important aspect of the battle, as far as parents were concerned, was that it had been over for two days. The Saturday papers had promised a "big push." And the fear—unspoken by Augusta but repeated time after time by her husband—was that the first real news to reach the Hattersleys would be brought by a telegram boy, as it had been brought, after Loos, to the Burtons across the road. All Sunday, Herbert hovered in the front window, while his wife scolded him for "making such a show." Sometimes she pretended that she did not know why he was pulling the net curtains aside. Sometimes she told him that they would know soon enough if the telegram was on its way. But she always gave her own furtive glance in the direction of Lenton Boulevard. So when Herbert discovered that the battle had taken place on Saturday morning and ended gloriously with "Several Thousand Prisoners Captured by the British and French. Number of Villages Taken. German Casualties Very High," he decided that a family that had not received a telegram by Monday night need disturb its curtains no longer. He had no way of knowing that, on the day which began under the early morning's green Very light, twenty thousand British soldiers had been killed. The dispatch of twenty thousand telegrams in two days was beyond the ingenuity of even Sir Douglas Haig and the Imperial General Staff.

The telegram arrived almost a week after Bert had been killed. When Augusta Hattersley heard the knock, she thought at first that it was Father Payne making his regular Friday visit. She rushed through the house, tearing off her apron as she hurried, and kicked at the rolled-up carpet that kept the draft from whistling through the gap between the door and step. As she slid back the two bolts she began to worry in case the new front-room armchair was still covered with the old sheet that protected it on days when special visitors were not expected. When she pulled the front door open, she did not recognize the temporary telegram boy who had been recruited to deal with the sudden rush of messages, for he wore only an armband to demonstrate his special responsibility. But she saw the red Post Office bicycle propped against the curb and knew what it meant. She opened the yellow envelope with methodical care. There was no need to hurry, no need to tear at the thick paper. She knew what the telegram said.

DEEPLY REGRET HATTERSLEY PRIVATE HERBERT 2042 1/7 SHERWOOD FORESTERS KILLED IN ACTION 7.1.16. ARMY COUNCIL EXPRESSES SYMPATHY

As soon as she had read the words, Augusta felt ashamed of opening the telegram on the doorstep. She ought not to be standing at the front door. It was a moment for privacy—to share, perhaps, with the family but with no one else. Yet Mrs. Paice was running across the road, drying her hands on a dirty gray towel. Before either of them could speak, there was the noise of a rarely opened window sliding up on its ancient sash cords and Mrs. Berry was shouting from her front bedroom at the telegram boy as he disappeared past the Grove Hotel, "Are there any more? Are there any more at the Post Office?"

Mrs. Paice sobbed without speaking. Augusta Hattersley, dry-eyed and silent, went through the house and into the yard to find Roy. "Run up to the Raleigh," she told him, "and fetch your dad."

"Are you ill, Mam?"

As soon as he asked the question, Roy knew the answer and knew why he was being sent to bring his father home. Snuffling onto the sleeve of his old jacket, he ran down the passage between the houses.

His mother shouted after him, "Be careful of the tram when you cross the boulevard."

For the first time in her life, Mrs. Paice went inside 59 Grove Road. Without invitation, she began to make tea in the kitchen. For Augusta there were still no tears. She asked Mrs. Paice to take a seat and went into the front room to draw the curtains as a mark of respect. She noticed that the old sheet was still over the new chair. Then Jenny Paice was hammering on the front door.

"Mam! Mam! There's a telegram boy at our house."

The same telegram boy carried six more War Office condolences to Grove Road. He made his last delivery shortly before Father Payne arrived at number 59. To the priest's surprise, the front door was opened without the usual grinding of bolts and dragging of carpets. Augusta did not want to invite him in. Despite the disrespect, she spoke to him on the doorstep.

"Father, Bert is dead. He was killed last Saturday. The telegram came just now."

"God rest his brave soul." The priest's reflexes had taken over.

"Amen," said Augusta mechanically, standing aside so that the priest could come in if that was still his wish.

Sitting in the front room, his cassock a startling black against the white sheet that still covered the new chair, he began to do his duty.

"You understand that he was blessed? Not having been to confession was of no consequence. Tonight he is in heaven."

"I understand, Father, that you did nothing to get him out of the army. I understand that he is dead and that he had no right to be out there at all."

As Father Payne walked down Grove Road the curtains in all the front rooms were being drawn as if it were already night.

The war to end all wars dragged on for another two tragic years, and when, at the eleventh hour of the eleventh day of the eleventh month of 1918, the Armistice was signed, the great men of Europe announced with suitable solemnity that the world would never be quite the same again. At 59 Grove Road in Nottingham they had known that to be true since July 6, 1916. On that day, life had changed utterly. Indeed, part of it had ended at the moment when the War Office telegram arrived.

At first, it was Herbert who gave every sign of suffering the most. For he, briefly, believed that he had lost more than a son on the

Somme. He thought of Bert's death in July 1916 as the death of hope —the hope of living a second life through the achievements of his firstborn. He had six more children to love and to admire. But he did not think that he could live through any of them as he had hoped to live again through Bert.

He barely remembered Frederick Hattersley's superstitions about the baby who had died at birth. But he began to feel his own sentimental version of his father's obsession with line and lineage. Nothing could make up for the death of the firstborn. He had heard his father say it often enough. He and Joe had never filled the gap which should have been occupied by the son who was dead and buried. It would be the same with him and Bert. For several months he really believed that his life was over.

Then to the anguish of Bert's death was added another agony. Augusta began openly to hold him in contempt. She did not disguise the reason. It was not just that he had failed to fight for Bert's release. It was the way in which he talked about his love for the son who died. He should have fought for the discharge and kept his feelings private. But he had done the opposite. It had all been left to her—the man's work which Herbert should have performed with a courage and determination which matched his boasts about being more a friend than a father. What was worse, for all his talk of broken lives, he would recover within weeks.

Augusta herself was sustained by one surviving ambition. Roy must and would become a priest, even though the thought of failing to win that last great prize frightened her. Without the prospect of that one achievement, she—unlike her husband—would really be left without hope. And, for a good Catholic, the death of hope is the death of faith.

There had been other deaths during the doleful years between the Somme and what the newspapers described as victory. None of the deaths was entirely unexpected, but each one possessed a particular irony. Robert Martin—who had enjoyed robust physical health if not complete mental stability—died from flu. Patrick, his obese and drink-sodden twin brother, recovered from a far more serious attack and was sent to Dublin—under the patronage of his niece Sister Assumpta—to a home for Catholic derelicts which was run by the Sisters of Mercy. His other niece, Clare, openly attributed his miraculous recovery not to divine intervention but to intestines made impervious to infection by a lifetime's immersion in Irish whiskey.

Emily Hattersley died in her sleep—peacefully, according to the maid who found her, the doctor who examined the body and the notice which was placed in the local paper. But Frederick, half-blind and paralyzed in right arm and leg, endured only the living death of the spare bedroom at the back of the house in Doncaster which was occupied by his daughter Mary. At holiday times, Mary always asked Martha if she would take him for a few days in order to "give us a bit of a rest." Martha, forgetting the obligations of her name, invariably found a plausible reason for rejecting her sister's request.

Bishop Brindle died at Mount St. Mary's Seminary in Derbyshire and was succeeded by Bishop Dunn. The new Bishop's first act was to strip his cathedral of the vulgarities which his immediate predecessors had added and which obscured the fine line of Pugin's design. His second was to arrange for a niche to be cut in the cathedral wall. It was constructed to meet the needs of a crippled matchseller who had been forbidden by the Nottingham justices to beg on the public highway. His third and most controversial initiative was the introduction of Gregorian chant to replace the theatrical music which had defiled the cathedral since the days of Bishop Bagshaw. The choir, with the exception of Clare Martin, resigned en bloc. A group of boys was hastily recruited to replace the disaffected sopranos and contraltos. Thanks to their aunts, Roy and George Hattersley were amongst them.

Each of the Nottingham deaths was followed by a burial which seemed the proper, if not perfect, epitaph for the life of the dear departed. Robert Martin was buried with his Old Master in the coffin beside him. Bishop Brindle's body was borne through the streets of Nottingham on a gun carriage, escorted by a detachment of Yorkshire Light Infantrymen. The route of the cortège from Midland Station to St. Barnabas's door was lined by a guard of honor made up of wounded soldiers.

Frederick was too ill to attend his wife's funeral. So the family place of honor in the front pew of the Calver Street Chapel was occupied by Herbert Hattersley, still wearing the black crêpe armband which Augusta had stitched onto his coat in 1916. He embarrassed his sisters by constantly turning around to stare at the congregation behind him. He was looking for his brother, Joe, who he hoped would suddenly appear at the back of the chapel in the manner of a minor character in a melodrama.

Winifred cried at the end of the service. And since crying was not in her nature, she wondered if she cried in memory of her sister or of her wedding to Thomas Spooner which had taken place in that chapel more than forty years before. She decided that she was crying because she was old. Augusta had agreed that Winifred could take Les and Roy to the funeral of the grandmother they had barely known —as long as their great-aunt paid their train fare. Roy was entranced by the elegance of the chapel's Georgian architecture and looked forward to describing it to Auntie Clare when he got back from Nottingham. On the way home, he told his father that he "wouldn't mind being an architect."

"Fat chance," said Les and added, without much conviction, "Mam says you'll be a priest."

"I don't know why you both talk so daft."

Herbert had temporarily abandoned fantasy about the future.

Herbert knew exactly what Roy was going to do. Tom Cross had once more come to the family's rescue and had offered Roy a job at Morley's which would have been beyond the boy's reach had he not spent a full year at St. Catherine's (Higher Grade) Secondary School. He was to become office boy in the dispatch department with the real prospect of becoming a clerk when he was twenty-one. His immediate duties would include ensuring that the special black stockings with exclusive white feet—which Morley's had sent to Windsor and Buckingham Palace since the days of Queen Victoria—were respectfully packed, loyally addressed and humbly dispatched by registered post.

For Bert there was no funeral. But his name was recorded in the Book of Remembrance at St. Mary's Anglican Cathedral and the War Office wrote to say that it would be inscribed on the memorial which was to be erected in France to commemorate "Commonwealth dead with no known resting place." His campaign medals never reached 59 Grove Road, though a parcel—containing the diary which he had made out of his sister's notebook, three letters from home and photographs of his mother and an unknown girl—was delivered to his parents shortly after Armistice Day. An invitation to take part in the Nottingham Victory Parade, addressed to his father alone, followed shortly afterward.

On the day of the planned triumph, Herbert Hattersley got up before it was light and left home over an hour earlier than was necessary to get to the mustering point on time. The parade was to form up in Shakespeare Street, the place from which, in 1914, Bert had marched off to France and glory. It was from those pavements that Herbert had caught the last sight of his eldest son. Waiting for the other marchers to arrive, he stood on the steps of the public library and marveled at how the world had changed in four swift years.

Standing there, heart heavy and eyes moist, Herbert genuinely intended to march with the Fathers of the Fallen, shoulder to shoulder with hundreds of other middle-aged men whose sons had died with the two battalions of Sherwood Foresters on the first day of the Somme. But before the parade began, he was joined by his cronies from the Grove Hotel. They told him that, taking into account his record, he ought to march with the old soldiers' contingent. So he took his place behind a hand-painted notice which read "Hussars and Household Cavalry."

Bishop Thomas Dunn was a compassionate man. So when he discovered the identity of the chorister whose broken voice rang, cracked and discordant, around the cathedral, he was deeply disturbed by the idea of expelling him from the choir. He watched the boy for several Sundays, and tried to calculate the character behind the pince-nez spectacles and under the thatch of fair hair which, disconcertingly, was parted nearly but not quite in the middle. The Bishop's anguish was increased by his observation of the youth's obvious enthusiasm. He decided that it was right to find something out about the boy's family background. He sent for his Secretary, Father James Kelly, and asked for details.

"He's the nephew of Miss Martin, the only survivor from the real choir . . . the old choir, that is. He's very keen. I don't know how his aunt would take it if we sacked him. And she'd be a terrible loss."

"We could make him an altar boy."

"He's been an altar boy, but he grabbed the chance to join the choir. His father used to be a singer of some sort."

"Do I know his father?"

"I doubt it, my lord. He's not of the faith. It's a mixed marriage. You do know his other aunt. Sister Assumpta, she teaches Class One. Very small and quiet."

"I don't recall the lad's mother." The Bishop had begun to panic. He could not possibly be unkind to a virtual orphan—no mother and a father who was spiritually dead.

"She's very sick, my lord. She used to do a lot of work here before her illness. But she's sick and . . . She's on your list for a visit when you've settled in."

Inclusion on the Bishop's visiting list made the choirboy's mother very special. The Bishop asked for more details.

"Her eldest son was killed in the war with the local Territorials. Joined under age. There was some unpleasantness with Father Payne at the time. The mother tried to get the lad out. But Bishop Brindle . . . As you know, my lord, Bishop Brindle was not a well man during his last years here."

Bishop Dunn was a graduate of the Academia dei Nobili Ecclesiastici, the college which specialized in Church administration, and he took the question of episcopal management extremely seriously. He was, he believed, particularly good with people. He made a firm decision. He would visit the family, console the mother and tell her surviving son that it was his bishop's wish not that he should leave the choir but that he should resume his old duties as altar boy. He smiled at the wisdom of his decision.

Father Kelly called at Grove Road to warn the family of the imminent visitation and found Augusta asleep on the horsehair sofa. At the sight of a priest, she tried unsuccessfully to rise to her swollen feet.

"Sit yourself down."

The priest was anxious to emphasize that she was to go to no trouble. His visit—like the visit of the Bishop which he had come to arrange—was to be treated with the utmost informality. To Father Kelly's distress, the swollen lady on the horsehair sofa accepted his proposal at face value.

"Could you ask the Bishop to call in between half past five and six? My husband won't be home by then and that would be best. He's not one of us and he'd find it strange to have a real bishop in the house."

"His Grace was thinking of about three o'clock. Three o'clock next Tuesday."

"Tuesday will do very well. But three o'clock won't do at all. My son Roy isn't home from Morley's until a quarter to six and I'd particularly like him to meet the Bishop."

"His lordship particularly wants to meet Roy," said Father Kelly with real conviction, adding slightly too late, "as well as you, of course."

"I thought he would." Augusta beamed with maternal pride. "I don't get to the cathedral very much these days, my feet being what they are. St. Paul's is more convenient. I can get to Lenton Boulevard in five minutes..."

Father Kelly was about to offer a helpful suggestion, but Augusta had not quite finished.

"...and Canon Hughes is very kind to me."

The implication that Augusta had not received equally helpful treatment from the whole Nottingham hierarchy was clear. But Father Kelly decided to ignore it and, instead, make another attempt to clutch the straw which he saw floating in front of him.

"Wouldn't Roy like to go to St. Paul's with you?"

Without knowing it, Augusta drowned his hopes. "Oh no, Father. He would not. He likes the cathedral. He used to be an altar boy. Now he's in the choir. I thought you'd have known that, being the Bishop's Secretary."

"I do, I assure you. It's the Bishop who is interested in finding out more about him."

Had it been possible, Augusta would have swelled with pride. "I thought he would," she said for a second time.

Bishop Dunn's interest in Roy—only moderate and highly specific when he arrived at 59 Grove Road—grew to a size which almost justified Augusta's expectations as soon as he met him. Herbert having not yet returned home, the Bishop was able to slump in the living room's only comfortable chair. He lounged—his biretta touching the antimacassar and his long legs stretched out against the hearth—believing that his posture emphasized how at home he felt in a working-class living room. Augusta feared that his attempts to drink his tea while lying down could only end in his dropping one of her best cups and saucers. As a result, the tension made anything like normal conversation impossible. Augusta stared at the Bishop's hands and the Bishop's Secretary stared at his own feet. When Roy came through the kitchen door, the living room was silent. At the sight of the black, red-edged figure at the far end of the room, he dropped the two ancient volumes which he was carrying.

At first—partly influenced by his Secretary's eagerness to pick them up from the floor—the Bishop believed the books to be the Bible and a missal. Roy reached them first. As he put them safely on the kitchen table Bishop Dunn read their real titles. The larger book

455

was a bound volume of the *Magnet,* a boys' weekly magazine which specialized in public-school stories. The smaller had its title engraved upon its spine in blood-red letters: *Stories of the Spanish Inquisition.*

Augusta, from the sofa, made a formal introduction. "My lord, this is my son Frederick Roy."

Bishop Dunn leaned toward Roy, offering his ring for the boy to kiss, and wished that he had extended the same courtesy to Augusta. He tried to dispel his disappointment about the books with the slightly conflicting consolations that *Stories of the Spanish Inquisition* had an oblique connection with the faith and that reading anything was better than reading nothing at all. Roy noticed the signet ring on the Bishop's little finger.

"Is that your coat of arms?"

The Bishop was taken aback but pleased by the boy's confidence.

"No, it's just the badge of a society I used to belong to."

"Have you got a coat of arms? I'm very interested in people's shields and family crests."

The Bishop, who had not yet acquired his episcopal bearings, felt as if he had been found out in some awful sin of omission.

"I've got a motto. *'Fiat Voluntas Tua.'* It means 'Thy Will Be Done.' "

"I know," said the boy from behind his pince-nez.

"It's a play on words, a pun on my name." Bishop Dunn felt a deep need to reestablish himself in the boy's esteem.

"I know," the boy said again. "It often happens in Latin. When General Napier captured Sind, he said to his wife, *'Peccavi.'*"

Father Kelly, who could not remember the accurate story about General Napier's Latin admission, was quite unnerved. He tried to guide the conversation. "His Grace wants to talk to you about being an altar boy again."

"Indeed I do," added His Grace himself, "and about a lot more besides. How do you know about General Napier and Sind?"

"I read it in a book."

"Do you read a lot?"

"All the time, my lord." Augusta was sitting up. "That's why his eyes are so bad."

"And how old are you, my boy?" Bishop Dunn was sitting up too.

"I'm nearly sixteen. I shall be sixteen on the twelfth of June, the Feast of the Taking of Gibraltar."

At least, Father Kelly was certain about some things. "That's not a feast day. Not in the true Church."

456

"It was a battle," Bishop Dunn and Frederick Roy explained simultaneously.

"They called it that for a joke," Roy added.

The Bishop looked grave. "I do want to talk to you, young man. About the choir and serving and other matters. Will you come and see me on Thursday night about this time?"

"Yes, please," said Roy, remembering his manners.

The boy and the Bishop spent an uncomfortable evening together. Bishop Dunn was a natural conversationalist—gregarious, cheerful and fascinated by human foible. His young guest was not. If the Bishop asked Roy a question, he answered it to the best of his ability and then fell immediately silent. If he had something to ask the Bishop, he posed his question, listened intently to the answer and then fell silent again. But although that first Thursday night was not a great success, it ended with an invitation to visit Bishop's House again on the following Thursday. During that brief and stifled hour, Bishop Dunn had "noticed something" about Roy, though he was not quite sure what it was. When he told his Secretary of his discovery, Father Kelly was silently skeptical. The Bishop was notorious for detecting virtues in young people of both sexes which others could not recognize.

After four consecutive Thursday nights, Bishop Dunn came to a firm conclusion about the special grace which lurked behind the pince-nez and lay under the hair parted almost but not quite in the middle. Roy had a rage for facts. His obsession was displayed by his proud recital of small nuggets of information. Often what he said was wrong. But it was usually near enough to being right to impress Bishop Dunn. Napoleon III was not killed in the Zulu War, nor was Garibaldi born in Argentina. Bonnie Prince Charlie did not become a cardinal and Thomas More was never Chancellor of the Exchequer. Bishop Dunn was, however, rightly impressed that a working-class boy, not yet quite sixteen, should even have heard of such historical figures. When he was corrected—gently by the Bishop but less so by his Secretary—Roy always nodded gravely. But despite his respect for the cloth, it was the authority of the printed word which he accepted without question. "I read it in a book" was for him all that needed to be said in defense of his controversial assertions. If he had read it in a book, it was certain to be right. His rage was not knowledge itself but the books in which it was printed.

Roy visited Bishop's House every week for almost six months and, ironically, the closer the friendship grew, the more formal the meetings became. Bishop Dunn sent for a primer to test Roy's Latin and confirmed his suspicion that the tags by which he was occasionally astounded were not supported by any grasp of grammar, vocabulary or syntax. Roy took North and Hilliard home and returned it in seven days able to decline *mensa* and conjugate *amo, amas, amat* without having any clear idea of what it was that he had learned. He did, however, welcome the idea that the Bishop's Secretary would coach him in the subject. Father Kelly himself was less enthusiastic about the idea, but it was not his place to argue. After a couple of lessons, he was forced grudgingly to agree that Frederick Roy was an unusual boy. The Bishop had no doubt.

"He has a talent for learning and a real desire to learn."

"I'm not sure about that. If he's clever at all, it's in a special way. He wants to learn, but it's all a bit aimless. He doesn't know why."

"I know why."

Bishop Dunn was not a man to keep a secret to himself for long. So he added, in order to heighten the tension, "And I know what he wants to do."

Father Kelly played his proper part. "And what is that, my lord?"

The moment for the revelation had still not quite arrived.

"We must get him some formal education. I've written to the President of Ratcliffe."

Slowly, Father Kelly was beginning to understand what the Bishop knew about Roy's rage to learn, why the boy must be given some formal education and what it was that Bishop Dunn believed Roy wanted to do. The more he understood the Bishop's train of thought, the more horrified he felt.

"But . . ." Father Kelly could get no further.

"But what, James?"

"Can he have a bishop's place if he's not bound for the Church?"

"He cannot."

"And he has a vocation?"

"He has, James."

"And he has told you so?"

"He doesn't know it yet himself. But the voices will call him. I'm sure of that."

"With all respect, my lord, you can't tell Ratcliffe that."

"I shall tell them that I have no doubt that he is destined for holy orders. And what I tell them will be the truth."

Father Kelly was still not satisfied. He asked if the boy's impious father had been consulted and was assured that both Sister Assumpta and her sister Clare were convinced that, after a few ritual complaints, their brother-in-law would not stand in the way of his son receiving a proper education. The Secretary expressed fears about money being available for the essential extras which a bishop's place did not finance and was told that the two aunts already mentioned (and a great-aunt who followed one of the modern heresies) would scrape a few pounds together.

"And what about the mother? What has she to say about all this?"

"James, his mother heard the call on the day when he was born. She has been waiting for the echoes to reach the Church ever since."

CHAPTER THIRTY-FOUR

MEN OF LETTERS

In the pale sunlight of early spring, Ratcliffe College was, at least in appearance, all that Roy had hoped and expected it to be. Ivy almost covered its walls, but the sharply pointed arches of Pugin's windows could just be made out through the tangle of gray-green leaves. The cricket pitch, which only came into view when Roy had walked almost the full half-mile of the gravel drive that led from Fosse Way to front door, was being cut for the first time that year. The ancient horse which pulled the rattling mowing machine had a green and white rosette in its bridle. College colors, thought Roy. He was already expert on the customs and conventions of the English public school. He had gained his knowledge—long before he was nominated as a bishop's scholar—from dog-eared, secondhand copies of the *Magnet* and the *Gem*. The *Magnet* told the story of Greyfriars while the *Gem* chronicled events at St. Jims. As Roy turned his attention to the details of Pugin's architecture (about which he had read in the *Tablet*) and recalled his happy childhood Saturdays spent buried in those boys' magazines, he felt himself to be a Greyfriars man at heart.

Like every proper public school, Ratcliffe had an iron-studded oak door and Roy knew that behind it there ought to be a porter's lodge.

He was not disappointed. A dark cubbyhole opened off the flagstoned hall, from which it was separated not by a door but by a counter. A shadowy figure was sorting letters into the rack on the far wall. The shadow, Roy decided, must be the porter himself—deferential yet domineering, pompous, patronizing and paternal. He addressed the man in his best voice.

"How do you do?"

The figure moved into the light. Porter he certainly was, for he wore the porter's regulation uniform of apron and grave expression. But he was also a monk.

"How do *you* do?" asked Brother Patrick Doyle and added, "Lovely day for the race."

In Roy's mind this observation produced immediate images of Harry Wharton winning the hundred yards' dash and Bob Cherry triumphing in the mile, with Billy Bunter, Fisher T. Fish, Hurree Jamset Ram Singh and Mr. Quelch looking on.

"Which race, Brother?"

"The human race."

Brother Doyle slapped his thigh and roared with laughter as if he had just thought of the joke. In fact, he had first made it back in 1885 and he had repeated it, at least once, on every day since its invention.

Roy tried to laugh, but failed. Brother Doyle showed no signs of awkwardness or disappointment.

"Welcome," he said. "Welcome, Hattersley, Frederick Roy."

"How did you know?"

"I can tell. I recognized you the moment you walked through that door. Studious, they said. After nearly forty years in this glory hole, I can recognize studious."

He did not add that, of the four new boys expected that morning, three—who had already arrived—were under ten.

"Do you know anybody here?"

"No, Brother."

"Well, we'd better find you a good shepherd."

Brother Doyle knew that, as was the College custom, a boy had been asked to keep a friendly eye on the newcomer. He described the hundred-year habit as if it were his own initiative not out of any desire to appear powerful in the new boy's eyes. In his experience, new boys needed reassurance and he was happy to provide it at once. Brother Doyle was available to do anything required of him—serving in the refectory, cleaning boots, keeping bathrooms clean and tidy. It was all God's work. But the part of God's work which he enjoyed the most was keeping boys cheerful.

"First, I've got to take you to see the President. He's called Father Cremonini."

"I know."

"Let's hear you say it."

Having only read it in a book, Roy could manage nothing better than a crude imitation of its complicated vowel sounds, and that only after several unsuccessful assaults on its first syllable.

"You've got to learn to say it properly. Don't get the idea in your head that it's foreign. Father Cremonini is as English as you and me. More English than me if truth were known."

Roy tried again and got it more or less right. Believing that he had qualified to meet the President, he picked up the battered suitcase which Aunt Clare had lent him. Brother Doyle pushed up the counter and seized the bag out of his hand.

"You've got to learn how things are done here. That's my job. We make a gentleman out of you here. A gentleman first and priest second."

Roy felt doubly embarrassed—embarrassed because he had gauchely picked up the case and embarrassed because his case was being carried by a man old enough to be his grandfather. The President was not ready to welcome the new scholar. Brother Doyle put the case down on the tiled corridor floor and Roy bent down in order to pick it up again.

"I've told you. That's my job. I'll take the case up to your dormitory. You just stand there and wait until the President has finished."

Roy assumed that the President was at prayer. For the image at Ratcliffe which the new boy had carried in his mind from Nottingham was a cross between Eton College and a Franciscan monastery—equally dedicated to work, worship and sporting excellence. His naïve view of life in his new school was the typical product of his complicated personality. In many ways, he was old beyond his years—with knowledge and understanding which few other sixteen-year-old boys could match. But he was also invincibly innocent. It was not so much that he resisted temptation as that he failed to notice it. He lived in a world of his imagination and remained gentle, myopic and reverential toward both learning and authority.

The President was asleep in his study—a fact which Brother Doyle had been right to keep secret. For Roy would have preferred his own explanation to the truth. He was infatuated with the complicated hierarchy of the Church and felt comfortable and secure when surrounded by its order and discipline. It was the certainty of Catholicism, as well as its ceremonials, which attracted him to Rome. So he stood obediently in the corridor wondering why the letter *B* was embossed, in extravagant Gothic letters, on the flagstones. The idea of moving from his appointed spot never occurred to him. He waited patiently for twenty minutes. Then Father Cremonini opened the study door and invited him in.

The President's study was dark and badly furnished. The regulation crucifix hung on the wall behind his desk and the regulation Bible lay open on the top of a bookcase which contained no books. Ratcliffe was not an academic institution and the President was not an academic man. He was head of a school which catered for the sons of the Catholic middle classes. And it provided places from which prodigies and paragons nominated by the Midlands bishops could prepare for the priesthood. It did not aspire to send its sons to Oxford or Cambridge or to compete at games with the great public schools. But it existed in the shadow of those historic institutions and it copied their conduct wherever its limited finances allowed. The traditions of classical education were a bridge between the theories of Dr. Arnold and the demands of the Pope.

The President, having asked courteous and concerned questions about the journey between Nottingham and Leicester, moved on to a discussion of Roy's place in the school.

"I'm told that you've learned Latin with remarkable speed."

It was an assertion to which Roy could, in honesty, only reply with a categorical "Yes." After a moment's silence, Father Cremonini tried again.

"It's important that you enjoy yourself here. It sometimes isn't easy to settle—especially for young men of your age. But you'll soon make some friends."

Father Cremonini was always apprehensive when a sixteen-year-old youth joined the school. Seven-year-olds cried themselves to sleep for a week and then forgot that there was a world outside the classroom and dormitory. But sixteen-year-olds were men with memories, and sometimes what they remembered of life before Ratcliffe made it impossible for them to accept the communal asceticism of a proper Catholic education. The Bishop had been categoric in the case of Hattersley, Fredericus Rex. The President had been assured that

463

he would "take to it like a duck to water." But Bishop Dunn was
notorious for adopting whole families of prospective priests with what
a previous President of Ratcliffe had described as "more kindness of
heart than clarity of thought." This young man looked suitably unworldly. He had begun to grow out of his suit, and the tight jacket
combined with his brand-new shoes to give an appearance of respectable poverty. But the President still worried about leaping the gap
between I. and R. Morley's stocking factory and a public school. So
he repeated his advice.

"There's a lot to enjoy here. I hope you'll make the most of it."

Hattersley, Fredericus Rex had no doubts.

"I will, Father, I will."

"It's customary..." Father Cremonini tried to make the point
gently. "It's customary to call me President. It's what everybody does.
One of the important things here is always to do the same as everybody else."

Roy felt no embarrassment at the gentle correction. He had asked
the Bishop's Secretary if there were a book which set out how he
should behave at Ratcliffe and was told that no such book was available. If he had been given a book with instructions, he would have
known exactly what to do. Since no book had been provided, the
ignorance was not his fault.

"Yes, President."

Father Cremonini noted, with relief and surprise, that Hattersley
used his proper title as if he had been using that form of address
since he was seven.

"I'm sure you'll fit in very well. I've asked a young man called
Baldwin to show you around. He's just your age. But he's been here
for years. He's a bishop's nominee too. One of Bishop Brindle's boys."

The President opened his door and revealed Baldwin, standing
almost to attention in the corridor outside. The introductions were
uneasy, for Hattersley F. R. was gauche and Baldwin would rather
have been rowing on the river Soar. They walked several paces down
the corridor without speaking. Then Roy's curiosity overcame his
diffidence.

"What are the *B*s for?" Roy pointed at the flagstones and the elaborate Gothic letters which were embossed upon them. He was impatient for an answer. "The *B*s on the floor, what are they for?"

Alfred Baldwin put his hands on Roy's shoulders and turned him
through ninety degrees so that, instead of looking across the corridor,

he was looking down its full length toward the statue of the Virgin at its far end.

"Look down now."

To assist in the operation, Alfred moved his hands from Roy's shoulders and grasped him by the ears and pulled until he adjudged that the head between them was at the proper angle for the careful examination of the paving stones. The elaborate Gothic *B*s turned into elaborate Gothic *M*s.

"This is the Lady corridor."

Baldwin tried not to laugh. For he wanted neither to hurt the new boy's feelings nor to be irreverent about any subject which was even remotely related to the Virgin Mary. But as they walked along the corridor together the schoolboy hysteria suddenly exploded. To his relief, Roy began to laugh as well. They laughed until they coughed and choked, and they leaned on the wall until they had recovered their breath. Then they began to laugh again and laughed all the way up the narrow spiral staircase to the first floor. The laughter created a bond between them and, in the Common Room, Alfred opened his tin trunk and brought out the half-melted remains of a block of chocolate. They shared it and the giggles subsided enough for them to talk again.

"What's your first name?"

Roy's answer was suitably precise. "Frederick. But nobody calls me that. Everybody calls me Roy."

"Well, I shan't call you Roy. If you were a sheepdog, I might. But Roy's not a name for a human being. I can't call you Frederick. We've got two of them already. What's your Latin name?"

"Fredericus Rex, King Frederick. You could call me King."

"I could. But I don't think that I will. I shall call you Rex. Everyone will call you Rex. You are my first christening."

Alfred licked his fingers and made a moist cross on Roy's brow. The anointment completed, the tour which began with Alfred and Roy as wary strangers continued with Alfred and Rex as firm friends. The new name was adopted without question or regret. For the *Magnet* had already revealed that the acquisition of a nickname was a sure sign that the recipient had been accepted in public-school society.

The transition from Roy to Rex was not, however, complete or comprehensive. The public-school boy was Rex from that moment onward and would not have answered to any other name in Ratcliffe's buildings or on its playing fields. But when the summer came and Rex went home, he became Roy again from the minute that he arrived in Grove Road. It was the beginning of the schizophrenia which was to divide his life forever.

It was a confusion of which, on that first day, he was wholly unaware. He instantly became a Ratcliffe man and believed that he would so remain, first and always. Only once, during his whole expedition around the school, did a thought of his distant family make him sad. And, even then, he felt not homesick but guilty.

The music rooms—four glass booths with dilapidated pianos inside their far from soundproof walls—made him think of his mother. Augusta longed once more to possess a piano and yearned to play the old upright which she had owned when she was a girl but which could not be fitted into the parlor at Grove Road. Inside the music rooms—"the birdcages," as Alfred told Rex to call them—were enough pianos to make his mother happy four times over. Rex felt ashamed that he was to enjoy so much when she enjoyed so little.

The sadness did not last long, for next Alfred took him to the school library. It was a second-rate library. But it was the only library which Rex Hattersley had ever seen and he could barely believe that, for the next year, the rows of battered books would be his for the borrowing.

"You can take two out every week. You can read whatever you like in here. But only two a week outside the library."

"Only two!" Rex was horrified.

"I'll borrow one for you, if you like. I don't read two books a week. I don't read. I only take one out because it's the rule."

"Don't you like reading?"

"Not much."

"Then why did you come here?" To Rex, Ratcliffe had become an institution for the promotion and encouragement of reading.

"I'm a bishop's scholar like you. I came here to be a priest, and if I have to read a page a day to get into a seminary, then I'll do it. But it doesn't come to me naturally. The thought of being up to my neck in books for another eight years . . ." The idea was so abhorrent that Alfred could not finish the sentence which put it into words.

"Is that what you'll have to do?"

"It's what we'll both have to do if we become priests."

Rex was visibly thinking. Under his strangely parted hair his brow

466

was furrowed, and behind his pince-nez spectacles his eyes were screwed up in concentration.

"Come on," said Alfred, who had only limited respect for cerebral activity, "it's writing-home day. Sooner I start, sooner I'll finish."

Rex decided that he, too, would write home and tell his mother that she need not worry about how he was settling down. He would, of course, sign his letter "Roy." But in his heart he felt "Rex," Rex of Ratcliffe, a man from the *Magnet.*

Like every other boy at Ratcliffe College, Rex wrote home each week and on every Friday morning he presented his letter to Brother Doyle for posting. Augusta Hattersley read the letters to the family over breakfast every Saturday morning, interspersing her own comments amongst accounts of how her son had learned to row, joined the cadet force and discovered the miracle of St. Augustine's *Confessions.* In fact, he discovered little more than a single aphorism. *Tulle lege. Tulle lege.* But since the injunction to take up and read was, to him, the secret of the universe, those four words made him a passionate Augustinian. Leslie and the girls were cross-examined on their brother's theological inclination, as they were cross-examined at the end of every other paragraph, and Herbert was required to confirm his interest by giving the occasional grunt. The letters always concerned the immediate past—lessons learned, meals eaten, exercise taken and books read during the previous seven days. But Augusta invariably deciphered what she believed to be coded messages about the future. Her son was following a course of instruction necessary for entry into a seminary. The idea that it would not result in his becoming a priest never entered her head.

One letter—received just before Rex was to turn into Roy for the Christmas holidays—caused Augusta particular excitement. Hattersley F. R. had been chosen to read a passage of Latin during the ceremony which marked the end of term. Augusta's spirit was lifted not by the honor which had been done to her son or by the scholastic success which it represented but by the words of the passage which he had chosen to declaim. It was, of course, from Augustine's *Confessions.*

Fecisti nos ad te et inquietum est cor nostrum, donec requiescat in te.
Thou hast created us for Thyself, and our heart cannot be quieted until it finds repose in Thee.

After that she had no doubts. She read the rough translation over and over again, finding almost as much difficulty with the juxtaposition of the words as with her son's strange, upright longhand.

"Can you imagine," she asked Herbert, "a more exciting letter to read than this?"

Her husband grunted to indicate that he could not. Within a week his judgment was to be confounded.

The letter which made his heart thump and a pulse beat in the side of his head arrived in the shop in Alfreton Road three days after Christmas. Willie Foster put it by the cash register on the counter and forgot about it.

He was hardly to be blamed. For the envelope in which it came was dirty, creased and almost covered with the barely recognizable names of roads and towns which had been crossed out because the intended recipient was "not known at this address" or had simply "left." It had originally been sent to Herbert at the Empress Works. When it arrived, the new master redirected it to the old family house in Asline Road. At Asline Road, it was posted to the Doncaster address which the previous owner had left for such eventualities. Frederick Hattersley never saw it. His daughter Mary—thinking that seeing Herbert's name on the envelope would upset or, worse, enrage him—hid it at the bottom of her work box without noticing the one feature of the envelope which should have excited her attention. She asked her husband for Herbert's last known address and he looked it up in an old pocket book. The information was almost twenty years out of date, so the letter was sent to Cavendish Street, from where Clare Martin had recently moved into a house more suitable in size to her spinster state. The new tenants—who had been born and brought up at the other end of the road—remembered the young man who had the fight with the burglars and recalled that he owned a shop on the way out of town. Having reached the destination, it lay on the counter until Roy Hattersley called into the shop on his way to the public library in Parliament Street.

Roy walked to the library on most evenings of his holiday and he usually made a detour down Alfreton Road. It was the only chance which he had to speak to his father, who left the house before he was out of bed, returned and ate silently when his work was done, left again within the hour and fell immediately to sleep as soon as he settled down in the armchair after his visit to the Grove Hotel. Normally, Roy and his father chattered away about what Herbert called "the old days" in Sheffield. But on the evening after the letter arrived Roy spoke only one word.

He recognized the importance of the letter as soon as he saw it lying on the counter. Winifred, undaunted by her failure to interest Bert in philately, had persuaded Roy to start a stamp collection of sorts. It mostly consisted of common British reds, blues and browns torn from the envelopes of family and friends. Under their postmarks, King George stared stiffly to the left beneath a ceremonial crown. But the stamp on this letter was different in one particular. Where the crown should have been, the stamp on the creased and crumpled envelope had one single word. Roy said the word as he handed the letter to his father: "Canada."

Herbert was not sure why, but he locked the shop door before he read Joseph's letter.

I hope you are well and prospering. I'm as well as can be expected, taking into account the weather, very hot in summer and very cold in winter when I can never get warm. A man in Winnipeg, just out from home, said that he had read in the paper that Father had died. So I'm going to come home. Not yet, in about a year when I'll have settled up out here. Probably about next Christmas. Is there any money due to me? I hope the works does well. I've not worked with the tools for years. So I'll be ho help there. I'm now in a different business.

Write and tell me the news. Is Mother still alive? My wife died ten years ago so I'll be coming home by myself.

Herbert Hattersley, being a man of both simple and generous disposition, saw nothing ironic in the letter ending with good wishes from his "ever devoted brother." He did, however, feel a brief surge of anger at the idea of Joseph—having made a Canadian fortune—staking some sort of claim to his father's will, the inheritance which had been built up by years of toil at the Empress Works. Then he remembered that his father was not dead, that the Empress Works was sold, that he had contributed to its bankruptcy and that there was no legacy for Joseph to inherit. Anger and resentment were replaced by sympathy and anxiety. Herbert understood how Joe would feel when his hopes were dashed.

Augusta did not even seem surprised that the brother-in-law, whom she had never met, had suddenly reappeared from across the world and out of the Hattersley family folklore. She immediately concerned herself with the practical details of Joseph's return.

"Will he want to stay here when he gets back? I don't know where we'll put him."

Her husband was scandalized by her lack of understanding.

"He won't stay here. He'll stay in a hotel, if he comes to Nottingham at all. But I doubt if he'll come this way. When he finds out how things are in Sheffield, he'll probably stay in London instead and deal with his business affairs down there."

"I wonder what business he's in, if he's not a cutler anymore."

"It'll be something big. Everybody knew that our Joe would go a long way."

"He doesn't write like a big businessman. He writes like a workman and on very funny paper. I wouldn't expect a big businessman to write in pencil."

"That's as may be. But you take it from me, Joe will be rich by now. Real rich. You never knew him. Everybody who did said he'd get on. And I'll tell you why he'll get on. He never let anybody or anything stop him doing what he wanted to do. Nobody or nothing."

Herbert—having proclaimed his faith in the ultimate victory of the indomitable human will—turned his attention to the difficult task of replying to his brother's letter. Inevitably, he asked for his wife's assistance—disguising his need for her help with the unconvincing pretense that he was thinking out loud rather than asking her to correct his grammar or check his spelling. Together they covered six pages. They described Emily's death, Frederick's illness and the sale of the Empress Works. They wrote of Herbert's marriage, Augusta's children and Bert's small place in imperial history. They even mentioned the success which Sheffield United were enjoying in the First Division of the Football League. They did not, however, mention Herbert's job. During the discussions which turned into arguments about what should or should not be included, the subject was not mentioned by either husband or wife.

The letter being finished and signed by Herbert alone, it was sealed down in its brown manila envelope and propped up on the mantelpiece so that Leslie would not forget to buy a special stamp on his way to work on the following morning. Augusta sat back exhausted.

"Well, that's another job done."

"He'll be as surprised to get my letter as I was to get his."

"I imagine he will."

"God, I'm looking forward to seeing him again and him meeting you and Les and Mu . . ." Herbert's voice trailed off in memory of Bert. "Anyway, we mustn't wish our lives away. Next Christmas is a long way off yet. It's only February."

"It's June I'm looking forward to," said Augusta.

Herbert, as was his habit when his wife said something which he did not understand, grunted.

At Ratcliffe, the important month was June. There were still three weeks to enjoy or endure before the end of term. There was a War Memorial Chapel to be built and the difficult transition to be arranged between the Oxford Junior Examination and the examinations of the Oxford and Cambridge Joint Board. Father Cremonini was about to relinquish the Presidency and be succeeded by Father Aloysius Emery. As a result of the President's retirement, the Bishop of Nottingham (who always visited the school immediately before the summer holidays) made a formal visitation. Ratcliffe received him with suitable ceremony.

On the path outside the front door, the school was drawn up in parade-ground fashion. The boys—with the exception of the Cadet Corps—wore their Sunday cassocks and stood in two irregular lines. The Corps formed a guard of honor on their left flank while the brothers made up a loose square to the right. The priests stood three paces ahead of the front rank of scholars, like company commanders, while the President enjoyed the lonely eminence of a commanding officer at a point exactly a yard away from the mark at which the Bishop's driver had been told to stop.

Unfortunately, the driver, who stopped precisely on his mark with his rear door exactly opposite Father Cremonini, drew up so close to the waiting President that the front bumper brushed against his soutane. Father Cremonini flinched visibly at the prospect of meeting his maker sooner than he expected and then leaped back as the door of the Bishop's car swung toward him. Only Brother Doyle laughed out loud.

There was much blessing and kissing of rings and there was lunch in the Upper School Refectory. Then Bishop Dunn addressed the whole school, using as his text not Biblical quotations, which would have been the choice of a conventional prelate, but the legend of the pelican as told by Saint Jerome. He pointed dramatically to the por-

471

tion of the wall between two of the oriel windows which was decorated with the school shield.

"The pelican in her piety," he cried, "the symbol of this school's devotion to the faith and the future."

In the fourth row of senior pupils, Rex Hattersley tried to remember the real meaning of the word piety. Pity? Reverence? Love of son for father or father for son? He determined to look it up in his dictionary as soon as the address was over.

After his address, Bishop Dunn was conducted to the President's study and offered a reviving glass of madeira. There followed a speech of thanks (which Father Cremonini thought both perfunctory and insincere) and the presentation of the diocesan farewell gift (a leather-bound history of the Italian Risorgimento), which the recipient took to be a calculated insult. The Bishop then got down to the serious business of the day—the final decisions about which boys should go on to seminaries and then into holy orders.

At first, the discussion went remarkably smoothly. It was agreed that McSweeney R. and Callaghan A. should be sent to St. Alban's Collegio de Inglese in Valladolid, that Williamson B. and Smyth V. should go to Ushaw in County Durham. Other boys were to be sent to Oscot and to Hammersmith. But, as always, the great decision concerned Rome. It was agreed that Quinn B., whose devotion was matched only by his intellect, was an obvious candidate for membership in the English College and that Baldwin A. (despite his aversion to study) qualified because of simple faith, passion to serve and extent of family bequests to the Church in and around Leicestershire. Eagan M. had a brother in the priesthood who was an alumnus of the College and was popular with everyone because of his good humor. After a brief discussion, his name was added to the list. Father Cremonini rose to wish the Bishop farewell.

As the President stood up he was engulfed in a feeling of relief that flooded over him like light from heaven illuminating a saint in a stained-glass window. His association with Bishop Dunn had ended. Never again would he have to show obedience to this absurd and irrational figure whose whims and fancies played as big a part in the government of the diocese as dogma and canon law. The President bent, in a stiff bow, to kiss the episcopal ring.

"Sit down for a minute," said Bishop Dunn, smiling nervously. "We haven't quite finished."

Father Cremonini did as he was instructed.

"Hattersley F. R." The Bishop spoke the name with slow deliberation.

"He's doing quite well, my lord. Fitted in remarkably, considering his background. He loves books and learns Latin for pleasure. Some of the other boys tease him because of his spectacles. But despite his eyesight, he's very keen on cricket and started to row—"

"Thank you, Father. No doubt his mother will be most grateful to read that on his end-of-term report. But it is not quite what I meant."

The irony—and the obvious pain which it caused the President—restored the Bishop's confidence. He stretched out his long legs across the study floor and tapped the ends of his fingers together.

"What I meant was, what is going to happen to him now?"

Father Cremonini knew exactly what the Bishop meant—meant but did not yet quite have the courage to say. He decided that the best way to combat the reckless irresponsibility was to act as if he were having a normal conversation with a sane man who would not even contemplate the idea which he knew was inside the Bishop's head.

"He'll take the joint examination next year when he's eighteen. He won't do spectacularly well. But, God willing, he'll matriculate. I would hope for a credit in History, perhaps even a distinction in Latin. Then I suggest a steady job. We'll find him something in a bank or a council office. Perhaps he could become a solicitor's clerk. He needs something with security, something steady."

It was Bishop Dunn's turn to stand up. "He's for the Church, Father President. Have no doubt of that. The only question to be decided is the seminary to which I send him. To which *I* send him."

Father Cremonini did not need to be reminded that the decision was the Bishop's and the Bishop's alone. "It is not for me to question your judgment, my lord, but with respect may I ask a question?"

"Of course you may." Bishop Dunn was offended by the implication that he was a bigoted man with a closed mind.

"Does the boy wish it?"

"He does. He made that clear to me before he came here."

"And will he accept the obligations? Does he even know what they are?"

The Bishop's irritation grew. "If you doubt my judgment, Father—or for that matter, my word—let's have the young man in and ask him."

The President took the Bishop's offer literally, and Hattersley F. R.

473

was sent for. He had, Bishop Dunn noticed, grown during his fifteen months at Ratcliffe. Rex's hair was shorter and was parted slightly more to the left, and the pince-nez spectacles looked less incongruous on a man of over seventeen than they had seemed on a boy barely old enough to wear long trousers.

"The Bishop wishes to ask you a question."

"Yes, my lord."

"The priesthood ... the priesthood ... we believe that you should enter the Church, that you are called to serve Christ and his flock."

"What have you to say?" Father Cremonini was prepared to risk further humiliation rather than fail in his pastoral duty.

"My mother wants me to become a priest."

The Bishop, still without doubts, went in for the kill. "But what about you?"

There was no reply.

Father Cremonini decided to seize the initiative and exploit the boy's obvious indecision.

"You must appreciate what it involves. Perhaps poverty, certainly chastity and lifelong discipline. Are you prepared for that?"

Bishop Dunn, afraid and furious, was about to answer the question himself, when Father Cremonini pressed the point home.

"And there are the years of study. Seven long years of continuous learning. Reading, reading, reading. That's how you'll spend morning, afternoon and night. Lectures in Latin."

"Yes," said Hattersley F. R. "That's what I want."

"The priesthood?" The Bishop was jubilant.

"The priesthood, yes."

"Well," said Bishop Dunn, "all that remains is to decide which seminary."

"That is purely your decision, my lord." Father Cremonini was not prepared to become involved with such madness.

"And I have decided. Rome."

"Rome!"

"You said he spoke Latin like a native." The Bishop slapped his thigh and tossed his head in a triumphant laugh. "I shall write to them today."

CHAPTER THIRTY-FIVE

SECOND THOUGHTS

It was cold in Rome and Rex was glad that he had traveled across Europe in his thick worsted Sunday suit. Eight new seminarians stumbled out of the station into the October dusk and experienced for the first time the sweet smell of the Eternal City in autumn. After twenty hours of cramped traveling, they were stiff in every muscle and they could still feel the marks left by the wooden benches of their third-class carriage. Anxious and exhausted, they walked out into the Piazza del Cinquecento and waited for the welcome which had been promised them as they left Victoria Station on the boat train. Rex began to wonder what they would do if, by midnight, there was still nobody to meet them.

Alfred Baldwin contemplated buying one of the penny buns which according to his phrase book were called *maritozzi*. He had not eaten since Dormodossolla, when the local Rosminians had bought cheese and wine for the four travelers from their sister house in Leicestershire. And since the Ratcliffians had thought it their Christian duty to share their meal with the rest of the compartment, the half-rations had done little more than whet his appetite. But Alfred—who had been hungry since the train had hurtled south and down through the Simplon Pass—was not sure if he could buy a single *maritozzo* for

475

himself, or if Christian brotherhood required him to buy one for each of his companions. He resolved his dilemma by remaining famished.

During the twenty minutes that they waited outside the station, their hopes were raised a dozen times as priest or monk appeared to be making his way toward them. Then, just as even the most self-confident members of the party began to despair, their savior appeared from inside the station and startled them with his calm, English greeting.

"We're here, Mick. Sorry. We started out late and we've been looking for you on the platforms."

"Are we glad to see you, Bill!"

Bill—a small youth with a self-confident pink face—embraced first Michael Eagan and then Alfred Baldwin.

The introductions began.

"This is William Ellis. He left Ratcliffe last year. Did you ever meet him, Rex?"

Before he had time to answer, the travelers who had not enjoyed a Ratcliffe education were announcing their names and offering their hands with the diffidence and respect owed to one their senior.

"Francis Cashman. How do you do?"

"Hugh Atkinson."

"I'm Bernard Quinn."

"Hugh Kelly, pleased to meet you."

"You can meet the rest on the way, Bill."

The pangs of hunger had grown too sharp for Alfred to endure. He bought a bun and began to eat it.

"What do we go in?" Michael Eagan assumed that they would travel in a horse-drawn bus of the sort that Ratcliffe had recently abandoned or in a motor coach of the type that Ratcliffe had recently acquired. William Ellis disillusioned him.

"You walk. We walk everywhere. That's lesson one. Walk and work. That's the real College motto. Anyway, we can't start out until I find Heenan and O'Dwyer. That's lesson two. You are never allowed to walk outside the College by yourself. Morning walks are compulsory. Wait at the front door until there's somebody to go with you. No picking and choosing. Go with whoever it is."

O'Dwyer, round and smiling, was sighted in frantic conversation with a porter. Heenan, sharp-faced and intense, was located trying to obtain information from the inquiry office. The party set off at a brisk pace down the Via del Viminale. By the time they got to the Piazza Venezia, the introductions were completed.

"Which one is Hattersley?" asked Bill Ellis.

Hattersley identified himself.

"Bishop Dunn has asked me to keep an eye on you for a bit. Says you might take a bit of time to settle in."

"Won't we all?" Michael Eagan was looking at the Victor Emmanuel Monument.

"I'll be all right," said Rex, embarrassed by what seemed like special treatment.

"No doubt. But Bishop Dunn's instruction must be observed. Most of his letter was about the virtues of order and discipline. He's heard of some journalist from Turin called Mussolini who's going to squash the Masons and he's full of it. Anyway, Dunn's Darlings have to stick together.

"Dunn's Darlings!" Rex did not like the description.

"Better than Dunn's Dunces. That's what one or two of 'em have been called."

Alfred Baldwin, being a Darling himself, explained the description to his unworldly colleague. "All it means is that the Bishop took a shine to you and sent you here."

". . . or to Valladolid," added Michael Eagan.

". . . clever or stupid," said William Ellis with the calm confidence of a man who was clever.

Ellis, Cashman and O'Dwyer began to discuss, from the heights of their seniority, whether or not there was intrinsic virtue in intellect— whether, for example, a stupid bishop could be a good bishop. Bleakly, Heenan explained that virtue lay in the way in which God-given gifts were used. There being nothing more to say on the subject, the conversation ended. Short of breath, Rex Hattersley walked on without speaking. He could feel the blisters beginning to swell on the palm of his hand where the soft skin rubbed against the rough handle of his old suitcase. But what did a blister or two matter? He was in Rome and had taken part in—or at least listened to—a theological disputation. The joy of it stayed with him right up to the entrance to the English College.

"All you need to do tonight is wash, eat and sleep."

"Thank you, Father." Francis Cashman, being the first new seminarian through the door, answered for them all and, in consequence, felt responsible when the tall erect figure with the close-cropped hair corrected him.

"Neither priest nor monk. Not father nor brother. I'm about halfway through here. Tonsured last spring. I'm so old because I was in the war."

"Sorry," said Francis Cashman and Michael Eagan together.

"No need to be sorry." O'Dwyer grinned as he offered an unhelpful explanation of their mistake. "It's his military bearing that makes him look like a cardinal. An understandable mistake."

"He was senior to a cardinal," said William Ellis. "He was a captain in the Machine-Gun Corps."

"Just so you know everything about me that's worth knowing, let me explain that my name's Humphrey Wilson. But these young hooligans call me Frick. Frick was a German general who was here in Rome. So since I fought against the Germans for four years . . ."

He let the sentence trail off so that his audience could judge the brilliance of the wit for themselves. Noticing Alfred Baldwin's impatience, Frick Wilson suggested that they might eat first and wash afterward.

"You're so late, you have to sit down in the kitchen. Follow me, quick march."

The picket paused at the kitchen door and Frick Wilson rapped out a military paradiddle on its center panel. For a moment there was silence. Then a voice from within called out in language which Rex could not recognize. Frick flung the door open and shepherded his flock inside. On the table in front of them, vast piles of food were flanked by huge carafes of wine. It was the sort of sight which should instantly have commanded the attention of a working-class boy from an English provincial town. But it was not the veal and the pasta, the huge tomatoes and the hunks of bread which transfixed him. In each corner of the strangely shaped room stood a nun wearing the pure white habit of the Elizabethan Sisters. Each nun stood facing the wall.

"Lesson three," whispered William Ellis. "They're not allowed to show their faces to a man. So be careful not to catch them unawares. One glance at you and it's a hundred Hail Marys. Then the washing up doesn't get done."

Rex ate, bewildered, and then Frick Wilson pointed him toward his room and bed. William Ellis was no longer there to give numbers to the lessons. But it seemed to Rex that he learned half a dozen new rules before he was ready to sleep. No one was to visit him in his room—except at times of ill health and then never singly. A half-liter of wine would be left outside his room early each morning. Since it was intended for medical rather than social purposes, if it was not drunk during the day a written explanation of the abstinence would be expected. He could wash in his enamel bowl as often as his free time allowed, but he could enjoy only one bath each week. He would be allowed twenty minutes under the shower or in the tub. At a prescribed time he would be required to join the queue in the bath-room for the purifying water.

He was ready for bed—inside the first pair of pajamas which he had ever owned—when an unknown priest appeared at the door of his cell.

"Clothes," he demanded. "Clothes."

"What do you mean?"

"I want your clothes. Pack them in your suitcase and give them here."

"What am I to wear tomorrow?"

The priest did not enter the cell, but threw from outside a bundle tied together with a rope girdle. It was made up of two cassocks (a summer soutane which he was to wear until the first of November, the winter alternative which was to keep him warm thereafter) and the shirt and shorts which were to be worn under them in all seasons. The shirt was made of calico and the shorts of canvas.

"Take care of the hat," the priest insisted. "It was made by Silves-trini and you won't get another. Wear it with the strings loose except when otherwise instructed."

Rex Hattersley slept badly. The College which he had thought to be a second home had welcomed him with a recital of the strange rituals which he was required to perform or witness. He had come to Rome with the clear intention of reading three books each week. And he was not sure if he was capable of such concentrated or continual study while wearing canvas underpants. When the rising bell rang to warn that it was six o'clock, he had been awake for over an hour. After mass, half an hour later, the thought of breakfast nauseated him.

Mass was said in the Martyrs' Chapel underneath the frescoes of the Virgin Mary and between the shells which decorated the walls in memory of the College's origins as a hostel for pilgrims on their way to the Holy Land. When mass was over, the new recruits filed into the Great Chapel and, while they awaited the arrival of the Rector, stared at Andreas Pozza's painting of Christ converting the heathen world. It was difficult to look at anything except the picture of the blood which flowed from the nail marks in his hands and feet, engulfed the whole world and set fire to England.

The painting was the initial subject of Monsignor Hinsley's address.

"My sons, we are a missionary institution and you must never forget that we were founded in the dark days of the Reformation to bring England back to the true faith and the true Church. That work has only just begun.

"I ask you to take your inspiration from the saints and martyrs who have sat where you now sit. Think of Julian Watts Russell, whose memorial glorifies this chapel wall. That tablet was taken from the Via Mentana, the exact spot where Julian Watts Russell fell fighting for the Pope against the secular powers who sought to steal the papal land and deny the Holy Father's authority."

Having touched lightly on the Cardinal Duke of York, Archbishop of Frascati—to whom he referred as Henry IX of England—the Rector moved on from the subject of distinguished Venerabili to the question of formal instruction.

"The following members are deemed in need of special Latin tuition . . ." Rex was gratified that he was not named amongst them. "Gentlemen, you are all expected at the Gregorian University at eight o'clock tomorrow morning. Please remember your afternoon siesta. It is necessary to your health as well as obligatory in the College rules. You will be Entered Venerabili in the Liber Ruber tomorrow, October the twenty-third in the Year of Our Lord nineteen hundred and twenty-one."

Rex sat in his pew for less than a minute after the Rector's address had finished. But, in those few seconds, more thoughts passed through his mind than he was accustomed to consider in a whole day. The prospect of seven years' study at the Gregorian University entranced him, as did the prospect of life under the gilded capitals of the Corinthian columns and between the ecclesiastical portals which decorated the English College. But, for the first time, he began to realize that something was expected in return for the lectures and libraries, the austere splendor and the atmosphere of scholarly detachment. He was not sure that he was capable of continual devotion to the mysteries which were represented all around him—mysteries which seemed only distantly connected with the Sunday school at St. Barnabas's Cathedral and the catechism which he had repeated to his mother until he was word-perfect. For the first time since he left Grove Road for Ratcliffe College, he felt homesick.

Herbert Hattersley described himself as "not much of a traveler" in much the same way—and for much the same reason—as he described himself as "not much of a scholar." Admitting incapacity and incompetence was far better than visiting places he had no wish to see or staring at books, newspapers and magazines he had no wish to read. But the letter which invited him to meet his brother, Joe, in Sheffield briefly changed his attitude toward both traveling and scholarship. On the day of its arrival, he rushed to the station to check on times of trains and to buy himself a ticket. And on the four evenings which separated the invitation from the reunion, he visited the reading room at the public library in order to study the serious pages of the serious papers. The brother whom he had not seen for thirty years was a man of the world. Herbert prepared himself for conversations about Commonwealth Preferences, the Gold Standard, the creation of an Irish Free State and America's withdrawal from the League of Nations.

He was first surprised and then disappointed that the reunion was arranged for Hen and Chickens Hotel in Castle Green. But—thirty years of separation having clouded his memory of Joe's character— he decided that the rendezvous had been chosen for reasons of sentiment. The Hen and Chickens had once been the public house of his dreams. He had always longed to drink in its town-center sophistication, with elbow on mahogany bar, foot on brass rail and gleaming black hair illuminated by its crystal chandeliers. But the Hen and Chickens was the haunt of little mesters, spade makers, owners of small engineering works and coal merchants. Any one of them might have told his father that he had been seen with a pint pot in his hand. Joe, Herbert convinced himself, remembered all that. He would have planned to walk down from his suite at the Victoria Hotel, making a detour on his way in order to telegraph London with instructions to sell stocks and buy shares.

Herbert was not quite sure what he should tell his brother about his own prospects, for his career was once more at the crossroads. Willie Foster was moving to Sleaford, where he was to be employed in the corn merchant's business which his father-in-law owned. Willie was confident that the new proprietor would want to retain the services of a first-rate cutler—albeit to perform tasks which were beneath a first-rate cutler's dignity. But Herbert's optimism had faded with the years. Nobody yet knew who the new proprietor would be. So, in case his evening earnings were about to end, Herbert had provided himself with a more or less convincing consolation. Leslie, his apprenticeship over, was bringing money home. Gussie was to be married next year. Roy was off his hands for good. He and Augusta could manage without the bit he earned in the shop—if they had to.

As Herbert waited in the best room of the Hen and Chickens his spirits rose as he slowly drank his first pint of the day. He decided that there was no need to mention the job in the shop to Joe. "I work at the Raleigh," he would tell him. "Raleigh Bicycle Company, the biggest cycle works in the world." Then, remembering his brother's transatlantic connection, he determined to modify his claim about the company to "the biggest cycle works in Europe."

Herbert recognized his brother as soon as he came into the bar parlor. The face was the same as it had been when he was five—older but the same shape. And even had he grown a beard, broken his nose or been covered in smallpox scars, the clothes would have proclaimed the man. He wore a gray homburg hat. When he hung it on the stand by the door, he revealed snow-white hair. The hat did not quite match the navy-blue pilot coat which reached nearer to the ground than was fashionable. But Joe had never been a smart dresser and since the coat appeared identical to the one which their father had worn as a sign of solid prosperity, Herbert's reaction was more envious than critical. Joe was clearly a man of property. He pushed toward the bar without stopping to remove his coat. Herbert assumed that his brother had recognized him and did not want to waste a moment before they were at last reunited.

"Joe! Joe!" Herbert jostled his neighbors at the bar in his anxiety to meet Joe halfway.

Joe stopped and slowly turned his head. One of the once bright blue eyes was clouded over with a white film. "God Almighty, is it you?" The accent was so strange that it seemed impossible that the voice belonged to Herbert's brother. "Christ, Herbert. You haven't half changed."

Notwithstanding the shock of the accent, Herbert grasped his brother's hand and pumped it for several seconds. He was not sure how to relinquish his grasp. So he stood as if they were waiting for the sodium flash of a posed photograph. Joe continued to express his astonishment.

"I'd never have recognized you, Herbert, not in a thousand years, tash and all."

Herbert began to feel a great gulf opening up between them—a gulf which he was desperate to bridge. At that moment he was balanced precariously on the tightrope which joined the two sides of the great divide. Joe's behavior during the next few minutes would depend on whether he made a successful crossing or fell into the strange abyss of detachment. The man whose hand he still held was a stranger. But a stranger who, as well as being his own flesh and blood, had once been his closest friend.

"How long have you been in Nottingham?"

Herbert swayed on the rope when he remembered that his exile had begun long before Joe had sailed for Canada, and he almost lost his balance when he recalled the long and detached letter which he had written a year ago with such care and difficulty.

"Anyway, Bert, it's bloody good to see you."

It was strange to think of himself as Bert again. For, these days, Bert was the little boy who had loved fishing, who had worked in the packing department of I. and R. Morley's and who had been killed in the battle of the Somme. But he had been Bert once, and the memory steadied him. He stumbled to the far side of the great divide and astonished the drinkers around him by grasping his brother in an unembarrassed embrace.

"It's good to see you an' all. God, it seems a long time."

"It *is* a long time. Lot a' water flowed down t'Don sin' you an' me were lads."

They both laughed at Joe's caricature of a Sheffield accent.

"Lord help us, Joe, you're back from thirty years in Canada and I've not offered you a drink."

"Whiskey," said Joe. "Whiskey and water."

They took their drinks to the corner of the bar parlor and sat at one of the cast-iron tables. It was just like old times. Herbert knocked his knee against one of the sharp legs and spilled his beer. Joe looked at him with affectionate exasperation.

"You haven't changed at all."

"Just as clumsy as thirty years since."

"You're not clumsy. You just don't think. Never did."

"So you used to say."

After that, the conversation was no problem as each brother attempted to tell his own story and only managed to relate a single fact before the other began an unrelated anecdote of his own. When their father was at last mentioned, Herbert fell silent. Joe's description of the back bedroom at his sister's house in Doncaster filled him with guilt and horror.

"He's half-dead, Bert. And they treat him as if he's gone already. A woman comes in to wash him. Mary won't do it. Good food, nice room, but no family."

"I tried to make it up with him, but he wouldn't . . ."

"They never speak to him. He just sits there. Not that talking to him's easy."

"Can't he speak at all? When I last saw him . . ." Herbert was anxious to make plain that he really had tried to do a son's duty.

"He can hardly get his words out. He can understand, most of the time. But he can't speak. He gets into great rages trying to make you understand. One of 'em will kill him sooner or later. How long since the stroke?"

"Best part of twenty years. Just before t'war began."

"And he's hung on. Strong as a horse."

"Was he pleased to see you? He never wanted to see me."

"I think so. It's difficult to tell. He's got it in for you all right. Wouldn't let me mention you. Once he called me Frederick. Still thinks about that dead baby."

Joseph and Herbert shuddered together, even though they were sweating in the moist heat of the crowded bar parlor. It was again Herbert's turn to buy the drinks.

"You must be hot, Joe. Shall I take your coat and hang it up?"

At first, the offer was refused. Then, as the sweat began to run down his face, Joe reluctantly eased himself out of the heavy worsted arms and let the coat fall onto the bench around and beneath him. The jacket which it had hidden was stained and threadbare and badly patched at the elbows and over the pockets. Herbert guessed that the trousers which it still covered were even more disreputable.

"I'm a bit down on my luck at present. Came over steerage. That's why the suit smells. I've made plenty in my time. But I've made it and lost it. That was my way. Last time, I lost it for good. That's why I came home."

"What about the coat?"

"It's Father's. So is the hat. Gave it to me yesterday. And this . . ." Joe handed Herbert a bank book. "Open it."

For a moment, Herbert hoped that his name would be printed

inside. But he was not really surprised to read "Joseph Hattersley Esq." written on the flyleaf in careful Victorian copperplate. He was not, however, prepared for the total on the bottom of the last page. Deposits and interest added up to eleven hundred and eighty-seven pounds, twelve shillings and sixpence.

"You can buy your own bloody drink." Herbert tried desperately to grin.

"I'm going to do better than that. I'm going to buy a pub. This pub. It's all arranged."

Herbert could think of nothing to say.

"Hard work, mind. It's going downhill. Times are changing. That's why I'm getting it for six hundred quid. Twenty-year lease. It'll see me out. The old bugger put money away for me for years. If I'd known about it, I'd have gambled it away in a couple of months. I suppose I was lucky that he didn't tell me."

Herbert vaguely recalled a meeting with a cashier in the bank who asked him questions about a mysterious account in his brother's name. What his father had said about putting money aside for Joe had been true. It was to be used for buying a public house. Herbert laughed out loud.

Joe put his forefinger to his lips. "For Christ's sake, don't let the barman know. Not with me looking like this. All done through solicitors this morning. I saw the advert on Tuesday, got my bank book yesterday and now it's all done. I'm buying some clothes this afternoon before I sign the deed." Joseph leaned forward and whispered conspiratorially, "There'll be four hundred quid left. Four hundred quid or more."

Herbert felt it was his place to listen.

"I'm buying a shop, a cutler's shop, in Nottingham. Least, what was a cutler's shop. It's an ironmonger's now."

As Herbert looked more than usually bewildered, Joseph decided to tell him the whole story.

"It's your shop, Herbert, the one you work in at nights. I can get it for four hundred. You can run it, if you want to. And we'll split the profit."

"Split the profit?"

"Three to one in your favor—part owner and manager. We'll own it between us. Your name'll be on the deed, part owner. I reckon I owe you two hundred quid from this little book. Do you want to do it?"

Herbert was speechless again.

"It's not charity. It's how they do things on the other side of the Atlantic. It's called incentive. As a partner you'll work harder, make more money for me. Do you want to do it or not?"

"Of course I bloody well do!" There were tears in Herbert's eyes.

"But general ironmongery, mind. Paraffin as well as scissors and a bit of sharpening and setting on the side."

"Aye. I know that well enough."

"That's that then."

"Except I need to know how you found out. Did Aunt Winifred tell you?"

"I've not spoken nor wrote to her for thirty years. Didn't even know that she was still alive."

"How did you know then?"

"The solicitor told me shop were for sale. Then when I got details, I guessed it were the place where you sharpen and set at night."

"And how did t'solicitor find out?"

"He found out from Jack Foster's lad. Did you not know? Our father gave him the money to buy it in the first place. Two hundred pounds he gave him. God knows why."

For some reason which he could not even understand himself, Herbert chose that moment to ask Joseph what had happened to his eye. But he did not listen to the answer. All he could think of was the two hundred pounds—two hundred pounds given to Willie Foster at a time when the Hattersleys of Grove Road were struggling to find twopence and would have thought of two pounds as a fortune.

He was vaguely conscious of Joseph saying, ". . . so I've just got to make the best of it." But his thoughts had moved on to the strange relationship between his father and Jack Foster which had led to young Willie's good fortune and his own betrayal. Jack, who had always prided himself on his independence, had been favored for bending to Frederick Hattersley's will. And his son had been re-warded because of the father's obedience. Herbert wished that he could feel proud that he had at least kept his self-respect. But he feared that if he had his time again, he would choose meekly to inherit. There was only one aspect of the affair about which he felt absolutely certain.

"That settles it."

"Settles what? You don't mean the job? You still want it?"

" 'Course I do. It's not that."

"What is it then?"

"I was going to go to Doncaster to see him. To see him before he dies. Despite the bank book—and not a penny for me—I was going to go and try to make it up. But not now. Bugger the old sod."

Joseph, the bank book in his hand, did not reply.

Augusta decided that, with Roy being away and little Gussie about to be married, the whole family could be adequately accommodated at 80 Alfreton Road. There had been a house behind the shop long before Frederick Hattersley had converted two of the back rooms into workshop and boiler house. One of them would be used again for the purpose for which it had been designed—a back bedroom. The machinery had all been auctioned off when Frederick Hattersley sold the business, and the new owner had made a home of a sort in the bare rooms which remained. Willie Foster had mended a couple of windows and decorated one of the downstairs rooms. He had spent money on improving the living room and had built a bathroom onto the back of the house, although he had not yet had the taps connected to the boiler which heated water in the kitchen. Upstairs there was a desperate need for paint and paper. But a family with three teenage sons could apply both without undue difficulty.

It took three months to finish the job. Clare Martin advised on color and texture and Tom Cross lent a hand with the heavy lifting. Winifred Gunn watched from a chair in the middle of the living room while Augusta, almost immobilized with dropsy, sat beside her and supervised the work of her three sons. Herbert did the papering and only once stepped from the ladder into the bucket of paste which little Gussie had made for him. Leslie wanted to try his hand at graining but was forbidden to tamper with the wet brown paint. George sandpapered woodwork and Syd scraped off old paper.

On the morning before the family moved in, Herbert Hattersley leaned his borrowed ladder against the front of the shop. He could not afford to decorate the windows with an enamel sign of the sort which had been his father's pride and glory. But he meant to have the family name outside the family shop. A signwriter had outlined the ten letters on the board which ran along the wall above the window. And the new proprietor and manager filled in the complicated shapes with dark blue paint until they clearly read "Hattersley and Sons."

There were still old customers to be served, and when the sign had been written, Herbert went into the shop to finish the day's grinding and setting. He was working on a pair of shears, when the owner of the drapery next door but three came through the door.

"Do you own it now?" he asked peremptorily.

"I do."

"And are you the Hattersleys whose lads go to St. Mary's School?"

"I am." Herbert wiped his palms on an old rag in preparation for shaking hands.

"They say you're Germans. All your lads have German names that you keep secret. *Karl* Leslie, *William* George, *Charles* Sydney. We don't want no Germans around here."

Herbert did not consciously throw up the hatch at the end of the counter or pick up the shears with malice aforethought. Nor did he make a considered decision to chase the draper out onto the Alfreton Road. Fortunately the policeman who happened to be passing knew him. They had often talked together late at night when Herbert, working at his bench, was the only sign of life on the road. So he understood what the portly middle-aged man meant when he ran from his shop brandishing a pair of gardening shears and shouting about his son who had been killed in the war. The policeman caught him in full flight and told him, "Steady on or you'll be in trouble."

"That bastard called me a German."

The draper, safely across the road, denied that he had made any such suggestion. "I only asked if he was. Only asked. It was a civil question."

Herbert lifted the shears again.

"Look here," said the policeman. "Provoked or not, I don't want any nonsense. Get inside, the pair of you." He turned to Herbert and addressed him in most unconstabulary tones. "You're old enough to know better, Herbert. Fancy letting an odd word like that get on your nerves. No more trouble, mind, or I'll have to take you in."

It was Herbert's bad luck that, on the following day, the policeman was passing just as the butcher from Derby Road came round to collect his sharpened knives and cleavers. And it was even worse luck that the butcher left his largest cleaver lying on the counter. Naturally enough, Herbert ran out to catch his customer before he drove off, and, equally naturally, when he saw that the butcher was already in the cab of his van, he waved the cleaver in the air to signal that it had been forgotten.

Despite the butcher's corroboration, it took the best part of an hour to convince the station sergeant that Herbert meant no harm. Then he was sent home with a caution.

"We don't like trouble around here," said the sergeant. "And we don't like those who bring it."

Once he realized that he was not going to be charged, Herbert's manner changed from injured innocence to outrage. "I'm a respectable shopkeeper paying rates in this town, an old soldier and a member of the Constitutional Club. I'll thank you to keep your impudence to those who are prepared to stand it."

He walked out of the police station feeling that the outcome of the incident had made the inconvenience worthwhile. He would not have said that before he owned—at least in part—his own shop.

CHAPTER THIRTY-SIX

ANOTHER CHURCH: ANOTHER MIRACLE

R ex Hattersley—uncertain about his faith and insecure about his future—found the news that he no longer lived at Grove Road almost too painful to bear. Throughout his confused first year in Rome, the memories of a happy childhood in a loving family had been the firm foundation which kept his precarious life from collapsing in complete despair. The memories all took the form of pictures and the pictures all had Grove Road for their background. When he thought of his mother, he visualized her either resting on the old horsehair sofa or half-hidden in a cloud of soapsuds and steam in the kitchen on washdays. The image of his father that he carried in his mind was a reflection of that florid face and immaculate hair in the mirror over the living-room mantelpiece. Syd and George wrestled and squabbled in the dust of the backyard and Aunt Clare—who had just popped next door with a message for Tom Cross—warned them that they would be in trouble when their mother saw the mud on their trousers. If they were no longer where he remembered them, he was not sure that he would remember them at all. The idea that his family was slipping away from him replaced doubts about doctrine as his principal anxiety, and attempts to imagine them in their surroundings took up time which had previously been employed in soaking up the majesty of Rome.

The doubts about doctrine were not the uncertainties which usually afflicted young prospective priests. Rex had faith in everything. The Bible he believed literally, and the word of every pope he accepted without question. The nearest that he got to heresy was his unspoken skepticism about the Seven Proofs of the Existence of God. Of course God existed and he did not need the evidence of rain falling downward—rather than perversely traveling in the opposite direction—to convince him that an ordered universe must be the product of a Divine Will. When he read, on instruction, Hilaire Belloc's *Reply to H. G. Well's History of the World,* he was fascinated by the description of the life of seals rather than by its repudiation of the Darwinian theory. The idea that man had evolved from monkeys was intrinsically ridiculous. Life on earth began when God breathed on clay and made Adam. There was no more to be said about it. He could not work out what all the theological fuss was about. Rex's problem was not the failure of belief but a reluctance to spend the rest of his life persuading doubters to accept the obvious. What was more, he did not enjoy communal life. He wanted to live peacefully with his family.

He began to think of himself as an impostor, and the feeling of guilt combined with the hatred of the regimented life increasingly alienated him from the College. He had come to Rome to read books. And the books were a continual delight. But more was expected of him than the assimilation of a million facts. He was a student of the Gregorian University by false pretenses, enjoying the delights of the Eternal City as the result of a fraud. He had no calling to reclaim England for Holy Mother Church. It would take up valuable time which might be spent on reading *The Lives of the Popes,* drawing diagrams of the battles in the Great Civil War or making lists of Napoleon's marshals, the clans which had fought with Charles Edward Stuart and the tributaries of the river Trent. Could a priest, he wondered, go to cricket matches? Most depressing of all, he knew that a priest must live alone in a gloomy presbytery.

Frick Wilson and Bill Ellis had noticed that he grew increasingly gloomy and, assuming that he suffered from the usual homesickness, had promised him that he would feel better in the summer after three months in Palazzola in the hills above Lake Albano. But the summer

491

came and went, and back in the routine of heavy meals, early lectures, brief walks, and compulsory siestas, Rex still felt a lost soul. It was in the Borghese Gardens that Michael Eagan forced him to face up to his melancholy.

"You ought to talk to the Rector."

"What about?"

"Hating it here."

"I don't hate it here. At least, not all of it."

"You hate too much of it. Too much for you to last out for another five years."

"I love most of it. I love the mass and the music. I love the lectures. I love living in Rome. I go on more expeditions than anybody. You didn't go to the Catacombs or with Father Thomas to the Baths of Caracalla."

"Why are you so unhappy then?"

"I'd just like to go home at night."

Michael Eagan tried to remain sympathetic, but he was nineteen. "I see. You want to go to the Gregorian University during the day, visit the antiquities in the early evening and then go home to a hardware shop in Nottingham. I'm not sure that we can arrange that."

"It's an ironmonger's shop. And that's not home anyway. What I'm saying is, I want to be ordinary. I'm not ready to be different from other people."

"Priests aren't ordinary and never can be."

"That's what I'm saying. That's why I shouldn't be here."

"You've got to talk to the Rector."

"I won't, not yet."

"It's too late. I've told Bill Ellis and you know what he's like. He'll have been to the Rector by now. There'll be a message for you at dinner. Bet you a shilling."

"I can't remember what a shilling looks like."

The note was passed to him the moment that grace completed the meal. It was neither a command nor an invitation but simply a statement of time and place. "Rector's study, half past nine."

Rex shuffled out of the refectory worrying about how he would spend the nervous twenty minutes before the appointed time. When he passed the Rector in the hall, he tried to avoid their eyes meeting. But he failed.

"It's a glorious night. Why don't we have a little walk and talk as we go? It's like an oven in my study."

492

At first, they walked without talking down the Via di Monserrato toward the Farnese Palace. Just before they reached the Piazza, Monsignor Hinsley asked the inevitable question. Rex was struck by the strange combination of an Irish priest's language and the accent of the English establishment.

"Are you troubled, my son?"

"Yes, Rector."

"Can you tell me about it?"

"I'll try, Rector."

"Are you having doubts?"

"Yes, Rector."

"It's important to set out what the doubts are. The mysteries are not easy to comprehend. If they were easy, they wouldn't be mysteries. It's best to talk about them."

"It's not that, Rector."

"What then, some of the new dogma? You must not believe that every truth was revealed to us in the time of Our Lord. It is only to be expected that a wicked world learns slowly. Take, for example, the revelation of infallibility . . ."

"It's not that, either, Rector. I believe all that. I can't understand how anyone can believe anything else."

Monsignor Hinsley smiled and grasped Rex's elbow. He had a profound respect for simple faith. The Heenans and the Griffins, the O'Dwyers, Ellises and Cashmans were the glory of the College—the men who were destined to become bishops or better from the day on which their names were entered Venerabili on the Liber Ruber. Those were the men with whom he took his regular evening walks, arguing with them about the liturgical reforms of St. John Chrysostom and the true meaning of Father Matthew's *Apostle of Temperance*. But how refreshing to meet a young man whose belief was uncomplicated by intellectuality, a young man whose humility made him doubt his capacity to fulfill the destiny for which Providence had so clearly intended him.

"I think I understand. You worry about whether or not you are worthy to serve the Lord."

Rex exhibited again the unworldliness which the Rector had so much admired—combining it with a demonstration of his irritation that instead of listening to a description of his problems, Monsignor Hinsley persisted in telling him what his problems were. Frustration made him frank.

"No, Rector. I don't think that. I'm not even sure what worthy means. I've never thought about it. It's just that I can't see myself as a priest. The other day you said it was a job as well as a calling. It's a job I don't want to do."

Monsignor Hinsley began to revise his opinion about the young man's natural humility.

"What other occupation did you have in mind?"

"I don't know. But I want something ordinary. Something with a house and a family. You know . . . I want to be ordinary, not looked at in the street. I want to wear normal clothes and ride a bicycle."

"We do not expect a vow of abstinence from cycling." The Rector did not mean to be unkind. He was hardening his heart in preparation for the most difficult of all the questions. "Is it matters of the heart? Women? Marriage?"

"Not more than anything else. Well, I suppose it is in a sort of way. I don't see myself living on my own. I want to be part of a family."

"My dear boy, we are your family now. What were you doing before you came here?"

"I was at Ratcliffe for eighteen months. Before that I worked for a bit. I was office boy at Morley's in Nottingham. Before that—"

"And do you think that you can go back to Morley's after two years here and almost as long at a great public school? Whether or not you are lost to us, you are certainly lost to them."

Rex felt weak with fear. He could not even outline a mental picture of his real family. His father now drank in a public house which he did not know. His mother cooked in a kitchen which he had never seen. George and Syd slept in a bedroom which he would not recognize. The Rector repeated what he believed to be reassurance. What he intended as balm was gall.

"We are your family now." Then John Hinsley noticed Rex's distress. "Is there nothing you like about us? No family is quite perfect. But surely we have some redeeming graces."

"I like the studying. I like the music. I like . . . I suppose that I'm just homesick."

"If you stick it out a little longer, one day you'll be homesick for us. We'll grow on you. You'll see."

Rex could not think of anything to say.

"Give us a chance." The Rector sounded genuinely humble. "When do you expect to be tonsured?"

"A year next November."

"Give us until then. And for the next year, throw yourself into everything. Get out into Rome. You'll never have another chance like it. If you tell me next autumn that you still want away, we'll not argue."

Monsignor Hinsley assumed that silence meant consent.

"Have you been reading about this man Mussolini? He's taking on the secret societies at last."

They had turned into Via della Cappellari and the Rector had noticed the municipal-election posters which defiled one of the ancient walls. Candidates' names were followed by initials which signified not academic distinctions nor military honors but membership in a Freemasons' Lodge.

"I think he's come to an agreement with the Vatican. Wouldn't it be wonderful if the Pope made peace with Italy after all these years? We invited this Mussolini man to Palazzola last summer. But his people wouldn't let him come. Said it was too dangerous to travel through the woods. The communists might murder him. I think he'll deal with them as well as the Freemasons . . ."

They turned across the gray front of St. Philip Neri and back into the Via di Monserrato. The walk was over. Rex was back inside the college.

Monsignor Hinsley's political prediction proved correct. For a year, the Italian newspapers were filled with the names of machinating politicians—Bianchi, D'Annunzio, Fata, de Bono, Lusignoli, Fara and Sante Ceccherini. Students at the English College—feeling the exile's pride in the institutions of home—were contemptuous of the instability of their adopted country and skeptical about the political respectability of the innumerable factions which competed for power.

Mussolini was an improbable hero—small, bald, fat and a journalist by profession. But he managed to assume the trappings of heroism. He also possessed a heroic turn of phrase. "It was on the banks of the Prave that we began the march that can only end in Rome." In the Via di Monserrato they were not sure what it meant. But it had a true romantic ring of the sort which is associated with braggadocio rather than real brutality, and it therefore came as a great surprise when the march on Rome turned from a metaphor into a full-scale revolution.

Mussolini's insurrection was a feeble coup d'état. Fewer fascists assembled than Il Duce anticipated, and the Black Shirt squadrons were dispirited by hunger and an unseasonable cloudburst which drenched them to the skin. But they had risen up against a pathetic government, and the columns, which had barely numbered twenty thousand when there was fighting to be feared, had swollen to four times that number by the time of the Victory Parade. In the Vatican, an ancient priest—recalling the war in which Julian Watts Russell had died—announced, "We defended Rome better in 1870."

Il Duce declined a second invitation to visit the English College, but there was a meeting between Prime Minister and seminarians, even though in Via di Monserrato they described it as a confrontation. Three of the senior men—Frick Wilson, Michael Farmer and Henry Maddox-Maffere—had crossed the Tiber and were walking in the Pamphili Gardens. Their talk, as usual, was of the war in which they had just served. And for some time their concentration was disturbed only by the song of crickets in the hard brown grass. It was a golden afternoon in late spring and the Villa Doria Pamphili gleamed like burnished ocher in the sun. A haze hung over the lakes and fountains, and the workmen—who had been dredging the weeds from the water—were eating bread and cheese in the cool shadow of the church of San Pancrazio.

The three students heard the sound of the motorcar's engine before they saw the horse and rider which the open-topped Bugatti followed at a respectful distance. It was the car, rather than the rider, which first caught their notice. The horseman, sitting stiffly on a snow-white mare which looked too big for him, was not an arresting sight. His head barely rose above his shoulders and his face was obscured by the shadows which fell upon it from a huge black bowler hat. The car, on the other hand, commanded their undivided attention, for the man who sat on the folded canvas roof with his feet on the back seat was carrying a shotgun. As the strange cortège approached the San Pancrazio obelisk the workmen stood up and, shuffling out from the shade, bared their heads in respectful salute.

"It's Mussolini," said Frick Wilson.

The three men stood on the grass at the side of the gravel path as the rider and escort approached.

"Hats off," shouted the man with the shotgun.

Frick Wilson and Henry Maddox-Maffere obliged.

"Hats off!" the man shouted again, staring at Michael Farmer. But Michael Farmer, staring back, seemed not to hear.

Slowly, as the Bugatti drew level, the man in the back seat raised his shotgun to his shoulder and took careful aim.

"Hats off!" shouted the driver.

Later that night in the College, they said that what followed was Maddox-Maffere's finest hour.

"Don't shoot!" he called, waving his shovel hat in the air. "Don't shoot! He's sick."

Maddox-Maffere tapped his brow with his finger and wondered if the rivulet of sweat that he felt running down the side of his face had been born in heat or fear.

"He's sick. It's shell shock. He means no disrespect. Shell shock." And then came the moment of genius. "Shell shock after the fighting. He was at Caporetto. He was with the American volunteers."

Il Duce gave a stiff little bow, one soldier to another. The shotgun swung away and the Bugatti passed on.

"May you be forgiven." Frick Wilson was more impressed than outraged.

"Bloody fool," said Maddox-Maffere .

"I only take my hat off to the Pope and the King of England."

As it turned out, Michael Farmer had only to wait a few weeks before an opportunity to perform the second gracious act arose.

King George came to Rome in May and his state visit provoked a great debate within the English College about how he should be greeted. The seminarians were royalist to a man. But there was some division of opinion about which royal house claimed their allegiance. On St. George's Day, mass was said in St. Peter's around the tomb of the Old Pretender, or James III as they liked to call him. Ultras amongst them referred to the Cardinal Duke of York, Archbishop of Frascati, as Henry IX. It was by no means clear what homage the College ought to pay to a Hanoverian king.

In the end a compromise was agreed. The College would collectively accept the invitation to the Embassy reception. But the seminarians would wear white roses when they were presented to Queen Mary. The white rose was the symbol of support for Bonnie Prince Charlie, worn by the faithful for a hundred years after Culloden as a symbol of their sub rosa support for the old dynasty and the old religion. The ex-servicemen wore their medals, too. They had fought for king and country and were not prepared to allow ancient arguments about the succession to obscure their patriotism.

Spring, the Rector said to himself, is always a difficult season. I shall be glad when the summer comes and we can all get to Lake Albano and Palazzola.

. . .

Rex Hattersley looked forward to the summer at Palazzola. He thought of it as the last phase of his life in Italy and he anticipated his last few weeks at the College with an impatience which had a cause he would hardly admit to himself. He had enjoyed his previous two summers on Lake Albano and he expected to enjoy the summer of 1923—as soon as he could escape south.

In the summer heat of Rome, the last days of June were intolerable and were only endured by the College as an experience of purgatory to be borne in the knowledge that the pure heaven of the Appian Hills was not far away. In the last week before the retreat to the lake, Rex hardly slept at all. Rome had discovered the motorcar and decided that its principal purpose was the popularization of the klaxon horn. If Rex attempted to sleep with his window open, the air which circulated in his little room carried the noise of a thousand motorists sending greetings, warnings and complaints to fellow drivers. If he closed his window, he could not breathe. The ancient dust blew from the streets into his eyes and nostrils and awoke within him the ancient Hattersley evil spirit—hay fever. He coughed and sneezed his way toward high summer and counted off the days to Palazzola.

At Palazzola the day did not begin until seven o'clock and formal studies ended at four in the afternoon. There was a tennis court, a billiard table and a swimming pool. The best swimmers—including Rex, who had learned to swim in the canal behind Grove Road and had spent many sunny afternoons naked in the Trent—were allowed to swim in the lake itself. Lake Albano was the crater of an extinct volcano which had mysteriously filled with water and, even more mysteriously, remained always at the same level without help from rivers or streams. The locals said that it was five miles deep in the middle, and their superstitions about what lurked on the bottom were reinforced when a fisherman capsized his boat and was never seen again. Rex swam out each morning toward the Pope's summer palace on the opposite shore and only turned back when he felt certain that he had reached the spot above the unfathomable deep.

"One day you'll drown," warned Hugh Atkinson.

"And," added Michael Eagan, "being in a personal state of grace, you'd go straight to heaven."

"You cannot be sure of these things." Francis Cashman took theology very seriously.

"If it's hell," said Frick Wilson, "I know what it will be like. I was there in 1916."

The greatest joy of Palazzola was the rowing. The English College owned two heavy boats which they pretended were racing shells, and in the early evening scratch crews raced each other from the landing stage, at the foot of the cliff below the chapel, to the pleasure beach a mile along the lake's rim. North competed against South, and Soldiers against Public-School Boys, and Newmanites against Manningists. Rex was so eager to row that he would lay claim to any crew which was incomplete—insisting that Ratcliffe was not his alma mater, Manning was right to exile Newman to Rednall and Nottingham was in the south of England.

He particularly enjoyed mass at Palazzola. It was, of course, the same mass which they expected him to say every morning of his life. But in Rome it was said under the angry gaze of Christ militant, who was converting the world by blood and fire. At Lake Albano it was celebrated in the cool white Cistercian chapel with the outlines of the sixteenth-century figures still palely visible on its medieval fresco. Rex felt most at home in the Church Serene and Certain which had worshiped in that chapel before the Reformation had disturbed the peace of its exclusive ministry. He was at peace at Palazzola. If only he could have lived in such quiet contentment, he would have wanted to stay in Italy forever.

It had been agreed that he should return to Rome the day before the rest of the College moved back into the Via di Monserrato. Everybody knew why he was leaving Palazzola early. Indeed, everyone—friend and foe alike—approved of the idea that if he was to leave, it was better that he should be packed and gone before the rest of the family got home. That way he would be quickly forgotten as the survivors moved closer together to fill up the void which his departure caused.

There had been little discussion of his early and permanent departure. Only William Ellis had talked of letting people down and urged him to consider his responsibilities. Michael Eagan had admitted that he did not understand and Francis Cashman had asked him to make sure that he was really doing what would make him happy. It had been a long time since anyone had mentioned the subject of his happiness and he was heartened by Cashman's concern. On the last night before Rex's departure, the four of them walked in the garden looking, as always, for fireflies and marveling, as usual, at an artesian well which drew water to the top of a cliff. Ellis asked which one of them was reading G. K. Chesterton's *Heretics*—one of the books recommended for light reading during the evenings at Palazzola. None of them was.

"I want to ask you about a bit of it, the bit I don't understand."

They sat in the cloister and waited for Ellis to bring out the book and, for the first time in three years, Rex felt one of the mystic brotherhood. It was, he knew, the natural reaction to leaving—a feeling which would desert him the moment that he changed his mind and decided to stay. But he was glad that Rome had meant enough to make him feel sad at the parting and that he would leave real friends behind.

Ellis sat on the wooden bench that ran along the cloister wall and leaned back so that the light from the windows fell upon the page.

"The common defense of the family is that amid the stress and fickleness of life it is peaceful and pleasant and at one. But there is another defense of the family which is possible and to me evident: this defense is that the family is not peaceful and not pleasant and not at one."

"Read it again," demanded Michael Eagan. "It makes no sense to me."

Ellis followed his bidding, and it was mutually agreed that the aphorism was meaningless.

"Showing off," said Eagan.

Rex was not sure. He had no idea what the passage meant. But he had been driven back into despair by the attempts to understand it. He no longer felt competent to comment on matters concerning the family. It was for that reason that he was walking to Rome next morning.

The stream of sweat had begun to run down his back before he had walked half a mile. His summer soutane felt no lighter than his winter cassock, and his hard canvas shorts cut into the backs of his knees. As well as the haversack which contained his Bible, change of socks, razor, towel and soap he carried the cardboard suitcase which Aunt Clare had given him when he left Nottingham. Unfortunately, it had split and was held together by a heavy leather belt which scuffed his knuckles when he gripped its handle. Rex hoped to complete his journey before the midday heat made walking dangerous, but he stopped after an hour to eat the bread that he had brought with him from Palazzola. In Nottingham, on the summer picnics which passed for holidays, he had always eaten his sandwiches and drunk his bottle of water as soon as he got to the first field. The habit was too strong to break. Fortified, he struggled on north along the Appian Way, his heavy shoes disturbing the dust which had once felt the soles of legionnaires' sandals as they returned from foreign wars. At Ciampino, he began to feel faint. But he marched on. He kept going for another hour, rested briefly and strode out again through the Roman suburbs. Suddenly his knees began to give way and he staggered toward the sanctuary of one of the great basilicas that ennoble almost every street in Rome. Rex was not in the mood even to notice its style and architecture. But even if he had paused to stare at its black façade, he would have thought of it as just another of the churches which cardinal after cardinal had built and rebuilt over the previous five hundred years—a confusion of classical and baroque; dirty, elaborate and oppressive. Inside it was Santa Maria Maggiore.

Forty years before, Frederick Hattersley had stumbled out of the January snow into the awesome nave of York Minster and, under the splendor of its great Gothic arches, he had felt himself to be in the presence of a God who was justly called Almighty. Inside Santa Maria Maggiore, his grandson and namesake felt a less spiritual emotion. The feeling of nausea and the fear of fainting were both forgotten. Between the long lines of Corinthian columns that ran from end to end of the church, the sun streamed in from the windows high above the nave. But on either side, beyond the pillars, were long corridors of mysterious dusk, where, thanks to a trick played by the architect, the sun could not reach. He could see—past the pillars and through the gloom—patches of light which he took to be side chapels. But he had no time to spare for them. Above him, past the curled capitals of the Corinthian columns, were great mosaic pictures which sparkled in the sunlight as if they were made of precious stones. He recognized only one tableau—the meeting of the brothers Jacob and Esau. Before he could concentrate on the other messianic figures, he had to shade his eyes from the reflected brilliance of the ceiling. It was decorated in a pattern which he half remembered from St. Peter's—a pattern which, when he first saw it, had reminded him of the golden rose which Derbyshire cricketers wore on their caps. But in St. Peter's, the rose was half-lost amongst all the other bosses and panels. In Santa Maria Maggiore, it was repeated time after time. Had Rex Hattersley realized that every panel had been made from Peruvian gold which Ferdinand and Isabella of Spain had given to the church, he would not have been more impressed.

He wandered, entranced, first down the sunlit side of each row of pillars and then in the shade. He stopped at every side chapel—Borghese, Sforza, Pauline and Sixtus V. It was the altar canopy which confirmed the instinct that he was in the most beautiful building in the world. For years he had nurtured a secret hatred of the four twisted and bloated pillars which Bellini had designed to guard the altar at St. Peter's. Now he knew that his judgment was right. Now he knew the sort of columns on which the canopy should be held. Through all the doubts which had tortured him for a year, he began to feel again the old attraction—his fatal infatuation with the sights and sounds and smells of the Church Beautiful. A religion that could create Santa Maria Maggiore must be worth some sort of allegiance. He stumbled back into the glare of the afternoon.

Outside, in the dry air of the Piazza dell'Esquilino, with his head throbbing, his feet aching and the knuckles of both his hands sore and bleeding, he completed the declaration of faith—for the first time he began to understand his relationship with the Catholic Church. It was not the mysteries which were important to him. It was the magnificence. And without the mysteries the magnificence—the service, the sacrifice, the splendor and the suffering—could not exist. Suddenly, he was afraid of losing his part in the splendor and the suffering, as he had once been afraid of losing his place amongst his family. He waited for a few minutes under the shade of the portico and watched the beggars play on the susceptibilities of the passersby. One vagrant wore trousers made for a man twice his size and accommodated their extra length by rolling them up in a cuff that reached almost to his knee. In its fold, he carried a tourist's guide to Rome. Rex smiled at another example of the Eternal City's infinite variety. He would, he knew, miss it all. Then he felt an irresistible desire to go back inside the church. The mass had begun. The priest wore the green vestments of an unexceptional day and they glowed emerald in the sunlight. Rex repeated the responses under his breath.

Rex reached the Via di Monserrato more than two hours later than he had planned and he assumed that the Rector would have abandoned his plan to talk to him that night. It seemed that he was alone in the College and he decided to soothe his sore back and aching feet by taking the long bath which the absence of other students made possible. But he knew that before he luxuriated in so scandalous a self-indulgence, he had a duty to make his peace with Monsignor Hinsley. So he wearily climbed the stairs to the library and wrote out a note of explanation and apology. His first effort had to be thrown away, for he smeared the paper with blood from his grazed knuckles. But the second draft, although grubby with sweat marks, was clean enough to take to the Rector's study and leave for examination the following morning.

To Rex's astonishment, the door was open and Monsignor Hinsley sat behind his desk in a pool of light which fell on him from a standard lamp in the corner of the room. The lamp was intended to illuminate the book which the Rector was reading, but the golden circle spread across the baize covering the top of his desk. At its edge —golden Royal Cipher gleaming against black background—was Rex's passport. Next to it was a third-class railway ticket marked "Londra."

There could, Rex realized at once, be no doubt about what had happened. Because of his behavior and demeanor over the year since he had told the Rector of his doubts, he had been adjudged unsuitable for ordination. His own opinion about his future was no longer of any consequence. The decision had been made. He had changed his mind too late.

"Sit down, Hattersley."

The Rector closed his book with a snap which reverberated around the study and echoed into the deserted corridor.

"I've got some bad news for you."

Rex hung his head. Ordination had suddenly become the objective of his existence, the unobtainable prize that was indispensable to his happiness, the destiny which he was going to be denied. The verdict was clear, but the Rector seemed strangely reluctant to pronounce sentence. When he spoke, he chose his words with painful care.

"Your mother. I fear that she is most seriously ill. Indeed, she is mortally ill. God rest her soul. Your aunt sent you a telegram. It arrived this morning. I think that you should go to Nottingham at once. I took the liberty of obtaining a ticket for tomorrow morning."

Rex remembered that his mother used to complain that he always wanted what he could not have. At that moment, he no longer wanted the Church. He wanted to be at home in the living room at Grove

Road, with his mother resting on the horsehair sofa and his father changing his collar in preparation for an evening at the Grove Hotel.

"Is it the dropsy, Rector?"

"I only know what was in the telegram."

Monsignor Hinsley handed Rex the yellow paper. "Return if possible. Mother fading fast."

Without reading the name which followed, Rex knew that Aunt Clare was the author of the message. Only Clare could have written "fading fast."

"I'm sorry, Hattersley. I'm very sorry."

"Thank you, Rector." Rex leaned across the desk to pick up his passport and ticket. But Monsignor Hinsley had not quite finished.

"Stay as long as necessary. It's more than two months before your tonsure. As long as you're back a week before then."

CHAPTER THIRTY-SEVEN

THE LIFE AND THE
RESURRECTION

R ex hoped that when he arrived in Nottingham—sunburned, but in every other way typical of the young men who walked its pavements—he would feel as if he had never been away. He was wrong. The town was much the same. But he lived in a part of it which he did not know. Indeed, although he could have walked blindfold to the old house, he had to ask a policeman which bus traveled along Alfreton Road. By the time Rex found number 80, he felt like a complete stranger. The trauma was so great that he either did not notice, or did not think it important, that the blinds were drawn in the front bedroom window.

The kitchen was empty and he was not sure which of the two doors that flanked the fireplace led into the living room. The door on the right, which he tried first, opened into a food cupboard. The tins of salmon, tomatoes, pineapple chunks, Carnation milk and sardines made him feel, for the first time, that he was at home. The door on the left led into a tiny vestibule, made even smaller by the coats which hung on its only blank wall. Straight ahead, there was another door. To the right, a flight of stairs rose almost vertically. On the stairs, his head on his knees, sat Syd, who spoke to his brother as if they still

505

shared the same bed every night. The matter-of-fact familiarity made it impossible, at first, to grasp what he said.

"Mam's dead."

"Where's Dad?" Rex heard himself replying in the same flat tone. At that moment, he felt despair, not grief.

"He's gone out to make arrangements. Aunt Clare's up there, and Assumpta. They won't let us in."

Great-Aunt Winifred, hearing the noise, appeared through the far door and, partly obscured by coats, addressed Syd.

"In there, young man." She grasped his shoulder and gave him a helpful tug in the direction of the living room. "I told you to stay in there with Muriel and George."

Syd having been pushed in one direction, Rex was led in the other and sat down at the kitchen table.

"She went very peacefully. Clare was with her. She says it was like falling asleep. A big sigh and she'd gone."

"When did it happen?"

"Ten o'clock this morning. We'd expected it for days."

"Why didn't you send for me before?"

"We thought it would frighten her. All the way from Rome! She would have known that she was going."

"I wish you had. I shan't see her now." Rex was embarrassed by the banality of his complaint. "Where's Dad?"

"He's gone to the undertaker's and to arrange things at the cathedral. Clare offered to do it, but he insisted."

"How long will he be?"

Rex was desperate for his father to return. Only his father would understand how he felt. Only his father would share his grief. Only with his father would he be able to show his anguish.

The left-hand door opened and George appeared, tearstained and silent. Muriel was one pace behind.

"I tried to keep him in the front room, but when he heard that Roy was back, he wouldn't stop."

"All of you go through into the living room. You too, Roy. I'll make you a sandwich. You must be famished."

Rex, who had turned back into Roy without even noticing the transformation, hugged his sister and then hugged his brothers in turn. He asked each one, "Are you all right?" and was assured they were "OK," "Fine" and "Not bad," respectively.

506

Then Muriel cried, "It was awful yesterday. We couldn't get her warm."

When Roy went into the kitchen to get his sandwiches, Aunt Clare was washing her hands in the sink.

"Do you want to go up and see her?"

"Let the lad have his tea first," said Great-Aunt Winifred.

Clare sat down with Roy at the table and began the serious business of telling her nephew all that he should know about the previous twenty-four hours.

"She went very peacefully. Just slipped away. She had no pain all week. Just got weaker and weaker. She said what a handsome man your dad was. He came into the bedroom at about six, before he'd had a wash or shave, and she said how smart he looked."

"Why didn't you send for me before?"

Roy was looking for accomplices to share his increasing feelings of guilt.

"We thought it would frighten her. Then she asked for you. So we—"

"Why did she ask for me?" Guilt was turning into panic.

"I think she just wanted to say how proud she was. When Canon Hunt came round on Wednesday—"

"Tuesday," corrected Winifred.

Clare, without acknowledging her error, continued, "When Canon Hunt came round last Wednesday, she said that she expected a letter from 'my son, the priest.' Canon Hunt laughed."

"In a very kind way," added Winifred. "And he said, 'Not quite yet, Mrs. H.,' and he laughed."

Clare finished the story. "Your mam glared at him and said, 'He will be, Father. He will be.' And Canon Hunt went on and on about of course he would be and there was no intention of suggesting anything different."

"It was the first time that we'd seen Augusta smile for days."

"I was waiting for her to say 'DV.' She always said 'DV' after she talked about something good happening. But she didn't say it. She'd decided that God had made up his mind, and that he was willing already."

Roy stared at the scabs on his knuckles and wondered if he really had walked to Rome from Lake Albano only two days before. The marks of Aunt Clare's suitcase were still on his hands. Without the tangible proof of his long day, he would have feared that the miracle of Santa Maria Maggiore was just a dream and his fears that he was to be expelled from the English College no more than a nightmare.

"I'm tonsured in two months."

Winifred was horrified. "They never shave your hair off! That's pagan."

"It's just a bit cut from the back. It's symbolic. That's all. Just marks the days I take real vows."

"I wish your mother could have been spared to see the day. You going into the Church was her great consolation. That's why she died so peacefully. God rest her soul."

Clare knew that there was a line from *The Sign of the Cross* that summed up the position exactly. Unfortunately, after thirty years she could no longer remember it.

"Do you want to go up and see her?" she asked.

"I'll go up when Dad gets back. I'll go up with him."

"Come up with me now."

Before Roy had time to argue, Winifred explained why he should not wait for his father's return.

"Your dad gets very upset. Blames himself and says that he didn't provide for her properly. He gets very worked up. It's best not to go up with him."

Roy had spent his first two hours at home concentrating on keeping calm—lightening the family's load as Monsignor Hinsley had told him, not adding to the burden. He had not cried when Syd and George had cried, sentimentalized when Clare sentimentalized, but had studiously copied Winifred's obviously counterfeit composure.

He was not sure if he was yet ready to see his mother's body and he was still recoiling from the thought of its being washed and laid out by her sisters. He had never seen a corpse and his only idea about how his mother would look came from the novels of Charles Dickens. He had an awful fear that her jaw would be tied up with a bandage and that her eyelids would be weighed down with pennies. When he faced the ordeal, he must face it alone. It would be better to face it at once. Slowly he stood up. As he walked, silently, toward the door he kept reminding himself that it was his mother who lay in the bed upstairs. Her soul was on its way to heaven.

At the kitchen door, he paused. "Did the priest get her in time?"

"Of course!" Clare was insulted by the question. "The doctor didn't get here until she'd gone. But Canon Hunt was here an hour before she went. She smiled at him. She knew it was the last rites."

Winifred, unmellowed by age, felt a Nonconformist resentment rising inside her. "You really are quite the priest already."

Roy blushed. "I'll go up now. I'll go up on my own."

He pushed past Syd and George as if he had not seen them, strode resolutely up the steep stairs and, on the little landing, opened the wrong door. Inside was a room which was familiar but not quite familiar enough to be comforting. It contained all the furniture from his old bedroom at Grove Road—the big iron bed which he had shared with his brothers, the rough chest of drawers with the cracked mahogany-framed mirror standing on its top, the small wooden bed which his father had cut down so that it fitted under the eaves and the wicker chair, now even more threadbare than when he had thrown his clothes across it for the night. But there was one thing strange about the room. It had pegged rugs against the beds. In Grove Road, the cold linoleum was bare.

Roy drew a deep breath before he pulled open the door which he calculated must open into the front bedroom. In the half-light, he could just make out the bed. He tiptoed to the window (as if respect required him to maintain the absolute silence of the dead) and lifted a corner of the curtain from the windowsill. He expected to feel fear and nausea, but he only felt love and pity. It was his mother lying on the bed—white, old and strangely small, but his mother nevertheless. Sister Assumpta knelt by the bed like a child asking for protection through the night. Roy knew that his aunt expected him to kneel beside her, but he kissed his mother on the forehead and left the room without looking down. He had never kissed his mother like that before and it seemed a wholly inadequate way of saying goodbye. But he could think of no other way to touch the still figure. He clung to the handrail as, knees shaking, he made the perilous descent of the stairs. Below him, Syd and George, hypnotized by the idea that their mother was still upstairs, lurked amongst the coats. They clung onto Roy as he reached the bottom step. With them, he cried for the first time.

Winifred (half-asleep) and Clare (feverishly awake) awaited his return in the kitchen.

"We'll cook chops when your dad gets home." Winifred pushed herself up from the table and went to the sink to start peeling potatoes. Food was the great healer.

"I better take my bag upstairs. Which bed is mine?"

But before either aunt could reply, Herbert was back—three stones heavier than when Roy had left for Rome and now so large that he dominated the room. Leslie and little Gus were with him, and Leslie reached out for Roy first.

"I'm glad you're back." He looked ashamed to be pleased about anything on such a day. "There was no pain at all. The doctor said there would be at the end, but there wasn't. She just slipped away."

Herbert, who had been momentarily transfixed by the sight of Roy, came to life and seized his son in a bear hug. His great belly pressed his watch chain against Roy's ribs. Each word was carefully articulated and accompanied by the smell of beer.

"She talked about nowt but you. At t'end it was you all the time."

Huge tears ran down the fold between nose and round, red cheeks and disappeared in a mustache which was not so carefully trimmed as it once had been.

"Have you made all the arrangements?" asked Clare, who had no faith in her brother-in-law's administrative ability.

"I have."

Leslie understood why his aunt asked the question. He gave the details. "The undertaker will be here tonight about six. We've got a nice coffin, real oak."

"With real brass fittings." Herbert had insisted on real brass fittings.

"They were a bit worried about getting the coffin downstairs on Tuesday."

"Why Tuesday?" Winifred was sure that Leslie would get something wrong.

"There's the vigil. She's in church overnight."

"Is Canon Hunt definite?" asked Clare. "She'd want Canon Hunt."

"Canon Hunt is definite. That's why it's Wednesday." Leslie added an afterthought. "And the Bishop will be there."

Herbert remembered another service at the cathedral when another bishop had baptized poor little Bert. That bishop had performed the last rites over Herbert's hopes of reconciliation with his father. He had buried whatever chance remained of the Empress Works being handed on—as was right and proper—from father to son. Bishops suddenly took the place of Germans in Herbert's personal demonology.

"The Bishop will be there, the bloody Bishop. Alleluia!"

It had become difficult to make out exactly what Herbert said. For he had abandoned the careful articulation, and his slurred speech was made all the more incomprehensible by his sobbing. But snatches of anger were occasionally audible through the maudlin gabble.

"Lot of help bishops were to her. It's been all work for her, work and drudgery. Work and drudgery and suffering. If it hadn't been for bishops, she would have had a bob or two and kept comfortable . . . Bishops worked her to death."

Muriel and little Gus started to cry, and Syd, who was not quite sure what was happening, joined them out of fraternal solidarity. George ran to stand behind Clare, who watched the exhibition with incredulous disdain. Roy fiddled with buttons on his jacket.

"Don't upset yourself, Dad."

Les put his hand on his father's arm. It was angrily shaken off.

"You can't remember what she was like before she was worn down. You can't remember her before, before . . ." He turned to his aunt. "You can, though. You can remember her before she was downtrodden. Tell him what she were like."

Age had not withered Winifred's contempt for humbug. "Don't talk such nonsense, Herbert. Downtrodden was the last thing Augusta was. If she was here now, she'd give you what for. Coming in the worse for drink at five o'clock in the afternoon. She'd have given you what for, m'lad."

There was a knock at the door. The undertaker had arrived early.

Roy made his mind up to change back to Rex as soon as the Channel steamer left port, and he decided that—in his true persona—he would break his journey in Paris and Milan. He had received explicit instructions to proceed straight from ferry to train and to remain in his carriage until he reached Rome. But the College knew neither the date nor the time of his departure and—having become an expert in the complicated character of sin—he convinced himself that a minor (and unexpected) act of disobedience was nothing worse than venial but that the failure to seize his chance to see Notre Dame and *The Last Supper* would put his immortal soul in peril.

He did not enjoy his illegal detours. In both Paris and Milan he felt totally insecure from the moment he left the train until he was safely back on board another east-bound express. As he scurried to his forbidden assignations with architecture and art he continually felt inside his pocket to make sure that his passport was still safe. When he felt the comforting shape of the Royal Cipher on the cardboard cover, he began to wonder if George Nathaniel Curzon, His Majesty's Principal Secretary of State for Foreign Affairs, had afforded him all the protection that he needed. Page five of the passport was stamped: "Not valid for the Klagenfurt Plebiscite Area." The prohibition was nothing to worry about. But he needed to worry about something and Klagenfurt would do.

Rex left England profoundly sad. But he arrived in Italy filled with a new hope which he could neither explain nor condone. He tried to convince himself that he had become so quickly reconciled to his mother's death because of the certainty that she had joined the saints in paradise. But he feared that the real reason was less to his credit. He had become more interested in the future than in the past. And his future lay in the Catholic Church. On his first night back in the Via di Monserrato, as he unpacked his battered cardboard suitcase, he felt the emotion of a traveler who had returned home.

At the bottom of the suitcase there was a small square parcel, a gift from Aunt Clare which he had promised not to open until he was safely inside his cell. Rex did not find the temptation to break his promise hard to resist. For he had no doubt that the package contained a pocket missal of the sort which priests carry for use in sudden emergencies. He waited to unfasten the string and tear off the brown paper until he had washed, eaten and convinced himself that his friends were glad to see him back. Then he opened the parcel. It contained not a missal but a cigarette case.

The first letters he noticed engraved upon it were "EPNS." He then pulled the neatly folded piece of paper from under the band of golden elastic behind which the cigarettes were to be confined. Under the note there was a second engraving: "From Aunt Clare. 11.30.23." Rex puzzled a moment over the significance of the date. Then he unfolded the piece of paper and read its laboriously composed message. "Silver for tonsuring, but I promise gold for ordination." Until he received his cigarette case, Rex had never even thought of smoking. He started the next day.

The gold which Clare promised was rolled, and it was presented (in the form of cuff links) on the day before Rex became Father Hattersley. After they were over, the four years between the two gifts seemed to have been one long, golden holiday. Work became easier as Rex's increased command of Latin made some of the lectures almost comprehensible. And, with the confidence which comes from seniority, he began to enjoy the evenings in the Via di Monserrato almost as much as the days in the Gregorian University.

He offered to play a part in the College production of *Trial by Jury*. But the voice which had first attracted Bishop Dunn's attention had not improved and he was allowed to do no more than shift scenery. When the more ambitious *HMS Pinafore* was produced, he was cast as one of the army of sisters and cousins and aunts who attended upon Sir Henry Porter KCB, First Lord of the Admiralty. He played football with the same enthusiasm and the same success, tackling like a tiger despite the necessity to wear his pince-nez in order to obtain even an approximate view of the ball's whereabouts.

But sports and frivolous pastimes took up only a tiny part of his leisure hours. His real enthusiasm was Rome itself. He made a list of all the great churches and visited them one by one, ticking them off his inventory and marking against the name the date on which the pilgrimage was made. Seminarians were not allowed to walk the streets alone. So each afternoon Rex stood at the College door until he could persuade someone to accompany him on his expedition. After visiting Santa Maria in Domenica, he insisted on crossing the hot, dusty Via della Navicella in order to explore Santo Stephano Rotondo.

"What will you do," asked Hugh Atkinson, "when you've seen all the churches?"

"He'll start on the fountains," said Alfred Baldwin, who had accompanied them only after much persuasion.

"There are still five hundred churches that I haven't seen."

Rex meant to make the most of every Roman minute.

The politics of the city, which were in turmoil, touched him only occasionally. The death of Matteotti—murdered by Mussolini's fascists and buried in a shallow grave—did not move him until he realized that he had been within yards of the kidnapping at the moment of abduction. He was far more outraged by the proposal to demolish the English College in order to build a covered market on ground which, for five hundred years, had been hallowed by saints and martyrs devoted to the redemption of England. When Mussolini changed his plans and the College was saved from destruction, Rex's temporary interest in Roman politics subsided.

He thought of home. But he did not think of the real home of civil war in Ireland, the General Strike and the Labour government. He thought of an idyllic England of county cricket, Corinthian football, noble statesmen and poor but patriotic families with portraits of the King hanging above the fireplace in every humble home. Sometimes, on his way back to the College, Rex would persuade his companions to make a detour past the Central Station, where he would search for news of the England of his imagination. He could never afford to buy a newspaper. But he would glance furtively at the pages of *The Times* and then repeat its headlines back in the Via di Monserrato. On one summer night, he copied the cricket scores onto the back of a picture postcard which illustrated (with an olive and white engraving) the delights of Palazzola: "Notts 418 for 8 v Hants 118 + 136 for two." He passed the postcard around the silent refectory with a pride which would not have been out of place if he had scored one of the centuries himself.

In the real world of Nottingham and Sheffield, other Hattersleys lived more humdrum lives. Joseph did not return the Hen and Chickens to the glory of its Victorian splendor, as he had once intended, but depressed the standards of its furniture and fittings to just the respectable side of spreading sawdust on the floor. As a result, the public house began to make money. A head barman was employed and the landlord himself spent more and more afternoons at local race meetings. He gambled on every race and rarely won. But since he limited his stake to sixpence, he returned home solvent. When customers asked him why he spent so much time on so unrewarding an activity, he always replied, "I like it." To Joseph, that was justification enough.

His brother, Herbert, could not make the same claim about shop-keeping. The occupation was wholly alien to his character. He could never resist the temptation to borrow coppers from the till and he did not even attempt to discourage his family from following his bad example. The result was financially disastrous. But Herbert survived because, one by one, his children ceased to be a burden upon him. When Leslie left home to marry Dorothy, Herbert could not pay the grocer for a month, for Leslie had been bringing money home. But when Gus married Mac, her father was significantly better off. So when Muriel began to court Mr. Moon, Herbert was not sure if he feared the loss of a housekeeper or welcomed the end of liability.

Bishop Dunn, encouraged by his success with Rex, found George a place at Panton College, Wragby, and gave his word that success with the Lincolnshire Silesians would be rewarded by a place at the seminary at Valladolid. The prospect of Ratcliffe and Rome was dangled before Syd. Three priests from one family was a record to which Bishop Dunn had often aspired but never achieved.

After more than twenty years of almost continuous physical deterioration, Frederick Hattersley suffered a second stroke. It was not so serious as the first but it killed him. His daughter Mary—who had kept him always clean, usually fed and sometimes happy—argued that the expense of a Sheffield funeral could not be justified, for he had been forgotten by the Methodists and cutlers of that city. Her sister, Martha—who had visited her father half a dozen times each year—insisted otherwise. In life, her father's wishes had counted for nothing. In death, they became law. So the funeral service was held at the Calver Street Methodist Chapel. There were fourteen mourners in the congregation.

Herbert was there. He closed his shop for the day, sewed black crêpe onto the arm of his brown tweed topcoat and escorted his Aunt Winifred to a pew which had been quite unnecessarily reserved for family. He found the whole occasion emotionally disconcerting, and his confusion was increased by Winifred's whispered commentary.

"It seems impossible that he's gone. I thought he'd live forever."

Her nephew did not understand that she spoke figuratively. "He's done very well. Ninety and a stroke near twenty years ago. Must have had the constitution of an ox."

Winifred decided that something more straightforward was called for. "Joe should be there. Joe doesn't care about any of us. When I think of my hopes for him . . ."

"He did very well by me."

Herbert's defense of his brother was interrupted by the beginning of the service.

When it was over, only half of the mourners followed the coffin to the General Cemetery. The arrangements had been made from Mary's house in Doncaster and a number of essential details had been overlooked. The verger had not been asked to clear the path between the gate and the grave, so the clergyman who led the cortège had to kick his way through twitch grass and bramble.

The mourners stood on the damp clay which had been dug out of the grave and cursed that no one had covered the loose earth with artificial grass, as was usual at respectable funerals. Inevitably, their attention wandered from the dolorous ceremony which was being acted out before them.

"Ashes to ashes," intoned the unknown clergyman, dropping a

handful of earth onto the coffin with a thud which reverberated around the broken columns and between weeping angels. Mary noticed a gravestone which had been smashed into pieces by the men who had dug her father's grave. She hoped that the damage would not be blamed on the family. The idea that they might be charged for some sort of repair was intolerable. Then she saw the strange inscription which was clearly visible against the moss and under the grime: "and Frederick his grandson, dearly beloved son of Frederick Joseph and Emily Hattersley."

Rex thought of coming home to Nottingham as a reunion with his younger brothers. He was apprehensive about reestablishing a relationship with his father. In the old days, before Ratcliffe and Rome, he had thought of his parents as a single entity. Now he was not sure how he would deal with life in Nottingham without his mother, and he feared that his father (who had lost the light of which he was but a pale reflection) would have been forced to abandon the easygoing irresponsibility which charmed his children but which had driven his wife to despair. George and Syd posed no problems. They would fill the gap left in his affection by his mother's death.

It was April when Rex got home and both George and Syd were on holiday in Alfreton Road. George was spending his last Easter in England before he left for Valladolid and Syd was about to begin his first term at Ratcliffe College. George did not want to go to Spain and Syd did not want to leave Nottingham. The Easter holiday was their last refuge and Rex's return provided the highlight of the movable feast and the focal point of their pleasure. To Rex it offered a hope of recreating the family which he had lost when he left for Rome.

At first it seemed that the hope would not be realized. For although George and Syd welcomed their brother home like a hero and savior, Rex discovered that his brothers were strangers. Both had been children when he left for Rome. In the seven years of his absence, George and Syd had begun to grow up. Their memories were not his memories, for they had lived a life in Nottingham that he had not shared. To his surprise, his feelings for his father had hardly changed at all and they were reinforced by Herbert Hattersley's defiance of the years. The face was a little redder, the belly much bigger and the ebullience—which had simultaneously infuriated and enchanted his family—was not quite so unconstrained. But he was the same man. George and Syd were different people. Rex would have to work to

516

get to know them. He set about the task with a methodical determination.

In the two weeks which followed Easter Monday, he worked hard at winning their affection. He took them to Trent Bridge to watch Notts County play football and he encouraged their atavistic instincts with stories of Ironmonger, the goalkeeper who had become part of the club's mythical past. The afternoon was spoiled by Syd's belated announcement that Ratcliffe had started to play rugby. They went together to the cinema and marveled that the moving pictures had found a voice. Rex bought cigarettes, handed them to George as a gift between equal adults and turned a blind eye to Syd's furtive smoking. At Clare's suggestion, they bought tickets for an evening of Catholic bravura in which G. K. Chesterton, Hilaire Belloc and Maurice Baring answered questions on "Church, State and the Counter-Reformation." Mutual bewilderment helped to bring the brothers together. But at the end of the holiday, Rex felt that he had still done no more than break the ice which froze George and Syd into a different world. He went to see Bishop Dunn, still confused about his new place in his old family. At least Clare behaved as if nothing had changed. Without consulting him, she had bought Rex a new black suit from Burtons. It was a size too big. But Clare insisted that it would be "just right" when its new owner "filled out." She was very proud that she had chosen a style which came complete with waistcoat.

"It'll look just right with a dog collar," Clare promised.

Rex thought that she would be interested to know that the Rosminians of Ratcliffe were the first order in England to abandon clerical bands in favor of what the boys at the school called "back to fronts." But he was only halfway through his story when Clare's eyes glazed over. Clare was for drama not dogma, romance rather than reality.

"Your mother would want you to look smart."

She handed him a five-pound note and added, without obvious correction of her previous thought, "You better buy some new underthings as well."

The term "underthings" added, by its originality, an air of mystery to the transaction. Rex briefly wondered if priests wore special pants and vests.

Bishop Dunn congratulated Rex on his suit and on the gleaming polish on his battered Roman shoes.

"Very smart. Very smart indeed. Your mother would be proud of

517

you." His mind leaped on to the real subject of their meeting. "What are we to do with you between now and August?"

Rex had no answer to the question.

"We're still not sure where to send you after you're ordained. It might be Mansfield. It might be Derby or Louth. Do you mind which?"

"I'd prefer Mansfield, my lord. It's nearer home."

Monsignor Hinsley had written to warn the Bishop that Rex retained a dangerous dependence on his family, but Bishop Dunn had dismissed the Rector's fears as the apprehensions of a man who had been out of England for too long. He decided, despite the confidence which he felt in his protégé, to take sensible precautions.

"You'd better move in here for the summer. Teach a bit in the school and live in the presbytery. Get used to us and our ways. Bill Ellis is coming to be my Secretary in June."

"Yes, my lord."

"Have a holiday in July. It's the last time that you'll ever get one without having to get up at six o'clock in the morning."

Rex thanked the Bishop for his concern and left. Walking home, he realized that he had played no part in making the decisions which determined his destiny.

Clare cross-examined him about his conversation at Bishop's House. "You should have told him that you wanted Derby."

Rex agreed, though he was not sure what was so special about the city. All he could remember about its history was the welcome it gave to Charles Edward Stuart in 1745. If Bonnie Prince Charlie had not decided to turn back at Derby . . .

"He's right about the holiday," said Clare.

Rex agreed again and forgot all about the idea until his aunt accosted him after mass ten days later.

"I've talked to Winifred and we're deciding about a holiday."

"What holiday?"

"A holiday for you, Syd and George. We're going to hire a boat."

"What?"

"Tom Cross thought of it. He went on one when he was a boy. It's not very expensive and you'll all have a wonderful time. We've booked it. It's a barge. A barge with sails. You get it at Bungay and sail about on the Broads in the sun."

They sailed about on the Norfolk Broads for seven days of rain and wind. They were badly prepared, unsuitably dressed and inadequately fed. Most of the days they spent dodging the swinging boom and bailing out the leaky cabin. At nights they huddled together while Rex told stories of the family's past, George offered his opinion on world events and Syd boasted of his sporting achievements. They loved the dangerous mornings when they set sail and the desperate afternoons when they could not find a mooring. But most of all they loved the damp evenings of sardines, tinned salmon, cigarettes and conversation which was theirs and theirs alone. Only rarely did their talk turn to the vocation which awaited them all.

"Have you any doubts?" George asked nervously.

"None," Rex assured him. "None now."

"You will have. You will have on the night before you're ordained. Everybody does. It's a wedding and all bridegrooms have doubts the night before. You'll see."

"Will you feel silly?" Syd was determined to take part in the discussion.

"Of course not. Why should I?"

"I would, lying flat on the church floor with my arms spread out like a bird. I'd feel . . ."

"Well *I* won't."

"Will Dad come to see you? I bet you'd feel silly if he—"

Rex ignored the wager. "I hope he'll come. He's been to church before. Did he ever go when I was away?"

"Not since the funeral," said George.

"Will Mrs. Wilson come?" Syd could not understand the signals which George was sending him.

"Who's Mrs. Wilson?"

Syd was eager to answer. "She's the woman Dad used to take out last year. He had a big row with Aunt Clare about it. She said they were going to get married, but Dad doesn't see her anymore. Though I saw her at the end of our road last week."

"Why didn't you tell me?"

"We thought it was all over by the time you got home." George wanted to be reassuring. "Perhaps it is."

"I hope it's not," said Syd. "I like her."

A month later, Rex lay on the cold, tiled floor in the Cathedral of St. Barnabas, his outstretched fingertips touching the fingertips of Hugh Atkinson, who lay next to him. He tried to concentrate his mind on the new life which was only the last vow away and to drive all trivial thoughts out of his mind. But, out of the corner of his eye, he saw his cuff inside the sleeve of his black clerical jacket. The cuff link which Clare had bought him gleamed in the light from the cathedral window. He tried to clear his mind of such unworldly feelings as the pride of possession. Then every other thought was driven out of his head by a sudden stab of cramp. The pain which ran down the backs of his legs made it impossible for him to confine his thoughts to the vision of Christ Risen and Triumphant which was to guide and govern the rest of his life. His mind kept turning to the sight he had seen as he made his slow way from the vestry to altar. His father sat proud and best-suited next to Aunt Clare and Great-Aunt Winifred in the third row of pews. Behind them sat George and Syd. George was giving ostentatious advice to Tom Cross about how to follow the order of service in the missal. But who was the blowsy middle-aged lady in the same pew? Could it possibly be Mrs. Wilson? The idea was intolerable. But worse still was the fear that some members of the congregation might believe her to be his mother. All holy thoughts were driven from his mind. After the service was over, he made his required visit to the Bishop. He was still seething at the thought of Mrs. Wilson.

"Come in, Father." Bishop Dunn savored the moment. "Come in, Father Hattersley. What a day! What a day to remember. Now you've made your decision as a priest—Derby or Mansfield?"

"Derby." Rex had no hesitation.

The Bishop was crestfallen. He had not offered an honest choice. "I thought you wanted Mansfield. I gave you Mansfield, because I thought you wanted it. I thought you wanted to be near home."

"It doesn't matter."

Bishop Dunn was offended by the churlish response. "Well, it's all decided. Mansfield it is, with Father Keogh. St. Philip Neri, but not an exact replica of the one at the end of the Via di Monserrato."

"No, my lord." Rex was not in a mood for jokes.

"And don't keep running home to Nottingham."

"I shan't, my lord."

Rex spoke with obvious conviction.

CHAPTER THIRTY-EIGHT

MEN OF PROPERTY

Winifred Gunn—who had been irresponsible in youth and reckless in middle age—matured into a wholly unreasonable old lady. She remained in Huntingdon Street long after she should have moved to a smaller house and she resented, as well as resisted, all suggestions that four bedrooms were in excess of her needs and an unnecessary burden on her dwindling strength. In the end, it was her great-nephew Leslie who persuaded her to buy a little house on the other side of Victoria Park. Leslie was careful—careful about himself and careful about others—and his reputation helped him to convince Winifred that the move would protect her from work and her relations from worry. In preparation for moving from eight rooms to five, offers of furniture were made to all the family. Herbert was given first choice. Without thinking, he said that there was nothing that he wanted.

"What about John's draughts table? You always used to like it."

The draughts table was dark oak, inlaid with squares of golden elm. A brass hinge fastened the round top to the pedestal. When Herbert's children were young, visits to Aunt Winifred's house were enlivened by swinging the table top onto its side and pretending that it was the helm of a great oceangoing liner. Winifred always indulged the fantasy by making noises which she thought sounded like wind and sea before Herbert drove the young navigators from the drawing room and carefully set the tabletop back in its proper position. Herbert would not risk his children damaging such an example of expert workmanship.

"I couldn't take it. It's too nice. You keep it."

"Of course you could take it. John would have wanted you to have it. And it will be useful. You can eat your tea off it when there's just you at home and you don't want to set the big table."

Herbert shuddered. It was not the thought of defiling the draughts table that frightened him. Winifred, not noticing, persisted with the distribution of furniture.

"Is there anything else you'd like? If you don't have it, somebody else will. I shall only get a few coppers if I sell it."

"Is there anything from Sheffield, anything you don't want? I got nothing when they sold up. Mary got rid of everything without even telling me. I'd like something from the old days."

"There's the clock." Winifred sounded reluctant to admit its existence.

The grandfather clock had chimed the hours of Herbert's childhood. First it stood in the parlor, then it dominated the hall. With Joseph he had laughed at the funny name on its decorated face, "Manoah Rhodes and Sons, Clockmaker of Bradford," and, like Joseph, he had been beaten for turning the brass finger below the dial from "Chime Two" to "Chime Eight" or "Chime Silent." The clock had belonged to Winifred's parents, who had bequeathed it to Emily. When Emily had died, Winifred had pocketed her pride and asked Mary and Martha if she could keep it in the family and, despite the bad grace with which they agreed, she had taken it into Nottingham and stood it in the corner of her drawing room like a holy relic. She had hoped that it would stay there for the rest of her life.

"The clock?" she went on. "I'd love you to have it. I didn't like to ask. It's far too big for my little house. I'd be very grateful if you took it off my hands, if it's not an imposition."

Herbert was incapable of pretending that he would accept the clock as a favor to his aunt. His enthusiasm for its possession prevented him from offering proper thanks. But his response left Winifred in no doubt about how much pleasure she had given him.

"It ought to strike. It keeps good time, so the ratchet must be working. Just a drop of oil and it'll be fine. I'll take it to pieces before I go. Once the weights are out, it's easy enough."

"Thank you, Herbert. That's put my mind at rest."

Winifred was anxious to change the subject. Herbert was not.

"Is it screwed onto the wall?"

Winifred had a more urgent question to answer. "I'm not sure what to do about Joseph. I ought to offer him something. There are some really nice things."

There was a moment's silence as nice things reminded Herbert of his mother. Winifred did not like moments of silence.

"Do you think he'd like anything?"

"Leave Joe alone. He won't thank you for offering. He likes to be left to himself."

"Surely he'd like to be asked, even if I've nothing he wants."

Winifred had not met the new Joseph. She still thought of him as a clever little boy, looking at Flags of the World in the back of Thomas Spooner's atlas. Herbert knew that the clever little boy had become a cynical old man, and he wanted to protect Winifred from the folly of treating Joseph like a child.

"Leave Joseph to himself. That's what he wants."

"Then I hope he won't complain if he's left to himself when he needs company. I thought that when he didn't come to your dad's funeral."

"He won't complain, not Joseph. He won't let on, even if he's lonely."

"He always was a strange one. Always sure that he knew best. Often used to go away to be on his own, just to enjoy his own company."

"Now he's like that all the time. At least, he has been the twice I've seen him. But he's been very fair with me. Set me up in the shop."

"Rubbish! He made a good investment. You're paying him pounds every month and he's doing nothing. The bit he gave you—your share in the shop—was yours by right. You're as stupid about him now as you were when you were ten years old. You're as good a man as he is any day. What's he become with all his brains? The landlord of a public house, that's what."

Herbert did not expect Winifred to understand. She had never understood, and was incapable of understanding, what was special about Joseph, whose genius was concerned with what he was, not with what he did or once had done. There was something within Joseph which made him victorious even when he sweated inside his father's old topcoat because he dared not display the stained and tattered suit which it covered. Joseph had an inner strength. He was his own man. That was the quality which Herbert envied. For Herbert belonged to anyone who passed judgment upon him.

"How long has he lived on his own?" asked Winifred.

"Years and years. And he seems to like it. There's nobody to bother him. He goes to where he wants and does what he pleases. It's not a bad life."

"You wouldn't like it."

Winifred at well over eighty had no more tact than Winifred at twenty-five. She persisted in talking about Herbert's prospect of solitude.

"When Syd goes away to school and Mu gets married, you come here for tea whenever you like. Don't sit in that house on your own, brooding."

Herbert's long-held opinion about his aunt's inability to understand him was confirmed. He was alone already—alone in a way which could not be changed by the presence under his roof of a growing son and a daughter of twenty-five. Winifred was remorseless.

"You'll hate it then."

"I hate it now." Unlike his brother, Herbert let his feelings show.

"Then why don't you marry that Mrs. Wilson, the one Clare told me about?"

Winifred had preserved her ability to surprise and her need to shock. Indeed, during her years as wife and widow, she had gone out of her way to increase her reputation for saying things which others would think best not said. The identification was added as if to suggest that there were several Mrs. Wilsons in Herbert's life.

"What did Clare tell you? It's none of her business."

"She said that she was sorry about being nasty to you about it."

"She hasn't said so to me."

"Perhaps not. But she is sorry, nevertheless. Believe me."

"It doesn't matter. I don't need Clare's approval."

"She knows that, but she still can't help telling you what she thinks. Got real nerve, has Clare. She's slept in Tom Cross's bed for thirty years and she still lays down the law about respectability."

"Is that what she said about Mrs. Wilson? That she wasn't respectable?"

524

"She said that the lady worked in a public house."

"Nothing wrong with that."

"Then marry her, if that's what you want to do."

"You always make everything sound so easy."

"I'm not saying that it will be easy. Doing what you want to do is often very hard. It's hard because you've got to stand out against other people. But I do know one thing. Doing what you want to do is usually right—right for yourself and right for other people. Far more pain has been caused by people doing their duty than by people pleasing themselves."

"You can't just—" Herbert was not allowed to finish his sentence.

"Why can't you? I've seen too many people ruin their lives by trying to do what was expected of them. Your father for one and your mother for another. How old are you, Herbert?"

"I'm fifty-eight and you're talking to me as if I were a lad of sixteen."

"That's an old woman's privilege. Answer me a question. Where will you be in twenty years' time?"

"Pushing up daisies." Herbert grinned for the first time.

"You certainly won't make out old bones. You've got ten good years left—less time than's passed since poor old Bert was killed. If you take advice from an old woman, you'll make the best of what you're offered."

Herbert seemed to be studying the pattern in the carpet. "It'll be easier when Syd's gone to school and Mu's married."

"That might be too late. Don't take my advice. Follow the example of your own son. Look at Roy."

"He calls himself Rex these days."

"I don't care what he calls himself. Look how happy he is. We didn't want him to be a priest but he didn't care. He's doing what he wants. It's the secret of life. It is . . . really."

Even without the nagging fear that he was about to acquire a stepmother, Father Hattersley would have found difficulty in adjusting to life in the industrial England of 1927. In Rome he had become— without ever realizing it—a special sort of snob. He had developed an unreasonable reverence for antiquity and a corresponding contempt for anything which was modern or up-to-date. As a result, he felt uneasy in the world of plus fours, the Charleston, bongos, pogo sticks, Charlie Chaplin, short skirts and the Prince of Wales. Society's ills—poverty, crime and disease—he blamed on the Reformation, a fall from grace which he tried to put out of his mind by the careful, though uninformed, examination of buildings which were designed before that unhappy event. In consequence he set off for St. Philip Neri, in the Chesterfield Road, Mansfield (circa 1925), with a sense of deep foreboding. Rex had no doubt that it was God's will that he should go to Mansfield. Indeed, God had made him ask to serve in that church and that town when he might have expressed a preference for Derby and Pugin's most perfect evocation of the standards and values of the English Middle Ages. Clearly, he had been sent to Mansfield to do penance for some awful sin. And he concluded that there must be a second, though equally unknown, offense which he was required to expurgate through the second anticipation of purgatory awaiting him in the Mansfield presbytery. Father Keogh, the parish priest, was Irish.

From the Chesterfield Road, St. Philip Neri looked all that he had feared it would be—a huge brick shoe box with a pitched roof which might have been designed for a different building. The presbytery was built in the same brutal style. Rex had to bend down in order to rattle the chromium-plated letter box which was set in the wood below the little panes of smoked glass that made up most of the door.

Father James Keogh was out. His housekeeper, Mrs. Kathleen Fitzpatrick, having been told to prepare a place for the new incumbent, had covered the dining-room table with enough food to feed five thousand of the faithful. Buttered scones jostled for space with ham sandwiches, jam tarts and slices of pork pie. Currant buns shared plates with custard slices and Scotch eggs. The massive fruitcake had already been cut and a blancmange wobbled beside it, unstable but intact. Mrs. Fitzpatrick poured dark brown tea into a huge rose-decorated cup.

"Come on, Father. Tuck in. Don't be shy. Father Keogh hates people who are shy."

Rex hesitantly took the cup and saucer from the housekeeper's outstretched hand and, absentmindedly, picked the spoon out of the saucer. He looked at the maker's name to see if it said "Sheffield."

"It's perfectly clean, Father. I assure you of that. Nobody has ever suggested that I don't keep a clean house. Father Keogh wouldn't like to think of you turning your nose up at things here."

"I do assure you . . ." Father Hattersley dropped the spoon.

"Well then, tuck in. Father Keogh likes people to have a healthy appetite."

Mrs. Fitzpatrick bustled out to put more hot water in the teapot, leaving Rex to worry if he had called her Mrs. Fitzmaurice or, worse still, Mrs. Fitzherbert. By the time the housekeeper returned, he had eaten two sandwiches, one jam tart and half a piece of fruitcake. His rate of consumption was adjudged to be unsatisfactory. Particular exception was taken to the way in which he had slighted the pork pie. Wrestling with the top of a mixed pickle jar, Mrs. Fitzpatrick defended its honor.

"It's all homemade. Father Keogh won't have anything that's shop-bought. What will he say when he gets back and finds that you haven't eaten a single piece of his favorite?"

Rex decided that it was best not to find out the answer to Mrs. Fitzpatrick's question. Stuffing his mouth with pork pie, he began to examine the decoration and furniture of the presbytery's living room.

The cheap leatherette easy chairs were of the sort that furnished every presbytery in England. There was the usual wireless in one corner of the room. It was connected to an aerial in the garden by a frayed wire which festooned one wall like a Christmas garland. A gramophone stood on a bamboo table. The record on its turntable was Count John McCormack singing traditional Irish airs—most of which had been written in England by Percy French during the early years of the twentieth century. At one end of the mantelpiece, wooden bookends held the companion volumes of Aquinas, Augustine and Thomas à Kempis. Their pale blue binding showed no sign of wear. A portrait of the Pope hung above the fireplace and a cheap print of Saint Theresa stared at it from across the room. A shillelagh was suspended under the picture of the Pontiff. Next to the Sacred Heart above the door, a plate (with a shamrock pattern) carried a message of welcome in Gaelic. Rex did not have time to savor his despair before Father Keogh arrived.

Rex thought that the parish priest was the squarest human being that he had ever seen. He had a square head with a square haircut, a square double-breasted suit and square shoulders that looked almost as wide as Father Keogh was tall. Above the square jaw were a square mouth and a square nose.

"Welcome. I'm sure this is not what you wanted, but welcome nevertheless."

Rex did not have time to deny the allegation of disappointment before the parish priest swept on.

"Is Mrs. Fitzpatrick looking after you all right?"

"She is, Father. Very well. Very well indeed."

To Rex's surprise, Father Keogh noticed the irony.

"She'll calm down when she gets to know you. She's bossy now because she's nervous. But she's a good soul. Don't get irritated during the first few days and you'll become good friends. Did she ask you about the bicycle?"

"No, Father."

"Have you got one?"

"I didn't know I needed one."

"You do indeed. Mrs. Fitzpatrick knows where you can buy one for thirty bob. No three-speed or anything like that, but it will get you around the parish. Do you box?"

"I do not."

"That can't be helped. Thank God you're a cricketer."

"I don't play much. I like to watch."

"Don't tell the lads that yet. After what His Lordship told me, I've made out that you can bowl faster than Harold Larwood."

"Won't they find out?"

"Not till next season, and you'll be accepted by then."

"What sort of lads are they?"

"Mostly sons of colliers or railwaymen. They'd be down the pits and at Langwith Junction themselves if there were any jobs going these days. Most of the boys in your Bible class will be out of work, apart from stealing coal from the sidings and poaching pheasants. But no doubt the English College prepared you for life in Mansfield.

"I'm used to hard times. Times were hard at home."

"Here they're not just hard. They're bitter. The fights on Saturday nights are mostly between colliers and railwaymen. The miners think that they were let down last year when the railwaymen went back to work in the middle of the strike. Poverty has made them good haters."

Rex wondered if the miners included hating the railwaymen in their confession and if the railwaymen confessed to betraying the miners. He wondered, too, if stealing coal and poaching pheasants were venial or mortal sins. But most of all he wondered if there were any women amongst Father Keogh's parishioners, or if the Catholics of Mansfield were, as their parish priest described them, all male. Life in Mansfield was clearly going to be as barbarous as he had feared.

"The way things are now will make your job especially difficult."

Rex nodded gloomily. His depression was heightened by the feeling that Father Keogh enjoyed giving him the bad news.

"Did His Lordship tell you about the special job?"

Rex shook his head. He had guessed that he was to have a special mission to the young and brutal.

"I want you to raise money. Two thousand pounds. That's what it will cost to decorate the church. You'll use my name, of course—mine and the Bishop's. But you'll do the running about. These days we can't rely on the Cliffords and the de Lisles. What they had left to give they gave to Father Payne for the building. Anyway, between me and you, the English aristocracy doesn't understand the importance of decorating the inside of churches. The Irish do. And this Irishman is going to make the inside of St. Philip Neri, Mansfield, look like a proper church, not a Methodist chapel. And you are going to do all the hard work."

Father Keogh laughed and clapped his hands in pleasure to think of the difficulties that Father Hattersley was going to face. Carried away by his own enthusiasm, he invited his assistant to examine the walls which they would decorate. As they walked along the corridor which connected church to presbytery Father Keogh blew coal dust from the surplices that were hung, for safekeeping, on its wall.

"You wouldn't have to do this in Rome, I suppose?"

It was the second mention of the English College, an institution of which Father Keogh clearly disapproved. Rex began to fear that the parish priest also disapproved of him. He gritted his teeth and determined to say something complimentary about the inside of the church.

Beyond the door, at the end of the corridor, was what seemed to Rex a different world. The Corinthian columns which flanked the nave bore broad Romanesque arches and, above the arches, deep windows lit the ceiling which curved under the ugly pitched roof. Behind the altar, the wall bent in a full half-circle and was divided into long panels by six marble pillars which were topped by gilded capitals. The dome above the altar was already decorated with mosaic. But the walls—between the marble pillars, beyond the Corinthian columns and in the side chapels that spread out from the nave like the arms of a cross—were bare plaster. Father Keogh waved at the wall between the marble pillars.

"Made for great holy paintings. I thought of two archangels and three saints. Raphael for preference. If we stick to Romanesque style we can't have a Virgin, not as the centerpiece of the picture anyway."

Father Keogh was not quite so carried away with his enthusiasm

529

that he did not notice that he had astonished Rex by his understanding of church architecture.

"What worries you, Father? Did you think I meant the real thing? I only aspire to cheap copies. Or was it the elevation of art above piety?"

"Neither of those things," answered Rex with absolute sincerity.

"Well then . . . what was it?"

"I was thinking of what the church would be like when you had finished."

Father Keogh's passion was irrepressible.

"Like a cathedral. Like a cathedral. You'll have seen a few churches during your years in Rome. I never had that advantage. But I'm going to make this church worthy to stand alongside them in paradise. That is, if you can raise the money."

The work was not always as congenial as Rex had first hoped. During the depression there were two ways of collecting cash. Coppers could be begged from devout Catholics who could barely afford the cost of their daily bread, or the same pious souls could be encouraged to spend their grocery money on games of chance. Rex found both activities distasteful.

It was not simply the moral propriety of his work which concerned him. He never enjoyed collecting from a collier who had not cut coal for eighteen months, and he hated watching a railwayman—with six children to support on two pounds ten a week—paying a shilling to take part in a raffle. But his real problem was personal. He found the work uncongenial because it was unsuited to his character. He blushed bright pink when he tried to sell a ticket and turned deep red when he asked for a donation. But he carried on, thinking both of the church which was to be and the martyrs whose wounds had been deeper than the stabs of conscience and the pricks of diffidence denied.

The one form of fund-raising which did not offend his reticent respectability was the whist drive, for which he developed both talent and enthusiasm. He did not enjoy playing. But he took pride and pleasure in arranging the tournaments. Late in the afternoon of each Tuesday and Friday, he let himself in by the back door of the parish hall and prepared for the evening's event. First he opened out the baize-covered tables, stood them in neat rows in the hall and (with equal care) placed four hard chairs around each one. He was careful to make sure that exactly half of each chair seat protruded from under the tabletop. A scorecard was placed on that part of the seat which was thus kept visible and a pack of cards (counted to make sure that it was complete) was placed exactly in the middle of the green baize tabletop. Finally, the curtains of the stage were pulled apart to reveal a plywood tea chest covered with a print tablecloth. Half a dozen books were piled on the tea chest. During each hand of the whist drive, a sign (signifying which suit was trumps) was leaned against the books. The knowledge that he had made the signs himself gave Father Hattersley particular pleasure. Father Keogh was equally impressed with both his assistant's artistic talent and the expense which had been saved by painting heart, diamond, club and spade on the tops of old shoe-box lids rather than buying the commercial equivalent from Redmayne's sports shop in Nottingham.

Each whist drive made an assured profit. A full house was always guaranteed. Indeed, on rainy winter nights a queue formed outside the parish hall half an hour before the first hand began, and two dozen or more disappointed parishioners were turned away. All that was required to make the event a financial success was the purchase of prizes which, in total, cost less than the cash taken on the door. In a good week, the prizes were donated by local benefactors and every shilling ticket that was sold contributed twelve pence to the parish funds. Including the five shillings that the ladies regularly made on the refreshments, the whist drive produced an income of almost eight pounds a week. Rewarding though that was, Father Hattersley was sure that he could do better. He put his proposal to the parish priest.

"Do you know that there are whist drives in town which charge two shillings and sixpence at the door?"

"Not whist drives like ours. They're commercial. Run purely to make money. And they give big prizes worth five pounds or more. Half the players are professionals."

"We could do the same. There's the demand for it."

"The parishioners would be priced out."

Nine full months of exceeding peace had made Father Hattersley bold.

"I don't mind taking money from Protestants. Do you? They can pay us back for some of the churches that they stole."

"It would spoil it for our people. I'd rather get a license for a bar."

Father Hattersley, who had barely heard of whist before he came to Mansfield, had become protective about the purity of the game.

"That would spoil it more. Men would come to drink, not to play cards. They'd spill beer on the tables."

"Let's keep things as they are," said Father Keogh.

"Couldn't we try just one? Just to see what happens?"

Father Keogh hesitated and was lost.

"I know where we could get a big first prize," Rex persisted. "To be honest, I've got it already."

At Rex's invitation, Father Keogh went out into the scullery. Leaning against the sink was a reproduction of Millais's *Bubbles* surrounded by a fair imitation of an ebony frame.

"Where, in the name of all that's holy, did you get that thing from?"

"My aunt won it in the cathedral Christmas raffle, but she won't give it house room. She says that it looks like an advertisement for Pears' soap. It's worth five guineas. I've got a bill of sale."

Once again Father Keogh revealed unexpected depths.

"A nice little boy with a nice cake of soap, worthy of washing the hands of the Pope. Except it's Little Lord Fauntleroy in a lace collar."

"It's worth five guineas."

Father Keogh's resistance crumbled.

"We'll try it and see what happens. Put an advert in the paper. 'Two and six a head. Valuable prizes.'"

Rex improvised upon the theme.

"'First prize valued at five guineas.' We'll make ten pounds clear."

The hall was full half an hour before the whist drive started. Rex— as always referee and master of ceremonies—moved from table to table, checking scores on request and making sure that when the winners of a hand moved on to the next table, they sat on the right chairs facing their new partners. More than half the players were strangers from outside the parish. But, although the atmosphere was more openly competitive than he would have wished, Rex enjoyed the evening enormously. His determination to run such whist drives regularly was increased by what he took to be encouragement from Joe Macdonald, a miner with blue dust marks in the scars across his cheeks.

"I've not won a single bloody hand. But I dare say you've made a fair bit."

As the last hand began Rex thought of the pleasure with which he would welcome Father Keogh to present the prizes. It was then that the tall gaunt man at the table nearest the door cried out, "Over here, if you please. Referee, over here!"

As Rex hurried toward him the tall gaunt man pointed at the lady sitting on his right. It was Mrs. Alice Taylor, shunter's widow and church cleaner. Father Keogh had given her a ticket out of gratitude for the extra hours she had worked in preparation for the painting of the wall behind the font.

"This lady," said the tall gaunt man, "has revoked. It's my game."

"It was just a mistake." Mrs. Taylor was in tears. "I really didn't know I had any diamonds. As soon as I saw them I said so."

"No doubt, but it's still my game, madam."

The complainant laid his cards on the table, face upward.

"I've won the first prize. Must have. I've won every hand."

Rex checked the card and confirmed that the tall gaunt man was the victor. There was only perfunctory applause when the winner stepped up to accept his prize. Father Keogh handed him the picture without the usual word of congratulations. He was still glum when, having bidden good night to the parishioners, he had his cup of tea in the presbytery. Rex expected some unpleasant reference to his education.

"Too clever by half. That's what we've been."

"Let's keep it in the family in future."

Rex was not quite ready to capitulate. "There was no row or anything. Just an atmosphere."

"That's what the parishioners don't like—the atmosphere. There's no pleasure in it. It's because the professionals are there. Men like him."

"Like the man who won? Who was he? I've never seen him in my life before."

Father Keogh remembered that his assistant had been in the parish for less than a year and had much to learn about the world and its wicked ways.

"Why should you have seen him? Less we see of him, the better. He's called Ernest Brackenbury. He comes from Langwith Junction."

CHAPTER THIRTY-NINE

LOST AND FOUND

R ex reluctantly accepted the authority of his parish priest and abandoned the idea of organizing the most remunerative whist drives in the whole of the Nottingham coalfield. He decided, without much difficulty, to put Ernest Brackenbury out of his mind forever—even though he had felt strangely excited by the way in which the presence of the professional card players had turned his amiable competition into a desperate conflict. The whist drives—having reverted to their traditional form—made only a modest contribution to the decorations fund, but contributed enormously to the life of the parish. When spring came and the whist season ended, the baize-topped tables were packed away with real regret and the battered cricket bag was pulled out of the parish-hall storeroom. At the last Bible class in April a rota was drawn up listing the boys who would carry it to the recreation ground on Tuesday and Friday evenings.

Father Hattersley first assumed that the lads would want to spend their time in organized practice. He knew that on Saturday afternoons many of them played for local league teams and he thought of organizing something similar to the "nets" which he had seen at Trent Bridge when the county players prepared themselves for a new season. His suggestion that the evening should begin with an exercise

534

designed to improve their fielding was dismissed with derision. The lads wanted a match. Without waiting to hear any more of the assistant priest's silly suggestions, they began to pick two scratch teams.

"Are you a bowler or batsman, Father?"

"I'll umpire."

"We'll all take it in turns to umpire. And we all field."

The rituals of the scratch game were too well established to be broken.

"I heard you kept wicket," said the boy who wanted to be wicketkeeper.

"Well, you heard wrong."

The time had come for the oldest boy to assume command and act like a captain.

"You're on the batting side, Father. Say when you want to go in. Jimmy Conlan and me is going in first."

Jimmy Conlan was rummaging in the battered canvas bag. He had thrown several batting pads onto the patchwork of grass and cinders which was to become the cricket pitch.

"I can't find any pads with bloody buckles still on."

"You only need one," said the captain. "You're not batting for Nottingham."

"I'm wearing two on this bleeding ground, and a box."

"There's only one box," said the captain. "I went through the bag before I brought it. There were two last year, but some bugger's stolen one of them."

Father Hattersley wondered who would steal such a thing. To take it during the winter seemed either wickedly premeditated or particularly perverse. His unspoken question was answered by a small boy who was looking ruefully at his fingers protruding through the split seams of wicketkeeping gloves.

"They'll steal anything around here."

"Well, where's the box that's left? Where's the protector?" Jimmy Conlan had emptied the cricket bag.

"I've got it on," said the captain, proving possession by tapping his groin and producing the hollow sound of knuckles knocking on tin.

"You'll have to give it here when I take strike."

"And catch the pox! Not likely," said the captain.

Jimmy Conlan was not joking. He threw his bat on the ground. "Then I'm not fucking batting—"

There was a horrified silence at the sound of the forbidden word.

Every boy on the recreation ground used it ten times a day. But to hear it spoken in front of a priest shocked them all. They turned toward Father Hattersley and waited for him to take the necessary stern action.

"You're not playing tonight at all, Conlan. Put your coat on and get off home. I'll decide on Sunday what to do with you next week."

Conlan started to argue. When the priest ignored him and walked away, he lost his temper. "It's all right for you. It doesn't matter if your balls get knocked off."

The shocked silence of the evening was punctuated with nervous giggles. The captain decided to exercise his authority.

"Don't be so bloody cheeky. Take your coat and bugger off and we can start the game."

Little shock waves were still running around the recreation ground when the match ended. Rex had not been called upon to bowl or required to bat and had avoided making a fool of himself in the field. Had it not been for the incident at the beginning of the game, he would have regarded the evening as a total success. Even as it was, he rolled down his sleeves with considerable satisfaction. Then he found that his left cuff link was missing.

In the gathering gloom, the boys searched for it with immense enthusiasm, little application and no success. After an hour, the hunt was called off and obviously fraudulent promises were made about the search being resumed in better light on the next morning. As Rex walked disconsolately back to the presbytery the boys offered their opinions on the tragedy which had befallen him.

"You'll never find it now, Father. It'll work its way down into the cinders under the grass."

"Was it real gold, Father? How much do you reckon it was worth?"

"Do you know a man with one arm, Father? You could give him a present."

Jimmy Conlan was sitting on the wall by the recreation ground gate.

"What's all the fuss been about?"

"The Father lost a cuff link, a solid-gold cuff."

The resentment had not faded. "I thought they weren't supposed to have property. I thought they were supposed to give it all to the poor. That's what we used to be taught at Bible class."

Rex remembered that his Aunt Clare had told him that if he became a priest, he would always be respected. He wondered how many other people would share Jimmy Conlan's obvious low opinion of priests in general. And he wondered if what Jimmy Conlan thought was true. He was God's eunuch, a pauper for Christ! There could, he convinced himself, be worse fates. But he understood why the boys in the Bible class never quite treated him like one of themselves. He was different.

The Bishop's letter was more of a shock than a surprise. Surprise it certainly was. But the idea of surprise contained within it at least the possibility of a happy outcome. When Rex saw the envelope—with his address on the front and Bishop Dunn's crest on the back—he had no doubt that it was the portent of some sort of doom. Bishops do not write to assistant priests unless they have exceedingly good or excessively bad news to impart. Rex's nervous disposition convinced him that he was not facing triumph but disaster. The envelope's contents increased his apprehension. For instead of stipulating the nature of his offense or describing the cause of the Bishop's displeasure, it simply invited him to tea at Bishop's House. Rex decided that his misdemeanor must be too terrible to put on paper. His uncertainty was intensified rather than removed by the cross-examination with which the Bishop began the dreaded conversation.

"How long since you were ordained? I should remember. May I be forgiven, I should remember."

"A year, my lord. Just over a year."

"Have you enjoyed your time at Mansfield?"

"Very much, my lord, very much indeed."

An agonizing pause preceded what Rex expected to be the beginning of a denunciation.

"In all my years, I have never said what I am about to say now to a priest of such recent ordination. Never. What do you think of that?"

"I don't quite know what to say, my lord."

The Bishop slid down in his armchair, stretched out his long legs in front of him, closed his eyes and—placing his fingertips together—began to change Rex's apprehension into bewilderment.

"There are three special reasons—apart from your abilities, that is. Firstly, Rome. Father Froes was himself at the English College. We are hoping for an endowment and that might just tip the balance. An endowment would be more than welcome."

"I see," said Rex, not seeing at all.

"That's the second point. Father Keogh says that you're a champion beggar. It's a gift you'll need to cultivate. Do you know how it got there in the first place?"

"Got where, my lord?"

"Got to Langwith Junction. Father Froes built it with his own money. And the presbytery. He went to Bishop Brindle and made him a straight offer to build a church if he could be parish priest. Not the sort of thing that I'd agree to, but we mustn't judge too harshly. That's why the congregation is so small. Should never be there. But we can hardly close it down. That's what the Wesleyans do."

Bishop Dunn opened his eyes to see if Rex was amused. Detecting no sign of merriment, he repeated his witticism in a more obvious form.

"Catholics open churches, Methodists close them down. Right?"

Rex had begun to follow the drift of the Bishop's rambling. Though what he seemed to be saying was barely possible.

"There's another reason. I've just heard from the President of Ratcliffe. Young Syd didn't want to go home this summer. Did you know that? Stayed at Ratcliffe until a week ago."

"I knew that he stayed at school until the end of August. He said he wanted to do extra work."

"His work is very good. At least, that's what the President says and I think we ought to take his word for it. As I understand it, he's had some sort of argument with your father. Anyway, he says he won't go home for Christmas. He wanted to go to Valladolid and spend his holiday with George."

Rex's concern for his brother emboldened him to interrupt. "Do you know what Syd's worried about?"

The Bishop was not to be sidetracked. "But we don't think that's a very good idea."

Rex contrived a reply which allowed him to repeat his question without sounding impolite. "Is that because you think it would only make the problem worse? I'm not quite sure what's bothering him."

"Neither am I. But I've no doubt that you'll be able to sort it all out."

The Bishop spoke with absolute sincerity. He regarded irrational optimism as a major virtue—a view which could be justified not so much by the number of saints who possessed that characteristic as by the army of martyrs who had died because of its possession.

"Anyway, that's not the main reason. The real thing is that you are the right man for the job. I'd better be formal for a moment. I'm sending you to St. Joseph's at Langwith Junction as parish priest. What do you think about that?"

Anxiety about Syd's apparent estrangement from his father blunted the sharp thrill of pleasure that Rex should have felt when he first fully realized that he was to have a parish of his own. He managed to say thank you, but he was feeling new concerns. He decided to call at the ironmonger's shop in Alfreton Road on his way back to Mansfield and find out if the reasons for Syd's unhappiness were what he expected them to be. But his host had other plans for his evening. Wholly unaware of the turmoil he had created inside Rex's mind, Bishop Dunn began to boom out his plans.

"Father Froes is coming here tonight. He'll arrive in about an hour. I thought that you might like to meet him and find out a bit about the parish."

Rex's reluctance was so obvious that even Bishop Dunn noticed it. The Bishop was proud of his generous disposition and always reacted strongly when his benevolence was rejected.

"Of course, if you've got something more important to do . . ."

"I've nothing to do at all." Rex knew it was the wrong answer. "It's very generous of you to invite me. Thank you very much, I'd love to stay. It's very kind."

The effusion mollified the Bishop. "Well, how would you like to spend the next hour? A little walk? Or would you like a cup of tea with your aunt? She'll be back in the convent by now. I could send for her. Or would you like an hour in the library?"

"The library please," said Rex quickly.

Father Hattersley spent the hour studying Butler's *Lives of the Saints.* Joseph Cafassa (23 June), Joseph Oriol (23 March), Joseph Tomassi (1 January). None of the biographies budged him from the hope that his Joseph, Joseph of 120 Langwith Road, Langwith Junction, was Joseph of Arimathea—the Joseph who had taken the crucified Christ from the cross, anointed the body and buried it in the Tomb which he had bought as his own last resting place.

But the reasons why Rex was attracted to that Joseph were not even mentioned in Butler. They were certainly legend, probably myth and just possibly connected with pagan folklore. There was no acceptable evidence to support the superstition that Joseph of Arimathea had traveled to Cornwall with Phoenician merchants, taking with him the Chalice in which the First Eucharist had been celebrated at the Last Supper. But Rex wanted to believe in the Holy Grail for which King Arthur's knights once quested. More than that, he hoped that that most fantastical part of the fable was true and that the young Jesus had once accompanied Joseph to England's green and pleasant land. Parry's setting of Blake's *Jerusalem* had become Father Hattersley's favorite piece of music. When he heard that King George had told a Sandringham orchestra that if they would not play it as part of their recital, their royal host would whistle the tune unaccompanied, he almost forgave his sovereign for being a member of the House of Hanover.

Father Charles Froes looked as if he could easily afford an endowment. His cheeks were pink and smooth, his gray hair formed up across his head in rows of identical waves and his fingernails were so clean that Rex found it hard not to stare at them. His enthusiasm for the church he had built was boundless, and he launched—within minutes of meeting his successor—into a description of what awaited Rex at Langwith Junction.

"There are four statues—Saint Christopher, Saint Anthony (holding a rather attractive lily), as well as the Virgin and our patron saint. Since we are a working parish, Joseph is holding the tools of his trade, a mallet and saw. During the General Strike they wanted Saint Christopher to carry a miner's lamp, but naturally I said no."

"Quite so." Bishop Dunn sounded shocked.

Rex, reconciled to being a priest in the parish of the wrong Saint Joseph, sat quietly and listened as the Bishop of Nottingham made repeated attempts to bring the conversation around to the subject of money and the possibility of Father Froes endowing his old benefice.

"The parish will remember you for many a year."

"I hope so, my lord. I hope so."

"It's a pity that we can't provide something tangible around which their gratitude could be built."

"I hope that the church itself will be my memorial."

"Quite so. But no doubt you'd like to see something to mark your retirement."

"If the parishioners wanted to make a little collection . . . But that's not a matter for me."

The fencing went on until half past nine, at which time Father Froes—who boasted a motorcar—offered to drive Rex home to Mansfield before he returned to the Langwith Junction presbytery. As he bade his Bishop farewell he fired his parting shot.

"I've been thinking of giving a little something to the parish myself. I'm sure you'll agree, my lord, that I ought to discuss it with my young successor here."

Enthused by the thought of an endowment, Bishop Dunn accompanied his guests to the front door. As Rex settled himself in the car he felt that the Bishop was looking at him as if he held the financial fate of the whole diocese in his hands.

Father Froes sat upright behind the steering wheel of his Austin Cowley and peered, myopically, at a point on the road immediately in front of his bonnet. But although he never looked at his passenger, he addressed him in staccato bursts of sound on the more depressing aspects of life at the Langwith Junction presbytery, which pride, rather than consideration, had prevented him from discussing in front of the Bishop.

"House is far too big. Too big to heat. Important to get cheap coal. Plenty about. Have to look for it in summer."

Rex made a mental note.

"Only twenty-nine at mass last Sunday. St. Joseph people started going to your place after it was rebuilt. Try to bring a few back with you."

Rex tried to think of possible defectors.

"Need new altar boys and servers. No young men in the parish who'll do it. No organist, either. Went to Leicester last March. Hymns don't go badly without music as long as I start them off. Not so bad when you get the hang of it."

Rex blushed at the thought of leading the singing.

"One other thing. Woman who wants to be baptized. Been after instruction for months. Getting more and more difficult to prevaricate."

Rex thought of the picture above the altar in the main chapel of the English College and wondered why Father Froes was so determined to prevent the purifying blood of Christ from spilling onto this particular lady. For seven years he had been taught that he was a missionary from Rome dedicated to reconverting England to the true faith. He was not in a mood for conversation, but he felt obliged to inquire what stood between this particular soul and the hope of salvation.

"Because she doesn't mean it. Not serious. Doesn't want to become a Catholic. Just says she does."

"How can you possibly tell?"

541

Father Froes recognized the criticism in the question. "I know her. You don't. You'll find out."

"Find out what?"

"That she won't get married."

"But how does that affect . . . ?"

Before the question was finished, Rex had lost interest in discovering the answer. Father Froes, however, launched into a rambling explanation of the lady's unsuitability for baptism.

"Twenty-five and thought to be good-looking—though I'm no judge of these things. Ideas above her station. Big noise in the tennis club. One day playing matches in Clownie and Cuckney dressed like Suzanne Lenglen. Next at Communist Party meeting. Running about for miners in the General Strike. Said she'd go to Ruskin College, that trade union place at Oxford. Rides about in her father's horse and trap. Calls the pony Kit. Understand now?"

"Afraid not."

"Use your head, man. Can you imagine a woman like that marrying an Irish collier of forty-five?"

"Perhaps she's in love with him. No accounting for tastes."

"Nonsense. Just wants to leave home. Thinks it's a way out. Won't do it when the time comes. She can play about with O'Hara but can't play about with the Church."

"Are you sure that she only wants instruction so she can marry?"

"I'm certain. O'Hara won't marry her until she does."

"You're stopping her getting married."

"Stopping her leading O'Hara on. That's all. His parish priest, not hers."

"Is O'Hara the man she says that she wants to marry?"

It was an absentminded question prompted by loss of interest in the subject but continued determination to be polite. Father Froes replied with a look of pitying contempt. To cover his confusion, Rex asked a second question.

"What is she called?"

"Brackenbury. Enid Brackenbury."

"I've heard that name before. I think that a man called Brackenbury came to one of our whist drives in Mansfield."

"Did he win?"

"Every hand."

"Her father. No doubt about it. Gambles on anything. Two flies on a window. Gambles on which reaches top first. Loses on horses. Wins at cards."

Rex remembered the feeling that there was something wicked—and therefore exciting—about the tall gaunt man who had won the picture of *Bubbles* in the imitation-ebony frame. His interest in the Brackenburys became genuine.

"Does he mind her getting married?"

"Of course he does. Sick wife. Needs somebody to look after her."

"Sounds pretty selfish to me."

"Not a bit. Much maligned man, Brackenbury. Just because he likes a flutter. Highly intelligent man. Could have been on the County Council. Sells good clean coal."

"Is that how you know him? The coal?"

Father Froes coughed. "That's one thing. And we have a mutual interest. Horses. Owned one once, a long time ago. Discuss blood-stock, that sort of thing."

Horses having entered into the conversation, Father Froes's mind inevitably turned to thoughts of money.

"Bishop expects you to ask for a gift."

"I'm sure he doesn't."

"Know damn well he does. Don't want to disappoint him." Father Froes gurgled in what was the nearest that he ever came to a laugh. "Tell him I will. Telephone when you get back."

"That's very generous, Father."

"Tell him what it is." Father Froes gurgled again. "Hired those Italian artists to paint inside of the church. Father Keogh told me about them. Knowledgeable chap. But likes to cause trouble."

Rex was not sure how he should respond. For he knew that it was not quite the gift for which Bishop Dunn had hoped. It seemed that Father Froes knew it too.

"Costs seventy-five pounds. All I can afford just now. Better for you if I'd given money. What Dunn wanted. Sorry. Won't be taken for granted."

His message having been delivered, Father Froes pulled his motor to the side of the road.

"Drop you here. Won't take long from here to St. Philip's."

Rex expressed his gratitude for both lift and donation and began the three-mile walk to Mansfield.

. . .

Herbert Hattersley sat in the living room behind the ironmonger's shop in Alfreton Road and tried to ingratiate himself with his youngest son.

"You don't need to walk in the pouring rain. I'll pay your fare."

He took a florin out of his pocket and slapped it on the table with a theatrical flourish. Syd was unmoved.

"I'll get wet anyway at the match. It doesn't matter if I get wet on the way."

"No need to get wet at all. Go in the stand."

Another florin was banged onto the table and, like the first two-shilling piece, was left lying there.

"I want to walk." Syd was already struggling into his coat.

"What about your dinner? If you go on the tram, you can have your dinner. It'll be ready in five minutes."

"I'll get some fish and chips on the way."

"That's it, isn't it? You don't want to sit down at the table with her."

Herbert managed to sound hurt, angry, incredulous, understanding, triumphant and despairing, all in a single sentence.

"No, it isn't."

"I know full well it is. You can't deceive me. I'm your father and you're the only son I have left now."

Syd was moved neither by the sentiment nor by the peculiar logic. "I'd better be off walking."

He left by the back door, rather than taking the short route to the street through the shop, and set out on the long walk to the Meadow Lane football ground. A hundred yards along Alfreton Road, he almost collided with his brother. Father Hattersley, head down and battling against the driving rain, could see nothing but the wet paving stones immediately in front of his feet.

"What's the matter?" Syd assumed that Rex's unexpected return was the result of some catastrophe.

"I heard something was the matter with you. Something at school."

"Who told you?"

"The Bishop."

Syd gave a low whistle. It was a confession that, despite his teenage cynicism, he was impressed.

Rex could feel the water squelching inside his shoes. "Let's go . . ." He could not quite bring himself to say "home" but he pointed in the direction of the shop.

"I'm going to the match."

"At half past one?"

"I'm walking."

"Then I'll walk with you."

As they walked Syd told his brother everything. He did not know why he so disliked Mrs. Wilson. He had liked her at first and she was kind, generous and anxious to please. But he could not settle at home when she was there. He was not even comfortable in the living room when she was serving in the shop.

"I shan't go there at Christmas. If there's only me and the Indians at Ratcliffe, I still shan't go home."

"If Dad says it's all right, you can come to me. I'm getting a house next month, a house of my own. I've got some news . . ."

Syd's mood had changed. "So have I."

He felt inside his drenched raincoat and pulled out a copy of Palgrave's *Golden Treasury,* bound in blue leather with gold tracing. The moment he opened it, great drops of rain fell onto the certificate which was stuck inside the front cover. Rex's first instinct, as the ink began to run, was to tell his brother to close the book. Then he realized that it was more important to read what had been written in careful copperplate: "To Charles Sydney Hattersley for his excellent work."

Together the brothers caught a tramcar to Meadow Lane. Rex bought two meat pies from a stall outside the ground, and they ate them sheltering from the storm in the lee of the wall which ran along the back of the empty terraces. During the forty-five minutes before play began, they talked about the old times—years which they had experienced separately but felt they had enjoyed together. By the time the match kicked off, they had told each other a dozen stories about their mother. Notts County beat Bolton Wanderers by three goals to one. It was a good afternoon.

CHAPTER FORTY

THE FIRST CHRISTMAS

F ather Hattersley, remembering his predecessor's advice, examined the contents of his cellar as soon as he moved into the presbytery at Langwith Road. He found several dozen empty bottles (burgundy, vinegar and communion wine in equal numbers) and piles of old newspapers which, on his closer inspection, he identified as copies of the *Sporting Life* dating back to 1918. Father Froes had practiced what he preached and planned his consumption of coal down to the last lump—which he had put on his living-room fire at ten o'clock on his final evening at St. Joseph's.

Rex took possession of the presbytery on a cold December morning when the clear blue sky suggested that it would be a colder night. He knew the name of only one local coal merchant and he had seen the address of Ernest Brackenbury's yard on a calendar which Father Froes had left hanging in the kitchen. Buttoning up his black gabardine raincoat, he made his way to 11 Langwith Road.

The yard was not what he had anticipated. The expected heaps of coal littered the frozen mud, and a dust-covered youth was filling hundredweight sacks with lumps of shining anthracite. But rusty agricultural machinery was piled in one corner, and opposite the plows and harrows were half a dozen battered old motorcars. Prices had been painted on their windscreens with the whitewash which was more commonly used to advertise grocery bargains on the windows of co-operative stores. Ernest Brackenbury was a secondhand-car dealer as well as a coal merchant.

From behind the house, which stood at the back of the yard, came the sounds of the countryside. Pigs snorted, hens cackled and the whinnying of a pony echoed from inside its corrugated-iron stables. A cock stood proudly on top of one of the coal heaps as if to symbolize the marriage of agriculture and industry which every pit village represented. Warily watching the collier's chanticleer, Father Hattersley approached the house. Humbly he made his way to the back door and tapped with his usual reticence. A female voice answered and seemed to say "Come in," but it was so faint that Rex thought it both polite and prudent to knock again.

"Come in!" The whisper had become impatient.

Despite the cold, Father Hattersley's bare hands were sweating and they slipped on the door handle.

"Come in!" Impatience had turned to annoyance.

Father Hattersley stumbled over the threshold.

"You should have walked straight in. Everybody knows that."

The reproof came from a hunched figure sitting so near to the fire that a flying spark might easily have set alight the dress which trailed on the floor. At first, Rex thought that he must be in the presence of a Brackenbury grandmother, for the figure was dressed in the uniform of a family ancient. Her knees were wrapped in a tartan rug, and an old-fashioned crocheted shawl was spread across her bent shoulders. In one hand, she held a long toasting fork—wooden but with steel prongs. She was using it to feed herself with small squares of bacon and beetroot sandwiches that had been placed on the table beside her. With the other hand, she attempted to turn down the wireless which had been playing so softly that Rex had not realized that Carroll Gibbons and the Savoy Orpheans were on the air. Her twisted fingers fumbled with the knob and, instead of the sound being turned down, the music exploded into the kitchen, and the old lady turned her head away from the sudden burst of sound. When he saw the face in profile, Rex believed for a moment of fantasy that she was the Enid Brackenbury of whom Father Froes had told him, for there were flaming auburn streaks in her gray hair and the hollow cheeks had retained a perfect complexion. For a few seconds, he tried to decide if she was twenty-five or seventy. Then he remembered that Ernest Brackenbury had an invalid wife.

"I'm very sorry. I was looking for Ernest Brackenbury."

"He'll be back any minute. Father Hattersley, is it? I'm stuck in this bath chair, but you're very welcome to put the kettle on and make yourself a cup of tea. I hope you'll wait."

"No. I'll come back. I really didn't mean . . . I thought . . ."

"You're very welcome to wait. He'll be here in a moment. So will my daughter. She's only just popped out for a moment to the shops. We ran out of something."

"It was Mr. Brackenbury that I wanted, not your daughter."

Remembering Father Froes's account of Miss Brackenbury's potential conversion, Rex was anxious not to give the impression that he was looking for new recruits.

"Is it coal?"

"Yes, it is. Father Froes recommended that I come here."

A frisson of resentment fluttered around the room at the mention of the priest's name. But before Rex had time to consider its significance, there was a thud on the kitchen door and the missile which had crashed against it bounded into the room. It was a wire-haired terrier—completely white except for a black patch over one eye, which reminded Rex (as it reminded everyone) of a pirate. Having raced around the room, barking in a falsetto which belied its buccaneering appearance, the dog came to rest against Mrs. Brackenbury's feet and looked up at her with adoration and desire to be fed small pieces of bacon and beetroot sandwiches. The terrier was formally introduced.

"This is Mick. He belongs to Enid. Never goes anywhere without her. She must be in the yard."

Rex leaned forward to greet his new acquaintance with a pat on the head. Mick, teeth bared, lunged and missed the hand of friendship by a fraction of an inch.

"He's very friendly. Wouldn't hurt a fly. He didn't mean to catch you. If he'd wanted to bite you, he would have got you all right. His father was champion ratcatcher of Derbyshire. Stroke him again. Show him that you like him and he'll be friends."

Mick did better with his second attempt. His teeth bit into and held onto the cuff of Rex's coat, and he began to shake the black cloth as if it were one of the rats which his father had killed with such distinction.

"Drop it, Mick. There's a good boy. Drop! Drop, I say!"

The dog began to make a noise like the engine of a small motorboat. It continued to tug at the sleeve.

"You can tell by his growl that he's only playing. Don't move, Father. Drop it, Mick! Drop! Drop! He thinks that you've come to attack me. Do you like dogs, Father?"

Before Rex had time to answer, the kitchen door opened and, screaming like a soul in torment, Mick abandoned his quarry and rushed to greet the new arrival.

"Are you being a bad boy?"

The first thing that Rex noticed about the girl in the doorway was that she was thin—a fashionable thinness which was intentionally accentuated by a fitted cloth coat with a great fur collar which spread out across her shoulders in order to emphasize the slender waist and hips. Then he saw her face under the felt cloche hat. Set in it were the biggest and bluest eyes that he had ever seen. He tried to recall Father Froes's complicated account of her marital intention. He could not recall why Enid Brackenbury wanted to marry O'Hara. But he had no doubt why O'Hara wanted her.

"This is the new priest," said her mother. "He's come about coal."

Enid Brackenbury offered her hand. Emancipated, thought Rex with disapproval. An emancipated woman like Aunt Winifred.

"I hoped to see your father."

"I've just seen him down the road. He'll be a few minutes yet. Have a cup of tea whilst you're waiting."

The pressure for tea had become irresistible, and Rex sat quietly in a corner of the Brackenbury kitchen holding a cup on his knee and fearing that he was eavesdropping on the conversation of the two women.

"That dog is still there," said Enid. "Tied up behind the shop."

"It's a shame, such a lovely dog. People like that ought not to have dogs. They don't deserve them. Did it look hungry?"

"It's as thin as a rake. It whines all the time. I think it's frightened."

"I've seen him hit it with a stick. We could have it, Enid. Why don't we offer him a good home?"

"You know that we can't, Mam. Mick would kill it."

549

"Do you like dogs, Father?" Mrs. Brackenbury remembered that she had a Catholic priest sitting in the corner of her kitchen but forgot that she had already asked him the question.

"Yes, I do. Very much." Rex felt that he could give no other answer.

"Then why don't you have it? It would be company for you in that big vicarage."

Enid's occasional enthusiasm for joining the Catholic Church had not encouraged her to master its peculiar vocabulary.

"I don't think that I could."

"Of course you could." Mrs. Brackenbury added her moral pressure. "It would be a Christian act. It's a beautiful dog. Just needs a good home."

The introduction of theology prompted Father Hattersley to speculate about the enthusiasm with which the dog's ill-treatment was discussed. It would have been a calumny to suggest that the women welcomed the opportunity to agonize over the suffering animal. But there was no doubting the pleasure with which they demonstrated their compassion and condemned the wickedness of the world. He decided that it was only a matter of time before they renewed their appeal for his assistance.

"I really must go. I'll come back again tomorrow."

"We can arrange for the coal."

Rex realized, to his surprise, that Enid Brackenbury was anxious not to lose the sale.

"I really hoped to take some home with me today. Just a bucketful if I could. There's nothing left in the presbytery. Perhaps I could borrow an orange box or something."

Enid giggled at the impracticality of his suggestion.

"Let's make an order out now and we'll send you the first bag down straightaway. Jack O'Hara can wheel it down to you in a barrow." She noticed that the priest started at the name.

"It's not that one, Father. Not the one Father Froes told you about. It's his little brother."

Rex backed out, hoping that his interest in the family was not too obvious.

"What about the dog, Father? What about the collie?"

"It's a very kind idea. Very kind indeed."

As he walked across the yard, he only just avoided slipping on a patch of ice.

The full order of the coal—enough to heat the presbytery for the whole winter—was delivered at ten o'clock on the following day. The dog—a purebred collie sheepdog—arrived two hours later. Enid Brackenbury had decided that a dog (in need of a home) and a priest (in need of a friend) were meant for each other and that fate had sent her to bring them together. So she determined to arrange the union by employing the unscrupulous methods which had been pioneered by the pet shops which she so despised. Her plan was to arrive at Father Hattersley's front door looking like Diana the chaste huntress with her hounds on leash. Chivalry would require the dog to be accepted for a "trial period" and then the match would be made. No human being—certainly not a priest with gentle manners and pince-nez spectacles—would be able to evict a long-haired collie which had spent several weeks ingratiating itself by licking hands, rubbing against legs, stretching out full length across the hearth and rolling over onto its back. Enid Brackenbury's plan did not work out in the way she intended. Before she could begin her complicated deception, Father Hattersley was on his knees, patting the collie's head and scratching behind its ears as if he had been brought up surrounded by dogs.

"I've been thinking about it all night. I meant to come round this morning and ask you if you really thought that I could have it."

Every word he said was true. But, as he spoke, he found every true word almost unbelievable. He had thought of nothing except the dog until he went to bed, and during the night he had dreamed of it. At half past six, as he had prepared to say mass to a congregation of two, he had prayed for the power to think of only holy things. But at every stage of the service the visions which had swum before his eyes were all of dogs. At the moment of transubstantiation he had decided what he must do. He would return to the local coal yard, seek out the proprietor's daughter and ask her if she would rescue the collie and pass it into his safekeeping. For whenever he thought of the dog, he thought of it being given to him by Enid Brackenbury.

Enid herself was crestfallen to find the conquest so easy.

"I had to pay the butcher five shillings. He said it was a pedigree."

"I'll pay you, of course. I didn't realize..."

At that moment, Father Hattersley did not possess fivepence. But if possession of the dog had required him to promise to raise a thousand pounds, he would have promised to raise the money.

"No, you won't. It's our Christmas present."

Father Hattersley looked up at his benefactor. The dog, anxious not to lose his attention, leaped up and—leaning its legs against his groin—assumed the position of a rampant armorial bearing. Rex winced and then blushed at the realization that, by acknowledging the discomfort, he had conceded the possession of genitals.

"They can tell if you like them," said Enid approvingly. Rex winced mentally again. The last time he had been given that reassurance, the dog under discussion had tried to bite the part of his anatomy which was closest to its teeth.

"He needs a drink."

Without waiting for her host's agreement or approval, Enid walked down the hall in the direction of the kitchen. As Rex listened to the sound of the running tap he wondered how she had become familiar with the layout of the house. She returned carrying a pudding basin which was so full of water that she left a damp trail behind her.

"I'm afraid that he's a bit timid. He's been badly treated. It will take a lot of love and care to make him feel safe."

"I hope that I've got the time to look after him properly."

"You'll have to give up other things. Taking on a dog's a big responsibility. He'll have to be your hobby now."

"Hobbies aren't much in my line."

"Don't you do anything for pleasure?"

"Being a priest is a pleasure."

"But except that?"

"I sometimes watch cricket. And in the winter I go to football matches. I read." The list seemed wholly inadequate. "I used to draw churches, old churches. In Rome I visited ninety-six churches in four years. I went to Southwell, just before I left Mansfield."

"We're going to a very old church on Monday to take the Christmas wreaths. Steetly Chapel. Have you ever been there?"

Rex shook his head sadly.

"My grandfather's buried there. So is my grandmother. But she died before I was born. It's near Worksop."

The dog was lapping away noisily. Rex could not think of anything to say, but wanted to say something.

"What sort of church is it?"

"Very small. Norman, I think. A big round arch over the door.

There are marks in the wall where Cromwell's cannonballs hit it. He thought that there were soldiers inside."

"I must go and see it one day."

"Father Froes used to drive us there in his car. Do you have a car?"

" 'Fraid not."

"Can you drive? My father would lend us one of those in the yard."

Rex was about to say " 'Fraid not" again when he thought that Christian duty might require him to drive the crippled woman and her daughter on their Christmas visit to the family grave. He could not drive and had never driven. But in five days he might, somehow, learn the rudiments of driving.

"Monday, did you say?"

"Or Tuesday. Wednesday would do if we could get a lift."

He was sure that he could learn to drive by Wednesday. Fate had offered him a full week to seize the opportunity. The decision to take it was made before he began to wonder what exactly the opportunity was. As the dog—having drunk his basin dry—leaped up on him again Rex decided that his enthusiasm sprang from a laudable determination to help the sick and a human, if slightly frivolous, wish to see another example of English church architecture.

"Wednesday. I could certainly manage Wednesday afternoon if we could be back by evening time."

"Of course we can. By the way, somebody will have to look after Peter. We wouldn't leave Mick at home all afternoon and they couldn't come in the car together. Mick would kill him."

"Peter! Is that what he's called? Peter! I've got the name of a dog and he's called after a saint."

Rex learned to drive after mass on the following Sunday morning. The butcher, who supplied meat to both the Mansfield and the Langwith Junction presbyteries, was the only vehicle owner known to him. And, unfortunately, the vehicle which delivered beef and mutton was a van which had seen better days. But the butcher himself was eager to spend a couple of hours coaching his parish priest—or at least more anxious to accompany him during his initiation into driving than to allow the lesson to be learned, as Rex had suggested, under the sole guidance of God. Enthusiasm made Rex an apt scholar, although he moved out of second gear only rarely and attempted to avoid reverse altogether. Indeed, he was so promising a pupil that the butcher—who made no deliveries on Mondays—allowed him a morning alone with his precious van. By Wednesday, Rex felt ready to drive out of the Brackenburys' yard, even under the gaze of Ernest Brackenbury himself.

Ernest Brackenbury was not at home.

"Dad's away for a bit," Enid explained mysteriously. "We can take whichever car we like."

Rex selected the model which seemed most closely to resemble the butcher's van, and the complicated business of loading up began. The cargo could hardly have been more inconvenient. Mrs. Brackenbury had to be wheeled across the muddy yard in her bath chair and lifted through the narrow car door. Since her knees were set in an immovable right angle, she could not sit on either side of the back seat but had to be spread along its full length.

"Keep hold of Mick!" she cried. "Don't let him jump on my legs."

Enid leaned forward to straighten the rug on which her mother sat, and released her grip on the dog's lead. It leaped into the car and Mrs. Brackenbury cried out in pain. Mick was pulled out with difficulty and two vast homemade holly wreaths were fitted into the arthritic triangle under the cripple's knees. Enid sat next to the driver with Mick on her knee. Rex drove slowly forward with the dog's hot breath against his left cheek. As they accelerated to twenty miles an hour on the open road he felt its rough tongue in his ear.

Steetly was even better than Enid had promised. But Rex was not allowed to enjoy it. Mrs. Brackenbury, who was unable to leave the car, insisted on parking at a place which gave her the best view of the churchyard. Since the vantage point was hard against the lych-gate, the pleasures of the afternoon were prejudiced by the knowledge that it had to end with the car backing out onto the narrow road. Mick escaped and, after urinating on the base of a Saxon cross, tyrannized the chickens in the neighboring farmyard. Even when order had been restored, Rex was not left to examine the simple Norman chapel uninterrupted. Enid wanted to talk about her relatives. She waved a gloved hand in the direction of her grandparents' gravestones.

"They brought me up, more or less. I loved my grandfather. He was a lovely old man. He lived down the Worksop Road. I used to sit on his knee in the arbor."

"Was your mother ill when you were a child?"

"As long as I can remember. Rheumatoid arthritis. Then there was my father . . ."

Rex thought it right to change the subject. "What did your grand-father do?"

"He defended us against my father. He was a wonderful old man. He wanted my mother to pack up and move back to Grove Cottage with him. He used to sit on the porch and tell me—"

Another attempt to shift direction seemed necessary. "Father Froes said that your father's family came from Sheffield."

"Well, Father Froes would know. He and my father were very good friends."

"I didn't realize."

"Let me tell you what sort of friends they were. They backed horses together. While Father Froes was losing all the money he had, my father was losing our housekeeping. We're not very keen on Father Froes, my mother and me. But he was right about Sheffield. He probably went with my father to a race meeting there."

Desperate to swim out of the deep water, Rex returned to the subject of ancestors. "Was your grandfather—your Sheffield grand-father—a cutler?"

"He was a caretaker, a chapel caretaker. He was caretaker at Calver Street Methodist Church."

"Good Lord!"

"I know. He was a real Holy Joe. No smoking or drinking. Sit still on Sunday. And his son became a mad gambler and a womanizer and a wife beater."

"That's not what I meant. My father went to the same chapel. Your grandfather must have known him. Perhaps your father and mine sat next to each other. Have you ever seen Calver Street? Inside, it's very beautiful—beautiful, that is, for a Methodist chapel."

"Weren't your parents Catholic?"

"I'm the child of a mixed marriage. Dad still says that he's staunch Methodist—so staunch that he smokes, drinks and never goes to chapel."

"Why didn't he convert when he married your mother?"

"I don't know. I never asked him. You don't have to, you know. As long as you stick to the rules and don't mind not having a Nuptial Mass."

"I expect Father Froes told you that I'm going to marry a Catholic."

"He mentioned something." It was not a subject which Rex wanted to discuss.

"Did he say that I wanted instruction?"

Rex nodded.

"My father persuaded him not to do it."

"That is a very serious accusation to make. It would be terrible if it were true."

"It is true."

"Of course, if you want—sincerely want—to enter the Church . . ."

"I shall, when Jack gets back from Ireland. He's helping his father with the cows. The old man has broken his leg."

"Why not start now?"

"I don't know, really. I suppose it all seems unreal while he's away."

Father Hattersley knew that it was his duty to hold out the arms of the Church and encourage the unbeliever to enter into its redeeming embrace. Rex Hattersley, on the other hand, found immense comfort in the suggestion that Enid Brackenbury was still not absolutely sure about the rock on which her life was to be built. The priest won the struggle.

"Well, I'll be glad to talk to you about instruction. I'll help in any way that I can."

"You can help after Christmas. My mother's going to see a specialist in Sheffield—for her ulcer. She has ulcers as well as everything else. I've never seen Sheffield."

"Neither have I, I didn't even go to my grandfather's funeral."

"But you've heard a lot about it." Enid grinned.

"I have indeed. The Wicker."

"The river Don."

"Bramall Lane."

"And the Moor. Will you drive us down the Moor?"

"I will certainly drive your mother to the specialist."

Rex decided that to refuse would be a denial of his ministry.

Herbert Hattersley regretted the arrangement which he had made for Christmas from the moment that it was impossible for his plans to be changed. At first, the idea of spending the holiday with Mrs. Wilson had seemed irresistibly attractive. He looked forward to being indulged—to sitting in his stockinged feet without fear of harassment, to leaving empty beer bottles on the kitchen table and to dropping food down his waistcoat without exciting disgust and contempt. The original plan was to spend the festive season in Mrs. Wilson's house in Woollaton Park. But then Herbert changed his mind.

"The kids won't be able to call round if it were there."

"They won't call round anyway," Mrs. Wilson observed with her usual cheerfulness. "They won't come round, because I'm here."

"Don't say that. They're all caught up in their own families. They want to spend Christmas in their own places."

"Then it's a good job I'm here. Or you'd be left on your own."

"Clare's asked me round. She's looking after Tom Cross and she's asked me round there. Winifred's going there."

"Well, I'm looking after you. I don't mind where it is."

"Let's stay at Alfreton Road, love."

Mrs. Wilson, being amiable by disposition, agreed and carried across Nottingham the vast amounts of food which she had hoped to serve from her own table. When she saw the extent of her preparations spread across the kitchen, Herbert's spirits improved. But his optimism did not survive a lonely Christmas Eve. Whenever carol singers knocked on the shop door, Herbert leaped up and rushed out in the undisguised hope that Leslie, Muriel or little Gus had come to call. When, at midnight, Mrs. Wilson kissed him on the top of the head and wished him a Merry Christmas he could no longer hide his depression. Two days of enforced celebration only served to turn depression into despair.

In the Langwith Junction presbytery, the happy morn was anticipated with almost equal apprehension. The lady who spent her Monday mornings washing Father Hattersley's shirts and scrubbing his floors arrived early on Christmas Eve and roasted a chicken before she rushed home to make her elderly husband's breakfast. In her hurry, she left the pantry door open and Peter, for once neither docile nor disciplined, pulled the bird from under its wire-mesh cover and triumphantly carried it into the living room. Rex felt reasonably confident that the tooth marks would disappear when it was hotted up on the following day.

Syd arrived from Ratcliffe College with a large and painful swelling over one eye. A cyst, dismissed as unimportant by the College medical officer, had been inflamed during the annual boxing championships. The ache under Syd's eyebrow was nothing compared with the pangs of remorse he felt whenever he recalled that during a sleepless night he had furtively smoked away the present which he had bought for his brother.

The late evening was the most difficult time to fill. Both of the brothers had been used to attending Midnight Mass and therefore having the last hours before Christmas regimented by the demands of preparation for the eucharist. But Father Froes had always insisted that a mass at midnight—with half a dozen communicants in the congregation—was a demonstration of weakness which amounted almost to blasphemy. As he ate his supper, still feeling guilty about breaking an imaginary fast, and attempting to make desultory conversation with Syd, Rex determined that next year there would be a Midnight Mass.

Halfway through the very long evening, Rex suggested readings from seasonable literature. Syd said that he had already read *A Christmas Carol* twice and he was clearly more mystified than amused by Mr. Pickwick's expedition to Dingley Dell. In desperation, Rex opened a poetry anthology and turned to "The Oxen" by Thomas Hardy. Syd spoke the lines self-consciously.

> *"So fair a fancy few would weave*
> *In these years! Yet, I feel,*
> *If someone said on Christmas Eve,*
> *'Come; see the oxen kneel...'"*

He did not move onto the last verse.
"Do you believe all this?"
"All what?"
"The oxen and asses kneeling at midnight."
"Read on. You don't have to believe it. It's just a nice idea."

Father Hattersley feared that he had betrayed the blessings of simple faith. But his greatest concern was about a material rather than a spiritual crisis. He was worried about his shoes. Rex possessed only one pair (relics of his last year in Rome) and they were so decrepit that the cobbler had refused to mend them for fear that new soles would tear the old uppers apart. The hope of new shoes for Christmas had been dashed by the extra expense of preparing for his brother's visit. The priest feared that when he faced mass next morning, the pressure on his toe caps would force his shoes to disintegrate when he knelt in prayer.

His anxiety was not, he convinced himself, caused by either pride or vanity. For he accepted, without embarrassment, that when he prayed at the altar—his back turned to the congregation—the parishioners in the front row of pews would see straight through the gaping holes in the leather to the socks—and perhaps even the soles of his

558

feet—which they were supposed to cover. But that was different from total collapse. His only concern was that nothing unseemly should happen in God's House.

However, Christmas at Langwith Junction, unlike Christmas behind the ironmonger's shop in Nottingham, steadily improved with the passage of time. The shoes did not fall apart and Syd, conscious that he had no present for his brother, agreed that what gifts there were should be opened after breakfast. There were more parcels than Rex had expected—an easily recognizable half-bottle of whisky from a parishioner who could not afford such generosity, unexpected tins of biscuits and dried fruit from local shopkeepers who hoped for the approval which would encourage trade, the Bishop's unmistakable diary and several parcels with Nottingham's postmark, which the brothers assumed were gifts from the family. As Syd was about to cut the first knot Rex leaned behind the sofa and pulled out the cricket bat which he had saved all year to buy.

"Careful," said Syd, when his brother caught the handle between the back of the sofa and the wall. He had found the badly hidden bat the night before and he could not counterfeit surprise. But his pleasure was as great as the pride he felt in being able openly to read the words on the blade. "Gunn and Moore. The Autograph Triple Spring."

They opened the small packages first—the pairs of identical socks from Leslie and his wife, Dorothy, the two cellophane-covered boxes of handkerchiefs from Gus and Mac and the cigarettes labeled "Love from Muriel and family." Syd barely had time to wonder if his sister was pregnant before Rex handed him a parcel with wholly unknown origins. It showed every sign of being a tin of biscuits.

There was corrugated cardboard beneath the brown paper, and tissue paper under that. Inside the tissue paper was a black papier-mâché box decorated with hand-painted flowers in a style which Clare, from whom the gift had come, called *chinoise.* For years it had carried her makeup from dressing room to dressing room and then, after her retirement from the stage, it had occupied a position of honor on her dressing table. As a child Rex had been fascinated by it. Now the box had been filled, almost to the brim, with pencils, India rubbers and a carton of charcoal. What Rex had taken to be a further part of his aunt's meticulous packing, Syd recognized as a tiny sketch pad. On the first page of cartridge paper, Clare had written her Christmas greeting:

Dear Boys,

At the bottom (in tissue paper) are gifts from your dad. Knife for Syd and scissors for Roy. I can't call you Rex! Enjoy the holiday and keep drawing.

Your loving and proud aunt.

Clare

Rex, at least, realized that the pocketknife and paper scissors had been taken at Clare's initiative from the shelves of the ironmonger's shop.

The parcel below the Spanish stamps was obviously a book. Rex took his turn to tear the paper and read George's note.

Happy Christmas to you both. Vows of poverty prevent expensive presents. It's the thought that counts! I know you've always coveted this. Sinful! Have it with my forgiveness! Love to young Syd. Saluté. George.

The book was an anthology of verse. *Mount Helicon.* It was George's school prize for "excellent work" during his last year at Ratcliffe. As the tears began to mist Rex's pince-nez Syd ran up to his bedroom and returned with his *Golden Treasury.*

"My present is the same. I've not had time to wrap it up."

"I'll keep it for you until you get a presbytery with a bookcase. It's a lovely book. I shall read it in bed tonight."

The chicken was a great success. Peter sat, endearingly immobile, until the meal was over. Then, regal and composed, he accompanied his new master on a walk across the fields to Shireoaks. The dog was much admired by passersby.

"What a lovely day," said Syd.

"Things can't ever be any better," Rex replied.

He was wrong. On the day after Boxing Day, Father Hattersley returned from mass to find a package on the presbytery doorstep. It was instantly recognizable as a shoe box. But he was astonished to discover that it contained shoes. The writing on the box was unfamiliar. It read, "We noticed on Christmas Eve. Please accept as our tithes. From the Brackenburys. We hope they fit." The shoes were a size too small and they pinched across his instep. Rex wore the shoes all day and kept them on throughout the evening in preference to his carpet slippers. The blisters which the shoes brought up on his toes rubbed against the sheets and kept him awake all night. The pleasure which the pain caused him was, he feared, unrelated to the martyr's crown.

CHAPTER FORTY-ONE

THE SALAMANDER

The errand boy's first thoughts were for his knees and knuckles. For it was those extremities which hit the dusty tarmacadam of Pelham Street when the old lady who had come out of Geo. V. Hutton's dressmaker's shop stepped off the pavement and into the path of his hurtling bicycle. For several seconds he just looked with silent horror at the raw flesh where his skin had been grazed away. Then he saw the old lady lying in the road. A trickle of blood ran out of one ear and down her neck onto the old-fashioned lace collar which had pushed out from under the fur that had hung across her shoulders. Worse still, her eyes were open. The errand boy realized that she was dead and began to howl.

The shop assistant who had sold the old lady a tweed coat for the exorbitant price of two and a half guineas bent over the errand boy and asked him if he was all right. His reply was incomprehensible. Lying with his bicycle on top of him, he was looking at the legs and feet converging on the old lady's corpse.

"Not all there, if you ask me," said the shop assistant, looking up and addressing the crowd which had begun to form. "She left her change. That's why I had to run after her. Walked straight into the road without looking. She must have been a hundred anyway."

At the hospital, to which she was taken not in hope but because routine required it, the Lady Almoner was unable to identify the body. A search was made of what—when it was new—would have been called a reticule. There was nothing in it to provide a clue to her identity except two postcards. One—a picture of the Swiss Guards at the Vatican—had clearly been sent to her in an envelope. For all that was written on it was the message "Merry Christmas and Love. Roy." The second had traveled alone. Its stamp, bearing the head of Queen Victoria, was still firmly in place. It was a reproduction of a painting, *Work* by Ford Madox Brown. But, although the colors were still clear and bright, the writing on the other side was so faded that only one word was legible. At the bottom of the address, SHEFFIELD had been printed in capital letters. The policeman who came round to the hospital to complete his accident report counted the five-pound notes which the handbag contained and offered his opinion.

"The old girl's worth a bob or two. Somebody will claim her, you mark my words. But if they don't, we'll put a little notice in a Sheffield paper. That'll have them come running."

The policeman—fearing that he might have to draft the notice himself—offered the Almoner a few comments on the undesirability of allowing senile old ladies to wander the streets without adequate identification.

"Old people won't always be bidden. They like their independence like the rest of us," the Almoner replied.

Winifred Gunn—who had died as she had lived, with little thought for her own safety and no concern for the convenience of others—would have endorsed that opinion.

As Agnes and Enid Brackenbury prepared for the following day's trip to Sheffield Ernest—loving father and faithful husband—made his single contribution to their plan.

"Bring us a paper back, will you?"

Enid was aggressively un-cooperative. "We may not have time. We've got a lot to do. We're not going joy-riding, you know."

"Not time to buy a paper? You're just being awkward. I'll ask the priest."

"He'll not be interested. He's never had a bet in his life."

"Christ Almighty."

"Don't use that sort of language in here," said his wife. "Save it for your cronies in Cobbler Jack's."

"Christ Almighty!" Ernest Brackenbury repeated the words with malicious deliberation. "All I'm asking for is a paper. I don't want you and the bloody priest to ride in the Grand National."

"We'll need some money," said Agnes.

"What for?" Her husband sounded genuinely astounded.

"For petrol," Enid answered. "For petrol, for one thing. We can't expect Father Hattersley to pay."

"We'll need more than that. There'll be bills to pay in Sheffield. We can't keep doctors waiting like we do the grocer and the milkman."

Mrs. Brackenbury's passion alarmed her daughter.

"Don't get upset, Mother. I've got enough for the doctor. Worksop sent it."

"Them again!" Ernest Brackenbury's mood changed to offended pride. "You're my wife and I'll provide for you without you going running to your precious brother and sister."

"Then provide," said Enid. "Provide instead of gambling the money away."

Ernest Brackenbury moved, almost imperceptibly, but his daughter flinched.

"Going to hit me again, are you? Like last Saturday?"

Her mother braced herself against the arm of her bath chair as if she were struggling to stand up. "Don't you dare. Or somehow I'll get out of this contraption."

"Will you indeed? Last Saturday, John O'Hara was going to come round and give me a good hiding. But he hasn't been yet."

"He would have done it if I'd had my way. But Enid was too proud to tell him. Too proud to admit that her father hits her."

The melodrama left Ernest Brackenbury unmoved. "And if what I hear is right, he won't have seen the bruises."

"You're foul," said Enid. "Foul."

Her father answered with studied calm, "No. I just want a Sheffield newspaper. That's all. That's how all this nonsense started." He put two ten-shilling notes on the table. "Here you are, don't drink it all away."

The inevitable argument about whether or not mother and daughter were prepared to accept money being offered in such a way was prevented by a timid knock on the door. Rex Hattersley, priest and chauffeur, had arrived. He showed every sign of being deeply grateful for the opportunity to inconvenience himself on behalf of an elderly invalid and her daughter, both of whom he barely knew.

Ernest Brackenbury switched to his jovial manner and led Rex into the yard to choose the car in which to make the journey. He seemed a far more agreeable man than the insistent victor of the Mansfield whist drive. Nevertheless, Rex was cowed by the way in which he walked through the mud with long confident strides. Before the potential donor had time to speak, Ernest kicked at the tire of a bottle-green saloon.

"This is the one."

He reached inside the door and pulled out a badly printed notice: "Singer Junior, £148.10s when new. This model (only one owner) £50."

"You'll like this." Ernest Brackenbury offered his opinion with the air of a man who had never been contradicted in his life. "Sit inside and I'll show you the gears."

Rex obeyed and, with Ernest Brackenbury sitting beside him, he went through the motions of shifting the gear lever from first to reverse.

"One more thing," said the instructor.

The pupil expected to be taken on a guided tour of the dashboard.

"It's about Enid."

The priest stared out through the windscreen. The nerves in his stomach throbbed in anticipation of the necessity to do his frightening duty. He prevaricated.

"What about her?"

"I reckon that she'll ask you today about being a Catholic. She'll tell you today that she wants to . . . to . . . to join."

Rex made a lightning psychological calculation and decided that he was more afraid of questioning Mr. Brackenbury's right to raise the subject than he was of defending his own duty to accept a new soul into his Church.

"If she does, I shall discuss it with her—of course."

"Do you know why she wants to become a Catholic?"

"I'm sure that she has many reasons. But I understand that she wants to marry one of my parishioners, John O'Hara."

"Have you ever met him?"

"I'm not sure what that has—"

"He's an Irishman of forty-five. He came here thirty years ago as a navvy when they were digging the railway cutting. And he still talks like a Paddy. He's a collier when he's working, which isn't often. Enid is twenty-five and full of herself. Can you see her in a pit cottage scrubbing the bare floorboards, washing his back and giving birth every year?"

"That would be a great blessing, Mr. Brackenbury."

"Not for her it wouldn't."

"She should be the judge of that."

"Do you know why she is doing all this?"

Rex was amazed by his own answer. "There are those who say she wants to get away from you, that she's afraid of you and so is her mother."

He vaguely recalled a line from Robert Browning which he had learned at school—"a fine sword filled up the empty sheath of a man." Nevertheless, he was profoundly glad when Ernest Brackenbury replied without obvious offense, "She's doing it to get back at me. She's doing it because she found out that I had a woman in Bolsover. She's ruining her life for that."

"What else should she do? Marriage is a woman's destiny. It is a sacrament."

"Not to John O'Hara it isn't. Look at what some women have done. That little Jennie Lee is a Member of Parliament."

"Surely you're not suggesting . . ."

"When A. J. Cooke came here during the General Strike, Enid sat in our kitchen and argued with him. She told him that the railwaymen would let him down and she was right. She was right and A. J. Cooke was wrong."

Father Hattersley was speechless. Astonishment turned into horror.

"And another thing. She doesn't believe a word of it. Never has and never will."

"How can you possibly know?"

"Because she's my daughter and because I've seen and heard her making her views plain. She was there when we buried Owen Ford and put the parson—the regular Church of England parson—out of work." Ernest Brackenbury gave a short, mirthless laugh. "When Owen Ford died—died of starvation, called consumption on the burial certificate—we gave him an atheist's funeral. They made us bury him in holy ground, but he had an atheist's rites. I spoke the words over the coffin and Enid read from Engels's *Condition of the Working Classes.*"

The conversation had become impossible for Father Hattersley and he decided to end it.

"I shall have to say what I think right."

"So shall I," said Ernest Brackenbury, turning the starting handle and firing the engine at a single swing. "So shall I. You can depend upon it."

For Rex, the visit to Sheffield was a disaster. Enid gave him constant and detailed advice about both his driving and the route which he should take, while her mother complained in turn about her back, stomach, head and knees. Mrs. Brackenbury suggested that he might take charge of Mick during the consultation, but much to the priest's relief, he was adjudged too unreliable to be trusted. So, after patient, daughter and dog disappeared up the steps of the consulting rooms, he drove in search of the places about which his father had so often spoken. At the end of the hour's free time which he had been granted, he had seen nothing except the dirty brick wall of Bramall Lane football ground and a long straight street of shabby shops which seemed to specialize in shoddy goods. He could not believe that it was the Moor about which his father had spoken as if it rivaled the Elysian Fields.

He arrived back at the consulting rooms at the time which Enid had told him and sat outside for twenty minutes before a maid came out with the news that Mrs. Brackenbury felt unwell after her examination and would not be able to travel for another half-hour. He declined a seat in the waiting room but accepted a copy of the local paper. In the hour before his passengers appeared, he read it from start to finish. On page five there was a police notice describing the appearance and the known possessions of an old lady who had been knocked down in Pelham Street, Nottingham. He felt guilty. It was a shameful way in which to find out that Great-Aunt Winifred was dead.

Rex did not tell the Brackenburys about his bereavement, for he felt incapable of dealing with the fulsome expressions of sympathy which he knew the news would provoke. He felt an obligation to be sad and tried genuinely to mourn her death. But for ten years Winifred Gunn had been a virtual stranger to him. His real concern was for his father. So, his passengers deposited at Langwith Junction, he drove on to Nottingham and the ironmonger's shop. Herbert Hattersley sat alone in the living room, reading the *Nottingham Post*. A half-empty pint bottle stood by the side of his chair. Rex could not see a glass.

Herbert was only slightly drunk, so his mood was not so much maudlin as philosophical. He blew his nose loudly as a sign of respect, expressed gratitude to heaven that his aunt had felt no pain and regret that she had died alone. Then, for the first time in his life, he said what he had always really thought about her.

"She was a great lady and wonderful to us when we were kids. But she was very modern. She was a suffragette before the war. And she used to wear fashionable clothes even when she was middle-aged. My mother always worried about the people she got in with—women who had theories about having babies or, more like, about not having them. And she'd say anything that came into her head. Spoke against the war in 1914. Very brazen was your aunt."

"Did you mind? I mean, did she shock you?" asked Rex, genuinely interested in one of his father's rare expressions of opinion.

"You've got to be respectable, haven't you? That's why I'm on my own now. Because I want to keep respectable, for what it's worth. It's always been important to me that my neighbors know I'm respectable."

Rex was about to agree when his father warmed to the theme.

"Your Uncle Joe was just like her when he was a boy. Still is, I wouldn't wonder. See where it's got him. He ran off to Canada, lost all his money and now he's just a publican—not a respectable shopkeeper but a publican. They were two of a kind. Welcomed trouble. It made Joe an outcast. He was years on his own. No family to rely on for help. Gambled everything and lost."

Father Hattersley made noises which he hoped confirmed his sympathy for the uncle he had never met and his unqualified belief in respectability.

For the rest of the winter and early spring, Father Hattersley—having purchased enough coal to keep him warm until the summer—saw very little of the Brackenburys. He did his best to put the whole family—Ernest, Agnes, Enid and the dog Mick—out of his mind. For when he thought of them at all, he felt even more nervous than he had felt in his first days at Ratcliffe and at the English College in Rome. He was uneasy. But he had no idea why he felt so uncertain of himself and so lacking in confidence about his future.

John O'Hara reappeared at Langwith Junction and attended confession with a regularity which was attributable to his character rather than to his conduct. Rex could not help staring at him as he sat in his pew or knelt at the altar rail waiting to take communion. He looked nearer to thirty than forty-five, and his pale face smiled what seemed to be a genuine smile of pleasure. He was, his parish priest decided, a genuinely happy man whose simplicity would have appealed to Bishop Dunn. "A good man," the Bishop would have called him, adding that simple goodness was all too rarely rewarded.

Without Peter, who went everywhere with his master and slept across the foot of Rex's bed at night, Rex's life at the presbytery would have been day after day of desolate isolation. So Syd's decision to spend his summer holiday in Langwith Junction—notwithstanding the departure of Mrs. Wilson from Alfreton Road—was greeted by his brother in the way that a beleaguered garrison might welcome a relief column. Then the good news came from Spain. The Rector of the Collegio Inglese had agreed that George should spend his six-week vacation (a privilege enjoyed by all fourth-year seminarians in Valladolid) not at a holy house or monastic retreat but in his brother's parish in Nottinghamshire. Rex began to make plans for August as early as April—cricket at Trent Bridge, trips to Sheffield to relive the family's history, excursions with picnic baskets, paint boxes and cartridge paper. He decided to buy himself a bicycle and to borrow two more when Syd and George arrived home. When, in June, he received the legacy which Winifred Gunn had left him, he had a better idea. He would use part of the fifty pounds to hire a motorcar for the summer.

"I've never hired one out before. There's been no call for it," said Ernest Brackenbury. "If it's just a couple of trips, I'll be happy to oblige. You've done favors. I'm not ungrateful."

Rex, who feared that he was being thanked for Enid's continued Protestant state—a condition for which he had no responsibility—was determined not to be under any obligation.

"I'd rather hire. I need it for a full month."

"All right then. I'll charge the hire-purchase rate." Ernest Brackenbury made his calculation out loud. "Five pounds down on the Austin Seven and five and twopence a week till it's paid off. Let's say a quid for all thirty-one days."

Father Hattersley handed over his pound just as Enid Brackenbury appeared, pushing her mother in the bath chair. Mick sat precariously on the invalid's knee. As soon as the women saw Rex, they began to cross-examine him about Peter without waiting for Ernest to finish his sentence about making out a receipt. Before Rex could give anything like a comprehensive reply, the conversation inevitably turned to the neglected dogs of Langwith Junction. Only when they had explored the full extent of local brutality did they show any interest in Rex's first visit to their house for almost six months. As soon as they discovered that Syd and George were to spend August in the presbytery, they took over the detailed planning of the holiday.

Agnes Brackenbury spoke warmly of the Dukeries—the part of Nottinghamshire in which she had been brought up—and she described the joys of walks in the grounds of stately homes, especially when accompanied by Uncle Ern, the head clerk in a woodyard who could estimate the number of coffins which could be cut out of a living oak tree. Enid reminded Rex that Langwith Junction was within walking distance of Sherwood Forest and the Major Oak. When a visit to Worksop was recommended, Ernest Brackenbury took a sudden interest in the arrangement. Rex felt that he was, in some way, waiting to pounce.

"You must call in to see Annie and Lot," said Agnes, speaking of the Mesdames Skinner and Hartill—her respectively real and adopted sisters—who carried out their business as tailors and dressmakers to the senior servants of the minor gentry in that town.

Ernest struck.

"Newcastle Avenue. They live on Newcastle Avenue, right next to St. Anne's Church. Built by Sir John Robinson, a brewer who made a fortune out of racing. Just shows. Christianity is not above putting a pound or two on the horses." He turned to Rex. "Do you know, Father, that the Church of England is the biggest slum landlord that there is?"

"Don't be provoked, Mother." Enid had other things to talk about. "There's the Bank Holiday tennis tournament."

Rex was about to inquire politely about the details. But Enid supplied them before he had time to ask.

"It's the big tournament. It's all Bank Holiday Saturday and Monday —if you get through. They draw doubles partners out of the hat. I would have won last year, but I had to play with an old man of forty. It's at Clowne."

"You could all enter." Mrs. Brackenbury had caught her daughter's enthusiasm. "I always go ... if I can find someone to drive me there."

"I can't believe that you'll play, Father. I thought you'd be for the men's games. I heard you were a cricketer." Ernest Brackenbury was enjoying himself again.

"I doubt if I'll enter. But I'm sure that Syd and George ...."

"Have they got whites? They have to wear flannels." Enid's mind was already on the tournament.

Syd had whites—two pairs of cricket flannels, as required of all boys at Ratcliffe College. They were not quite big enough for George, who was more Rex's size than Syd's. But George struggled into a pair and, like his little brother, paid his shilling entrance fee for the Clowne Tournament. He was drawn with a lady who wore a skirt that swept the grass and played with a racket which had a fish-head handle. They were knocked out in the first round. Enid was drawn with Syd and did not disguise her disgust that fate, having matched her with a geriatric one year, paired her with a schoolboy the next.

The mixed doubles started in the middle of Saturday afternoon. As Syd and Enid won their first-round tie their anxious supporters watched from outside the wire netting which surrounded the court. Mrs. Brackenbury sat in the bath chair. Despite the heat, her knees were covered as always by a tartan rug. Mick, fastened to one wheel, snapped at flies and occasionally at Peter, who lay panting in the sun. Rex, his dog collar limp with sweat, followed every point through the blur of his moist pince-nez.

They stayed there until play finished at eight o'clock. And since Syd and Enid won both their matches, they took up their positions again at ten o'clock on Bank Holiday Monday morning. They were still there when Syd and Enid won the finals at six o'clock. The silver cup was balanced next to Mick on Mrs. Brackenbury's knees and the victorious party made their triumphant way to the car. The Austin Seven was not big enough to accommodate five adults, two dogs and a folded bath chair, so Syd and George caught the bus back to Langwith Junction. Syd insisted on calling in on the Brackenburys in the hope of taking the cup to the presbytery for the rest of his time in Nottingham. But by the time they arrived, it was already on the mantelpiece. John O'Hara was in the Brackenbury living room. He was obviously delighted by Enid's success. "Are you really going to play at Cuckney? I'll come and watch you there, if it's a Saturday."

Mrs. Brackenbury looked at O'Hara with undisguised hostility. "I think that these four young people can have a lovely summer. That car takes four people very nicely."

"What about you, Jack? How much time will you get off?"

Rex was relieved to hear Enid taking an interest in John O'Hara's plans.

"I'll be working five days, sometimes six. But I hope you'll not let that stop you. It's very good of you, Father, to help her; she'd be a fool to miss the chance."

"Help her?"

"With her education, Father. It doesn't matter to me, having no schooling myself. But I know it matters to her. And we're both very grateful. Any time you can spare for the books, I'll make sure that she's there."

Ernest Brackenbury snorted his incredulous snort but immediately put Rex's mind at rest by demonstrating that his skepticism concerned not the existence of his daughter's extramural education but O'Hara's enthusiasm for its success.

"If you're so keen on her getting educated, why are you dragging her off to the Miners' Welfare to watch you play billiards when she could stay here and talk to the Father and me?"

"She can stay if she wants."

"No, Jack. I'll come with you."

"It's their loss." Ernest turned to Rex. "They say you got friendly with Mussolini when you were in Rome."

"I saw him once. I saw him from a distance of ten yards. I was walking and he was in the back of a car. Nearly ran over me."

"You'll never convince them of that in the miners' lodges. They say you're a fascist sympathizer." Ernest Brackenbury smiled with such amiable malice that even Father Hattersley was convinced that his reputation was not destroyed.

"That's miners for you." Mrs. Brackenbury forced her way into the conversation. "They'll say anything about anybody."

By the end of the summer, the worst that was being said about the brothers was that George, who was dark and handsome, carried a knife and that Syd, who owned his own cricket bat, was on Nottingham's books at Trent Bridge. Whatever damage such renown did to their reputations was a trivial price to pay for the joys of that August.

Each morning, Enid and Mrs. Brackenbury made sandwiches and packed them, together with the cakes they had baked the previous night. Usually—because of Rex's duties or Mrs. Brackenbury's health —the three brothers and their friend could not leave Langwith Junction until midday, and often—because of Enid's obligations to her mother and Rex's duties in the parish—they had to be back by early evening. But no matter how short or long, each day was glorious. They drove to the great houses of Derbyshire and gawped up at their long windows, walked across the hills of South Yorkshire until they

572

found exactly the place to sit and read. Syd drew churches in charcoal. George painted trees in watercolor and Rex sat quietly thinking while Enid talked to him without requiring his participation in the conversation.

There were days of particular glory. Enid saw a grotesque squatting Buddha in a Derby junk shop and, before anyone noticed, ran into the shop and bought it for half a crown.

"Bet you daren't keep it in the presbytery."

"Bet I dare."

"With that stomach," Syd said, "they'll think it's Bishop Dunn."

And they laughed with joy at the intimacy of their friendship.

Twice, during the last week, they went to Beeston and hired rowing boats on the Trent. Rex became Leander instead of the cautious older brother who held back the young and more adventurous spirits because of his own timidity. He could row better than either Syd or George and he took a heathen delight in demonstrating his superiority at one physical activity. On the last Friday of the holiday, as he pulled out into the center of the current, he thought that never in his life had he been so happy. But as he tied up at the jetty at the end of his afternoon he felt nothing except despair that the holiday was about to end.

On the morning that the holiday ended, Enid came round to the presbytery to say goodbye. Syd, as the youngest of the brothers, had the honor of presenting the parting gift. It was four slim matching books of poetry—Keats, Browning, Tennyson and Palgrave's *Golden Treasury*. It was the Palgrave which had given them the idea. For Enid had been openly envious of Syd's school prize when they had taken turns reading from it on one wet evening. Rex—on the pretext of visiting the cathedral while the others explored the castle—had searched the bookshops of Nottingham for something suitably similar. When he found the four kid-bound anthologies, he decided at once that they were too expensive and that he would buy them. Hours were spent examining the texts for suitable quotations to inscribe on the flyleaves. George claimed that he had done best by finding, in *Idylls of the King,* "Enid made sweet cakes to give them cheer." He insisted that Tennyson be regarded as his gift alone. Syd claimed Keats, and Rex—left with Browning—could find no suitable quotation. For the book seemed filled with love poems. But he insisted that they all sign the Palgrave and added,"From the Three Musketeers."

573

Enid wept when Syd handed over the gift and said that it had been the best summer of her life, better even than the summers with her grandfather in Grove Cottage.

"I wish it didn't have to end."

She spoke to all three brothers, but Rex replied as if she had spoken only to him.

"But it must." There was not a trace of doubt in his voice.

"Why? Why must it be?"

Syd and George were in the yard, tying their suitcases into the open car boot. Enid repeated her question.

"Why must it?"

"I think that you know."

"No, I don't. You don't want it to end and neither do I."

Rex pushed Peter into the kitchen and closed the door. "We'll miss Syd's train."

With uncharacteristic rudeness, he bustled his way from the living room and into the yard.

Enid waved them a pretty goodbye, and Syd and George whooped and waved back as the Austin Seven stuttered away down the road to Nottingham. At the station, Rex saw his brothers into the train, which would stop first at Leicester and then in London, bade them a perfunctory farewell and left the station before they had pulled away from the platform. Within ten minutes he was at Bishop's House. Father Ellis, the Bishop's new Secretary, gave him the welcome appropriate to an old friend.

"Is there some sort of trouble?"

"Of course not, Bill. I just want to talk to the Bishop."

"Is it urgent, Rex? I really shouldn't just barge in and say, 'You've got a visitor.' It's a bit unusual."

"I need to see him, Bill. I really do."

Bishop Dunn had to work hard to preserve his avuncular reputation. "I hope that you've no bad news for me. Not ill or anything? I was a bit surprised that you came without warning."

"I'm well enough, my lord. But I need your help."

"It's yours for the asking, presuming that what you ask is in my power to give."

"I need to leave Langwith Junction."

"Need to leave or want to leave?"

"Need to leave, my lord."

"How can that be?"

574

"There is a woman, a young woman. I believe that I am attracted to her in a way that a priest should not be."

"Have you done anything wrong?"

"I have done nothing wrong, my lord. I have not even thought many sinful thoughts. But I have begun to feel the sort of affection that I vowed I would never feel. I'll go anywhere. I don't need to have my own parish. Perhaps I should go abroad. I do need to leave."

"You vowed to suppress your feelings. You didn't say that you'd stop being a man. You couldn't possibly have made such a promise. All you swore was to put thoughts of love and marriage out of your mind as soon as they appeared."

"I cannot do it. Not if I stay at St. Joseph's."

"If you leave now, like this, you'll never trust yourself again. I'm not even sure that I shall trust you."

"I do not trust myself now, my lord. That is why I must leave."

"Have you ever heard the legend of the salamander?"

Father Hattersley despaired; even at such a moment of doubt and difficulty, Bishop Dunn continued to posture. "It came out of the fire. I doubt if it can help me. I'm in the fire now and asking you . . ."

Rex decided that his impertinence should be abandoned in mid-sentence. If Bishop Dunn noticed the priest's irritation, he did not take offense.

"The legend of the salamander has a great deal to teach you. I don't mean the story. I mean the legend engraved on its back. I can't remember the words exactly. But they are to the effect that we defeat evil by going to meet it, not by running away."

"I can't beat it, my lord. I've lost already. I must leave."

"You cannot say that."

"You want me to stay?"

"You must stay. You must stay and do your duty."

"Then pray for me, my lord."

"I do. I pray for you every night." For once, Bishop Dunn regretted his flippancy. "I pray for you every night because I think of you as my son. I discovered your calling. I made it possible for you to be a priest. I gave you a parish. I love and admire you. I am proud of you and I trust you. You must go back and overcome this thing."

As Rex knelt to receive the Bishop's blessing the picture he had in mind was Charles I, saint and martyr, waiting to feel the executioner's ax on the back of his neck.

"The Lord will guide you. I am sure He has guided you before and He will again."

Rex drove slowly back to Langwith Junction, feeling too shaken to risk any speed greater than twenty miles an hour. He went straight into the church and knelt before the statue of Mary. He tried not to rebel against the authority of his bishop, but he knew that as well as praying for the grace to accept his vow of obedience he was also asking a special favor. He was asking the Virgin at least to understand the temptation he would face and to accept, as Bishop Dunn had been unable to accept, that it would not easily be overcome. At least in one of his prayers, he was able to echo the Bishop's sentiments. He asked for a sign—the sort of sign that had been sent in Santa Maria Maggiore on the day in Rome when he had thought of leaving the English College. As always, the world and its problems intruded into his meditation. Suddenly, worried about Peter locked lonely in the presbytery kitchen, he rose from his knees and completed his observances with unsuitable haste.

Peter bounded out of the kitchen, tail wagging in an extravagant greeting. As Rex had feared, the bowl which he had left filled with water had been drunk empty. Barely pausing to pat the dog's head, he walked toward the sink. At the far end of the kitchen, a tweed sports jacket hung on the back of a chair. A pair of carefully pressed gray flannel trousers had been laid across its seat, and on the trousers there was a neatly folded check shirt. George had forgotten to pack the casual clothes which the Collegio Inglese had given him at the beginning of the holiday.

Rex pulled off his black suit jacket and pulled on the sports coat. It fitted him perfectly, as he had known it would. Then he held the flannel trousers against his leg. They were a half-inch too short. But the turnups could be turned down and ironed flat. Rex carried the clothes upstairs and hung them in his own wardrobe. Then he took his bank book out of Aunt Clare's papier-mâché box, which stood on his chest of drawers. He still had almost forty pounds. He was sure that he could persuade Ernest Brackenbury to sell him the Austin Seven for less than that.

His prayer had been answered. He had been sent a sign. As he heard the noise of his dog panting in search of him up the stairs he remembered that Peter had possessed the keys to the Kingdom of Heaven.

· · ·

For the rest of the autumn and during the early weeks of winter, Father Rex Hattersley and Miss Enid Brackenbury pretended that the joys of August would never end. Their meetings were neither secret nor furtive. Enid pursued her education and Rex improved his mind with regular visits to the local public library and tours around buildings of historic or architectural interest. Often, Rex's background commentary on what they did and saw was less than perfectly accurate. So when they visited Southwell Minster, they searched in vain for the tomb of General Allenby, a soldier much admired by Rex for his piety and for an allergy to cats which was hereditary in the Hattersley family. But Enid did not mind the wasted time. And when, because he was both unworldly and absentminded, Rex committed some terrible faux pas, she did not even notice. In the garden at the Hop Pole in Ollerton, he asked to pay for a pot of tea and added an inquiry about the result of the football match between England and Spain. When the waiter handed a piece of paper, which bore the figures seven and one, he believed it to be the bill rather than the score and offered his silver-plated cigarette case in lieu of the cash which he did not possess. Enid simply opened her handbag, took out a half-crown and paid the two shillings and threepence which she knew the tea to cost. In his company she was contented.

As the weeks passed they grew more adventurous and bought tickets for *Rose Marie* at the Lyceum Theatre in Sheffield, where they sat side by side in the upper balcony, apparently unaware that the rest of the audience was not made up of Catholic priests and unmarried women. Even the clothes which Rex wore that night—his brother's sports jacket, a shirt too tight to button at the neck and the tie which George had been awarded in recognition of inclusion in the Panton College first fifteen—did not provoke any comment from Enid. Rex, who was desperate to avoid compromising discussions, gladly assumed that—being used to Church of England vicars and Methodist ministers—she was not surprised to see another sort of clergyman abandon the livery of his trade.

Only Mick took real exception to their friendship. And the dog had good cause. Before Rex and Enid met, there was a long walk over the fields and common land each night. But thanks to the influence of Rex, the evenings were taken up with talk. Mick would not have got out at all had it not been for the regular arrival of John O'Hara, shortly after the Miners' Welfare closed. John, with half a dozen pints inside him, always expressed his gratitude for the trouble that the priest was taking over Enid's education and settled down to marvel at the erudition which was on display in the Brackenbury living room. He was persuaded to go home only when Mrs. Brackenbury suggested that Enid accompany him to his lodgings in order to "let Mick stretch his legs"—a euphemism which never failed to cause O'Hara pleasure. As soon as the suggestion was made, Rex always remembered some pressing reason for his immediate return to the presbytery. Often he was reminded that Peter was locked in the kitchen without water. Occasionally he recalled that there were candles to be set in place in preparation for the following morning's mass. The discovery of omissions which he must immediately rectify clearly caused Rex great distress. He always left white with emotion.

The evening's discussions usually concerned books, for Enid and Rex Hattersley had found previously unrecognized literary merit in the romantic novels of the day—Ian Hay's *Knight on Wheels,* James Hilton's *Lost Horizon* and Jeffery Farnol's *The Amateur Gentleman.* But occasionally Enid and Rex talked about politics, and if Ernest was at home, he joined in. Ernest Brackenbury believed—with some justification—that he was an authority on both political theory and practice. Enid, who was contemptuous of him in general, treated his opinions on those particular subjects with a respect which almost amounted to awe. Rex, on the other hand, usually approached the discussion of politics with a studied diffidence. But when the coal merchant argued for rationalism, socialism and the dictatorship of the proletariat, Father Hattersley thought it right to express polite disagreement. Ernest sometimes continued his intentional provocation until the priest's dissent turned into suppressed rage.

"How John Wheatley can stay Catholic beats me."

Rex did not reply. Indeed, he seemed not to hear.

"Only success of the whole bloody government. Built all those houses. But wants to fill 'em with thousands of unwanted kids."

Rex refused the bait for a second time.

"How does he justify it? That's what I'd like to know. Minister of Health! How can a Minister of Health—a Labour Minister of Health —justify bringing all those unwanted children into the world?"

Rex looked as blank as if he had been addressed in Swahili. But Ernest was not to be denied.

"Come on, Father. How can you justify it? And the women? Downtrodden. Treated like cattle. How can you justify that? How are you going to justify it to Enid here?"

"I'm not sure that I can."

Ernest Brackenbury was still trying to digest the answer when John O'Hara arrived. Mick yelped in anticipation of his evening exercise and Father Hattersley remembered—with an excess of emotion— that he had left the presbytery door unlocked. When Ernest was alone with his wife, he began to express an astonishment which Agnes's innocence of theology did not enable her to understand.

"Did you hear that?"

"Hear what?" Mrs. Brackenbury's only interest was in being helped to bed.

"Hear what he said about thousands of unwanted children being brought into the world. He's supposed to say that it's God's will and a woman's blessing. He's supposed to be the defender of his faith."

"Perhaps he didn't want a row." It was a feeling which Mrs. Brackenbury understood.

"He's supposed to want a row. If you ask me, he's a very strange priest is that one. It makes you think."

"Think what?"

"Think about him and our Enid. What they're up to. It wouldn't be the first time that a priest forgot himself."

"How can you even think such a thing? He's always behaved like a perfect gentleman. It's all in your filthy mind. About your own daughter too. You ought to be ashamed of yourself."

"You've been shut up here too long. You've forgotten what real people feel like. You've forgotten what real people do."

Mrs. Brackenbury began a sniffle but pulled herself together before it turned into a sob. Defending her daughter was more important than feeling sorry for herself. "I haven't forgotten that there are some decent people in the world. I know there's bad and I know there's good. Don't you worry about that."

"I don't worry. I don't worry about what you think about me and I don't worry what she's up to either. I'd much prefer her to ..." He was not sure how to describe the superior condition. "Much prefer it to her marrying that lump O'Hara. So would you if you had any respect for her."

"That's a terrible thing to say. Anyway, there's nothing to it. If there was I'd know about it. A mother knows these things."

Ernest snorted his disbelief.

"She would have told me. There's nothing that girl doesn't tell me. No mother and daughter could be closer."

"Don't be so soft. She wouldn't tell anybody. She may not know it herself."

The conversation had moved on to a level which was too spiritual to ensure his wife's discomfiture. Ernest Brackenbury returned to basics.

"If they're tupping every day in Sherwood Forest, do you think that she'd come home and tell you about it? Do you think she'd come home and say, 'Mam, I've been in the bushes with the priest'? You must be daft, woman."

"You're just horrible and I shan't listen to you anymore. I'll tell you this, though. Whether she told me or not, I'd know."

"How could you?"

"If there's anything between two people, they look at each other in a special way and they touch each other when they think nobody's looking."

"And you've been looking, have you? That means that you suspected something too."

"And another thing. What she said to me proves it. They never talk about the future and they never talk about themselves. They never talk about where they'll be or what they'll be doing in a year's time. She told me so herself. They just talk about what they're doing today."

"I thought he was supposed to be making a Catholic out of her."

"I don't know about that. I just know that they don't do anything wrong."

Ernest Brackenbury—who never imagined for a minute that they did—decided that the sport was over.

"I wouldn't mind if they did. I'd say good luck to them. Let 'em be happy while they have the chance."

They stayed happy until early December.

CHAPTER FORTY-TWO

THE LAST MIRACLE

Neither Enid nor Rex had ever believed that their happiness could last for long. For a time, each of them felt protected by the rules of conduct which they had tacitly agreed and which Mrs. Brackenbury had rightly insisted guided their behavior. But while they enjoyed an entirely proper pleasure in each other's company, that pleasure was so intense that each meeting was itself an impropriety. Enid had no idea how the strange relationship would end and carried it on from day to day. Rex increasingly believed that it would end in tragedy and carried it on nevertheless. Rex's fears were, for once, justified.

It was a tragedy which, by the standard of world catastrophes, would barely be described as tragic. And it was a tragedy wholly of Enid's making. Early on one cold November morning, she made a rare call at the presbytery. Her reason, or perhaps her excuse, was to offer Rex a dozen "new-laid eggs" which the Brackenbury hens had produced in a sudden excess of fecundity.

"They're fresh and we can't use them. Heaven knows why they've had so many. Perhaps it's the weather."

Rex stood awkward but delighted, longing to ask her in but fearful of doing so.

"They need to be kept somewhere cool."

Enid did not share the priest's inhibition. First she advanced into the hall. Then she moved toward the kitchen and the cubbyhole in the corner which was called a pantry. On such days, the pantry's temperature was imperceptibly lower than that of the rest of the house. She pushed the kitchen door open. Peter, excited by the sound of voices, bounded out into the hall and through the still-open front door. The gate which divided presbytery from road was open too, for Enid, with new-laid eggs on her mind, had no time to spare for anything so prosaic as lifting latches and turning knobs. The lorry, pounding down the road from colliery to Brackenbury's coal yard, never even saw the dog which, having caused a little judder under his front wheels, lay bloody, mangled and dead in the gutter.

Rex was the first one out of the presbytery door. When Enid reached him, he was kneeling in the road next to what was left of Peter. She tried not to look at the heap of blood-soaked fur, from which the dog's head—still intact—looked up at his master with the devotion which had made Rex feel loved during their brief life together. Somehow, Rex had got blood on his hands, and as he nervously touched his face it was smeared down his cheek and across his jaw. He was crying and Enid realized that he was paralyzed by grief. Enid's only desire in the world was to look after him—to look after him then and forever and to protect him from the unavoidable pains of the world. At that moment, she had no doubt that her ambition was beyond realization. What she said was no more than a lament for her inability to meet his overwhelming need.

"You need somebody to love, somebody or something. You really do."

Rex awoke from his trauma and spoke as if a long nightmare was over.

"I love you. I loved you the first moment that I saw you."

"I love you too. You know that."

Their instinct for respectability was too strong to allow the conversation to continue. Silently they stood up, Rex bewildered and Enid for the first time afraid.

"Let's bury Peter."

Enid—partly to calm her fears—took charge. She led the way down into the presbytery cellar, brought out old sacking and the remains of an ancient packing case and, swallowing down her nausea, removed the body to the back garden. Rex dug a shallow grave and the corpse was interred.

"Wash your face," Enid commanded, "whilst I make some tea. Then we'll talk."

As Rex scrubbed his hands and watched the vortex of pink-tinted water spiral out of the cracked porcelain washbasin, he assumed that he was about to begin the most important discussion of his life. Enid, he told himself, had decided both what must be done and how they were going to do it. He was sure that her decision was that they would never part. Suddenly he was not afraid.

"You know that we can't see each other now."

Rex was almost speechless with shock. "But I thought . . . You said . . . I love you."

"That is why we can't see each other anymore. It was all right when we pretended—pretended to ourselves. But the pretense is over. Now we have to face facts."

"The fact is that we love each other."

"The fact is that you are a Catholic priest."

"I don't have to be. I became a priest and I can stop being one. I wasn't born a priest."

"Weren't you born to be one? Isn't it God's will?"

"For God's sake, leave the theology to me. You don't believe any of that stuff anyway. Out there in the garden, as we were burying poor old Peter, I couldn't help thinking of you at some atheist funeral that your father told me about."

"That sort of thing just makes it worse. I may not believe in papal infallibility, the Immaculate Conception or whatever you like, but you do . . . Don't you?"

"I don't know whether I do or not."

"When did you start to have doubts? When I told you that I loved you?"

"I've had doubts all my life. Every priest has."

"Well then, you'll have to keep your faith like every priest does. That proves it. We have to finish. Now."

Suddenly Rex was filled with a terrible fear that Enid did not love him after all and that all her talk about his priestly obligation was just an excuse to end even their friendship.

"It's O'Hara, isn't it? You want to marry O'Hara."

"I suppose that I will marry O'Hara. But I don't want to. I want to marry you. I just have enough sense to know that it's impossible."

"Why do you want to marry him?"

"I said that I didn't want to. But I shall. I shall marry him because he's a good man and because I must get away from my father and take my mother with me. I can't go on being frightened—being frightened for her as well as for me. And I can't go on worrying about where the next pound comes from."

"I can take you away. If things are so bad we can go tomorrow." Rex spilled out the next thoughts that came into his head without considering the consequences. "You've never said things were so bad before. I didn't know that you were frightened or that you're short of money. You never seemed to be frightened, or short of money for that matter."

"I could have guessed. I knew you'd say something like that. You're backing away already. It's one of the reasons we can't do it. Nobody with any sense would take us on. You're not going to do it. You'd be crazy."

"I'm not backing away. I only said that I didn't know. You never told me."

"I never told you because I didn't want us to talk like this. I knew you'd say come away with me. I knew you'd mean it at the moment. And I knew that you wouldn't do it when the time came. It's cruel to talk about it when we both know that it's impossible. It's cruel to us both, because I know that you love me and that you'd do it if you could."

"I could."

Rex was white with something very like anger. The second time, he shouted his contradiction.

"I could."

"Think of what would happen. You've got no money, no job. I've got a crippled mother. The Church would come and take you back."

"No, it wouldn't. And I can get a job."

"You'd be an outcast. Syd and George would disown—"

"Syd and George would understand. They like you."

"They enjoyed their summer holidays. That's all. But they are both Catholics and they are going to be priests. You walk out of the Church and they'll never speak to you again."

"No, they wouldn't . . . I mean, yes they would. Syd and George would stand by me."

"You see what I mean. Stand by you. You talk about it as if it were like being sent to prison for stealing."

"No, I—"

"Yes, you do. And you're right. You'll have no friends, no job, nowhere to live, no money. And you'll have to be with me and a sick old woman. Whatever you say now, you won't do it. The Bishop will persuade you. Your father will persuade you."

"My father! He doesn't like me being a priest."

"He'll like you getting your name into the paper less, I tell you. You won't do it."

When Rex did not reply at once, Enid feared for a moment that she had convinced him that it was impossible. His response, when it came, did very little to reassure her.

"I can do it if you help me. I can't do it on my own. But if you help me I can. I can do it if I arrange it properly. Leaving without... without... without behaving as if I don't care about the harm I do."

Enid knew that she had to risk a desperate gamble.

"I can't help you. You have to do it on your own. If you want me— want me enough to live through the scandal and the poverty—you'll do it. But I'm not going to persuade you."

"I don't want you to persuade me. I want you to help me."

It was not a moment for logic.

"It's all the same. If you mean it you'll do it on your own."

"Now? Today?"

Enid's nerve faltered for the first time. She made a tactical retreat.

"Not today. I'll tell you what. We're not going to see each other until after Christmas."

"Why not?"

"Because my mother and I are going to Worksop. That's why. You know that. I told you weeks ago. If you're ready for us to go away together then—"

"We'll plan it bit by bit, won't we?"

"No, we won't. You have to do it on your own. We're back on New Year's Eve." Her nerve bent again but it did not quite break. "But we'll be at Worksop all the time. Come there. They'll help. Come there when you are ready."

Enid knew that it was important not to cry. She walked toward the door, hoping to look calm and detached.

"I'm sorry about Peter. You ought to get another dog. That's always the best way when a dog dies."

Rex was supposed to answer that he loved her and that if they lived together he would not need the surrogate affection of a collie.

Or, at worst, he was intended to reply that after Christmas they would share Mick under the same roof. But the best response he could manage was a simple expression of what he felt in his heart.

"I don't want another dog. After Peter, I don't want another."

Without another word, Enid walked away, trying to persuade herself that Rex was devoted to the memory of the dead dog simply because she had given it to him. By the time she got to the coal yard gate, she was almost convinced that before the end of the year Father Lochinvar would have ridden, if not out of the west, at least from the presbytery at the other end of Langwith Junction.

For almost a week, Rex Hattersley sat in the presbytery immobilized by fear, uncertainty and resentment. Each morning, he was able to force himself out of bed only because of the knowledge that if he once missed mass, the decision over which he was agonizing would, in effect, be taken. He ate incessantly, feeding his neurosis with toast, tea cakes and tinned salmon. He remembered the parish visits which he had promised to make. But he did not make them. Unopened letters lay on the hall table. His bed was left unmade. All his energy was concentrated on worrying about what he might do, fearing that he had lost Enid forever and pitying the solitary existence that condemned him to making the great decision without benefit of loving friends. Enid, he told himself time after time, should have helped him. And time after time he got near to thinking that if Enid loved him she would not have deserted him at such a moment. But the thought that Enid did not love him was unbearable, so he quickly moved on to thinking of who else he could ask for help. The answer was always the same.

Syd was too young. George was in Spain. Clare would talk exclusively about his mother's high hopes and beliefs in his vocation. His father would tell him to do what he liked (which was no answer at all) and ramble off into reminiscences about his boyhood in Sheffield and his singing triumphs in smoking concerts and at annual dinners. The Bishop would tell him to do his duty. He could think of no one who could talk to him about what really mattered—whether or not he could face the first scandal and then the life of an outcast. It was then that he remembered Joe. At least Joe knew what it was like to turn his back on family and friends. Next morning, Rex abandoned all thought of breakfast and drove to Sheffield immediately after mass.

He was apprehensive about even pushing open the door of the Hen and Chickens, and his nervousness was justified. For as he sidled in a hush fell over the bar parlor and the customers looked at him as if he were the first priest to have crossed the threshold. Halfway between door and bar he lost his nerve and almost turned and ran. But he told himself that if he did not have the courage to buy a drink in a public house, he could not hope to face and survive the hostility of the whole Catholic Church. So he gritted his teeth, edged toward the bar and strained to hear what the man in front of him ordered. It seemed to be called a "magnet," so unlikely a name that Rex simply waved in the direction of his neighbor's glass. A bottle, with a magnet on the label, was produced from under the counter.

"It's our pleasure," said the barman. "On the house."

Rex sipped nervously, coughed and leaned toward the barman as if he had a major secret to impart.

"I wonder if the landlord could spare a minute."

The barman replied, wholly unconvincingly, that he was not sure if the guv'nor was in, and disappeared. When he returned, he lifted the flap in the bar and—with a courtesy which amounted almost to deference—invited Rex to follow him into the private quarters.

The landlord was standing in front of his fireplace rattling change in his trouser pocket. He did not remotely resemble his younger brother. Rex had always assumed that Joe would be indistinguishable from Herbert—with a face a little redder, a nose a little fuller, a waistcoat a little tighter and the check of his suit a little louder in deference to the publican's calling. Joe Hattersley was tall, thin and whey-faced. He had a consumptive cough, a wall eye, and he looked almost as nervous as Rex felt.

"What can I do for you, Father?"

Rex was immediately apologetic. "I should have warned you I was coming. I'm your nephew. I'm Herbert's son."

"Christ Almighty. And I thought that you'd come to touch me for a donation. Is it Bert, has the old lad passed on?"

"He's very well. I'm sorry if I gave you a shock." Although Joe showed no signs of trauma, Rex persisted with a second apology. "I should have warned you, I really should, rather than shock you like this."

"Not a bit of it. It's just a surprise seeing you in your togs. I know Bert's sons are all priests. But seeing you in the dog collar and everything. Are you George?"

"I'm Roy, though these days I'm called Rex. I got the nickname at school."

It was Joe's turn to apologize, but not for his mistake about the name. "I'm forgetting my manners. Sit down while I get you a drink. Can I call you George?"

"I'm Rex. George is still in a seminary in Spain."

"Jesus Christ. It gets worse and worse. You'll wonder what sort of chap your father's brother is." Joe did not seem to understand that the blasphemy made it worse still. He waved his hand in the direction of a chintz sofa.

"Don't worry," said Rex, who could always win an apology competition. "It's my fault. I should have warned you. It was very rude."

"It still doesn't excuse me. I haven't offered you a drink. From what I hear, whiskey's the priest's tipple."

As Joe took a whiskey bottle and two glasses from a cupboard Rex braced himself for the assault upon his palate.

"I'm glad old Bert's okay. I don't see much of him. But I'm still fond of the old lad."

"He doesn't like living on his own. I'm not even sure that he looks after himself properly."

"Unless he's changed since he was a lad, he'll soon find somebody to look after him." Joe realized that he had said the wrong thing, but he decided it was best to pretend that he was paying his brother a compliment. "Bit of a lad, your dad. Didn't like his own company much. Never spent many nights with a good book."

Rex felt that he had to rally to his father's defense. "He always talked a lot about you." It was the best that he could manage on the spur of the moment and he hoped that the implied rebuke was clear.

"I bet he did. All Hattersleys talk about their relations. They keep interested by never seeing them. Did he tell you about our dad killing the rabbit on the Chapeltown Road?"

Before Rex could admit that he had heard the story a hundred times, Joe had moved on.

"Did he tell you—?"

The conversation was going in the direction which Rex had hoped for and he leaped in to accelerate its progress. "About you running away? Yes, he did."

"I didn't run away. I left. That's different."

Rex bounded on, helter-skelter, in pursuit of his quarry. "I've got a young man in my parish who says he can't stand living at home and

588

must go away to marry a girl he met. I've told him turning your back on family and friends must be terrible, cutting yourself off, becoming an outcast . . ."

"I didn't have any choice. I'd have suffocated if I'd stayed at home. I didn't care about leaving all that behind me. I thought I was going to make something of my life. I didn't care."

"And you've never regretted it?"

Rex needed Joe's judgment to have no regrets.

"Of course I did. I regretted it after about six months. And I've regretted it ever since. I was a bloody young fool. If I'd stayed at home I'd be rich now instead of running this rat hole. I'd have made that factory work. I threw it all away. Christ. Of course I regret it!"

"So you'd advise my young parishioner to sit tight?"

"I never give advice and I'm never asked for it—apart from which horse is likely to win the three o'clock at Doncaster."

Rex was so disappointed that he sat, head bowed, looking at his shoes and remembering who bought them for him. When Joe suggested "a bite to eat" in the bar, he simply nodded and followed his uncle to the wrought-iron table at which Herbert had sat on the day of the great reunion. Rex banged the table and spilled the drink, true to family tradition.

After a few moments of silent mastication, the landlord announced, "I'll tell you one thing."

Rex looked up, expecting more discouragement.

"This young lad, this parishioner. If he *needs* to do it—cut loose I mean, start all over again—he'll have to be ruthless. He'll have to do it without bothering about anybody else. He'll have to do it without worrying about who he hurts. If he waits for his father to understand or for his brother to agree, he'll never do it. That's how it was with me. I thought that I couldn't live without starting up on my own. If your young man can't live like he is, or without I don't know what, he can't afford to shilly-shally. He has to make up his mind and get on with it or he'll be lost."

"But you regretted it."

"Your young man may not. He may have better reasons than I had. He may have more sense than me. He may be leaving for something that's worth it. I don't know, do I?"

Rex thanked his uncle and began to make his way out of the public house. To his surprise Joe followed him across the barroom out into the road.

"Didn't your father tell you that I was the clever one?"

Rex did not have time to wonder what his uncle meant.

"If you want any help, let me know. I've told you, I'm a bit short of family at the moment. If you need anything, let me know—anything, that is, except advice or money. In my experience—"

"Thanks," said Rex, "but I won't. You've been a great help already."

Rex reacted to Aunt Clare's letter with a decisive alacrity which he attributed to the stern advice that he had been given in the Hen and Chickens. He wanted to be on his own on Christmas Eve. Indeed, the success of his whole plan—perhaps of his entire life—would be jeopardized by the presence of a fastidious old lady running her finger along the tops of doors and complaining about the dust. The message on his postcard was both grateful and categoric.

> You coming to Midnight Mass was a lovely thought. But I fear it isn't possible. I'm staying here till next day and then going to Nottingham. I hope to see you there. Perhaps you'll come next year.

The reply came by return of post. The whole letter was emphatic. But some of the words were printed in capitals for special emphasis.

> I know about Nottingham. You can drive me there. Syd says you've got a motor. This is your FIRST Midnight Mass in your OWN parish. SOME FAMILY MUST BE THERE. Can you meet me in Mansfield? I'll bring my own sheets.

Until he read the second letter, Rex had not realized that his aunt had contemplated staying in Langwith Junction for the night. His second postcard was more categoric than the first, but it did not contain the note of panic that Clare had detected in his first reply. The idea of his aunt in the back bedroom was absurd. Clare must not be allowed to transform it from annoying fantasy into dangerous reality.

> The presbytery is quite unsuitable for visitors. No hot water or heating upstairs. I do not have a housekeeper. You'd be lucky to get any breakfast. I look forward to seeing you on Christmas night.

He knew that his postcard ought to end with a blessing. But Rex could not quite bring himself to treat his aunt as if he were a priest rather than a nephew. Although he had doubts about the propriety of simply sending his love, he was certain that his aunt would not persist in her determination to visit Langwith Junction. For almost a week, faith in Clare's fastidiousness seemed wholly justified. For Rex heard no more until Christmas Eve. Then, at three o'clock, a telegram was delivered to the presbytery. It read, "Arriving Mansfield Station six o'clock. Hope you can meet."

Rex met, but only with great inconvenience. Pastoral visits which he had meant to make in the early evening were crushed into the late afternoon and a message was sent to the Miners' Welfare that he would not, after all, be able to join them for the Christmas raffle draw. Clare, weighed down with accoutrements which she thought necessary to make her brief stay tolerable, showed no sign of remorse about the difficulties which she had created. When her nephew told her that he had disappointed the few Catholic miners in his parish by his failure to put in an appearance at their celebrations, she suggested that they go at once to the social club and attend the event together. Rex accelerated and steered resolutely toward the presbytery.

Clare Martin and her nephew were still surrounded by luggage in the presbytery hall when the front door began to shake under a fusillade of urgent knocking. Rex being hemmed in by two suitcases, his aunt edged the door open. A large, pale-faced workingman stood on the step.

"Can I see the Father, quick? It's urgent."

Believing that at least last rites were in demand, Clare pulled the door open and stood back. Rex, seeing John O'Hara standing on his doorstep, looked like a man on whom a terrible blow was about to fall.

"What is it, Jack, what's happened?"

"I arranged for you to draw third prize, Father. If you don't get to the Welfare straightaway, somebody else will do it. I don't want them to say you let them down."

Rex, turning from white to pink, told his aunt that he would be back in ten minutes and suggested that she leave the cases in the hall until he returned. Clare made no attempt to join the expedition. She felt immensely proud of the love and respect in which her nephew was obviously held by his congregation. She was happy to await his return in the presbytery living room.

The mantelpiece was crowded with Christmas cards, and Clare began to read the names which were written inside them. She found the Bishop's Fra Angelico and was delighted to read, "I am proud of you. I knew that my faith was justified." Frick, Bill and Michael added nostalgic footnotes about Rome. Her own card, containing the message that a mass was to be said for Augusta at the cathedral, she moved from the second row to a place of honor beside the clock.

Syd had decorated his Ratcliffe College card with illuminated script with which a medieval monk would have been impressed. It was, Clare, thought, in happy contrast to the pictures of stagecoaches and drawings of Christmas revelers sent by local business in the obvious hope that their greetings would encourage future custom.

One card contained a scandalously commercial message. It read, "Expect coal delivery as promised. Earlier the better." At first she could not make out the signature. Then, to her surprise, she realized that the coal merchant was a woman. The card was signed by Enid Brackenbury.

DATE			